WHEN THE EYE SEES ITSELF

ERIC BORGERSON

Polylyric Press

When The Eye Sees Itself

First Edition: January 2018

Polylyric Press
1717 E. Vista Chino, # A7-108
Palm Springs, CA 92262
Email: info@polylyric.com
Polylyric Press is an imprint of Polylyric, Inc.
For information about Polylyric Press or its authors, go to polylyric.com or call 800/294-9258.

ISBN 978-0-9980696-3-0 (hardcover)
ISBN 978-0-9980696-4-7 (softcover)
ISBN 978-0-9980696-5-4 (eBook – EPUB)
ISBN 978-0-9980696-6-1 (eBook – MOBI)
ISBN 978-0-9980696-7-8 (eBook – PDF)
Library of Congress Control Number: 2017959232

Cover illustration by and © Alexandra Kronz Kaethler.
Cover design by Jessica Bell.
Formatting: Streetlight Graphics
Printed in the United States of America.

For my parents

PART 1

Anna pushed her way between the last two supplicants and drew a breath to plead for entry.

"Papers," preempted the body-armored officer standing in her way at the gate.

"I have to meet a friend." She pulled identification from her satchel. "A Citizen. I pass through this port three times a week."

The cop glanced at her papers and handed them back without looking at her. "Then you know that Vulnerables are barred from Citizen venues without a certified travel pass and an authorized escort."

Her skin prickled. Calm and cool, *she thought. Not ten miles beyond this institutional obstacle lay the capital city she was trying to reach, its skyscrapers and millennia-old ruins deceptively luminous from a distance. She pulled another document from her bag. "I have a sponsorship letter from the friend I'm meeting. She is from a prominent family, so you might want to make a quick call before you jeopardize your badge."*

The cop met her eyes and smacked the tip of his baton on a sign posted on one of the crumbling cement pillars flanking the gate: "Citizens And Properly Documented Transitees Only Beyond This Point." Several paragraphs of rules and statutory citations followed.

"No pass. No entry."

Anna's heart raced. "Listen you stupid robot,*" she began.*

The officer snapped alert and examined her with sudden interest.

"Let me see those papers again."

Anna backed away, shoving everything back into her satchel. "Forget it. I'll apply for a pass."

He spoke into an audio device clipped to his collar. "We have an Aggressive trying to gain access through a Vulnerable sector."

Anna heard gasps and a few muffled cries as the crowd of Vulnerables shrank away.

"Great." She scanned the terrified faces. "You simpletons, I'm one of you and this whole thing is bullshit, can't you see that?"

Her challenge merely hastened their retreat and Anna feared she would have no route into the safety of obscurity.

Just as she was considering panic, a bottle shattered next to the cop's head and the crowd blew into responsive chaos. Anna seized the distraction and plowed through the disintegrating scene, rendezvoused with her bottle-heaving savior, and fled.

Later, she searched for a functioning public macrophone near her house in the Vulnerable district where she was confined. The first two she passed had been smashed. The third one functioned, but was covered in graffiti. Apparently she wasn't the only Vulnerable having a tough time fitting in. She dialed up Wendy, her friend in the Citizen venue she had been trying to access.

"At least you can depend on those noodles for one thing," she said after recounting the ordeal. "They were too spooked to get in my way."

"Thank God for that," Wendy replied. "Good thing you weren't in an Aggressive sector."

Anna looked around at the signs of unrest. "I'm starting to wonder how different it would be."

"I should have come to get you."

"Who has time for that? Besides, I don't think it would have worked with this cop. He was by the book. I still would have needed a pass."

Anna turned her head to the side to read the graffiti: "The classification system is fraudulent and must be destroyed." True, *thought Anna,* but how?

"What will you do now?"

She scanned to make sure no one was listening or saw her reading the subversive sentiment. "Make an appointment with an advocate I found on the Micromedium, and have him get me a real pass so I can meet with him at his offices in the city."

"Then you will be on their radar."

"Better than being trapped here forever."

Wendy sighed. "At least there you're safe."

"Why don't you move out here with me?"

"No thanks."

"Uh huh."

"You could end up a hell of a lot worse off."

Anna chewed her lip. "Yeah, that's the catch."

"Why don't we get you a new identity?"

"I can't afford that, and I don't want to have to play that game for the rest of my life."

"You think your other options would be easier?"

A woman walked by. Anna tried to catch her eye for a friendly greeting, but she was either too drugged or depressed to notice.

"You know how to cheer a girl up."

"Hmm," said Wendy. "Would you rather have some pretty lies?"

"If you can make them convincing."
"Maybe the advocate can help you sort things out."
"I doubt it."
"Try to have an open mind?"
A police radio crackled.
"Anna?"

1

Advocate Leo Baksh absorbed the young woman's opening summary which, though scant, revealed details meriting investigation.

"How long have you felt this way?"

Anna reclined in the tattered high-back chair and considered the question, wondering whether the complexity of an honest answer was within this man's intellectual and emotional reach.

Her fingertips adjusted strands in the armrest's coarse fabric.

"It's hard to say," she hedged. She brushed a swath of thick black hair back from her face, revealing skin which, though pink and healthy, looked as though it rarely suffered unfiltered exposure to the sun.

She swept her eyes over the advocate, a man older than she but still young, who faced her in a similarly comfortable and threadbare seat. He was presentable enough, with curly hair the same color as hers and rich, olive skin. She lowered her protective barrier and allowed a torrent of sensory data through, sifting for clues to his perspective and agenda.

Leo didn't push. Through years of representing Vulnerables in a classification system baffling to even the most balanced and privileged of its subjects, he had learned the value of letting others sort their thoughts and feelings unprompted.

Anna abandoned her vain quest to read Leo's mind, blunting the blast of sense impressions. She shifted to a search of her own memory and feelings, calculating a safe response truthful enough to be of use by her potential advocate.

"Since my ninth year of school, at least."

Leo let the answer echo in both their minds as he studied her. Putting a potential client at ease while generating enough discomfort to motivate disclosure was a challenging ridge to traverse. Her gaze remained steady yet hopeful about this potentially critical episode amidst a lifetime of cruelties and soul wounds. He decided on a gentle nudge:

"Suddenly? Or did it become more significant at that age, in that social context?"

Here it is, Anna thought. The choice. Try to argue I was misclassified at birth? Ask for protection? Let them tinker with my mind? Claim I'm living proof that the line dividing Vulnerables from Citizens needs another round of revision?

"Ms. Dao?"

Anna returned her focus to Leo and probed back. "To what extent will my answer to that question determine how or if you will help me?"

Smart and cautious, he thought. Regardless of where she is properly classified, her strength was evident. Whether she would devote it to her survival as a Vulnerable or had the other traits she'd need to fight for change in the classification structure was worth exploring.

"It is a preliminary question," Leo said calmly. "I need to get to know you before we can assess whether we'll work effectively together and toward what goal. I'm not making any assumptions and I will include you in my thinking when I start approaching conclusions. Fair?"

Anna glanced around, wondering what the disorder and ill repair this man surrounded himself with said about his professional skills. She narrowed her eyes. "Sounds great for you but when can I pick your brain so I can approach my own conclusions?"

Leo suppressed a laugh at the tiny magma seep. "I promise to tell you my own story and answer your questions before either of us makes a decision."

Anna frowned. She hadn't expected this, though her anticipation was an amorphous compound of hope and a cynical expectation that she would be disappointed. As the conversation unfolded, she bumped against a reality she had studiously sought to avoid during weeks of run-up to this meeting. If she were seeking help from an advocate, she would have to let that person share her personal thoughts and private history. In her experience of people preoccupied with classifications and their repercussions, sharing that kind of information gave away the precious little control one had over one's destiny.

Snapping out of her reverie, Anna jutted her chin. "You first." Her smirk registered somewhere between flirty and hostile.

Leo's amusement faded, though he checked an urge to test her with sarcasm. Taking one slow breath through his nose and smiling faintly with his eyes, he replied, "Since I'm the advocate and you apparently want my help, I'm afraid you'll have to ante up first. If that's too much for you, I wish you the best and invite you to come back when you muster the guts to address whatever impelled you to ask for my time."

Anna unfolded her arms and dug her fingers into the chair's disintegrating upholstery, coiled to give this comfy Citizen a tongue lashing he'd never forget.

Leo added, "Before you storm out of here I will tell you this: I was classified as a Vulnerable until I was almost twenty-five."

Anna's head swiveled back and forth in a tight spasm of disbelief. "You couldn't have a job like this unless you were a full Citizen."

Leo didn't respond.

"That's like what, twenty years ago?" she said, trying to regain composure as this unseemly revelation rippled through her mind.

"Ten years, thank you," Leo replied, acknowledging the jab but declining the bait.

Anna sat poised on the edge of her chair, rocking with palpable ambivalence. Finally, she jumped up.

"Fleeing?" Leo asked with what sounded annoyingly like mirth.

She mirrored his guarded amusement. "For now," she said, "I need to think." *And see what I can dig up on you.*

Leo took in the young woman's barely veiled ferocity. "You know where to reach me. In case you weren't informed, I represent Vulnerables. Aggressives are the province of Mr. Fehring, in the other wing."

Her mouth agape at the man's temerity, Anna squinted and threw her hands on her hips. She was furious at the suggestion she might have Aggressive features and even more irritated that an angry defense would confirm the absurd point. When she thought her voice might perform as instructed, she said calmly, "Thank you, Mr. Baksh. I'm aware of your putative area of expertise."

Leo watched her.

"I'm not an Aggressive," she insisted as though he had challenged her. "I told you in my message that I'm classified as a Vulnerable."

Leo replied, "Classification and reality are two different things. Often they correspond, but sometimes they don't."

Anna straightened her loose fitting sweatshirt and reached for her backpack.

"Which is why the government offers us the option of mind-screwing reprogramming," he paused. "Excuse me," he corrected with mock contrition, "I mean 'education, evaluations, and therapy.'"

Anna froze.

"It's also why we have all the suffocating so-called protections, not to mention the barbaric punishments," he continued. "It's why there are so many protests, and why the Department of Adjudication is choked with litigation. Fortunately for me, all of this creates the need for advocates," he concluded with emphasis, "which brings us back to the purpose of your visit. Why did you come here today, Ms. Dao?"

OK, he's not completely stupid, she thought. He's attempting to appear skeptical about the classification scheme, so he might possess critical insight. But does he? Can he grasp a little real-life complexity? Contradiction? Messy truth? Can he be trusted?

"This remains between us?"

"Unless you tell me you have harmed a Vulnerable or are planning to commit a crime, I will not report anything you tell me. Unless you tell it to someone else, it couldn't be used against you in any proceeding."

Anna knew from her own research that, formally speaking, he had accurately described the rules of their engagement. She also consulted her own over-developed instinct which tended toward thinking he might be trustworthy. From the moment she walked in the room, Anna struggled to screen out perceptual data from the advocate. She had to do this all the time, with everyone, to maintain any semblance of her own identity. Sense impressions always seeped through her barriers though, no matter how hard she fought it. With this fellow, she perceived a broader than usual range. He radiated a pleasing combination of mental acuity and kind sensitivity but also dark undercurrents. The tolerable, almost familiar blend was more than she could say for most people.

She said a silent prayer that she wasn't setting herself up for a defeat to dwarf all the agony she'd endured through her young life. "I'm not even sure how to explain why I'm here or what I want."

Leo did his practiced best to conceal the relief that spread through his chest and replied, "Why don't you start by digging a little deeper and telling me when these feelings—you describe them as being like you have no barrier to other people's experiences—truly began."

After regarding the advocate in tense silence, Anna sat down and told him her story, haltingly at first, then in fits and rushes and periodic silences borne of fear she had revealed too much.

2

LEO'S MEETING WITH ANNA WAS the last appointment at the end of Friday after a grueling week of client interviews, hearings at the Department of Adjudication and the Board of Classification, testimony before a panel at the Council of Delegates, research in legal and psychological doctrines applicable to his clients, urgent calls from family members, some but not enough exercise, a little too much beer, and a late-night emergency trip to the vet with his cat.

Exhausted, Leo felt a rush as he walked out the front door of the building that housed his office—a once lovely but inadequately maintained and unavoidably post-prime structure which, though stylish in a Bohemian sort of way, did not exactly scream "polished professional" to those unacquainted with his considerable fortitude and intellectual gifts.

The afternoon was waning into dusk. The setting sun reflected like squares of copper from skyscraper windows downtown and bathed the stone ruins they towered over in peach light. Leo took a moment to appreciate the city's beauty, then was walking toward his car when his macrophone chirped. A glance at the source ID revealed someone from his ancestral home. He shook the device in his fist. "Can't I have one goddamn minute of peace?" He silenced the ring and let the call go to voice mail.

Still muttering, he settled into his car, stuffed a handful of unopened mail from the passenger seat into his briefcase, turned over the ignition, and eased into the rush-hour throng, heading for the pub to meet his buddy John. Inching along, he activated his macroaudio receiver and flipped through stations until he found a good tune. He sang along and groomed in the rearview when forced to sit idle at stoplights, but his mind was skipping over unpaid bills, neglected work, lost love, and family struggles.

Leo's awareness bled back into the physical world as traffic flowed more freely. When he pulled up to a stoplight in a sketchy neighborhood between his office and the more affluent commercial district where he was headed, a riot of graffiti on a cinderblock wall at the corner caught his eye.

"Exterminate the Vul parasites!" proclaimed the uppermost expression, spray-painted in angry black script. Someone had added in dark green "And the Citizen gluttons!" Another commentator had crossed through all of that and written "Destroy the classification monstrosity. Revolution now! Restruct!" Under that, in red paint dripping with what would be comical morbidity were it not for the content: "Torture the torturers to death."

Leo felt a chill as he reread the last line until a beep advised him the light had turned green. He waved an apology and, as he started forward, a Capital Public Works truck pulled up to the curb. Through his rearview, he saw a cleanup team jump out with airless spray guns and cover the warring outbursts with an off-white coat applied in overlapping sweeps.

The capital, like the rest of the country, was enjoying a period of relative prosperity under the current progressive national administration of Chief Executive Belinda Mosgrove after a decade of austerity and resulting economic stagnation under her conservative predecessor, Belford Thorsch. The city was in positive flux, with a mix of demolition, construction, and cosmetic refreshment gradually sprucing up the dilapidated environment that characterized much of downtown and its environs. Despite those efforts, unoccupied office buildings with broken glass remained in some neighborhoods near Leo's office. Municipal crews were ubiquitous. Of late their role had shifted predominantly from fixing park benches and patching stucco to systematic suppression of political speech. Blatant displays of social tension used to be rare, but were more frequent and radical in recent months.

"Torture the torturers to death?" Leo whispered as he drove. This upwelling of radical expression excited him on one level. He considered himself an activist too, though working within the system. The rising anger and defiance also made him nervous. He supposed that was the objective, though he wondered whether the more extreme activists had a coherent end in mind.

Discomfort from this minor rent in the city's patchwork civil veneer wove into the rumination that had occupied Leo's mind since leaving the office and he began to fret. His consternation amped up when the macroaudio station had stopped playing music and was broadcasting a manically upbeat commercial: "Whether you're a shy Vulnerable or a cranky Aggressive, our certified therapists and educators will have you ready for your Citizenship exams in six months or we'll give you your money back!"

"That's right folks, you can buy your own lobotomy!" responded Leo as he snapped off the set and pulled into a parking lot. "Just a little mind fucking and you'll be fine," he added, checking to be sure he hadn't locked his keys in the car before heading across the street.

The Heartwood Pub, a cozy after-work watering hole frequented by twenty-to-forty-somethings featured hardwood floors, stained-glass panels, and a finely tooled and ornate old rosewood bar with beveled, gold-backed mirrors extending along one side of the capacious front room. Evening light peeked through the plate glass front, illuminating faces Leo found friendly and familiar. The patrons' voices were like a gentle stream flowing over smooth stones.

Leo relaxed his mind and swept his eyes over the crowd until his attention snagged on John, who held up a hand in motionless wave. Leo turned sideways to slide between two tables, one full of boisterous women he saw there on Fridays, the other occupied by a couple with barely touched drinks, engaging in an intense, apparently unpleasant exchange. He swapped greetings with one woman at the busy table as he slipped by, then turned his attention to John, who awaited him with a grin. John's smile always tickled Leo. Goofy and optimistic. Someone who didn't know better could almost mistake him for naïve.

"You look trashed," John said as Leo settled into a chair and craned his neck to see the evening's choices of brew.

"Kisses to you too, asshole," replied Leo. They made brief eye contact and lifted their heads in a silent chuckle. The familiarity of their routine over twenty years of friendship soothed Leo. "Tough week."

"I was under the impression they were all tough," said John, taking his eyes off Leo and raising a hand to catch the attention of their waitress, Wendy.

"They are," said Leo. "I'm getting worn out."

Wendy approached the table, smiling. "Good evening, guys."

Wendy was a gift. Her hair, deliberately unkempt—rather resembling a wad of hay kicked across a windy road—screamed "Screw your convention!" yet her manner was always generously pleasant, notwithstanding Leo and John's obvious enmeshment in mainstream professions. The three of them were almost friends.

"What'll it be?"

"I'll have the doppelbock," said Leo.

"Excellent choice," Wendy responded and turned to John.

"What's good tonight?" he asked, beaming at Wendy with boyish innocence.

Wendy glanced at Leo. "Don't let him fool you. He was here last night and sampled nearly everything, I think. No?"

"I don't know what you're talking about," said John, flashing Leo a quick smirk. "You trying to get me in trouble with the boss here? Didn't anyone ever teach you that employees of drinking establishments are supposed to be discreet?"

Wendy rolled her eyes. "You want me to surprise you?"

"Yes, please."

She snapped alert with a deranged grimace. "One pint of the experiment it is," she piped. With a wink, she was off.

John and Leo turned back to one another with eyes wide. "That may have been a mistake," said John. "So are you worn out as in you need a good night's sleep? Or worn out as in you need antidepressants and a career change?"

"Jury's deliberating," Leo said, glancing around the room. When he looked back at John, he saw his friend studying him.

"Has something changed?"

"No. Yes." He picked up a cocktail napkin and threw it back down. "No. Nothing ever changes. That's the problem."

"You help make important things change all the time. If nothing were changing, why would you be worn out all of a sudden?"

Leo pulled out a pack of cigarettes and passed one to John before sparking one up.

"It feels like all I do is make suggestions for wallpaper changes in prison cells, and from taupe to beige at that."

"Gosh, that sounds bleak."

Leo's nostrils flared but he knew it would be silly to take offense. "It's hard not being able to singlehandedly usher the world to revolutionary utopia."

"I would imagine."

Wendy soon returned, expertly wielding a tray full of pints.

"One doppelbock for you," she cooed, placing Leo's beer down with a conspiratorial wink. "And one mystery formula for you," she sternly proclaimed, the corners of her mouth turned down in revulsion and her eyes full of fright. She lowered John's glass as though it might be radioactive. "Medics are standing by," she whispered as she tossed back her bramble of locks and, with a guttural half-laugh, swerved her tray toward the next table.

They eyed the beer suspiciously.

"Drink up, sport," Leo said, taking a swig off his pint.

John raised his glass and sniffed at it, sneering and looking confused. Leo watched with rapt attention as John took the thinnest of sips, then gaped at Leo with disgust.

Leo raised his eyebrows.

"Tastes like cat piss and compost."

"I'm afraid I've never tried either of those," said Leo.

"Cat piss, compost . . . and flowers. And cough syrup."

"Yummy. Let's get a pitcher."

John took Leo's amusement as a challenge and swallowed two big gulps, then shrugged and smacked his lips. "Pretty good."

Heads turned their way as Leo howled. "Oh my God" he cried, shaking his head. "You're an incorrigible dipsomaniac."

The men were momentarily distracted by a reciprocal upwelling of revelry from the table of women who had witnessed the exchange.

"Back to your long-suffering inadequate messiah crisis," said John, pausing for Leo to feel the little blade slide between his ribs. "Tell me what you've been working on and why it feels colorless."

John and Leo had been friends since high school, attended the same college, surfed kaleidoscopic wormholes on psychedelic carpets through the electric-guitar ether together, organized and marched shoulder-to-shoulder in political protests, dated a few of the same girls, and even had sex together once. Twice if you include the time they spent with a young woman they rented a flat with one summer. But they were smashed when that happened, so they agreed it didn't count. Having left no stone unturned, their friendship was solid and committed.

"Same crap I always work on," replied Leo. "Helping Vulnerables."

John had forsaken graduate school, opting to spend several years traveling and writing freelance articles published by major newspapers. After growing tired of life as a global transient, he returned home to a desk job at a medium-sized paper and earned tenure as a recognized journalist. His exceptional talent and unwavering sense of entitlement to stunning success enabled his rapid ascent to a first-tier writer position for the country's largest and most highly regarded paper, the *Capital Times*.

Leo, mercurial by nature and prone to brooding, lacked a similar sight for paths of gold. Not that he failed to achieve his own measure of success, but his triumphs typically involved drudgery, constant anxiety, and at times bone-crushing depression. John always said that this showed Leo was a stronger person and a better student, but Leo never found this comforting.

Wendy swept by the table, her features inquisitive. "He likes it," hollered Leo over the babble. She swerved back and, as though fatigued by the antics of a smart but devious child, said, "Why am I not surprised?"

Tipping her head back to ponder, she recounted, "I've heard people call it vile, foul, or at best, interesting. I even heard 'lawsuit' amidst one guy's torrent of vitriol. But congratulations," she said to John, "you have the dubious honor of being the first person to like it. We have some mop water in the back we could bottle up for you in a jiffy if you're still thirsty."

John took the berating in stride. "Why in God's name are you still serving it and what possessed you to choose it for me?"

"Don't get all huffy with me, buster," Wendy said with her head high. "I believe I was just informed that you like it." Then, quietly, "Our brewmaster is experimenting with more exotic recipes—this one is supposed to be 'rich and smooth, with base notes of cumin and the faintest hint of sage, delightfully accented with the ethereal aroma of jasmine.'"

John tapped Leo's arm. "Cat piss, compost, and flowers. An earthy cosmic dream."

"Another round?" chirped Wendy.

"I'll take a pale ale this time," said John, "and another for my friend."

"Something to eat?"

"Yeah," said John, pointing at Leo. "Nachos."

"And some of those grilled pesto mushroom caps," added Leo.

"And calamari," said John, rubbing his tummy.

Wendy gasped in mock shock. "You pigs! One trough coming up." With a stern glance at each of them, she glided away, shifting her expression at the last moment to the pleasure of a shared joke, reflecting the warmth she enjoyed with these two—not so profound as to be called love, but something good and wholesome that they all valued.

"I should marry that woman," said John as he watched Wendy saunter away.

"You flatter yourself," replied Leo.

"Speaking of self-flattery, what's triggered your current bout of omnipotent impotence? Out with it."

Leo fiddled with his glass. "I'm not sure you'll understand."

John dropped his chin and stared at Leo. "Oh, come on," he sighed. "Don't start with this." Cocking his head from side to side, he recited the time-worn refrain: "I can't possibly grasp your terminally unique dilemma because I don't know what it's like to not be a Citizen."

"That's pretty much it in a thimble," Leo said, sipping his beer and avoiding John's eye.

"For fuck's sake, don't you ever tire of that self-serving dirge? I knew and loved you through the whole thing. Before, during, after, now. Cut the crap."

Leo felt reciprocal annoyance rising in his chest and mentally cycled through several retorts, ranging from amplified bitching about his own emotional challenges to a deconstruction of John's undeserved and poorly appreciated privilege. He refrained from these dramatic maneuvers, however, partly because they were defensive and partly because the irritated expression on John's face told him a false move could end this evening prematurely and unpleasantly.

They remained at alert, both tense and on the edge of a snotty outburst, then eased off and slowly shifted to frustrated but relieved smirks.

It was an old spat.

Leo scanned the room as he calmed himself, noticing Wendy in a heated exchange with a rough-looking character, all muscles and crude tattoos with a shaved head and angry face. An Aggressive by the looks of him, and probably not lawfully present in the Citizen venue. Wendy jerked her head toward the door and spoke through clenched teeth.

John turned around to see what Leo was staring at, but the intruder had slipped away.

"Nothing," said Leo. But he wondered.

Wendy dropped off their new beers, cordial but distracted. John and Leo noticed the variation in her demeanor, but John hadn't witnessed what preceded it. "She's busy tonight."

"Yeah," said Leo, shaking his head. "Anyway, It's not just self-pity," he said, returning to their discussion. "My past affects my relationship with my work."

"Of course," said John, relieved as Leo shifted to this more fruitful track. "I haven't lived through what you survived but I do try to stay informed. I watched you go through it and, as you may recall, I'm rather bright."

They both snorted at these understatements, and the remnant of the conflict dissipated.

"I've always thought the classification system was bullshit," Leo said. "It's stacked in favor of Aggressives, or, at least, the Aggressive principle."

Leo was born into a Citizen family, but was reclassified early in his youth as a Vulnerable due to what the authorities deemed his pathological sensitivity. After spending his childhood in this protected but disparaged status, he went through years of education and therapy to balance a more measured expression of his sensitivity against an appropriate level of assertiveness and foundational anchoring. In his early twenties, the Board of Classification found he had developed a balanced and temperate blend of Vulnerable and Aggressive traits and deemed him fit for Citizenship.

"I'm grateful they let me in, believe me. I enjoy Citizenship and its privileges."

"Cheers," said John as they clinked pints and took a swig.

"But the reprogramming was hell."

"I know it was, Leo."

The process of so-called guided development Leo had endured involved torments he had feared would destroy him. The reprogrammers, as the teams of evaluators, educators, and therapists were colloquially known, refused to accommodate his hypersensitivity or let him hide or be shy. One assumed their intentions were virtuous, but their obsession with protocol often blinded them to the nuances of individuals they were "helping." In their zeal, they put him through violent fights and other harrowing physical ordeals that would be difficult for even people of ordinary temperament to endure. As traumatic as those were, Leo faced even greater difficulty when he was forced to verbally spar in front of jeering panels and withstand withering verbal assaults, angry tirades, and criticism until he was mute and humiliated, then ordered to stand up and do it again. This brutal form of therapy was designed to shatter a person and rebuild him from the ground up on a solid foundation. Reprogrammers considered Leo a success and featured his case—mercifully anonymized when published—in training manuals for up-and-coming reprogrammers.

"I thought I would collapse or go mad."

"But you didn't."

"Not exactly. Part of me had to die to survive. Truth is, killing that part of me was their goal and I'm not sure it was a fair trade. The best of me, my innocence, was slain on the altar of 'balance.'"

Sensing the marked shift in tone at their table, Wendy discreetly set their platters, plates, napkins, and utensils down without a word and walked away.

"I think I'll marry her," said Leo.

"You don't like girls," said John with a slight grin, though his eyes reflected the seriousness of the larger discussion.

"That's not quite true."

John rolled his eyes. "Back to topic. Maybe what you're calling innocence was just a little boy who needed to grow up."

Leo acknowledged the point with a shrug. "Don't get me wrong, learning to plant an anchor and hold my own in debate and conflict has made my work possible—it's a dimension of life I couldn't access before the training. Becoming fit for Citizenship did bring benefits."

"Not to mention the nachos," said John, scooping a heap on his plate.

"Yeah, not to mention those," said Leo, taking a scoop of his own. "Though the anti-discrimination laws gave me limited access to places like this."

"But I could almost never drag you out to spots where Citizens hung out because of the monitoring and because it stressed you out too much."

"Yes. True. Exactly."

"So?"

"I've been living as a Citizen for ten years and helping other Vulnerables. It's a decent life but it's numbing on some level. Disorienting. Depressing."

"How?"

"This woman came to my office today. A new client. Twenty-three years old, attractive, smart. Also scared, skeptical, cynical. She had initiated the contact with a voice message saying she was a Vulnerable who needed a consultation regarding her status and preferred to discuss the details in person. Her appointment was today, right before I came here."

"Ah," said John, sensing proximity to pay dirt.

Leo popped a greasy pesto mushroom in his mouth and said, "She was a real firecracker." He swallowed the treat, moaning as though this weren't the ten thousandth time they'd shared a plate of these little hors d'oeuvres.

"I could tell immediately she might bolt like a wild horse if I questioned her too forcefully, so I gave her room to disclose at her own pace and searched for points where I could prod her to open up more.

"She wasn't buying much of my shtick, I'm afraid. She was quick to push back and test me. I stood my ground in a way she found sufficiently playful because she took a gamble and trusted me with her story. I'd like to take credit for that but I think it says more about her courage. And desperation.

"At first, all she would say is that she 'had no barrier to other people's experiences.' When I asked her how long she had felt that way, she started bobbing and weaving until we worked through her initial distrust. She almost bailed."

John exhaled a breath of amusement as he listened to Leo and imagined the scene he described, aware of the legal context and noting the deeper strength Leo always exhibited when focused on his work.

"Before she told her story, she had already displayed an unusual array of signals. Though she identifies and is classified as a Vulnerable, she is fiery, combative, adept. She wasn't afraid to set me back on my heels or question me. But when I stood my ground, she let her fear and uncertainty show. She needed to believe in my strength and stability so she could trust me to handle her disclosures responsibly, yet she also needed to know I was sensitive enough to appreciate her torment.

"I took a gamble and told her I was a Vulnerable until I was twenty-five, but I refused to tell her more until she described her situation. She didn't know what to make of that."

"I bet."

"She told me her mother was a Citizen and her father was a Vulnerable."

"That's unusual."

"Very. A Female Citizen with a male Vulnerable is a rare pairing—5 percent of the coupled population. Of course, they can't legally marry."

"Mm hmm."

"The courts are split over the status of such a couple's children. In this Adjudicative Quadrant, they are presumptively classified as Vulnerables, but that's mainly because of their social stigma, not any empirical probability of heritable Vulnerable traits."

"Wouldn't surprise me."

"Her situation is further complicated because she displays both Vulnerable and Aggressive features, so any route she takes toward Citizenship would be dangerous."

History and politics were a shared passion for these two, with John focusing on economic perspectives through his journalism and Leo focusing on law and advocacy. Anna's case set them both to reflecting on the origins of the classification system and its development into the current categories, criteria, and related allocation of rights, privileges, and punishments.

Its earliest roots consisted of laws designed to protect the physically weak from exploitation and coercion by the physically strong. A thousand years prior to this evening at the pub, the strong used the weak at will, inflicting forced servitude and horrific violence and sacrifice with impunity.

The early laws emancipated first the slaves and then the servant class, providing a crude set of protections and penalties intended to address gross-level abuse within a larger feudal economic and political system, but no system of Citizenship per se.

With the development of a market economy, attendant emergence of an entrepreneurial class, and broader distribution of increased wealth, the distinctions grew complicated.

After the creation of the Council of Delegates about 400 years ago, the concepts of Vulnerability and Aggressiveness were refined. Extremely weak or physically disabled individuals were still classified as Vulnerables, but Vulnerability evolved to encompass relative fragility, powerlessness, or the inability to self-defend. It included psychological and sociological considerations as these fields of analysis developed in the academic and professional worlds.

At the same time, the legal definition of the other extreme—Aggressiveness—evolved to include tendencies to abuse more subtle and abstract forms of power.

In between these two poles developed the concept of Citizenship, with Citizens defined as having a healthy, balanced, and temperate blend of the two principles—a functional midrange.

"Which is almost everyone," pointed out John. "Society is composed of Citizens."

"Officially, yes," said Leo. "The overwhelming majority are Citizens."

"We help the outliers join in," added John.

"Yes and no," said Leo.

The categories were treated as rigid and clear, with rights, duties, and penalties allocated accordingly. The government and society in general strove to help Vulnerables and Aggressives develop into Citizens. In that sense, Leo acknowledged that John was technically correct.

Reality was less tidy. The Vulnerable and Aggressive principles were at play in all three categories. The law strove to define if and when Vulnerables needed protection, and whether Aggressives deserved isolation or required corrective treatment. The thresholds were subject to interpretation and constant evolution due to a complex array of forces.

"We have a web of overlapping bureaucracies now," said Leo. "The Council of Delegates, the Department of Adjudication, and the Board of Classification are just the official main players. The Association of Psychologists, academics in nearly every other field of social science, public health, medicine, and law weigh in on where and how the government should classify individuals."

"Not to mention commercial interests," added John.

"Don't even get me started on that," said Leo, giving John the stop sign.

Pressure by Vulnerables or Aggressives to broaden the criteria for Citizenship always met with resistance. For every social movement, legislative proposal, classification petition, or court case seeking to expand the definition of Citizenship, a well-funded counter-movement voiced fear of social instability or profited from the infrastructure that administered and enforced existing categories.

"Most people are Citizens. But that hasn't been true for me or people I help professionally. It's not what I think about or how I experience the world. Even though I'm officially a Citizen, I feel like an outlier who could be redefined back into an excluded class should the political winds shift, and I'm not alone."

"You worked your ass off to become a Citizen," said John.

"But what has it gained me? The right to petition the courts or classification board on behalf of others so they can be stigmatized or assimilated? We aren't making any progress as a society. We keep refining the classifications and shifting the boundaries, but the whole system, the allocation of wealth, legitimacy, and power, depends upon a set of attributes and definitions that perpetuate subordination and exploitation. Even the privilege of Citizenship is predicated on an exploitative and violent world view."

"No," countered John. "It is designed to create a world of balanced people and stop exploitation."

"Officially, yes," rejoined Leo. "But does it? That's what's killing me. I'm not sure that's the real goal."

"Then this woman walked in," prompted John.

"A complex, fascinating, emotionally injured, justifiably furious woman comes to me for help. Being presumptively born a Vulnerable is a surmountable challenge, given the antiquated reason, but she also has a severe inability to filter out others' experiences. I don't know the extent of it, but from what she described, she has a nearly psychic perceptivity."

"I visited countries while I was freelancing where she would fit right in," said John, "but classifying her here is a challenge. Interesting."

"If this extreme Vulnerable trait were uncovered during her evaluations, it would enmesh her in an endless mire of proceedings and appeals that could lead her nowhere but to a glorified asylum."

John frowned in acknowledgement.

"Or worse, her Aggressive features could catch the wrong evaluator's attention and get her ripped out of her unsatisfactory but protected life and forced to live—or die—with the Aggressives."

"That wouldn't happen," said John.

"That does happen," replied Leo. "Naturally, she is scared to risk that or trust anyone enough to disclose her issues. She is too vulnerable to handle life comfortably among conventional stressors, yet to interact with her one-on-one is to be battered by Aggressive traits.

"If we could do a net balance of all her characteristics, they would cancel out and place her into the Citizen range. But it's not that simple. She has a pronounced but unprotected Vulnerable trait well beyond average in intensity. No analytic or diagnostic system is refined or calibrated enough to give a valid result that the gatekeepers of Citizenship would consider."

"But this is what you do," said John.

"It feels futile. Even if I officially help this woman, am I actually helping her? Or am I holding her hand and lending legitimacy to a system that will either pathologize her personality or tear her apart through reprogramming?"

"You can use her case to push for refinement of the Citizenship criteria.

That would help her and others like her, which would help us all have a richer, more diverse, enlightened community of Citizens and a better system of law," said John.

"Tell that to the Citizens Action League."

"Fuck the Citizens Action League."

"Easy for you to say."

Leo stretched his back muscles, realizing how wound up he was despite John's cool counterargument. "We can always take on the classification system, but do you have any idea what that would entail for her?"

"For her or for you?"

"Both."

"Leo, why did you choose a career as an advocate?"

"I thought I could leverage the lessons from my own experience through the power of Citizenship and an advocate's license to help other Vulnerables."

"Right."

"But."

"But what? You have helped a lot of Vulnerables. You've won protection for people and you've won cases that changed the classification system. You should be proud of that."

"Like I said, it feels like changing wallpaper in the prison cell."

"That's self-indulgent whiny bullshit. We didn't create the world and we don't rule it, but we can decide what we contribute to it. Your work matters. It improves lives and it helps advance the larger culture."

"Perhaps," said Leo, unable to shake his malaise. Even after this speech, he felt uninspired by his work and no less distressed.

Realizing with a cringe that he had hogged the conversation with his own issues, Leo turned his attention to John.

"Thanks for listening," he said in a belated and inadequate expression of gratitude for the gift of John's patient attention.

"No problem," said John.

"How are you?" Leo asked, embarrassed. "How goes the book?"

"It's been accepted for publication by Sapient Imprints."

"What?" Leo shouted, glancing with embarrassment at the heads turned his way. "Why the hell didn't you tell me?"

"You were lamenting the failure of your divine plan for the emancipation of humanity."

"I'm sorry," said Leo. "I want to hear how this happened."

"I want to tell you," said John, checking his watch, "but it will have to wait because I need to run."

"But we just got here."

"We've been here for an hour and a half. I'll call you," John replied, his eyes focused across the room as he gestured to Wendy for the check.

"It's on me," Leo said.

"That's not necessary," said John, who made more money and managed it responsibly.

"Please," Leo insisted. "My treat."

John acquiesced, more appreciative than he let on that Leo considered paying for their meal a priority among his mismanaged and mysterious expenditures.

"Seriously, thanks for letting me get all that out and talking through it with me."

"It's cool. These are significant issues. I'm interested and I'm with you. Stay strong."

John gathered up his briefcase and jacket and walked out tall and confident, turning heads in his wake. The dashing figure he cut was tempered by an awkwardness one could not ignore.

"That's a cute shirt you're wearing," said Wendy to alert Leo she had stopped at his table.

Leo looked down to see what he had on, a dark blue button-down patterned with tiny green fleurs-de-lis. "Thanks. I like yours too."

"Everything OK?" she asked as she collected Leo's payment.

"Oh, yeah," he replied.

Her grim smile showed that she would ask more if the context were different. Leo returned her gaze, restraining his curiosity about her interaction with the rough-looking visitor. Rather than breach etiquette, they kept their thoughts to themselves, and Wendy moved to another table as Leo stood to leave.

3

Lauren Drey checked her attire as the elevator lurched to a halt at the thirtieth floor. The doors slid open to reveal a glass entryway across the hall, emblazoned with a blue, silver, and white government seal identifying her employer, the Department of Domestic Intelligence.

She had been a DDI agent for twelve years, yet the official welcome gave her a rush today. Running a leisurely thirty seconds behind schedule, Lauren was unusually brusque with the front office staff and stopped at her own office to grab a stack of files before heading for the conference room. She and her partner Melissa Benton had unwound at the Heartwood Pub over a few beers the night before. Lauren was less focused than she preferred after the spontaneous weeknight indulgence.

She scanned her case summaries before the morning strategy session. Once a week, Lauren and her fellow agents met with George Mills, chief of the DDI Capital Region, to brief each other on key developments in their investigations. The sessions were often tedious and redundant, but sometimes the brainstorming and unsolicited advice from other agents yielded breakthrough insights. The meetings were worth the effort and, in any event, were mandatory.

Today, however, was unique in Lauren's career. The chief had asked her to brief her colleagues on a set of related cases involving issues and technology so new that the legal contours of her investigation were being defined even as she collected information. Her briefing would intrigue the agents, she was sure. She hoped they would produce insights she could use.

As she opened the soundproof door to the conference room, pre-meeting banter tumbled through like the bustle of city traffic. The room flooded with morning light and everyone looked animated and ready to begin. Shunting aside nervousness, Lauren sat resolutely at the long conference table next to Melissa and across from James Malone, an agent whose ruthlessness was both admired and regarded with trepidation throughout the DDI Capital Region.

Lauren slid a scrap of paper to her partner listing the four cases she thought merited discussion, and Melissa signaled her agreement with a curt nod.

The agents' voices subsided as Chief Mills called the meeting to order.

Lauren's attention wandered as agents summarized their investigations. Usually she enjoyed contributing a thought or two, but already stretched thin by a large and emotionally treacherous caseload of her own, she pulled back and let others brainstorm.

She was rudely dislodged from her reverie by an elbow to the ribs from Melissa indicating it was her turn to submit cases for discussion.

"Sorry, I, uh, we, Melissa and I, have four cases that are presenting unique challenges right now," she said, pulling out the relevant files and summaries she had prepared.

Lauren and Melissa worked in the Vulnerable Exploitation Unit. Melissa focused on locating people who were being physically and emotionally abused. Lauren now focused primarily on what they had provisionally (and inadequately, in her opinion) dubbed "virtual exploitation," a phenomenon taking place on the Micromedium and spreading so rapidly that neither the law nor scientific understanding could keep up. Today was her chance to bring her colleagues up to speed. After consulting with scientists for weeks to prepare for this briefing, she had one ready to patch in via macrovideo feed. She hoped he and she together could explain the material in terms the other agents could understand.

"Each of these cases involves exploitation of Vulnerables using revolutionary new quantum neural interface technology," Lauren began. "As you know, we have tracked Vulnerable exploitation fantasy groups on the Micromedium for years. There have been fictional depictions of Aggressives abusing Vulnerables for decades, both in mainstream entertainment over the Macromedium and in harsher, less socially acceptable and sometimes illegal forms on the Micromedium.

"Most of our cases have resulted in prosecution of individuals who were conspiring to inflict or broadcast violence or psychological abuse on a Vulnerable or group of Vulnerables. The greatest difficulty for the courts was distinguishing between performances of fantasy abuse scenarios and broadcasts of actual abuse.

"The cases we're currently investigating involve something more nefarious. We think the participants are using new technology to form a neural link and jointly experience recorded incidents of actual abuse."

"Videos of Vulnerable exploitation are already illegal, Agent Drey," said James Malone without looking at her. He began reading papers from his own files.

Lauren turned a cold eye his way. The two had worked together for years, and he possessed unrivaled prowess in unsavory tasks, though it did little to ease his colleagues in social interactions. Lauren's feelings toward James sometimes strayed from indifference to annoyance and even full-on aversion. He was smooth as polished marble on the surface, but Lauren's gut told her she wouldn't like what she would find if she looked more deeply. For that reason and because she refused to let him cow her with arrogance, she remained collected. As best she could, anyway.

"Right," she answered after a beat, resisting the temptation to comment on his manners. "But there's more involved here and I'm not sure there is a legal category for it. The technology is changing so fast that our ability to track it lags behind the events we're investigating."

"Take your time, Agent Drey," urged Chief Mills. "Walk us through it."

Lauren glanced at a page of bullet points and started with familiar territory. "The basic technology is already known to us. Recent advances in neural scanning have enabled us to map patterns associated with aggressive behavior. Old-school MRI scans and early experiments involving EEG electrodes placed directly on the brain tissue have been superseded by more precise and less intrusive Quantum Field Resonance Imaging, or QFRI nodes placed on the skull of experimental subjects.

"From extensive clinical research, our forensic team has charted aggressive neural patterns and thresholds which we've been correlating with categorization standards. Eventually, this may become the primary tool for categorizing people as Citizens or Aggressives, though we're a long way from having the scientific and political consensus it would take to make that happen.

"In the meantime, the advocate general has been working on arguments to get the technology validated for use in court as evidence of a criminal defendant's culpability. Combined with proof of aggressive behavior, we think the QFRI data will prove persuasive for categorizing defendants as Aggressives and getting them properly jailed or institutionalized."

"Most of us have read the briefings on these developments, Ms. Drey," said the chief. "How does this affect this new area of investigation you're describing?"

"The same QFRI technology is at the heart of these cases but is employed in a completely different way. If the reports we're getting are accurate, people are using the equipment to literally link their minds together for a shared fantasy abuse scenario. As with the old-style conspiracy cases, the activity is deviant and potentially indicative of deeper pathology and criminal propensity but is probably not currently illegal, provided it is a fantasy and does not involve exploitation or abuse of a Vulnerable."

"However," interjected Melissa, "we are told that these neural interface sick-fests are augmented and intensified by multimedia recordings of actual incidents of abuse."

"So?" said James.

"Moreover," Lauren resumed, "these recordings reportedly also use quantum neural technology—reading and recording both the aggressive rush of the abuser and the fear response of the abused Vulnerable and then incorporating them into the QFRI pattern transmitters used in the neural interface fantasy sessions."

"So not so virtual," said the chief.

"Not so virtual at all. Indirect yes, but concretely connected. The fantasy abusers are feeding off the original abusive act itself."

"I still say, so what?" said James.

"The perps may be ingesting the victim's life energy," said the chief.

"How?" James asked. "Sounds like a vivid recording. Entertainment gets more vivid all the time."

"Would you want someone consuming your consciousness?" asked Lauren.

"If they could do it without taking it away from me, I couldn't care less. It might be flattering. Or hot, depending."

Chief Mills scanned his agents' faces, which registered between amusement and disgust.

"From what we've learned, it's more than a recording," said Lauren. "We think the perps and victims might become entangled in a way that harms the victims."

"How the hell could that be?" asked James.

"It's complicated."

"OK," said the chief, "I'm sure we'll learn more as we go. For now, let's hear about your cases."

Lauren resumed, "We've been monitoring an anonymized virtual chatroom where perps hook up. Aggressors congregate there and search for others to link together and share an abuse experience. They are careful about how they issue invitations or broadcast their interest, but the intent is obvious. We have seen one frequent flyer, or at least we're pretty sure it's the same actor. He uses different virtual identities, but both his virtual names and his expressions follow a pattern. He, and we assume it is a male because he presents as such but we don't know for sure, asks something to the effect of 'is there anyone here who gets a charge out of talking about Vulnerable punishment—just fantasy of course.'

"We have assumed identities in the virtual chatroom and have engaged him a few times. He has alluded to use of virtual abuse recordings, saying they are 'very realistic,' but has never said he has recordings of actual abuse. When we ask if we can see one, he says 'sure if you want to form a nodal link'—slang for a QFRI-mediated and enhanced neural interface through the Micromedium. The problem is, forming a neural link is a risky procedure under the best of circumstances. To form one with the purpose of sharing an enhanced recording of actual Vulnerable abuse would be both complicit in what we believe to be a crime and likely mentally harmful to an agent."

"Wait," interjected Renée Stephens, an agent from the Violent Crimes

Unit. "Can we back up a second? How are the links established? How are they experienced?"

Renée's shiny, straight, jet-black hair was hooked behind her ears and flowed to the middle of her back. With alert brown eyes, a long and narrow face, and high cheek bones, she was a handsome woman, tough but kind. Anyone who viewed her sensitivity as weakness usually discovered their error the hard way. She wasn't as tightly controlled or coldly dispassionate as many of her colleagues. This created friction at times, but the chief viewed her personality as a useful variable in inter-agent dynamics. Even James knew Renée was a good cop, though he would take that belief to his grave.

"At this point, I would like to bring in Dr. Ishwar Palam via macrovideo link," said Lauren. "Dr. Palam is an expert on this technology. I have conferred extensively with him throughout these investigations, and he can answer your technical questions."

"I thought you understood this material," offered James.

Lauren refused his invitation to go on the defensive. "What I understand I learned from Ishwar and his colleagues."

"Let's give this expert our attention and courtesy, agents," instructed Chief Mills. "That includes you, Malone."

James eyed the chief but didn't respond.

A wall-mounted macrovision screen at the end of the room blinked to life, showing the renowned physicist, a comely fellow, fiftyish, with dark skin and an unruly shock of ebony hair pierced with threads of silver. He greeted the agents enthusiastically. Palam spoke in a rich accent, all r's and t's to Lauren's ear, though she had grown accustomed to his manner during their acquaintance.

After introductions, Lauren invited Renée to repeat her question.

"Dr. Palam, thank you for assisting. My question is how are these links established and how are they experienced?"

"Well," began Ishwar, "to form the links, participants employ devices originally designed to allow computer end-users to issue mental commands to their Micromedium network terminals."

"I thought those devices could only implement crude instructions, like clicking an icon," said Renée.

"That was true, initially," he replied. "The early scans using EEG electrodes on the brain tissue and functional MRI, or fMRI, equipment that tracks changes of glucose consumption in the brain were successful in mapping the neural activity associated with simple motor functions. Those followed discrete and identifiable patterns.

"When more sensitive electrodes were developed for placement on the external skull, it became possible to develop relatively nonintrusive tools that enabled end-users to issue crude commands by training the mind through focused visualization to form a neural pattern recognizable by the program running on the interface connected to the electrode sensors. It required extensive training of the end-user, but it worked.

"Later research with the electrodes on the brain gradually yielded insight into more subtle and complex neural patterns, including ones associated with language. These experiments were crude, enabling the programs connected to the sensors to determine with about eighty percent accuracy when test subjects were thinking yes as opposed to no.

"The lid was blown off with the advent of both quantum computing and quantum field resonance imaging. A small minority of neuroscientists have long asserted that consciousness cannot be explained by reduction to neurosynaptic links, no matter how numerous, because signals take too long to cross the cleft between neurons via chemical reactions through neurotransmitters. These scientists posited that something deeper was going on within the neural architecture at the quantum level that might, with advances in technology, be measured directly."

Lauren interjected, "Though it is now widely available, the origins of the QFRI technology are shrouded in national security cloaks impenetrable even to us so far. We have theories but no way to verify them yet. The first QFRI machines were large, like the old-school MRI scanners, requiring subjects to lie still. Two years ago, a company involved in manufacturing this equipment, Interlink Technologies, developed an approach that uses nodes placed in an array around the skull. Microaccelerators emit charged subatomic particles through the brain and sensors detect them from the other side of the skull, producing a neural quantum field. Literally an image of the mind." She gestured to Dr. Palam.

"The resulting fields are staggeringly complex," he resumed, "as complex as consciousness itself. Presumably, if they could be deciphered, it would be like reading thoughts. Unfortunately, it's raw data so far. Some patterns have been correlated with EEG and fMRI data and identified as associated with basic motor movements and crude speech, as well as with aggressive behavioral propensities. The QFRI sensors are immeasurably more sensitive and precise than the older technology, but deciphering their complex data still requires an accurate theory of the mind, which we are no closer to having than we were with crude images from the older technology."

"It's the same problem but with a new worksheet," said Lauren. "A more detailed way of mapping the same basic functions."

"What does this have to do with not-so-virtual abuse experiences?" prompted the chief.

"The interesting thing is that although the quantum field brain scan output is indecipherable, it can serve as a medium for two scanned individuals to share a perceived experience," answered Lauren.

No one spoke for a beat as they contemplated this.

"Do you mean to say that their minds are actually linked?" Renée asked, shocked that Lauren meant her initial summary literally. "They can hear each other's thoughts?"

"Through interfaces and the Micromedium, which become parts of the shared experience," said Palam, "but, yes, their minds share a real-time, experiential link."

Before continuing, Lauren noticed the agents exchanging expressions of surprise, wide-eyed despite their years of experience with the bizarre and horrific.

"We have not definitively identified the provenance of this technology, but our consultants suspect that research on cranially conjoined twins likely served as one source of information for its development." Noticing expressions of perplexity, Lauren turned the floor back to Palam.

"Several sets of conjoined twins whose brains were partially fused have been closely studied over the course of the last thirty years. The pairs had mostly distinct brains, but they shared enough tissue that separating them created so great a risk of death that their parents, and later they, opted against it.

"The clinical observations of these people make fascinating reading if you can persevere through dry academic formatting and language. Observers found that twins whose brains were linked via their thalami experienced each other's physical sensations on some level and appeared to be cognitively linked.

"For example, when one is blindfolded and the other receives visual stimulation, the blindfolded one shows activity in her visual cortex. Children joined in this way frequently lapse into speaking in unison. They usually both say I when speaking about either's experience and rarely say we. One child can view a program on macrovision and the other will laugh at the funny parts. They will get up silently and walk across the room so that one can retrieve a cup of water and hand it to the other to drink.

"As these children grow up, their brains develop a greater ability to screen out each other's input. Consequently, by the time they are old enough to describe their subjective experiences, they are not consciously sharing sensation and thought in the same way as the objective data suggested when they were children.

"Nevertheless, studies showed that when one conjoined twin was kept distracted and the other silently read test material such as pairings of numbers and images, the other twin could identify the pairings at a higher level of success than if neither of them were shown the pairings in advance. On some level, the information was being transferred, even if they weren't aware.

"Other experiments suggested that sensory data also continued to be shared, though beneath the level of conscious awareness. Interestingly, the twins often reported overlapping or interrelated dreams, even into adulthood."

Lauren surveyed the room, pleased that Dr. Palam had her colleagues' full attention.

"How interesting," said James in a tone that indicated otherwise. "How does this connect to your cases?"

Lauren ignored James and invited Palam to continue.

"Our current hypothesis is that the QFRI-mediated and enhanced interfaces are modeled on data from the conjoined-twins studies, and they create a virtual thalamic bridge," said Palam. "We believe that connecting the participants' thalami enables them to mesh their conscious minds and, while still being two people, experience a shared perceived reality much as conjoined twins do naturally."

"If the neural scans are too complex to decipher—as complex as the brain, which we crudely understand—how can technology exist to create such a sophisticated link?" asked the chief.

"That's what we wanted to know," said Lauren, nodding back to Dr. Palam.

"We think the link allows the quantum neural maps of the participants' minds to interpenetrate through the interface. To be more specific, each brain can apprehend the QFRI projection of both brains through the link," he replied.

"How?" asked James, interested despite himself.

"We don't know," admitted Palam, "but that doesn't mean it isn't happening. Think of it as a computer taking a high-resolution image of a masterpiece painting. It may analyze it in terms of shading and shape and certain visual criteria like brush style and texture and maybe even identify the artist. What it can't do is explain the effect the image has on a human being who sees it. It can transmit the data, the person can receive it and be moved by the artistic brilliance of the piece and its creator, yet we can't describe why or how.

"Or consider an analog recording of a symphony," he continued. "Vibrations from instruments disturb air molecules to produce sound waves. They travel through the air and vibrate a membrane attached to a magnet and cause an electromagnetic pattern in a coil known as a microphone. The electrical signals are attached to a device that, when stimulated, carves grooves into vinyl, or makes a pattern on a magnetic medium.

"When played back, those grooves or magnetic patterns vibrate a needle or affect a magnetic head. A device turns that vibration or pattern into an electrical signal, which affects a magnet that vibrates a membrane known as a speaker.

"This vibrates air molecules, and those vibrations travel through the air as wave patterns that strike the listener's eardrum and move tiny bones on the other side that stimulate nerve receptors. Those send neuroelectric signals to the listener's brain, which interprets them as sound. The brain understands sounds as fitting together into a pattern we call music.

"Let's say a great master composed the symphony, a renowned orchestra performed it, the recording and playback equipment are high quality, and the listener has good hearing and appreciates classical music. The listener will likely have a complex experience upon receiving this auditory data. He or she may be moved by the beauty of the music, impressed by the skill of the performance, awed by the genius of the composer, and so on."

"No theory of music intermediated between the vibration of the instruments and the experience of the listener," observed Renée.

"Exactly," said Palam. "No theory of music. No theory of sound or electromagnetism. There was an analogical chain of connections between the creation of the music and the listener's experience of it. It's as though pipes were connected between the violins and the listener's brain. The mind apprehended them as music through whatever that particular mind associates with such patterns of sound.

"Or think of radio. Complex sound was transmitted wirelessly via patterns in radio waves, received, and converted into sound again long before we had a comprehensive theory of sonic vibrations, electromagnetism, or the perception of sound to explain it. The transmission occurred through an analogical medium or interface.

"We think the QFRI interface, though geometrically more complex than the perception of analogically transmitted sensory stimuli, works according to similar principles.

"The QFRI interface uses a high-resolution, broad-spectrum Micromedium channel to create a quantum field interface that two minds can detect via the neural nodes attached to each head. It broadcasts the quantum configuration of each brain into the interface and allows each mind to experience both fields directly."

"Like a radio connection between their brains," said Renée. "A direct link."

"A quantum field connection actually, but yes," said Palam, "a direct link. As with conjoined twins, we think the brains of both participants adjust to accommodate both sets of input. At first, it is probably confusing. It may be that the shared fantasy and the use of the QFRI recording of the abuse, which is also fed into the interface and boosted, helps the minds align so they believe they are having a shared perception. Almost a shared mind but not quite. They are still partially aware of being two people, but in the coordinated pursuit of the fantasy scenario, they align sufficiently to build off each other's and the external stimulant's input. It is as though their minds have interpenetrated each other, together experiencing the intensified content of the QFRI-enhanced recording. From our informants' descriptions, the participants build the shared perception to peak intensity together. This probably follows a standard neural pattern of addictive behavior—hyperstimulation of pleasure and reward centers in both brains—leaving them neurally depleted and hungry for more.

"We also suspect that the connection involves an element of quantum entanglement, that their minds become interlinked at the quantum level. But we don't understand what part that plays or the potential implications."

James said, "So we have two sick fucks addicted to linking minds through a neural interface and getting off on an artificially intensified abuse scenario. I ask you again, isn't this already covered by the statutes prohibiting videos of Vulnerable abuse?"

Lauren and Melissa glanced at one another through their peripheral vision. "Well, James," began Lauren with exaggerated patience, "as I said, our informants tell us that at least some of the virtual abuse scenarios are recordings of actual violence. Further, we're told those recordings are being made with QFRI sensors that collect impressions of both the actual Aggressor's rush and the actual Vulnerable's fear and pain. Our two hypothetical chatroom buddies are the market for these illegal recordings, whether they pay for them or not. This creates an incentive for production of more such recordings, and ones of greater intensity. Also, the Vulnerables whose abuse is recorded are forced to live with the knowledge that their abuse is being repeatedly used by Aggressors for illicit consumption."

"But that's true of all videos of Vulnerable abuse," James persisted.

"We think this is worse. The QFRI intensification makes this form of sharing particularly addictive. We also suspect it harms the participants by desensitizing them to the suffering of others and promoting the development or amplification of baseline Aggressive propensities and maybe behavior. As I said before, we don't understand this technology well enough yet to know all the ways it might harm the depicted Vulnerables or the participants."

"How could it harm the Vulnerables in ways that are not already prohibited by the laws against videos of Vulnerable abuse?" asked James.

Lauren turned to the chief, who had been briefed on all aspects of her investigation. He signaled his permission to proceed.

"We don't have a definitive answer to that, but the physicists and neuroscientists we've consulted have speculated that the phenomenon may have a feedback effect on the victim."

"Meaning?" asked James, his interest piqued.

"The perps' minds may affect the victims remotely."

"How?" Renée asked.

"Dr. Palam and his associates think that everyone whose minds contribute to the shared experience, including the people in the recording, may become entangled on the quantum level, such that the experience flows in all directions.

Probably not consciously, but under the surface. The perpetrators may unwittingly intrude themselves into subregions of the victims' minds."

"Repeating the incidents of abuse?" said Renée.

"Inflicting new acts of abuse, actually," replied Lauren, "but yes, by consuming the recording of the original act through a medium that may further harm the victim."

"In other words, they're proxy-mindfucking the victim's subconscious?" said James.

"To put it crudely," said Lauren.

"Sounds like a crude act," said James. "Why sugarcoat it?"

Lauren responded with a quick shrug.

"What are the effects?" asked Renée.

"We have yet to examine a victim," said Lauren. "The neuropsychs think it could manifest as post-traumatic stress disorder. Nightmares, depression, panic attacks, disproportionate reactions to stimuli, disrupted relationships. Who knows?"

James thought for a beat. "If the victims are affected in this manner, what would happen to an agent who tried to intervene undercover?"

Lauren was quiet a moment. "We don't know."

"That's reassuring," said Renée.

"Unless there are more questions for Dr. Palam, why don't we let him get on with his research," said Chief Mills. Thanks were extended and the screen went dark.

"OK," said the chief, "tell us about your other cases."

Lauren turned to Melissa, who had to shift from absorption in the dynamics around her to realizing she had the floor.

"There are multiple investigations with a possible nexus to the lead case and the phenomena Lauren and Dr. Palam have summarized," Melissa began. "First, we have a lead on a possible producer of the recordings. Second, we have a lead on an Aggressor who appears in a recording that is circulating."

"How can you know that if your agents haven't formed a neural link?" asked Renée.

"We are relying on a description by two informants and information gleaned by one of our agents in a chatroom session. The final lead involves Polytronics Inc., a tech company we think may be manufacturing some of the components."

"Should that technology be illegal?" asked James, returning to the challenge he had begun earlier. "I don't see how Dr. Palam's speculations about possible subatomic feedback constitutes a new offense. Where is the crime here, other than the video itself, which is already illegal and aggressively prosecuted? Are you suggesting that this nascent field of neural interfacing is criminally punishable?" he prodded. "Because if you are, you're headed for a big fight. Think of the Micromedium gaming industry. Do you honestly believe you can convince the delegates or a court to outlaw a technology with that kind of economic potential?"

He waited to see whether anyone else seconded his concerns. Seeing he still had the floor, he continued, "This sounds like a new frontier in science, computer technology. Hell, even consciousness. Identity! What is the illegal part of what you describe, other than the content, which is already prohibited?"

"Our legal counsel is preparing a report for our liaison to the Delegates Intelligence Committee," interposed the chief. "We believe new legislation will be necessary to adequately define the offense at issue here and provide the means for prosecuting and punishing it. The Office of Legal Counsel is requesting input from our department. The question is how to package it so that we can get a statutory basis to proceed. The floor is open. James? No one believes you don't see a crime here. You've outlined the problem. Our current understanding of the injury is too intangible to sell. What's the solution?"

Soaking up the ego stroke, James languidly stretched his arms and pretended to yawn. Lauren stared at him without expression. "Well?"

"You two are obviously way ahead of me on this," he began.

Lauren resisted the urge to roll her eyes.

"The way to pitch it is this: The crime involves theft of the Vulnerables' experience, the replication of the Aggressors' abusive behavior, and the simultaneous virtual perpetration of the same offense and consumption of emotional energy stolen from the Vulnerables. The neurally connected junkies are part of the crime because they are feeding on the neural energy of the victims and perpetrators. These recordings are more than images. They contain part of the consciousness, the *being* of the victims and the perps, even if nothing is being transmitted back to the victims at all."

"Yes," agreed Lauren. The other agents signaled accord. "The neurally connected junkies, as you call them, are feeding like vampires off the victimized Vulnerables. They are consuming vivid neural impressions, albeit indirectly and enhanced, but actual neural impressions, from the victims. That needs to be defined as illegal and stopped."

"If something worse is happening at the same time," chimed in Melissa, "we'll be stopping that too until we learn how to track and measure it."

"Exactly," replied James with a wink.

Lauren darted a glance at Melissa and thought she detected a smile. She couldn't fathom Melissa's apparent fondness for James. Melissa had once told her James possessed layers of potential she doubted even he had noticed yet.

"Do you have any idea how many people have thought that?" Lauren had asked. "It's part of his trap. Can't you see that?"

"I'm talking about something deeper than that, the place he tries to hide when he deploys it," Melissa had replied. Lauren didn't know what that meant and didn't want to.

"All right," said the chief. "James, Lauren, and Melissa, write up your thoughts on the legislative aspects. Anyone who wants to weigh in, direct your input to one of them. I insist you exercise great caution in your investigations. We could try to hinge charges on the existing laws prohibiting videos of Vulnerable abuse, but I agree with James that this would be politically reckless. Proceeding half-cocked could prevent progress if it precipitated a well-coordinated or potent pushback by industry and Citizen activists. First we secure the clearly defined statutory authority. Then we start tearing this ugly web apart."

4

HOME FROM THE PUB AFTER a stop at the grocer, Leo struggled with a stack of files, bags of groceries, and a fistful of mail as he keyed his way through to the entry hall of his apartment. A bag of trash he had stashed by the door but failed to take out awaited him, as did dust balls twirling on the floor in the front door's wake.

Franz—Leo's ancient, devoted, and, to hear Leo tell it, brilliant cat—rubbed against his legs, beginning the nightly campaign for dinner and, if luck shined like most nights, a few bonus treats. Leo flipped on a dim hallway light and murmured loving inanities as he scanned the letters for anything exciting or threatening, eventually culling out two pieces of work-related correspondence and what looked like a card from his friend Jeaneane. He dumped his cargo on the kitchen table and headed for the answering machine, which years of such nightly rituals had relegated to the counter below the cabinet where he stashed the cat food.

Four messages awaited his attention. Hitting play too quickly to consider whether he wanted to listen to them, he opened the cabinet and selected a can of stinky fish for Franz as the first recording began.

"Advocate Baksh, this is Rebekah Frith, Adjudicator Hutchinson's clerk in District Four. I am calling to advise you that the reclassification review hearing for Petitioner Jeffrey Beeson has been rescheduled for Thursday, May 5 at 2:00 p.m. due to a conflict with another matter. Please confirm that you have received this notice."

"Great," said Leo, juggling appointments in his mind to accommodate this shift and cringing as he realized he must have put his home number on the pleadings in Beeson's case. He made a note to check the greeting on his answering machine, praying it wasn't too unprofessional.

The second message was from a travel agent Leo could neither bring himself to place reservations with nor cut loose because he needed the perennial hope of escape.

He stopped halfway through spooning food into Franz's bowl as the third message, this one from Jeb, Leo's ex, started playing. Leo considered deleting it, but the impulse never prevailed. Franz impatiently ducked under the spoon to eat as Leo tensed to listen.

"Hi, Leo. Sorry to intrude but I need to pick up the rest of my things. I think we should set some ground rules about future communication and contact, if we're going to have any."

"Good idea" said Leo to the unhearing machine, "so why the hell are you calling?"

"I hope you're OK," the message continued. There was a long pause. "Bye." Leo shook his head and hit delete.

The decision was mutual. Leo agreed to it because Jeb had already imposed unilateral decisions—the most significant being that he was free to cavort with others and lie about it—that made staying with him intolerable. Once Leo moved past the initial recriminations, he acknowledged that Jeb's decisions did not come out of nowhere. Leo's compulsive but ambivalent absorption in his work and associated ambient domestic chaos took an emotional toll that had pushed Jeb away for years. Then again, Jeb was unhelpful to such an extent on the home front that Leo often felt sabotaged.

He awoke from this well-worn rumination to the metal handle bouncing between his fingers as Franz licked fish oil off the spoon, hinting he was ready for the remainder of the can.

"Sorry, baby," said Leo, scooping the rest of the aromatic slop into Franz's bowl as the final message played.

"Hi," breathed the selfsame Jeaneane, whose card Leo eyed with interest but had yet to open. "I was wondering if you'd like to be my date tomorrow night for the opera. Giuseppe was supposed to take me but his mother dropped in unannounced and trashed our plans for a change." Leo saw her *talk-to-the-hand* gesture in his mind's eye. "Apparently her company is so scintillating that she is not governed by ordinary bounds of common courtesy." A mock gasp. "Did I say that?"

Leo smiled.

"Anyway," she continued, "the tickets are for great seats. I haven't been to the opera in an age, but it would be fun to go with you. I haven't had any real time with you in weeks. Please say yes. Maybe we could do dinner and drinks. And then I could move in," she concluded with a playful giggle. "Just kidding, handsome. Call me."

Not a fan of opera but most decidedly a fan of time with Jeaneane and dressing to the nines on rare occasion, Leo mentally accepted this unexpected invitation. His thoughts still on Jeaneane, he tore open the card.

> Hiya. I want you to know that you are brave, brilliant, loving, and gentle, and your friendship is a priceless treasure to my heart. You've been in a funk for too long and it's time to move on. I know some of it, but I sense more than sorrow over Jeb is troubling you. I'm here. xxoo, Jeaneane.

Leo and Jeaneane met at an advocate's office where both had cut their teeth after attaining licensure upon completion of their studies. Brief conversations around the copy machine grew into full-blown friendship upon discovering they shared a desperate unhappiness at the firm and a common faith that life should be better than the fate the battle-scarred veterans running the place had chosen and inflicted. Both dreamed of a career that left room for meaningful relationships and creative pursuits. Unfortunately, such considerations were viewed as genteel self-indulgences in the culture of the firm, so it became clear that a change of employment would be necessary if Leo and Jeaneane were to pursue the balanced lives they envisioned.

Their friendship also hung upon girders of mutual emotional recognition borne of childhoods lived without the privileges of Citizenship. They grew to trust one another, to share their tender hopes and fears, to provide loving environments to each other's heartbreaks, and to encourage each other in the quest and hope for a balanced life.

Leo was the first to leave. His performance had been exemplary and he was well liked, even loved, by his colleagues and managers. His departure was greeted with regret and disappointment but not anger, and he received a warm send-off as he took his leave and tried to set up his own practice.

Jeaneane stuck with the firm for another two years, futilely trying to negotiate terms of engagement that left room for other aspects of life she considered essential. Leo relied on her for guidance as he stepped out on his solo professional path, availing himself of materials and collective knowledge she had access to due to her membership in a large, mature practice.

At the same time, Jeaneane leaned heavily on Leo for emotional support and personal counsel as she trembled under the weight of an overly burdensome professional life. Usually this was fine, though he sometimes wondered whether she would have an easier time were she a tick less self-focused, but he didn't know how to say it without jeopardizing their friendship. Others who had braved the subject made no headway, earning scars and banishment for the effort. Unless he discovered an effective approach, Leo decided to endure Jeaneane's sometimes troubling propensity to forget that other people had needs of their own.

As she struggled between her desire to leave the firm and her simultaneous craving for approval from its authority figures, he often wanted to shake her and scream "They can't fix you!" but he would realize he couldn't fix her either—or himself for that matter—and the best gift he could offer was a nonjudgmental ear.

Eventually it became unavoidably clear that, though her colleagues loved Jeaneane, the culture of the firm was not resilient enough to accommodate her demands.

So she left. Not as Leo had, to brave a solo practice, but for an arms-length contractual arrangement with another firm. The relationship was not a happy one, but it afforded Jeaneane enough control over her life and limitations on work that she maintained, if not ideal employment, at least a tremulous peace with her new colleagues.

As the years progressed, they referred work back and forth or helped each other when one or the other hit a thin patch or was caught in a bind. More often than not, Jeaneane called upon Leo for help because Leo usually needed the income and possessed different skills. Jeaneane was gifted in rainmaking, fearless confrontation with even the most intimidating adversaries, and spectacular courtroom theatrics, whereas Leo possessed sharper research skills, greater knowledge of the law and current political developments, and superior talent for written advocacy. They made a great team and often discussed forming a partnership, but their respective emotional needs kept him working alone and her attached to a larger organizational structure. They didn't want to ruin their friendship by becoming business partners.

Still full from the snacks he devoured at the pub and nauseated from the beer, Leo put away the groceries without interest in a formal dinner and ditched his work mail for the relaxing comfort of a shower.

Clean and grounded, he climbed into bed and dialed Jeaneane's number. Voice mail. *Of course.* "Hi," said Leo as he straightened out the bed clothes and moved aside coffee cups and papers so he could check the alarm clock. "I'm home. Got your voicemail and lovely card. Thank you. I can't tell you how right on time they were. As to your invitation, my answer is an unequivocal yes"—he sang in a faux operatic falsetto—"Let me know when the show starts and let's meet for dinner first. How about something spicy? Call me. Smooches."

Leo turned out the light and drifted off into an exhausted sleep.

For several hours after her initial meeting with Advocate Baksh, Anna Dao vacillated between barely acknowledged hope and pangs of fear she had set in motion events that would make her life unlivable.

She replayed the conversation in her mind until she had probably overwritten the memory beyond accurate recall.

In none of her compulsive revisitations of the exchange, however, did she turn up any indication that he was being deceptive or harboring a malicious agenda. His disclosure of having been a Vulnerable until he was twenty-five was surprising and interesting. Anna sensed he was perceptive and sensitive. *Also depressed*, she thought. She suspected he was adept at keeping that deep, dark undercurrent of anxiety below the surface of his own awareness. She made a mental note to investigate further.

After hours of circular rumination, she resolved to wrench her focus from deciding whether she could trust the advocate to thinking about how they could most wisely direct their joint efforts.

According to reviews she found on the Micromedium, he came highly recommended. Despite the shoddy office accommodations, she thought with a chuckle, remembering patches of peeling paint and sagging plaster. He was reputed to be skilled and zealous, both in cases invoking legal protections and public resources for Vulnerables, and in fighting for expansion of the definition of Citizenship through litigation and lobbying for legislative changes.

Which way should they go? Change the system? Or let it change her?

Anna chewed on her lip as she thought about the prospect of "guided development" by the government. All Vulnerables were entitled to government protection. They were also given publicly funded therapy and education designed to foster eligibility for Citizenship, but that option made her nervous. The privileges of Citizenship would be attractive to any but the most passive and contentedly dependent of Vulnerables, which Anna certainly was not. Yet, to pursue Citizenship as currently defined would entrust her fate to reprogrammers whose motives and technologies she distrusted.

She didn't tell Leo this but she had tried therapy when she was younger and it went horribly wrong, leaving scarred memories of a device forcibly strapped to her head, blasting something dark and horrible into her mind.

"No!" she commanded herself. She shook her head to banish the thought.

Stories also circulated about Vulnerables who went for reprogramming and found themselves not among the ranks of Citizens but reclassified as Aggressives, a worse form of exclusion than a lifetime coddled and protected, even if deprived, as a Vulnerable.

These were the loci of Anna's reluctance. She knew of few people like herself. A Vulnerable by birth, perceptive and sensitive bordering on psychic, and bereft of filters to protect herself from experiencing others' suffering and dysfunction. Also, an incendiary temper and sometimes violent if she felt threatened. *Occasionally overtly cruel if we're being honest with ourselves*, she thought. None of that should be a surprise given what she'd been through, but the law didn't grapple well with contradictions.

Her bed sheets feeling like a straitjacket, Anna tried to imagine surviving among the Aggressives. "Hell no," she thought aloud. To be exposed to illness and brutality with her level of sensitivity and volatility would almost certainly spell disaster.

But she wasn't faring well as a Vulnerable either. Her "condition" of extreme hypersensitivity was not formally recognized as an axis of Vulnerability, so she had few tools to protect herself from the intrusions of others.

There were protests demanding legal protection of sensitive types from subtle forms of Aggression, as well as activists trying to force the doors to

Citizenship open wider. Anna, with her unusual characteristics, could serve as a test case for either agenda.

She mentally ticked off three possible paths.

One option was to seek protection for a new form of Vulnerability. She could invoke accommodations that would insulate her from the chaotic and aggressive tendencies of others. She was already protected from physical jeopardy. If she could enshrine her form of sensitivity as a protected class feature, she could construct a safer and less painful life for herself, and at government expense. "Comfortable and safe," she said to the darkness. "And suffocating."

If instead they fought to modify the criteria for Citizenship, they'd have to persuade the Department of Adjudication, the Board of Classification, and maybe even the Council of Delegates that her sensitivity was counter-weighed by temperate Aggressive features to render her fit for Citizenship, even though the criteria would have to be expanded in both directions to accommodate her and people like her.

There would be resistance to this for countless reasons, including conservatives' fears that allowing an increased range of Vulnerable and Aggressive traits would destabilize the Citizenry. "Conflict with the Cleagues," she spat, using a common epithet for members of the conservative Citizens Action League.

Her last option was to undergo "guided development" toward fitness for existing standards of Citizenship, so she could avoid terrifying legal and political fights, but she might surrender to mutilating intrusions into her mind and heart. "Butchers," she muttered.

All three paths risked exposure of her explosive side, which could raise questions of whether she was properly classified as a Vulnerable in the first place and gain her not Citizenship but reclassification as an Aggressive. "Suicide," she promised herself, "and maybe take a few others with me."

Either path requiring legal changes would put her in the crossfire of the social movements. She was after a habitable life, not notoriety or fame, though helping beat back the Cleagues was a seductive consideration, she mused with a snigger.

Reprogramming was the path of least resistance, but also the one Anna most feared. *This must have been the option Advocate Baksh chose*, she thought. Having selected that route for himself, would he have the steel to help her if she opted for a confrontational course? She untangled herself from the sheets and returned to cycling through the options.

Anna wrestled with these thoughts until she drifted into a fitful sleep, where her unsettled musings gave way to troubled dreams of winding hallways and heavy bands of metal wrapped around her head. "You!" she awoke screaming in the night, but there was no one to comfort her. She gulped down a couple aspirin and a sleeping pill. "Leave me be," she pleaded to the darkness, then willed herself back to sleep.

5

As Leo and Anna slept, a hacker across town assembled equipment in a cluttered basement illegally wired for electricity and Micromedium access, placed a wired array of QFRI nodes around the crown of his skull, and tested the interface with a few commands. Satisfied that it was functioning, he submitted the day's passcode to enter a well-encrypted virtual meeting place and confer with associates he knew only through fictitious monikers.

A roster appeared on the left side of his screen:

Infiltr8org

Hackizen

Aggresserable

Sleeperagent

Subterraneum

This ad hoc group had parleyed for several months. At first they stuck to subversive political banter. Once they had established a rapport and trust, they coordinated their technical skills to make incursions into government and private sector infrastructure.

Liam, known to his virtual compatriots as Infiltr8org, was not affiliated with any social movement in his visible life. On the sly, he contributed his formidable skills, resources, and connections to political efforts he deemed worthy.

He opened the meeting with the group's partially tongue-in-virtual-cheek mantra:

Infiltr8org: The classification system is fraudulent and must be destroyed.

This anarchist sentiment appealed to all of them, though they had deep differences over methodology and long-term objectives. Some were convinced that only direct action, including violent strikes against the legal and political structure's weak points, could awaken the Citizenry from its hallucination of stability and trigger fundamental change.

In Liam's view, the more radical path was to lay bare the government's lies and reveal the truth of it: The classification system relied on perpetuation of the Aggressive–Vulnerable dichotomy, and it prized the Aggressive principle above all other values, even as it pretended to condemn it.

He was certain the system would collapse under the weight of its own hypocrisy. It just needed an array of social movements strong and durable enough to push the old order over the threshold into full breakdown. To do that, they needed information.

Liam believed violence was counterproductive. Not only would it undercut their authority to critique the Aggression inherent in the existing structure, what good was destroying infrastructure and scaring Citizens? Who would this inspire to build the next chapter of history, and where would they live if the cities were ruined?

Each of the virtual meeting participants was experienced in the old electrode sensor interfaces, but had graduated to QFRI devices once several shipments of the components were intercepted and distributed to safe spots for anonymous collection.

These were basic interfaces, limited to transmitting commands into Micromedium terminals. Liam and the others knew people were using more elaborate QFRI nodal arrays to make direct neural links between their minds, but they viewed this as madness. No one in this group was interested in revealing more thoughts than he or she chose to disclose, so they stuck to thinking text onto a shared page. The result was something between chat and real conversation, cloaked in anonymity.

It was well known in the hacker community that people were using Elidrine to enhance their use of the QFRI arrays. But Liam and the others had seen what Elidrine could do to a person, so it was forbidden in this virtual meeting place.

Liam mentally issued another text entry into the meeting:

Infiltr8org: I have a new contest for you.

The list of room occupants shifted to active mode as their cyber ears perked.

Because they respected each other's anonymity, no one asked why Liam seemed to have an unlimited supply of funds. Besides, he doled out rewards for jobs well done.

Unbeknownst to them, Liam was the scion of a Citizen family that enjoyed a stunning accumulation of wealth, amassed through ownership of companies engaged in the lucrative business of imprisoning Aggressives and institutionalizing Vulnerables under government contract.

He found the double irony amusing. The private prison industry was funding subversive activity geared toward toppling the system it depended on for its existence and profitability, and a ragtag group of snot-nosed, self-styled anarchists were steadily enriching themselves through the ill-gotten profits of the oppressive bastion they claimed to revile.

He suspected his fellow meeting participants would not share his amusement, so he kept this little detail to himself.

> **Infiltr8org:** This is a big one.

Big indeed, even for these would-be revolutionaries. Reports kept surfacing that the Department of International Intelligence (DII), the global-scale cousin of the Department of Domestic Intelligence (DDI), was subjecting terror suspects overseas to sophisticated forms of torture. The government did its best to suppress and discredit all such claims, but they continued to leak by way of the Macromedium and even more strongly the Micromedium.

What more damning indictment of the system's hypocrisy could there be than the use of torture by a government whose authority rested on its purported triumph over unbridled Aggression?

> **Sleeperagent:** Let's hear it.

> **Infiltr8org:** I want access to the DII Micromedium hub.

> **Hackizen:** Funny.

> **Subterraneum:** Anything else? Keys to the government treasury and access codes to the nuclear stockpile?

(Laughs all around)

> **Infiltr8org:** We dance around it, but let's get real. That's the weakest point in the whole façade.

> **Subterraneum:** Weak point my ass. More like the steel girded, nuclear armed, hack-proof encrypted fucking fortress the entire façade is tacked on.

> **Infiltr8org:** Exactly.

> **Aggresserable:** Impossible.

> **Hackizen:** Crazy.

> **Infiltr8org:** You disappoint me.

(Silence)

> **Sleeperagent:** I suppose you would give the info to a moderate group. Which one? Respect? Spectrum? Pro'gression?

Respect was a coalition of political and social service groups seeking to have a more elastic definition of sensitivity recognized as a Vulnerable trait and protected at law, though it would still preclude Citizenship.

A more ambitious group called Spectrum was fighting for expansion of the criteria for Citizenship. They sought inclusion of sensitive personalities encompassing a wide range of Vulnerable traits, recontextualized into a broader concept of Vulnerable–Aggressive balance.

Pro'gression was an organization of moderate Aggressives who also sought expansion of the criteria for Citizenship, but from the other end of the classification system.

Even though they had overlapping goals, Spectrum usually tried to distance itself from Pro'gression because Vulnerable requests for recognition or protection were more palatable to the mainstream than Aggressive complaints about unjust restrictions or oppressive prison conditions. This did not endear Spectrum to the more radical Aggressive activists, and Liam believed it weakened both movements. He suspected the rift could be overcome with the right bait.

The socially conservative Citizens Action League opposed all three movements.

Infiltr8org: It will depend on what we find and what they're willing to do with it.

Hackizen: The moderates wouldn't know what to do with that kind of information. Give it to someone who will use it.

Infiltr8org: In other words, give it to Restruct.

Hackizen: Yep.

Restruct was a loose-knit group of Aggressives without a uniform political agenda other than a mission to tear down the Classification scheme. Some who claimed affiliation with Restruct had a habit of blowing up crowded Citizens' venues and attacking energy and Micromedium bottlenecks, so they were regarded as extremists.

Infiltr8org: Terrorism is not the answer. It destroys everything, including the path forward.

Hackizen: Don't be naïve. The crazy acts of a few psychos do not make Restruct a "terrorist organization." The reason Restruct is equated with those whack jobs is because the Cleagues use fear to discredit any movement they view as a genuine threat.

Sleeperagent: Not all of us think they're psychos.

Sleeperagent tended in a more radical direction than the others, or at least did so more openly. Usually, they ignored these comments.

Aggresserable: You underestimate the potential influence of the moderates, Hack. They have connections to key players in the government, not to mention the faith communities.

Hackizen: All the more reason they can't be trusted. The religionists construct prisons of the mind that make the real ones seem natural. Why do you think the Cleagues are in bed with the Congregation of the Way?

Aggresserable: Religion is a battleground of perception like any other and you are a fool if you neglect it. We need pushback on that front too, and the moderates are mature enough to realize it.

Hackizen: Let us pray.

Aggresserable: Don't be a child.

Hackizen: Why don't you pull your head out of your ass and see some real light?

Infiltr8org: Knock it off!

Hackizen: You can't possibly expect us to take the risk of compromising the DII hub if all you're going to do is waste what we find by giving it to the moderates. You might as well give it to the Cleagues and be done with it.

Infiltr8org: Perhaps, but when the public hears "Restruct," it hears "destruct" and that produces fear and retrenchment.

Hackizen: What I hear is "restructure" or "reconstruct." That's what we need to do and we won't get there by risking our lives to funnel crucial info to people too dazed by irrelevant arguments over God to use it.

Aggresserable: Do you want to tear everything down, Hackizen, or build something new?

Hackizen: I want to do something that has an impact, not something that pretends to.

Infiltr8org: You know damn well that's true for all of us. The question is how to destabilize the classification system in a way that yields something better. Revealing that the government simultaneously condemns aggression and inflicts torture could open people's eyes. What bigger contradiction is there?

Respect, Spectrum, Pro'gression, who cares, if the information gets out?

Hackizen: They'll just get assimilated.

Infiltr8org: Not if they're armed with serious enough details about the DII. That would be unprecedented. It could change everything.

Hackizen: Maybe. But the chances of that don't justify the risk of breaching the DII hub.

Sleeperagent: On the other hand, if we go in, you can't control what we do with the data, can you?

Liam anticipated this.

Infiltr8org: You won't be going in. You find me a way to breach the barrier. I will go in alone.

Hackizen: How convenient.

Infiltr8org: We disagree about how the info should be used and you're worried about the risk. The fewer of us who penetrate the hub, the better for all of us. I'm paying you to find the doorway and I'm undertaking the risk to gather the data. That gives me the privilege of controlling dissemination. Take it or leave it.

Hackizen: We could do it without you.

Infiltr8org: Be my guest. I'm sure someone else will happily take the prize.

Liam didn't like playing that card but he wanted to end the political argument and lock in the mission.

Sleeperagent: How much? To get you in the hub?

Infiltr8org: One million credits.

(Long pause)

One million credits, wisely invested, could amount to independent wealth, leaving the victor free to pursue activism and techno play without the risky financial raids that were necessary when one did not maintain ordinary employment.

Subterraneum: We will have to work together. It is risky.

Hackizen: Risky? It's psychotic. We could all end up in prison. Or worse.

Infiltr8org: That's true. It's also precisely why this hack is so important. People are suffering at the hands of this branch of our government, yet our public continues to believe that we live to abolish Aggression.

If you work together, the purse will be 1.5 million credits, shared among the winning team.

That should stimulate some healthy competition, Liam thought with a smirk. Greed will drive them to work on their own until they figure out it's too difficult or too dangerous, then they'll combine the fruit of their efforts. Once that happens, it will be a matter of days.

Knowing his fellow hackers were buzzing with thoughts about how to approach the problem, Liam bade them farewell.

Infiltr8org: We've been hooked up too long. I need to trash this spot and clear out. Watch your backs and sweep your prints, everyone.

He disconnected from the interface and destroyed all evidence he had been in the abandoned basement that served as his uplink for this dangerous meeting.

6

As Leo opened his eyes, the dread was already upon him, grabbing hold before he crested into consciousness. It was like this every day.

His mind sifted up nuggets of hypothetical danger. His eyes darted over imperfections in his bedroom ceiling as he constructed lists that bled into one another and looped back upon themselves, a Möbius strip of obligations and peril. Irrational, but the fear was so palpable it didn't matter.

"It's Saturday, Leo," he said aloud after several minutes of this daily compulsion. A wave of relief bathed his neurons. The demons holding his mind's eye receded into the background, and he shifted into awareness of his physical surroundings.

Leo's eyes rolled down from the ceiling to his own chest, where he discovered Franz regarding him through two slits. The cat was sprawled across Leo's midsection, one foreleg stretched languorously across his chest and his chin plastered against Leo's sternum.

"Morning," croaked Leo. Franz acknowledged the signs of life with a great yawn, his lips peeling back to reveal chipped teeth, a raspy tongue contracted into the shape of a wave, and a puff of oceanic stink.

"Pew," said Leo, as Franz swallowed twice and settled his chin back on Leo's chest. "We should get your teeth cleaned, pal."

Franz stretched a paw onto Leo's mouth. Leo doubted Franz could understand his words, but he was equally sure the cat was telling him to shut up because it was too early for Leo's prattle.

Gently dislodging Franz, Leo threw back the covers. The chilly morning made him want to stay in bed, but the courts and offices were closed, so getting up was worth a few shivers. "Saturday," he said with a stretch.

Franz, gifted with a rich tonal vocabulary, sang out a trilled arpeggio and headed for the edge of the bed. In his seventeenth year, the cat resembled a stuffed animal with the fur rubbed off. He debarked the mattress in the usual manner of his feline seniority by aiming for the floor and sliding down the bedspread on his brittle old claws.

As Leo stood up and threw on a robe, Franz coaxed him with a throaty chirp and turned toward the bedroom door.

"I'm coming," said Leo.

Franz glanced over his shoulder and delivered another bark.

"Yes, baby, time for breakfast."

Franz croaked again, advanced into the hallway, and turned back to be sure Leo was following.

It occurred to Leo that he was being beckoned like a dog to perform his assigned function. He patted himself on the head as he followed Franz into the kitchen and dutifully served up breakfast. They had taken care of each other this way for a decade and a half. Leo did not know how he would handle losing Franz to the inexorable ravages of time, but the critical juncture was approaching.

Leo ground up some coffee and set the pot to brewing, then flipped on his macroaudio set. The Macromedium was being eclipsed by the Micromedium, but Leo wasn't sure this was a good thing and he patronized the old networks and technology.

An ad for an upcoming movie commenced. Strings played in the background as a narrator's voice thundered in deep bass:

"She was a Vulnerable trapped among Aggressives."

A woman's voice erupts in an urgent whisper: "It's too dangerous. They'll kill you if they find out who you are."

The narrator continues, "He was a Citizen cop under cover."

A man growls through clenched teeth: "I'm willing to take that risk to get you out."

The narrator: "In a world where secrets mean survival and trust is for fools, he was her only hope."

"You don't know them like I do. Go while you still can," cries the woman.

"I'm not leaving you behind!" the man retorts in whispered rage.

"To save her he would have to risk everything," the narrator pauses, "and change a civilization."

"For God's sake," said Leo, rolling his eyes. The music shifts to a tone of motion and intrigue as the narrator continues:

"From the maker of *Infliction* comes a story of courage, redemption—"

"Let me guess," Leo said as the soundtrack waned into one mournful violin. "Love."

"—and a passion stronger than fear," the narrator cooed.

Leo cursed as he spun the dial to a news channel and pulled a pile of papers toward him.

He ignored the sports report underway and plowed the papers into piles by level of urgency. Bills would wait. Ad circulars and fliers from the Citizens Action League went into the trash. He organized the week's newspapers in chronological order and set them aside. He shuffled together papers relevant to a project he had undertaken for Jeaneane, then put the two business-related missives from yesterday's mail in front of him and got up to pour a cup of coffee and rinse out Franz's bowl.

Leo started his private practice out of his home and had rented a separate office for the past two years, so he sometimes received professional mail at his home address. This resulted in anxious intrusions into what he was trying to build as his sanctuary away from work. For reasons that fared poorly under rational scrutiny, he had never cleaned up the division between his home and work environments.

Sipping his coffee, Leo braved the first letter, sent from the Board of Classification. His minor trepidation turned out to be unwarranted, as the envelope contained a hearing officer's recommendation that one of Leo's clients be granted reclassification.

Emboldened by that victory, he proceeded to the second letter, which proved less cheerful. A notice from his licensing board ordered him to pay his dues plus the late fee, or his license would be suspended. "Fabulous," he said, tossing it atop the pile of bills.

He cradled the cup of coffee and sorted the papers for Jeaneane's project, a fairly straightforward assignment to research a law at issue in an upcoming hearing and write a discussion for inclusion in her trial brief. He had already printed out legislative materials and academic articles. Today's task was to organize them and write the analysis.

"Piece of cake," he said aloud, and polished off the cup.

The headlines blared on the audio broadcast. "This just in from the capital!" shouted a newscaster, whose unprofessional level of agitation yanked Leo to attention. "There has been a massive explosion at a power grid station in the city's Eastern District."

The broadcast cut to the voice of a breathless emergency worker: "We have hundreds of casualties and we're pulling people out of the rubble around the edges. We can't even penetrate the blaze yet. There's at least four blocks on fire ..." People could be heard crying in the background amidst a blare of crisscrossing sirens.

"Holy shit!" Leo hollered in disbelief. He rushed to the window and saw smoke rising in the distance.

Several government officials were interviewed. Their answers ranged from dismissal of the incident as a natural occurrence to calls for calm as an investigation proceeded.

A random smattering of Citizens was interviewed, and the possibility the government spokespeople had yet to voice was given a name: terrorism. Domestic, that is. Aggressives, of course.

The commentators chewed over the possibilities. Inevitably, the action was associated with the Restruct movement. A couple of analysts challenged everyone to avoid jumping to conclusions but they were shouted down. The segment closed with an announcement that the chief executive was meeting with the Department of Domestic Intelligence heads and would address the public within hours.

The news turned to the economy. Leo poured coffee, half listening to the ongoing broadcast as he powered up his Micromedium terminal and started outlining the document he had promised Jeaneane.

Several hours later, he had a rough draft done and broke to shower and dress. Franz, ensconced in the warmest corner of Leo's couch, squawked at him as he passed. Leo nuzzled his forehead, which earned him a moist nose kiss, a few affectionate yaps, and a rattle of purrs.

When he returned to the kitchen table smelling of soap and dressed in jeans and T-shirt, Leo turned his attention to the news. Chief Executive Belinda Mosgrove had apparently been speaking while Leo showered and was wrapping up her assurances to the public.

Leo supported Mosgrove, who hearkened from the progressive party, though he sometimes thought she hewed excessively in the direction of compromise, which he might have been inclined to forgive had he known the whole story. Mosgrove had inherited an impossible situation and her election had given people a badly needed sense of hope in the institution of her office. Her predecessor, Belford Thorsch, was a brutish populist who had harnessed prejudice against the excluded classes to gain office, then exploited his position to advance the interests of foreign corporate profiteers in whose companies he was invested. Credible evidence indicated that a foreign power where many of the companies were based had manipulated the election that launched Thorsch into office. When the Department of International Intelligence tried to bring these improper influences and associations to light, Thorsch, who was remarkably thin skinned and insecure for a man of his stature, engaged in embarrassing attempts to discredit the intelligence community. This alienated International Intelligence Director Trent Hobson, and triggered a culture of distrust within the agency that persisted beyond Thorsch's administration.

Although Hobson officially reported to the chief executive, tensions with the DII were already strained when Mosgrove assumed office. She made a great show of respect for the intelligence community after she took her oath, and the public clung to the hope that her leadership had mended the schism initiated by her predecessor. Outside the public's eye, however, she and her advisors had grave concerns about the DII leadership, and she strove to build bridges with conservatives in the Council of Delegates due to their potential influence over Hobson and the intelligence apparatus he steered. This often ticked off progressives who had supported her run for office believing they had given her a mandate for forceful battle with the conservatives.

Regardless of any reservations about her politics, Leo was impressed by the rich voice and crisp diction she deployed in times of crisis. Had he been viewing her on macrovision, the effect would have been even more impressive. Mosgrove always cut a commanding presidential figure, her silvering hair a striking contrast to glowing mahogany skin and onyx eyes. Her face was long and angular, and her mature beauty combined with her polished intelligence to convey authority whether one agreed with her or not.

The end of the chief executive's speech and the commentary that followed took pains to avoid accusing Restruct. However, they strongly suggested evidence the explosion was a terrorist act in protest of restrictions placed on non-incarcerated Aggressives. It was further noted that certain Restructors considered this a pressing issue. The public was left to connect the dots.

"Most helpful," said Leo. "Thank you, everyone."

The phone rang and Leo checked his watch, realizing he still did not know when and where he was meeting Jeaneane for the evening festivities. Serendipitously, it was she:

"Hi," she said, elongating the vowel affectionately.

"Hey," Leo responded.

"How are you?"

"Not bad. I just finished a draft of your document."

"Thanks for turning it around so fast. It's a huge help."

"No problem. Truth is, it's right on time. My advocate dues are late and I need the cash."

Slight pause. "You should have said something, I could have loaned it to you." Leo wasn't sure whether he heard a cooling in her voice or was just being self-conscious. Jeaneane's unspoken judgment irked him, given her own deficiencies she didn't realize everyone saw. He knew how hard she could be on herself, though, and who was he to call her out?

"I appreciate that," he said. "But it's better this way. I have enough debts."

"I understand that," she said, "but your dues are important and aren't the late fees outrageous?"

"Yeah. Anyway, the extra work is definitely a help."

"Next time speak up," she scolded. "I know you're good for it."

Leo eyed the pile of bills. "Thanks."

"How about that new fusion place down on Fifth Street? It kicks ass."

Leo remembered seeing an ad for the place. "Sounds great. What time?"

"Meet me there at 6:30."

"Done."

"Bye," she said.

"Wait," said Leo. "What do you think about this explosion business?"

"Explosion?"

"It's all over the news. Power grid station explosion. Mosgrove is all but saying it was Restruct protesting the new restrictions on Aggressives."

"I didn't realize there were new restrictions," she said. Jeaneane did not invest much time in following the news. Leo found this vaguely troubling, but withheld comment.

"New ID requirements, search rules, travel restrictions. It may be a major attack. I can see smoke from my apartment."

"Wow."

"Turn on your audio. It'll cycle over again."

"I don't need that today. It's been a long week. I'll let you fill me in, OK?"

"See you tonight then," Leo said, shaking his head.

They finished the call and Leo spent an hour skimming the week's newspapers. In light of the report that a power station had likely been attacked, the previous week's news seemed ominous: Fierce rhetoric from the government about suspected terror plots. Security force pledges to rigidly enforce the new standards for Aggressives. Article after article about attacks on Vulnerables, breaches of Citizen venues, and prosecution of Aggressives. Articles about political demonstrations organized by Respect, Spectrum, and Pro'gression. A scathing editorial by an unnamed author purporting to speak on behalf of the Citizens Action League.

Leo reached saturation and tossed out the papers.

Later, Franz cuddled him for warmth and love while Leo navigated to a social quadrant on the Micromedium. He seldom put himself out on the Micromedium to meet others these days. Following Jeb's trail of deceit into such venues uncovered his ex-partner's feckless betrayal, divesting the social sites of the allure they'd once held. He had met Jeb in a virtual place, and he later wondered whether that choice had portentous implications he'd ignored to his peril. His inability to answer that query made him wonder why he was dipping a toe back in now.

But dip he did.

He logged into the old site where he'd met Jeb all those years ago. It was now considered passé, but it felt familiar and relatively safe, even if it did puncture his heart. He was used to that. It reminded him he was alive.

He dusted off his old virtual identity and entered a textual greeting:

Asad: Evening, gents.

He received a few friendly verbal slaps on the back from familiar monikers. Clicking around to see who the new people were claiming to be, he stumbled on an individual named "Anaku." After trading jokes and playful fencing, Leo said he had to run because he had a date.

Anaku: What sort of set do you have?

Asad: Set?

Anaku: Headset. Interface. Old school or quantum?

Asad: I'm not sure what that means. I'm using a keyboard.

Anaku: Wow. I didn't know they sold those anymore. Is your terminal steam powered too?

Asad: Funny. It's old equipment but it serves my needs.

Leo told him what kind of work he did. Anaku, who said he was an artist, told Leo he needed new Micromedium interface equipment.

Anaku: Haven't you tried the electrode interfaces? Those were out when you said you were on here before.

Asad: Yeah, but they were more trouble than they were worth. By the time you got it to enter "yes" or "no" correctly, you could have had a whole exchange by keyboard, logged off, gotten laid, and slept for eight hours.

Anaku: True. But the quantum arrays are a whole different world.

Asad: I type fast. Besides, I suspect they're beyond my reach. I represent Vulnerables, not the prison industry. Not shopping for new equipment right now.

Anaku: Artists don't rake it in either, at least not ones whose unparalleled brilliance has yet to be discovered.

Leo smiled.

Anaku: I know a way to get them cheaply.

That struck Leo as odd, though it did arouse his curiosity. He handled it playfully.

Asad: Do I detect the scent of thievery?

Anaku: It's more about getting tools from where they're abundant and unnecessary to where they're scarce and will be used for the greater good.

Asad: I see.

Anaku: I'm serious.

Asad: Maybe you can tell me about it sometime. But not tonight. I'm late.

Anaku: Drop me a hit sometime. Use this:

Anaku sent Leo the coordinates for his Micromedium node.

Asad: Thanks.

Anaku: Will you hit me?

Asad: Don't know yet. I enjoyed talking.

Anaku: Is Asad your real name?

Asad: In a manner of speaking. Is Anaku your real name?

Anaku: It's what I'm called.

Asad: In the real world?

Anaku: This isn't real?

Leo could see the conversation fork into splayed tines from that interesting juncture, but he didn't have time for the options:

Asad: Have a good night.

Anaku: You too.

Leo shut down his Micromedium terminal, scratched Franz, who dug his claws into Leo's leg in pleasure, then dressed for his night out with Jeaneane.

7

RAIN PATTERED ON THE SIDEWALK, reflecting the signals and passing traffic in intersecting ripples of light. Leo lost himself in thought as he followed the dancing patterns and waited for Jeaneane who, as always, was late.

He felt cool fingers on his forearm and turned to see the woman herself, who smiled as their eyes met. "Hi," he said, and they kissed. Jeaneane took Leo's arm and he escorted her into the restaurant.

"Sorry I'm late."

"It's OK," he replied. "It was peaceful watching the rain."

"The cab driver was a fucking moron," she proclaimed, her profanity quite at odds with her appearance, which verged on angelic.

The maître d' looked amused as he guided the ersatz couple to their table.

The room bubbled with cheerful conversation. Leo felt a little rush of excitement as they made their way between the tables in the hip but unpretentious joint. He did not sense the condescending attitude he sometimes encountered in upscale Citizen venues. The décor featured a blend of stone floors, rough wood, and hammered metal, warmed by indirect lighting, and softened by water falling in steady sheets over vertical glass panels placed at angles to divide the room into faux-intimate subregions.

After seating Jeaneane, Leo took his place and scanned the menu. "I've never dined here," he confessed. "Everyone says it's the shit."

"They speak the truth," she confirmed, flashing him a peek over the top of her menu.

They settled on an array of finger foods from around the world: A couple of salads. Skewers of duck drizzled in a balsamic glaze. A tray of spicy fried curry dumplings.

"Exotic," he said.

"They do a pretty good job," she answered. Jeaneane deployed an air of bored sophistication more frequently in recent years. She strove to obscure any remnants of her small-town roots, which amused Leo, who grew up in the city's environs and considered its dwellers ironically provincial.

He unfolded his napkin and regarded his friend.

Jeaneane's mane, resembling spun gold with the faintest vein of copper, was piled atop her head in a twist of curls, held in place with an ebony stick adorned with silver and sapphires. With viridian eyes and alabaster skin, she was like Boreal sunshine refracted through glacial ice. Her exceptional beauty, animated by her intelligence and sarcastic wit, both warmed and chilled. It captivated and endowed anyone it was bestowed upon with a sense of privilege and worth, a power she wielded deftly.

She was stunning, dressed in low-cut crushed black velvet that accentuated her curvaceous splendor.

"Is my makeup screwed up?" she asked, noticing Leo's appraisal.

"Au contraire," he assured. "I don't think I've ever seen you look so lovely."

She pressed her lips together and put her hand on Leo's, beaming love through her emerald eyes.

They laced fingers briefly, then turned to the waiter as he approached their table.

"Can you believe all the cops on the street?" Leo asked after they had placed their order.

"Oh. My. God. I'm glad you warned me. I listened to the news after we talked. They said they were deploying police in the major cities and transportation hubs, but it's unreal, isn't it?"

"I've never seen anything like it," he agreed. "The activists must be making more headway than the media have been letting on."

"Or the Cleagues are fanning the flames of overreaction. They never let an opportunity go to waste to push for martial law."

"Could be," Leo conceded. Jeaneane didn't follow the news like he did, but she was a bloodhound when it came to politics. She knew well-connected people and paid attention to the rumor mill of the intelligentsia.

"I've heard that Restruct is trying to hijack the Micromedium," she offered. She obviously thought this was delicious scandal.

"Good for them," said Leo.

Jeaneane leveled him a cold stare and remained silent. She considered radical sentiment rather indecorous. Besides, she liked an indulgence now and then. Who could shop or read gossip columns on a hijacked Micromedium?

"I don't know," he fidgeted under the sudden drop in temperature. "I don't mean that. I'm spinning my wheels lately and any change sounds good."

Jeaneane's attention had wandered to a handsome and reciprocally interested guy several tables away. *As loyal as ever*, thought Leo, then chastised himself for judging. What harm was there in a little flirt? Jeaneane sometimes lunched with a fellow like this, then ruled him out as "her mate," which was perplexing since she was living with someone who thought he enjoyed that status. Leo hoped his silence would retrieve her from the anonymous flirtation and remind her that a real-life discussion was pending.

Jeaneane turned back, looking proud. Leo stared at her until she realized she had dropped the conversation. "Sorry, what did you say?"

"Spinning my wheels," he repeated.

Jeaneane jumped back on track. "I can relate," she said. "Anything in particular?"

Leo told her about his meeting with Anna and his conversation with John at the pub. Jeaneane said she understood his ambivalence. "I'm sorry," she said in a tone indicating she was anything but. "John would have more authority on the subject if he'd ever had life served up by means other than a silver tray." Jeaneane was not a big fan of John.

"How about you?" Leo asked as their dinner was served and wine poured, knowing the topic would vaporize her minor dudgeon over John. "How's life at the firm?"

"Frustrating," she replied with a sigh. "They don't appreciate my work. They treat me like a flunky and fight me when I try to restructure my schedule or work on more prestigious assignments. It's been like that my whole life. Everyone was jealous of me. Any time I dared ask for recognition or voiced a need, I was treated as undeserving and selfish."

"Sorry, sounds painful," he said, hoping they would avoid tarrying in this quagmire. "How about the work itself?"

"The cases are interesting," she replied, accepting his invitation to shift gears. "Mostly lawsuits involving industrial pollution. I'm also defending a few criminal cases and representing some complainants in assault cases," she said. Leo urged her on.

"One of my clients has been a Citizen for five years. Before that she was a Vulnerable. She's suing her employer for assault. Bizarre case. She said he strapped a band around her head before he attacked her, and that he was wearing something similar on his own head."

"What were they?"

"I don't know. The case was investigated by the police, but the prosecutor declined to proceed, allegedly because there wasn't enough evidence to convict."

"As if that ever stopped them," Leo said.

Jeaneane agreed. "We have medical records corroborating her claim that she was struck during working hours, but there isn't any other direct evidence besides her testimony."

"Is it enough to support the lawsuit?"

"Possibly, at least to initiate it. She thinks the headbands may have been recording devices of some sort."

"Cameras?"

"She doesn't know. The company manufactures Micromedium interface technology, but she did graphic design for marketing and had never seen images of the things."

"Subpoena their product lists and specifications and have them examined by an expert. Haul in a few of their execs for questioning."

"We tried."

"And?"

"They convinced a court to quash our subpoenas."

Leo frowned. "On what grounds?"

"Are you ready for this?" She reached across the table and placed her hand on his forearm. "On grounds of national security and state secrecy. We were not even allowed to see the contents of their motion," she finished in a dramatic half-whisper.

Leo rocked back in his seat. "A simple assault lawsuit by a low-level employee is being blocked through a concealed ex parte motion on grounds of national security and state secrecy?"

"That's correct," she pronounced. "The judge also imposed a gag order."

They locked eyes and sipped wine as they contemplated the scale of this development.

"I'm speechless," he observed.

"We're appealing the ruling on the subpoenas, but something big is at issue here."

Leo felt a tug at his memory and told Jeaneane about the Micromedium chat he'd had earlier that evening.

"You're going back there? After everything that happened between you and Jeb?"

"It's not easy to meet people," he said, feeling like he shouldn't have to defend himself. "It's not like when I was in school and there were people in my life all the time. My work always brings me into contact with the same people."

"The real world is a better way to meet people," said Jeaneane.

"People connected to the Micromedium are in the real world," Leo parried.

"Yeah, alone in the real world, hiding behind wires, force fields, and fictitious identities," she said in riposte.

"I was testing the waters. I talked with this guy, at least I assume he's a guy, named Anaku who told me I needed to get something called a quantum array, which he said is much better than the old electrode arrays."

"Those things were too much hassle," Jeaneane said, pointing at a mixed-grain and dried fruit salad she just tasted and widening her eyes in approval.

"That's what I said and he said these quantum things were 'a whole new world.'"

"That's interesting."

Leo sampled the salad and agreed with Jeaneane's assessment. "I remember some articles on experiments involving quantum fields and the brain, but I haven't read anything about technology for individual use or Micromedium interfacing."

"Me either," she agreed. "Sounds like it might be a lead. Thanks."

"See, Micromedium socializing has its benefits."

"Uh huh, like cheating spouses and scam artists. What did you say his name was?"

"Anaku," Leo replied, savoring the shape of the word as he pronounced it.

"That's unusual. Are you going to talk with him again?" she asked, making little effort to conceal her distaste over the origin of this connection.

"I haven't decided but probably."

"I'm not encouraging it but if you do, try to find out more about that technology."

"Will do."

"Thanks. I plan to talk to my local delegate about the case. We're also hiring an investigator to sniff around."

When they left the restaurant, the rain had stopped so they walked to the opera house.

"You're looking quite handsome this evening," Jeaneane said as she wrapped herself in a shawl and took Leo's arm.

"Thank you," he replied with a quiver of the head as though straightening a necktie. He felt rather handsome tonight. Olive complected with a shock of sable curls, thick black lashes, and eyes like chipped obsidian, he was usually regarded as good looking. He also knew how to dress when the occasion called for it. Tonight, he wore a well-tailored coat, a thin black sweater, silk trousers, and he sported a fresh haircut he'd secured on his way to dinner. They made a chic couple, if he did say so himself. Admiring glances from passersby confirmed the point.

As they strolled toward the concert, Leo tried to pick up what he had started sharing earlier about his vexing ambivalence toward work. Jeaneane didn't respond, and she was staring past him with a mesmerized smile. He turned to see what had captivated her attention and saw her fixing a strand of hair in the reflection of a storefront window. He stopped talking.

"I'm sorry, did you say something?" she asked after a silent beat as though waking from a dream.

"No," said Leo.

When they arrived at the opera house, Jeaneane said she needed to use the restroom, but the line for the woman's room was absurdly long and the men's room, per usual, was wide open. "Guard me," she said and stalked into the men's room. Leo gauged the disbelief in those who caught her move and hustled into the restroom with an astonished yelp. He stood guard by a stall and avoided other men's eye contact as Jeaneane relieved herself. They left the restroom together with her arm imperiously draped over his, defying anyone to challenge her. No one did.

Although Leo and Jeaneane viewed each other as attractive, there had never been ambiguity or confusing sexual tension in their friendship. This allowed a closeness that might produce claustrophobia or excessive conflict in a romantic relationship. As friends, they shared nearly everything. It also allowed Leo to tolerate Jeaneane's solipsistic lacunae, which would have been intolerable in a lover.

He asked after her love life as they settled into their seats, and listened as she described disappointment with her current partner that was reaching a critical threshold. Jeaneane loved deeply. Flirtatious lunch dates notwithstanding, when she started a relationship, she went all in, hoping they could stay the course until the end. The breadth of her emotional range, her brilliant mind, fierce independence, and dagger-like tongue often intimidated her partners. She had yet to find a man who both cherished and tolerated her. She felt like she was reliving her lifelong plight of being told she wanted too much.

"You don't want too much," Leo reassured her. "You settle for too little. One day, a man strong enough and smart enough to handle all of you will fall to his knees and thank the universe that he has been allowed the privilege to love such a goddess. Until that happens, you haven't met your match."

Jeaneane rested her head on Leo's shoulder as the overture commenced. Leo breathed in her exquisite fragrance and laid his head over hers.

"Thanks," she said softly. Leo hugged her to him and settled in for the musical histrionics that were about to begin.

"I've never been big on opera," he confided.

"The soprano's supposed to be phenomenal," she whispered.

She was that and more, and Leo was moved to tears by what turned out to be a world-class performance.

8

"LEO."

"That's folksy," spoke the caller, "but I don't recall our agreeing to use first names yet."

Leo stopped stuffing papers into his briefcase and turned his attention to the macrophone he had just answered.

"Ms. Dao," he said, recognizing his new client's voice.

"It's Anna."

"Leo," he said, again, smiling.

"I've spent the weekend thinking."

"OK."

"I'm ready to discuss options."

"Excellent. I can't do it right now, though. I'm on my way to a Board hearing."

"I didn't expect to become the center of your universe. I just said I'm ready to talk." On her end of the call, Anna cringed.

Neither spoke for a moment.

"Let me try this again."

Leo chuckled to himself and waited.

"I'm clear on what the options are, but I'm hoping you can give me some guidance."

Aware this polite display of deference was only partially genuine, Leo replied, "Be glad to, and then you can tell me whether you think I've got the backbone to represent you."

Anna laughed despite herself. "That's not how I would have put it," she said.

"I just bet. I can free up an hour this afternoon at two if you can make it then."

"Today?"

"Problem?"

"No, that's great. I figured it would be a few days."

"We can wait if that's what you prefer," he said through a deliberate yawn.

"Two o'clock will be fine, Advocate Baksh."

"I thought we'd established that it was Leo, but if titles give you confidence, feel free to keep it formal, Ms. Dao. I'll be big bad Advocate Baksh. Want me to wear a tie? I could find a name tag with the court seal on it too."

"Are you always a smart ass?"

"When I'm talking with one."

She looked at the phone and stifled a laugh.

"See you at two, Leo."

"Bye, Anna."

Leo spent half the day waiting in the Board of Classification hearing department for his case to be called. After fourteen items on the 10:00 a.m. docket finished, his finally came up. The proceeding took five minutes.

"Two-and-a-half hours of waiting for a five-minute appearance," he griped to a colleague in the hall afterward.

"Sounds about right," replied the other advocate with a roll of the eyes.

"It's a wonder the system functions at all," said Leo, turning toward the exit.

"This is functioning?" asked the other rhetorically as they emerged into an overcast afternoon. They smiled bleakly at one another in a wordless farewell and Leo headed for his car.

After driving across town and finding another parking place, Leo stood in line for forty-five minutes in the clerk's office at the Department of Adjudication. Messengers and clerical staff surrounded him as he filed documents in one of his cases, not sure whether he should feel embarrassed or proud that he had no secretary or assistant to relieve him of these menial tasks. The agent at the clerk's desk who stamped in his filing made her opinion on the subject apparent through an attitude of open disdain.

Leo wanted to ask how it felt to be a human conveyor belt but he knew this bureaucratic gatekeeper could royally screw his cases if he pissed her off. Ashamed of his defensive elitism, he accepted her sour disposition and mustered the fortitude to wish her a good day. To her credit, she nodded in response, which, for her, was practically a lap dance.

Leo felt oddly touched by this dismal approximation of civility as he walked away from the desk. He shook his head, muttering, "Leo, you're pathetic."

When he returned to his office at 1:45, Anna was waiting on the steps.

"You're early."

"Wow, you were serious about the tie," she said, giving him the up and down as he ascended toward her.

"It's not for you," he reported, "I had a hearing, remember? But you must admit, it's pretty convincing." He stood up straight and turned in profile, raising his hand in expository grandeur.

"Impressive," she said, with a round of air applause.

He snickered and held the door for her. She gave him a sidelong expression of concern for his sanity as she entered the building and stood by the door to his office. She pedaled her feet and rubbed her hands together like a flurry of fine sandpaper for warmth as Leo fumbled with the keys.

"Don't most advocates have support staff?"

"That's not how I work," he said as he entered the anteroom to his office.

"How's that," she asked. "Efficiently?"

He was creeped out by her perceptivity.

"We're back to stage props?" he deflected. He stepped to the right and bleated "Advocate Baksh will be with you shortly."

He opened the door to his office, turned up the heat, stashed his briefcase, ditched his tie, ran his fingers through his hair and, leaning back into the anteroom, said, "Oh, Clive, please send in my next appointment."

After this, he stepped out and stuffily intoned, "Advocate Baksh will see you now," gesturing for her to enter his office.

"You are a complete freak," she said as she skittered past him.

He held the grandiose gesture of welcome and followed her with his eyes as she passed, then sat opposite her, the picture of innocence and mystification over her expression of bafflement.

They were still for a moment, then bobbed their heads in a chuckle, equally surprised by the course of this interaction.

"I could use some coffee," said Leo, harnessing the flow. "Care for a cup?"

"Coffee would be great," said Anna, settling into her chair.

Once the pot was brewing, Leo returned to face her and tented his hands.

"What are the options?"

"There are three," she said, numbering them off with her fingers. "Seek protection for a new axis of Vulnerability, submit to guided development for reclassification under existing criteria, or fight to expand those criteria to accommodate me and people like me."

"I agree," Leo confirmed, privately impressed by the accuracy and succinctness of her summary.

Anna described thoughts on all three approaches but withheld her deepest concerns.

Leo observed her carefully as she spoke. She seemed drawn to the safety of protection, but she displayed distaste for the smothering prospect of reprogramming.

Which left fighting to change the rules for Classification.

"It sounds to me like you have a clear preference."

"In theory," she affirmed. "But I'm not sure I have it in me to fight a war like that."

"Plus you're not sure I have it in me to do battle on your behalf."

Her expression turned quizzical. "I'm guessing you must have gone through the reprogramming."

Partial dodge, thought Leo. "Yes," he acknowledged, "I did."

"Was it the right decision?"

"To be honest, I don't know. How do you take your coffee?"

"Black."

Leo's office sported a little kitchenette in a recess along one wall. A sliding wooden door designed to conceal it looked as though it might be frozen open by the accumulated dust. Properly maintained, the feature would have been cute. Anna peeked as he pulled two dirty mugs from the sink and washed them out. He poured them full and handed one to her, then sat back down to face her. She made sure he saw her scrutinize the mug for cleanliness.

"No recent cases of dysentery," he assured. She wiped a hand across her forehead in theatrical relief.

They warmed their hands on the steaming cups and regarded one another.

"You've entered my life at an interesting juncture," he said, taking a calculated risk of disclosure.

"How so?"

"I have been questioning the path I chose. The benefits of Citizenship are legion, but I found the reprogramming ... how best to put it?"—he looked over her head—"violative," he decided, reestablishing eye contact. "I was forced to give up aspects of myself which may have been strengths, were the world sane enough to recognize them."

"Like what?"

She studied him.

"Deep sensitivity," he said at length. "Similar to you."

Fear of disappointment rippled across her features and touched his heart.

"If you had it to do over again, would you make the same decision?"

"I don't know but it's not a realistic question."

"Why not?"

"Because it's impossible to mix who I am now, what I've learned and how I've grown, with the choice I had to make at an earlier stage of my development."

She nodded comprehension.

"Also, the legal and political landscape is ripe for a challenge in ways it was not fifteen years ago when I had to choose."

"Because of the activists?"

"In part, yes. Also, years of decisions by the Board of Classification and the Department of Adjudication that have effectively expanded the criteria for Citizenship, even if incrementally. And evolution of the popular culture."

"But the Cleagues are stronger now too."

"True."

He paused to gauge her vibe. Easing into fraught terrain, he continued, "The more important factors have to do with you."

"What do you mean?" she asked, knowing full well what he meant.

Her voice had tensed and she was gripping her mug tightly.

"The other way I was similar to you was my temper," he said.

She flinched.

"I don't know you well, and I haven't seen evaluation results yet. Nevertheless, my initial take on you causes me concern that you could end up reclassified as an Aggressive if you chose any path other than expansion of the criteria for Citizenship."

Anna's tension broke and she cradled the warm mug more gently. "That's my worst fear. I don't think I could survive it."

"I understand."

"Couldn't that happen if we lost a fight to change the rules for Citizenship, too?"

"Theoretically but highly unlikely. It's a quirk in the law. If you seek protection or reprogramming you're putting your classification at issue and run the risk of a determination that you belong in a different category. If instead you challenge the classification scheme, it sets in motion a different type of adjudication, one addressing the propriety of the Classification categories themselves. The focus is on the system, not you, even though you are the one raising the challenge. It would take a separate petition from the government to reclassify you. That would be viewed as retaliatory. We could stop it and get you an award of damages if they tried it."

Leo saw a spark of interest.

"As to whether I have the guts to be your advocate on a quest to expand the criteria for Citizenship, I offer this:

"First, while I have mixed feelings about having gone through reprogramming, I unquestionably gained strengths through it that serve me well as an advocate. I am good at holding my ground and I do not shy away from conflict.

"Second, I have won many battles of this type, though they admittedly involved a narrower range of traits than you possess."

She took a sip of coffee and listened.

"Third, I'm pissed off by the ways the reprogrammers psychologically brutalized me. That anger harmonizes with your goals, it doesn't conflict with them."

She raised her mug in a mock toast.

"If you think that by representing you I'd be fighting a battle that I wish I'd fought for myself on some level, you're right. But that would work for you, not against you."

Leo let Anna absorb these points.

"OK," she said.

"There's another aspect it's important for you to consider."

She turned an ear toward him.

"There will be publicity. Your case could put you in the crossfire between the conservatives and the various activist groups."

"I realize that," she said, "and I don't like it."

"I don't blame you. I won't bullshit, it could get ugly. But you could use it to your advantage if you overcome your resistance to it. There are groups who would mobilize considerable pressure on your behalf."

"Which the Cleagues would match or exceed with their filthy hate-mongering."

"That is a possibility," he agreed. "I will do everything I can to protect you, including getting an injunction to insulate you from harassment if it comes to that."

She chewed on her lip.

"I don't think we can hope for your case to proceed without drawing attention from the activist factions. The best and most realistic approach is to expect it and play them against each other in your favor."

"Cynical," she said.

"Strategic," he countered.

"Do you have contacts in these groups?"

"I do. I have direct contacts among the so-called moderates, meaning Respect, Spectrum, and Pro'gression. Let's just say I know how to get information back and forth to people in the Restruct movement, but let's also say I didn't say that."

"What about the Cleagues?"

"The Citizens Action League considers people like me a threat to their greedy choke hold on government and commerce—I mean a danger to the wholesome stability of the pureblood Citizenry from evil contamination by the unwashed horde," he said, slowing his speech and exaggerating his enunciation as the sentence unwound.

Anna cracked a lopsided grin.

"You don't like 'Cleague,'" she asked, pointing a playfully accusatory finger at him.

"For a person in my position, use of derogatory epithets is—"

"Inappropriate?"

Leo saw the challenge in her features. "Not expedient," he corrected.

She turned down the corners of her mouth, impressed. It was official. She liked the advocate, and his guileless appearance could be a useful weapon. Having her enemies underestimate their adversary might prove advantageous.

She asked about the activist groups, and Leo gave her an overview of their respective agendas and constituencies. They talked about possible forms the protests around her quest might take, and ways they could influence and leverage them.

"I like the sound of Pro'gression," she said, referring to the group of moderate Aggressives.

"Why does that not surprise me," he said, playing the fatigued parent, troubled by the potential fallout Anna's aggressive tendencies could have for their joint endeavors. "Promise me you'll never say that to an evaluator, a reporter, or a judge."

She held up her hand as if taking an oath.

The conversation lulled into a pause and Leo topped up their mugs. They sipped their coffee and ruminated. Anna heard water dripping in the sink.

"Why don't you take some time and think about it."

"I don't need to," she said.

He raised an eyebrow.

"I want to challenge the Classification criteria."

Leo cautioned her about rushing into a decision, saying he was not interested in filing her case if she planned to abort when it started heating up. "I don't expect you to know with certainty that you can stay the course," he explained. "But don't say you want to proceed unless you're prepared to make a commitment."

"When I decide to do something, I do it."

This he believed.

"But I can't afford to pay you."

"Despite efforts by the conservatives to cut off funding for this kind of litigation, as things stand I can get the Board of Classification to appoint me to represent you at public expense, if you qualify financially."

She said she doubted that would be a problem. Leo tried to ease her with a gentle smile.

"If you can make that happen," she said, "then let's do it."

"You're sure?"

"Yep," she answered with one determined slap on the armrest.

He studied her face and found no sign of ambivalence.

"Alright," he replied at last. "Then we fight."

Mischief lit Anna's eyes. "We fight," she agreed.

They clinked mugs to seal the decision.

9

LIAM BLEW ON THE OIL drum serving as his makeshift desk and squinted to protect his eyes from the resulting plume of dust. Rays of sunlight from cracked windows high overhead streaked through the swirling motes and warmed the side of his face. The abandoned warehouse he had chosen, redolent of motor oil, rust, and mildew, made up for its lack of comforts through its unmolested remoteness.

He didn't like using the same site twice to connect with his hacktivist compatriots, but it had been months since he last used this spot and he was pretty sure no one had been here. The Micromedium link was hot and there were no signs of tampering. He needed to suss out some new sites for one-time hookups, and he needed a secure site when the time came to attempt incursion into the Department of International Intelligence hub. For purposes of the brief update scheduled for today, this spot would have to do. Wired up, he launched the meeting:

Infiltr8org: Greetings, revolutionaries.

Liam suffered a barrage of cynical commentary on his estimation of the group's likely historical significance, then the hackers settled in for a serious discussion.

Hackizen: We knew it would be complicated, but it's beyond anything any of us has ever seen.

Infiltr8org: Let's hear it.

Hackizen: This is what we've determined so far: Standard encryption and password protection is the outer wall of the fortress.

Aggresserable: Not even that. More like a paint job on the outer wall.

Hackizen: Right. It's state of the art but it's for show. Pathways loop around into each other and back upon themselves.

Infiltr8org: And under the paint?

Hackizen: Not certain yet, though we have suspicions. At first it seemed like random noise but eventually we saw patterns.

Infiltr8org: What kind of patterns?

Hackizen: Too complex to define or analyze.

Subterraneum: Almost organic.

Hackizen: Yes, organic is a good word for it. Like natural shapes.

Infiltr8org: Organic arrangements of what?

Hackizen: Numbers, words, lines, symbols, curves, patterns of blank space, gradations in complexity, color, density.

Infiltr8org: You could see this using the standard Micromedium interface?

Hackizen: Yes.

Infiltr8org: What did the underlying code look like?

Hackizen: Unintelligible.

Infiltr8org: What about at the hex or binary levels?

Hackizen: You won't believe me.

Infiltr8org: Tell me.

Hackizen: We were simultaneously viewing output from the same portal on each of our terminals. But when we took a simultaneous snapshot of the same chunk of output and parsed it, we each saw a different result.

Infiltr8org: That's ridiculous.

Hackizen: It is nevertheless true.

Infiltr8org: Did you analyze it?

Hackizen: No. We compared results and confirmed the differences, but none of our tools could analyze the data. It didn't fit any recognizable coding pattern.

Infiltr8org: What does it mean?

Hackizen: We have several ideas but no method to test them.

Infiltr8org: This is giving me the creeps. Perhaps we should abort.

Sleeperagent: No way. You set the purse and we may already have been tagged in some way.

Infiltr8org: That's what I mean. Don't stress about the money. I will compensate you for the work you've done so far, regardless of whether we proceed.

Sleeperagent: We've seen too much to turn back. If we get in trouble without getting hold of anything useful, that would be a complete waste of everything. Of us. Do you want to be responsible for that?

Infiltr8org: Of course not, but anomalous behavior of this scale means we have no idea what we're dealing with or how to protect ourselves. We can't even do risk assessment.

Hackizen: Patience. Let us tell you the rest first. We think the garbage patterns we saw in the initial output may be the standard Micromedium interface's representation of complex QFRI data.

Infiltr8org: But why isn't it comprehensible? Our terminals can read our QFRI interfaces.

Hackizen: Only because we have them narrowly focused for simple speech commands. This is more complex.

Infiltr8org: As in quantum neural interface data?

Hackizen: That's our hunch.

Infiltr8org: They have a neural QFRI field protecting the DII Micromedium hub? As in, it's wrapped in a consciousness?

Hackizen: That's our working hypothesis. It

could consist of multiple interpenetrated mind fields.

Infiltr8org: If the Micromedium interface can't decipher it, the code is unintelligible, and its content is somehow linked to the observer, how can we use it?

Aggresserable: We can't. Trying to decipher the code is a waste of time. Besides, we think the code is an artifact of a more complex phenomenon when a quantum field neural link takes place. The code is the terminals' attempt to represent the field. The field is a natural phenomenon that extends through the Micromedium. It's like an analog extension of the mind itself. The code is the terminal's attempt to describe its contours, but the thing itself is of a higher order than the code. If it is neural QFRI data as we suspect, the way to use it is to interface with it at the quantum field level.

Infiltr8org: Form a nodal link. Connect your minds to it.

Aggresserable: Yep.

Infiltr8org: Who knows what kind of damage could result from that? We might as well storm the DII headquarters wherever they are with water pistols and signs that say Torture Me.

Aggresserable: We should not attempt it if the link can't be controlled from our end. But there may be ways to minimize the risks of detection or harm to ourselves.

Infiltr8org: Enlighten me.

Hackizen: I know several people who have chopped up the arrays. I'm told there are ways to partially disguise one's signal, buffer feedback, and tunnel through the fields to the underlying hardware.

Infiltr8org: This is the DII we're talking about.

Hackizen: I realize that, but we all know how this

works. My contacts are every bit as smart as the DII sellouts. There is no monopoly on information technology..It's an open field. These guys have made significant progress reverse engineering the equipment.

Infiltr8org: There is no technical monopoly, but it's a question of resources. The DII has unlimited funds and infrastructure.

Hackizen: These people are quite well equipped as well.

Infiltr8org: From what source?

Hackizen: If I knew I wouldn't say. Not even here. Not even to you. For our purposes, I can tell you that they have an advanced understanding of the QFRI technology and they are willing to share it. For a price.

Infiltr8org: I have nothing against subcontracting in principle, but bringing others in greatly increases our exposure. I also don't like the sound of the associations you are suggesting.

Hackizen: We won't bring them in. I will deal with them and we will use the information without their involvement. They know nothing about this group's existence or mission.

Infiltr8org: It's still risky.

Hackizen: Everything in life is risky. In this case, the risk would fall on me.

Sleeperagent: How do you know they're not government agents?

Hackizen: You'll have to trust me. I've known these people for years. They are antisocial techno geeks who live for solving puzzles. To them it's a lucrative game. The source of those funds is most decidedly not the government. They're good at what they do and they may hook us up.

Subterraneum: I say we get the info and test it out in a low-risk environment, like the social sites. We can make an informed assessment after that.

Infiltr8org: I am open to that if you all agree not to attempt a run on the DII hub. We also all need to be sober about the magnitude of the risk we're taking.

Aggresserable: This mission entailed high risk from the beginning. We're all on board.

Infiltr8org: Everyone?

(Assent all around)

Infiltr8org: Alright, Hack, make the appropriate inquiries and let me know the price. This is an additional expense and I don't expect you to deduct it from the purse. I trust you to take all necessary precautions, protect the group, and cover your tracks. We'll transfer the funds through customary channels. In the meantime, NO INTERFACING WITH THE DII HUB. Anything else?

Hackizen: Not at present.

Infiltr8org: Let me know when you have an update.

Aggresserable: Ciao.

Papers pirouetted on swirls of stale air as a light rail coach beeped up to the subterranean platform where James Malone waited. Plexiglass doors hissed open, and he squeezed aboard the bloated car, stood nose-to-nose with a suited Citizen, and glared. When the man held his ground, James whipped out his badge, and both the other man and other passengers yielded him an unfair chunk of the precious standing space.

Having claimed the extra footage to which he considered himself entitled, James reviewed his notes on pending investigations and arranged the day ahead. Ever since the briefing on the neural interface virtual abuse investigations, he had systematically streamlined his caseload to focus on this new phenomenon.

He worked with Lauren and Melissa to cull through suggestions by various staff and developed a report for the Office of Legal Counsel. Given the volatile political situation and fear among the Citizenry over the recent terror attack, they would soon have a clear statutory mandate to investigate these cases, followed by restrictive protocols and legal standards to worry about.

James believed there was much to be discovered through this new technology. He planned to give it a private taste before the investigatory formalities limited his access. He also intended to lead the dragnet when the investigation began. The more adept he was at using the technology, the further ahead of his peers he could remain and the more he could control the course of the investigation. He didn't care if Lauren was the official lead, provided he was the one with the actual, if invisible, steering wheel.

The train pulled into the Capital Civic Center station. James rode up the escalator into an ancient plaza, surrounded by what the tourist bureau touted as a thrilling montage of preserved colonnades and friezes interposed with ultra-modern government buildings gracefully designed in homage to the ruins' antiquity. A collapsed dome atop the remnants of a superannuated forum where the first proto-legislature met was mirrored in an adjacent glass-and-steel symbolic reference to its intact glory, towering over the Council of Delegates' modern rotunda. Some viewed the contemporary government buildings as masterful artistic references, accenting and blending with the historic relics. Others saw them as a crass aesthetic joke.

James could not have cared less. He quickstepped into the DDI regional headquarters, flashing his badge and grumbling to the security agents. All entrants were subject to search, even high-level agents. In reality, no one took that seriously. The DDI was the nation's security. What did a door guard have on them? James was infamous for finding ways to punish security staff that obstructed him. He also was known to fix things for those who cooperated, and more than one security guard had been liberated from pesky legal problems or annoying personages after looking the other way when James entered or exited the building carrying items that ought to have been inspected. Rumor had it that James was instrumental in one employee's ascent from a guard active in the union to the head of labor relations for the company. No one knew what strings had been pulled or pressure brought to bear, but the guy had been one of James's favorites. His promotion was abrupt and unexpected by his peers.

James feigned casual boredom as he entered the DDI Capital Region offices, scanning his notes and mumbling snubs to the staff as he passed. He pulled the door shut behind him as he dove into his office, activated the lock and soundproofing, deployed a scatterbug to foil eavesdropping devices, then opened an encrypted Micromedium vocal communication channel and entered the coordinates for his contact at the Department of International Intelligence, an individual who identified himself as Baikal. James had done his own sleuthing and suspected Baikal's name was Sandoval, but kept this to himself.

International had an official liaison to Domestic and vice versa, but they weren't James or Baikal. This was a back-channel connection. James had never sought authorization for the relationship and felt no duty to disclose it. A certain modicum of secrecy was necessary for effective intelligence work, even with one's own department. He had often sharpened his edge at Domestic by fortifying his investigations with information surreptitiously gleaned from International. Other agents occasionally looked askance when he pursued a lead for which it appeared supernatural perception would have been required, but he kept anyone from inquiring too aggressively by finding ways to share credit for the windfall. No one knew he was regularly conferring with a DII operative.

He had never met his connection face-to-face. Baikal made the first contact, luring James with information on a huge arms-smuggling investigation, then hooking him with the biggest gun bust in James's career by tipping him off to a key meeting within the national borders. The DII agent helped James fabricate an informant, and the case brought such fanfare and funding to the DDI Capital Region that no one wanted to know any more than they had to, including the chief himself.

This recent round of communications, however, was initiated by James. There was a growing incidence of people employing a QFRI Micromedium interface technology to engage in illicit neural links. James wondered if the DII agent knew about the equipment and its uses.

As luck would have it, Baikal was quite familiar with the technology in question and could arrange for samples of the highest quality to come into James's possession if he so wished. James was most favorably disposed to such a development. The DII agent said he would gladly oblige, but had a small favor to ask in return.

The agents spoke for a full hour. At the end of the conversation, James knew when and where he could pick up his QFRI array, supporting software and tutorials, and several other items he would need.

James terminated the connection and drummed his fingertips on the desk, clenching his jaw in concentration as he whirled through possibilities.

He picked up the phone and dialed out on a secure line. This call would be logged, but the contents would be shielded. After two rings, Fredrick Luttrell, the recently minted director of labor relations for SecurePort's security services answered.

"Luttrell."

"Freddy, this is James Malone."

"Yes, Agent Malone," answered the former guard. "Is something wrong?"

James relished the deference.

"No, Freddy. Everything is fine. How is the new position?"

"It's a dream come true, sir. A lot of responsibility but I can handle it."

"I'm sure you're fine," James assured him. "How has that tax lien worked out?"

"Disappeared off my credit report, Mr. Malone. No more collection notices. I was afraid to call them about it, in case it would, you know ... "

"Resurrect it?"

"Yeah. Cause trouble."

"You don't need to worry about that. No need to call anyone. They'd just tell you there was no record of a tax debt. No point in putting questions in anyone's heads, is there Freddy?"

"That's what I was thinking."

"Very prudent. Good instincts."

"Thank you, sir." The uncertainty in Luttrell's voice made James sneer.

"Let's hope that good judgment applies to other areas of life as well."

He let the comment echo in Luttrell's mind.

"If I were to ask you a few questions, do you think you could keep them under your hat?"

"Yes, sir. Anything."

"I need to rely on you, Freddy. If I found out I trusted you foolishly, it would make me unhappy. Is that clear?"

James could almost hear the man sweat. "Of course," he replied after a beat.

"Am I correct in understanding that your firm provides both security and janitorial services?"

"Yes, Agent Malone," he answered proudly. "We are the primary provider of both security and custodial services for most national and local government facilities."

"Does that include the Board of Classification and the Department of Adjudication?"

"Yes, sir."

"How about the chambers for the Council of Delegates?"

"Special division but yes the Council of Delegates too."

James's eyes widened.

"No kidding. Are you everywhere? What about the chief executive's office?"

"No, sir. A special military unit provides security for her, as I'm sure you know."

"Yes," James acknowledged, his mind spinning on other subjects.

"How about the Department of International Intelligence."

"I think they provide their own security, sir," he said politely.

"I imagine they do," James said, tapping his fingers.

"Freddy, I will need your help. If you don't want to work with me, I won't cause you trouble, provided you do not disclose that this conversation took place. You have my word. However, if you decide to work with me, this promotion would just be the beginning. I would make sure you and yours were well taken care of."

James inspected his fingernails as he let this percolate. Luttrell owed him his pelt and they both knew it.

"I am happy to help you any way I can," the security official offered.

"I thought perhaps you'd feel that way," James replied. His attention was caught by Lauren Drey who was waving to him through the narrow window next to his office doorway. He held apart his hands to indicate he would be on the phone for some time. She looked exasperated and held her thumbs and pinky out with other fingers folded in the universal symbol of a phone against her ear and jerked her head at him. He dismissed her with a thumbs up and swiveled his chair to face the other way.

"You've been with the firm a long time, no?"

"Twenty years."

"Has your promotion undermined your relationship with the guards you knew through the union?"

"I don't believe so. We're between contract negotiations right now, so no one hates me yet." Luttrell tittered nervously.

"Excellent. Do you have access to a company roster showing assignments and security clearances?"

"Yes," he replied. "Security and custodial services are separate divisions, but the government security clearance procedure is the same for both and we coordinate the staffing through an integrated database for labor-relations purposes."

"Perfect. Please transmit a copy of the roster, assignments, and security clearances for all employees to these coordinates." James read him a secure Micromedium locale and an encryption code. "How difficult would it be to spoof the security barriers at the work sites and gain access for other operatives using your employees' clearances?"

"It would depend on the sites and shifts and how many other security or custodial personnel were on duty," answered Luttrell, his discomfort rising along with his wish that he had never indebted himself to this DDI agent.

"Please give some thought to how we might accomplish that. Put together a short list of individuals we could safely recruit and trust in both security and custodial services. The rewards for assistance will be ample, as well as the penalties for any attempt to thwart us."

"I'm sure."

James could practically hear the man shiver. He resisted an urge to growl.

"Freddy, this is a matter of national security." He rocked in his chair. "You can back out now," he fibbed, "but if we move beyond this point, you will have to stay the course. No exits."

"I understand, sir. I will assist you however I can."

"I knew I could count on you."

James sketched out the mission they would execute together, which Luttrell understood as involving the installation of certain equipment at key sites throughout the government infrastructure.

"It sounds dangerous," said Luttrell. "And"—James could hear him swallow—"illegal."

James sniggered. "As I said, it's a matter of national security. You let me worry about the risks and legalities. The less you know the better off you will be. If push came to shove, you could take shelter under my authority," James said, amused by his own extemporaneous fiction.

"Is this an official DDI mission then? Shouldn't I go through proper vetting for that?"

James clicked his tongue with disapproval and let Luttrell twist in the void until he was sure the erstwhile security guard was wondering where he'd misstepped.

"Hmm," James drawled, "something must be wrong with this connection because it sounded distinctly as though you were trying to tell me how to do my job."

"No, sir."

"I thought not. Let me be blunt. You're not an agent. You're no one, Freddy, you know that don't you? Nobody. All that you think you are I have lent you for my convenience. I am now using you for a specific, limited function. Keep your mouth shut and your feeble mind focused. Do you follow?"

After a pause, Luttrell said, "You can trust me, sir."

"I hope so," James snarled. "For your sake. If anything goes awry on this project or if I find out you've flapped your trap, you will yearn for the days when your so-called problems consisted of tax liens and a dead-end career as a doorman."

There were hisses and pops as Luttrell fumbled with the receiver. "I understand."

James let the silence burn, then eased his tone. "Glad to hear it. I look forward to working with you, Mr. Luttrell."

They arranged a time and place for their face-to-face meeting.

"I'm logging this as a call about rumors I've heard that your employees are planning an illegal strike," James said. "Thank you for your assurances that the firm will take all necessary measures to preserve the stability of government security services."

"It's been my pleasure," replied Luttrell. "My notes are in accord."

Having taken care of his unofficial business, James was prepared to deal with his colleagues and began by calling Lauren and doing his best to placate her. They agreed to meet and discuss the draft statute a delegate proposed to submit on behalf of the Office of Legal Counsel, defining the crime of "QFRI-enhanced and mediated parasitic abuse." He then deactivated the scatterbug, unlocked his office, and commenced his official workday.

When he walked into the conference room where Lauren and Melissa waited, they abruptly cut short their conversation.

"Agents," he greeted.

"James," Melissa said.

Lauren gave James the once-over. "What was so important and private?"

"By definition that would be none of your damn business," he replied, slapping a notepad on the table.

"I know we have equal rank, but the chief has ordered you to report to me on this investigation."

"Let's not get carried away. I have substantial seniority over you, and I do not report to you. You are the lead on this investigation and I am happy to assist. But you have no weight to throw at me and if you try, you'll be one agent short on this project."

"Should we discuss this with the chief?" she asked, sharpening her consonants.

"Do let's," he shot back with equally pronounced diction.

Melissa examined her colleagues with impatience. "Are you done?"

James and Lauren remained locked in tension a moment longer.

"Yeah, for now," said Lauren.

She distributed the proposed statute.

"Please analyze this and put your thoughts in writing. I'll integrate our feedback into a draft response. I won't transmit it without everyone's agreement."

James stuck the document in a folder, crossed his arms, and waited for the next item on the agenda.

Lauren turned to the developing investigation. She informed her colleagues that Chief Mills, at her request, had asked the Department of International Intelligence liaison to consider whether the DII could procure QFRI arrays for the DDI agents' use.

Electricity fluttered over James's skin but he didn't let it show.

Lauren summarized the latest intel from informants who monitored the virtual abuse chatrooms. She also briefed them on information the Office of Legal Counsel had gleaned from partial access to classified court papers in a lawsuit against Polytronics Inc., one of the companies they suspected of manufacturing the QFRI arrays. The case had started as a simple assault accusation, but had been blocked on national security grounds. It was a jurisdictional multi-car pileup involving the DDI, DII, and the advocate general.

"The things I can verify as germane to our investigation are that this company appears to be manufacturing relevant devices, the DII is aware of it and is probably the customer, and an incident of abuse has been hushed." She said it appeared DII was pulling rank, with the help of the advocate general's office, and that even the DDI was being frozen out. They agreed to monitor the situation as the legalities were thrashed out, and Melissa volunteered to set up an information feed on the case from the Office of Legal Counsel.

They turned next to the issue of greatest interest to James, the question of whether they should attempt an undercover neural link with a virtual-abuse chatroom participant once they had the technical means and legal mandate to do so. They all agreed such a tactic would prove invaluable to their investigation, provided they could conceal an agent's identity at all in a neural link and somehow assure the agent's safety.

The group generated a list of technical questions about the technology and its uses for submission to the DII liaison and tabled the discussion until they had more information.

They divvied up monitoring of the various surveillance targets and agreed to collect information until further developments on the legal, technical, and interdepartmental fronts paved the way for the investigation to proceed to the next level.

Lauren snapped her notebook shut and volunteered to summarize the status of their work at the next departmental brainstorming briefing. The agents then adjourned, with James heading one direction and Lauren and Melissa another as they left the conference room. Lauren looked over her shoulder and shuddered for reasons she couldn't explain. James was his usual surly self, but something about his intense glare when they talked about the neural interfaces gave her the willies. She shrugged it off, thinking he was the best equipped of the three to undertake such a reckless task. Submerged in wordless impressions, she parted ways with Melissa without acknowledging her farewell, and entered her own office to carry on with the day.

10

JOHN FORESHORTENED HIS STRIDE TO accommodate Leo's shorter legs and lesser fitness. Leo had been jogging regularly in recent months, and when he called John to say he had decided to fight with Anna to change the classification criteria, John had suggested they discuss it over a run through Memorial Park.

Unfortunately, Leo was finding that although he had improved his aerobic fitness, he lacked sufficient breath to both talk and run.

Once John felt he'd pushed his friend past where he would have stopped on his own, he suggested they finish their lap and grab a soda at the snack shack.

"Sounds perfect," said Leo, relieved.

Autumn was in full swing but there were days like these where the tattered threads of summer could still be cherished. John and Leo bought cold drinks, walked to the edge of the botanical garden, and perched on an old, rough-hewn wooden bench looking down upon a slope studded with fragrant, late blooming flowers fluttering in the afternoon breeze. Butterflies and bees helped the flora make love as John and Leo relaxed into post-exertion euphoria. The afternoon air was warm in the sunshine, caressing in light puffs, and tinged with enough cool moisture to make the skin celebrate the fresh gift of life.

"How nice," said Leo, breathing deeply.

"Yeah," agreed John, with a reciprocal breath.

Leo asked after the publication of John's book. Caught up in his own story, John was grinning like a kid by the time he described signing the contract for the book's publication.

"That's fantastic," Leo said, touched by his old buddy's simple glee. It was refreshing that someone so accomplished could still be that excited by a new achievement and Leo said so. John shrugged and smiled.

They shifted to Anna's case and Leo described their decision to fight.

"That's great," said John, regarding Leo with warmth, both aware that the decision meant as much about Leo overcoming obstacles as it did about Anna.

Leo also brought up the alleged terror attack on the power station and John shot him a glance that said, "You don't even want to touch that mess." Leo's expression assured the contrary and John frowned as he weighed whether and what to disclose.

Leo and John both worked under rules of confidentiality, with Leo strictly prohibited from discussing his cases and John constrained to protect his colleagues and their sources from exposure. But sharing with each other felt more like having a conversation with an extension of oneself than a breach of confidentiality. Leo had the added safeguard that the contents of his conversations with clients were protected by a privilege only they could waive. Even if something leaked, it technically could not be used against his client if she had not disclosed it. Such leaks could lead to investigations that turned up other damaging information and tracks could be covered to conceal the original source. Leo knew this, but his trust in John and his need to share with him sometimes overrode technically proper professional judgment.

For John, spilling information to which he was privy could spoil a scoop, endanger a reporter, or tip off a misfeasor before the journalistic (and eventual prosecutorial) trap had snapped shut. He trusted Leo too, and brainstorming with him had led to investigatory breakthroughs on several occasions. He considered it worth the risk. Still, he was mindful of how much he shared.

"Jill Blatsky is working that story. The more she digs, the smellier it gets."

"Smelly how?"

"The government has done everything but call it a terrorist attack by Restruct. Except the guy they nabbed has no history of extremist activity. He was born a presumptive Aggressive and never petitioned for reclassification. His neighbors and coworkers say he is peaceable and hardworking and—this is the real kicker—severely cognitively impaired."

"If he'd petitioned for reclassification he would have been deemed a Vulnerable."

"Right, but according to the government, he's the mastermind of a sophisticated terror attack on a piece of major infrastructure."

"Not likely."

"No. Second, that was no power plant."

"Hmm?"

"It's all been locked down, but a couple of scared first responders have described the site to Blatsky. She brought in a forensic expert and it sounds like an accident involving superconductors operating at high voltage and low temperature."

"Which means?"

"Some sort of supercomputer. Maybe a particle accelerator."

"Defense?"

"Don't know. When Blatsky started poking around, a deputy advocate general put heat on the editor, then got a court order prohibiting us from publishing the information."

Leo's skin crawled. "Let me guess, national security and state secrecy."

"Exactly," said John, eyeing Leo.

Leo described Jeaneane's assault case and the government blockade that had stopped it on similar grounds.

"Crazy," said John.

"The court imposed a gag order," added Leo.

John threw up his hands in exasperation. "You can't have a free society when the government can stifle the press."

"I agree," said Leo, "but anyone who thinks this is a free society has been seeing too many movies."

John partially conceded the point with a side-nod. "The public doesn't even know the government is keeping all of this under wraps."

"I suppose that is the nature of secrets but I agree. How can the Citizenry know whether the government is under control when its actions are systematically shielded from public scrutiny?"

Leo scuffed at the gravel as the men fretted.

"How's Jeaneane?" asked John after a bit.

"Dissatisfied at work. Close to ending her relationship, I think."

"Status quo then?"

"Be nice."

"She'd find life a lot more fun if she'd pull about fifty feet of barbed wire out of her ass," said John, stretching his legs, and peeking at Leo.

Leo muffled a groan. Years earlier, he had introduced John and Jeaneane in an ill-fated attempt at matchmaking. Inevitably, they slept together but did not hit it off. Leo privately titled the drama "Clash of the Monster Egos."

"I think the barbed wire may be a strength when she's working."

"No doubt. Uptight and wretchedly ill-tempered can be a useful demeanor when you're crushing skulls in the courtroom."

"That's not fair. She's brilliant, passionate, beautiful, and she has a tongue like a sword."

"I didn't say she isn't hot. I said she's cold."

Leo covered his mouth. "Yes, she is both of those things," he conceded.

He was always defending one of them from the other. He used to confide in each his concerns about his friendship with the other, but accusations of betrayal crushed him from both sides. He opted for fierce loyalty to each, which was difficult but less complicated even though they professed to despise each other as only the truly entangled can.

"I've also never known anyone so in love with her own reflection," added John.

"She has a lot to love in that department," replied Leo, thinking that he'd caught John adoring his own reflection in a store front on not-so-rare occasion.

"That doesn't make it any less embarrassing," said John.

"True," replied Leo, suppressing a smirk.

John shot Leo a glance, but Leo shrugged innocently.

Satisfied that the objectionable retort he sensed in the air would not be forthcoming, John turned his attention to the flowers. The two sorted their thoughts, surrounded by a euphony of bees buzzing, birdsong, children's laughter, and the squeak of rusty swings.

The sun dipped below the tree line and both men felt a wave of goose flesh.

"Better get moving," said John. Leo tossed their cans into the trash as they rose to leave.

"Nice shot."

Picking up the thread of conversation about Jeaneane's case while they walked back to their cars, John told Leo he'd heard about the QFRI interfaces from a colleague who was working on a story. "If they're half as good as people say, they could revolutionize journalism. Typing and dictating are a colossal waste of time. No one at the paper has seen one. They're not commercially available."

"Then how are people getting hold of them?"

"Someone is distributing them, but it's not an officially sanctioned release."

Leo told him he had "met" a guy who claimed he could access them.

"Get ahold of one if you can without putting yourself in danger," prompted John, eyes alert with journalistic hunger.

"Danger?"

"Danger. As in, part of a criminal enterprise. Or the target of a government investigation into leaked classified technology."

Leo considered these warnings.

"Be careful with this guy. If you can get him to give you any information about himself, I can run a check on him."

"That would not be polite."

"Screw polite, Leo. You got off easy with Jeb, a lying cheating dirtbag. You never know who you're dealing with on the Micromedium."

Leo felt an embarrassing urge to defend Jeb but said nothing.

They approached their cars, parked one behind the other at a curb.

"Just promise me you'll be careful."

"I promise."

They hugged and John kissed Leo on the cheek. This greater-than-usual display of affection startled Leo. John ruffled his hair.

"Good luck with the case."

"Oh, thanks," Leo replied, his attention tugged back to Anna and the work ahead.

"Keep me posted, counsel."

They climbed into their respective vehicles and John tooted his horn as he pulled away. Leo flicked his lights in response and headed for home, his head filling with strategic considerations in Anna's case and scraps of the pleadings he needed to start drafting.

When Leo arrived at his apartment, he learned he had been out too long for his feline companion's taste, which cost him a customary brief subjection to the cold shoulder. Fortunately, a smorgasbord of treats and lots of cooing earned a few cross squawks, followed by friendlier chirps and full blown purrs.

Hauling the bag of bones into his lap, Leo popped onto the Micromedium and drafted a short greeting to Anaku, which he sent to the appropriate coordinates. He eased Franz onto the feather comforter on his bed and jumped in the shower.

Franz was coughing when Leo came out, which had been happening with greater frequency in the past year. "Poor baby," Leo said softly, remembering like it was yesterday when Franz was a kitten and darted around the house like a cartoon character, a little furry bullet of love and joy. Leo prepared an herbal remedy that the overpriced alternative veterinarian had prescribed, and fed it to Franz with a dropper. The cat disliked the flavor and put up a fight, but he also sensed he was being nurtured and kept his claws and what were left of his teeth out of the struggle. He calmed down as the medicine took hold. Curling up on a pillow, he dozed, gurgling purrs when a sound nudged him back to the waking world.

Leo gathered up his running clothes. As he was throwing them in the hamper, a friendly ding told him he had received a micromissive. He flopped on the couch and activated the screen, delighted to discover that Anaku had already responded and invited him to a private chat.

Leo made himself a hot toddy, wrapped up in a throw his mother had knit for him, and entered the coordinates for the private, virtual conversation. Using his microsocial name he said:

Asad: Hi.

Anaku: Good evening.

Asad: Do you live here in the capital?

Anaku: We're all everywhere all the time when we meet like this, are we not?

Asad: I suppose. Or maybe we're nowhere and no one.

Anaku: So you're a nihilist.

Leo steadied the keyboard on his lap.

Asad: No, not at all.

He shared that he'd been out running with an old and dear friend and that he was settled in for a cozy evening at home.

Anaku: Sounds nice. I rarely have cozy nights.

Asad: How sad. I imagined being an artist would afford you quality alone time.

Anaku: My art is rather unconventional.

Asad: I thought all true art was by definition unconventional.

Anaku: Touché. Calling what I do "art" is unconventional, though accurate. I am a social artist of sorts. A catalyst.

Asad: What is your medium?

Anaku: Power and information.

Asad: What sort of "art" do you create with that?

Anaku: The most important kind. The art of transformation.

Asad: Transformation of what?

Anaku: The world, I hope.

Leo snorted. Ambitious fellow. Must be young.

Asad: Is that all?

Anaku: No, that's just the most succinct synopsis I can offer in response to your questions.

Asad: Is this your idea of getting to know you chitchat?

Anaku: Chitchat bores me.

Asad: Why did you want to talk with me?

Anaku: You interest me.

Asad: Why?

Anaku: Because of the work you do, for one thing. Whether you realize it or not, you are a social artist too.

Asad: You may overestimate the significance of my work.

Anaku: Maybe you don't appreciate its larger context.

Leo thought this sounded condescending. Who did this guy think he was? He considered delivering a quick dissertation on the sociopolitical significance of his work (or lack thereof), but kept his hands off the keyboard.

They fell silent for a time. Leo was the first to resume typing:

Asad: When we first spoke, you mentioned the quantum array interfaces.

Anaku: Yes.

Asad: You have access to them?

Anaku: Yes.

Asad: How?

Anaku: I direct them from where they are to where they're needed.

Asad: Right. Very redistributive of you. I hear they are not commercially available and may be classified technology. How do you have access to them?

Anaku: They are more widely available than you think, regardless of their official status. I am doing my best to make them available to people who can use them.

Asad: But how do you get them?

Anaku: Through associates.

Asad: And those would be?

Anaku: More detail than I am willing to share with someone I've just met.

Hard to argue with that, Leo thought, hoping he hadn't put him off by digging too hard, though he could see John in his mind's eye waving a caution sign and whispering to get more information on this guy.

Leo took a different tack and asked why Anaku would want to make the device available to him.

Anaku replied that he believed widespread distribution of the arrays would result in greater transparency and insight.

Asad: Into what?

Anaku: Reality.

Leo asked how much it would cost. Anaku said cost was not an issue.

Asad: Social artistry is lucrative after all?

Anaku: My sources and volume of income are rather personal, Leo.

Leo's skin prickled.

Asad: How do you know my name?

Anaku: A fellow in the room told me the other night. I confess that I learned a bit about you before I greeted you the first time.

Leo was suddenly uncomfortable and said he did not appreciate feeling disadvantaged.

Anaku: Let us eliminate the disparity. Form a neural link with me through the quantum arrays.

Asad: What does that mean?

Anaku explained that it meant they could touch minds. Leo was shocked by this claim and found it difficult to believe but didn't disclose those thoughts. Instead, he wrote:

Asad: You don't want to tell me who your sources are, where your money comes from, or what you're trying to accomplish, but you are willing to 'touch minds' with me?

Anaku: Yes.

He didn't elaborate.

Asad: Sorry but that sounds like more intimacy than I'm comfortable with.

He was also intrigued and didn't want to close the door on the possibility, so he qualified:

Asad: Until I know you better.

Anaku: I understand.

Leo had precisely nothing by which to identify this guy, but he was dying to check out the array. Hoping he'd find a way to justify such a reckless course, he asked:

Asad: Can I try it out for operating the Micromedium terminal?

Anaku: You should start with that to learn how to use it, regardless of whether you want to try its more profound capabilities.

Asad: Is there any danger?

Anaku: No adverse effects have been reported so far, but it is a new technology. It does involve streaming subatomic particles through the brain. I can't say with certainty that there are no long-term effects. Studies indicate it is no more harmful than electromagnetic radiation from wireless Macromedium devices.

Asad: You've used it a fair amount?

Anaku: Several hours a day for more than two years.

Leo noted to himself that access to innovative technology for that long meant Anaku must have a connection either to the government or the manufacturers or designers, any of which would surely involve a security clearance. Anaku must have known he'd deduce this.

Asad: And no problems?

Anaku: No problems.

Asad: I appreciate the generous offer, but I don't feel comfortable being indebted to you. I don't know you or anything about you.

Anaku: You wouldn't owe me anything. You would be doing me a service by participating in the dissemination of this technology.

Leo considered that and wrote:

Asad: How would that benefit you? Can you monitor me while I use the array?

Anaku: It is not my intention to invade your privacy. If you're concerned about that, there are privacy settings and protocols that can reduce the risk of monitoring.

Asad: Reduce?

Anaku: Yes. Nothing on the Micromedium is immune from eavesdropping.

Leo rested his fingertips on the keypad and wrestled with how to proceed.

Asad: How does that help you gain 'insight into reality'?

Anaku: It is not I, but you who will see reality more clearly.

Asad: And that's what you want?

Anaku: Yes. Everywhere. Everyone.

Asad: Aren't some things better left secret?

Anaku: Not in my opinion. No.

Asad: Not sure I agree with that.

Anaku: That's fine.

He made no further comment.

Leo knew John and Jeaneane would both be concerned by his next move, but his hunch was that Anaku would not try to harm him. He didn't know whether this was wishful thinking but he stopped that line of inquiry and said he would like to try out the array.

They planned for Leo to pick up the equipment, software, and tutorials for their use.

Asad: Will you be there?

He hoped the answer would be yes.

Anaku: No. You know where to reach me if you have questions or want to explore a little more.

Leo found this offer stirring but resolved to defer further exploration until after he had taken the array for a thorough test run as a Micromedium terminal interface.

He thanked Anaku profusely.

Anaku: Not at all. Let me know your impressions when you're comfortable sharing them.

Leo said he would, thanked him again, and signed out.

Franz squawked as Leo sauntered to the bedroom and crawled under the covers. He lay down, wondering if this new device would be helpful as he worked on Anna's case and hoping he had not obligated himself to the wrong person.

He left a voice message for John telling him he had arranged to collect a quantum array and promising to tell him all about it as soon as he figured out how to use it. He then left a similar message for Jeaneane, and lay facing Franz, petting him and mentally replaying his conversation with Anaku until he dozed off.

11

Over the next several months, life became much busier for Leo and Anna.

Leo filed a petition with the Board of Classification to modify the criteria for Citizenship to accommodate Anna and similarly situated individuals. On its own, this drew no media attention. As expected, the conservative Citizens Action League publicly opposed the petition, and media lenses instantly snapped into focus.

CAL president Alistair Coyle appeared via macrovision in a paid public service announcement to denounce the petition. Coyle was a regular on the macrocircuit, weighing in on political and legal issues his constituency considered important. This kept them happy, him visible, and the CAL front and center in the perennial struggle over Citizenship and its thresholds.

Coyle was a sturdy man in his late sixties, with thick, black-rimmed spectacles and thin, grey hair, oiled back from a forehead so square it mimicked the macrovision screens framing his projected image. Clad in white, starched shirt with black coat and tie, he was sobriety made flesh, his appearance alone enough to leave some feeling justly admonished before he even commenced to speak.

"Fellow Citizens," he began, "I come before you today on behalf of the League to alert you about a troubling petition recently filed with the Board of Classification.

"The ill disruptors within our borders do not want to get well, fair Citizens. They do not want to work and accept our help to earn their way to full standing among us. They do not want to live according to our rules, no matter how many centuries of prosperity and peace have proven them just and right.

"No, brothers and sisters, the disruptors are jealous of our balance and quietude. They want to throw open the gates and obliterate the standards that have given us our strength. The petition of which I speak has been filed by a disturbed young woman named Anna Dao, a rare schizoid type afflicted with extreme traits in both the Vulnerable and Aggressive spectra. Her petition is dressed up to appear fair and reasonable." Coyle held up a copy of the document and donned an expression of innocence. "Just an expansion of the temperamental range within our ranks. How could anyone object to that?" He paused. "Make no mistake," he continued with a sharper edge. "If the petition were granted, the results are as predictable as they would be dire: social upheaval, surging violent crime, businesses pushed to failure when forced to accommodate the weak and unstable. Police in our workplaces, churches, and schools to protect us from deviants history has shown should be confined and segregated until they are well.

"Talk to your delegates, dear Citizens. Submit letters to the adjudicator who hears Ms. Dao's petition. Remind them that there are time-proven, legal paths to Citizenship, and that their job is to preserve them. Ours is a civilized society where no one is left out, provided they are willing to do the work.

"Thank you for your fidelity, fellow Citizens, and may God bless us all with temperance and strength."

Well-funded, politically connected, and endowed with a sophisticated public relations and communications infrastructure, the Citizens Action League gained an advantage in the court of public opinion with this opening salvo in its public relations blitz. Leo had not only anticipated this, he had hoped for it. It put Anna's case on the media map, which saved him the trouble and expense of getting it there himself. The conservatives' offensive could be spun as histrionic, bigoted, and paranoid, and their thrust could be harnessed to propel the very changes they sought to obstruct.

Leo avoided responding to the Citizens Action League's campaign until he had his own organizational infantry in place, which took a few days and required considerable diplomacy.

Respect, the organization seeking greater protections though not Citizenship for Vulnerables, would not endorse Anna's petition because it fell outside the group's mandate, but pledged to provide support where it could.

Spectrum, the Vulnerable organization working for expansion of the criteria for Citizenship, and Pro'gression, the moderate Aggressive group seeking expansion of the criteria from the other excluded end rarely joined forces because each viewed the other as carrying a stigma that undermined its prospects. Pro'gression didn't want to deal with the conservatives' fears about Vulnerables' dependency on public assistance for protection and therapy. Spectrum didn't want to deal with conservatives' fears about an uptick in crime if Aggressives were allowed into Citizen neighborhoods unsupervised.

Leo worked every backchannel connection he had in each movement, lobbying them with the argument that Anna, with both a nearly clairvoyant sensitivity and a fiery and combative temper when threatened, had features that made her a potentially powerful lever for both movements. She carried the hope of simultaneous expansion at both ends of the temperamental spectrum.

Both groups could claim victory if her case were to succeed. People within both their constituencies who were excluded from Citizenship might gain access to Citizenship through the same broadened door.

After a lot of convincing and help from allies, he persuaded Spectrum and Pro'gression to publish a joint statement of support for Anna's petition, which was a huge boon. Never had the two groups publicly joined hands. Their unity made the case even more threatening to the conservatives, regardless of Anna herself.

As the date for the hearing on Anna's petition approached, the Citizens Action League began organizing demonstrations outside the Board of Classification's hearing department, decrying the case as a host carrying a sociopolitical epidemic.

Spectrum and Pro'gression squared off against the conservatives at every rally, doing battle via placard and guerilla theater over subjects ranging from fairness in the courts to the opinions of God on Anna's petition, regarding which each side apparently had exclusive yet mysteriously conflicting reports.

Individuals associated with the radical Aggressive group Restruct started popping up at rallies. They proclaimed support for Anna and tried to sidle up next to activists from Pro'gression, but then began using megaphones and handbills to call for revolution at any cost.

"This petition is not enough," blared an unscheduled speaker at a demonstration in front of the Board of Classification headquarters. "The doors don't just need to be broadened, they need to be blasted off the hinges! Citizenship is a fraud! Burn the classification system to the ground! Revolution now!"

A Pro'gression activist yanked the Restructor's megaphone out of her hand. "You're playing right into the hands of the Cleagues, you fucking idiot!"

"She probably works for the Cleagues," chimed in a Spectrum compatriot. "Those morons are dangerous, stay away from them."

"I'm not the one working for the Cleagues, you stupid whores!" replied the Restructor. This fired up the less stable among the Pro'gressors, which could have sent things down a destructive course had cooler heads not prevailed.

The moderate groups, more numerous and better organized, overcame their own combative constituents and drowned out the Restructors with boisterous chants of tepid demands, like "Let her in!" "Due process for all!" and "Breadth is strength!" They also issued press statements disavowing any association with Restruct, which did not endear them to the radical Aggressives.

Leo fretted over the public skirmishes between the moderates and Restruct. He believed it should be possible to craft a comprehensive Progressive agenda that all the social movements could constructively embrace, and he agreed that the rift played into the conservatives' agenda. He could conceive parts of a unifying platform, but he had no time to develop it while advocating for Anna. The harsh political truth was that Restruct was a liability for her case, though he privately feared their exclusion would impede more long-term goals her petition was designed to advance.

These were academic concerns, however. The match, once struck, ignited a brush fire that flared beyond his influence.

For Anna, the months leading up to the hearing on her petition were traumatic, despite Leo's efforts to support and protect her. He kept her sheltered from media hounds by securing a protective order from the court and he arranged her transportation through means that insulated her from direct contact with the clashing demonstrations. The public never saw her face, but there was no way to protect her from the publicity. The culture warriors used her name and life as talisman, weapon, and evil portent, and she watched in horror as the parasitic and sensationalist media vividly amplified and commodified these opportunistic political maneuvers.

At the same time, she went through a private hell as evaluators subjected her to intrusive psychological and neurobiological testing. She had to endure these evaluations as the case progressed in order for the advocates to refine their arguments regarding whether and how the Board would have to modify the criteria for Citizenship to accommodate her. Excruciatingly detailed assessments of her profound sensitivity, intense volatility, and the relationship between the two drove the arguments on both sides.

Leo filed a prehearing brief, arguing that Anna's broad, balanced, and nuanced blend of Vulnerable and Aggressive features provided an optimal vehicle for modernizing the criteria for Citizenship in a manner consistent with centuries of evolving jurisprudence, forging a Citizenry that was increasingly textured and inclusive.

To exclude her, he contended, would perpetuate ugly and obsolete stereotypes ill-suited to an educated, scientifically developed, and intellectually honest society. It was time to refine the criteria to fit the subtlety and breadth of the human psyche and spirit for the benefit of all, especially the Citizenry itself.

Government Advocate Alicia Cheung submitted a brief in opposition, arguing that Anna's extreme combination of defenseless sensitivity and defensive volatility would make her and people like her walking bombs. Unable to stand their ground in situations tolerable to more appropriately temperate individuals, people like Anna would inevitably find others' words and actions wounding, then reflexively and disproportionately lash out. They would become victims who snap-morphed into violent criminals, creating instability the classification rules were designed to avoid.

The government relied heavily on the historic reasons for exclusion of the minority classes—Vulnerables because they needed protection from everyone and Aggressives because everyone needed protection from them. Individuals like Anna have a path to Citizenship, Cheung argued, a compassionate, sane path of guided development through education and therapy to help them mature into alignment with existing criteria for Citizenship. Anna Dao, not society's stability, needed to yield. If she wanted to change the rules, she should submit her request to the Council of Delegates and let the legislators work it out, Cheung concluded, not try to warp the existing law in her image through a judicial proceeding.

Once the parties had submitted their written arguments and began waiting for their hearing, the rhetorical war between the Citizens Action League and the shaky coalition of moderate activists gathered heat. Amidst the turmoil, Leo screwed up his courage and issued a public statement. His voice quavered at first and he felt blinded by the camera lights, but he had written his comments carefully and, once he started speaking, he grew confident:

"On behalf of my client, I ask the public commentators to exercise restraint and keep in mind that a human life is at issue here, one belonging to an individual none of you have yet had the privilege to meet.

"We are confident that the forthcoming proceedings will reveal that my client's petition represents a quantum step toward greater fulfillment of the values that make Citizenship something to be proud of. Through her, our community will grow deeper, broader, and will rise to a higher manifestation of its own true greatness.

"I urge those who seek to discredit my client's case to remember these things. First, to foment fear before the truth has been revealed is irresponsible and inconsistent with the most basic criteria for Citizenship. Second, the virtues of the Citizenry are its inclusiveness, defense of the vulnerable, responsible stewardship of power, and generosity of spirit.

"I would like to believe that those are values we all have in common, regardless of political predilection. Let us keep them in focus as this important case proceeds."

The words were temperate on their face but had the desired result. In the media coverage that followed, CAL President Alistair Coyle scolded the advocate for suggesting they were intolerant fearmongers or questioning the legitimacy of their commitment to the values of Citizenship. Spokespeople for Spectrum and Pro'gression scoffed at the conservatives' complaint because Leo had not made such accusations and would have been justified if he had.

Leo avoided the fireworks, refusing to make further statements or produce Anna for either public worship or pillory. The more the Citizens Action League cried foul while persisting in its opposition to Anna's petition before the Board even heard it, the shriller they sounded.

Alicia Cheung shrewdly sidestepped the cross fire and issued a terse statement that the case would be adjudicated in due course.

John used his considerable influence at the *Capital Times* to persuade colleagues covering Anna's case and the demonstrations to subject the conservatives to subtle ridicule. He spoke often with Leo during the precarious prehearing public melee, helping him strategize and keeping a supportive hand to his back.

Leo also consulted with Jeaneane, though their conversations usually tended toward satisfaction over "sticking it to the Cleagues." The controversy surrounding Anna's case, the collision of the social movements, and the media hype became so pervasive as the hearing approached that even Jeaneane, with her apparent allergy to reading the paper or following the news, was up to date.

"The case is hot," she told Leo. "Quite a shitstorm. Nice work."

Leo found his sudden notoriety as Anna's advocate exciting but also nerve wracking. He was too embarrassed to discuss that with John or Jeaneane, neither of whom had any reticence about public attention. At best, they would respond with condescending protests of understanding, which he could not stomach. He also strove to conceal his anxieties from Anna who, of all people, needed for him to be strong. This left him feeling alone, and sometimes at night he felt hairline fractures spidering down the girders of his mind.

When such episodes precluded sleep, he found palliative distraction in learning about the quantum array he received from Anaku. Over the weeks leading up to Anna's hearing, he loaded up the supporting software into his Micromedium terminal, figured out how to configure the array to his physical specifications, and ran tutorials. Some taught how to focus his attention, others how to calibrate the equipment and software to recognize his neural patterns.

The process reminded him of training old voice-activated dictation programs, except that instead of teaching the equipment to associate words and commands with sound patterns, he was training it to associate them with neural patterns. Unlike easily controlled speech, focusing his thoughts and screening out extraneous noise was challenging. Interacting with the equipment and observing its responses helped him zero in his intentions, which in turn made the equipment more responsive and accurate. The feedback loop was pleasurable. The hard work produced a mental concentration that screened out his chaotic thoughts about Anna's case and associated subjects, and generally calmed his nerves. After a few hours of practice, he was fatigued and relaxed enough to sleep.

By the eve of Anna's hearing, Leo had become adept at using the array to navigate the Micromedium and engage in textual exchanges using his mind. He celebrated by describing the learning process to Anaku through a micromissive written without ever touching a keyboard.

Anaku replied with a single word: "Excellent."

Leo felt an excited rush. He was certain the new technology would be of enormous significance, both to him and to the world. In this, he was correct.

12

While Anna's case boiled, Liam O'Brian, a.k.a. Infiltr8org, conferred several times with his hacktivist cadre. The individual who went by the moniker Hackizen met and, for a hefty sum procured by Liam, trained extensively with the shadow group that had reverse engineered the quantum arrays. Though he gave Liam's group progress reports along the way, it took six weeks before he could provide a comprehensive briefing. Hooked in via quantum neural interface, the hacktivists thought their words onto the shared virtual page:

Infiltr8org: What did you learn?

Hackizen: More than you want to know.

Infiltr8org: Can we spy on the field surrounding the DII hub undetected or not?

Hackizen: Yes, at least theoretically. It is possible to tap into a quantum neural field without being detected.

Aggresserable: Possible is good.

Hackizen: I said theoretically possible, but complex and difficult.

Infiltr8org: OK, let's have it.

Hackizen: Three components: hardware, software, and mental training. All risky. None easy.

Infiltr8org: Proceed.

Hackizen: Step one, hardware. We can configure the arrays to dampen our signals so they are less disruptive to the target.

Subterraneum: Sounds like something we could learn.

Hackizen: Definitely, but it's not enough on its own. It is impossible to completely suppress your quantum neural field and spy on someone else's because you can't tap another person's mind without interpenetrating your field with theirs. You must generate a field strong enough to contact the target's, but weak enough to minimize the chance of being detected.

Sleeperagent: Should be doable.

Hackizen: It's harder than it sounds.

Infiltr8org: So configuring the array to dampen the field is a start but not enough to avoid detection.

Hackizen: Right, so step two: tweak the operating software. We can warp the field output so that the projected image of our hypothetical eavesdropper's mind is out of phase with the target's. We run into the same balancing issue here as with the hardware, though. Too much phase disparity would make the link impossible because the eavesdropper's conscious mind must directly contact the target's to perceive it, but too much direct contact would alert the target.

Sleeperagent: That sounds harder.

Hackizen: It is.

Infiltr8org: What's the solution?

Hackizen: This is where it starts to get weird.

Subterraneum: Am I the only one who thought we passed that point a while back?

(Laughs all around.)

Hackizen: The next trick is to aim the quantum field intersection point beneath the surface of the target's conscious mind. This is trippy and hazardous. If the spy's field is too narrowly focused on the target's subconscious, the feedback can get surreal and disturbing. There is a reason we have boundaries between our conscious and unconscious minds. If you tap into someone's nightmare realm, it can fuck you up, and I don't mean temporarily.

Aggresserable: Did you ever try it?

Hackizen: Yes, and I saw some freakish shit in a few of my practice targets' mental hell realms. Some of the images still infect my dreams.

Infiltr8org: That sounds dangerous, Hack. I didn't expect you to risk injury to gather intel.

Hackizen: I'm tough. It was worth it. With practice, you learn how to aim at the lowest reaches of the target's conscious awareness, just above the threshold of subconsciousness.

Sleeperagent: How?

Hackizen: Partly science and partly trial and error. You must start with a map of where the neurosleuths think the boundary between conscious and unconscious mind lies in the brain, and aim your field to the corresponding location in the target's field.

Aggresserable: I know something about this. Those maps are crude approximations. No one knows where consciousness resides in the brain. It's probably distributed and resilient.

Hackizen: Could be. Nevertheless, stealth contacts have been achieved by focusing a phase-shifted spy field at the portion of the target field corresponding to the target brain's outer thalamic loops.

It wasn't easy but I improved with practice. Tweaking the hardware and the software is synergistic. When both are in balance, it's possible to briefly contact another individual and gather impressions from her, if you don't linger.

Aggresserable: The target doesn't notice?

Hackizen: The target detects a disturbance but initially perceives it as coming from her own mind. Like I said, the subterfuge can only be deployed briefly. The target's mind will sift out the stimuli and realize a contact had occurred. As you might imagine, this can trigger panic. Rumor is it can even cause a psychotic break if the target suffers from an organic instability.

Sleeperagent: Lovely. These risks wouldn't be limited to us?

Hackizen: Nope.

Infiltr8org: We'll weigh that out later. Finish your briefing. How do we contact another neural quantum field undetected long enough to get something useful?

Hackizen: Step Three: highly disciplined mental training.

Aggresserable: What kind of mental training?

Hackizen: The eavesdropper must learn how to keep his mind sharply focused, void of thought and emotion, and open to the target field.

Subterraneum: How can you operate the interface if your mind is empty?

Hackizen: Through tightly controlled, nonverbal intention. You point your mind like a laser.

Infiltr8org: You'd have to be a monk in a cave somewhere to pull that off.

Hackizen: It is the most challenging component. It's not impossible though. We can speed up the learning process. I'll tell you about that in a minute, but first think about this: If we can breach the DII's quantum neural sheath, then things really get interesting. It is theoretically possible for an eavesdropper to use her own mind field to trace the target field back to its emitter array. If we could get that far undetected, it should be possible to manipulate the array itself.

Sleeperagent: Are you serious?

Hackizen: Yep, and it gets better. In theory, we

could configure the eavesdropper's and target's arrays to enable a direct connection between them via quantum tunneling.

Subterraneum: We could hack a hardline through the neural shield into the DII hub itself?

Hackizen: Exacto.

Infiltr8org: That's more than I expected you to find, Hack. I'm stunned. We have to find a way to do it.

Hackizen: It'll take time and patience, which are not the strong suits in this group.

Aggresserable: Speak for yourself.

Hackizen: I am.

(laughs)

Hackizen: We all must become proficient at deploying a disguised intrusion into the quantum neural field surrounding the DII hub. That alone is next to impossible. If we get past that, we can explore and analyze the structure of the DII sentinel field. *Then* can we begin to construct a strategy for piercing the field and tunneling through to the arrays.

Subterraneum: And the DII hub itself.

Hackizen: Ultimately, yes. Theoretically. You understand?

The group agreed that they should each train in all three techniques and ascertain who had the greatest proficiency at the mental discipline component before they decided who would hazard the tunneling task.

Infilt8org: We should figure that out before anyone even tries scouting out the sentinel field.

Everyone agreed. Liam was confident that he would surpass his friends on the mental discipline vector not only because of their volatility and disorder, but also because he had practiced meditation for several years as part of martial arts training he had undertaken to calm his nerves and focus his mind. He didn't share any of this during the early discussions. He stepped up his training to keep an edge on the others, certain that when they engaged in the exercises Hackizen described, he would be the indisputably optimal choice for the mission. In any event, he held the purse strings and was unwilling to place the others at risk of losing life, liberty, or worse. One way or the other, Liam intended to be the person who tunneled into the DII hub.

Once Hackizen had briefed the group on what he had learned, they talked about how to train for penetrating the DII field under cloak. Hackizen distributed detailed instructions on the hardware and software configuration for the others to study.

> **Sleeperagent:** Except for Hackizen, none of us has even tried a neural link, much less attempted one without the knowledge of another party. How can we do that without putting ourselves in danger?
>
> **Aggresserable:** We should try it with each other first.
>
> **Subterraneum:** No offense but I don't want you guys experimenting on me, and I doubt you want me experimenting on you.
>
> **Infiltr8org:** It's best that we maintain limited knowledge about one another in case one of us is arrested.
>
> **Subterraneum:** You mean abducted.
>
> **Sleeperagent:** Same difference.

No one disagreed.

In the end, they decided that each would develop basic proficiency with the neural linking process by investigating it with someone they knew and trusted personally. Once they all understood and had experienced this extraordinary phenomenon, they would reconvene. Each of them was also to study the equipment and software configuration specs and commence a rigorous course of mental training.

The reverse engineers who trained Hackizen had given him a short list of qualified teachers whose discretion they vouched for and whose skills, both in mastery of their own minds and in the art of teaching, they regarded as highly advanced.

> **Hackizen:** One advantage to working with a certified teacher is that the sessions would be confidential and shielded by legal privilege.
>
> **Sleeperagent:** For what that's worth.

Infiltr8org: It could be worth a great deal.

In truth, he shared Sleeperagent's belief that official niceties would be of little use if the group's objective were ever suspected, but there was no point in planting seeds of doubt before they began. They had to train somehow.

Hackizen: We should use separate teachers so that our paths don't cross and no single teacher will encounter multiple puzzle parts.

Sleeperagent: We can't stop them from talking to each other.

Hackizen: No, but they are competitive and they have ethical duties of confidentiality. We're less exposed than you fear. Most of the stuff that comes up sounds like noise.

Aggresserable: If we're working with different teachers, won't it mean we're learning different techniques?

Hackizen: How much difference does that make? The goal is to focus and quiet the mind, however it's achieved.

The group set an initial ninety-day period to try out the arrays for neural interfacing, master the technical material, and undergo training in mental discipline. They would take practice runs at cloaked neural espionage, using the harmless medium of the social sites.

Hackizen: Before we try that, I'm told it is possible to accelerate the mental training by participating in social sites where they do neurally joined group meditation.

Hackizen gave them the coordinates of two sites his associates said were reliable, both in authenticity and confidentiality.

Hackizen: These groups are devoted to accelerated awakening of the mind through neurally connected, joint practice. They don't care about people's life debris, if a participant is serious about the training.

Sleeperagent: Sounds risky. I don't like it.

Hackizen: Don't try it until you've achieved solid, sustained concentration in your individual training. These teachers can induce a stable meditative state within weeks. Practicing in a neurally linked group will accelerate your learning geometrically with little risk. Don't rush into it.

Aggresserable: Before we sign on for this, I would appreciate knowing something about how these people you know came by this knowledge.

Sleeperagent: Me too.

Subterraneum: Ditto.

Infitr8org: Hack, is there anything you can share that would put us at ease?

Hackizen: I'm willing to tell you my suspicions. The more I learned from these guys, the more certain I became that they were tapping into an information source beyond their own circle. I tried to ingratiate myself and earn their trust, but I couldn't get anyone to spill their source.

Sleeperagent: Doesn't that make you nervous?

Hackizen: Yes, and I intimated as much.

Infiltr8org: How did they respond?

Hackizen: They answered that if a source existed, they had the collective sense and expertise to ensure that it was not a threat and that whatever they learned from it was sanitized before its use so no danger would result to anyone who applied the resulting techniques.

Aggresserable: Do you trust them?

Hackizen: I don't trust anyone. If I had to guess, I would say their work is funded by a foreign government, a well-connected domestic antigovernment group, or both. I don't believe they simply reverse engineered the arrays. They must be accessing highly classified intel.

Aggresserable: That would require someone within the government or connected to it.

Hackizen: I agree.

Sleeperagent: What could motivate someone to leak that kind of information?

Hackizen: I can imagine lots of reasons. Dwell on it and your head will spin off your neck.

Infiltr8org: If this is front-edge intel, it gives me hope for our mission, but not knowing the source makes me nervous. You didn't pick up any clues at all?

Hackizen: In the middle of my training, I walked in on one end of a conversation I wasn't supposed to hear. I caught a few words, but I couldn't tell whether they were technical terms, monikers, or names.

Subterraneum: Can you remember any of it? Maybe one of us will know what it means.

Hackizen: There was one word I heard several times but couldn't catch, something like *ahkoo*. The guy on my end discovered me and severed the conversation before I could get the context. I was lucky I didn't end up in a ditch over that little gaffe. I couldn't ask for clarification.

Infiltr8org: Does that mean anything to anyone?

No one responded.

Infiltr8org: We should proceed cautiously. No matter how far we get, we should abort if anyone detects signs we are being tracked. Be alert.

Their training agenda established, the hackers scheduled weekly check-ins to compare notes and coordinate their progress and observations

Liam was pleased with the cadre's industriousness, especially Hackizen's, and told them so, both verbally and through an advance bonus untraceably transferred to accounts they could access at their leisure.

13

James Malone was aware of the ruckus surrounding Anna's case but did not care about it. Modifying the thresholds for Citizenship would create, at worst, a minor inconvenience to the Department of Domestic Intelligence. The status of people under investigation might need shuffling. Even if the Cleagues were right and expansion of the criteria for Citizenship precipitated an uptick in violence and instability, it would mean more funding for law enforcement. "Job security," James periodically proclaimed when skimming a story about the escalating culture wars. Ordinarily, he would leverage developments like these to seek expanded authority to infiltrate the political groups and conduct surveillance of their members. Today, however, there was more enticing fare on the menu.

James carefully managed his involvement in Lauren's investigation into the neurally mediated parasitic abuse. He occasionally bucked her authority to maintain a consistent persona and avoid suspicion, and he conducted enough interrogations of his own to appear as though he were genuinely assisting the investigation. The only thing he truly cared about was to be the lead agent when it came time to enter the neural interface abuse sites undercover. In pursuit of that objective, he stole time to master the fundamentals of operating the quantum neural array Micromedium interface.

He had a natural aptitude for the new technology. Mental focus had never been a problem for Agent Malone. Among the many testimonials to this fact was a trail of romantic carnage in his wake, dozens of women and a few men who hungrily, often obsessively, sought to know the vulnerable soul they thought they saw peeking from behind the hard, thrillingly intelligent, and coldly driven persona. James was aware of the seductive power he wielded through permitting glimpses of tenderness, then pulling away as an admirer tried to see into him more deeply. He was a master at the art of enticement and denial, forever the wounded wolf pup who needed the right nurturing to help him heal, whose love, once he felt safe enough to share it, would be the stuff of legend. With scientific precision, James's tender core was always maddeningly out of reach, retreating like a mirage as soon as his prey yielded to the urge of pursuit. He prided himself on the ability to lure even the most independent and cynical of quarry into his trap. The thrill was subjugation of their resistance and self-respect. Once he achieved that, he moved on to greater challenges, slamming shut doors of emotional granite, leaving his sometime lover to a solitude of shock, rage, and despair.

James's icy detachment served well in the professional arena too. He excelled at debate in criminal justice classes on subjects others found disquieting. This caught the eye of a DDI recruiter and earned James a foot into the agency with a job as an investigator's assistant. From there, his career ascent was rapid and calculated. Work became the scaffolding of his life, the thing he always fell back on for support when other areas were less satisfying. He cleared his mind from romantic matters with unwavering focus on an investigation the way a wine taster clears his palate with a sip of water and bite of bread. Whenever he'd satisfactorily compromised his current lover's personhood, he used acute attention to his cases as the tool for erasing her from his mind and life. This ability to compartmentalize and screen out thoughts and sensation proved instrumental to James's enviable professional reputation and freedom from untidy emotional entanglements.

Learning to command the Micromedium terminal using the quantum array came easily to him. He trained his mind and the equipment to work together and within weeks had dispensed with conventional interfaces.

Except when he was within sight of his colleagues, that is.

By the time Lauren had secured a set of basic quantum array interfaces through proper procedure via the DDI–DII liaison, James was already reading about how to form neural links and scouting out the social sites. By the time Lauren briefed her colleagues on basic configuration and use of the arrays to issue commands to the terminal, James had settled on a site and was primed to venture his first mind link.

He would have progressed more rapidly were he not also commanding an illegal, clandestine mission at the behest of his backchannel DII contact, Agent Baikal (whom James continued to believe was Sandoval). Using Fredrick Luttrell and SecurePort, the security firm where James had placed him as director of labor relations, James systematically coordinated the installation of eavesdropping equipment throughout every major national government venue to which they had access.

When James collected his own advanced quantum array and associated materials Baikal had arranged for his use, he also picked up the first of many shipments of devices for installation in the courtrooms of the Department of Adjudication, chambers of the Council of Delegates, hearing rooms at the Board of Classification, local police interrogation rooms and investigatory offices, and various administrative locations throughout the government. He almost flinched when he saw the scale of what was afoot. His initial hesitance promptly dissolved when Agent Baikal promised access to the most classified intel regarding uses of the arrays and an unlimited budget for deploying his temporary agents. He also chose to take solace in Baikal's assurance that the operation was a critical matter of national security because the DII had reliable evidence of a treasonous conspiracy at the highest levels of government. Baikal promised to provide James with leads to career-making busts that would eclipse anything he'd done before and, combined with the DII's political influence, result in his eventual appointment to the directorship of domestic intelligence, not to mention a statue erected in his honor at the DDI headquarters rotunda.

Fame took a back seat to conquest and punishment in James's hierarchy of desired pleasures. Nevertheless, he could think of few costumes more lethally intoxicating than the directorship of domestic intelligence. Adorned with that persona, James could subvert nearly anyone. The thought made his pupils dilate.

Using Fred Luttrell's access and connections, James relayed schematics of each target venue to Baikal. In return, he received detailed instructions for installing and configuring the surveillance devices. Luttrell recruited a loyal cohort of compromised SecurePort employees through old union contacts and, coached and equipped by James, hooked them with a combination of threats and handsome inducements. Half were security agents and half custodial employees. James also brought in other operatives whose loyalty he'd cemented through life-changing intercessions in sticky government matters, monetary awards, and placement in precarious situations whose continuation or collapse were within his control.

With a combination of compromised SecurePort staff and outside operatives using stolen SecurePort employee clearances, James and Luttrell set about systematically implementing nothing less than a government-wide surveillance intrusion.

All the setups involved quantum field emitters and detectors, arranged to scan neural activity at various levels of specificity. Some devices were configured to surveil quadrants of a room to gauge the level of a crowd's group temperamental state. Others were set up for a more concentrated focus.

In the courtrooms of the Department of Adjudication, the installations were precise and specific. Large QFRI nodes, shaped like bells attached via pivot mounts to an assembly containing a power source, computer, and a data transceiver, were installed above ceiling panels and under the floors. Smaller nodes, resembling large thimbles attached at their caps via pivot mounts to junior versions of the control boxes for the larger nodes, were installed at each advocate's podium, and in the walls around the adjudicator's bench, the witness seat, and the jury box.

For each podium, three nodes were placed below where the speaker's head would be located during a proceeding. Similar configurations were installed around the adjudicator's and witness's seats, and a cat's cradle shaped array of the devices was placed around the jury box.

Shielded nuclear batteries powered all the nodes, so they would neither depend on nor draw suspicion through consumption from the building's power grid.

Once the units were situated, the operatives remotely activated them and launched preinstalled configuration software. The nodes, or compact particle-accelerator guns, emitted streams of subatomic particles upon activation, instantly detected one another, and aligned according to preset specifications based on the room schematics James had supplied to Baikal.

Wide particle streams crisscrossing through the room between the large nodes in the floor and ceiling could track the location and movement of the room occupants. When an individual stepped up to or into a station such as an advocate podium or the witness box, narrow particle streams running between the smaller nodes at each station and the larger nodes in the ceiling would scan the person. The small nodes at the station would then align their particle streams to intersect through the individual's brain on their way to the larger nodes in the ceiling, generating a rudimentary quantum field resonance image of the person's mind. Once the nodes had zeroed in on the target's brain, they could track it if it was within the range between the small nodes at the station and the larger nodes in the ceiling.

If the particle streams had been visible, they would have resembled an old-school, laser-based alarm system, its beams crisscrossing the room like a web. When DII agents processed data from the surveillance installations, they could have it represented in a form much like this. For people in the bugged rooms, the nodes and particle beams would be undetectable.

Data from the devices streamed through a nuclear-battery-powered central hub equipped with a satellite uplink at each of the government venues. The resulting information would be much less specific than the detailed quantum neural resonance field images produced by the cranial QFRI Micromedium interface arrays. James wondered how the comparatively crude data mined through these large-scale room arrays could be used, but Baikal told James such knowledge was above his pay grade.

It took eight weeks for James's task force to mine the short list of major national government venues with QFRI surveillance devices. Once the operatives were trained, James had Luttrell set them up in a more self-sustaining and compartmentalized command structure so they could accelerate and expand the process and minimize the risk of compromising the whole operation. None of the operatives knew who James was and Luttrell knew nothing about James's DII contact.

Once he had delegated coordinating the installation raids to Luttrell, James focused his work with Baikal on covering the operatives' tracks and thwarting any suspicions that could lead to discovery of the installations. This was unpretty work of a variety James coolly enjoyed. When Luttrell reported to James that one operative may have breached confidentiality by hinting to a co-worker with a nudge and a wink that a secret operation was underway, the individual vanished. This disappearance aroused fear among the operatives, which James surreptitiously inflamed with rumors the DII had shipped the snitch overseas for interrogation about the recent terror attacks. The unnerving fact that no reports of the disappearance ever appeared in the Macromedium news outlets bolstered the spook value of this scenario. Conspiracy theories pulsed on the Micromedium, but there was nothing definitive. Together, these shadows had the desired effect of sealing the lips of the other participants and chilling the curiosity of other SecurePort staff.

When James was ready to brave his first neural link, data from the surveillance arrays was streaming to a command center somewhere, though he knew neither where nor for what specific purpose. His hunger for knowledge of all things hidden was strongly aroused, but he disciplined himself to leave well enough alone. The cost-benefit analysis favored dutiful cooperation.

Agent Baikal was so pleased with the pace and effectiveness of the deployment that he gave James access to information about the quantum arrays he was sure Lauren would not receive through normal channels. It was for knowledge like this, James reminded himself, and hope for potent career prospects on the horizon, that he allowed himself to be used as a conduit for the DII agent's staggeringly subversive intrusions. *Harnessing the quantum arrays will make my prostitution worth the sacrifice to my dignity,* James thought with a laugh.

Of this, he became more certain with each detail he learned about the new technology.

14

THE OUTDOOR BAZAAR NEXT TO Memorial Park was like a watering hole in the savannah for people living in the capital. It provided nourishment to body and spirit, and served as a social venue for both Citizens and members of the excluded classes. Strong police presence discouraged bad behavior, but the cops did their best to stay in the background.

The offerings were dazzling: Textiles from all over country and world, wares of local artisans and farmers, cafés, bakeries, restaurants, and bookstores. People often loitered for hours, purchasing nothing more than a cup of tea or a pastry, and gorging on the colors, music, and pulsating human mosaic.

The day before the hearing on Anna's petition, Leo took a break from his intensive preparation and strolled through the public marketplace, hoping it would clear his thoughts and refresh his spirits. For the most part, the bazaar did not disappoint: Leo strolled among the offerings, his senses awash in silken fabrics rippling in the sunlight, rainbow strands of semi-precious stones, aisle after aisle of glazes, carvings, paintings, glasswork. Wisps of resinous incense blended and clashed. Leo closed his eyes and thought to himself that the crowd's overlapping conversations sounded like a marimba percussing on the breeze, but the sublime perspective was short lived.

"Those shoes were the only thing I wanted to buy," griped one disgruntled tourist to her companion as they passed by Leo's ear. He opened his eyes to view the source of this first-world complaint and was greeted with a waft of cigarette smoke.

Leo craned away from the fumes and his eyes fell upon vendors pedaling traditional crafts like the apparently timeless wooden geese with bonnets. *God how depressing*, he thought. He pivoted to admire a strand of turquoise beads and was savoring an oily sip of coffee and critiquing his own attempts to filter out stimuli he found distasteful when he heard a familiar voice. Wendy, the waitress from the Heartwood Pub he and John frequented, was standing across the square from the row of booths where he had lingered. She was wearing dark glasses, but Leo could tell by the abrupt cessation of her speech and the way she snapped her face toward him that their recognition was simultaneous and mutual. Another woman, muscular and fierce, all sharp angles to Leo's eye, was holding Wendy's hand. She turned toward him too, but didn't look friendly.

Leo started to raise his hand in greeting, and Wendy began to open her mouth, when out from behind a group of strangers strode Anna, still chattering full tilt over the joke she had been sharing with Wendy and her companion. Leo pulled his hand down instinctively, and Wendy's mouth snapped shut. "I'll be damned," he said softly. Sharing his instinct that he and Anna should not be seen together publicly, Wendy shrugged and tilted her head, her blond bristles twinkling in the sunlight. Anna followed Wendy's gaze and spied Leo, then put her hands on her hips in mock exasperation over her inability to shake him. Leo choked back a giggle and turned away.

Anna's face was miraculously still a public mystery, but Leo's wasn't. They could not risk him drawing attention to her by openly socializing, much as he wanted to say hi.

He left the square and wondered how he should spend his final evening before Anna's hearing. He decided he could satisfy both his professional responsibilities and his curiosity about Anna's relationship with Wendy by reviewing his notes while relaxing at the pub. This was Thursday so Wendy probably had stopped by the bazaar on her way to work.

The Heartwood Pub was situated within walking distance on a transitional street between the bazaar and a charming part of town where dining and clubbing tended toward late-night hours. He passed a store selling high-end kitchen implements, several art galleries, and a spice shop. He imagined buying a small fortune worth of fun gadgets he didn't need, allowing time for Wendy to beat him to the pub. He stopped by his car and riffled through Anna's file, selecting a thick hearing notebook, a legal pad, the prehearing briefs, a few pens, and some divider stickers. He threw everything in his briefcase and headed for the Heartwood.

The joint was abuzz with loquacious patrons revved up from a day at the bazaar, starting the weekend early with a night on the town. Leo inhaled the homey, sweet-and-sour blend of yeast and savory victuals while scanning the room for an out-of-the-way table.

Wendy emerged from the kitchen, buttoning a strap on the cook's apron she wore over a dress that was hand painted pink and green in a plaid design which somehow, due to its splashed-on irregularity, telegraphed smart-assed irreverence. She ran her eyes over him, pausing for a nanosecond on his briefcase, and then tipped her head toward a table against a wall by the front window.

Leo acknowledged with a wave and made his way past tables of revelers, into a chair with his back against the wall so he could see both the room and out the front window.

Wendy made her way over. "Satisfactory?" She was still straightening her garments as she stood facing him across the table.

"Perfect."

Leo wasn't sure how best to initiate the conversation he desired.

"Are you on duty already?"

"Not for another five minutes, but I'll make an exception for you, Advocate Baksh."

Leo chuckled at this feigned formality. "That's very kind, Ms... ."

Wendy tilted her head, waiting with demure interest.

"I'm afraid I don't know your last name."

She playfully snuck a response behind the back of her hand: "Malone," she whispered, "but please, call me Wendy."

"Wendy, I wasn't asking if you could wait on me, but if you could join me for a round."

Wendy pointed at herself in inquiry.

He pointed at her to confirm. "I'm Leo."

She furrowed her brow and glanced over her shoulder. "I'll do both. Let me get Tye to cover my tables for a few minutes and I'll grab some stuff for us."

"Will that be OK? With your boss, that is." Leo glanced vaguely around the room, but didn't see anyone acting in charge.

"Oh sure," she answered, flicking away the question.

"Great, um, I guess I'll have—"

"Leave it to me," Wendy cut him short. "I think I know what you like." And she was off.

Leo wondered if her parting shot had more than one meaning but didn't dwell on the thought. Concerns about the hearing began to intrude. He started to open his briefcase but realized it would be rude to have work spread out when Wendy returned. In a few minutes, she came back carrying a pitcher of deep golden brew and two glasses, deftly balanced on a tray.

"Broiled mushrooms and some hot artichoke dip are in progress, but let's start with this," she said, laying plates with a baguette, goat cheese, and a bowl of olives on the table.

"Wow," Leo said. "That's beautiful. And quick."

"I know the kitchen staff," she noted in mock confidence, placing the tray on an empty table nearby and flowing into the chair opposite his in one graceful movement. "So," she said, tearing off a piece of bread, spreading it with cheese, and placing it on Leo's plate.

"So," Leo replied, pouring beer, first for her, then for himself.

For a moment, it seemed like this interaction could go anywhere. Anywhere at all. Leo imagined them embroiled in a raging political debate, crying over family sorrows, or doing the dance that people do and tumbling into bed.

The reason he asked Wendy to step out of their standard roles toward greater intimacy, however, was to explore her connection with Anna, so he strode resolutely in that direction.

"You know Anna Dao."

Wendy finished arranging bread on his plate. "You mean your client. Yes, we met in our sixth year of school at one of those Citizen/Non-Citizen cultural encounter things they used to do."

"Really?" Leo said with surprise apropos of nothing.

"Truly and for real," she confirmed.

"I know you each in different contexts and had no idea there was a connection."

She spooned a few olives onto their plates.

"I guess that seems significant to me because I seem significant to me."

Wendy shrugged a silent giggle. "She likes you."

Leo resisted the urge to ask whether Anna was satisfied with his representation, but Wendy considerately saved him the indignity. "She trusts you, and she's glad you're representing her."

"Glad to hear that."

Even though they both apparently knew Anna, Leo could not discuss her case with Wendy unless Anna authorized him to do so. It was clear Wendy understood this, because she adroitly kept the conversation directed toward public aspects of Anna's circumstances. "I like the way you've been managing the publicity."

"Thanks, but I would hardly call what I've been doing 'management.' Feebly trying to hold back the tsunami, at best."

"Bullshit."

Her word choice and serious tone took Leo off guard. They nibbled olives and took a sip of beer, studying one another.

Leo drew a breath to ask whether Wendy could tell him anything helpful about Anna's upbringing, but Wendy took the lead.

"Anna's case is"—she stabbed an olive with a cocktail fork and held it up—"important." She popped it in her mouth and chewed, observing Leo.

Leo felt like he was on a game show and was supposed to discern clues from that single word. "Yes," he replied, "on many levels."

Leo waited for her to say more.

"I don't know where this is going," she continued, eyeing him as though assessing what he could handle, "but I do know that a lot will turn on the Board's decision."

He tipped his head from side to side. "Can you be more specific? Something beyond the customary pissing match?"

Wendy looked over her shoulder, waved to Tye, and pointed to the kitchen.

"All I can tell you is that a decision against Anna would be disruptive. *Extremely* disruptive."

Her portentous tone surprised him. This conversation had taken a bizarre turn and he didn't know what to make of it. He realized he did not know her at all, and he wondered about her life beyond the pub. How much of a mess he had gotten into by taking on Anna as a client?

"Restruct?" he ventured, hoping he sounded nonchalant.

Her face went slack. "Surely you know that 'Restruct' is fiction."

He felt as though he had stumbled off a sandbar into a chilly undertow. "Excuse me?"

She closed her eyes and shook her head as if to say she didn't have time to teach the rudiments. "Please be careful on the day of the hearing and while you wait for the Board's decision. What kind of security have you arranged for Anna and yourself?"

The odd turn in this encounter fished from Leo's memory the shiver he felt the night he and John had stopped by the pub and he noticed Wendy speaking with the tattooed fellow. He also wondered about the forbidding woman he had spied her with near the bazaar. Wendy's life clearly extended into less sunny dimensions he was being granted the privilege to glimpse. This intrigued him.

Leo said he worked with a firm that provided secure and anonymous transportation for Anna but that he had taken no special precautions for himself.

Dropping any vestigial pretense of cheery simplicity, Wendy said, "It is imperative that you protect yourself. Hire a bodyguard, and make sure he or she is an explosives expert. Watch your back. Check your car. Get someone to clear your house before you go there. This case is important," she repeated, the scale of her true meaning becoming disturbingly apparent.

Leo could not conceal his shock. "Who am I protecting myself from?"

Wendy set down her fork. "It's complicated. I don't know the whole story or all the pieces but things are not as they seem."

Leo urged her on with his attention.

"The Cleagues predict Anna's case would lead to instability, right?"

He nodded.

"Who benefits most from instability?"

"Benefits?"

"Stands to gain the greatest advantage."

He considered the question. "It depends on your perspective and time frame. Short term, those arguing for tighter restrictions would get the most mileage."

"Exactly. The Cleagues. There's nothing they would like better than to see the rest of us clamped down under martial law."

"Then why are they fighting Anna's case so ferociously?"

"Perhaps to set the stage."

Leo frowned as he mulled over the implication of her words.

"Set the stage for what?"

"A crisis. Maybe an attack?"

Tye arrived with the mushroom caps and artichoke dip, nudging plates aside.

"Thanks, hot stuff," said Wendy.

"It'll cost you."

"Promises, promises."

Tye looked playfully besieged, then headed for the next table.

"Surely you're not suggesting the Citizens Action League is planning a terror attack if Anna loses?"

Wendy let the question hang. "No. Not exactly."

"Then I'm confused."

Wendy's expression showed she wasn't buying his claimed naiveté. "As I'm sure you are aware, there are people out there who think tearing everything down is revolutionary."

"Yes," said Leo, "they must know some magic that will transform the ashes into utopia."

Wendy snapped her fingers. "I've always found that part mysterious, too."

Leo grinned. "I thought you said Restruct doesn't exist."

"I said it's a fiction. There are people who self-identify as Restructors, but there is no central organization."

This was in accord with what his contacts had told him.

"So it exists, but only as an idea that the conservatives use to scare people. Most of the so-called Restructors view themselves as radical Aggressive anarchists and have thought no further than throwing wrenches into the system."

Leo considered this, trying to assemble an image from the pixels Wendy was illuminating. "You think the Citizens Action League is controlling the radicals people call Restruct?" He was amused that Wendy's cynicism eclipsed even his own most jaded theories.

"Control, no. Influence for their own purposes?" she shrugged.

"That's implausible," said Leo after a beat. "It violates all their cardinal objectives. Stability, temperance, security."

Wendy examined him with pity. "Just be careful. Things are not what they seem."

Leo desperately wanted to know where Wendy was getting her information. He doubted she would tell him but decided it couldn't hurt to ask. "How do you know—"

Wendy stood before he could complete the question and excused herself to check in with Tye. When she returned, her tone was lighter. "I'm sorry," she said. "You kindly invited me to join you and I've spooked you with visions of political apocalypse."

Leo smiled with his lips but not his eyes and they ate together in silence for a time, exploring their own thoughts and sizing each other up.

"I'm sorry but I can't tell you more," she said, answering the unfinished question.

"Understandable," Leo responded. "You have no reason to trust me with," he wiped his fingers on a napkin, "potentially compromising disclosures."

Wendy gave him a shrewd grin. "If I didn't have reason to trust you, I wouldn't have told you any of this."

"You do realize that if something were to happen after this conversation, you would be a material witness in the resulting investigation."

"Not unless you reported it to law enforcement or the media, which I'm trusting you won't do."

"Upon what do you base all of this trust?"

"Anna trusts you and I trust Anna's instincts."

Wendy started stacking plates.

"Besides," she continued, "I am adept at playing stupid when dangerous characters ask impertinent questions. And," she said in a near whisper, "I'm not above lying or reciprocating the gesture if someone tries to throw me under the bus."

Leo choked at this audacious challenge.

"Furthermore," she daintily dabbed her lips with a napkin, "You'll find I'm a much more useful resource across a table full of tasty bites than through glass at the jailhouse."

Leo shook his head in silent flabbergast.

"Circumstances may warrant further discussion in time," she concluded.

"Fair enough," he surrendered, and they both exhaled, relieved to table the subject.

Wendy checked her watch and her colleague across the room. "I have taken advantage of Tye's goodwill."

"Go," said Leo. "I hope we can have a lighter chat next time."

Wendy dismissed the comment as she rose. "I'm made of tougher stuff than people realize," she said airily, tipping her head with the charm Leo recognized. "Though I do know how to have fun, at least when the world isn't being so serious."

Leo gave her a grim smile. "I can relate on both counts."

"Yes, I believe you can." The tenderness in her voice told Leo she had observed him more than he realized, or perhaps had picked him apart with his hyper-perceptive client.

This reminded him that the women's friendship was what he'd come here to investigate. "Have you shared your safety concerns with Anna?"

"No," she replied. "She has enough to worry about as it is."

As do I, Leo thought.

"Now stick your nose in those notes."

Leo gave her a little salute. She crouched and added into his ear, "Give them hell tomorrow."

With that, she turned to the task of clearing the table and, with a glint in her eye, left to hoist a few patrons from her overburdened coworker.

Leo pushed away the remains of his beer and caught Tye's attention to gesture for a cup of coffee. Then he opened his briefcase and spent an hour reviewing documents for Anna's case. Wendy's words of foreboding and political intrigue circled beneath the surface of his thoughts like a shark after blood.

He finally surrendered to the inevitable and headed home. On the way, he called John and relayed his exchange with Wendy. John obliged Leo with exclamations of astonished delight over the personality facets Wendy had revealed. Leo hoped John would dismiss Wendy's theory as preposterous, but John was less accommodating on that score. "Anything is possible."

"But it makes no sense," said Leo. "The Cleagues predict that instability would result if Anna won. It would make more sense for them to orchestrate an attack if she were victorious than if she lost. If she loses, they should claim their position vindicated and celebrate their success."

"Wrong angle," parried John. "They want to prevent any violence in response to a victory in Anna's case. If there were a terror attack after a decision in Anna's favor—"

"They would say it proves their point," Leo said, "and they'd flaunt their moral purity by condemning the attack."

"But it wouldn't meet the smell test."

"No one would suspect the Citizens Action League of a heinous crime," Leo persisted. "Not even I would suspect that, and I can't stand them."

"Most people wouldn't accuse the Cleagues themselves. But the public would be more likely to suspect someone politically aligned with them than someone sympathetic to Anna's case. Bad PR to say the least. The war of public opinion is fought over perception, not facts. They could not afford to risk that sort of taint and you can rest assured they know it."

"True."

"If Anna loses, the calculus changes. What do the Cleagues want? Power. Their power depends on exclusion and their arguments for exclusion depend on fear. What better proof of their claim that the forces supporting Anna's case are hell bent on destroying the Citizenry than a terror attack in retaliation for denial of her claim? Public relations gold for the Cleagues, my friend. If Anna wins, the Cleagues must step lightly and work against the perception they are greedy bigots. If she loses, they could seize the moment and attack the movements at their roots."

"I don't believe they're that ruthless," said Leo. "Maybe I am naïve but I can't believe the conservatives are that cold blooded and nihilistic."

"I'm sure most of them aren't, but it fits into a coherent strategy. It's plausible."

"I suppose." Leo rubbed his eyes with fatigue. "I'm headed home and I don't find it sufficiently probable to warrant abandoning Franz and staying in a hotel."

"If there's anything to Wendy's theory, you're perfectly safe at this stage of events. If anything, they would want you healthy so you could deliver the loss they plan to exploit."

"How comforting."

"But you should take her advice and hire security while you await the decision."

"I cannot afford that. The Board is paying for Anna's secure transportation but I doubt it would do the same for me."

"Ask. If it can't be arranged, I know a guy who protects our sources. I could work something out."

"I can't accept that, John."

"If you can't get coverage from the government, I will insist."

Leo said he'd think about it and thanked John for the offer.

"Get some sleep, counsel. You've exhausted your mind on collateral issues. You need your wits about you tomorrow. Let's talk after your hearing."

At home, the sole threat to Leo's safety was a cross geriatric feline. Taking John's advice, he went to bed without listening to voice messages or checking for micromissives. As soon as his head hit the pillow, his mind resumed its racing. In the midst of what would be a sleepless night, he logged onto the Micromedium to a message from Anaku: "Good luck. Be careful."

Leo passed a hand over his face to wipe away his fatigue and apprehension. Abandoning the futile hope for slumber, he got up to caffeinate and prepare for the hearing.

15

Leo approached the Board of Classification headquarters between two rows of riot police holding apart warring phalanxes of protestors. Voices blared through megaphones on either side amidst tattered and conflicting chants. Leo pointed his attention forward, but could not avoid hearing pieces of the demonstrators' rage: "Vul parasite! Greedy Cleague hypocrites!"

He smelled smoke and heard drumming, and just before he mounted the steps, he saw flames. His focus broke and he turned to view a strikingly recognizable likeness of Citizens Action League President Alistair Coyle burning in effigy. Leo and the cop he faced exchanged rattled expressions before Leo passed through the building's stately archway into the cooler realms of governmental order.

He steadied his nerves while he walked to the hearing department and prepared to rendezvous with Anna. When they spotted each other, her expression bore the same combination of fear, determination, and relief he felt. No matter how things transpired, at least the anticipation would be over.

Due to the social unrest that surrounded Anna's case, the Board's hearing officer agreed to exclude all media from the hearing.

The advocates stood at their podiums and when Hearing Officer Closun Mbeza entered, Leo's mouth went dry and his hands slickened with sweat as he tensed for civil combat. When the hearing finally commenced, however, it was surreally divorced from the chaos outside. Mbeza said the parties' briefs had thoroughly explored the relevant law and arguments. The only issue he wanted the advocates to address was whether Anna's claim fell within the Board's jurisdiction or was more properly a matter for the political process.

Leo elaborated upon his assertion that Anna's case flowed naturally from centuries of case law refining the criteria for Citizenship. Government Advocate Cheung argued that Anna's quest sought a fundamental revision of the concept of Citizenship, which must be addressed through new statutes, not a petition under existing law.

"If it please the hearing officer," Leo pressed, "I would like to call Ms. Dao as a witness in support of her claim. Her testimony will discredit the government's abstract mischaracterizations—"

"No," interrupted Mbeza. "This hearing is adjourned."

Stunned, Leo turned to his opposing counsel expecting to see his surprise mirrored, but Cheung looked smug.

The hearing officer, who had stood to leave, appeared startled. Leo followed the adjudicator's gaze to the viewing area behind the advocates' podiums and saw a woman rise to her feet. Jeaneane, who apparently had slipped in after the hearing was underway, skewered the hearing officer with unwavering, ice-cold fury.

Leo saw a flutter of robes as Mbeza fled the room.

"That's it?" asked Anna.

"Not a good sign," Leo replied as he threw papers into his briefcase. "He'll dodge on jurisdictional grounds. Fucking coward." The government advocate adopted a mien of open amusement.

"Then what?" Anna persisted.

Leo held his hand over his eyes, then turned to her calmly. "We appeal, or lobby the Council of Delegates, or both."

He stepped over to the other advocate's table and was about to ask whether she would be representing the government on the inevitable appeal when Jeaneane reached across the bar and gripped his wrist. She tipped her head toward the other side of the room and when they were outside the other advocate's earshot, whispered, "Why didn't you move to disqualify him?"

"On what basis?"

"Didn't you get my message?"

He'd never checked his voice messages from the previous night.

"No, sorry."

Jeaneane flicked away the apology. "The investigator in my assault case has been surveilling the headquarters of Interlink Technologies, the company where my client was assaulted."

"The one whose case the government blocked on state-secrecy grounds?'

"Right. One frequent visitor turned out to be Cormack O'Brian, president and CEO of Protection Inc."

"The prison contractor."

"Prisons and treatment wards. Yes. Purveyors of confinement for both Vulnerables and Aggressives."

"OK."

"I asked him to tail O'Brian. We knew Interlink was involved in Micromedium interface technology and I wanted to find out what the connection was."

Leo glanced over at Anna, who sat at the advocate's table, intensely focused on Jeaneane and Leo. Leo held up a finger and turned his attention back to Jeaneane.

"What does this have to do with my hearing?"

"My investigator photographed O'Brian handing an envelope to an elderly gentleman last night. When he showed me the picture, I recognized him as Hearing Officer Mbeza."

"Odd but hardly enough to move to disqualify."

Undeterred, Jeaneane continued, "Among the many details my investigator turned up when digging into O'Brian's life trail was a web of connections to the top leadership of the Citizens Action League."

"What kind of connections?"

Jeaneane enumerated them on perfectly manicured nails.

First finger: "Alistair Coyle, president of the Citizens Action League, is on the board of directors for Protection Inc."

Leo shuddered at the recent memory of Coyle's likeness wrapped in flames. Jeaneane attributed the gesture to general revulsion for the conservative leader and did not comment.

Second finger: "O'Brian has been required to disclose several massive donations to the Cleagues' endowment."

She held up a third finger: "Protection Inc. and the Citizens Action League have retained the same lobbying firm to advocate against expansion of the criteria for Citizenship and in favor of more severe prison sentences for Aggressives and broader grounds for institutionalizing Vulnerables."

Leo considered this intel as he admired Jeaneane's opalescent polish and knack for theatrics, large and small. "These facts alone do not constitute a breach of adjudicatory ethics," he said. "The Citizens Action League is not a party to this proceeding, let alone Protection Inc."

"Oh, please."

"Not officially," persisted Leo. "The adjudicator is permitted to have personal relationships in his private capacity."

"Not with an agent of so fiercely partisan an organization that has publicly taken a position on a case before him, and not on the eve of the key hearing."

"We don't know that O'Brian was acting as an agent of the Citizens Action League."

"We know they are organizationally, economically, financially, managerially, and politically entwined and coordinated," retorted Jeaneane. "We have a photo of O'Brian handing Mbeza an envelope on the eve of your hearing."

"We don't know what it contained. Your investigation has uncovered an unholy alliance between the prison profiteers and the socio-political conservatives. Interesting to know some of the details but the basic fact is no surprise. The raw fact that O'Brian handed Mbeza an envelope is not enough to disqualify."

"You could at least have questioned his impartiality and made a record of the issue. You still can. Move to reconvene the hearing."

Leo cradled an elbow with one hand and tapped a finger on his lip with the other as he mulled over Jeaneane's information and suggestion.

"You think she knows?" Jeaneane asked, jutting her chin toward the government's advocate, who was packing her papers in a leisurely manner. "She didn't seem surprised by how things went."

"No, she didn't," he agreed. "The adjudicator was shaken by your open scorn."

"Yep, and he is not known for breaches of judicial temperament. There's no way he could know what I know. But he looked afraid he'd been caught. At something anyway."

"Yeah, but maybe just at planning to take the cheap and easy way out."

Jeaneane grabbed Leo's arm to see his wrist watch. "Damn it. I'm going to be late to my hearing now."

"On?"

"The order quashing our subpoena in the assault case. And the gag order. We have a hearing in the Department of Adjudication Appellate Division in half an hour."

"Are you crazy? What are you doing here? Go!" he said, shooing her with his fingers.

"This is an historic hearing," she replied. "You're the advocate. How could I miss it?"

Leo raised an arm in presentation toward the empty adjudicator's bench.

"Pretty tepid for an historic hearing."

"Start working on the appeal," said Jeaneane. "See what Prince John the Muckraking Parasite—I mean World Class Journalist—can do with what I told you."

Leo slapped a hand over his eyes.

Jeaneane picked up her briefcase, fluttered her fingers in greeting to Anna, shot the government's counsel a snotty glare, and hustled out the door.

"What was that all about?" Anna asked as Leo returned to the advocate's table and began packing the remainder of his things.

"Tell you later," he replied, his attention on the government's advocate, who had run out of busy work to justify her continued presence in the room.

"Would you like to jot down a notice of appeal now?" said Cheung. "You could post-date it and save on postage."

Leo smiled coldly at the taunt. "This will be a long haul, and I have great stamina," he replied. "See you in the appellate division."

"See you there," she confirmed as the advocates hauled their briefcases off their desks and the three of them headed for the door. When they stepped into the hallway, Cheung gave Anna the once-over, then elbowed Leo and said, "You may have the stamina to fight this out, but does she?" She leveled a sneer of underwhelmed appraisal at Anna before turning on her heel and stalking away.

"Nice," said Anna.

"She's the pillar of justice we're supposed to entrust with our hopes for security and peace."

"What's her problem?"

"Same as everyone else," he replied. "She's human. Give people too much power and they lose sight of their own sense of decency. Believe it or not, she's among the more cooperative of the government advocates."

"That's pathetic."

"Yep. Anyway, let's talk this evening. I have to go say something to the reporters. Cheung and I will keep them distracted while you slip out the back."

"What will you say?"

"Something generic. That was my colleague Jeaneane Spence in there. She gave me some information that may call into question the adjudicator's impartiality, but I want to think carefully about whether and how to use it. I don't want to piss him off or tip our hand."

"What kind of information?"

"Not now."

Leo flagged Anna's courier and told him to leave by the back service exit in five minutes. Anna would be concealed behind tinted glass and spirited away during his comments to the press.

As they were about to part, Anna surprised him with a quick hug. "Thank you," she said, her hands on his shoulders. "Good luck with the reporters."

"Don't thank me yet," said Leo. "Our rocket just left the platform, and that was a choppy launch."

"We knew this wasn't gonna be a short journey."

"It would have been nice to start with the advantage. Get going. I'll draw off the reporters in four minutes."

Anna turned with a toss of her hair and started down the hall. Just before she rounded a corner out of Leo's sight, she peeked back and gave him a wave. He held up his hand in reply, then turned toward the front entrance.

Advocate Cheung was talking to the security guard as Leo approached.

"How do you want to handle this?" he asked.

"It's a tempest out there," she replied, an expression of acute seriousness playing over her ordinarily dispassionate visage. "Are you open to coordinating remarks? We should keep things as calm as we can. I'm no more interested in a riot than you are."

Leo concealed his surprise. "Glad to hear that," he replied. "There's not much to report yet."

"True," she said, her tone inscrutable. The gloat she had displayed in the hearing room was gone as the advocates prepared to face far less academic repercussions of the case they had begun to fight.

The security detail had cordoned off an area for reporters outside the physical reach of the protesters. Leo and Advocate Cheung exited the building together. Reporters barraged them with questions.

Leo spoke first: "This is the opening hearing in what we knew was likely to be a protracted series of proceedings. We are relying on Hearing Officer Mbeza to exercise reasoned judgment in his analysis of the important issues before him. No matter how he rules, I don't think anyone expects this to be resolved with his decision."

Ms. Cheung echoed Leo's diplomatically neutral statement. "This is essentially the commencement of these proceedings. We had an orderly hearing, focused largely on jurisdictional issues," she said, exchanging a glance with Leo and hoping their decision to disclose this fact would give the public time to digest it before the hearing officer ruled, thereby decreasing the risk of serious disruption by taking away the element of surprise. "The parties will decide how to proceed when the hearing officer issues his recommendation."

"Does that mean the Board's going to duck the petitioner's claim?" shouted one reporter over the din.

Leo and his adversary had prepared for this. "Neither of us is speculating on the Board's thinking."

"Did you address the merits of her claim?"

"We'll comment further after we receive the ruling," said the government's advocate.

With that non-response, Leo and Advocate Cheung said they had no further comment, shook hands professionally, and went their separate ways without responding further to the cacophony of questions and attempted provocations.

Despite their efforts to minimize the turmoil, word of the advocates' comments spread among the boisterous crowd. The conservative activists started chanting, "Dismiss! Dismiss!" An uncoordinated upwelling of anger from the factions supporting Anna coalesced around the chant, "Mbeza, where's your spine?"

"Lovely," said Leo under his breath. "Very helpful." Though in truth, he shared the sentiment.

Police escorted Leo to his car and cleared a path for him to leave. He focused straight ahead as he slowly drove through, ignoring the placards that waved on both sides. He turned on the macroaudio to drown out the din, but was confronted with his own voice as the stations broke from regular programming to broadcast the advocates' comments. He shoved some music into the player and ratcheted up the volume as he cleared the crowd. *Won't be hanging out in any public venues this evening*, he thought.

Although he knew the feelings ran deep around Anna's case, he was unprepared for the intensity of the public conflict. As he pondered the mass response to her petition, Leo became increasingly convinced that the details of Anna's case mattered less than its apparent suitability as a catalyst in a larger struggle over power in the country. He thought about the Citizens Action League's ties to the private prison contractor, and he wondered about activists on his side and what invisible forces might be influencing them.

"What have I gotten myself into?" he asked with a shiver as he pulled up to his apartment building. He was grateful he parked in a secure garage with direct access to the building. Even with these standard security protections, he felt relieved when he opened the door to his place and greeted Franz without incident.

Leo listened to messages he'd neglected the day before, as well as a slew of atta-boys from after the hearing. He also forced himself to follow through and call Anna. He filled her in on Jeaneane's information and they agreed to mull it over and talk again in a couple of days.

"This isn't even about me," Anna sagely opined. "I don't think it's even about my petition."

"We knew your claim would be controversial," he partially countered, though he could not muster much sincerity because he agreed with her.

"I knew your claim would spark a response," he said, "but it's a bigger fire than I expected. The tension between these factions has been building for a long time. Your case is the ignition. It's probably more about the timing than anything."

"Just my luck," she said.

"Our luck," Leo corrected, as much to comfort himself as his client. "We can always withdraw the petition if it gets too ugly."

"I thought you told me not to start this if I wasn't going to see it through."

"I did."

"Don't you dare chicken out on me."

Leo huffed. "I expect our team to take the medal," he said, "or go down fighting."

Neither spoke for a moment.

"Get some rest Advocate Baksh," she said at last.

"You too, Petitioner Dao."

Leo fed Franz, took a hot bath, and tried to put the difficult day to rest.

Protests over Anna's case continued, and anxiety mounted among Citizens and excluded classes alike as they awaited Hearing Officer Mbeza's decision.

Leo consulted at length with Jeaneane and John about the potential impropriety Jeaneane's investigator had photographed and related information regarding Cormack O'Brian's organizational ties. With Anna's blessing, he held the card until the ruling. When the time came, they decided they would leak a story to the press on the condition of anonymity. A public scandal might do more to torpedo Mbeza's ruling than a formal motion to disqualify him on grounds of bias. Neither Leo, Anna, Jeaneane, nor their media liaison would have to dirty their hands. Who knew what a talented investigative reporter might turn up?

It was three weeks before Mbeza issued his decision. To no one's great surprise, the hearing officer dismissed Anna's petition on grounds that her claim exceeded the Board's authority. Echoing the government's argument verbatim, the hearing officer advised them to consult the Council of Delegates for a requested change in the definition of Citizenship.

The parties' advocates received notice of the ruling two days ahead of the public announcement. Leo conferred with Anna, then with Jeaneane and John, and proceeded with the leak impugning Mbeza's professional integrity. John had worked ahead with his editors and promptly set one of his most rabid subordinates on the trail. The *Times* planned to publish an initial story alongside an article on the decision the morning after it officially became public.

Two days later, as the Macromedium and Micromedium frothed with news of the ruling, Leo went to the appellate division at the Board of Classification headquarters to initiate Anna's appeal.

Once he finished, he stopped at a café across the street to sip a cup of coffee and collect his thoughts. The barista was accustomed to serving adjudicators and advocates and was too smooth to comment on Leo's case, but the radio was reporting on the ruling in the background as she served up his coffee and, rather than avoid his gaze, she faced him and raised her hands in a *what can you do with these idiots* gesture. Leo reciprocated with a shrug of thanks for her polite condolences.

He turned away from the counter, walked to a table, set down his cup and was halfway seated when a blinding light flashed through the café's plate glass front, followed by a thunderous tremor that toppled his table, sent his drink flying, and showered the patrons in a torrent of shattered glass.

Leo was facing perpendicular to the window, which saved his sight, though not the skin on the left side of his face and neck. The concussion knocked him to his knees and he cried out as shards of glass peeled the skin off his bones when he landed. He tried turning his lacerated face away from the explosion's source, but his attention snagged on peripheral movement. Squinting through the heat and tornado of pulverized remains, he saw an enormous piece of what had been the Board building's vaulted entryway arcing toward the café.

He threw an arm in front of his face and crouched down. People scattered to the sides of the ruined venue, some dragging others, voices crying and screaming, as the projectile completed its trajectory, crashing through the debris of outdoor tables, cratering the sidewalk, and ejecting a spray of cement, tile, and earth in all directions.

Leo pulled his arm away from his face and felt his eyebrows and eyelashes singe from the fire blazing out of the gaping hole in the face of the Board headquarters across the street.

He took stock of his own condition and concluded he was ambulatory and could both see and hear, albeit through badly ringing ears. Others in the café were less fortunate. Some had been blinded by the flying glass. Many, including Leo, were bleeding badly. He locked eyes with the barista who, fortunately, had been facing away from the front of the building when the bomb exploded and had dropped down below the counter as soon as her nervous system registered the initial flash.

"We have to get everyone out of here," he shouted, "and we have to get some help." She winced at Leo's grisly appearance, but vaulted over the counter. Between the two of them, they led the less damaged to help the most gravely injured move away from the immediate blast zone. Police and emergency medical personnel swarmed over the scene as Leo and the cool-headed barista helped the last of the victims stagger over the rubble to safer ground.

Having discharged instinctive duties, Leo slid into shock. A triage paramedic examined him and asked about his condition, but Leo babbled about people inside the Board building. The paramedic beckoned a colleague to take over so he could move on to the next casualty. Leo was strapped onto a stretcher, then lost track of events as he strobed in and out of consciousness.

The explosion at the Board of Classification was one of three bombs detonated within a five-minute period in the capital. A second device destroyed a Citizens Action League administration building, and the third went off at the central offices of the national government's advocate general.

The bomb at the Board of Classification was positioned in the hearing department, apparently placed in a utility closet adjacent to the chambers of Hearing Officer Mbeza. Miraculously, he was out of the building at the time, but his law clerk was killed in the explosion. Several other staff members were also killed, and dozens were injured, some critically. The toll would have been worse, but the board had no hearings scheduled that day and most of the other hearing officers and their legal staff were off duty.

Two people were killed at the Citizens Action League administrative building, a minor fixture in the organization's extensive infrastructure that housed offices of the group's religious evangelical wing. The building was mostly empty when the attack occurred, minimizing the loss of life, but the symbolic significance of the target was impossible to ignore.

No one died or suffered serious injury at the government advocate's offices. Security was so tight at the building that the terrorist placed the device in a service entry at the back of the building. Nevertheless, the brazen attack on the government's chief office of litigation struck at the heart of the Citizenry's sense of collective security.

Leo spent a night at the hospital receiving treatment for his lacerations and a blood transfusion.

The moderate activists—Respect, Spectrum, and Pro'gression—issued a joint statement soundly condemning the attacks, and even spokespeople claiming to represent Restruct rejected the incident as an act of senseless barbarity.

Their statements were overshadowed by the public face of the Citizens Action League. Victimized by the attackers and vindicated in its predictions of disaster in the wake of Anna's case, the group embraced the role of media darling. Alistair Coyle appeared on national macrovision and streamed across several Micromedium channels. He was even more earnest and somber than usual, and spoke with pious brevity:

"Honored Citizens, it is with heavy hearts that we grieve the terrible consequences of our fellows' misguided deviation from time-honored principles that have kept us safe and secure for so long. I will leave it to the experts to identify the perpetrators of this unspeakable act and its causes. For now, on behalf of the Citizens Action League, I ask that you forsake any aggression in your own hearts and pray for these deluded souls who wish to destroy our great nation."

Conservative pundits ran with the theme, arguing that the message of the attacks could not be clearer. This was a full-scale assault on the country's foundations—civic virtue, the rule of law, and the community's faith in a righteous and loving God. What, they asked, was the triggering event? A Board of Classification decision dismissing Anna Dao's petition. What more proof did the Citizenry need that the forces supporting her quest were pernicious threats to the civilization she sought to contort in her image?

Liberal analysts raged against this calumny, arguing it was absurd to attribute to Anna, her moderate petition, or her peaceful supporters the horrific atrocities of criminal extremists who lacked even the courage to take responsibility for their craven acts of violence.

While the ensuing debates raged, the Departments of Domestic and International Intelligence opened coordinated investigations. The editorial staff at the *Capital Times* focused its resources during the first seventy-two hours after the explosions to coverage of the attacks. On the third day, as the death tolls and other details materialized from law enforcement inquiries, the paper finally ran its article on the potentially compromising relationship between Hearing Officer Mbeza, Cormack O'Brian of Protection Inc., and upper management of the Citizens Action League. The story was buried on page six.

Two pages deeper in, a one-column article reported that the Department of Adjudication Appellate Division lifted the gag order in Jeaneane's assault case. The story reported that the case, which involved Interlink Technologies, a manufacturer of Micromedium interface technology, had been blocked on grounds of national security and state secrecy.

Overwhelmed by the political firestorm the bombing had ignited, obsessed with the lurid details the DDI and DII dished up in their press releases, and reluctant to cast aspersions on public officials when the government was under violent attack, none of the mainstream Macromedium newswires picked up either of these stories.

Alternative news hounds on the Micromedium caught them in their teeth, however, and began gnawing away in the information firelight's smoldering periphery.

16

LEO APPEARED TO ABSORB THE initial trauma of his injuries, the catastrophic impact of the attacks on the public's perception of Anna's case, and the stillbirth of the media leak about Mbeza's relationship with Anna's detractors with relative grace.

"Good drugs, huh?" prodded John, unfooled by Leo's attempt at conventional explanations for his poise. He perched on a wobbly stool in Leo's bedroom, having stopped by for a visit.

Leo considered a defensive argument but knew it would be pointless. "Yeah, opiates."

"Sweet. Got any extra?"

Leo reached into the nightstand drawer and tossed John a bottle of pain meds.

"You think this will hold you over?" John asked in shock at the volume of narcotics the doctor had prescribed.

"For a month, if I need them," Leo said. "I've already cut from four a day to two. I'll stop after another couple days."

"Good boy," said John, holding a pill between his teeth as he unscrewed the cap on a soda from the ice chest next to Leo's bed. "Cheers." He washed back the pill and burped, shook out a couple more and stuck them in his pocket, then lobbed the bottle back to Leo.

"I know you still feel like crap and no one expects otherwise right now. But as soon as you feel ready, you've got to make a public statement about the attacks. They're crucifying Anna and it's total bullshit. Her case is vanilla pabulum. It's ridiculous to pin those events on her."

"I wouldn't say her case is quite that bland," said Leo.

"You know what I mean," replied John. "She's not psychotic or violent. Her petition is reasonable. She's everyone's favorite invisible poster child and demon du jour. It's total crap. Sorry bud, but you're still the person paid to say so."

Leo placed the pills back in his nightstand and adjusted his pillows. "I know."

"Give yourself a few more days if you need it. Start preparing your remarks if you get bored. Lay off the pills, OK? I'm glad you're calm, but you're a little too calm. There's a difference between calm and blissfully stupid."

Leo glared at John and drew a breath to speak, but John cut him short.

"I'm not judging you. I can't imagine how traumatizing it would be to go through that. But you're still on duty and you should deal with the feelings. Ease in that direction, OK?"

Leo registered the gentleness of John's input. "OK."

John patted Leo on the shin, then took his leave.

Leo disciplined himself over the next two days to wean off the pills. The physical pain from his injuries had waned to a level he could tolerate with over the counter stuff, but that didn't help his jangled nerves. He knew that it was inappropriate to treat emotional discomfort with narcotics, but he needed relief. Not knowing where else to turn, he gingerly placed a quantum array around his injured pate and logged into the Micromedium, hoping that the concentration required to use the equipment would afford some respite. This proved partially true, but Leo had become so adept with the array's basic functions that using it no longer eclipsed his anxieties. On instinct or impulse, he hit Anaku at his Micromedium coordinates.

Anaku responded within ten minutes. He knew about the recent events and Leo's role in them, and was supportive as Leo described his distress.

> **Anaku:** I could help you work through this more effectively if you would join me in a neural link.

Leo hadn't yet braved the quantum array's more esoteric uses. Even though his mastery of the equipment's rudimentary functions left him hungry for more, the prospect was daunting.

> **Asad:** Wouldn't it be better to wait until I'm in a more settled state?
>
> **Anaku:** It would help you get to a more settled state. It can be incredibly therapeutic with the right person.

Leo repositioned the array, which was uncomfortable because of his wounds.

> **Asad:** And you're the right person?
>
> **Anaku:** I believe you'll find that I am, yes.

Sensing that he would benefit from contact with Anaku's stability—and curious about the possibility of a quantum neural interface—Leo agreed to try it.

To effect the link, Anaku advised, they would have to open a separate, higher capacity Micromedium channel, parallel to the link they were using for their text chat and routed through a hub equipped with ultra-fast quantum computing processors. Leo followed Anaku's instructions carefully for configuring both the array and the Micromedium terminal. Once they had coordinated their settings, Anaku advised Leo to increase the strength of the signal from his array.

Leo did as instructed and for several minutes sensed nothing. After four upward adjustments, however, something unusual happened. At the edges of his consciousness, he felt a presence. Not visual, not aural, yet still perceptual. Like peeking into an unfamiliar part of his mind.

He communicated through the text channel, mentally commanding the terminal to write:

Asad: I think I'm feeling something.

Anaku did not respond textually, but Leo sensed something subtle at the fringes of his awareness, like a whisper on the wind. He detected a pattern but he couldn't bring it into focus. Trying to follow it felt like grasping at a fleeting memory, appearing and disappearing like the fringes of a cloud in the outer reaches of his mind.

He perceived echo-like formations, traces of sound, color, fragments of language-like pattern. Not auditory, exactly, more like hints of meaning, but he could not discern words.

Stimuli washed from the periphery toward the center of his awareness in gentle waves. Susurrating patterns intermingled and overlapped like intersecting ripples from raindrops on the surface of a still lake. At times, points of focus emerged from the field of shifting vibrations. A consonant? A shimmering color? He couldn't understand it, but it grew stronger and more distinct.

It felt like random thoughts forming in the background of his own mind beneath the surface of his awareness, but it had a different quality. He tried to identify the sensation. A different shape? Color? Emotional tone? Energy? A different *feel*. Nothing captured the totality of what he was experiencing.

The echoes grew louder. Clusters of language-like thought aligned into forms resembling words. He strained to decipher the rippling patterns. Out of the miasma, he heard—or rather experienced as thought—the word "almost" buzz into coherence, layered among incomprehensible word forms resembling an audio recording played backward. This disintegrated into reverberating murmurs and indecipherable cross-patterns that resolved into the word "levels" and later organized into the word "alignment."

Leo ratcheted up the setting on his array one more notch.

In a beat of his heart, the neural link coalesced, like the view through a lens rotated into focus. Not completely at first, but into coherent enough form that Leo knew with certainty the thought that followed did not originate in his own head:

"There."

The word appeared in his mind. Not as a voice, though it had a vocal quality, but as a clear, crisp thought, escorted by an array of nearly overwhelming though not unpleasant sensory stimuli. Anaku's presence was palpable and as close as Leo's own thoughts and feelings, yet it was unfamiliar. It was part of his mind, but it was not of his mind. Leo's heart pounded with exhilaration and acute fear.

"Relax. It takes a minute to adjust."

"That wasn't my thought!" thought Leo, his resistance verging on panic.

"No, it was mine. Concentrate on your breath. Deep, slow breaths. Count them."

Leo complied. His fear notched down with each respiration, and Anaku's presence grew more vivid.

"It's not something you can force," spoke the thought-voice. "It's more a matter of allowing."

Leo consciously relaxed his mind and yielded to the bizarre sensation. His tension and resistance eased.

Nothing in his life or imagination prepared him for what unfolded. He was himself but he was not alone. He could grasp thought both from himself and from Anaku. Each felt as though it arose from his own mind, but he could distinguish them. He and Anaku were joined, yet not merged. Leo felt Anaku's being interpenetrated with his own. He had never experienced anything so intimate. He felt exposed to someone he barely knew, yet Anaku's presence was calm, warm, even loving.

"Is it always like this?" Leo asked with his mind.

"It's different with every person," Anaku replied.

Leo felt safe, which he didn't determine with his intellect. It's something that just was. His being trusted Anaku's.

Then there was a shift. Instead of words, Leo became aware of full-scale mind's-eye experiences. He would've called them memories or fantasies if they'd originated with him but they most decidedly had not. Anaku showed Leo a series of impressions: the room Anaku physically occupied, a sculpture on his desk, the face of a woman Leo had never met, and a beautiful valley on a tropical island, shrouded in mist, with a rainbow plunging between cliffs feathered in ferns and bathed in tendrils of falling water. Leo sighed at the beauty and richness of the images, soothed by the warmth of Anaku's energy and thoughts.

"Or what he's sharing of them," Leo's own mind interrupted. He partially withdrew from the link, though he could not disconnect without turning down the array. He became anxious as it occurred to him that Anaku must be witnessing everything he was thinking and feeling. As if on cue, Leo's subconscious compulsively spewed up mortifyingly personal debris—the petty theft he committed as a young teenager, sobbing in humiliation during his reprogramming, intimate moments from his past relationships, trifling resentments and jealousies, secret desires. "Goddamn it!" he shouted as these revelatory details tumbled through his mind.

A kind, non-judgmental sensation of amusement emanated from Anaku, as though Leo could hear him laughing, though he had never experienced Anaku's voice.

"Don't worry. Everyone does that in the beginning," Anaku said through the shared mind.

"I've never been so embarrassed in all my life," Leo replied, abashed.

A pulse of warmth emanated from Anaku, followed by a clear thought: "Relax. We are all complex beings, riddled with inconsistencies and contradictions. It is possible to cultivate a focused awareness that cuts deeper than those details. The more you learn how to do that, the more you can control what you want to share. Besides," he continued, "that was all quite tame, to be honest."

Anaku allowed Leo to contemplate those thoughts. He observed and experienced Leo absorbing them, then issued another mental invitation: "Think about what you'd like to show me. What's troubling you?"

Memories from the explosion started intruding into Leo's awareness. He consciously tried to suppress them. "Everything you've shown me is so beautiful. These things are ugly."

"I can handle it," came the reply thought. "You need to share it. That's why you wanted to establish this link."

Leo heard his own protesting thoughts but recognized they were defensive untruths. He sighed in frustration as he grasped that Anaku had been party to the chain of thoughts.

"True," he confessed in surrender to the futility of trying to hide.

"Show me."

Leo turned his thoughts to the day of the explosion. Sprays of glass. Using a tablecloth to beat the flames off a screaming woman. People crying, coughing, choking, dying. He shared all his memories with Anaku.

"That's horrible," responded Anaku. "No wonder you're suffering."

Leo felt surrounded by kindness, as though Anaku lifted the emotional weight of those memories off his heart. Part of Anaku's strength became his own.

"Wow," Leo said aloud. "Thank you," he said with his mind. He turned his thoughts to the political warfare raging in the wake of the ruling in Anna's case, then dwelt on his trepidation at the thought of entering the fray. Anaku's quiet, attentive presence thrummed. After Leo cycled through the crux of his anxiety, Anaku partially differentiated his mind and responded:

"You're suffering from the erroneous belief that you can and must control all of that. All you can do is decide how you want to respond to it. The situation is much greater than you or your client. It's bigger and more complex than your wildest imaginings. You have a critical role, but it's one piece in a much larger puzzle. Manage your part. Let go of the rest. You can study it with interest, but don't blame yourself for it."

Anaku reinforced this feedback with a nonverbal picture of the situation, a perceptual and emotional gestalt, open and spacious. Leo found the perspective cooling, refreshing, invigorating. He relaxed and shifted toward this vantage. His mind partially conformed to it, but this momentary surrender triggered fear, and he pulled back.

"Easy," came Anaku's thought. "I'm not trying to control you. I'm offering you a perspective. Take what resonates. Leave anything that doesn't. You retain your own power of discernment."

Leo relaxed. Despite the difficulty in distinguishing the origin of his experience, the link was precipitating wise insights. The whirlwind of his own mental chatter subsided. For a couple breaths, he yielded to the profound interconnectedness with Anaku.

Anaku's intentional focus peered around in Leo's mind and emotional energy field.

"I understand all of the stressors you've shown me," thought Anaku, "but there's something else here." Leo felt Anaku's point of concentration search toward a dark and fearful place that Leo usually perceived in the lower center of his chest.

"What is that?" Anaku asked, delicately but firmly probing closer to the spot Leo always sought to avoid, ignore, bury. "What is," he paused the question and zeroed in, "*that*," he asked, as the finely honed focal point of his conscious mind touched the center of the emotional singularity that tormented Leo from within.

Leo shuddered with a sob as Anaku penetrated the place of his solitary torment, a place he could not describe, much less let anyone see. Tears rolled down his cheeks at the simultaneous relief from this loving contact with the locus of his deepest wounding and panic at being indefensibly vulnerable and exposed. "I don't know," he whispered aloud and in his thoughts.

"Ahh," came the compassionate, responsive thought as Anaku withdrew his attentional focus from this buried darkness in Leo's heart. "Then that, my friend, is where the work lies." Anaku surrounded Leo in what felt like radiant love. Leo's hurt place sank below his conscious awareness, but he knew the contact had caused a shift.

For a calm stretch that followed, they shared desultory perceptions on music, peak life experiences, and visions for a better world. They broached fundamental philosophical questions, agreeing that a shared exploration could prove intriguing but should wait for another time when they were rested and had integrated the material from today's session.

Anaku gave Leo the coordinates for some neurally interfaced, group meditation sites, and suggested he check them out. "It will help you gain insight into that dark place and develop tools for dealing with it without being overwhelmed by it."

He instructed Leo how to disengage safely from the link, warning that he would experience a sense of loss when the connection was severed but directing him to contemplate the impressions left on his mind. "You'll find comfort and peace in that, if you focus on it."

After they said goodbye, Leo wondered at the revolutionary phenomenon he'd experienced. Though the connection was technically severed, Anaku's presence remained. Unsettled by the sensation that he had absorbed part of Anaku's mind—or been changed in ways that made Anaku's mind part of his—he contemplated the possibility that the converse might also have occurred, that his mind had become part of Anaku's. He wondered how true that was and what it meant.

After reflecting on the adventure, Leo explored his feelings around engaging with the public over Anna's case. His anxiety was greatly reduced. Anaku's words and the perceptual perspective that accompanied them still pulsed in his mind. The meld had bestowed an alternate way of viewing the situation. By shifting to that vantage, he could tap Anaku's strength and make it his own.

Leo's resolve solidified and he called John. "I'm ready to face the media."

John could tell there was no need to ask if he was sure. "When?"

"As soon as you can set it up."

John said he'd make the arrangements.

A brief surge of habitual stress struck after Leo hung up from setting the wheels in motion. His thoughts wandered to the bottle of pain pills in the nightstand and he considered availing himself of the pharmaceutical relief, but rejected the option out of fear it might dull the new sensations he'd absorbed.

"No way," he said aloud. He relaxed on his back, and Franz stretched out on his chest, a paw on each side of Leo's head making a slight scratching sound as he kneaded the pillow next to each of Leo's ears. They touched noses and the cat purred as Leo lovingly stroked his soft, thinning coat, his fingers bouncing over the ribs and knobby spine protruding from beneath. Franz's purrs fell into a lulling rhythm with Leo's calming breath. Together they circled slowly through the strata of their minds, down to the healing realms of sweet, peaceful sleep.

Department of Domestic Intelligence agent James Malone sat at a desk in his private, home office with a crown of QFRI nodes strapped to his cranium. He turned up his array another setting, and jerked his head back involuntarily as he felt the other man's mind become almost as one with his own. "And ... contact," came the thought from Here4U2(Ab)use, an individual James had met in an off-beat social site and convinced to join him in his maiden neural link.

"Incredible," James thought in return.

"Yes. Isn't it? You say you're into abusing Vulnerables."

"Are you really a Vulnerable?" the James part of the shared mind asked doubtfully.

"I am for you," came the shrewdly ambiguous reply. "You can give me all you've got. No limits."

James's upper lip curled into a sneer. "Close enough." He focused his mind and thrusted at the link partner with a spear of cold, angry hate, accompanied by a grisly memory of beating a detainee he'd gotten carried away with during an interrogation when he was a rookie. He developed more subtle and controlled interrogation techniques when he matured as an agent, but these memories held special relish for James. It was nice to find a venue where he could relive them so palpably.

He felt Here4U2(Ab)use recoil in shock and genuine fear. *Clearly more than he bargained for*, thought James. The other man did not disagree, but he also did not leave. James could taste the man's terror, experience it as though it were deliciously almost his own.

Goosebumps covered James's neck and limbs, and his sneer morphed into a smug grin.

He was about to deliver another blow when a disturbance tugged at him from beneath the surface of his awareness.

"What was that?" snapped his mind. He checked his settings but found nothing amiss.

"What was what?" came his partner's timid reply.

Excited by subduing this boastful chatroom veteran, James yearned to turn back to the game. He zeroed his mind to a silent, stable point and listened for unusual input, but there were no more disconcerting anomalies. He must have detected a subconscious impulse from his link partner, but he instinctively set aside a sliver of his attention to remain vigilant.

"Nothing," the James part of the shared mind replied finally. "Let's continue."

Across town in an abandoned service chamber, located beneath a capital subway line, a small-boned and compactly built but muscular young woman with intelligent grey eyes and a militaristic buzz cut ripped a quantum array off her head and hurled it across the room. As it rattled against the cement, she turned to a corner and vomited. Once she'd regained her composure, she tapped the space bar on a keyboard that was linked to a chat session running parallel to the carefully attenuated quantum neural link she'd unceremoniously severed.

The virtual room occupants switched to active mode and she began to type her report:

Sleeperagent: It's harder than we thought.

PART 2

Extending thirty floors below Memorial Park in the nation's capital, guarded by state-of-the-art anti-missile technology and girded against penetration by so-called bunker-busting munitions, the Department of International Intelligence headquarters is one of the country's most protected sites, second in security only to control centers buried in mountains to survive a nuclear attack.

At this fortress's most inviolate lower reaches lies a spacious room. It is softly lit, acoustically insulated, with tightly controlled temperature and humidity to minimize sensory distractions. Nine stations resembling luxury international fight pods, ergonomically optimized for long-term occupancy, surround and face the chamber's center in a circle. In eight of them, individuals recline comfortably with eyes closed, each wearing a quantum array wired through a local conduit into the DII mainframe.

These DII neural sentinels and other members of their corps trained for years and endured a vetting process so strict it screened out thousands of skilled applicants. They are the elite of the elite, chosen for their exceptional intelligence, mental focus, emotional stability, and unwavering commitment to the security of the department and therefore, they believe, of the country and world. Through the arrays, they maintain an interpenetrated quantum neural field. Though they remain individuals, each experiences the joined mind as though its reach were his or her own. Together they envelop the DII Micromedium hub in a seamless caul.

The sentinel agents work in staggered, eight-hour shifts. Once an hour, a relief agent settles into the ninth pod, dons an array, and tunes into the field, and the others adjust to accommodate and align with the new mind as it interpenetrates with their neural link. When the expanded field is stable and clear, support technicians dial down the array connected to the agent whose shift is ending, her signal fades from the joined awareness, the remaining agents adjust to compensate for her departure, and the field remains perpetually intact.

The field this core group maintains is the innermost of three nested layers. Another wired circle of agents, physically located in an adjacent room, maintains a second neural field surrounding the first. A third group maintains the outermost field, which surrounds the inner two. Though the layers are not literally spherical, that's how the agents visualize them and how they function: as three concentric spheres encircling and shielding the DII Micromedium hub.

An attenuated quantum neural chord connects between the fields, allowing agents from one layer to communicate with those of another without blurring the distinction between the two. Coordinating through these links, the three layers work together to control access to the DII hub, protecting it against attempted intrusions and determining whether to grant connection requests.

When approaching the hub, a party seeking access through conventional Micromedium equipment and communication protocols would encounter a labyrinth of passwords and encrypted loops to nowhere and, beneath that, indecipherably complex output, as Liam's compatriots found when they first surveilled the site. The sole means for anyone, including a field agent with security clearance, to interact with the hub is by obtaining permission to create a data portal through the sentinel caul, and the only way to do that is through a quantum neural link.

The agents that form the outermost layer perform the bulwark of protection and filtration, assessing mind-to-mind requests for access throughout their shifts. Many are legitimate connection queries by DII operatives or outposts. With the quantum arrays becoming more widely available, however, the agents increasingly must grapple with attempts to hack the department hub, both by amateurs and sophisticated entities.

When it comes to the amateurs, the agents screen out most spurious hails by enforcing a strict password and handshake protocol, listening selectively and limiting communication to those ostensibly authorized to at least submit a request. A would-be hacker who somehow obtains the introductory sequence can capture the sentinels' attention, but then must face their direct scrutiny. The agents summarily dispatch such fraudsters, then follow up with a quantum pulse to the point of origin, delivering a traumatic but non-lethal jolt and disabling their equipment. Anyone posing a real threat would be tracked down and arrested, but none have merited such pursuit.

More efficient security techniques are in the works to stem the rising tide, such as making the shield opaque to all but applicants whose arrays are modulated with the hub's according to pre-established configuration specifications. But the filtration technology is not yet ready for deployment.

Occasionally, a foreign espionage agency makes a more sophisticated access attempt using forged credentials and a fictitious identity, but the sentinels are coldly adept at detecting subterfuge. Though it is theoretically possible for security leaks to occur by way of a false persona flawlessly performed through a neural link to the sentinel shield, the agency's risk assessment technocrats consider it unlikely and do not believe it has ever occurred.

Legitimate access queries proceed thusly: The outer sentinels sort applicants and forward duly validated requests to the middle sentinel field. Since the outer field filters most of the noise, the middle field has greater resources to scrutinize the requests that pass the first level. It if concurs in the authorization, it forwards requests to the inner sentinel field.

The innermost field is superordinate to the outer two, directing their operations when necessary and serving as final arbiter for access requests. If the agents forming the inner field give final authorization, the hub pierces the shield with a Micromedium data conduit and connects to the applicant's node. Other hub systems then monitor the links through conventional means and sever any behaving anomalously.

The outer layers also perform most of the screening labor to conserve the inner layer's resources for a different, critical function: It silently, patiently, attentively monitors the shield for irregularities, disturbances, attempted subsurface intrusions. The primary function of the innermost field is to lie in ambuscade, silent and motionless, like a heron stalking prey until it knows it can strike with lethal precision. The agents forming the inner field, the most focused of their corps, near sociopaths in their cold detachment, quietly wait.

And listen.

17

ROWS OF IDENTICAL MINIATURE, SLIGHTLY warped simulacra of Leo standing on the stairs reflected at him from dark glasses adorning the national police officers guarding the macrovision studio he was about to enter.

It had been nearly a month since Hearing Officer Mbeza rejected Anna's petition. The dead from the attacks that followed were all accounted for. Leo bore a couple of small bandages on his healing wounds. Multiple investigations continued to sift through the evidence and purported tips, but the nation's best and brightest had yet to make a definitive attribution of responsibility. Theories roiled from every quarter and exacerbated acrimony between the political factions, creating an atmosphere of paranoia and crisscrossing insinuations of blame.

Desperate to serve up some flesh to the increasingly outraged public, the Department of Domestic Intelligence turned from obvious theories to more speculative possibilities. Anyone found to have been near the explosions faced questioning. Despite the presumption of honor that accompanied Leo's Citizen status and advocate's license, the authorities turned their attention to him. Apparently, a remote detonation device was discovered in the rubble in front of the café where Leo was injured. Hadn't he been in the Board of Classification headquarters minutes before the blast?

John and Jeaneane pressed Leo to demand legal representation during the interrogation, and Jeaneane volunteered to serve as his ad hoc counsel. Confident that the truth of his innocence was all the protection he needed, Leo took the high road and waived the right to an advocate when he met with the DDI investigators.

He bore up well under questioning. His genuine outrage over the attacks, the fact that he was injured and made no attempt to flee the jurisdiction, and his willingness to submit to questioning unrepresented by counsel favorably influenced his interrogators' assessment. Also, DNA traces on the detonation device did not match the sample he voluntarily provided.

Leo was forthright with the DDI agents in all but one respect. When asked whether he had an explicit or circumstantial warning of the attacks, he said, "Other than the volatile public conflict around my client's case? No." The agents asked a few follow-up questions, but Leo demurred.

He felt conflicted over this deception but he had promised Wendy he would not tell the authorities about her warning on the eve of Anna's hearing. He did his best to convince himself she wasn't involved and that her prescience was borne of keen political instincts and proximity to gossip mills he was insulated from due to his professional status. Even if that were true, he knew there was a possibility questioning her could lead the investigators to valuable clues. However, he took her at her word that she would give up nothing if the DDI hauled her in, and he shuddered at the thought of what the agents might do to overcome her resistance. He also had not forgotten her grisly admonition that she would be a better source of information alive and free than incarcerated or worse. Nor had her thinly veiled threat to take him down with her if he betrayed her entirely slipped his mind.

If he became convinced later that she was involved in the attacks, he would have to make an even tougher choice. Absent such conviction, he opted to preserve her confidence, even if it meant telling a lie to characters as dangerous as these. He prayed that this decision would yield fruit of the wholesome variety.

The DDI agents never designated Leo as a suspect, but they directed him to stay in contact and let them know before he did any traveling. Although they assured him their inquiry was confidential, someone leaked it to the *Scope*, a tabloid publication reviled and slobbered over by the Citizenry and excluded classes alike. Once the rag broke the story, John's paper, the *Capital Times* was obligated to run a column emphasizing that Leo was not a suspect.

Activists from Respect, Spectrum, and Pro'gression decried the development as a brazen, illegitimate, politically motivated attempt to divest Anna of her counsel by slanderously associating him with the attacks. In response, the moderate activists seized on the all-but-ignored article in the *Capital Times* from three weeks earlier, reporting rumors that Hearing Officer Mbeza was compromised by representatives of the confinement industry and, in all likelihood, the Citizens Action League. Demonstrations were banned in the wake of the explosions, but the groups began a Micromedium campaign demanding an inquiry into Mbeza's associations. The conservatives cried foul. The moderate activists cried conspiracy.

Amidst this fray, Leo was about to make his first public appearance since the attacks. Media outlets had hounded him for weeks to give an interview. He considered holding a press conference with all invited. In light of the false and dicey not-quite-allegations against him, however, and the fury over the not-yet-substantiated scandal involving Mbeza's ties to the conservatives, he decided working with an interviewer he could trust not to crucify him would be wise. He selected a nationally broadcast, live news-and-variety show, hosted by a seasoned journalist respected for her intelligence, supreme skill as an interviewer and, most importantly to Leo under the circumstances, her civility, fairness, and unshakable dignity.

Leo examined the rows of National Police that flanked the studio entrance, and the fractal of mini Leos mirrored back at him from the cops' lenses. He cleared his throat and handed his ID to the officer in front of the building's entrance. The cop removed his sunglasses, examined Leo's ID, turned cold eyes up to Leo without moving his head, looked back at the ID and again and Leo. Without a word, he opened the door and turned aside so Leo could enter.

A young man, handsome in an overly enthusiastic and still-becoming-himself way, met Leo on the other side of the entrance. The fellow's ID tag bore the word "intern." *As if that isn't apparent enough*, Leo thought with a smirk.

"Advocate Baksh! Jamie Tesh."

Leo shook his hands with the exuberant youth.

Jamie pointed in the direction they were to travel. "It's great to meet you."

"Nice to meet you, too," replied Leo, embarrassed by the stars in the kid's eyes but touched by his innocent glee.

"Sorry about the security gauntlet," Jamie continued. "I wanted to greet you out there but they wouldn't let me."

"Don't worry about it," said Leo. "Not the cheeriest lot, but it's like that everywhere. I expected it. You obviously let them know I was coming. Thank you."

Jamie lowered his eyes diffidently at this acknowledgement and didn't reply.

After an awkward moment Leo said, "How does this work?"

"Work?"

"My appearance. What's the procedure?"

Nudged by this cue, Jamie hit his stride and launched into the schedule ahead for Leo, spilling out the details in a river of words. "I'm supposed to take you up to meet Ms. Corbett so you can say hi. Then you go down to makeup. Ms. Corbett will meet with you again an hour before the broadcast to go over the interview layout. Another guy, Phil Sanders, will soften you up before you go on camera."

Leo half expected him to start hopping up and down and skipping as he spoke.

"And then," the intern twirled his fists one over the other in a disco roll and threw his hands at Leo, "You're on."

They continued walking.

Leo felt his insides tighten and an icy wave swept over him from head to toe as he anticipated being interviewed on live macrovision.

Jamie eyed him peripherally. "It will be OK. Everyone gets nervous but Phil Sanders is great at helping people relax. You'll be great."

Leo cleared his throat.

Jamie, an inch shorter, twenty-five pounds lighter, and a good ten or twelve years younger than Leo, put his hand on Leo's shoulder and stared with grave intensity into his eyes. "I know it," he proclaimed in conclusion with what Leo assumed was supposed to be a commanding tone.

Notwithstanding the intern's silly heavy-handedness, Leo found his sincerity disarming and he relaxed despite his own cynical amusement. "Thanks," he said, omitting the "kid" he thought silently, which he suspected would sour the moment unnecessarily.

"Besides," Jamie continued as they approached their first destination, "you have the whole stinking, writhing, lying, self-devouring monster by the tail, so all you have to do is be who and where you are and everything will be fine."

Leo turned to the intern with eyebrows raised.

"Sir," Jamie said, flashing Leo a quick, sarcastic smile, followed by total deadpan.

A laugh burst out of Leo like a popped balloon.

"That's my personal view, not Capital Macrovision's official position."

Jamie opened the door for Leo to a studio abuzz with cameras and a hive of busy staff preparing for the broadcast. Leo was still adjusting his assessment of the young man as they approached the anchor's door. The intern held Leo's gaze as he knocked and said over the din, "It's Jamie. Advocate Baksh is here to meet you, Ms. Corbett."

When the door opened, Leo felt relaxed and open. The studio clearly had sound reasons for hiring Jamie and assigning him to this task.

"Advocate Baksh, Lynn Corbett," said the woman before him, extending a hand in greeting.

Leo had watched *The Morning Show* for years and had long admired Lynn Corbett. Despite being only partially made up for the broadcast, Lynn's off-camera presence was as palpably intense as her media version, though not in the same way. *It's her eyes*, Leo thought. *This woman is for real.*

"It's an honor to meet you," he replied, shaking her hand firmly. "I'm a big fan."

"That's very kind," she said, placing her other hand over Leo's and holding his gaze. "I hope you still feel that way after today's broadcast."

These words might have been threatening were they not delivered with warmth and humor.

"I hope so too," said Leo, with a tinge of playful terror.

"I'm looking forward to interviewing you, Mr. Baksh."

"I'm looking forward to it too," said Leo not quite convincingly, "But I'm a little nervous. Please call me Leo."

"I'm sure it will go fine. We're good at pulling these things off. My associates will have all the nervousness beaten out of you by the time we go live," she assured. "I'm Lynn."

"We need to get you down to makeup," intervened Jamie.

"I will come down an hour before the broadcast so we can chat about the interview," said the anchor amiably.

"Very good," said Leo. "Until then … then."

He cringed at his awkwardness and they ducked their heads in a giggle as Leo turned to follow Jamie to the next stop.

"She can't say this," Jamie told Leo in a tone of secrecy, "but she's totally behind you. We all are. Well, I can't speak for everyone. But everyone I know is. And anyone who isn't is an idiot and doesn't matter."

Leo was starting to like this kid.

A few paces later, Jamie opened a door to a large dressing room containing several stations where stylists prepared guests for their macrovision appearances. Jamie hollered to an individual who faced away from them that Leo Baksh was here for prep. Without turning around or pausing in his conversation, the stylist jabbed an index finger twice toward a chair in front of a sink and mirror to his right. Jamie held up his hands as if to say, "What can you do?" and directed Leo to the chair. Leo slid into the seat and Jamie hopped on a stool nearby.

Finishing his conversation with a boisterous cackle, the stylist turned to the new arrivals. He wore his hair in a great, unkempt mop, and was draped in pastel silks. "How do you do?" he said, sweeping his arm in a great arc and presenting his hand to Leo. "I am Gustavo and I will be your stylist today."

Leo responded with his most winning smile. He took Gustavo's hand, which packed a much more muscular grip than he expected and replied, "Leo. Pleasure to meet you."

Gustavo held Leo's hand and gaze. Leo felt uncomfortable with the prolonged scrutiny but he wanted this to be a good interaction so he permitted it. Gustavo's features signaled approval and he reciprocated Leo's grin and relaxed his grip.

"Likewise," he said. Turning to Jamie, he said with much less warmth, "You. Go."

Jamie started to protest but Gustavo gave him a desiccating glare. Jamie turned to Leo and said he'd be back in half an hour.

"Forty-five minutes, boy!" barked Gustavo.

Without replying, the intern turned and walked away. When Gustavo returned his attention to Leo, Jamie mouthed exaggeratedly from behind his back, "Thirty minutes" and held up three fingers, then his index and thumb in the shape of an O. Leo did not permit himself to smile.

"That boy gets on my nerves," said the stylist. "All limbs and dorky in the way."

Leo bobbled his head from side to side. "That was my first impression. I think there's more to him than that."

Gustavo crossed his arms. "Yes," he said at length. "Bright boy. Good boy. I still don't like him. Someone should keep him in check. Might as well be me," he concluded with a head-to-toe flourish.

The stylist crossed his arms. "You're a big star today."

Leo said he was no one special.

"Oh please," said Gustavo. "You and your client are what's going on right now."

Before Leo could respond, the stylist had grabbed him by the chin and eyed his face.

"So handsome," he said and clucked his tongue. "And these curls," he exclaimed, running his fingers through Leo's hair and releasing his chin to cover his own mouth and wheeze an appreciative gasp.

Leo blushed.

"Great coloring," said Gustavo. "You're a natural for macrovision."

He turned Leo's head and examined his wounds. His expression turned sad. "Does it hurt?"

Leo said the surface pain was mostly gone but that he still suffered nerve pain.

Gustavo's face grew fierce. "Barbarians," he spat.

Leo yielded patiently to the inspection. "Can you cover it up?"

"Cover it up?" Gustavo leaned back. "Sweetheart," he grabbed Leo by the chin again, "have you been reading the papers? If anything, we should accentuate them. You need all the sympathy you can get. Trust me. You don't want to cover them up."

Gustavo told Leo his natural complexion was perfect for the cameras and only needed a little "accentuation" to compensate for the glare and bleaching effects of the lights. Through the stylist's surface frivolity, Leo saw Gustavo's competence, and the hour of fixing up for the cameras passed in a flash. Leo was dishing comfortably with Gustavo by the time Jamie appeared to escort him to his meeting with the anchor.

Gustavo shooed Leo off over his shoulder. "You're gorgeous. Break a leg. Give them hell. You can do it. Go. Go."

Jamie escorted Leo to the set where Lynn Corbett sat, the picture of poise and elegance, her legs overlapped at the ankles, knees together and demurely angled slightly off center, hands folded in her lap, spine straight, and her face relaxed in a warm half-smile.

Leo felt a slight rush, part excitement, part terror, as he took in her telegenic grace.

She gestured smoothly to the adjacent couch, angled away from hers at 120 degrees, both facing an arc of cameras and lights.

In his jacket pocket, Leo fingered the pain pill he'd brought in case his injuries flared up but mostly for emergency nerve control. He pulled out his hands, hung them resolutely at his sides, took a slow breath, walked over, and sat facing the anchor. He emulated her poise, minus the elegant feminine placement of her legs.

"Perfect," she said. "When you walk on, do it just like that. You're a natural."

"I was copying you."

"Well, I'm a natural, and you are apparently a good study."

Leo snickered as the wave of nervousness passed.

Lynn Corbett gave him an overview of how she planned to conduct the interview and a heads up about potentially challenging questions. She invited him to give her fair warning about topics he considered off limits, though she could not promise she wouldn't press him. They agreed on the range of subjects and identified the potential points of tension.

Corbett would put him through his paces, but she would neither attack him nor strand him. It was a safer prospect than he would be facing with any other journalist under the circumstances and he made a silent note of thanks.

After Leo finished his chat with the anchor, Jamie escorted him to a waiting room furnished with supple leather upholstered love seats, beverages on ice, and a wall-mounted video monitor showing the countdown to the broadcast.

"What's your pleasure?" asked Jamie.

"A sparkling water, please."

Just then, in walked Phil Sanders, the guy Jamie said would soften Leo up. Two inches shorter than Leo's 5'9", jowly, and bald with white around the temples, Sanders introduced himself and gestured toward the seats. He and Leo sat across from one another on either side of a glass coffee table.

Sanders took control, questioning Leo about whether he'd ever been on a macrovision broadcast (he hadn't), whether he enjoyed his work (sometimes), and how he was feeling about the imminent interview (nervous). He took Leo through a few breathing exercises and made him do some stretches.

"Good. Now, pretend I'm Lynn and you're you and we're on camera."

The wall monitor burst with the opening music for the show and applause as the broadcast began. Sanders muted the volume.

"Introduction, blah, blah, blah. What's happening with your case?"

Leo started to describe the procedural posture of Anna's appeal, and Sanders rolled his eyes back into his head and started to snore.

Leo stopped.

"Shorter and sweeter. This isn't advocate's school. Pretend you're explaining it to a reporter who knows nothing about the law."

"I thought that's what I will be doing."

"It is."

Leo gave a short lay description of Anna's case.

"Better. Now, why did you set all those bombs and kill all those people."

"I didn't," Leo snapped.

"Really?" said Sanders, raising his eyebrows and elongating his enunciation in theatrical skepticism. "Then why are you so defensive?"

"I'm not defensive. I'm sick of being accused of something I didn't do."

Sanders covered his mouth and shook his head. "Are you hearing yourself echo?"

"Yeah."

"No good," said Sanders. "Try again."

Leo thought for a moment and calmly said, "I assume the question is a joke, albeit one in poor taste. I'm as angry about those attacks as anyone."

"Better," said Sanders. "Keep your cool no matter what she asks. She will not try to mess you up, but she may give you opportunities to show your strength. Use them. Otherwise, you'll mess yourself up. Understand?"

"Yep."

Sanders ran Leo through a few more provocative questions. Satisfied with Leo's responses, he turned to coaching for the appearance itself.

"You've got about five minutes."

Leo felt a wave of nausea.

"How are you feeling?" asked Sanders. "Heart racing? Sick to your stomach? Palms sweaty? Throat dry? Maybe a little faint?"

Check, check, check, check and check, thought Leo, taking stock. "All of the above."

"Completely normal. Take a sip of your soda."

Leo complied.

"You must have made lots of court appearances. Think of it like that."

"I'm a nervous wreck before court appearances."

"Perfect. You've had lots of relevant experience. Did any of them kill you?"

"No."

"God, that's a relief. You had me worried there for a minute."

Leo swatted at Sanders.

"Everyone gets nervous but you're young and healthy. You won't have a stroke. Worst case scenario, your mind will go blank and you will look like a neurotic idiot."

"How comforting," said Leo, tickled by Sanders' audacity at articulating this very real possibility.

"But that won't happen. You're going through the worst part right now. You a swimmer?"

"Not professional."

"Right. But you swim."

"Yeah."

"You know how when you're getting ready to dive into the water you don't want to because you know it's going to be an uncomfortable shock when you hit the cold?"

"Mm hmm."

"And then you dive. Lo and behold, the cold water is an uncomfortable shock just like you anticipated. But then—"

"You swim and you adjust."

"Yes, you adjust and glide through the water smoothly. But you don't get to skip the cold part."

"Court appearances are like that."

"So is this. Let's go."

Sanders walked Leo to the edge of the set. They were at a commercial break and stylists were touching up the anchor. Gustavo appeared from out of nowhere and patted perspiration off Leo's forehead. He gave him a couple of light slaps on the cheek, daubed his faced with powder, finished with a tap of the soft brush on Leo's nose (accompanied by a wink), and he was off.

"Three, two, one ..."

"And we're back. Our next guest is Advocate Leo Baksh, representative for Petitioner Anna Dao in a case that has been the focal point of great controversy and is also blamed by some for the recent spate of unspeakable violence that has plagued our capital. Mr. Baksh was seriously injured in the attacks following the rejection of his client's petition. This is his first public appearance since these events and we are pleased to bring you this exclusive interview. We appreciate his courage and graciousness in meeting with us today. Please join me in welcoming Advocate Baksh."

As Corbett was finishing her introduction, Sanders caught Leo's eye and said, "Deep breath, hold it, exhale slowly, slowly, slowly. Now breathe in again and exhale slowly as you walk on. Give 'em hell." He nudged Leo on stage amidst the audience's cued welcoming applause.

Tension filled Leo from his core outward as he walked on the set. He locked his gaze on the anchor's eyes and forced himself to smile as he sat on the couch, just as he had rehearsed.

Lynn Corbett's smile mirrored none of the anxiety Leo was sure he must be exuding like toxic radiation. Instead, with seasoned prowess, the anchor welcomed him in honeyed tones.

"Advocate Baksh, thank you for joining us today."

Leo felt a pulse of gratitude for her warmth, authority, and calm.

"Thank you for having me."

Leo's mouth was dry and he found his mind was overloading. He wasn't sure he would hear the anchor's questions.

Off camera behind her, Sanders mimed diving into a pool and the intern was giving him two geeky thumbs up of confidence.

Leo almost laughed and turned back to the anchor.

"As we all know, your client's case has drawn a bit of controversy," began Corbett.

"A bit, yes," Leo nodded and the audience tittered.

"Before we talk about that, let's make sure everyone has a clear understanding of your client's case and where things stand legally."

"Sure."

"Let's begin with Ms. Dao's petition. Forget for a moment what the pundits are saying and the conflicting versions on the street. What is she seeking?"

This question could not have been more centrally located in Leo's sweet spot of expertise, yet he faltered as he summarized Anna's claim. He got the information right, but his throat constricted twice in the middle of a word and he felt humiliated for being so nervous.

Sanders remained on the sidelines, first miming the act of swimming, then standing erect and taking a deep, calming breath.

Leo noticed he wasn't breathing at all and forced himself to follow Sanders' suggestion. As he inhaled, the anchor, deploying some of the perceptivity and grace that accompanied her greatness, prompted Leo with a follow-up question that showed him he was being too technical.

Leo exhaled as she finished the question, felt his core relax a notch, and resumed his overview of Anna's case in more digestible terms.

"She's asking the Board to refine and expand the thresholds for Citizenship on both ends to allow her and people like her—acutely sensitive and passionate, yet still balanced and strong—to join the Citizenry."

"Why doesn't she instead simply temper her personality to conform with existing standards?"

The audience erupted in cued applause.

"Such intrusive and unjustified manipulation of her mind and heart would be anything but 'simple,'" replied Leo using air quotes. "Contrary to the misinformation that's been so irresponsibly published, the reach of her Vulnerable and Aggressive traits is not extreme and perhaps more to the point, it would not be in the interest of the Citizenry to suppress the evolutionary challenge her case presents."

"Explain."

Leo focused as his conviction about Anna's case merged with his legal training and verbal aptitude. He modulated his voice and relaxed into the role of advocate.

"The hype about Anna Dao misses the point in two ways. First, Ms. Dao is a balanced, dynamic, vibrant, creative, perceptive, and highly intelligent individual. Anyone with a sane mind and wholesome heart would be proud to have her as a neighbor, colleague, or friend.

"Secondly, this case ultimately isn't about Anna. It's about who we are as a people and who we want to become. Do we want to calcify existing legal descriptions of legitimate personhood? Chain ourselves to a past defined by antiquated notions of the range of healthy human expression and experience? Or do we want to build on the achievements of our past and bring our community to a higher and more refined expression of its own greatest features?"

"Some have argued," said the anchor with a tone of firm, patience persistence, "that your client, or let's put her aside, that what she seeks goes beyond what you're calling expansion and refinement. Some are arguing that the so-called expansion would shatter the values of temperance and balance that give our society and political system its strength."

Leo flicked away the argument with his fingertips. "People are saying and doing a lot of things, most of them off point and unhelpful. Our more principled opponents contend that keeping the definition of Citizenship narrow and resisting efforts to expand the range of Vulnerable and Aggressive features avoids destabilizing a system that has served us well for a long time."

"As in centuries," said the anchor.

The audience responded with light applause.

"As in a millennium, from one perspective," parried Leo. "But that's exactly the point. It has not survived by rigidly clinging to the past. It has survived by evolving. Critics of my client's claim say they want to preserve traditional definitions of Citizenship. I ask them which ones? The original ones where all you had to do to be a Citizen was stop beating your serfs? The definition of Citizenship and the thresholds governing protection on one end, imprisonment on the other, and membership in the middle have evolved over those centuries based on our deepening understanding of human psychology and social behavior.

"Just as that understanding of who we are and what makes us tick continues to evolve, so must our legal standards governing allocation of rights, duties, protection, privileges, and punishments. Otherwise, we are adhering to a set of legal definitions increasingly at odds with our understanding of who we are."

"Won't granting Citizenship to people whose levels of sensitivity and volatility some see as pathological undermine stability?" asked the anchor.

"It will bring challenges," said Leo. "Anything worth reaching for brings challenges. We've risen to them before and we can do it now.

"But let me put it to you like this: The risk of instability from refining legal definitions to accommodate contemporary understandings of what it means to be a healthy person would be nothing compared to the social instability we risk by forcefully maintaining a legal system based on increasingly obsolete and irrelevant definitions of who we are. Nothing foments social unrest like a government based on archaic and repressive values."

The audience responded with a discordant mix of applause, whistles, boos, and hissing. Leo and the anchor turned and regarded the spectators.

Across town, hoots sounded from the newsroom as John watched the interview in his office. He clenched a fist. "Contact."

Jeaneane, who had forgotten Leo was appearing but who had yielded to a nagging urge to turn on the show, caught the last exchange. She grabbed a cup of coffee, swept her house gown beneath her, and set her attention on what appeared likely to be a spicy interview.

"Let me make sure I understand," said Lynn Corbett. "Are you suggesting that violent retaliation for a ruling against your client is something we should expect, even accept?"

"Oh, come on," groused Jeaneane in her kitchen.

"Not at all," said Leo flatly.

The audience grumbled. The anchor held up her hand to silence them. "Are you saying the conservatives are the ones causing social unrest?"

More grumbling from the audience. Louder this time.

Leo narrowed his eyes at the anchor with what could be viewed as incredulity or even mild contempt.

"Ms. Corbett, I think we both know that's an overstatement and mischaracterization of what I just said."

Unflappable, the anchor responded with a shrewd smile. "I believe it's time for a break. We'll be back in a moment so Advocate Baksh can set me to rights."

The anchor placed a hand on Leo's arm and the two began an inaudible and friendly conversation as the station cut to a commercial.

"Careful," she said for Leo's ears only.

"I'm sorry," he said. "I didn't mean any disrespect."

"Not that," she said with a dismissive wave. "I asked for that. I've beaten up bigger guys than you so don't worry about me," she added, poking his ribs with a scarlet fingernail.

"But mind your step if you criticize the conservatives for increasing social violence."

"That wasn't my point."

"I know it wasn't, but that's what people will hear if you aren't very careful."

Leo took that in. "I hear you. Thank you."

"Don't mention it. You're doing well, by the way."

Leo was about to protest that he felt he'd been a stammering fool, but

Phil Sanders stepped between them. Stylists swept around Corbett. Sanders reached down, grabbed Leo's wrist, and looked up in faux perplexity, counting off numbers with the fingers on his other hand.

"I'm no math genius, but I'm definitely getting"—he tipped his head to the side—"not zero. You must be alive."

"Very funny." Leo yanked back his hand. "Alive but embarrassed."

"Por qué?"

"Because I choked up and made a fool of myself."

"Oh, good God," retorted Sanders. "That, my friend, is considered a hiccup. You might need a few more rehearsals before you steal Lynn's job, I'll grant you."

The anchor craned her head around Sanders and arched an eyebrow, then turned back to her cadre of support staff.

"You got in a groove there," Sanders continued. "Just ride that. You're doing great. Remember, calm and cool. You can say stuff that pisses them off and get away with it if you do it with a smile. They hate that."

Sanders scuttled off and everyone prepared to resume.

"Three, two, one."

"We're talking with Advocate Baksh, representative for the controversial reclassification petitioner, Anna Dao. Just before we took our break, Mr. Baksh was going to scold me for misquoting him," she said playfully. "So, you are neither saying that the attacks are justified nor that the conservatives are responsible for social unrest."

"That's correct."

"Then what are you saying?"

"I'm not interested in assigning blame because I don't think it's productive or realistic. We're dealing with a complex array of factors here. My point with regard to Anna Dao's petition is that continuing to rigidly enforce legal standards that are out of sync with an evolving understanding of our psychology and temperamental range is more destabilizing than refining and modernizing those standards."

"Why is that?"

"Because people chafe under a government deaf and blind to their natures and needs."

"What about the needs of the existing Citizenry?"

"It is our position that the Citizenry will be enriched by greater inclusiveness and temperamental diversity. My client is not violent. She is profoundly sensitive and passionately expressive. Allowing her and people like her the full status of Citizenship will add color, depth, and enriching contrast to our community. That will make us stronger and more dynamic. To refuse to accommodate the range she represents would imprison the Citizenry in a narrow behavioral structure that will become intolerable to the excluded classes and the Citizenry itself."

"I think you'll find people who disagree."

"I already have, but I respectfully submit that history is, and will be, on our side."

"That remains to be seen, doesn't it?"

"Of course."

"Now, theory aside, let's turn to the issue of the recent terror attacks."

"Alright," Leo said solemnly.

"The *Scope* and the *Capital Times* reported that you were questioned by agents of the Department of Domestic Intelligence regarding the explosions."

"Yes."

"Can you tell us about that?"

"I will not speculate regarding an ongoing investigation. I cooperated with the inquiry because I, like everyone fit to live in the light of day, want to see the perpetrators caught and confined."

"Some have suggested that you may have been involved. Others have characterized those suggestions as a bad faith attempt to sabotage your client's case. What do you say to these competing claims?"

"I am not going to sewer-wrestle with extremists, no matter what their political angle. I'm also not going to indulge my accusers with a lengthy defense. I'll tell you this for what you think it's worth: I had nothing to do with the attacks. I deplore all forms of violence and abuse of power. I was gravely injured, both physically and, though it's unseemly to state it publicly, psychologically by the violence. I will assist the investigation in any way I can. I will not let the attacks or their exploitation by political opportunists stop my client from proceeding with her just and meritorious petition."

The audience clapped approval.

"Are you represented by counsel?"

"No."

"Why not?"

"Because I have nothing to hide and I have confidence in our law enforcement agencies."

This drew even longer applause.

John approved, though he heard notes of incredulity from the newsroom.

Jeaneane, in her kitchen, made a finger-down-the-throat gesture.

"Who do you think is responsible for the attacks?" probed the anchor.

"I don't know and I'm not going to speculate."

"But you have your suspicions."

"We all have our suspicions. But making public comments based on personal suspicions is largely why we're embroiled in a state of public hysteria."

"Hysteria's a strong word."

"I don't think so."

"You say unfounded opinions are largely responsible for this hysteria. What else is involved?"

Leo took time to calculate his response. "We would do well as Citizens, collectively and individually, to step back and take a good hard look at ourselves."

"All of us?"

"All of us."

"Are you alluding to the Citizens Action League?"

"Not specifically, but unless something drastic has happened to the language or the nature of reality, I believe they would be included in 'all.'"

The interviewer smiled. "What would we see?"

"I wouldn't presume to predict," said Leo with a slight grin.

"Are you being evasive?"

"Not at all."

"Hard to argue with that advice."

Leo sighed. "I'm sure someone already is."

After another commercial break and brief recap, the anchor turned to another point of controversy:

"What are your thoughts about the allegations that Hearing Officer Closun Mbeza may be compromised by associations with Protection Inc. and perhaps the Citizens Action League?"

"I am not able to comment on the truth or falsity of those disturbing allegations," said Leo. "It is looking like there will be a formal investigation. If the allegations were proven true, I believe it would wholly invalidate Mr. Mbeza's ruling in Ms. Dao's case."

"What steps are you taking?"

"None at present. I am assuming the hearing officer's integrity is above reproach absent conclusive contrary evidence. He is an honored jurist and is entitled to a full and fair process."

"No irregularities in the hearing?"

Leo considered the question for a long moment.

"Our position with regard to the hearing will be set forth in Ms. Dao's appeal. We believe the hearing officer improperly abdicated jurisdiction and my client was erroneously precluded from presenting the merits of her claim."

"Which means?"

"He ducked."

"Is that evidence of impropriety?"

"On its own, no. We contend it was an error in legal judgment."

"Is it *consistent* with the claim he's biased?"

Leo shook a finger at the anchor. "If I were to say yes as a matter of logic, my answer would be misconstrued as suggesting his ruling was *evidence* of bias, which I do not claim. I will leave it at no comment."

"That's a pretty meaty no comment."

"No comment."

John laughed in his office, as did Jeaneane in her kitchen.

So did most of the studio audience, though a ripple of discord was also audible.

"Leaving aside the question of the hearing officer's objectivity," the anchor said, shifting gears, "the activists are raising a larger question regarding the private confinement industry's involvement in determining whom we deem Citizens and whom we institutionalize or imprison."

"Yes."

"What are your thoughts about that?"

"It's a complex and delicate issue." He paused to formulate his approach. "I think it's fair to ask whether policy decisions bearing on membership in society and the physical liberty of its subjects should be influenced by the profitability of locking people up."

"Surely no one is suggesting we should confine people because it's profitable," parried the anchor. "Someone has to provide these services, be they government employees or private contractors. Don't these providers have a right to protect their interests?"

"Absolutely. That is one place the issue gets complicated and where many discussions of it go off the rails."

"Explain."

Leo squared his shoulders. "As difficult as it is, there is a place for confinement in a civilized society. There is also nothing inherently wrong with a private company providing confinement services, if it does so both humanely and cost effectively."

"Some would say that's a big proviso."

"Yes, it is, but bear with me."

"Continue."

"As for the public sector, I support the right of employees, including prison guards and Vulnerable treatment center employees, to organize and bargain collectively for fair wages and working terms and conditions."

"OK."

"But here's the thing: The prison guard unions and a conglomerate of private confinement companies, the mightiest of which is Protection Inc., aggressively lobby the Council of Delegates against expanding the criteria for Citizenship, promote broader grounds for confining Vulnerables and imprisoning Aggressives, and seek longer periods of confinement."

The anchor pushed back. "But aren't people working in these institutions well situated to weigh in authoritatively on these subjects? They are on the front lines, so to speak, in dealing with the confined population."

"That is true," answered Leo. "I'm sure there is a great deal of relevant experience and expertise, both among the public and private employees of these institutions, and within the institutional structures themselves."

"So?"

"The problem is that they also have a strong pecuniary interest in preserving and expanding the grounds for confining people. This is how the guards make their livelihood and the contractors make their profits. It would be disingenuous to suggest the positions they take are immune from those raw financial interests."

"So what do we do?" asked the anchor. "Bar them from lobbying?"

"That's another area that makes the issue complex," replied Leo. "No, I don't think barring these entities from voicing their positions is consistent with a free society. Moreover, it would be naïve to believe that formally barring these powerful, wealthy, and well-connected entities from lobbying would prevent them from exerting significant influence on the formulation of public policy in their areas of interest."

"Then what's the answer?"

"I don't think there is a simple solution, much as people might wish there were. The most effective way to respond to the issue would be for the public to get more involved."

"Are we back to looking at ourselves?"

Leo faced the audience and held a hand toward Lynn as though presenting a victor. "Yes," he said, turning back to her, "we need to ask ourselves what sort of society we want to build, what we are trying to accomplish by confining Vulnerables and imprisoning Aggressives, and how we want to pursue those goals."

The anchor bowed her head regally.

"Let me be clear," Leo continued. "The discussion must consider the legitimate interests of the people and institutions that provide these important public services. It is as much a mistake to disrespect those interests as it is to let them drive the policy. However the rules for confinement develop, we need to honor the livelihoods of those who are running our institutions and prisons and find a role for them in the evolving regime."

"The confinement policy should determine how we compensate the providers and not the other way around?" asked the anchor, skillfully focusing Leo's point.

"Essentially, yes," replied Leo. "Honoring our public servants is important. They have every right to protect their livelihoods. But their monetary interests should not determine who gets to be a Citizen and who is institutionalized. Robust public involvement is the key to keeping the various interests in proper balance and perspective."

"I'm not sure your comments will win you friends on either side of that debate."

"Perhaps not, but that's because I'm willing to say what neither side wants to concede: They both have a place at the table."

"Never a popular position when the parties are so polarized," said Corbett.

"No, but one that holds hope for a path forward, which we desperately need," replied Leo.

"Where does your client's case fit in all of this?"

"My client seeks refinement of existing standards."

"So you've argued," said the anchor. "Is there a permissible way for the private confinement contractors to voice an opinion?"

"Yes. If and when the Board's appellate division entertains briefs, anyone with an interest in the case can submit non-party briefs for the panel's consideration."

"So there's no need to bribe the judges," prodded the anchor.

A hint of a smile passed across his lips. "No," he replied. "No one needs to bribe anyone. They can file a brief and contribute to a healthy, principled debate."

"No need to blow anything up?"

Leo's features turned dark. "No. It's impossible to communicate anything honorable or worthy of consideration through violence. All it does is tear us apart and tear us down, leaving nothing in its wake but fear." Leo's voice betrayed an embarrassing upwelling of sorrow, as he finished by saying, "Please, no more bombs."

The anchor harnessed the solemnity and, despite Leo's visible discomfort, let the tension linger. With flawless timing and masterful grace, she closed the interview by saying, softly, "So, your message today is to look at ourselves and get involved."

Leo swallowed as the emotional tide ebbed. "Exactly," he answered, his voice steady.

They regarded one another calmly.

"There you have it folks, Advocate Baksh, thank you for joining us today."

"It's been my honor, Lynn, thank you."

After the show closed, the studio staff showered Leo in words of congratulation and encouragement. Gustavo gave him a hug and a peck on the cheek. George said he looked good for a dead guy.

Lynn Corbett told him he did splendidly, but also said Leo should brace himself for attacks by the Citizens Action League.

"No thanks to *you*," said Leo, eying her with faux enmity.

"Oh, come now," she replied without contrition. "I made it possible for you to punch them without scraping your knuckles."

"Won't you take heat for that?"

"No," she said with a satisfied sigh. "If you review the tape you'll see I still left you at the center of the target. I think I saved us both a measure of grief. You're the one in the hot seat, but I left you some wiggle room."

"Thank you," said Leo, taking her hand, "for everything. You're a master."

"I try," she replied. They were still for a moment before releasing their hands and bidding one another a silent farewell.

Jamie escorted Leo to a side exit to avoid press and demonstrators. "I told you you'd do great," said the intern.

"Yes, you did. Thank you for that. Thanks also for helping me with my nerves."

Jamie turned to Leo with a wry grin as they reached the exit. He threw a *ta-da* gesture and said, "I'm full of surprises."

God what a dork, thought Leo. "You certainly are."

Jamie pulled out a surprisingly professional business card: Jamison Tesh, Media Relations Specialist.

"It should say 'aspiring', but that wouldn't make an impressive introduction."

"True," said Leo. "It's all a matter of timing and perspective, like so much in life."

Jamie nodded gravely.

"Thanks, Jamison," said Leo, emphasizing the grown-up version of the intern's name and slipping the card in his breast pocket as Jamie's eyes followed.

"Don't lose that," said Jamie. "You might need a media specialist in your line of work."

"I'll definitely call you if something comes up," promised Leo.

"Call me anyway," Jamie answered without missing a beat as Leo was walking through the exit.

Leo turned in response, but all he saw through the crack of the closing door was the intern's bemused deadpan, followed by a wink just before the latch clicked shut.

Cheeky brat, Leo thought as he descended the stairs, amused and flattered despite himself.

Leo turned up his collar, donned an uncharacteristic hat and a pair of shades, and circumnavigated the crowd outside the studio unnoticed.

When he slid behind the wheel of his car, he took a minute to decompress and found he was filled with tumultuous waves of conflicting emotion. Pride and excitement over the positive feedback the studio staff gave him, but also deep, stinging pangs of uncertainty over the adequacy of his performance, discomfort over his increased visibility, and trepidation over the potential fallout from his comments.

He ground his teeth and fretted. This was how he usually felt after a public appearance. Like an imposter, an interloper whose insufficiency people were too polite or embarrassed to talk about in his presence. After a few cycles, this well-worn routine exceeded Leo's tolerance. "You did it," he scolded himself aloud. "Enough."

He grabbed his mobile device, which had messages from Jeaneane, John, his folks, and a few others but nothing from Anna. "That's weird," he thought aloud.

As he started the car, he promised himself he would take the rest of the day off as a reward and celebration. He took the pain pill from his pocket and swallowed it with some cold coffee still sitting in his cup caddy. He caught the move for a self-honest moment in the rearview, but nipped any critical thoughts before they had a chance to bud.

On the way home, he skipped through the voice messages. They were a surfeit of praise.

18

PATRICE, KNOWN TO LIAM AND his associates as Sleeperagent, sipped the remainder of her tea, rinsed the cup, and settled onto a cushion in the nook she had arranged for her mental training. This was an experiment, in many ways. She generally preferred a Spartan aesthetic. As if it wasn't enough that her apartment was situated in an Aggressive district due to her status, she had chosen a loft in an industrial part of town, with a view of smokestacks, ducts, and conveyer belts. The only foliage she saw were obstinate weeds straining through cracks in the cement. She was one of those weeds, she sometimes told herself. They were her kind.

When she forayed into the meditation training she and the others had agreed to undertake, she overcame her initial resistance and set up a softer, more colorful practice space. Bamboo in a slate planter, a woven mat, and an altar with objects that helped her relax and focus, like a rock she found in a river as a child and a shard of pottery with "Awake" etched into its cracked glaze. No incense, however. It was already too close to a cliché for her taste. One had to have limits.

Patrice adjusted the settings on her nodal array and Micromedium terminal and listened with her mind for the quantum field signals of other participants in the neurally joined meditation group. She had been skeptical about the usefulness and safety of the circles at first, but after several sessions, she was hooked.

Her initial attempts at solo training were not what she expected. All the images she'd seen of people in meditation depicted them as serene and relaxed. When she tried a few simple exercises, such as sitting with an erect spine, eyes nearly closed, and focusing her attention on her breath, she discovered a bucking bronco of chaotic, repetitive thoughts and feelings which reared up repeatedly no matter how resolutely she turned her attention back to her breath.

Persistent by nature, Patrice read up on technique, discovered that her experience was standard fare, and redoubled her efforts. Nevertheless, her progress toward achieving stillness was so slow that she wasn't sure she was reaping any benefit from the practice.

A few weeks into this foray, she visualized her discursive thoughts as invaders she was observing and shooting down in a video game. The errant thoughts almost acted embarrassed when exposed, and vaporized into nothingness.

Occasionally, if she persevered, her mind surrendered and fell silent like a brilliant sky revealed through dissipating wisps of cloud, and she momentarily experienced a calm, lucid awareness. Her mind just *was;* it had no object, thought, or agenda.

The experience was so novel and liberating that she tried to grasp it and analyze it. As soon as she did though, the fragmenting, mirrored labyrinth of her discursive mind displaced it.

It was a lot of work for little payoff, but those elusive moments of spacious clarity were so profound that she wanted to continue. When she tried to eavesdrop on a neurally connected exchange in a fetish social site, her revulsion so disturbed her focus that one of the participants detected her presence. That would not do if she or the other hacktivists attempted a run on the DII Micromedium hub. Not if they intended to succeed. Or survive.

She reluctantly approached one of the group sites Hackizen had learned about from his training with the quantum array reverse-engineers. She discovered that pursuing the practice with others accelerated both its pace and intensity. Each participant grappled with his or her own chaotic mind and with the other participants' roiling mental detritus as well. At first, Patrice thought this would overwhelm her. She also feared she would compulsively reveal endangering facts about the hacktivists' mission, not to mention embarrassing private thoughts that she routinely edited before speaking in a social setting.

When she braved her first neurally joined session, her mind spewed out the same random froth that plagued her solo sessions. So did everyone else's. To her relief, it was impossible to tell where the threads of ambient cognitive noise originated. As this material surfaced into the participants' shared awareness, Patrice experienced it as an expanded version of her solo practice. Oddly, she could not say whether the random thoughts stemmed from the lower reaches of her own mind or someone else's.

Occasionally, something so far outside her life experience would float up that she assumed came from another participant. She couldn't be sure though. Sometimes while sitting alone she would drift into a partial sleep state. Dream images seeped into her awareness, but she could examine them because she maintained her concentration even as she strode the boundary between sleeping and waking life. This was similar, even with thoughts she found foreign.

She experienced the threads of life stories as background racket, like the sound of a macroaudio receiver from another room. As the participants mostly hailed from the same period and interconnected matrix of cultures, the mental noise was remarkably consistent and nearly impossible to differentiate, especially since the joint objective was to let it flow through ungrasped.

She felt less exposed than she feared she would.

Synergistic with the safety of anonymity, Patrice was surprised to discover that neurally joining with others in a group practice yielded a much deeper, more stable focus. Each participant's resolute intention and effort to stay centered reinforced all the others' reciprocal contributions, producing sustained concentration none of them had achieved individually. When she sat alone after these sessions, she took the strengthened discipline with her, resulting in deeper, more stable, and prolonged periods of quiet awareness.

In accordance with the site's protocol, Patrice paid attention to her breath and relaxed her mind as she made the final adjustments to her equipment and eased into the neural nexus connecting the room's participants.

The teacher leading this group is an advanced practitioner. Participants configure their quantum array settings so that the teacher's signal is stronger than the others', allowing her to introduce more dominant thoughts into the shared mind. She guides the group through simultaneous controlled breathing exercises to bring their concentration into alignment. After several cycles, the participants' minds synchronize to the same rhythm.

The teacher next guides the participants to focus their minds in synchrony around a mantra. It is different each time. Today, the syllables are oh-mah. The group silently thinks this mantra, slowly, over and over, at a beat established by the teacher.

After ten minutes, the teacher instructs the students to let the mantra fade and direct their minds on the center of the shared awareness. Not as a physical space but a conscious intersection of their joined minds.

This is extremely challenging. With a mantra, there is a handle for the mind to grasp, even if it arises and ceases repeatedly. To focus the mind without such an object requires absolute concentration while completely letting go. To the rational mind, it is a paradox. When the group members manage to pacify the clinging of the thinking mind and turn their awareness to a shared point of pure consciousness, they simultaneously and jointly experience a deep, luminous silence.

For a moment. And then the discursive noise bubbles up like swamp gas.

When this happens, the teacher either broadcasts the mantra, which the students resume until they regain alignment. Or the teacher thinks, "Now." The word-thought rings like a bell, bringing the participants' shared mind back to the present, allowing the random background thoughts to dissipate.

The students' efforts mutually strengthen, and they experience longer periods of crystalline silence. It is simultaneously deeply relaxed and acutely alert, containing nothing and everything at once, reflecting back their joined consciousness like a flawless, polished mirror.

Still, random, chaotic thoughts and feelings always churn below the surface. The practitioners experience this incipient roiling more as sensation than thinking, though edges of cognition periodically become apparent. Parts of words, sounds, images, and sharp emotions connected to bits of narrative. Periodically, the story fragments become so salient or sticky that they catch someone's attention and cause the group's focus to waver.

After a stretch of quiet concentration during today's session, Patrice noticed overlapping, rapid-fire images, sounds, bits of songs and thought fragments erupting into the shared mental space: Did I turn off the stove? How can I still be so fat? Man, she was hot. I have to get that goddamn thing fixed. Oh shit I forgot to pay the electric. God I suck at this. Why the hell won't you call? Yeesh that was humiliating ...

In the midst of this melee, Patrice perceived an image of Advocate Baksh on macrovision being interviewed by Lynn Corbett on *The Morning Show.*

"What a dupe."

She wasn't sure whose thought it was but she agreed with it.

"Trust the cops? Prison industry and reform activists cooperating? Is he stupid or just naïve?"

"Now!" comes the thought-command of the teacher.

The shared awareness quiets. The focus stabilizes. The teacher leads the group in a mantra cycle, reinforcing the participants' concentration and loosening the allure of the thoughts that had begun to take hold.

Leo, wired in from his home terminal, falls into rhythm with the group, slowly and repeatedly thinking "*Oh-mah*" in synchrony with the others, like rowers in a galley working together to move a great ship gracefully through a mighty sea.

The group mind focuses, and his sense of a separate self fades and merges into one mind with a central point, as though the circle shared a single, primordial space, undifferentiated, perfectly aligned and whole.

Then, a niggling thought pops up from the lower reaches of someone's mind. It feels like his but one can never be certain in this setting:

"Dupe?"

This sets off in Leo a round of fretting, defensive hostility, and self-questioning that pulls him from the calm alignment and disturbs the surface of the shared consciousness so acutely that the others become aware of themselves as separate entities and the connection fills with cognitive noise.

Patrice perceived the questions about Leo Baksh's performance. She also experienced several images not of the screen, but from on the set facing the anchor who conducted the interview. She found this confusing, almost as though she were in a dream and had stepped through the Macromedium screen and into the studio.

"You think you could have done better?"

Was she asking this of herself? Good question. Could she?

The meditation group leader tried to reestablish the group's focus, but concluded after several exercises that they had accomplished all they could for today's session and that further effort would do more harm than good.

"We're restive today," she told them with her mind. "That's how it is sometimes. It may not seem like it, but the committed effort to stay focused when thoughts keep snagging us is good practice. Good work, everyone." She guided the group through closing rituals and admonished them to spend time in individual practice. The participants dialed down their arrays and disconnected.

Leo removed the crown of quantum nodes from his head and reflected on the thoughts about his macrovision appearance, wondering where they originated. He decided all that mattered was which one he believed, regardless of their provenance. He had chosen his positions during the interview for sound strategic reasons, whether others recognized it or not. He reminded himself it was impossible to please everyone, including himself much of the time.

Over in her apartment, Patrice stood to stretch and thought about what it must have been like to be interviewed on national macrovision. Unfamiliar ripples of anxiety panged in her chest as she contemplated being questioned by Lynn Corbett about the terror attacks in front of the world.

Leo moved to a cushion for a session of silent practice on his own.

Patrice sat back down, folded her legs, and focused on her breath.

Each strove to pierce thoughts and abide in still awareness with minimal success.

As Leo sought to balance and focus, an image of himself on macrovision rose from the depths of his mind and snagged his attention. Try as he might to let the pestering image pass, he caught on it and his mind splintered into associated thoughts and feelings.

An image of Leo on macrovision similarly arose in Patrice's mind and pulled her attention from the breath.

After repeated, unsuccessful efforts to let the image go and return to their respective attentive foci, Leo and Patrice shifted methods and concentrated on the image to investigate it.

Rather than dissolve, as distractions often did when observed, the image of Leo on the macrovision screen became more vivid to each of them and stretched in its frame, like the skin of a drum vibrating in slow motion.

As Leo and Patrice peered down further into their own minds, the phenomenon grew in dimension and intensity, enticing them deeper into its dynamic center, until each had the unsettling sense of passing back and forth through the screen, from the perspective of interviewee in the studio to audience watching the broadcast, to interviewee, to audience, as though an invisible pendulum were stretching the screen from one elastic extreme to its opposite and back again. The sensation was frighteningly acute, precipitating a dash of vertigo and nausea in each of them.

Unable to banish or turn away from this vivid experience, each made its oscillation the meditative focus until the mesmerizing phenomenon resolved, dissolving cycle by cycle and easing away, into the gently undulating rhythm of the breath.

19

ANNA PEERED AT LEO THROUGH dark glasses and the window of his car.

He still hadn't heard from her three days after his interview and didn't know what to make of her silence. As the days passed, self-centered paranoia that she was disappointed in his performance gave way to healthy fear that something might be wrong and he cast aside his infantile pride and called her.

She answered and assured him she was fine. She didn't mention the broadcast and Leo forbade himself to ask. After some awkward small talk, she told him she'd like to see him face-to-face. He offered to meet her at his office that afternoon. Instead, she asked whether he might be up for a drive the following weekend because she needed a ride down the coast to a retreat center where she planned to take a class. He said a road trip sounded like an excellent proposal, and they selected this corner, discreetly remote from her home, for him to collect her.

Leo had to pass through a checkpoint to enter the Vulnerable district where Anna lived. He could have sent her a pass to meet him on the other side, but that would have been more complicated. Once she was in his escort, the authorities would give her only cursory inspection.

The protected district was clean, though less affluent than the Citizen districts where he lived and worked. He hadn't visited Anna's neighborhood, but this one was typical: one-story, simple but well-maintained homes, a humble breakfast joint, a gas station. No trees. Clean but on the bleak side. Nothing remarkable other than the ubiquitous cameras and police phones prominently displayed in both Vulnerable and Aggressive Districts. Usually the ones in the Aggressive venues were vandalized and covered in graffiti while the ones in the Vulnerable districts were unmolested. A couple of the cameras and phones on this street, however, looked as though they had been smashed with a baseball bat. Unusual.

He always experienced a blend of relief and suffocation when he traveled back into the Vulnerable enclaves. It felt safe on one level, both because his family had relocated there for a time after the government reclassified him in his youth, but also because there were safeguards in place to protect the populace from harm or disruption. That same fact also made it oppressive. The Citizen venues might be less predictable, but that meant they were less scripted and controlled too. Conservative efforts to clamp things down notwithstanding, the Citizen realms felt freer.

Leo popped open the lock, and Anna swung into the passenger seat, unwrapped a scarf from round her head, and strapped in.

"Long time," he said.

"Been a bit," she agreed.

Anna slid the sarcastically large sunglasses down her nose and scrutinized Leo over their rims.

"Nice smart asses, I mean glasses," said Leo.

"You are healing nicely," she replied with a stifled laugh and raised her eyebrows for a response. Anna had spoken to Leo a few times since the explosion but this was her first time seeing him.

"Parts of me better than others. Some days better than others. Overall, yes. I think so."

She waited for more details, and when they weren't forthcoming, slid the sunglasses back up her nose and sat against the passenger door so she could face Leo as he drove. The two felt an instinctive affinity for one another.

"I was kidding about the glasses," he offered.

"I got that."

"They're quite, uh ..."

Anna offered him her ear.

"...glamorous."

"Yes. Well," she said, brushing nonexistent lint off her sleeve. "I'm aiming for the media-weary heiress look."

"Nice," he said, eyeing her peripherally, "But the backpack may foil the cloak."

She pulled down the lenses long enough to stage whisper, "Old money needn't boast."

"I wouldn't know."

"Alas, neither would I," she sighed.

Leo set coordinates in his navigation device, and they were off.

Anna combed tangles from her hair with her fingers while Leo navigated toward the coastal highway. As they crested the first rise on the edge of the city and saw green hillocks presaging the windy journey ahead, each felt excited and relieved.

"It's been way too long since I got out of the city," said Leo.

"Same here," said Anna. "I love this route."

"Me too. My folks had a cabin down south when I was a kid."

"Had?"

"Yeah, for a little while. It was fun."

"What happened to it?"

"Long story."

Leo invited Anna to select music, unsure whether she would consider anything in his collection to qualify as such. She flipped through the stack, politely neutral in her reactions, and chose an obscure jazz recording that Leo purchased after a concert at a coffee house several years earlier.

"I'm impressed," she said holding up the cover before she inserted the data into the macroaudio player.

"You know him?"

"Of course."

"Of course," echoed Leo, feeling old.

"I mean I know *him*," explained Anna. "He dated Wendy a few years ago."

"Oh?"

"Yeah. Brief and intense. Didn't end well. But she wasn't mad enough to throw away all the recordings he gave her."

"Unpublished tracks?"

"Yep. He's kind of a prick but a beautiful artist. I love his stuff."

"Me too," said Leo, as the caressing beat commenced. "So, what is this class you're taking?"

Anna put away her sunglasses and turned to face him again. "Martial arts."

Leo adjusted the temperature as he absorbed this.

"I know you're worried about implications for my case, but I've already started the training and I think it's good for me."

"That's important," said Leo. "Good to hear. Tell me more."

After a moment's reflection, she concluded his vibe matched his words, so she gave it a go. "It's helping me across the board," she began. "It has a meditation component, which is providing an anchor."

He said that made sense.

"It also has an action component which"—she chewed her lip—"it's hard to describe."

They squinted at the glare as a wooded stretch of road ended and Leo turned onto the coastal highway. Complex chords danced off the speakers.

"It's a fighting art, but the objective is to prevent harm to yourself and your opponent. It's like a dance. When I perform a kick or strike and accompanying shout it's"—she mimed truncated versions of strike-forms as she searched for the right word—"almost a musical release of anger."

She wondered whether that made sense to him.

"It's anger but it doesn't tear me up on its way out or fester in my guts. It passes like wind through a flute, and then it's released." She flicked her hands apart like she was setting something free. "Afterward, I feel like I've been"—she turned within a moment—"purified. Cleansed."

"Wow."

"Yeah. It makes me feel less exposed. Less overwhelmed by other people's trips. In control of my power."

They traveled along the curving highway. Like molten diamonds, the ocean's slick surface reflected the sun in sparks of searing white. Leo cracked the window and they could hear waves crashing on the rocks below, thundering oracles for the cliffside they traversed, as seagulls rode updrafts along the craggy precipice and laughed.

A motorcycle buzzed by in the opposite direction.

"Sounds healthy."

"It is. It's stitching me together."

He reflected on Anna's words, thinking about her case. Thinking about her. "We should harness that to add momentum to your claim."

"They'll just say I'm making my body into a lethal weapon."

"They might. But we can model some persuasive arguments on what you've described. Let's let it percolate and see what we can come up with."

Anna absorbed that for a moment.

"That wasn't the reaction I expected from you."

"Maybe you don't know me as well as you think."

"Probably not," said Anna. "People don't even know themselves as well as they think."

Leo wondered if this was meant for him or herself.

"True," he said after a beat.

"I don't know you at all," she continued, "but I feel like I do."

This touched Leo. He felt the same way.

"I've been experimenting with meditation too," he offered.

"Oh?"

"Nothing of the action component you describe. Silent sitting, mostly."

"We do that too as part of the training before the exercises."

They compared notes and gossiped about what spastic messes they were.

"Thoughts pop up out of nowhere," said Anna. "Like camera lights flashing in a stadium. Where do they come from? So random. Drives me nuts."

"Same here," said Leo. "Like there's a wild horse galloping around in my head, and some idiot gave it permission to speak."

"It never shuts up," said Anna.

"Almost never."

They fell quiet.

"Yes, almost never," she agreed, and they chatted about the brief stretches of stillness and silence each had experienced.

"Those make me feel like I'm crazy the rest of the time," said Anna. "All that noise I call my life is a sliver of what's going on."

"I know what you mean. No wonder the world is so screwed up."

"I read an article where a physicist said all the stuff we can detect and measure, everything that the sciences have told us makes up the physical universe is five percent of what's actually there," said Anna. "There's not enough matter to make the gravity required to hold the galaxies in their shapes, and the universe is expanding faster and faster. They call the big question mark 'dark matter' and 'dark energy,' which is code for we have no fucking idea."

"I've heard that too," said Leo. "It's crazy."

"I think the other ninety-five percent is what we tap into when we have those silences in meditation. It's what the spiritual masters are always harping about. You know life is an illusion, blah blah blah."

Leo raised his eyebrows. "The silence is what they're calling dark matter and energy?"

"More like the silence is the doorway into the reality behind the illusion. The ninety-five percent isn't dark at all, it's obscured by our fixation on the surface."

Leo reflected on these thoughts. "That's profound."

"Ain't it?"

He gave her a sidelong glance. "Yes, it is."

Spiritual questions aside, they also agreed that the practice was having beneficial effects on the rest of their lives, which was encouraging, but weird, since most of the time it felt like nothing was happening when they sat on the cushion other than futile efforts to stop getting lost in trains of useless rumination.

"I suppose recognizing that is progress," said Leo.

"So they say."

The album ended and Anna chose something even more ambient, a sleepy electronic composition suitable for a modern museum installation.

"That piece always makes me feel cool and lonely," said Leo.

"Would you rather something else?"

"No. Leave it. Those corridors need light too."

She snapped shut the case. "Blue light," she said.

"Definitely," agreed Leo. "Cold, blue light."

With that, Anna settled in her seat to gaze upon the passing beauty as they let the music shine its healing chill into the depths of their lifelong, solitary sorrows.

"It touches those places without making me all weepy," she said.

"Exactly."

She pulled a notepad from her bag and jotted down the identifying information for the recording.

When the long track finished, Leo told Anna about the neurally joined meditation groups he'd been exploring.

"You mean you're wiring your brain into one of those quantum mutilation devices?"

"Excuse me?" Leo said, stung by her response, which snapped out like the tip of a whip.

"Are you getting jacked up on Elidrine first too?

"What? No. Elidrine?" Leo was momentarily silenced by the incongruity between the sublime experience of the group practice and the polluted suggestion of using drugs with the equipment. "No. It's nothing like that."

He started to describe the experience of joining with the others in meditation, but Anna stopped him with the thinnest rudiment of courtesy. "Look, whatever you're doing, I hope it's helping. People are doing fucked up shit with those things. Please just"—she made a scooting motion with her fingertips—"keep it to yourself."

Leo was dumbfounded.

Anna ejected the music and started snapping through the recordings for something else.

What the hell? thought Leo. "I'm sorry," he began. "Did something—"

"It's OK," Anna said, holding up her hand. "It's OK," she repeated, throwing her open palm toward him in the universal *Just shut up* gesture. "Let's talk about something else."

"But—"

She turned to lock his gaze, defying him to continue. Tipping her head toward the road, she yanked the steering wheel to keep them from flying off the ledge as the highway turned.

Leo, shaken, brought his attention back to the road. He drove without speaking for a few minutes, then swallowed and said, "OK."

Anna decided against further music. "I'm sorry."

"Me too." He wasn't sure what he was apologizing for, other than upsetting her.

She put her hand on his but the no-go sign could not have been clearer. He kept mum.

She patted his hand and sat back against the passenger door again, ready to commence a more pleasant segment of their trip. "I'm sorry I didn't call you about your interview on *The Morning Show*," she said, causing Leo a bit of emotional whiplash, but also relief she was broaching the subject they'd been avoiding.

"Did I do something that offended you?" He cringed inside as he awaited the response.

"God, no," she replied. "I couldn't watch it. I knew how nervous you would be, which I couldn't screen out while I watched you. I also knew she'd be asking you about me and about all the crap everyone has been saying and," she threw up her hands, "I couldn't deal."

"It went OK, I think," Leo began.

Anna dismissed the interruption, "I recorded it and waited until Wendy had seen it so she could give me the highlights and I could decide whether to watch it."

"And?"

She adjusted her garments and let him squirm. "Wendy thinks you're super smart and a hell of a lot savvier than you look."

"Gosh, thanks."

"Welcome," replied Anna. "I tuned in to some commentary from the talking heads."

Leo felt a chill. He had been trying to avoid listening to the commentary.

"I assume you have been following all of that."

"I've managed to avoid it."

"Fool. Let me fill you in."

He didn't respond.

"I expected the moderates to be cheering us, and the conservatives to be gathering torches and pitch forks."

This was Leo's expectation as well.

"For kicks I went straight to the most conservative news show, and they were saying things like 'voice of reason,' 'peacemaker' and, my favorite, 'should run for office.'"

Leo hooted at the absurdity.

"I considered firing you on the spot."

"I may have to fire myself."

"Then I checked out a Micromedium forum for the moderates. The fact that the conservatives were praising you was enough to poison the opinions of some. They used words like 'dupe—'"

Leo flashed on his bizarre experience that started with this annoying word in the group meditation.

"—'naïve,'" she continued, "and don't take this the wrong way but, well, 'whore.'"

"There's a right way to take that?"

"Matter of taste, I suppose."

"I see," said Leo, rolling his eyes.

"The voices of more seasoned spokespeople disagreed. They used words like 'sly,' 'strategic,' and again my favorite, 'should run for office.'"

"You've got to be kidding."

"Nope."

Anxious about his performance and fearful that they would relay criticisms he'd rather not hear, Leo had avoided calls from John and Jeaneane during the days following his appearance after accepting their initial accolades. He now assumed they carried tidings of these unforeseen developments.

"So," she said, elongating the vowel, "I watched the interview."

Leo's hands were sweaty on the steering wheel.

"You nailed it. No offense, but you did a lot better than I thought you would."

"I was a nervous wreck."

"I could tell you were nervous. Who wouldn't have been? I would have gone into cardiac arrest but you handled it."

"Lynn Corbett and her staff are good at making it happen."

"That doesn't surprise me. People usually end up relaxed and articulate on her show. They can't all be that pulled together."

"True."

"You took on tough issues and spoke honestly without disrespecting anyone. That's why you've become a wild card. They still don't like me but they like you."

"But everyone knows where I stand on these issues."

"Yes, but everyone stands somewhere and most can't talk about them intelligently or civilly. Don't be surprised if you start getting offers from the dark side."

Leo turned to her without expression.

"When you do, remember who you are, Advocate Baksh."

"You're being dramatic."

"No. I'm not. Lastly, thank you for defending me so valiantly."

"I thought that was my job."

"It is. And you did it. Well. On national macrovision. You upstaged all those haters, and pulled it off with style and grace." She finished by grabbing his arm and flipping her hair onto his shoulder. "My hero!" she gushed, then pushed him away as she flopped back in her seat. "How's that?"

"Ample," said Leo. "Thanks."

"Welcome," she replied airily. "Seriously though. Thank you, Leo."

"I'll send you my bill."

She waved away the absurdity. "Screw that. Send it to the Board."

They giggled, and Leo delivered a middle finger to the agency on both their behalfs.

The digital ring of Leo's mobile device interrupted their amusement. Anna pawed around in the back seat to find it for him.

"Let it go to voicemail."

"That's a bad habit," said Anna. "I'm surprised you're getting a signal out here." She eyed the screen as she handed it to him. "Unidentified."

Leo glanced down at it before answering. "A strong signal. Must be good atmospheric conditions."

"I thought clouds were better for reception over distance," said Anna.

They both peered perfunctorily out the front windshield at the flawless blue sky they already knew was there, and shrugged at one another.

"Leo Baksh."

"So professional," whispered Anna, donning her sunglasses.

"Mr. Baksh, glad you answered. Hope you don't mind a call on the weekend. Cormack O'Brian."

Leo reflexively eased off the gas.

"Mr. O'Brian. How—"

A dozen adjectives sped through Leo's mind, most of them impolite.

"Unexpected?" prompted the president and CEO of Protection Inc.

"To say the least, yes."

Anna pulled off her glasses in disbelief. "Cormack O'Brian?" she whispered with exaggerated enunciation.

Leo nodded, dazed.

She dipped her head and leveled a palm at him, as though serving something up. Leo could plainly read the meaning behind her gesture: "What did I just say? Dark side."

Anna redonned her glasses and stared out the passenger window as Leo grappled with the unwelcome intrusion.

20

"Mr. O'Brian, to what do I owe the pleasure of this call? And to whom? Which is to say, how did you get this number?"

Cormack O'Brian settled back in the leather comfort of his town car. "I know how to make things happen, Mr. Baksh. Today, I wanted to talk to you, and voilà."

"That doesn't answer my question."

"Your question seeks information I'm not at liberty to disclose, Mr. Baksh. The part about where I got the number, that is. As to the reason for my call, I'll tell you straightaway: I want you to work for me."

"Thanks but I already have a job."

"You're cut out for bigger things than begging judges for crumbs," said O'Brian.

He lit a cigarette and awaited the advocate's reaction.

"I hardly know where to begin in responding to that," said Leo.

"Begin wherever you like," encouraged O'Brian.

"Let's see, how about how dare you for starts."

"Come now, where's this mettle you displayed so adroitly on *The Morning Show* last week?"

"Do you mind?" snapped O'Brian's son Liam, who rode shotgun. He grabbed Cormack's cigarette and flicked it out the passenger window. Cormack glared at Liam, but acquiesced.

"You've wrapped what is supposed to pass for a compliment around a deliberate insult," answered Leo. "If further discussion is what you have in mind, you're off to a poor start. Sir."

O'Brian chuckled gutturally at this honorary postscript. "Very well, I will endeavor to be more genteel."

"If by genteel you mean socially appropriate, then please proceed."

Plucky kid, thought O'Brian. *That's good.*

"Forgive me, I spend most of my time dealing with unpleasant characters."

"Are you referring to your prisoners or your employees?"

"I meant the politicians in the Council of Delegates," said O'Brian, dodging the bait.

That tickled Leo's ribs. "I see," he said. "That I can understand."

"I'm sure. May I call you Leo?" O'Brian asked kindly.

"Of course."

"And I'm Cormack. Leo, I won't waste your time beating around the bush. You are a gifted young man. You're smart, articulate, good looking."

Liam turned to his father, slack faced, and shook his head.

"More than that, you're wise, insightful, balanced."

Liam slapped a hand over his eyes. The elder O'Brian socked him in the thigh.

"Thanks, but why would I want to sell my gifts to the private confinement industry?"

"You wouldn't be selling them to the industry. You'd be sharing them with the world."

"I see." Leo said, amused. "How would working for Protection Inc. allow me to do that?"

"You don't even know what position I have in mind. Your reaction is rather a letdown. I expected something more ... mature."

Leo was silent a moment. "You're right. I'm sorry. But you called me on my private line by way of a number you obtained through means you will not disclose, on the weekend, uninvited. I don't consider that appropriate. Nevertheless, my apologies for being impolite. You're a man of great stature and I mean you no disrespect."

Cormack thought he heard the tinkling of female laughter in the background. "Are you alone?"

"Excuse me, but that's none of your business."

"Absolutely true," O'Brian said after a beat. "Apology accepted. My apologies for intruding. I like to show off. It's one of my shortcomings. One reason I need an associate."

When Leo didn't respond, he continued, "Listen, I won't keep you. I just wanted to open a channel. All I ask is that you try to keep an open mind. One of your strengths, yes? Let me send you a detailed proposal. We have more in common than you realize and we could work together to help build a better world."

"Actually," Leo replied, "given the troubling rumors regarding your possible relationship to my client's case, it would be best if we did not speak again. I will have to disclose to the inquiry panel that you contacted me."

"Be my guest," said O'Brian. "I've done nothing illegal or improper. As for any concerns about conflicts of interest, you would have to refer your client to other counsel if you worked for me."

"I do not foresee making any such choice."

"Just think about letting me tell you more. When you do, chew on this: I agree that we need to reform the rules for confinement and broaden access to Citizenship."

Leo absorbed this in silence.

"Good day, Leo."

He terminated the connection.

"Man, you know how to pile it on," said Liam.

"I meant every word."

"Right."

"Son, there is more to me and more to this world than you recognize."

"That may be true, Dad, but Leo Baksh is a progressive, activist advocate. You want him because you think he can help stem the tide, and it's a tide, Dad, an oceanic shift, calling for reforms that will catapult Protection Inc. into bankruptcy."

Cormack threw his head back and howled at the comedy. "Protection Inc. is one of the strongest companies in the world. It's in no danger. You're right that I want Baksh's help in part to discredit claims that we are acting against the public interest. What you do not understand is that I want him even more because he can help us grow in directions that will bring our critics on board, not silence them."

"Dream on."

"That's what I'm trying to do, my boy. Dream, and then make visions into reality."

Liam turned away.

"Your problem is that you think too small," said Cormack. "You're looking at cracks in the paint. Take a step back and you'll see a thriving metropolis."

"I see the walls quite clearly, Pop," Liam assured. "Better than you know."

"Let's not fight," said Cormack.

After cycling through mental retorts, Liam succumbed. The old man pulled him into a sideways hug.

"Who all is coming to this shindig?" asked Liam.

Cormack had invited his son to accompany him to the semi-formal garden party ostensibly hosted by a society matron for seasonal social purposes. In truth, Liam knew, the main function of the gathering was for the Citizens Action League to reinforce its political infrastructure, and for its associated luminaries to rub elbows and strategize. Though Liam despised the values these people shared, he would not forsake a front row seat to their scheming, and accepted without hesitation.

Though his father knew full well of Liam's political objections, he welcomed his son's cooperation as a display of filial fidelity. Father and son each had a complex view of the world and, while they occasionally jousted, sometimes spilling a drop or two of blood, they respected each other's minds and were equally invested in the relationship. Cormack didn't know what Liam's agenda was, but suspected the boy fancied he was doing a bit of political reconnaissance. Cormack felt his son's views could use a good steep in the real world. Having his affable and attractive firstborn accompany him to the fête also sent the sort of message the conservatives favored. Attending together was to their mutual benefit, even if for conflicting reasons.

"I haven't seen the guest list, but it's going to be a largish group. The Merriweathers will be there. They paid for that new treatment center for mentally ill Vulnerables."

"I remember," said Liam. "They also fund a lot of arts organizations."

"Less practical, but yes."

Liam shook his head at Cormack's appetite for profit over culture.

"Reverend Cecil Rhodes of the Congregation of the Way. National Police Chief Alex Fortas."

"How relaxing," interjected Liam. "The rationalizer and the muscle."

"They are both quite personable, Liam."

"Uh huh. Who else?"

"All of the CAL's top brass."

"A veritable Cleague fest, then."

"I forbid you to use that filthy language in my presence."

"Dad, please." He rolled down the window and spat.

"Don't let that word cross your lips at the party."

"That's exactly what I had in mind."

Cormack knew the boy was too smart to make such a social mistake, but Liam's sarcastic protestations of incomprehension were standard script.

"Please tell me Belford Thorsch will not be there stinking up the place."

"No," said Cormack, "the League cozied up to Belford while he was in office because it would have been foolish not to, but now that he is out of power, his former glory isn't enough to overcome his lack of social grace."

"I assumed his money would earn him a spot among your buddies at the CAL. Isn't that why you still talk to the jerk?"

"He is a gifted businessman with influential associations."

"Right. Like dictators and international corpocratic mobsters."

Cormack sighed. "Son, there is so much you do not understand."

Liam bit his tongue. "I'm glad he won't be there. Who else is coming?"

"I'm sure there will be several influential families from Rhodes' congregation," O'Brian continued.

"Mmm, church girls."

His father chuckled. "Mind the champagne and your hands, young man. But yes, church girls," he said, winking.

"Same to you," Liam replied. "The list is improving. Who else?"

"There is a rumor that Justice Brannice may stop in."

"High Adjudicator Brannice?"

"So I hear."

Liam faced forward. "Isn't that a wee conflict of interest?"

"Not at all. This is a social gathering."

Liam guffawed.

"It is a social gathering," his father persisted. "There will be no one present involved in a case currently before the court."

"What about future cases?"

"No one at this gathering has given any financial support to High Adjudicator Brannice."

"What about vice versa? By showing up she's tipping her hand."

"Nonsense. Adjudicators are people, Liam. They are pledged to uphold principles of judicial objectivity. Sharing an afternoon with friends won't determine whether they are capable of that."

"If the activists heard about it they'd crucify her."

"There's no reason that they should," said Cormack, throwing his son a cautionary glance. Liam returned the eye contact but refused to offer up the assurances he knew the elder O'Brian sought. No point in foreclosing options and saying things that might later turn out to be lies. Liam disagreed with his father on many topics, but he also loved him and did his best to be honest with him. Sometimes, this required silence. If that meant he wasn't serving up the whole truth, at least he wasn't feeding him falsehoods.

They turned onto the gravel drive and began curving between rows of ancient live oaks to their host's stately mansion. Cormack said, "And of course, the grande dame herself, Evelyn Malone."

"Will Wendy be there?"

"I don't know, son."

"I suppose she wouldn't fit in."

"I don't think that would stop Evelyn from inviting her."

"Nor her from attending," added Liam. Cormack winked at Liam and they headed for the festivities.

A crisply uniformed attendant greeted them at the estate's grand entrance and escorted them through the main floor to a ballroom where the hostess held court.

Liam glanced around the magnificent chamber. Floors of cat's-eye marble. A vaulted ceiling adorned with trompe l'oeil sky. Elegantly understated crystal fixtures that seemed to fall like rain. Enormous potted palms. A concave wall composed of arched, fifteen-foot pane-glass windows, opening onto a great terrace and, beyond its steps, a botanical garden rivaling the finest of municipal arboreta. A chamber orchestra played at one end. Waitstaff milled among the guests, distributing sparkling libations and canapés.

"Cormack, Liam," called Evelyn Malone, her voice a rich alto seasoned with a touch of palsy. Its timbre bespoke maturity, strength, and authority, wrapped around a deep vein of love. Cormack and his son stepped forward and Malone hugged them each in turn, her embrace regal but genuinely warm.

"It's lovely to see you," she said, gripping one arm of each with hands like gnarled wood wrapped in coffee-stained crêpe paper.

"Evelyn, you remain the soul of elegance," said Cormack, meaning it.

They were old friends.

Evelyn Malone once stood somewhere in height between Cormack's 5'10" and Liam's six feet, but she seemed to have withdrawn to a point in her center over the years and now stood shorter than both. Undaunted, she still towered over them and everyone else in the room, but without making anyone feel small. Her hair, thick and pure white, swept up into a roll at the back of her head. A dress of silken azure complemented her sparkling blue eyes. Over her shoulders lay a finely wrought shawl of black lace, interwoven with tiny threads of green and turquoise. Around her neck, a strand of pearls glistened in rainbow orbs against her delicate skin.

"You are as handsome as ever, dear man," she replied, "as is this strapping fellow I would hardly have recognized since last I saw him were he not the living image of his father."

Liam repressed a groan and responded with a slight bow.

Evelyn nestled between them, hooked an elbow in Cormack's arm on her left and Liam's on her right, and escorted them into the crowd. She passed them off gracefully, as though surrendering each to another dance partner, and resumed making her rounds.

Liam snagged two glasses of champagne from a passing waiter and tried to strike up a conversation with an attractive young woman. When he offered her a bubbling drink, she shot her hands up as though warding off an evil portent and told him coldly that she did not "partake of spirits." From the corner of his eye, Liam saw Cormack moving toward him with the Reverend Cecil Rhodes in tow. Gesturing toward them with his chin, Liam said, "My father."

"Mine too," she replied, the temperature of her manner still at sub-freezing. Liam took this as his cue and turned for the terrace, barely making his escape before the paternal duo descended upon the stillborn conversation between their offspring.

As he strode across the patio, the garden unfolded before him in layers of emerald. When he approached the edge of the top tier, he saw a slope that descended beyond the lowest step, to a small lake shrouded in trees.

He stood mesmerized by this idyll for a long moment. Then, his eye snagged on a mop of blond chaos atop an appealingly strong-soft form clad in a sheer black cocktail dress, elbow on knee and chin on palm, absorbed in the same view he had just discovered. Liam's pulse quickened and his stomach dropped through his feet. He tipped his head forward and strode down the stairs to her.

"Care for a drink, miss?"

She tore herself away from the view, turning her head to the side and up to identify the would-be suitor and leapt to her feet.

"Liam!"

She threw her arms around his neck and kissed him twice on the cheek. He accepted these affections with arms outstretched behind her so as not to spill the champagne. Or hold her.

"Hi Wendy."

She stepped back and accepted a glass. They chimed a silent toast and took a sip, never releasing each other's gaze.

"I cannot believe you have stooped to attending such an event," she said, her amber eyes dancing with mirth.

"Hello, kettle? Pot calling," he responded, and took another a sip.

"I'm related," she said in retort.

"So am I," he replied. "I'm here with dear old Dad."

"Of course," she said.

"Is Patrice here with you?" he asked, glancing around as though she might materialize.

Wendy responded compassionately, if a bit wearily. "No, sweetheart. She's doing something else today."

"Too bad. I hoped I might meet her," he said, half meaning it. He swallowed and said, "How are you? Both of you. Individually and together I mean."

He cringed at his own awkwardness, and she giggled.

"We're ... OK."

"Pretty lukewarm, Wendy. How are you really?"

"I'm OK. Patrice is—"

She stopped, unsure whether he was over her enough to discuss this. He twirled his fingers in a *Go on* gesture.

"—distracted," she continued. "Stressed. To be honest, she's been gone a lot lately. It's her prerogative, don't get me wrong. I don't own her. But there's something going on and she swerves when I ask her about it. She says she's been pursuing a spiritual practice, but shouldn't that be making her more relaxed and present?"

"Depends," said Liam. "If this is too personal, please say so and I will understand, but are you satisfied being with her?"

Wendy and Liam were friends before and after they were lovers. They both called what happened in between love. To Liam that meant forsaking others and moving in. To Wendy it meant pirouetting together like butterflies before flitting off to new horizons. It wasn't that she didn't believe in marriage, she told him, but she had been disappointed enough times to have chosen a lighter path. Not forever, she hoped, but they had to end their romance. Easier for Wendy than for Liam, who found out the hard way what most people in Wendy's wake had discovered: one of the most alluring aspects of her personality was her gift for evading capture.

Wendy was perturbed that Liam turned the conversation from her relationship with Patrice to his own insecurities. She knew the two were related for him, however, so she buried her annoyance. "You mean because she's a she, or because she's not you?"

"Both, to be honest," he said, and looked down.

"Liam, you are a wonderful man. I love you and I hope we will always be friends. You'll find a partner who cherishes you and she will be so lucky to have you. I wasn't that person. It isn't about gender. I'm not set up the way you are when it comes to that. You know that."

"I know it with my head but I don't understand it."

"You don't have to relate to it to hear that it's true for me, do you?" she asked, searching his eyes for deeper comprehension.

He didn't answer that question. Instead, he asked, "Do you still screw around?"

She tapped her shoe. "Not that it's any of your business, but if you mean do we have an open relationship, then yes, sometimes."

"Is there room anywhere for us? In some other form than we tried before? As friends?"

Wendy tipped her head to the side, her eyes reflecting the sadness she saw pouring out of his like an open wound. "If we were meeting today for the first time and I didn't know your tender heart like I do, the answer would be as fast as we can get to a room," she replied kindly. "But we're not meeting today and I do know your heart. You're not cut out for that and we have too much history for that kind of story," she said, cradling his chin. She stood on her toes and kissed him gently on the lips then pivoted next to him, pulled his hand around her waist, and tugged him back toward the party.

"Doesn't my great-grandmother look like a queen?"

"She is a queen," replied Liam, "or a goddess."

As they crested the top tier, a tall slender man stepped in their way. Svelte, dressed in a perfectly tailored suit, and strikingly handsome in a chiseled, not-quite-made-of-flesh way, he regarded them with steely grey eyes which, though beautiful, carried not a hint of warmth. His intrusion jolted them to a stop.

"James," said Wendy, "you startled me."

"Both of us," said Liam.

"Sorry, baby sister," said James Malone. Faint ripples of warmth penetrated his eyes, like wisps of geothermal vapor seeping through a glacial crevasse.

"Any other entrance wouldn't be you. Liam, you remember my brother James?"

"Of course," said Liam, extending a hand.

James shook Liam's hand without looking at him and said to Wendy, "God, Great Grandmother looks like death in a dress, doesn't she?"

Wendy groaned in familiar exasperation.

Having failed to elicit a better response, he continued, "Still slinging swill for stinking street trash?"

"Still destroying people's lives for the police state?" she shot back, annoyed that he could hook her.

"More or less." His features softened and he embraced her. "You look good."

"You too," she said shaking her head.

Liam said he'd get more drinks and slipped away.

"You could have been a little more courteous to Liam," said Wendy after he left.

"If he wasn't man enough to keep you, why should I bother?"

"For someone with your education and power, you're disgustingly ignorant," she said with a defiant leer.

"Not ignorant, baby girl, just good."

"At?"

"Everything I do."

"Time to try something new," she whispered as Liam returned with glasses for three.

"Liam, forgive me for being so rude," said James, playing a little charm like a face card. "I hope you are well."

"Yes thanks, James. Doing OK. You?"

"Fine. Your father?"

"Still furnishing the world with lodging for the people you bust," said Liam.

James eyed him. "Keeping you in fine duds in the process, it seems."

"True," Liam conceded.

They clinked glasses, unsmiling. Wendy shivered and rubbed her arms.

"But he doesn't just lock up criminal Aggressives, he hospitalizes Vulnerables, too, does he not?"

"Something like that," said Liam. "Speaking of Dad, I'd better go perform my role as deserving heir to the empire."

"Let's give him the whole show," said Wendy. "Want some arm candy?"

Liam offered his elbow and Wendy slipped through her slender arm.

"Will you be here later, Jimmy?"

James smirked at the appellation. "Yes, I'm staying the night. Go for a swim later?"

"Perfect."

She and Liam turned to go inside, and she blew James a kiss over her shoulder. He pretended to catch and release it in wonderment, like a butterfly. Wendy saw the glint of love in his eyes as he looked back at her just before she turned away.

Liam and Wendy spent the next two hours tagging along with Cormack O'Brian, meeting and eavesdropping on conversations among the conservative elite. Liam found the detached euphemisms they conversed in comical. He rarely heard "Vulnerable," "activists," or "terrorist" even though these were the primary topics of discussion.

The religious attendees and Citizens Action League representatives gathered into circles around leaders with feet in both organizations and plied one another in sugared tones as they nibbled hors d'oeuvres. Without saying it, both groups reminded National Police Chief Alex Fortas that his political future rested in their hands, as if this were not apparent from the means through which he had secured his appointment. Two conservative members of the Council of Delegates made a brief appearance, which caused quite a splash, but Cormack didn't bring Liam when he paid his respects. Liam assumed this derived from Cormack's well-founded concern that the younger O'Brian couldn't resist the urge to deliver a barb or two if given the chance.

Liam noticed an individual he couldn't place talking intently with Alistair Coyle, the president of the Citizens Action League. Wendy said she didn't know the man's name but heard someone say he was an entrepreneur in Micromedium technology. This piqued Liam's curiosity, but he never got within earshot of a conversation or finagled an introduction.

Liam was surprised to discover that Reverend Rhodes and his flock, although using fairly traditional religious vocabulary, seemed like kind people who believed that existing criteria for Citizenship provided the optimal framework for a happy and spiritually healthy life, not just for Citizens but for those who strived for Citizenship. Nevertheless, he found their rigidity and claims to piety repugnant.

When he probed a few on political issues, most were resilient to a point. Nearly all cited scripture in saying the "disruptors" didn't understand God's plan, which apparently was manifest through the current iteration of the state. Liam found the defense of the status quo frustrating. Nevertheless, some of these people were sincere, not cynical and duplicitous as he and the other hacktivists, particularly Hackizen, had fiercely believed. One young woman even said Liam's challenges were consistent with her beliefs but she slipped away before he got her name.

He wasn't sure how, but these discoveries seemed important. Aggresserable's comments on the folly of disregarding the Cleagues' spirituality may have had some merit, he mused. He was contemplating this thought and scanning the crowd for the young woman who had displayed such breadth of perspective, wondering who could identify her, when he felt furrowed fingertips lightly caress his forearm and turned to find Evelyn Malone regarding him with curiosity.

"Having a good time, dear?"

Wendy had wandered off.

"Yes ma'am. Thank you. It's a beautiful gathering. Everything is perfect."

"I'm glad."

She took his arm.

"So," she said, "what is the eldest son of Cormack O'Brian planning these days?"

Liam did not immediately respond. "With regard to?"

She shrugged and cocked her brow. They walked toward the great lawn's edge, gravel crunching beneath their feet with each slow step.

"I'm taking stock right now. I'm single, no thanks to your great-granddaughter."

"Don't ever think it's for lack of love. You know better than that, don't you?"

Liam thought in silence. "Yes, Ms. Malone."

"Call me Evelyn. We're family even if not by blood."

"That's a great honor to hear, ma'am. Evelyn."

"Nonsense," she said. "Let's sit a moment."

She swept her arm toward a bench under a flowering cherry tree. They sat down and Liam continued. "As for work or a career or whatever, I'm having a hard time deciding."

"You object to your father's business."

He wondered whether he dared speak the truth, then decided it would be absurd not to. Evelyn was no fool. "I can think of nothing more crass and cynical than imprisoning people for money."

"It's more complex than that," she said in response, which did not surprise him, "but what you say is terribly important."

He didn't expect to hear that.

"The ship your father steers exists," she continued. "We can't wish it away, nor the system of laws and customs he navigates it through."

"I'm not sure which is ship and which is ocean, that's half the problem."

Evelyn nudged him with her shoulder, amused by the smartly put point. "Things change slowly."

"Not always."

"No, but often when they change too quickly, they are replaced with something far worse."

"What worse thing could replace a system of imprisonment for profit?" he said, having fearful ideas of his own but curious about her view.

"Try a totalitarian regime," she replied. "A military dictatorship."

He knew Evelyn was a force to contend with, but they had never discussed politics.

"Then what do we do?"

"Yes, what *do* we do?"

"The classification system is based on lies," he said.

"Yes and no," replied Evelyn. "It evolved out of a struggle between oppressors and the oppressed. It still reflects that in important respects, though it's become more abstract."

"I don't consider confinement abstract," he said.

"Neither do I," she agreed. "Nor do I consider torture as such."

Evelyn held his gaze and tipped her head forward, as if to say "yes, that's what I said."

"But," she continued, "the rules governing who gets fixed, hospitalized, imprisoned, tortured—and who bears the dubious honor of inflicting those ills—are becoming increasingly abstract. On one level, the rules reflect a straightforward ongoing struggle to define a just and honorable civilization. On another level, they are manipulated as scrims to camouflage the movement of institutional power."

Liam turned to face her. Goddess indeed.

"And?"

"Your father's company represents enormous institutional power."

"I'm not sure I know what you're suggesting."

She patted his hand. "Sit with it, dear."

"Don't you think more is involved than institutional power? Belief is what holds people together in institutions. Isn't it a war of beliefs?"

"Yes," she agreed. "And of perception," she added, knocking his forearm with her knuckles.

"How do we change that?" he asked.

Voices pierced their conversation with calls for the hostess, warning that High Adjudicator Brannice was about to be announced. Evelyn told Liam she had to see to her other guests.

Liam jumped to his feet and helped the elder stateswoman up as several high-ranking guests approached.

Before he let her go, Liam lobbed a friendly challenge. "No offense, but if you believe in working with ugly institutional power, why didn't you invite Belford Thorsch to this event?"

Mischief rippled across Evelyn's features. "Keeping one's enemies nearby is important," she said, "but that doesn't mean I wish to fraternize with spoiled trash. One must have standards."

Liam couldn't help but laugh at her deft return. She winked at him and took the arm of her assistant to rejoin the other guests.

As he watched her walk back to the manor with her entourage, Liam saw his father speaking with James Malone. He craned his neck to keep them in sight, but the milling guests severed his view. When the crowd thinned enough for him to look again, neither was there.

Hours later, after all the guests had left, Evelyn stood on the second-story veranda outside the master bedroom and saw the lake ripple in intersecting circles as her great-grandchildren, James by blood and Wendy by blood and adoption, swam in the moonlight.

"So different," she thought of the two, and sighed.

She went back inside and entered a security code into a keypad discreetly situated behind a tapestry, and stood back as a panel slid open, revealing a small alcove. She stepped in, settled into a plush chair, placed a crown of quantum nodes around her white carapace, and closed her eyes.

21

"All right, let's begin."

The chatter subsided as the Department of Domestic Intelligence agents in the Capital Region office heeded the chief's call to commence the weekly brainstorming session.

"Let's start with Domestic Security. Bimal?"

Bimal Gurung, head of the region's Domestic Security Division, is a stout man in his mid-sixties with a coffee-and-cream complexion still remarkably smooth due to its plump foundation. His few remaining strands of graying hair are neatly groomed, and he wears thick, utilitarian bifocals. With more seniority than Chief George Mills, Bimal is deceptively soft spoken, his gentle persona belying a steel core.

"We remain focused on two major investigations," he began, "neither of which is proceeding to my satisfaction, despite exemplary work by our agents.

"First, we have come to a virtual standstill in our inquiry into the disastrous explosion last year in what Belinda Mosgrove's press secretary, and therefore the media, erroneously called a power station in the capital."

"Why are you unable to proceed?" asked the chief.

"Jurisdictional power grab by International."

"Why would International try to push us out of that investigation?" asked Lauren.

"It's hard to know for certain why the DII does anything it does after the damage Belford Thorsch did." Bimal was referring to Mosgrove's populist predecessor, who had alienated the DII and its director after International released damaging information about foreign influence on the election that put Thorsch in power, as well as Thorsch's ties to foreign corporations whose interests he promoted while in office.

"The DII still reports to Mosgrove like we do, and it has a legal duty to share intel and coordinate with this agency," said Lauren.

"Trent Hobson has obviously taken some troubling lessons from his run-in with Thorsch," said the chief, referring to the director of international intelligence. "Despite her efforts at rapprochement, Ms. Mosgrove remains the unfortunate beneficiary."

"As do we all," said Lauren.

James clearly didn't share the others' concern with International's secrecy and assumption of autonomy beyond its legal mandate in the wake of the Thorsch scandal. "Shouldn't we leave that investigation to the DII's expertise and consolidate resources on other matters?"

Lauren frowned.

Bimal eyed James. "Perhaps ultimately," he replied, "but I'm not prepared to make that recommendation. I'm troubled by our inability to get answers from anyone, including International, about the facility, the event, or the mysteriously in-absentia suspect.

"Most of what we've pieced together has come from draft media reports that DII advocates blocked from publication through the gag order they secured. The reporter working on the case, Jill Blatsky of the *Capital Times*, has willingly shared her summaries, but refuses to identify her sources. John Hanes, who ascended to acting editor in chief, is backing Blatsky. We threatened to have them jailed and they responded in one voice that they would happily reiterate their refusal in the Department of Adjudication."

James scoffed. "Call their bluff."

"That would enmesh us in a battle that would divert resources from our main objective, gathering information about the attack. While it is no secret that Hanes tends toward a liberal agenda, he is a well-respected and connected journalist. Jailing him would precipitate litigation implicating freedom of the media and the balance of power between branches of the national government, not to mention limits on our investigative power."

"More reason to take them on," persisted James.

Bimal regarded James calmly. "Eventually, perhaps, but this is not a good test case. Nothing in Blatsky's detailed notes suggests her sources have committed a crime or know who did. If they were protecting a suspect, it would be another situation. My chief concern is with the attack, not with curtailing the power of the press to protect its sources. I do not want to get mired in that legal quicksand."

"Do you trust a news hack to conduct a competent interrogation?" asked James.

"In fact, in the case of Blatsky, frankly yes, I do. Sometimes it is most efficient to let people do their jobs and allow information to flow freely."

James's lip twitched but he remained silent.

"What have you found out?" asked Lauren, nudging the ball away from James.

"As we have discussed in previous briefings, the facility assuredly was not a power station. No utility company claims it. It was not registered with the

Department of Power. The company that owns the land is a dummy corporation with a fictitious board whose source has been expertly concealed.

"After her initial interviews with first responders, Blatsky retained a team of experts in physics, computer science, and Micromedium technology to review her sources' descriptions. The experts said the equipment appeared to include super-cooled superconductors, massive magnets, and what they guessed is a new generation data processor, probably a quantum processor."

"Which means?" asked the chief.

"Whatever it is, it likely includes a particle accelerator and a supercomputer."

"Whose is it and what is its purpose?" asked Lauren.

"We have tried to send agents to the facility's environs," replied Gurung, "but the site is cordoned off by International, and whatever physical connections it may have had to the Micromedium or power grid have been removed without a trace."

"Maybe it wasn't online yet," offered James.

"Likely not, or we would have had at least some aberrant Micromedium data its presence would explain. We have been unable to identify evidence of it in any Micromedium backups. However, it must have required an enormous amount of power even to test it, not to mention blow it up. Yet we have neither found evidence of massive consumption from the grid nor identified an independent source."

"It must belong to International or the military or some sort of joint entity," said Melissa.

"That is our working assumption," agreed Bimal.

"What does the DII liaison say?" asked Lauren.

"You know her as well as I do," said Bimal.

"In other words, she said DII will brief us on a need-to-know basis, which means never."

"She threw in a few words like 'national security' and 'classified' but yes."

"Wouldn't it be more in the interests of 'national security,'" said Lauren using air quotes, "for our agencies to cooperate and share intel?"

Bimal kept his visage neutral. "One might reasonably so believe." He considered Lauren the finest of her generation of agents, though he would never publicly play favorites.

"Perhaps that was what the DII liaison had in mind when she"—he paused and closed his eyes a moment to choose the right word—"telegraphed that International may turn over its suspect to Domestic, and that we may be strongly encouraged to give the advocate general grounds to seek his conviction as a domestic terrorist."

Lauren cocked her head, incredulous. "Where is he now?"

"At an undisclosed location."

James snorted.

Lauren glared at him. "If the media accounts have any validity, he could not possibly have planned and executed such a destructive attack on a piece of infrastructure that valuable and protected, whatever it was."

"If International opts to refer him to us," Bimal replied, "it would strongly request that he be portrayed and documented as a supremely devious member of a conspiracy whose other members remain at large and that the infrastructure be identified as a power station."

"International can go to hell," snapped Lauren. "That would be fraud, plain and simple. What the hell is going on here?"

Bimal Gurung held Lauren's eye, the sobriety of his expression acknowledging the validity of her outrage.

The chief, who stood with one foot on a chair and an elbow on his knee, had observed the conversation without visible reaction. "We will evaluate the case if it is referred to us," he said, closing the topic.

Lauren threw up her hands in frustration.

Continuing the transition, the chief said, "Lauren, unless I'm mistaken, you've been getting a little more help from the DII liaison, and I want you to summarize it in a minute. Before we switch to the virtual abuse investigations, Bimal, what is the status of your investigation into the recent bombings?"

"I regret to report that we have made little headway in that investigation, either. For such a drastic set of acts, we have few credible leads. We have ruled out nearly the entire initial batch of subjects. The most interesting live thread, and it is not a strong one, involves a barista at the coffee shop across the street from the Board of Classification headquarters."

"Is this person in custody?" asked Melissa.

Gurung directed attention toward Renée Stephens of the Violent Crimes Unit.

"No," answered Renée. "Local police questioned her after the attack. She remained at the site to render aid to the injured, spoke freely with the investigating officers, had been working at the café for six months, and had local contact information, so she was allowed to leave."

"Was she injured?" asked Lauren.

"No," said Renée. The agents exchanged glances around the table.

"Where is she now?" asked Melissa.

"We don't know," said Renée.

"Who is she?" piped up Pradeep Gopalan of the Fraud Unit, to everyone's surprise. Pradeep was always impeccably attired, and some viewed his angular features as rivalling James's. Fortunately for him, James considered no man his equal and chose to view Pradeep's courteous manner as unthreatening passivity. Pradeep usually focused on white-collar investigations but was trying valiantly to honor the chief's request that the agents help each other across unit divides.

"Turns out we don't know," said Renée.

"Some subject," said James.

"Best we have at present," replied Bimal.

"What about her employment record?" asked Pradeep.

Renée passed the floor with a gesture to Bimal.

"It is for a young woman named Allison Flanders who, we found out after an extensive search through altered records, died ten years ago at age eighteen. We're trying to trace how the barista acquired the identity. It may have passed through a fraudulent Citizenship ring."

James shifted in his seat and scanned his colleagues around the table as Bimal continued.

"We know these groups sometimes hijack life histories from deceased Citizens and through means we have not deciphered, alter official records to delete the death so that a non-Citizen can adopt the resurrected identity."

"Don't the decedents' families ever cause problems?" asked Melissa.

This crossed into Pradeep's area of expertise, so Bimal offered him the floor.

"Not if the imposter lives far enough away and keeps a low enough profile. It's one of several techniques the rings use to forge Citizenship. It is the easiest method to pull off but the least flexible. It also entails assumption of a new identity, a high price to pay.

"It is much more difficult, though if successful, far less disruptive and restrictive, to alter the would-be Citizen's own records. This is not easily accomplished because it requires changing the history of an ongoing records stream, not to mention peddling a story to friends, family, neighbors, and colleagues that will allay suspicions. One also has to avoid triggering an investigation, which probably involves bribes."

"No small task," said Lauren.

"No, but it can be done, at great risk and for a correspondingly immense price."

Pradeep noticed James staring at him with an intensity that made him uncomfortable. Pradeep glanced around the room to see if anyone else had noticed, but before he had completed his inspection, James said:

"Where does this leave the investigation into the attacks?"

When Pradeep turned back toward James, he was no longer eying him, and appeared relaxed.

"We have a short list of people we have not ruled out," Bimal said, passing a sheet to Lauren on his left. "Each of these was either reported to have been near one of the sites, had a file with us due to subversive political activity, or both.

"We have two individuals in custody on rather … creative terror conspiracy charges based on illegal weapons and a cryptic map found in their automobile when local authorities stopped them for a traffic infraction. We do not believe they were involved in planning the recent attacks, but agents had previously opened files on each of them based on reports that they had made radical statements at public protests. The prosecutor probably could not make the terror charges stick. Nevertheless, the subjects may provide valuable information about the Restruct movement, if given the right incentives."

Lauren read the list of names, as did Melissa. When it reached James, he said, "What about Leo Baksh?"

Bimal raised his eyebrows. "We have no reason to believe he was involved. He was cooperative and everything he said checked out. The only thing even remotely linking him to the attacks is his representation of the petitioner whose loss in the Board of Classification the terrorists may have been protesting."

"Isn't that enough to keep him on the short list?" asked James.

"Certainly not," said Bimal, without the slightest change in his inflection. "It might be significant if there were anything else linking him to the attacks. Standing alone, however, his is a legal and constitutionally protected function. If we started prosecuting advocates because crazies don't like rulings in their cases, we would end up shutting down the Board and the Department of Adjudication. That would prove contrary to our agency's goal of keeping the country functioning under the rule of law, which should be reason enough—"

James looked amused but did not speak.

"—but it would also trigger a backlash that could cost us our jobs and scale back the authority of the agency, which should concern even the most self-centered of us."

James let this slide. "But there is more. He was in the Board of Classification headquarters minutes before the attack. At the time of the explosion, he was in the café across the street where the remote device was found."

"He was at the Board's headquarters to file a notice of appeal in his client's case, which was timely and appropriate," replied Bimal. "He was injured in the attack and stayed to render aid. He has cooperated throughout the investigation and has never requested legal representation. The DNA on the remote device did not match the sample he voluntarily provided."

"Whose DNA was it?" Melissa asked.

"It didn't match any known records," Renée answered.

"Were there matches elsewhere in the café?" the chief asked.

"There were some potential matches from the drain in the employee sink," Renée said. "But there were too many sources, and they were too degraded."

Bimal eyed James with a cool, steady gaze. "Do you have any information about Advocate Baksh we should know, James?"

James returned the stare and was silent a long moment. "No," he said finally.

Bimal observed him for an uncomfortable stretch. "If that changes, advise one of us immediately."

James bristled under the directive tone, but responded with a curt nod.

"In the meantime, he's off the list," Gurung concluded.

"There is another potentially significant detail in this investigation," Renée said. "The hearing officer whose decision the explosion appears to have been delivered to in protest was not in his chambers at the time of the attack. His research assistant was killed.

"When we questioned research assistants for other hearing officers, two told us that Hearing Officer Mbeza and his late assistant had disagreed over Anna Dao's case. The assistant was about to lose his job because he refused to draft the analysis Mbeza preferred."

James snickered. "These dipshits blew up their own ally while their villain lunched elsewhere?"

"That's one scenario," replied Renée, frostily.

James tipped his head. "Are we chasing down conspiracy theories now, Renée?"

"If you mean do I think these incidents were the product of a conspiracy, yes."

"You know that's not what I—"

"If you're insinuating that I'm making assumptions about the conspirators' identities or objectives," she said, "then no, James. Are you?"

"It's not my case," he said, holding up both hands, as though simultaneously pleading innocence and fending off an attack.

Renée shook her head. "I'm merely presenting you with facts we don't have an explanation for yet. They may or may not prove significant."

"Maybe it's just how things worked out," said James.

"It may well be," said Renée, "but we don't have enough information to reach any conclusions yet. Until we do, I'm not ruling anything out."

When James did not respond, Bimal wrapped up the briefing. "We will update you after additional interviews and surveillance."

"If anyone has suggestions for this investigation, contact Renée or Bimal," the chief said. "Lauren, you have the floor."

Lauren absorbed the information Bimal and Renée had disclosed and accepted the chief's change of subject.

"If you've been reading your weekly legislative summaries, you know the quantum parasitic abuse bill the Office of Legal Counsel drafted sailed through the Council of Delegates virtually unopposed and awaits the chief executive's signature, which we expect any day.

"Predictably, some delegates raised privacy concerns. Two outliers even questioned whether the neurally joined consumption of QFRI-enhanced abuse recordings should be categorized differently than conventional illicit abuse recordings. Their objections did not carry the day. However, the proponents compromised by giving the statute a short half-life. It contains a sunset clause that will result in the law expiring in two years if it is not renewed. We'd best speed along our investigations and conduct them cleanly if we want to retain this authority."

"How does the Office of Legal Counsel think the statute will fare in the courts?" asked the chief.

"That depends on several factors," answered Lauren. "We believe the chances of its being found constitutional will turn, in part, on what our investigations uncover. Concerns about privacy and virtuality will likely fade into the legal background if we find sufficiently offensive perps."

"So much for the principled rule of law," Renée said.

"I'm a cop, not a politician or an adjudicator," replied Lauren. "My goal is to stop this disease in its tracks. If showing the courts scary pictures helps me do that, that's what I'll do."

"I share your desire to thwart this phenomenon," said Renée. "I want to protect Vulnerables too. I just think the determination of whether the crime is sufficiently tangible to justify enhanced punishment should be based on objective criteria, not ick factors."

"I'll leave that to the advocates," said Lauren. "My job is to bust the abusers. You can rest assured the defense bar will do its best to shoot down this statute. In the meantime, I intend to use it."

Renée nodded once, acknowledging Lauren's position without agreeing with it.

"How is the investigation proceeding?" prompted the chief.

"Apace," answered Lauren. "The DII liaison provided our team with QFRI array equipment, software, and tutorials. All three of us completed initial training. Rigid mental compartmentalization and emotional," she pointed a shoulder toward James, "detachment are assets when utilizing this equipment, so it will come as no surprise who has proven the most adept in our initial experiments."

The agents responded with guarded amusement.

"James has formed neural links in several mainstream social sites."

"James?" invited the chief.

"Piece of cake," he replied. He gave them an unsatisfyingly terse summary of the experience, then answered a barrage of questions. When those subsided, he said, "It can be confusing at first. Sometimes you can't tell where thoughts are originating, but it gets easier to maintain a sense of your own part of the link with practice."

"How will we determine culpability if we can't distinguish the origin of thoughts?" Renée asked.

"I know my own mind," said James.

"Will that be enough to identify incriminating thought-action by the subject in court?"

"With proper testimonial foundation, it should be," Lauren answered.

"I'm a good witness," said James, which Renée acknowledged was an understatement. James was unshakable on the witness stand.

"Assuming passage of the statute is imminent, how do you plan to proceed?" the chief asked.

Lauren replied, "We have been monitoring two sites where we think consumers and distributors of the soon-to-be illegal QFRI-enhanced abuse recordings hook up. We have constructed several virtual identities through which James will enter the sites undercover."

"In the first phase, he will establish a presence in the group and conduct surveillance.

"In phase two, he will establish relationships with targets of interest and display receptiveness to partnering with them to jointly experience one of their illicit recordings.

"Unfortunately, we are told that the room participants may not trust him enough to form a link and share an abuse recording unless he has one to trade."

Renée's eyes widened.

"James will first try to build trust through using his," she looked him over, "creative and unusual intellect."

"If that succeeds, it means what?" Renée asked.

"Ideally it means that, in phase three, a perp will provide an abuse recording and form a neural link with James. They will experience it together. Through information he gleans and our monitoring of the Micromedium connection, we will trace the target's signal, identify his location, and secure an arrest warrant."

Renée shifted in her seat. "James, are you sure you are willing to risk the potential impact of that on your psyche?"

James turned a cold glare on Renée but did not indulge her in a response. He turned back to Lauren.

"Of the three of us, the psych team suggests James is best equipped to compartmentalize the experience and retain sufficient dissociation to preserve his cover and minimize the risk of harm to him."

"I see," said Renée, "and if the subjects of this investigation do not invite James to dissociatively experience these abuse scenarios with them?"

James eyed Renée and noted her tone.

"If the perps offer to share their collections on the condition that James prove his bona fides by distributing one in exchange, he will accept the invitation," said Lauren.

"And distribute a QFRI-enhanced recording of an actual incident of abuse?"

"Yes."

Renée turned from one to the other. "How will he do that if no one gives him one first?"

Lauren replied evenly, "We already have three recordings to use."

Renée furrowed her brow.

"Where did you get them?"

Lauren avoided Renée's eye. "From the DII liaison."

Renée regarded Lauren with open surprise. "Where did International get them?"

Lauren fiddled with her papers.

"Excuse me," Renée objected. "I think this falls under need to know."

"Presumably, they were intercepted in international transport."

"Presumably?"

"I don't control the DII liaison any more than you do, Renée," Lauren shot back.

"Let me get this straight," Renée said. "The Department of Domestic Intelligence, in the name of stopping the new 'QFRI-mediated parasitic abuse' phenomenon, is going to distribute a batch of QFRI-enhanced recordings of actual abuse of unknown origin provided by the Department of International Intelligence."

"We would use them if necessary as bargaining chips to capture people already in possession of, and intent on distributing, such materials," said Lauren.

"And in the process, *distribute* them," persisted Renée, incredulous.

"Ideally we would apprehend the subject before he or she passed the recording on to a third party," said Lauren.

"What kind of vegetable do you take me for?" snarled Renée.

James snickered.

"Agents," said the chief sternly, "Take a breath."

They complied. For a moment.

"I hereby respectfully object to this proposed strategy," Renée said. "It is reckless at best. It may make this office the lynchpin of a criminal enterprise."

"By definition, that is not true," said James, sounding almost bored. "We have statutory and constitutional authority to undertake measures that would be illegal if performed by a civilian, in the course of investigating and interrupting a criminal enterprise, as long as we don't induce someone to commit a crime he or she had not already expressed a willingness to commit."

"Don't lecture me with academy claptrap, James. I took the same classes you did. What about indirectly inducing people to commit crimes?"

"Spare me the sanctimony, Renée. The agency has used guns, drugs, and undercover hookers for decades. This is no different."

After a moment, Renée said, "True, but this strikes me as different, if not in kind, then by a degree so great it amounts to a difference in kind. You have sold this law to the delegates based on the argument that these recordings contain part of the *being* of the victims. The recordings on that theory are harmful in and of themselves. How can you justify distributing them?"

"They are only harmful if consumed during a neural link," Lauren replied. "That consumption is where the harm occurs. Our objective is to stop the people who are participating in or enabling that consumption."

Renée jabbed an index finger at each of them in turn, saying, "You are enabling that consumption. Why don't you cuff each other now and spare the world your chest of horrors?"

"Hormonal issues, Renée?" James asked.

Everyone in the room turned in disgust to Malone.

Renée stood. "Request permission to be excused from this"—she refrained from using harsh language but her snarl still made the final word sound like a curse—"meeting."

"Permission denied," responded the chief. "Please sit down. You are raising important concerns here. James, see me after the meeting."

Renee complied but the tension was palpable. James constrained outward signs of his amusement to a blank stare.

"Have you reviewed the contents of these recordings?" Renée asked.

"No," said Lauren. "It is only possible to experience them in the context of a neural link, but the DII provided written synopses. The recordings range from thirty seconds to two minutes. Each involves a person being abused. One verbally, one through threats of physical harm, and one through infliction of physical pain."

"How nice," said Renée, "and do we know the identities of the participants?"

"No."

"I see. So, for all we know, these could be recordings of a DII agent torturing interrogees."

Melissa and Lauren glanced at one another peripherally.

"Torture is illegal," said James, examining his fingernails.

"We all know government agents are torturing detainees outside the country," said Renée through clenched teeth. "Hell, maybe one of your recordings captures a DII agent torturing the mentally retarded individual they want us to prosecute for blowing up the nonexistent power station," she shouted in exasperation. "How perfect would that be? Victim, terrorist, martyr, and avenging angel all wrapped up into one."

"Oh for fuck's sake, what goddamn difference does it make who the participants are?" shouted James. "We have what we need to snag the bastards who are using this shit. Enough! Renée, if you want to start a campaign against DII human rights abuses, please, be my guest and resign so you can begin the crusade."

Bimal Gurung cleared his throat. Everyone turned toward him except James who peeked at him from the corner of his eye.

"Fellow agents, I am gravely disappointed by the lack of professionalism and basic respect displayed at this meeting. Agent Malone, our colleague Agent Stephens is raising concerns of the most serious nature that reflect the basis of our legitimacy as a law enforcement agency. Moreover, as this is new technology, we don't know what sort of national security risks might result from dissemination of these recordings."

James turned to Bimal in open disbelief.

Bimal held up his hand preemptively and continued. "That said, we must proceed under the assumption that the recordings from a fellow law enforcement agency are a better bet than recordings from common criminals. We must further assume that the DII would not provide us with tools inimical to our national security.

"Renée, I believe we can trust our colleagues to use the recordings only if necessary to complete the investigation and identify and capture perpetrators of these crimes. I trust we can also rely on them to do their best to ensure that any tactical distribution occurs only in a context wherein immediate apprehension of the criminal and recovery of the recordings before they are further distributed is reasonably assured."

Renée started to respond, but Bimal held up his hand. "It's not a perfect world. There is always a balance. Your concerns are valid, but if there is no other way to draw out these actors, it must be done."

"I still object," she said calmly.

"You have the right and duty to do so if that is what your conscience and professional judgment dictate," he said.

James gave Renée a round of silent applause.

"As for you Agent Malone," Bimal said, raising his voice for the first time, which caused James to freeze in place, "I for one will be following the course of this investigation. If the flippant juvenility you've displayed toward your colleagues is any indication of your attitude toward the stakes in this investigation, then I strongly advise you to adjust your course." He delivered this with consonants sharpened like tiny whips and finished with an ugly sneer, to the amazement of all present, the discomfiture of some, and the delight of a few, though they were careful not to show it.

James surveyed the room, completing the circuit by turning to the chief, who clearly had no intention of admonishing Gurung for his borderline threat. Even though he wanted to belt the sorely deserving smart mouth, James held his tongue.

Once he let James's silence lay bare the nature of the exchange, the chief turned back to Lauren.

"Anything else?"

"Yes," she resumed, maintaining her poise despite the fireworks. "As we reported in previous briefings, we have compiled extensive interviews with several abuse victims whose ordeals we suspect were recorded for illicit use by the quantum junkies. We will be on the lookout for any recordings related to those people or incidents.

"Melissa also met recently with Jeaneane Spence, the advocate representing the former employee of Interlink Technologies, whose assault case against her former supervisor has been at the center of our other little jurisdictional pissing match with International."

She nodded to Melissa, who took the floor, brushing a long, frizzy, dark-brown lock of hair over her ear and sitting up straight. Melissa's voice was a deeper pitch than Lauren's. Odd, as Lauren had the more forceful personality.

"Jeaneane Spence is nobody's fool. She is smart, assertive, and ferociously protective of her client. I would not want to back her into a corner if she were not cuffed and shackled first. And she's a knockout. No doubt a master with the jury."

Renée and Lauren were amused. James was intrigued.

"It appears that Interlink Technologies is part of a consortium of companies that is manufacturing Micromedium interface equipment."

"Quantum arrays?" asked the chief.

"Not according to their public disclosures," replied Melissa, "but we suspect so, yes. Interlink's board of directors has members in common with another company we've been surveilling, Polytronics Inc."

"By the way, both have directors in common with Protection Inc., the private confinement contractor," Lauren interjected, then returned the floor to Melissa, who continued.

"An individual working at Polytronics has described material we believe to be quantum array components. Having common corporate directors does not mean Interlink is similarly engaged. But Spence's client said the supervisor strapped a band around his head and a similar one around hers before he assaulted her. The item she described sounds quite different from the nodal arrays DII gave us, but we are entertaining the possibility it's another form of QFRI device."

"Why would the alleged assaulter take the risk of using his company's product in an illegal act on an employee?" asked Renée.

"Other than the usual psychopathological or pharmacological possibilities," replied Melissa, "perhaps he assumed, accurately it turns out, that the DII would find a way to block attempts to hold him accountable in court."

"I don't see the DII doing something as stupid as authorizing the use of a crime on a Citizen to test equipment."

"I didn't say DII authorized it. I said maybe the perp knew DII wouldn't let the case go public," replied Melissa.

Renée acknowledged the distinction. "How did the DII arrange that?"

"Spence said she couldn't tell whether the deputy who asserted state secrecy was implementing the advocate general's policy or was acting under the direct influence of the DII."

"And we don't know either?"

"Not as yet."

Renee was visibly troubled, but said no more.

"Spence's practice includes criminal defense," continued Melissa, "so it's no great shock that she is wary of law enforcement agents. However, she is frustrated that the court has blocked her subpoenas and depositions, apparently at the behest of the DII. I think she hopes we can help with that or, if not, that we may pursue the assaulter criminally. I didn't encourage either hope since I doubt we could accomplish either objective, but I did not dispel them either. As a result, she agreed to make her client available for an interview. We meet next week."

"Nice work," said the chief.

"Objections, Renée?" James asked.

She crossed her arms and ignored him, asking Lauren instead, "When does Agent Malone begin his participation in the illicit QFRI-enhanced abuse recording trade?"

"The undercover sting operation," Lauren corrected, "is good to go as soon as Mosgrove signs the bill."

The chief asked, "Anything else from your team, Lauren?"

"Details of course, but that's where things stand."

"Other comments?" When no one else spoke, he turned the meeting to the Fraud Unit where it carried to its end without further scuffles.

After the meeting, the agents heard James and Chief Mills shouting at one another in the chief's office, but could not make out what they were saying.

22

LIAM SNAGGED HIS JACKET ON a piece of gnarled wire as he squeezed through a tear in the chain-link fence.

"Damn it."

He pulled the fabric free, ripping a hole in his sleeve. *Should've used the worn-out one*, he thought. But it was getting chilly, and he needed the insulation from the newer parka. With gloved hands, he pushed the patch of torn fence back into place, picked up the aluminum utility case and crowbar he'd set beyond the hole before climbing through, and turned toward the decaying structure.

Rapidly reclaiming what had once been an industrial-park-grade chemicalized lawn, a thick mass of scrub stood sentinel before the condemned building. It would have been easier to approach via the crumbling parking lot, but the gate sections of the fence were better fortified and more conspicuous than his point of entry on the side.

Liam slashed his way through the bushes, collecting additional snags on his coat and scratches on his neck and wrists. Eventually, he reached what was left of a paved walkway ringing the building and moved more freely to the doorway he intended to traverse. He nudged the corner of his crowbar behind the padlocked hasp with a rusty squeak. Two firm yanks later, it clattered on the sidewalk. He was in.

He pulled a flashlight out of his pocket and moved toward the main lobby where schematics he had loaded on his mobile device told him he would find a utility stairwell to the upper floors. Rats skittered out of his path, squealing protests over his interruption of their years-long dominion. Cracked plaster and God knew what else crunched under Liam's boots as he prowled through the hallways and entered the building's main lobby.

The remains of a corporate sign, pitted and running but still legible, towered on a cracked marble wall behind what was once an elegant reception and security desk: "Interlink Technologies: linking you to the universe and beyond."

Liam shook his head at the hyperbole. "To the Micromedium will suffice, your corporate majesties."

He maintained an automated mapping program that constantly monitored the local Micromedium architecture. Although this building was condemned and abandoned after an earthquake eight years earlier, the program indicated it still had a live wire in an office on the third floor.

Following the map on his mobile device, he moved from the reception desk to an inconspicuous door around the corner. He forced his way into the stairwell, which stank of rust, mildew, and vermin thanks to years of water leaking from above. He shined his light up the metal staircase, which was twisted from the earthquake and badly corroded from the moisture. Holding the flashlight in his teeth, he tested the stairs. Reasonably confident they could hold his weight, he climbed, bracing himself in case a step collapsed. He maneuvered his way from treacherous flight to treacherous flight without cutting himself or falling to his death.

The water and decay worried him. He wondered if the scouting program had made a mistake. To his relief, when he exited the stairwell on the third floor and made his way down the hall, he found the office dry and the Micromedium node both hot and uncorrupted. It was odd that the node was never severed, but the Micromedium had grown for so long that it was like a frayed fabric with loose threads along every edge and hole. This particular line was connected to a branch sufficiently broad for his purposes despite its age, because its owner was a cutting-edge developer of the technology.

There was no sign anyone had disturbed the site for years. A thick layer of dust covered everything, punctuated by footprints and spoor from animals of various size and shape, none of them human. The large office window had a crack, but was otherwise intact. Liam couldn't decide whether it would be more dangerous to close a blind or risk someone seeing light from his Microterminal. He compromised by propping up an old projection screen that covered the window to the halfway point. After hunting up a broom, he swept clear a work area around the node. A desk and old office chair were beyond rustic but still structurally sound, so he threw together a makeshift station. Switching from heavy leather to fine polymer gloves, he powered up his Micromedium terminal and wired up his quantum array.

Before he connected to the Micromedium, he launched a program to anonymize his signal and enable him to tunnel through the local quadrant to another intersection. If things went badly, his trail should end at a remote site and the DII should be unable to capture any information that would identify or lead them to him. *That's the plan anyway*, he thought. "Don't let me down, baby," he said aloud when the program alerted him that it had disguised his signal and was ready to tunnel to a remote site and connect to the Micromedium.

Liam donned the equipment, plugged his terminal into the node, and mentally commanded the terminal to execute the connection sequence. Once he was linked to the Micromedium, he opened a broad quantum channel to take the group's first swing at penetrating the DII sentinel field.

As he had confidently predicted, Liam's hacktivist compatriots agreed he was the best suited to brave the attempt on the hub. Each of them had become adept at configuring the hardware and software for surveillance on others' neural links. Each also had made great strides in the mental training. Liam alone had achieved multiple successful sessions of reconnaissance links in the social sites without the target detecting him or becoming suspicious.

This was due in part to his ability to remain open and emotionally nonreactive even when he was privy to surreal and upsetting phenomena. The others found themselves snagged by the fields they were surveilling, which disturbed the target's awareness. It was a bit like losing an invisibility cloak while eavesdropping on a private conversation between people in the privacy of their bedroom. The fright increased the disturbance and, with it, the spy's exposure.

Though Liam was sensitive by nature, he had disciplined his mind for years as part of his martial arts training. That, combined with his cool determination to pierce the sentinel field and reveal the hub's secrets, gave him the focus he needed to surpass his cohorts at the cloaked quantum neural espionage. So, the group chose him to make the run. Or so they believed. Liam never intended to let any of the others undertake the risk.

They also agreed that it would be foolish to open a text channel to their virtual meeting place while he attempted to pierce the DII field or even afterward from the same physical location. He dared not think about their existence during the mission. If the DII traced his signal, he wanted an impenetrable firewall.

With sober well wishes, the hacktivist cadre bade him good luck when last they "met." They waited uncomfortably for him to surface in their virtual meeting place after the mission with news he had been successful and was still alive and free.

Liam focused his mind through a breathing exercise, mentally piloted his quantum neural signal to the vicinity of the DII hub and, as he approached the sentinel shield, emptied his consciousness of all verbal thought. He detected the shield in his mind's perceptual field as a presence—a combined sense that was kinesthetic and visual, yet neither distinctly.

As he drew closer, he heard in his mind's ear a cacophony of voices—a babble of supplicants seeking access to the hub. He almost saw them, a horde at the wall, some knocking, some politely conversing, some approaching with great fanfare and pomp, others trying impotently to traverse the barrier by brute force. Nearly all were coldly rebuffed.

He witnessed this for twenty minutes. During that time, he detected one signal within his perceptual range fold into the field and disappear. When that happened, he visualized diving under the field as though it had a lower terminus. He stilled his mind and turned his attention to the task of riding underneath the signal of the successful applicant, silently stalking the entity, as though holding his breath and swimming deep under water, guided by the shadow of a swimmer traveling on the surface.

When the applicant's movement slowed to a standstill, Liam tracked it and, to avoid panic, focused on his breath before opening his mind's perceptual field. What he experienced nearly caught him in a rush of emotion. Wary of letting it unmask his presence, he focused more acutely and opened wider still.

He perceived himself to be hovering within a great, deep-blue membrane, shimmering and luminescent, as though composed of electromagnetic energy. It appeared almost flat, but when he explored the outer edges of his perceptual reach, he sensed that it was vast and curved, like a translucent planetary mantle.

Far in each direction, the membrane thickened in circular patterns, as though the sphere were composed of great circular plates, curved and fused into one another, but differentiated into separate foci at the center of each melded piece. Like a soccer ball whose parts bled together instead of bumping along their edges into polygons.

From the outer surface of the membrane he had entered, he still faintly perceived the cacophony of would-be penetrants.

He turned his attention to the individual he had stalked to gain entrance, and listened with his mind to the person's interaction with the field. Interrogatory thoughts emanated from the spherical sheath, with answers from the applicant, including a call and response for what sounded like an access code. Liam tried to open deeply to this, hoping it would leave an impression on his mind for future recall. He had trained himself not to use rehearsal as a memory device when engaged in neural espionage because he knew the target would perceive it as an echo, which could draw attention to his presence.

He faintly detected other, similar conversations taking place. Experimentation told him he could home in on those exchanges too, but he focused his mind on the person he already had tracked.

The questions and answers, involving a DII investigation in the country's eastern region thousands of miles from Liam's physical location, ran their course and the neural field shifted. He sensed a difference in tone as the mind-field he was embedded in communicated with a less detectable but similarly toned other. He relaxed and reached with his awareness in pursuit of that communication stream and perceived a thread-like filament between the layer he occupied and another spherical shell toward the center of the phenomenon, which Liam took to be closer to the DII hub itself. After a moment, he perceived another filament forming, like an electrical arc, from the inner surface of the layer where he was situated across a gap to a deeper layer. Then he observed the applicant's signal move toward the filament's point of origin.

Liam again visualized the field as a vertical body of water and himself swimming down far below the applicant. He tracked the signal as it passed through what seemed like a great tunnel, far above the quiet depths where he moved, until both he and the signal he tracked crossed through to a smaller and more perceptibly curved spherical membrane.

Another round of call and response ensued and again he could hear other, though fewer, conversations. He focused on the signal he had tracked. As in the outer layer, the colloquy was followed by communication with a deeper layer, a coded protocol Liam could not decipher, and then another filament for the applicant to travel yet deeper.

Liam dove and tracked that applicant to this third, smaller, inner layer. He opened his mind to listen and heard a deep silence, punctuated by a terse exchange and intense scrutiny of the applicant. Liam sensed danger deep in his psyche but detected it before it surfaced into conscious fear. He focused his mind on a still point at its center until he felt his awareness stabilize and clarify, like a silent chime from a flawless bell.

Wired together thirty floors underground at the DII headquarters, the agents forming the inner sentinel field collectively sensed a possible anomaly, a faint undulation in their shared neural field, like a ripple on the surface of a still lake from an eel gliding along the sandy bottom, out of sight in the murky depths.

Liam perceived the neural field to fall silent and sensed scrutinizing attention, like search beams of the mind, crisscrossing through the spherical sheath. He maintained his crystalline stillness and sensed an attentional beam pass through him. He did not permit his focus to waver, allowing his mind to observe, not evaluate or react. The beams seemed to slow and converge in his vicinity, but they passed through him and, after several more sweeps, no longer aimed in his direction.

Liam focused back on the target in time to hear the neural field plainly express, "Identity verified. Access approved." Then, what appeared to be a thin, metallic pipe penetrated the sphere from within and continued out the other side toward the outer layers. After a moment, the pipe buzzed with energy. He tried to focus on it, but all he detected was a flow of power, like electricity through a wire. It appeared separate from the neural field, and he couldn't eavesdrop on it. Once the conduit penetrated the neural shield and went live, the individual's signal Liam had tracked into the inner layer vaporized, its energy absorbed into the continuity of the neural field.

Liam felt exposed but he did not detect more attentional scan beams from the field. Gradually, he opened his mind wider, visualizing it merging with the inner sphere and coextending with it throughout.

He held this perspective and listened with his mind until he observed eight distinct sources, each corresponding to one of the circular thickened areas he'd perceived before. He inspected them each in turn, his mind blank and receptive.

Suddenly, he felt the field rend in one region, allowing a new circular panel to materialize. The other panels shifted to accommodate this ninth source, and the field stabilized. Liam heard with his mind a protocol he could not completely follow but the gist of which was plain enough: shift change. Once the field was stable and quiet, a different portion of the sphere begin to fade, and the remaining foci adapted to close the region occupied by the departing source.

Before the movement was complete, Liam chose the circular focus that had seemed the least acute during his examination of the pre-shift-change eight, and aligned the center of his mind with the center of the circular source. He knew from group practice that when he shared a meditative point of focus in this manner with others, it was as though they were one mind. He hoped the same would hold true here. As he completed this alignment, the shift change wrapped up, and the field stabilized anew.

He knew the inner sphere was listening, just as he was, but he did not allow himself to consider whether the sentinels could detect his presence. Instead, he deployed an advanced technique, turning his attention on the source of his own attention. This can seem like a cat chasing its tail at first, but with practice, it is possible to pierce through to a non-dualistic perceptual state.

Liam entered this state and his neural array aligned with the array of the sentinel, whose point of intersection with the shield Liam now co-occupied via the fused quantum neural field.

The hacktivists theorized this would cause the two arrays to entangle on the quantum level, such that they shared a quantum state and were no longer two, despite their physical separation on the macro level. If this state persisted, they reasoned, manipulating one array would simultaneously manipulate the other. Theoretically, they could use this quantum linkage to create a data stream between the hacker's computer and the DII hub via the arrays through the phenomenon of quantum tunneling without the sentinels knowing it. They hoped to do this by running the secondary stream through the entangled quantum state itself and use it to access the DII hub via the sentinel's array. As the eye cannot see itself, the quantum neural field cannot perceive its own signal, so it should not detect the quantum tunnel for which it is, itself, the medium.

At least, that was the theory.

Liam abided in stillness, his mind sharing a central point with the sentinel's. His Micromedium terminal recorded this event as a neural field snapshot. The data was far too complex to analyze. The hackers were debating whether they could use such a recording to configure the array, replicate the entangled state, and create the tunnel without any of the hackers being wired in at the time. Hackizen doubted it, but Liam programmed his equipment to take the snapshot automatically if he made it this far just the same.

He remained in the meditative state until his Micromedium terminal detected the protracted stasis and powered down his array. The sphere, extending from the center of his mind out in all directions, faded. Liam became conscious of feeling cold. When he opened his eyes, his awareness filled with sights and smells of his derelict hacking station where, he registered with brief bemusement, he had been sitting throughout the entire experience.

Liam disconnected from the node and confirmed that his Micromedium terminal had captured a snapshot of the entangled quantum profile. He also ran a diagnostic program to check for signs of intrusion into his equipment. Reasonably satisfied that no one and nothing had tracked him or reverse-hacked his terminal, he powered down, unhooked his array, and packed up his devices.

Just before he stepped out of the room, he deployed a fogging device containing chemicals designed to degrade genetic material. If anyone entered this room, it would be clear someone had recently occupied it, but Liam ensured there were prints of neither the finger nor ribonucleic varieties.

Night had fallen as he passed back through the rent in the chain link fence. He scanned the area with infrared-sensitive glasses and with a device to detect electromagnetic fields, but found no signs of surveillance. Though if he had, there would have been little chance for escape. Still, he felt safer knowing the coast appeared clear as he headed for his car, parked in an alley nearby.

Though he was exhausted, Liam knew the others eagerly awaited word. Despite his desire for a hot shower and a drink, he traveled to his linkup site at the abandoned warehouse on the outskirts of town. This was the third and, he promised himself, the last time he used this site. He knew that entailed risk, but he was too spent to scout out a new spot. The warehouse was still undisturbed when last he used it. He felt safer going back there than risking a mistake while checking out a new place when he was tired.

After hooking up, Liam donned his array and opened a text channel, then logged into the hacktivists' virtual meeting place. It took several moments for the others to heed the alerts that Infiltr8org was back, redon their arrays, and switch from dormant to active mode in the shared virtual site.

Hackizen: `Code please.`

Liam recited a complex alphanumeric sequence to confirm he was not a DII agent hiding behind the moniker Infiltr8org. Though they respected Liam's mental discipline, it was always possible a neural link would have revealed the code. They asked him several follow-up questions, and his answers assured them it was their fellow. The possibility remained that he was supplying answers under torture to an agent wired in under his fictitious identity, but they had no way to rule this out and had to proceed under the assumption he would find a way to reveal it. Detecting no such indication, they accepted that this was the real article and remained vigilant.

The hacktivists each voiced relief at Tr8's survival and peppered him with questions. Liam summarized his experience from start to finish, and the others soundly chastised him for taking it so far when he was supposed to surveil the field and report back.

> **Infiltr8org:** That's all I did. I couldn't stop to think about it without risk of exposing myself or what we were doing.
>
> **Aggresserable:** Why do you think you perceived the sentinel field as such a specific spatial form? Why spheres?

This set off a flurry of speculation, with the simplest theory being that the sentinels visualize the fields as a set of nested spheres to help them organize and coordinate their interpenetrated signals.

> **Infiltr8org:** The shield was more powerful than anything I experienced one-on-one or in the small group neural interfaces while I was training.
>
> **Aggresserable:** Maybe they're using stronger equipment.
>
> **Sleeperagent:** Or maybe at that level of coordination, there are emergent properties we didn't experience in the informal setting, such as a higher order of strength and stability.
>
> **Subterraneum:** Could be. Maybe the spherical visualization works synergistically with those features. Spheres are naturally stable and cohesive structures.
>
> **Hackizen:** Who knows? This is all speculation. The important thing is you navigated through the shield on the sly.

Infiltr8org: Yes, and I did that in part by visualizing it as something I could swim under. It's malleable.

Hackizen: That was risky. I bet if you'd projected an image too different from theirs, it would have backfired.

Infiltr8org: Perhaps. But approaching it that way let me stay below the surface of the sentinels' awareness, maybe because it kept me focused beneath my own thoughts.

Hackizen: Makes sense. These are minds forming the fields after all. Human minds have a lot in common. You're still lucky it worked.

Infiltr8org: It was pure intuition. I did what it felt like I needed to do to get in.

Aggresserable: I wonder why you couldn't hear the codes applicants were using to gain access when you approached the shield.

Sleeperagent: Why couldn't everyone for that matter?

Infiltr8org: When I first approached, I think my field interpenetrated with the shield just enough to tap into the noise. But I wasn't neurally linked with any of the others and I don't think they were linked with one another. Everyone was trying to communicate with the shield at the same time and it was repelling most of them.

Aggresserable: Why could you hear the exchange so clearly once you got in?

Infiltr8org: Once I was inside the field, there was greater conductivity and less background noise.

Sleeperagent: How do you think they maintain the exterior shell or whatever it is that insulates the interior of the membrane from the chaos outside?

Infiltr8org: No idea. Perhaps highly refined mental training.

Hackizen: I'll see if I can get any information from the guys who reverse engineered the arrays.

Sleeperagent: Bad idea. Too specific.

Infiltr8org: I agree. If we need to know it in the future, you can fish around. Let's work with the information we have. We know we can gain access and merge with a sentinel source. How shall we proceed?

Hackizen: The theory is that when you aligned with the sentinel in a state of non-dual awareness, your mind became indistinguishable from the sentinel's mind. On the quantum level, they were not two. They were, in a real sense, one quantum state and that's what we want to exploit to tunnel through to the DII's equipment.

Aggresserable: What about their arrays? I thought we were banking on them becoming entangled too.

Hackizen: We are. It will take at least two of us working in tandem to tunnel through to the hub: one to penetrate the field and merge with the sentinel source in a non-dual state, and another to remotely operate that person's terminal to establish the data stream through the entangled arrays.

The group set to talking about how they could create a stable connection to the DII hub through a neural link, which would have a short duration, because forming one is exhausting and because the sentinels, and presumably their arrays, work on rotating shifts. They ran through several ideas and agreed to discuss the matter further during subsequent meetings.

Aggresserable: It looks like Tr8's gamble in going as far as he did has paid off. We know it's possible to merge with a sentinel source, and we know how the field is structured.

Sleeperagent: It was reckless and premature. We agreed you would surveil the site and report back. None of us, not even you, had fused with the mind of a target in a non-dual state. To try that for the first time in the DII shield was irresponsible.

Hackizen: I agree. We also should not have tried that before we knew how we would execute the tunnel.

Infiltr8org: Look, no harm resulted. We would have had to make another run to execute the tunnel regardless.

Sleeperagent: Don't jump to conclusions. We *hope* no harm resulted. I hope to God you didn't sound any alarms at DII headquarters.

Subterraneum: Or become so entangled that they are listening to this conversation through your mind.

Silence.

Subterraneum: I was kidding.

Aggresserable: Have any of you experienced anything after linking neurally at the social sites that you would attribute to persistent entanglement?

Hackizen: Not that I noticed.

Subterraneum: Maybe some dreams.

Sleeperagent: Some odd experiences in solo meditation. A sense that I'd absorbed others' perspectives and was still connected on a subconscious level after the group session ended.

Aggresserable: I've had similar sensations, but I attributed them to memory of the group practice.

Sleeperagent: That may be all it is, but it's vivid.

Aggresserable: Tr8?

Infiltr8org: I haven't experienced anything like that, but I will watch for it and tell you if I do.

The hacktivists reflected, then arranged times to meet again to plan their experiments and nail down their strategy for the next run on the DII hub.

Hours later, back home and steamed to the bone by a hot shower, Liam crawled into bed and succumbed to exhaustion.

Late into the night, he dreamt of a circle of colossi, white stone giants reclining in a ring, with great gleaming metallic crowns, turning slowly in a deep-blue sky, far overhead.

He floated up to the space between them and examined each in turn. Eight in all, their eyes were closed and their faces bore expressions of intense concentration.

His attention snagged on a familiar one. He started floating toward the giantess, a sense of panic rising in inverse square proportion to the decreasing distance, as though his emotions were gravitationally related to this rapidly approaching entity. He shook his head and fought in vain to stop his accelerating advance toward the icy visage when the sleeping giant's eyes suddenly opened.

Great white orbs with black sapphire irises edged in blinding light near their centers, like event horizons surrounding pupils made from singularities of infinite mass, locked onto Liam's gaze, and mirrored his shock.

A cold chill shot through his core as though his life force was being pulled into the black voids. As he drew closer, the enormous being rocked toward him, the space between her eyebrows contracting into a frown, her light-devouring eyes narrowing to a glare of cold, intense suspicion …

Liam woke screaming. He covered his mouth and heaved breath through his nostrils, the image of the figure's deadly scrutiny burning in his mind as he grasped at waking life.

23

LET ME SHOW YOU, HE wanted to say, the words almost across his lips. Instead, when Jeaneane had excused herself to answer the phone, Leo re-chopped the onions he had entrusted to her and had them sizzling in olive oil along with some minced garlic when she returned.

"Mmm, smells great," she said, drawing a smile from Leo, who found it funny that the perfume of these three ingredients, the foundation of most dishes he cooked, could dependably elicit such a response.

Then again, Jeaneane's version of cooking usually consisted of heating up frozen finger food in a toaster oven. Gourmet finger food, mind you. The items in her fridge were usually limited to wilted, mixed-green salads, a gummy bottle of salad dressing, an open can of pineapple slices, and a tub of cottage cheese. Perhaps some dusty bottles of well-chosen beer and wine in case of guests. To go with the finger food. What else did a girl on the go need? Nothing as far as Leo could tell, though he knew she was sensitive about her culinary repertoire, so he always raved over her reheated fare, which seemed to satisfy her.

Tonight, however, Leo had hauled over a box of groceries, herbs and spices, cast iron cookware, and wooden spoons. They'd scheduled a date chez Jeaneane for dinner and a movie, and Leo was the evening's chef. Jeaneane was single again and Leo wanted to help her rechristen her newly solitary abode.

"Thanks for cooking," she said brightly, crunching on a carrot.

"My pleasure," he replied. Leo loved to cook, but living alone, he rarely felt inspired to make much more than a simple soup or stir-fry. It was much more fun to cook for friends, and Jeaneane was an appreciative diner.

Leo threw in chopped brussels sprouts, sliced tomatoes, chanterelle mushrooms, fresh herbs, a small minced hot pepper, ground black pepper, sea salt, a dash of honey, a few drops of balsamic vinegar, and a splash of red wine. He set the mélange to simmer as he threw pasta in a pot, tossed together a moderately exotic salad with sweet, savory, and tangy components, and smeared garlic butter followed by ivory-colored shavings of hard cheese on sourdough bread bound for the broiler.

Ten minutes later, he assembled the meal in one graceful sweep and laid the colorful and aromatic plates on the table as Jeaneane lit candles and poured wine.

Jeaneane's hillside apartment reflected discriminating but unostentatious taste. The main chamber, one wall of which sported a picture window with bird's eye views of the city, served as both dining room and living area. The hardwood floor was partially blanketed by a faded-red, woven-cotton rug bearing a simple black pattern. A few small, fine paintings she'd collected while traveling adorned the walls. The room was sparely but elegantly furnished with rough-finished vintage wooden dining table and chairs. A teak-framed divan buried in a cloud of cushions and down pillows wrapped in skin-soft cotton demarked the boundary of the living area and faced an entertainment center discreetly tucked behind a sandalwood screen at the room's end. A cracked-teal-glazed raku ceramic vase held fresh flowers atop a carved ebony tea table in the corner. Somewhat neglected but tenacious houseplants rooted in an eclectic collection of pottery sat in dishes on the floor and windowsill, providing a living frame to the urban view as they reached for light.

Stacks of papers from Jeaneane's cases, held in place by her compact Micromedium terminal, overhung the edges of an end table next to the couch. Little toys inevitably squeaked and jingled underfoot when one crossed the room, revealing the existence of her reclusive Siamese cat, who allowed an elite few to touch her, one of whom was Leo.

Jeaneane's environment was cluttered but not messy, rather like the woman herself.

The table dressed, Leo and Jeaneane slid into their chairs, unfolded napkins, and chimed a silent toast. Candlelight refracted through the golden nectar and limned the edges of fine glassware.

Leo's sensory channels buzzed warmly. He'd been in a groove of late: working hard on Anna's appeal and other cases, massaging his home and office into relative order, nurturing his body with wholesome food, and sticking to a consistent regime of running and swimming. His developing meditation practice synergized with these good habits and he had never felt so alive, nor toned along as many axes simultaneously, despite his heavy professional burdens.

"What a beautiful meal," Jeaneane said softly.

"Sorry it's not more elaborate," he replied. "Just something simple."

"It's perfect," she assured. After they'd taken a few bites and she'd properly raved about Leo's skills in the kitchen, she asked, "What's your news?"

The day before, Leo had received a potentially life-changing call from the senior partner at his former firm asking him how he would feel about being nominated for appointment as a legal advisor to a member of the Board of Classification Appellate Division. His feelings were ambivalent, though he didn't say so. The partner asked him to get back to him within a week.

Jeaneane's eyes lit up upon hearing the news. "That's fantastic!"

"Thanks," he said flatly.

Her glee faded.

"Anna," she said.

"Anna," he confirmed.

If Leo took the job working for the entity adjudicating Anna's appeal, he would have to withdraw as her counsel and sever himself from her and her claim.

"That's not the only reason I'm less than whelmed."

"What else?"

"The commute," he said. "The time commitment. Loss of freedom and control over my time. Probably wretched government office facilities. Working for a political appointee and conforming to his politics and style."

"But you could influence his analysis," countered Jeaneane. "The firm wouldn't recommend you if they didn't think you would have a positive impact on the Board's decisions."

Leo granted the point and listened.

"You also have to think about the doors this could open. Maybe a judgeship at the Department of Adjudication in a few years? Maybe political office?"

"No thanks."

"I don't blame you on that one," she said, bobbing her head and holding up a hand in an *I hear ya, brother* gesture. "Still, this move could give you options. Sounds like you are viewing it as restrictive, but you might be missing the larger picture. It could open worlds for you, Leo."

"I don't think I'd like it."

Jeaneane sipped her wine, scrutinizing Leo and feeling out his mood. "How can you know if you don't try?" she asked at length.

Leo remained attentive and sipped his wine.

"It would require you to grow," she continued. "Maybe you'd grow into it," she said, raising her eyebrows and shrugging one shoulder. "Maybe you'd grow beyond it," she said, switching her shrug to the other shoulder. "Maybe it would show you what kind of career you don't want. It definitely wouldn't be a dead end."

"Would you take it?"

Jeaneane took a bite of salad and looked up into her mind as she munched. "No," she said after delicately dabbing her lips with her napkin.

"Why not?"

"Because I'm an advocate at heart. I couldn't stomach the role of an adjudicator's advisor. I'm not neutral. I couldn't pretend to be."

"Are you questioning my principles?" he asked, his manner both teasing and warning.

"Of course not," she said, her tone conveying the unspoken *silly boy*. "I think you could do a better job of operating in an adjudicator's context. You're more patient than I am."

Leo folded his arms, unsure whether this was a compliment or a calumny.

"I would get too pissed off to play the game of building consensus among the adjudicators. You would do a better job of coming up with a way to frame an issue that is deliberative and judicial in tone, yet advances the Board's case law in a progressive direction."

Leo was skeptical. He was well acquainted with Jeaneane's skill at wrapping acerbic critiques in velvet.

"It's a compliment, stupid," she said after a moment. "Don't expect me to slobber or put down my own supreme mojo," she added, twirling her fork up in a theatrical helix, as though casting a spell.

Leo held up his hands in surrender, satisfied that she would never deign to suggest that he possessed more advanced skills in law and advocacy for any reason other than love.

"OK. Then thanks."

"You're welcome, scholarly one." Her friendly sarcasm gave way to open sincerity. "You'd be a great legal advisor to the Board. We need people like you in those positions."

"I'm worried about the vetting process too."

As a Citizen, Leo was unquestionably eligible for appointment if he were otherwise qualified and the chief executive's administration selected him, but a persistent bias against reclassified Citizens remained.

"You can't let that stop you," said Jeaneane. "Look at what Anna's enduring."

"True enough," he replied, embarrassed by the point. Leo was also worried about his proposed appointment amplifying the recent social unrest around Anna's claim. "If I thought I could draw the fire away from her and her case, I would do it without hesitation. But I'm worried the conservatives would widen their attack and spin my advancement as spreading contagion, which could hurt her."

They wove scenarios about how it might play out.

"I hate to say it," Jeaneane said when they had exhausted the possibilities, "but John could provide good advice in this department."

"He's pretty busy with his new job."

"I'm sure Lord Hanes can take time from his duties as acting editor of the *Capital Pap-Peddlers*, I mean *Times* to advise his friend at so momentous a juncture."

Leo suppressed a sigh.

"If he can't, then why you continue to invest in that friendship is beyond me."

"Easy," said Leo. "I didn't say he wouldn't make time for me, but I feel bad asking for it when he's under so much pressure. But you're right. I'll talk with him."

With that settled, they sidelined the political issues. Leo asked how Jeaneane was handling her recent breakup. She responded with anger and disappointment, accented with harsh complaints about her ex and his mother, which was understandable enough.

Leo cringed, however, when this devolved to haughty critiques of her family, colleagues, and loved ones. He maintained a neutral visage and listened as she trashed her friends, their relationships, and their careers. As he always did when she was on one of these tears, he nudged her to consider the situation from a more compassionate perspective. This tripped her up briefly, but she inevitably returned to malicious gossip mode, her judgments usually preceded by "I'm sorry but," and followed by "Know what I mean?" which were Leo's cues to recite scripted yaps.

He loved Jeaneane, so he played a supporting actor in her excoriation play as best he could until he ran out of patience. Yet, as no one appeared to be off limits in her inventory of others' deficiencies, the question often nagged him: *What in God's name does she say about me when she's with them?* He wanted to believe she exempted him from such ill use, but if her treatment of everyone else was any indication, it didn't look good.

Leo never dwelt long on such thoughts. What was the point? He was in charge of him, not her. The friendship was rich and rewarding. God knew he wasn't perfect either. She had put up with him for years and been a loving and supportive friend, whatever she might say about him to others. Small price to pay for being close to her.

Yet Leo was sometimes troubled by how abruptly she could erect an ice wall between herself and others, including her clients when they did not progress or perform to her satisfaction. In less charitable moments, he viewed this as Jeaneane's inability to relate to people in struggle because, contrary to her favored narrative, her life had always been quite privileged. In kinder moments, he sensed that it derived from a sense of powerlessness to fix people's overwhelming dysfunction and need.

On several occasions he had heard her say, "I'm sorry but …" before bestowing her royal damnation upon someone she had been trying to help. In an instant, her loving support gave way to cold condemnation and complete abdication of responsibility toward the hapless reject.

He suggested that well-enforced boundaries might make such relationships more habitable and eradicate the need for impenetrable barriers and total abandonment. Unfortunately, she was unreceptive. Leo, not a master of boundaries himself, was in no position to judge.

He was particularly troubled tonight because he was about to ask whether she would take over Anna's case if he pursued the new position. He felt protective of Anna like his own heart and he feared what could happen if she fell short of

Jeaneane's expectations. He also felt Anna could hope for no mightier champion than Jeaneane.

After they had finished their entrées, Leo and Jeaneane cleared the table and Leo served dessert: a fresh lemon-passionfruit-ginger sorbet with a touch of mint.

"You made this?" she exclaimed, savoring the tingly, sweet, tart, twice-cool ambrosia.

"Quite easy, actually."

"Oh. My. God." She said in staccato homage. "You have to teach me. This is something I'd like to have on hand."

After dessert, Jeaneane cued up the movie, a romantic comedy with a palatably cynical vein.

Leo brewed tea and, before they settled in to watch, he returned to the subject of Anna and put the question to Jeaneane. She ran her nails through her golden tresses and pulled her hair into a ponytail, holding Leo's gaze as she thought.

He handed her a cup of tea and joined her on the couch.

After taking a sip, she nestled into the pillows. "Of course it was my first thought. But I don't have any experience with reclassification petitions."

"Other than your own."

"You know what I mean. Mine was when I was young. Before advocate's school. I haven't kept up with the procedures and case law like you have."

"But your clients have reclassification issues."

"Sometimes, and when they do, I refer them on, as you well know."

Leo had handled several cases on referral from Jeaneane.

"I understand your concern," he said, "but you could get up to speed faster than you realize. We've thoroughly briefed the issues in our filings with the hearing officer, and I've already drafted an opening appellate brief. You would learn most of what you'd need to know by reading those. I can also give you some excellent practice manuals for learning the Board's procedural quirks. Once you digest those, I could answer any remaining questions. You would do an excellent job."

She acknowledged his vote of confidence with a demure dip of the eyelashes. "I appreciate that, but I still wouldn't have your experience."

"You'd have *your* experience, and your supreme mojo, as you put it, in the courtroom. You are a force of nature. There is no other advocate I'd feel as safe entrusting with Anna's case."

She kissed her fingertips and touched them to his lips. "I'll think about it. You don't have to answer right away, do you?"

"No. I need to do more thinking too. Let's give it a couple days."

He tried to think of a way to address Jeaneane's impatience with others' challenges and her tendency to jump ship when things didn't go according to plan.

"One other thing," he said as she was picking up the remote to start the movie. "Anna is sensitive and can be volatile."

"That's the point of her case, isn't it?"

"Yes, but things sometimes go sideways with her. She goes off the grid for days at a time. Things set her off that you don't realize will have that effect."

Jeaneane eyed him, detecting an unspoken issue.

"I can't tell you more unless she authorizes me to," he continued, "I want to trust that you will stay the course with her, even if you don't like her."

Jeaneane tipped her head at him. Leo could see the wheels of her mind spinning through dozens of possible replies, but she chose a diplomatic path: "I consider that fair warning and I will weigh it as I consider your request."

Both ruminated on this, recognizing they were on delicate terrain.

"I need to meet her," she said, finally.

"I agree."

"Have you discussed this with her?"

"No. None of it. I didn't want to raise the subject until I had alternatives to offer."

"I can't agree to represent her without meeting her."

"I understand. Look, read the briefs. Give it some thought. If you are open in principle to representing her, I'll let her know about my possible nomination. I need to measure her response before I decide what to do. I would rather not broach the subject with her unless I can bring her to meet you. That will give her a chance to begin adjusting to the idea of working with new counsel, even if it is not ultimately you."

"Makes sense," she said after a moment. "OK, send me the briefs."

Leo exhaled relief, and they settled in for the movie. Both found moments amusing, but they were distracted by their own thoughts—about failed relationships and Anna Dao, among other things—and neither really tracked the film.

24

For Leo, the next six months felt like an amusement park ride that starts with a stern warning to keep your head back just before lurching to breakneck velocity and vertiginous loops.

To no one's great surprise, Jeaneane and Anna hit it off famously. They saw their own fire, wit and, uncoincidentally, wounds in each other. Anna surprised Leo with strength and maturity when he told her about his job prospect. He hadn't indulged himself in expectations but was concerned she might feel abandoned. Instead, she approached it as a friend, acknowledging that it would be hard for her, but focused mainly on what the move would mean to Leo and his ability to work for changes they both valued.

Preparing to sever their relationship was sad for both of them, but Leo took comfort in knowing Anna's loss was offset by the gain of a friend and mentor. He also believed Jeaneane would feel empowered by duking it out in the reclassification system that had hampered her in her youth.

Once it was clear Anna and Jeaneane meshed, Leo reached the decision in consultation with John to pursue the new position.

"You would be a fool to pass this up," John assured him. "It's the next obvious move for you. Take it." As was his style, John played to Leo's strengths. Leo appreciated his advice because he knew John was aware of his weaknesses, too, and the courage it took to refuse them control.

Under normal circumstances, the position of legal advisor to a Board member received little public attention. The adjudicators, not their legal staff, ordinarily bore the brunt of partisan wrangling. As Anna Dao's advocate and as the subject of political jockeying after his appearance on *The Morning Show*, however, Leo was an unusual case. As he feared, the activists came out swinging.

Far from giving unanimous support, the progressives split into factions, with some opposing the nomination on the theory that it reflected a cynical divide-and-conquer assault on their most powerful piece of litigation. To Leo's surprise, some people he had previously allowed himself to believe respected him now vehemently opposed his appointment, and on the pettiest of grounds. Among them were not only Citizens Action League spokespeople who had hinted he should run for elected office, but Protection Inc.'s president and chief executive officer Cormack O'Brian who had, until public disclosure of Leo's nomination, been actively recruiting him for employment.

"This man is a reformed Vulnerable," O'Brian had the nerve to say when questioned during a magazine interview on the confinement industry. "He can't be objective. He may well lack the fortitude to grapple with the pressures of the position, given the enormously contentious nature of the cases before the Board."

Leo was flabbergasted, but John said it fit with everything they knew about O'Brian.

"He's a greedy control freak, Leo. He recognized your assets and wanted to add them to his portfolio. You were potentially useful because he probably believed you could lend his company a veneer of respectability and objectivity. I suppose it is also possible he wants his company to grow in ways you could help him formulate, though I find that unlikely. Either way, he almost certainly believed that, as his employee, you would be safely under his control.

"Having you ascend to a position of influence within an independent adjudicatory body whose decisions affect his interests is a different situation altogether. He probably would have been on board for funding a run for political office if you'd taken that route, because we all know those favors cost. But appointment by the chief executive with no means for O'Brian to control you? Not cool."

Leo knew John was right, but O'Brian's bait-and-switch still pissed him off.

"That's what he wants," said John. "Get mad and you get weak. Staying calm and focused will expand your power and he knows it."

Leo had been walking from a café to his car during that conversation. As he rang off, a wheedling elderly Citizen who did not recognize him handed Leo a petition. Leo ignored the inarticulate signature gatherer and turned his attention to the text of the proposal which began with the headline STOP THE VUL INSURGENCY and called upon the chief executive to reject the appointment of Leo Baksh as legal advisor to the Board of Classification "to preserve the integrity of the Citizenship review process from infiltration by agents of the revolutionary Vul–Agg syndicate."

Leo handed the man back his clipboard, resisting the urge to shout, "I'm Leo Baksh and there is no such syndicate, you ignorant fool!" Instead he restrained himself to, "Thanks, I'm not interested." That sealed it. He would stay the course, come what may.

His determination proved invaluable because the vetting process was lengthy and intrusive. He had to endure a detailed strip-mining of personal information and endless interviews with ever higher-level officials within CE Belinda Mosgrove's administration before Mosgrove finally approved the appointment.

Mosgrove's director of appointments appeared via macrovision in a recorded statement to announce the decision:

"Chief Executive Mosgrove is pleased to announce the appointment of Advocate Leo Baksh as legal advisor to Board of Classification Chief Appellate Adjudicator Harlan Durell.

"Mr. Baksh's exemplary professional credentials are a matter of public record and speak for themselves.

"To those who have raised archaic claims that Mr. Baksh's reclassification history makes him unfit to serve, the chief executive offers this reminder: We are a society governed by the rule of law and the principle of fairness. We do not discriminate on the basis of classification history. Mr. Baksh's status as a Citizen is above reproach. Achieving Citizenship by reclassification from the community of Vulnerables testifies to his strength and commitment to our shared values.

"Ms. Mosgrove and the Board administration are confident he will be a fair and impartial advisor and will serve the public with diligence, impartiality, and integrity."

The surprisingly public endorsement from the executive administration for such an appointment shifted the complaints about Leo to gripes about the chief executive and her progressive party, neither of which, to the conservatives' dismay, were politically vulnerable.

"A brilliant move," John decided after further analysis over beers served on the house by Wendy at the pub. "It expands your influence, which will satisfy the progressives when they let it sink in. It also separates you from Anna's case, which takes wind out of the conservatives' sails. Meanwhile, this places you under her eye and partial control, so she can see what you're made of and decide how much use you might be over the long run. Well played by Madam CE."

And so it was done.

While Leo was fording the vetting process, Jeaneane prepared to take over Anna's case, consulting with him as she learned the ropes and rewrote the appellate brief in her own voice. Upon Leo's appointment, she substituted in as Anna's new counsel.

In contrast to the friction Leo had experienced with Advocate Cheung, Jeaneane developed a collegial rapport with her.

"I bet," said John when he heard this. "Different roles, same nasty temperaments. Evenly enough matched that they might have to focus on the merits of their cases for once."

"I hope so," said Leo. He saw Jeaneane's ferocity as coming from higher evolutionary frequencies than Alicia's, but he had no interest in arguing the point because his main concern was that Jeaneane would be effective for Anna.

In tandem with the chief executive's cooling-off measures, Jeaneane and Alicia jointly requested a four-month continuance of the briefing schedule in Anna's case. Jeaneane hoped this would allow time for the public's association of Anna with Leo to fade and for the activists to turn their sites onto other issues.

During this holding pattern, Jeaneane had to make her first major strategic decision in the case. The panel investigating the allegations of improper influence by and through Cormack O'Brian on Hearing Officer Closun Mbeza concluded that no violation of adjudicatory ethics had occurred and that the hearing in Anna's case had been procedurally sound and free of constitutional defect.

Jeaneane was furious. After some painful soul searching and consultation with, among other people, John Hanes (to her distaste), she concluded it would be unwise to belabor the ethics challenge. She had partially torn off Mbeza's mask while leaving her own intact. To fight about it further would risk exposure of her role in initiating the allegations, which could jeopardize her ability to continue representing Anna.

She reluctantly decided, with Anna's blessing, to focus on getting Mbeza's ruling that the Board lacked jurisdiction over Anna's case overturned on appeal. If they succeeded, this meant the case would go back to Mbeza, unfortunately. Even though the ethics panel had rejected the allegations of impropriety, however, Jeaneane wagered he would be unable to shake their taint and associated scrutiny of his conduct. That would have to be enough.

Leo considered this a wise choice. Seeing Jeaneane carefully titrate her fury enabled him to relax and trust that his former client was in good hands.

As these events were transpiring, the chief executive signed into law the new crime of QFRI-Mediated Parasitic Abuse, and the Department of Domestic Intelligence team headed by Agent Lauren Drey revved its investigation into high gear.

Agent James Malone trolled the Micromedium fetish sites undercover, spending several hours a day wired in at the office using a designated fictitious identity. Unbeknownst to his colleagues, starting weeks before the investigation officially began, he also spent several hours every evening at home in the same pursuit, off the record and with a different virtual ID.

Things went along without a hitch until Lauren noticed a discrepancy between James's master inventory of abuse recordings and the individual reports he prepared after each investigation session. She drew it to his attention:

"James, this recording does not appear in any of your reports."

James concealed his shock. He had burned the candle so low that he'd made the uncharacteristic mistake of including on his official inventory at work a recording he had obtained at home.

Without covering his tracks, that is.

In truth, he collected many of the recordings listed in the official inventory during off-the-record, after-hours sessions, but he meticulously modified the official reports to include an ostensibly kosher source for everything. This time, he'd let one slip.

James scanned the inventory item Lauren had flagged and responded with tightly controlled cool. "Let me check my notes. I'm pretty sure that came from the same session where I received that street fight recording, but I'll verify it and amend the report."

Lauren examined him through a squint, but she couldn't penetrate the surface of his strategically neutral affect. She let her skepticism show through the length of her silence, a fact James did not miss. "Please send me the updated report when you complete it."

He wanted to tell her to get screwed but he knew this was not the time. Instead, he delivered a mock salute and pivoted to leave.

Before he was out of earshot, Lauren added, "And please preserve your notes."

James kept walking and, if he heard her, did not respond.

Lauren sensed something was amiss and noted the incident in her private log. She also asked Melissa to monitor for further inconsistencies.

As the tachometer turned clockwise for Leo and Lauren, the hacktivists, spooked by Liam's recurrent nightmares, pulled their throttle in the opposite direction. No one knew whether Liam's dreams indicated the existence of a persistent, subconscious connection between him and the sentinel he had formed the non-dual meld with. Nevertheless, they decided it would be wise to leave the neural shield alone while they took stock, experimented, and planned.

The hackers continued mental training and espionage at the social sites. Aggresserable and Sleeperagent succeeded in forming a non-dual link with a target. Tracking Sleeperagent's progress remotely, Liam tunneled through her entangled array and commandeered her target's computer. Hackizen accomplished the same feat through Aggresserable's link.

Inconveniently, they found they could only do this through, and for the duration of, a live neural link. Once the hacker's mind disengaged from the target sentinel's, so did the corresponding arrays. They needed to establish a persistent channel into the DII mainframe, one that did not require Herculean mental and technical feats to maintain.

Hackizen proposed the most promising strategy, but it would be difficult and risky:

One of the hacktivists would surreptitiously penetrate the sentinel field and form a non-dual link with a field source, as Liam had done. Hackizen would tunnel through the entangled arrays and hack into the DII hub. Once inside, he would find the current code the DII agents needed to hail the sentinel shield and request access to the hub. He would also implant a fictitious profile into the DII hub's agent-identity database.

One of the other hackers would then use this identity and code to approach the sentinel shield from the outside and overtly request access to the hub. As the sentinel field scrutinized the applicant in consultation with the DII hub's database, Hackizen would monitor the process to be sure no security protocols detected the ruse.

With Hackizen working from inside the DII hub by way of the quantum tunnel through the entangled arrays, and another hacker working in tandem from outside the shield as a counterfeit applicant, they would induce the hub to authorize a data stream through the sentinel field, like the one Liam had spied during his run.

This conduit, however, would connect to a Micromedium node accessible to the hacktivists, not a DII agent.

The finishing touch would be to insulate the fictitious identity and associated data stream from DII hub diagnostics and verification programs, making it invisible to the hub's own view.

If they could achieve that, their access to the hub would be limited only by the hackers' programming expertise, which was constantly improving. Success would hinge on whether the hacktivists could outsmart the DII's own programmers.

As they finalized plans for the mission, the cadre realized that it might be their final act among the quick and free, so they took their time preparing. If it turned out to be their lives they were tendering, they wanted to make damn sure the purchase was worth the price.

Meanwhile, *Capital Times* investigative reporter Jill Blatsky, with the tacit approval of Acting Editor in Chief John Hanes, continued her investigation into the explosion of what the government had partially misidentified as a power plant.

She eventually contacted an employee working for a construction company that had helped build the facility. According to the source, a similar station was under construction 150 miles south of the capital. He didn't know what it was for or what it contained, but he could describe some of its parts. Blatsky took the list he generated to her experts, who gave her a shorter list of items that would soon go online: a small nuclear power plant, a particle accelerator, and a supercomputer of the quantum variety.

This project's purported locale did not show up on satellite maps. Remarkably, nothing appeared in any public records, and her consultants saw no sign of its presence on the power grid or the Micromedium. Yet if what her source told her was true, it was simply a matter of time before it plugged into the outside world, and Blatsky's technical assistants were poised to detect it.

25

DETERMINED TO MAKE A GO of his new job, Leo equipped Franz with an automatic feeder and plenty of water, resolutely embraced the commute, and reported early on his first day, feeling optimistic. When he saw his dimly fluorescent-lit, windowless little box of an office, he tacked up mementos from the life he was leaving behind, placed a couple of potted plants on his desk, and convinced himself he would adjust.

When Mosgrove's administration appointed Leo, the sole member of the Board of Classification Appellate Division without a legal advisor was Chief Adjudicator Harlan Durell. Harlan had voiced enthusiasm about working with Leo when they met during the vetting process, and Leo had accepted his new position with high hopes.

The initial portents were inauspicious. Wide-eyed hello-and-nice-to-meet-yous from other legal advisors and clerical staff seemed a tick manic, suggesting to Leo they had more to say about his new boss. He wanted to ask, but looking like a paranoid freak on the first day would not exactly maximize his influence with colleagues. So, he bit his tongue and returned their salutations. It would come out eventually. Things always do.

A rotund, grey and balding, ruddy-faced, jolly-eyed fellow twenty-five years Leo's senior, Harlan had clearly survived some hard knocks, which Leo noted with positive regard. The chief adjudicator was reputed to be "smart" but "eclectic" and "a bit scatterbrained." Ostensibly manageable traits, but Leo soon learned the hard way that the tongue-in-cheek descriptors were code for a far less charming reality: The man was impossible to work with. A psychological typhoon, leaving walls and skulls embedded with shrapnel in his torrential wake.

He was also unbelievably needy. Like Leo, he had a poor sense of appropriate boundaries. Unlike Leo, however, who had a hard time saying no, the chief adjudicator had difficulty taking no for an answer or recognizing others' rights or reasons to refuse his endless and often absurd demands.

Other legal advisors analyzed cases for the adjudicators they served, made recommendations and, after focused and intelligent discussions, wrote draft decisions in accordance with their adjudicators' informed opinions. They also worked with other legal advisors to determine how the adjudicators could form a majority analysis on a case.

This is not how things went with Leo and Harlan.

It turned out that Mosgrove had appointed Harlan to the post of chief among his peers not due to their confidence in him or his innate abilities but because she owed a political favor to someone who was willing to accept Harlan's promotion as payment. She had appointed Leo as legal advisor, at least in part, to compensate for Harlan's deficiencies.

Harlan was so insecure about his administrative duties as chief adjudicator that he focused on them to the exclusion of his caseload—and he wanted company in this paralysis. Rather than allow Leo to write summaries and recommendations for his cases, Harlan expected his legal advisor to play audience as he drafted correspondence. Durell would sit at his keyboard and recite a line as he typed it, periodically turning to Leo with eyebrows raised. When Leo suggested alternative wording, Durell would talk over him, continuing unabated in his recitation and belabored typing. With his skills wasted on this violently boring task, Leo's disinterest devolved into irritation and, eventually, depression.

When, on rare occasion, Leo got Harlan focused on their cases, Harlan usually reclined in his chair and generated rhetorical questions for his own aggrandizement that had little to do with the relevant law, rarely stopping to hear Leo's responsive attempts to guide him back to the matter at hand.

For Leo, the relationship turned into a tedious sport: He would monitor for a gap in the chaos large enough to sneak through a message crafted to snag his boss' curiosity or irk him enough to stall the verbal geyser. Then, Leo would throw a file in front of Harlan and propose a course of action. Inevitably, Harlan's mind would wander before he had grasped the point, and Leo would have to wait for another opening to resume the topic. Meanwhile, the cases piled up and other adjudicators rolled their eyes and griped.

It was maddening.

Harlan arrived late and left early every day, as did other adjudicators and their advisors. It was an unspoken perk of the positions. Harlan was so nervous about his inflated sense of administrative importance, however, that he required Leo to stay from early morning to late evening to "send the right message to the rest of the staff."

To make matters worse, Harlan compensated for his own gross inefficiency and absence from work by calling Leo at all hours to drone about matters he would not let Leo help him understand, thereby accomplishing more and more of absolutely nothing.

When Hurricane Harlan blew into the office, he tortured Leo and the clerical staff by huffing around as though they were in a state of emergency, yanking everyone off task for the duration of his esteemed visit and leaving their work swirling in his cyclonic trail as he blew back out. He would then sabotage their efforts to get things in order by phoning in to interrupt every five minutes with idiotic demands that drove the collective endeavor even further behind.

Leo treasured the uncommon days when Harlan pompously announced he was attending a meeting that did not include legal advisors. By the time Leo harnessed the blessed silence and hit a groove in sorting the mounting backlog of casework, an anxious Harlan would emerge from his summit, insisting that Leo play audience to a fretful monologue about administrative minutiae no one cared about, least of all his fellow board members or the chief executive who had appointed them. Leo sometimes barely restrained himself from screaming, "I'm not your fucking mommy. But since you want me to be, then for the love of God, shut up and let me tell you how to do your job."

Instead, he marshaled his patience and did his best to compensate for Harlan's perpetual state of self-absorbed cluelessness. Nevertheless, Leo's frustration contributed to an embarrassing dynamic of old-married-couple bickering. Add to this a lengthy commute, and Leo began to pop springs.

It took scarcely two months of this charade for Leo to realize he'd made a mistake, but by then he felt it was too late to reverse course.

Partly this was because, inconveniently, Leo had come to care about his boss. Notwithstanding his annoying personality, Harlan had a great, loving heart and he took his role seriously. He wanted to wield his office responsibly and fairly. He also valued Leo and wanted to help him advance his career. Though his endless prolixity did little to advance the cause of adjudicating his cases, it did reveal a surprisingly astute and progressive political perspective, which Leo assumed explained his presence in the chief executive's orbit. The guy was neither stupid nor naïve. Just a colossal mess with no self-awareness and a stunning inability to receive input from outside the swirling vortex of his own mind.

No master of boundaries himself, Leo gave beyond what was comfortable or appropriate, which Harlan rewarded by demanding more, and sometimes Leo snapped at him. Harlan's narrative then became that Leo was hot-headed and rebellious. Being painted crazy by the whack job who drove him there felt to Leo like he'd stepped into a mad comic script whose characters inflicted torture through malevolent irony.

Like Anna, Leo had a volatile side that long predated his encounter with Harlan Durell, but it was difficult to remember that when the person triggering its resurgence was himself so grandiosely dysfunctional. Sympathetic witnesses reinforced this imbalanced assessment, which kept Leo's critique off of his own part in the drama. The other board adjudicators, their legal advisors, and all the clerical staff shook their heads when Harlan passed through barking ridiculous orders. Each of them, at one time or another, had taken Leo aside to whisper their condolences and assure him that they appreciated his efforts to help Harlan focus and do his job.

The Board's head office manager, a politically conservative, charming, and intimidatingly competent individual, had held her twenty-year post through multiple chief executive administrations. When speaking to Leo about Harlan, she did not mince words:

"He's a freakin' lunatic. No one can work with him. We all know you have an impossible job. But so far, you're doing it. My main concern is to make sure you stay."

To accomplish that goal, she threw money at Leo. He had received a substantial raise after six weeks, and was making nearly twice what he earned in his private practice. Though he felt uncomfortable admitting it to himself, the relief in pressure the extra money bought in other areas of his life partially offset the stress of working with Harlan.

Leo had a significant albeit bizarre role in the Board's important work, and the position was crucial to his career and financial stability. So, he soldiered on. The choice made sense, but came at a far greater price than he anticipated.

The first casualty was his exercise routine. He tried to carve out time during the work day to maintain it, but it always ended up seeming far less important than the illusory emergency of the moment. He left home too early in the morning to exercise before work. At night, he was too exhausted and too burdened with loose ends from work and mounting piles of chores. It was hard enough to make time for sufficient stretches of sleep.

Next to go was his meditation practice. For a while, he had persevered in the morning before work. Eventually, fatigue made it impossible. He fell back to mini practices with his eyes open in the car after he'd had coffee as he drove to work. When the insanity at the office mounted, he tried to take short breaks for brief sessions of conscious breathing. It helped, but he eventually stopped even this minimal effort, so overwhelmed was he by the discordant storm of details that accompanied his work life with Harlan Durell.

Without the emotional and physical anchors of exercise and meditation, Leo experienced mounting stress in both body and mind. The long commute and lack of adequate sleep triggered a relapse in the pain of his injuries from the café explosion. To numb that and keep going, he started taking pain medication again.

To his temporary relief and long-term peril, he found the meds also relaxed his mind and helped him find Harlan less irritating. He worried less about the success of their shared mission. He stopped fretting about the backlog, enjoyed the company of his coworkers, and focused on individual cases. When Harlan called compulsively, the medicated Leo took it in stride and returned his attention to the task at hand with less intermediate mental noise.

Counterbalancing these perceived benefits, he was annoyed to discover the opioids made it all but impossible to use the quantum array to operate his Micromedium terminal at home. This proved problematic because he could dispatch more tasks using the efficient interface than he could with an antiquated keyboard.

He tried slowing down on the pills, but even with partial abstinence, his facility with the array decreased. After a day of stress, commuting, and neck pain, he would usually say "screw it" and swallow some relief. He persuaded himself that increased efficiency and peace at the office outweighed the lost benefits of using the array at home. His colleagues got by without the new technology, why shouldn't he?

He had stockpiled the pills after his injury, just in case. Once he started taking them again, the line between types of pain being treated became harder to discern. Eventually Leo stopped thinking about it and popped the pills like candy, tossing them back with cup after cup of coffee as he thumbed through papers.

He didn't realize the profound effect this was having on his brain chemistry until he abruptly ran out one cruel Friday morning. He made an appointment to see his doctor the following week. By Sunday, he had discovered why the opium poppy and its semi-synthetic derivatives, soft and kind as they seemed in the beginning, were the villains of legend. He writhed in a form of hell he had seen depicted in edgy movies but never experienced: the brutal and unforgiving scourge of opiate detox. His eyes watered. His nose seemed like it would run off his face. His lungs were raw and congested. His muscles gnawed, guts wrenched, skin crawled, joints ached. He could not sleep to save his life. Whenever his skin touched the cotton sheets, he felt like someone was dragging cheese graters over his nerve endings. To top it off, he was besieged by waves of panic, dread, guilt, and remorse, about what he could not say because he was in too much physical distress to hold a coherent thought.

He spent most of Sunday night lying in the tub under a warm shower illuminated with candle light until even that felt like a wire brush against his screaming senses.

By Monday, the best he could do between countless trips to the toilet was cling to his sweat-soaked sheets, tremble, and whimper in physical and emotional agony. Franz forwent feline aloofness and lay against Leo's side whenever he was still. Even the cat's soft fur felt like sandpaper and, with apologies and regrets, he pushed the poor old fellow away.

It was all he could do to call in sick. Harlan could hear the misery in Leo's voice and extracted a promise he would see a doctor, which Leo intended to keep.

By Wednesday, he had stolen a few fitful hours of sleep. Nevertheless, he gobbled aspirin, drank coffee even though he felt like throwing it up, showered, shaved, and donned clean clothes for his appointment.

The doctor eyed Leo attentively as he described the relapse on his injury-related pain.

"Have you been suffering from a cold, Mr. Baksh?"

"Yes," said Leo, "or perhaps a touch of the flu." He tried to sound sincere and relaxed. The doctor prescribed a short course of medication, plus referrals to a physical therapist and a chronic pain clinic. Leo knew this meant the doctor was concerned about his use of the pills, but for now, relief was in sight and nothing else mattered.

As he stood in line at the hospital pharmacy, Leo noticed a prissy nurse at the window speaking with a stalwart individual standing next to him. "There's one," said the nurse, pointing to a woman two lines over from Leo, "and there's one," he said, pointing to a sweaty young man two places in line ahead of him, "and there's one," he said, pointing to Leo, then looking away with a smirk when he noticed that Leo had seen him.

"One what, you smug little twit?" Leo wanted to scream, but he already knew. The nurse turned toward his companion, who listened conspiratorially and darted glances at the patrons in line but seemed less vampiric than his informant.

Leo gobbled down two pills at a drinking fountain outside the pharmacy entrance before leaving the hospital. He muttered resentfully to himself, imagining that the nurse was craning his neck to witness this confirmation of his suspicions.

Fifteen minutes later, as he was driving home, Leo felt the medicine seep like a healing nectar into his blood and tissues. The aches, pains, chills and heat flashes, clammy skin, raw nerve endings, scratchy mucous membranes, churning guts, and racing thoughts melted sweetly away, like the greasy remains of winter snow under a warm spring sun. As the persistent ache in his lower back vanished, Leo wriggled his spine into the car seat and sighed with relief. In a smooth, thirty-minute transfiguration, he morphed from the sickest and most desperate he'd ever been into a state of peaceful, vigorous bliss. It was like a miracle.

And he knew he was in big, big trouble.

He showed up for work the next morning a new man. He had lost a few pounds from the days of dope sickness, but had regained his color from the new supply. Everyone voiced pleasure at his recovery.

He made the twenty-one-day supply of pills last seven days. By the middle of the following week, he ran out again. By Thursday afternoon, he felt sick and unbearably exhausted. He needed out of his office and fast. Harlan consented but eyed Leo suspiciously. He urged Leo to talk about what was happening, hinting that he had been "every kind of – aholic" in his past and was there to talk. Leo dismissed the suggestion without denying its implications and headed home, where he resumed his detox nightmare from the week before.

Three-quarters of the way through a tortured, sleepless night, he dug around and found tranquilizers and muscle relaxants his ex-partner Jeb had left behind. They were expired, but Leo took one of each. It turned out nothing could overcome the insomnia resulting from the damage he had done to his epinephrine–norepinephrine balance, but Jeb's old pills did knock down the anxiety a notch.

When dawn peeked through his bedroom window, Leo abandoned the futile attempt to sleep and tried to distract himself from the discomfort by dealing with stuff he had let pile up at home. He told himself the debris was a result of his focus at the office, though his runny nose and sick stomach were at odds with the official narrative. The first thing he braved was a stack of unreturned and increasingly irritated calls from Jeaneane who wanted to talk with him about Anna's case and other matters.

She was cold at first when she answered, but upon hearing Leo's stuffy nose and hoarse voice, became concerned.

"You sound terrible."

"Just a virus," he deflected, glad for the increased warmth.

After talking over various and sundry, including Anna, they agreed to grab a bite the following week and catch up.

Leo spent the day trying unsuccessfully to make himself comfortable or nap. Finding neither an option, he returned to his pile of tasks in the evening, hoping it would yield some respite from his anxious rumination.

There were a bunch of other messages besides the ones from Jeaneane, most of which Leo skimmed and skipped. To his astonishment, the last one was from Jeb, inviting him to join him and a friend at a club that night.

Leo could think of almost nothing he wanted less than to be outside in the cold, inside being pummeled by noise and crowds, or in the presence of Jeb. Nonetheless, a voice told him maybe Jeb would have something to ease his discomfort, or at least some good advice on where he might find it. He almost opted for a shower and a bed but his desperation won out. After shocking himself alert with an ice-cold shower—intensely painful but ironically therapeutic—he threw on what he hoped was an appropriate outfit and headed for the club.

When he pulled into the parking lot at the designated venue and climbed out, a chill breeze lacerated his already cold and damp skin, making him shudder. His stomach churned angrily and he wondered whether he could do it. *I'll give it an hour.*

The club was situated in a converted warehouse. An outer door gave access to a chilly vestibule, where a young hipster sat behind what looked like a bank teller's window from a ghost town collecting payment for entry with an air of contempt. Leo had little patience for the lad's self-importance, but figured his own degraded appearance would make a snide retort pathetic, so he accepted the condescension and sauntered in to the sweaty venue. As he passed through the inner door, the temperature lurched from frigid to furnace. He preferred the heat, but the smell of bodies and smoke did not calm his queasy stomach. Nor did the flashing lights or pounding beat soothe his raw nerves. He was about to bail when directly before him stepped Jeb. The two hadn't seen each other in over a year.

Jeb was the first to holler: "No offense, but you look terrible. Are you sick?"

Leo felt wounded even though he knew Jeb spoke the truth. He considered marching out but opted for honesty: "Yes. I've become addicted to prescription opiates. I'm puking and shitting my way through the latest round of attempted detox."

Jeb smiled sadly at Leo and pulled him into a gentle hug, speaking more softly into his ear, "God, baby, you're like a sour rag."

Leo responded with something between a laugh and a sob.

As they stepped back, Leo saw another fellow in his peripheral vision stepping toward them. *Probably Jeb's new boyfriend*, Leo thought as he turned to face the intruder who turned out to be none other than the intern who had escorted Leo through his odyssey at the macrovision studio half a year and more earlier.

"Jamie Tesh, I presume," said Leo, amused by the young man's presence but unable to decipher the situation with his beleaguered neurons.

Jamie's expression turned from excitement to confusion to open concern as he beheld him. *I can only imagine what he must be seeing*, Leo thought. Pale, thin, drenched in cold sweat, shivering despite the heat, nose raw from blowing it fifty thousand times.

"He's dope sick," Jeb wasted no time to tell Jamie.

Jamie received the news without expression.

"Yes. We know each other," Jeb then said to Leo.

Leo mutely tried to process these details, but wanted to curl up on the floor. Or perhaps throw up. Or both.

"Come on," said Jeb. "Let's go to my car. We'll get you feeling better, and then we can explain."

To Leo's embarrassment, his teeth were chattering when they reached Jeb's car, even though he was dressed warmly. The other two wore skin-tight club T-shirts and jeans, but were pink-cheeked and warm from dancing.

Jeb unlocked the passenger door from inside and Jamie reached in to unlock the back. Before Leo could creak his aching self into the front passenger seat, Jamie had thrown his jacket over Leo's shoulders.

"Thanks," said Leo.

Jamie winked and closed Leo's door. Then he crawled into the back seat, yanked his own door shut, and squeezed between the front seats so they were a cozy little trio. The scene would have been most odd to Leo under the best of circumstances. In his sleep-deprived, detoxing state, it was downright surreal.

Jeb started the engine and cranked up the heat.

Leo examined Jeb and cataloged his impressions. Naturally slight of build and stature, with a narrow face, nearly pigment-less skin, and fine, sparse hair, Jeb remained less than handsome. Leo had found him attractive but that was because of his keen mind, sense of humor, and stunning creativity, not because he was much of a physical specimen. He had filled out noticeably since last Leo saw him, which suited him. *Though he should bear some demonic birthmark on his forehead to warn people he's a compulsive liar*, Leo thought with a touch of bitterness. He turned to Jamie.

Jamie returned Leo's eye contact and smiled. Jamie was calmer than before. Maybe this was because Leo was in such a non-intimidating state, but it seemed to emanate from Jamie himself. Leo smiled back.

"I don't have any hairs of the dog that appears to have pissed all over you, I'm sorry to say," said Jeb, "though I'm sure you realize that's the last thing you need, even though you probably want it more than life itself right now."

Leo shivered. His opiate-hungry veins were disappointed, but the flickering persistence of his native wisdom was grateful for the honest and true assessment.

Jeb continued, "This will help you feel better and get through the detox."

He handed Leo a white tablet.

"What is it?"

"Elidrine."

"Is it safe?"

"Quite a bit safer for you than the death syrup you've been guzzling, from the looks of you."

Leo fiddled with the pill, unsure what to do.

"Using a little Elidrine to pull you out of the opiate's gravity won't kill you," said Jeb.

"You have to be careful, though," interjected Jamie, obviously concerned, yet deferential to the longstanding history between the other two. Leo wondered what he would say if Jeb weren't present.

"I know you're used to being in charge, Leo," Jeb sighed, "but you're a mess right now, so do as I say for once and take the goddamn pill. It will make you feel better."

Historically, due to Leo's generally greater life competence and what he considered Jeb's laziness, Leo barked the orders. Jeb ostensibly complied but passive-aggressively rebelled in other ways, which drove Leo nuts. Jeb's sudden assumption of command was a refreshing break from their suffocating old dynamic. Leo tossed the pill in his mouth, and Jeb handed him a bottle of water to wash it down.

"While you wait for that to kick in, have a toot of this." Jeb produced a glass pipe into which he popped what looked like a shard of quartz crystal.

"What is it?" asked Leo as Jeb handed him the pipe.

"Same thing," he answered. "Just quicker delivery. Instant relief."

Jamie shrugged uncertainly.

"Used sparingly, it's no worse than most bad things," Jeb said. Leo wasn't sure what to make of that.

Jeb retrieved the pipe from Leo and heated it with a needle-like blue flame from a torch lighter, rolling the bulbous end containing the rock back and forth. It melted and vaporized into white smoke, which Jeb sucked into his lungs and held as he handed the pipe to Leo.

Leo studied him as the drug took effect. Jeb's expression did not change, but his face became flushed, even under the parking lot lamplight. He exhaled, evidently feeling exceptionally well. The car filled with a smell like ozone and burning sugar that turned Leo's stomach.

"Keep it hot," Jeb advised, pointing to the pipe.

Leo put the tip of the glass stem against his lips and Jeb ignited the miniature torch with a metallic click. Leo rolled the little globe at the end from side to side as Jeb had demonstrated, until the apparatus was again filled with acrid, white vapor.

"Hit it," commanded Jeb.

Leo pursed his lips around the pipe's stem and pulled. As he did, air entered the vaporizing chamber through a small aperture and the smoke swirled inside the pipe like a miniature planetary gas storm, then traveled up the stem and into Leo's lungs, entered his circulatory system, and crossed the blood–brain barrier into his suffering cerebrum.

The sensation was not as abrupt as he expected, but his mood shifted from down, to neutral, to positively upbeat. Energy rushed through his body and his stomach lurched from the caustic chemical taste. Oddly, it was not unpleasant.

The same became true for the other symptoms of his opiate detox. He still ached and felt sick—even on some level emotionally raw—but the Elidrine flipped a switch in his brain to a different configuration. It wasn't that the symptoms were gone. It was more like they didn't matter. How could that be?

He realized he was blithering all of this aloud.

"Keep it moving," Jeb said, gesturing toward Jamie.

"Oh, sorry," said Leo and passed Jamie the pipe. Jamie took a hit and passed it on to Jeb, who commenced another round, and then another, and another.

As the pipe went round, Leo regaled them in one long stream of excited speech about the difficulties of working with Harlan, his struggle with the opiates, the frustrating way they interfered with his ability to use the quantum interface, but how they made his life at the office tolerable, soothed his pain and calmed his nerves, and how they left him so terribly sick.

Someone had turned on the car's audio device and Leo moved to the beat, feeling euphoric, focused, energized, and fearless.

"Shall we?" asked Jeb.

The three of them jumped out of the car, bound for the club. Leo was no longer cold. He felt the urge to kiss and hug both Jamie and Jeb, as though they were old friends. The tiniest thread of reason kept him from acting on this impulse.

The next four hours blurred in a light stream of purple, green and strobe, as Leo and hundreds of others worshipped the beat with gyrating half-nude bodies in the ancient and perennial rite of ecstatic tribal dance.

Whether it was the Elidrine or the exercise, by the time they left, Leo felt as though he had washed some of the opiate sickness out of his body. His mouth was dry though, and he clenched his jaw as they walked back to Jeb's car.

Jeb reached into a bag in his trunk and retrieved a small pouch, which he handed to Leo. He produced a bottle of blue pills, opened it, threw in a handful of white pills, and gave it to Leo along with a bindle of white crystals.

"Here," he said. "Take the blue ones at night so you can sleep. Take the white ones in the morning so you can push through the rest of the opiate detox. Snort or smoke a pinch of the crystals if you feel like crap."

Glancing around the parking lot, Leo shoved the pills into the pouch.

"Listen to me," Jeb said in a tone that forced Leo to comply. "Two weeks. Do not use any of this for more than two weeks. These will get you free and clear of the opiates but won't trap you in their own pit if you don't use them longer than that. This will help you back on your feet."

"I can't afford to miss any more work."

"You won't have to," said Jeb. "Elidrine also substantially enhances your ability to use the QFRI interface."

This piqued Leo's attention.

"For God's sake be careful."

Leo crossed his heart. "Thanks."

Jeb gave Leo and Jamie each a peck on the cheek, jumped behind the wheel and was off.

Leo turned to Jamie. "You didn't come together?"

Jamie shook his head but made no move to take his leave. He frowned as Leo put Jeb's little pharmaceutical cocktail pouch in his pocket.

"Listen," said Jamie. "Jeb means well. And, technically, he's right that you can use those to get past the pain pills. But there are better ways."

"Ways that don't involve me missing more work?"

"Probably not. But ones that don't carry their own risk of something even worse than what you're already enduring. Elidrine is dangerous."

"You just used it too," said Leo, looking Jamie up and down.

"For the first time in six months," countered Jamie, "and I won't use it again for at least that long. I did it tonight to be on the same wavelength as you and Jeb."

Leo soaked this up. "I cannot miss more work without arousing potentially career-damaging attention. I also cannot let another day pass without tackling my backlog of casework. I can't. If I went that route, I might as well quit. I'm not prepared to do that."

"Even one week?" Jamie rejoined. "You would be like a hundred million times more effective when you got back—"

Leo giggled through his nose at this hyperbole.

"—and you could sustain it. This," he said, waving at Leo's pocket, "is a risky short-term burst. It's putting off the inevitable."

Leo frowned. "Jeb said this will help me skip some of the unpleasantries and get back on track. I will be careful. Promise."

"I have keys to a cabin in the woods," Jamie blurted. He caught himself and modulated his tone, continuing, "It's warm and dry and off the grid. It's in a grove by a lake. My grandparents own it. It has one of those wall-mounted perpetual water heaters that never runs out, plus a wood stove, and lots of feather quilts. The freshest air you'll ever breathe."

Leo made a silent whistle. "Sounds cozy."

"I can get time off. Let me take you there for a week. I'll take care of ... I'll keep you company and help you through this. The healthy way."

Leo was struck speechless at the audacity and good-hearted kindness of this unexpected offer.

Jamie let the silence stretch. "You could bring some work along if that would help. When you started feeling better, you could do some of it at the cabin."

Gravel crunched as cars rolled off the lot.

"It's a beautiful offer," said Leo, "But I can't accept."

Jamie looked as though he had arguments in reserve, but raised a hand in surrender and pursued it no further.

Leo's head was clearing as they stood talking in the cold, but as the drug wore off, he shivered and felt sick again.

"Did my charming ex tell you I'm evil incarnate?"

"No, he said you deserved better than you got from him but that you don't realize it and you sabotage your own happiness."

Leo rolled his eyes. "Relatively insightful. Also characteristically backhanded and conveniently self-absolving. Anything else?"

"He said you hate being an advocate but don't realize it and you keep doing it because you're trying to prove you're a good person, which everyone but you already knows, and if you knew it, you'd let yourself do something you love."

Leo scoffed. "I suppose there is an element of truth to that, but there is a lot more to it, which Jeb can't see because he has no sense of social responsibility."

Jamie nodded with an expression of grave understanding, in response to the seriousness of which Leo repressed the urge to laugh.

"Anything else?"

"Not really," said Jamie.

This clearly wasn't true, but Leo didn't push. "You guys never told me how you knew each other or how you ended up here tonight."

"I know Jeb from a drawing class we both took and ..."

Leo waited.

"I asked him to call you."

Leo's eyes widened.

"You never called me. And you didn't give me your number."

"It was nothing personal. My life has been busy. Generally, when you give someone your number and they don't give you theirs, it's up to them whether to have future contact."

"I realize that," said Jamie. "Are you mad then? That I—"

"Set a little trap for me?" said Leo.

Jamie frowned, trying to think of a better characterization for what he had done but decided a trap was apt.

"Yeah."

Leo laughed. "I should be. Bet you didn't expect me to show up a gory mess, did ya?"

Jamie waved away the suggestion. "Just looks like you've gone through a rough patch. If anything, the vulnerability makes you more ... visible, not less"—he swallowed—"beautiful."

Jamie gauged Leo's expression, then visibly resolved to hold his gaze.

"Listen, kid," said Leo, which caused Jamie to wince, "It's a good thing I feel like crap because talk like that could get you into trouble." Leo flirted as best he could while feeling disgusting in an effort to honor the young man's tender overtures. "I have to get home and lie down."

Jamie raised his eyebrows.

"Alone," preempted Leo. "Trust me, my apartment smells worse than I do."

"So come to my place."

"I have to feed my cat," said Leo, amused but undeterred from his intent to end this evening cordially and soon. He hugged Jamie and stroked his cheek before they parted, an intimate but noncommittal gesture.

"Thank you for the kindness, for luring me out tonight, and for the incredibly sweet offer to help me through this. But I have to push through and I can't take a break."

Jamie looked sad and worried, but he made no further attempt to persuade Leo. "It's an open offer," he said. "Call me if you change your mind."

"I'll call you anyway," said Leo, which earned him a sly grin. "It won't be soon. But when I get some breathing room and am in a better space, maybe we should ... see what's up."

Jamie blushed. Leo felt his pulse quicken, which surprised him.

"You fixed OK for wheels?"

"Yep, my car's over there," said Jamie, pointing a thumb over his shoulder.

"OK, then. I need to bid you good night," said Leo. "I'm spent."

Leo saw Jamie running through possible responses. To Leo's relief, he restrained it to "Goodnight, then."

Leo turned to leave, but paused to listen over his shoulder as Jamie called after him, "Please be careful with that stuff. Two weeks."

"Two weeks," Leo affirmed, then headed for his car.

26

WITH ONE FOOT ON THE window sill as cantilever, James Malone reclined in his office chair and gazed out at the Civic Center. Tourists from all over the world paid handsomely to view and photograph this arresting tableau: dramatically illuminated stone remnants of the ancient rotunda, echoed in steel-and-glass by the architecturally controversial contemporary chambers of the Council of Delegates that towered above. James didn't see even see it. On his chest and mind lay the Department of Domestic Intelligence's briefing, circulated in lieu of a brainstorming session this week because most of the agents were on field investigations and could not take time to meet.

Two items from Bimal Gurung and Renée Stephens regarding their joint Domestic Security and Violent Crimes Unit investigations into the terror attacks commanded James's attention. The first pertained to the exploded "power station" and the facility they believed was under construction to replace it. According to the report, in the past twenty-four hours their team had detected clear signs the new facility was operational and connected to the Micromedium.

Hairs stood up on the back of James's neck as he read this because its timing all but confirmed what he had suspected for months: The facility was related to the neural QFRI surveillance incursion he had helped implement at the behest of his contact at the Department of International Intelligence, Agent Baikal.

James regularly summarized his colleagues' work for Baikal. Regarding Lauren Drey's abuse investigation, the DII operative instructed James to keep an eye out for exceptionally disciplined and ruthless Aggressives. If he found people who had the personal focus to indulge in vindictive pursuits without getting lost in them, Baikal wanted James to tell him before he prepared a report for Lauren. Such individuals could prove useful assets for the DII's counterterrorism operations, Baikal explained. With advance knowledge and an opportunity to put the pieces in place, the DII could use any ensuing charges and prosecution as leverage to recruit such persons into the DII's service as an alternative to imprisonment and disgrace.

James agreed to this but he found no one who fit these specifications. Other than, perhaps, himself. He chose to withhold that thought until he decided a change from Domestic to International was in his professional interests. For now, he preferred the benefits of service as undercover DII conduit to Domestic. It afforded flexibility and access to information from both agencies. He wasn't officially in charge of anything, but he knew more than any of his colleagues at Domestic and he had information that could gravely harm International. Played the wrong way, this would cost him his life. Handled wisely, it gave him a great deal of power.

Baikal also rewarded James's willingness to spy on his colleagues by giving him a small set of intense QFRI-enhanced abuse recordings that the official DDI–DII liaison had not made available to Lauren. James fabricated sources for the recordings in his reports and peddled them at the fetish sites, where they were in high demand. These recordings and his unusually acute and potent neural aggression made James's virtual identities immensely popular. He traded recordings with ease and found willing partners for neural interfacing and abuse experiences every time he logged in.

James had firmly embedded himself into the perverse virtual community under his two fictitious identities. In fact, he was practically its hub. Regarding his official role, it wasn't a matter of finding someone to arrest under the new statutory authority. It was a question of choosing which to select for such treatment from the scores he'd compiled records on and explored the twisted rush with.

However, it was Bimal and Renée's investigation into the alleged terror attack on the misnamed "power station" and what they surmised was its replacement facility under construction that most attracted Baikal's interest. The International agent demanded as much detail as James could provide about what his colleagues knew. He also tried with limited success to have James thwart their investigation with questions at briefings designed to send them down blind alleys or confuse their focus.

Baikal neither confirmed nor denied that the facility belonged to the DII, but James was not stupid. Investigative reporter Jill Blatsky's experts opined that the thing included a particle accelerator and a supercomputer. The surveillance equipment James's ad hoc organization had installed was producing tremendous volumes of quantum neural field data. To process all of that for whatever purpose it was being collected would require enormous computing power and God knew what other technology. James knew neither its purpose nor how it functioned, but he suspected the facility was a superhub for the surveillance signals.

This knowledge put him ten steps ahead of his colleagues, who knew nothing about the surveillance intrusion or its possible significance for their investigations. His curiosity screamed to feed them something they could use to test his hypothesis, but he dared not.

Shortly before he read this week's briefing from the other DDI agents, James spoke with Baikal, seeking further instruction on installing the QFRI surveillance arrays. Baikal said the installation phase was complete and to await new directives once the equipment was functional and had been tested, which would be soon. Now, two days later, Bimal and Renée report the facility they've been monitoring has gone live.

"Bingo," James said aloud, "you sonofabitch, Sandoval," which he was all but certain was Baikal's true name. The corroboration satisfied him long enough to turn his thoughts to the next question: For what purpose? Domestic counterterror surveillance? Monitoring of potential national security threats within the government?

Both plausible.

In the climate of fear the periodic terror attacks produced, conservative politicians, law enforcement officials, and intelligence agencies met little resistance when acclimating the populace to an ever-increasing surveillance state.

Still, why invest in such extraordinary technology? Aren't plain old audio bugs, cameras, and data sifters sufficient for those purposes? Why widespread collection of neural data?

James didn't know, but he intended to find out.

The other item on Bimal's and Renée's report that intrigued James had to do with the more recent bomb attacks on the Board of Classification headquarters, advocate general building, and Citizens Action League offices. The report consisted of a single line with no explanatory detail:

"We have a lead on the barista."

James read the sentence several times in a vain quest to extract information.

"Who might you be, my little lady?" he wondered aloud, then stared back out the window and into his thoughts.

27

HOME FROM HIS NIGHT OUT with Jeb and Jamie, Leo felt sick and bone tired. He knew sleep would elude him, so he swallowed one of the blue pills Jeb had prescribed.

He fed and comforted Franz, who was showing clear signs of feline depression from his nearly constant isolation, punctuated by stints of Leo bedridden and ill. As the tranquilizer pulled him down, Leo picked up the old cat, crawled into bed, and slept soundly for the first time since he'd run out of medicine.

He awoke at noon Saturday, grateful for the sleep but still unwell, feeling raw and inflamed from the walls of his blood vessels to the surface of his skin, as though his bodily fluids had been replaced by caustic molasses.

"Ick."

Franz yawned and began beckoning Leo to the food bowl.

Still detoxing and hung over to boot, Leo lay there trying to decide what to do until anxiety about unfinished work tipped the scale in favor of motion. So he followed Jeb's advice and swallowed a white pill. Then he rose to feed the cat, but the blood rushed out of his head, nearly causing him to pass out. He plopped back on the bed with his head between his knees until his skin stopped crawling and his vision cleared. Through the fog, he heard Franz meowing plaintively from the kitchen. "Poor baby," he said to the empty room. "OK, Franz," he hollered. "I'm coming."

Leo stumbled into the kitchen and fed the cat, which was absurdly difficult. He guessed this was what great old age must be like. "Now there's something to look forward to," he said to Franz, noticing before he had completed the sentence that Franz was living the feline version of this eventuality at that very moment. "God, we're a pair, aren't we?"

Franz purred as he ate.

Still feeling like death, Leo pawed through the pouch Jeb had given him the night before and found it also contained a little glass pipe and a torch lighter. Leo wasted no time transferring a small crystal into the rig and torching it to vapor. As he sucked in the Elidrine smoke, he wondered whether Jeb had his best interests in mind. That thought was short lived, however, disintegrating into neural static amidst the energy shock wave that pulsed through Leo's body and mind.

At first, he was unfocused, hopping from one task to the next, sorting mail, cleaning house, organizing work. Eventually, he settled on one of Harlan Durell's cases. It was an interesting one, involving Aggressives who sought "guided development" back to Citizenship after they were released from prison. The legal issue was whether such individuals should be allowed to secure conditional permits to live among Citizens during the reentry process, or had to endure exile among unreformed Aggressives until eligible for full Citizenship.

There was a split among the hearing officers' decisions. Some read the relevant statute as authorizing Aggressives to live among Citizens during their post-incarceration period, on the condition they scrupulously obeyed all laws and participated in good faith in the reprogramming. Other hearing officers believed there was no lawful basis for such provisional permits and that persons released from prison had to live in Aggressive ghettoes until they proved themselves fit for Citizenship.

It was an important issue because ex-convicts had a demonstrably higher likelihood of success if they completed their therapy and education among Citizens than if they had to do it while surviving among unrepentant Aggressives. Nevertheless, the political conservatives vehemently opposed having parolees in their neighborhoods. Their fears were validated when the media sensationalized rare but grisly cases where an Aggressive living among Citizens while going through reprogramming lost control and perpetrated a crime. The statistics favored the permits, but the hype didn't, and fear was proving more persuasive than facts.

After reading the briefs and record evidence in the appeal, Leo donned his quantum array to summarize the case and do some initial research into the relevant legal and historical precedents.

Calibrating the interface and connecting to the Micromedium had long ago become second nature to him. As he completed the process this time, however, he was astounded. In his Elidrine-enhanced state, his mind was focused like a needle. He concentrated with precision on his writing, efficiently producing a full summary of the case. He had great stamina for research, browsing for uninterrupted hours through mountains of archives related to the issues in the case. He deftly switched between reading and writing, compiling a detailed set of notes as he blazed through the research. All of this he accomplished using only his revved up and sharply honed mind. Not once did he touch a keyboard during what turned out to be a marathon work session.

Best of all, this enhanced focus on his work alleviated his anxiety. Leo found himself concentrating, performing at a superhuman clip, and feeling relaxed and energized as he did it. "Now that is how it's supposed to feel," he thought aloud as he momentarily surfaced for air.

The effects of the white pill overtook the waning effects of the smoke and carried Leo for ten hours. He worked like a machine, never stopping to eat, drink, or even urinate. He was single-mindedly focused on his work.

As the drug began wearing off, his edge blunted somewhat and the QFRI array became less responsive. Eventually, he noticed Franz crying for him. It was well past feeding time. Leo doffed the array and unfolded his body from the desk where he had remained upright and motionless for hours, his dehydrated joints and tendons creaking and popping.

"Sorry baby," he croaked hoarsely at Franz as he scooped food into one bowl and water into the other, which by the looks of it had gone dry some time ago. He tried to pet the cat but received cross squawks. Leo opened the fridge and chugged some orange juice. His brain felt shell-shocked and depleted. Checking the clock, he decided he should sleep. So he took a nighty-night pill and crashed.

Sunday was a repeat performance.

Monday, Leo arose early, popped a wakey pill, hit the pipe a touch, showered, shaved, organized the substantial chunk of work he had completed, and prepared to leave for the office.

As he was about to depart, he realized Franz was not in bed with him when he arose. He found the cat curled up in some unfolded laundry on the couch. Attempts at affection were rebuffed, but Franz deigned to allow Leo to feed him before he left. Leo felt terrible about his derelictions and promised Franz he would be home early. The cat ate without the usual morning chirps and did not acknowledge Leo as he was leaving.

Three hours after Leo arrived at the office, Hurricane Harlan blew in with attendant gale-force bluster. He was not pleased with Leo's repeated absences, and Leo could tell a stern lecture was on the agenda. He preempted it with his memo on the Aggressive provisional permit case. Harlan eyed the cover page and flipped through the hefty document, turning down the corners of his mouth in acknowledgement. Leo bowed slightly in response and left his boss to read.

Ten minutes later, Harlan interrupted Leo with premature questions and comments. "Keep reading," Leo responded, which shut Harlan up for an average of five minutes before he interrupted again. "Keep reading," Leo commanded each time. Eventually, Harlan completed the document, walked into Leo's office, slapped the memo on his desk, clapped him on the shoulder and said, "We're gonna make history, buddy." Leo gave a hats-off flourish. "It's a once-in-a-career case," Harlan continued. "How soon can you draft a proposed decision?"

"Give me a week," said Leo.

Harlan roared out of the office and, for the first time since Leo started working in his new job, let him attend to his task in peace.

Drafting the proposed decision consumed Leo for not one week, but one month. He worked at the office by keyboard and late into the night and on weekends via QFRI interface at home.

When the two-week supply of Elidrine Jeb had provided ran out, Leo was underway full tilt on Harlan's now-flagship case and could not imagine slowing down. The Elidrine enabled him to work more effectively and efficiently, and for longer hours than he had ever achieved before.

The proposed decision was billowing into a monster as Leo girded it with the best logic, overwhelming precedent, and masterful scholarship he could muster in advance against whatever attack the conservatives devised on the inevitable appeal.

He didn't want to deal with any lectures from Jeb. He didn't want to deal with Jeb at all, in fact. This left him in a bit of a quandary, however, because he didn't know where to get more Elidrine. Searching for a supplier, Leo wended into some sketchy regions of the Micromedium social sphere. After mucking around in sundry bizarre sites where folks ranging from self-proclaimed anarchists to people peddling false Citizenship papers congregated, Leo finally located a supplier, arranged a meeting and, for a hefty pile of credits, bought himself a cache of pills and crystals.

Having found he could work for absurd lengths of time on little sleep with Elidrine, Leo opted against the blue tranquilizers. He grabbed an hour or two of sleep here and there when his neurons, even jacked up on Elidrine, ceased to perform adequately. That appeared to be enough.

His primary concern was to get the document done and into Harlan's hands. The boss had exercised great restraint, allowing Leo to work on the case without other distractions, but he was starting to tap his foot.

Leo continued to use Elidrine and work on Harlan's case. As the days wore on, he started shifting from focused to hyperfocused, sometimes dwelling for forty-five minutes on a single sentence, his mind cycling in an endless loop in search of the perfect word. While he toiled obsessively at the decision, people at his office noticed his improved dynamic with Harlan. They also noticed Leo had lost weight, spoke in rapid bursts, always looked exhausted, and had begun to neglect his grooming. A couple thought they had smelled unusual fumes outside the door of a vacant office where he sometimes napped in the middle of the day. No one said a word, but they worried.

On his way home from the office on Friday of his fourth week working on the conditional-permit case, Leo dozed behind the wheel from prolonged lack of sleep, dehydration, and starvation. With three fingers on the steering wheel, glass pipe between thumb and forefinger, and torch lighter in his other hand, he hunched down and sparked up the Elidrine, barreling down the highway and scanning his environs for cops as he inhaled the smoke to stay awake. The pipe burned his fingers, so he threw it on the floor and gripped the steering wheel with trembling hands, alert now, though more depleted than ever.

He examined himself in the rearview, gaunt, drawn, his forehead creased in perpetual concentration. "You are way out there on the edge, Leo," he said to himself with a thick tongue in a raspy voice that echoed strangely in his torqued mind. Enough of his judgment remained intact to know his current state had crossed the line to madness, but he was in too deep for an abrupt change. He promised himself to take a break when the decision was written, and hit the accelerator so he could get home and resume work.

Leo spent most of the weekend fixated on minutiae in the draft decision. He polished, tweaked, and revised hour after hour after hour. This continued unabated until an insistent pounding pierced his trance. He reluctantly pulled off his quantum array to identify the source of this rude intrusion and heard the voice of Jeaneane.

"Leo, it's me. Open up goddamn it."

He looked at the clock and around the room and felt a flash of panic. He considered pretending he wasn't home, but Jeaneane clearly had no intention of permitting any evasion.

She pounded harder.

"I'm not leaving. Open the door."

Leo scooped the Elidrine paraphernalia into a drawer, ran his fingers through his hair, walked to the front hallway, and sheepishly opened the door.

Jeaneane regarded him in silence. Her face was rigid with anger and Leo felt her eyes scan him down to his marrow in one icy sweep. Without speaking, she pushed her way past him into his apartment. "Oh my God. What the hell is going on?"

Leo turned to what she was seeing and realized his apartment was a stinking catastrophe. He followed her as she marched from room to room. Newspapers and mail spilled off tables and onto the floors. Dying houseplants lay in withered tendrils from hanging pots and windowsills. Coffee cups with reeking dregs and dots of mold populated every room. A sticky cascade of coffee grounds had congealed on the counter, cabinet, and kitchen floor from a disregarded spillover. Flies circled an overflowing garbage can and a heap of empty, unrinsed cat-food cans accumulated at its base. Jeaneane opened the fridge and saw three pizza boxes containing dried-up remains, missing a single slice from each, at least one of which was moldering away on a plate amidst a sink full of dirty dishes. There were burn marks on tables, the kitchen counter, and Leo's desk. The place reeked of rotten food, a sickly sweet chemically smell, wet towels and cat box.

Jeaneane started calling Franz, who stuck his nose out from under the couch.

She clicked her tongue and cooed at him before turning to examine Leo with confusion and open disgust.

"What the fuck is going on?"

"I've been focused on drafting a decision for Harlan in a case—"

"That's not what I'm talking about," she snapped. "What is"—she waved her hand around the apocalyptic room and at Franz—"*this* about? I've been trying to reach you for three weeks."

"Not much besides work," he stammered. "Sorry, didn't realize you called."

With an expression of absolute bafflement, she followed her nose to the bathroom and found Franz's filthy litter box.

She stomped past Leo and into the kitchen, grabbed a plastic bag, then stormed back into the bathroom and started to dump Franz's box. Humiliated and ashamed, Leo took over the task and Jeaneane returned to the living room, where she soothed and kissed Franz. "Sorry, baby," she said softly.

She walked back into the bathroom. "Tell me what's going on. Are you on drugs?"

Leo's nerves were depleted to the point of collapse, and he withered under Jeaneane's fury.

"No," he said. "I've just been working too hard."

She grabbed him by the shoulders and yanked him toward the bathroom mirror.

He tried to turn away.

"No." She wiped the sweaty curls back from his forehead and gripped them into her fist, then lurched him back toward the mirror with one vicious jerk. "*Look.*"

Leo beheld his reflection. Eyes vacant and bloodshot, sunken in dark circles. Face thin and bony. Skin scaling and unshaven. Hair a filthy bedraggled mess. He barely recognized the madman who peered back.

He turned his eyes to meet the reflection of Jeaneane's, which held him paralyzed with their stony rage. She let him roast and freeze under her gaze for a long moment. Then, her expression thawed to sadness and disappointment, and she released her grip and left the room.

Leo followed her into the living room. She swept debris off the couch, picked up Franz and placed him in her lap, twisted her own hair back into an untied ponytail and stroked the cat.

"Jeb called me," she said. When Leo didn't respond, she continued, "Which should show you how serious this is since he knows I loathe him."

Leo frowned. "You knew what was happening before you came here and shook me around."

She turned to him, daring him with her eyes to pursue this tack. He took the warning and fell silent.

"No," she said, "I didn't. Apparently some guy named Jamie?" she looked at Leo and he nodded. "He hounded Jeb to call someone who cared enough about you to come kick your tires. Jeb wouldn't tell me anything other than that he had seen you and you didn't seem well. Since I had been calling you for three weeks because *I need to talk with you about Anna*," she hammered, "and since Jeb would not risk hearing what I think of him by calling me unless the situation were dire, I wanted to see for myself."

"What about Anna?" asked Leo.

Jeaneane shook her head. "I don't feel like discussing that with you right now."

Her words stung.

"I don't know what you're on," she said coldly, "but you are fucked up."

He refused to let himself cry. "I know," he answered, contrite yet irritated by her tone.

"I'm sorry," she continued, "but whatever you're going through is no excuse for neglecting Franz like this."

He knew she was right.

"I'm tempted to take him with me."

"No," Leo protested, afraid she might do it. "He doesn't do well with being out of his space. He's too old."

Jeaneane spat, "His *space* is buried under fifty feet of garbage and drug psychosis!"

He wanted to ask her who the hell she thought she was to make such assumptions and pronouncements but her instincts were accurate. What was there to say?

"I have to finish drafting this decision," Leo assured himself as much as her after a moment. "It's almost done."

"It is done. Turn it in as is and take some time to get your shit together. Where is it?"

He printed her the most recent iteration. She grabbed a pen and, as she read it, flagged a flurry of typos. When she finished, she said, "It's spectacular, but it's a mess. Sloppy mistakes on every page. Go make these changes and send it to Harlan. I'll order something to eat."

The thought of food turned his stomach but he complied.

Two hours later, after a shower, lots of fluids, and a meal, the two talked about Anna over tea.

"She's hiding something from me," said Jeaneane.

"What do you mean?"

"When I read the psych evals, I got the feeling she was dancing around something, some trauma."

"Yes."

"When I tried to corner her about it, she got nasty."

"I had a similar experience," said Leo. He told her about Anna's angry outburst during their road trip down the coast. They tossed back and forth speculations but decided they had to let Anna share when she was ready.

"I'm worried it will come out the wrong way and screw her case," said Jeaneane.

"That's possible," said Leo. "The best thing to do is invite her to be open with you and create as safe an environment as you can for her to share. Beyond that, it's up to her."

Jeaneane was frustrated, but offered no protest. Leo hoped she could follow this advice and work with the result.

After helping Leo clean up and confirming he had sent Harlan the draft and would take Monday off to rest, hydrate, and nourish, Jeaneane kissed him and prepared to leave.

"Who's Jamie?" she asked as he helped her on with her coat.

"No one," said Leo. "A kid working at Capital Macrovision as an intern when I did my interview at *The Morning Show*. He's got stars in his eyes, believe it or not," he said, gesturing around his still-tattered abode.

She wrinkled her nose. "Well, if he's friends with Jeb, I'd stay away."

"I don't know what his relationship with Jeb is, but he's nothing like him. He's a nice, dorky kid," he added, thinking to himself that this was a superficially accurate but neither fair nor sufficient summary.

"Well, apparently you can thank him for this visit," she rejoined. She hugged him and whispered in his ear, "Please get it together," patted him on the cheek, and left.

Leo lay in bed and listened to all the messages he'd been avoiding. Increasingly annoyed and worried calls from Jeaneane. Several calls from John, the last one sounding genuinely concerned. Calls from his family. One from a bizarre computer synthesized voice telling him he had several micromissives from Anaku.

"How the hell did you do that?" Leo asked aloud, shaking his head as he deleted the message.

Toward the end, there were calls from Jeb. One said, "Stop being an asshole and let me know you're OK, Leo." The next one said, "Jamie Tesh tells me you left without giving him your number. Again. Idiot. In case you haven't noticed, Leo, he's completely gone on you, despite my efforts to tell him what a pain in the ass you are. Just kidding. Sort of. He's young but he's wise and more mature than I am, though I'll slap you if you ever remind me I said so. You could do a lot worse. Don't be stupid."

"Who said I was looking?" Leo said to the recorded Jeb, annoyed.

The message continued, "I'll respect your decision not to give him your number if you call me by five o'clock today. He's annoying the shit out of me to make sure you're all right."

This was followed by a call from Jamie. "Sorry, I know you didn't give me your number and this is a total breach of seduction etiquette, but I want to know you're in one piece."

Who the hell does this guy think he is? thought Leo. *What a pest.*

The next call was Jeb: "You're a selfish prick. I'm sicking über hag Jeaneane on you."

That was the last call.

Leo recorded a message for Jeb that asked how he dared insinuate himself into Leo's relationship with Jeaneane. When he reviewed the message before sending it, however, he lost his righteous bluster and deleted it. Instead, he left a short message thanking Jeb for his concern, apologizing for being off the grid, and telling him he was OK.

Leo slept like the dead that night. Next morning, he awoke filled with desperate cravings. To steady his nerves before calling Harlan, he smoked the last pinch of Elidrine.

Relieved when Harlan didn't answer, he left a message saying he had completed work on the draft after toiling all weekend for the fourth weekend in a row and that he was taking the day off to rest. He asked Harlan to leave him be for the day, read the draft, and write questions as they arose so they could discuss them on Tuesday.

He rode out the dregs of the Elidrine by sorting through papers and scrubbing the kitchen. By midafternoon, he was crashing hard and knew he could not return to work the next day. He lay in bed and fretted over this as fatigue and anxiety mounted like twin nemeses in his path.

He slept a couple of fitful hours and awoke in a panic. Desperate for a hit, he crawled around on the floor with a flashlight and picked out a few shiny specks that might have been Elidrine fragments from the rug. The pipe contained enough residue for one little toot, which he greedily ingested, along with the vaporized debris from the floor, some of which clearly was not Elidrine because it burned his lungs and triggered fits of coughing.

He wired up the quantum array and skulked to the fringy social sites, hoping to find some advice on how long the withdrawal from Elidrine would take. This gist of people's responses was that he could expect to sleep for a week, followed by several more of severe depression and unendurable cravings. As this would not do given Leo's professional responsibilities, most advised him to taper off. He decided this was his best option, but he had run through his funds. Luckily, his supplier told him his credit was good and they arranged a meeting.

Later in the evening, dosed and especially energized due to having slept the night before, Leo returned to the same Micromedium social quadrant to thank his supplier. After they exchanged pleasantries, despite his solemn oath to taper off, Leo hit the pipe again—hard. His mind activated but unfocused on work, he browsed the social sites and stumbled upon some fetish rooms that attracted his drug-warped mind like the gravitational pull of a black hole.

He stuck his cyber nose into one entitled, "Aggressives Who Punish." Without revealing his presence, he skimmed the list of room participants' monikers. Each evoked an Aggressive who took pleasure in inflicting pain or a Vulnerable who craved abuse. Leo felt an odd mixture of anger and intrigue.

He monitored the room's text chat. The participants were looking for compatible partners for a neural interface session. Leo wondered whether any of them were who they claimed to be. Something in him stirred at the thought of experiencing the virile rush of a true Aggressive's forceful energy.

Leo had known Aggressives during his life. Had suffered their verbal abuse and bullying. Had felt inferior to them. Belittled by them. Yet he had also always found them seductive on some level. They appeared to embody what he lacked. The thought of touching that titillated him. He wondered if he could do that without getting hurt. Could he pull off identifying as a Vulnerable and get one of these Aggressives to let him peek into his or her mind? The mind of an Aggressive was both forbidden and fascinatingly foreign. The thought of directly experiencing it was intoxicating and intriguing, and Leo decided he wanted to try it.

An insistent pinging told Leo someone was trying to communicate with him, which was odd because his monitoring of the room was currently cloaked. When he activated the icon, a chat box appeared. It said:

> **Anaku:** Where have you been and what do you think you're doing?

This was the last person Leo wanted to talk to in his current state. So he responded:

> **Asad:** Busy.

He closed the chat box, and muted the alert so he would suffer no further interruptions.

After contemplating possible sobriquets for the adventure, he decided upon the virtual name VulNeedsLesson. He took a gut-wrenching hit of acrid smoke and, under his anonymized fictitious identity, openly entered the room.

His screen promptly filled up with private text chat boxes inviting him to hook up for a session. He chatted with each in turn until he settled on a person with the screen name Domin8U whose cold edge ticked Leo off.

Domin8U claimed to be a male Aggressive who relished punishing Vulnerables who knew that's all they were good for. Leo knew he couldn't verify the male part, but he didn't care about that if the Aggressive part was genuine, which should be apparent enough if the person were real on that score. As they spoke, Leo savored the thought of inducing this cocky prick to display his aggression. What attracted him wasn't the idea of being hurt. It was the thought of the Aggressor unwittingly being used for Leo's own pleasure, even as he imagined he was dominating and punishing Leo. That thought, dominating the self-professed dominator without him even knowing it, sizzled Leo's Elidrine-drenched neurons. Leo didn't know if he could pull it off but decided to give it a shot and disconnect if it got painful.

They formed a link. Combined with the focus and stimulus of Elidrine, the Aggressive's forceful mental projection was electric. The game was delicate but the Elidrine allowed Leo to focus acutely. He strictly compartmentalized his mind, tailoring his thoughts to serve his performance as a submissive Vulnerable, but simultaneously observing the exchange with another part of his mind. Observing and consuming.

Leo and the other played a cat-and-mouse game until Domin8U unleashed the full measure of his vicious aggression on Leo, surrendering to his forbidden impulse to attack and abuse. The energy pummeled the outer reaches of Leo's mind like a beating, but he never let it compromise his inner sanctum. Instead, he modulated the Aggressive's neural energy and let it light up his own neurons. It was sharp, clear, hot, and fierce. Leo had never felt such an illicit rush. It was Elidrine to the degree of Elidrine.

When they were done, Leo felt sick but also sated. To use this would-be abuser for his own satisfaction slaked some old yearning he could not quite name. Leo questioned whether this was healthy, but it felt like he was learning something important and potentially healing. He viewed the event like a searchlight shining down into the caverns of his own buried wounds. He could see more deeply into himself through this encounter, he was sure. That had to be a good thing. Didn't it?

Leo found little sleep that night and had to use more of the drug upon arising to make it to the office. Harlan was aflutter over the draft decision Leo had written at his behest. The chief adjudicator proudly distributed it to his colleagues for review. He took Leo out for a lavish celebratory lunch (which Leo barely touched) and showered him in praise and gratitude.

Leo was delighted that his boss was so pleased. He hoped the rest of the Board members and their legal advisors would be similarly minded. Later in the day, he overheard one legal advisor say to another, "It's rather *long*." Nevertheless, he was confident they would recognize that the decision's heft and thoroughness would stand the test of time if the Board could muster the consensus to embrace it. If the others signed on, the case would establish Harlan's legacy and secure Leo's professional future.

Leo logged back into the fetish site that night after work and found the same participant. Once they had formed the neural link and exchanged compliments on the previous night's romp, Domin8U asked Leo if he wanted to take it to a higher level. Leo asked what that meant, and Domin8U said he had a collection of recordings that were enhanced with a QFRI overlay, such that they could directly experience recorded acts of abuse together. Leo was shocked and asked whether the recordings were real. Domin8U sensed Leo's reticence and assured him they were realistic fantasy performances. He regaled Leo at length about the increased intensity this would lend to what they'd already experienced.

As he listened to these thoughts, Leo was hitting his pipe. Part of his mind said no, but the drug compromised Leo's ability to act on sane judgments, most problematically his judgment that he should put down the pipe.

He agreed and, before he'd given it another thought, was on the receiving end of an Aggressive rush exponentially more magnified than the one he had consumed the night before, as Domin8U fed off the recording and unleashed his fury on Leo.

Leo focused on modulating and experiencing Domin8U's aggression. The recording involved someone screaming at a blindfolded person tied to a chair. Leo found it repugnant but he viewed it as unreal, and it did not interest him. Domin8U's energetic response to it, however, interested him greatly.

James Malone settled back in his chair after the rousing session, removed his array, and toweled the sweat off his brow.

"Wow," he said as his respiration calmed and he regained his composure.

He tried to decide between keeping this person on tap for when he needed a release and marking him for official investigatory pursuit.

"Too hot for comfort," he concluded aloud after sober assessment of his own arousal.

The decision made, he launched a tracing program to hunt down the identity behind the moniker VulNeedsLesson.

"A lesson is exactly what you're going to get, my little Vulnerable friend," he said, "but not before we have a little more fun."

He snickered as sweat trickled down his body in briny rivulets.

28

THE STURDY YOUNG WOMAN DUCKED lower into the hillside park bushes and scarcely breathed as she held binoculars with shaking hands and watched the DDI swat team swarm into Gillian Moss's apartment.

"Serves you right, you phony whore." The truth was she feared she had made a terrible mistake, the latest in a series that had long since ceased to align with her original purpose.

It's his fault, she thought bitterly. Crazy ever to have gotten involved with that greedy pig. "Marta, you stupid fool," she scolded herself as she put down the binoculars and pressed the heel of her hand into her forehead.

Three days earlier she had paid Cormack O'Brian, president and chief executive officer of Protection Inc., a surprise visit.

"I told you never to come here," he snarled, shoving her into his office.

"You promised to keep them off me but they're sniffing around," she said after he closed the door.

"Has anyone implicated you in the"—he paused in a preposterous display of delicacy—"activities?"

"Since I'm standing here before you, it would appear not," she coldly observed. "But they've started talking to people I know."

"If no one knows anything about your involvement," he said in a fatherly tone, "there should be no pro—"

"Listen to me, fucker," she said. "These people are not stupid. How the hell do I know what they know? They have those brain flayers now. Who knows what they can find out? You need to fix this. Now. Or, I swear to God," she said, pointing a finger in his face, "I'll take you down with me. You hear me? If they catch me, I will be sure they catch you, too, even if I do it with my dying breath, capiche?"

O'Brian replied with icy hostility, "Now you listen to me, my dear, and listen well: I will excuse this outburst because you are under intense pressure and don't mean what you're saying."

"I sure as hell—"

"Shut up," he snapped. "You are perilously close to a line you do not want to cross."

Marta stood her ground, undaunted. "I'm not the only one who knows you bankrolled this, Cormack. Kill me and someone else will take you down."

"Don't count on it, sweetcakes. To finger me they'd have to jeopardize your whole stinking cesspool of brain-damaged radicals. It would be an obvious ploy to frame an upstanding Citizen for the terrorist acts of a band of disaffected anarchists. They wouldn't stand a chance."

"Don't be so sure," she replied with a defiant sneer. "I've left a trace of this," she tipped her head to the side, "appointment."

Her presence in his office gave teeth to her threats and they both knew it. She was getting desperate, and desperate people could make big messes.

"Let's dispense with the empty threats, shall we my dear?" Cormack responded after a beat. "We've worked and played so well together until now. Let's not spoil things, hmm?" he said with an index finger under her chin.

She turned her head to the side, dislodging his finger. "I am not your dear. Nor will I be your sacrificial lamb."

"Lamb?" Cormack howled at the absurdity. "Missy, you organized a major terrorist attack. Save the innocent victim shtick for someone who doesn't know you." They stood in frosty silence. "Let's slow down," he said after a moment. "What we need is a simple diversion to throw them off the scent."

She did not respond, but held his gaze and took a seat facing his desk.

Cormack slowly laid his eyes over every inch of her. Neither the torn T-shirt, leather jacket, jaggedly tailored skirt, combat boots, nor comically strident tattoos obscured Marta's healthy curves, which he ogled without pretense of tact.

She glared at him.

"We need someone we can toss to them who will grab their attention but won't lead them back to us," he resumed, after feasting, to his satisfaction for the moment, on her harsh beauty.

She shook her head. "I don't want to throw those monsters any meat."

"Throw them one of your political enemies."

She crossed her arms and leveled him a smirk.

"How droll," he replied. "I wouldn't quite fit the bill. Besides, you must realize by now I'm not your enemy."

"Yes you are, you swine. We happened to have a confluence of tactical interests. But you are and shall always be the essence of greed. I'm here to help you trigger your own demise."

Cormack laughed. "By blowing up the obstacles to my enrichment? Vive la révolution."

"Fuck you."

He raised a hand to slap the filthy words out of her mouth, but she held her head up defiantly and offered him her cheek. Unwilling to give her the satisfaction of a barbaric display, he lowered his arm and took a seat behind his desk.

"Your newfound concern for the sanctity of life is most touching," he said. "But it makes the task more complicated. You need someone dirty enough to distract them, but clean enough to have a reasonable chance of getting through it alive and clueless enough to avoid leading them back to you. Or, more importantly, me."

She sat and thought, her jaw set.

"You radical Aggressives get all mushy when it comes to turning each other over to law enforcement," said Cormack. "But if they're on your trail, you have to give them something good."

She remained mute and tapped a finger on her arm.

"It's a simple matter of survival," he concluded in a tone which she guessed was supposed to be soothing. "You must know someone."

She wrestled with herself at length, then made up her mind. "There is one possibility."

He held one ear toward her by the tip of a finger.

"You know this barista they're looking for?"

He steepled his fingers and gave her his full attention.

"I know who she is."

Cormack was surprised and, to her satisfaction, impressed. After she convinced him that the barista was uninvolved in the attacks and didn't know who was, he agreed with her instinct. They discussed a few options and decided an anonymous tip from an untraceable number using an electronically disguised voice should do the trick under the circumstances.

That settled, Cormack said, "Now, come over here and show me what you're wearing under that skirt."

Marta concealed her disgust. Determined to retain influence over this useful resource, she also was perversely attracted to the beast, though that didn't lessen her revulsion, a dissonance which usually heightened the intensity of these lurid sessions. Relieved to have a plan, she indulged the request.

As she walked around the desk, Cormack added, with a cruelty that rolled off his tongue like poisoned honey, "The barista is a perfect solution. I'm sure your father would be proud."

Cormack had ensnared the enticing young ruffian by intercepting her after eavesdropping on a visit with her father, who was serving a life sentence at one of Protection Inc.'s high-security prison facilities. Over dinner, he ascertained that she appreciated the utility of a good barter, had manipulable political predilections, useful connections, and other charms, and that she was open to trading them for the influence and money with which he could power her schemes and provide her with cover, not to mention improve conditions for her father.

Hardened by years of Cormack's brutality, she absorbed the lash without a flinch.

"Not nearly as proud as he will be when you stop serving my purposes and I slit your throat," she answered, dropping her jacket on the floor and climbing into his lap to face him.

"Unless I slit yours first," he replied, peeling off her top. "But it won't come to that," he whispered in her ear and brushed his lips down her neck. "You'll see."

Now, three days later, Marta saw Gillian Moss begin the nightmare in her stead.

"Sorry girl," she said aloud as they hauled the woman out in cuffs. "At least you have a shot at seeing the light of day again."

Three hours later, she was on an international flight under a false identity, bound for a tropical locale where Cormack owned a seaside cottage under an assumed name. By her third in-flight cocktail, she had stopped worrying about Gillian Moss. "Just until the dust settles," she said before dozing off.

Through one-way glass in the interrogation room, Renée Stephens, Bimal Gurung, Chief George Mills and James Malone stood together and watched the young woman chain smoke.

"The identity she was using when we arrested her was named Gillian Moss," said Renée. "It's one of several. We don't know how many."

Gillian turned toward the glass and looked from side to side, as though she saw them observing her. Tall and slim, she was rather boyishly figured with large brown eyes, a slightly upturned nose, a tiny mouth, and a pointy chin. She wore her dark brown hair in a pixie cut. Almost extraterrestrial in appearance, she was attractive nonetheless in her self-possession and poise.

"What's her story?" asked James, intrigued.

"Says she had nothing to do with the attacks and has no idea who did," answered Renée.

James studied her. "Why did she run?"

"Says she was afraid of getting in trouble for using false identities and serving as broker for others to do the same."

"Naughty girl," James almost whispered.

"She has used the Gillian Moss identity for at least three years. That persona is a full Citizen, a card-carrying member of the Citizens Action League, and active in Reverend Rhodes' Congregation of the Way."

James peered at her, sure he had seen her before.

"She says she used the Moss identity to assist Citizen families in purchasing changes of identity for people who needed to bypass the reclassification process for various reasons."

"Lucrative business," said James. "Why would she be working as a barista?"

"Claims she had earned enough from the fraudulent-identity brokerage to start a new life," said Renée. "The barista identity, a Ms. Allison Flanders, was her exit strategy. Gillian Moss planned to send retirement announcements to her clients and move to the East Coast, where her life trail would disappear. Meanwhile, she would step into the barista persona full time and put together an ostensibly lawful life path using her laundered fortune."

"But unfortunately," interjected Bimal, "She was in the wrong place at the wrong time, and her barista persona went from obscure to front page in one explosive moment."

"Bad luck," said James.

"Bad luck, indeed," said Bimal.

"If it's true," added Renée, "which is where we're hoping you come in, James."

He tore himself away from examining the detainee, folded his arms, and gave Renée his full attention.

"Whatever price she pays for the crimes she claims she committed will pale in comparison to what she faces if we can hang the terrorism stuff on her."

James agreed.

"We tried to call her bluff by telling her we have equipment that would allow an agent to peek into her mind to see whether she's lying."

James registered mild surprise. "And?"

"She was unfazed. Volunteered to let us look."

"Oh?" said James, turning back to eye Gillian Moss, various and sundry, with renewed interest.

"We told her it takes some training," said Renée, "but she said, 'um, I don't think that will be a problem.'"

James reacted with a single breathy laugh, leaving a circle of condensation on the glass. "Is that so?"

"Since you have the most experience using this equipment," Renée said, completing the pitch, "we hoped perhaps you would interrogate her further using a neural link."

In truth, though she did not tell him this, Renée felt ambivalent about bringing James and the QFRI equipment into her investigation, but she needed to act fast. The chief, in a move that would cost him, had given Renée and Bimal one afternoon to conduct an interrogation before he alerted DII that Moss was in DDI custody. As soon as that happened, International would try to wrest jurisdiction from Domestic. Renée wanted to extract information as quickly as possible before the tug of war over the suspect began. If Bimal shared Renée's hesitance, he did not voice it. Together they decided to utilize James if he were willing, which Renée surmised he would likely be more than.

Haunted by concerns about James's conduct in Lauren Drey's parasitic abuse investigations, Renée hoped seeing him in action with the QFRI array might put her fears to rest or give her the fire power she needed to object formally.

James's initial response was notably circumspect. "I can do so as a practical matter," he said, "and not to spoil the party, but do we have authority to use the technology for this?"

Renée put a hand over her mouth to conceal a smile. Everyone knew James was no civil libertarian. *Surely you're not afraid of being sued or jailed are you, big guy?* she wanted to prod, but turned to the chief instead.

"The Office of Legal Counsel is of the opinion it's covered by existing authority governing lie detector technology," said the chief.

James scoffed.

The chief held up his hand. "Regardless, this is a terror investigation. Circumstances as exigent as these override privacy concerns. Ms. Moss has also consented to the procedure and appears to be familiar and experienced with the technology."

James darted a glance at the detainee.

"The calculus might change if your experience using this equipment indicates it would harm the interrogee physically or mentally in ways other than those associated with exposure of private details," Bimal interjected, handing James a sword with two edges, one of which could slice off Lauren's investigations.

James met Bimal's eye. "No. But it is extremely intrusive. I would be looking into her mind."

"Which is exactly what we want you to do," said the chief. "I'm authorizing it. If anyone takes heat, it will be me. I will protect you if necessary. You have my word."

James turned to Renée without expression and deadpanned, "Then yes."

Her suspicion confirmed that James's primary concern was his own ass. Renée searched his features for ambivalence but saw none.

"Thank you," she said.

"Not at all," replied James, concealing his excitement.

Bimal Gurung had studied these interactions with attention to James's body language and tonal inflection. James was a master of self-control, but Bimal had an even keener perceptual sense. His instincts told him James was hiding something.

"Do you know this woman, Agent Malone?"

James turned to Bimal, privately deciding the man was a problem. "No," he said flatly.

Bimal filled the room with his silence.

"But she does look familiar," James conceded.

"Where have you seen her?" pressed Bimal with curiosity.

Up your pompous ass. "I don't know," he replied.

Bimal looked James up and down once, then turned away. "Proceed."

James clenched a fist, then consciously relaxed it.

"Familiarize yourself with the file first, please," Bimal said without looking at James. Then, turning to him, he continued in a kinder tone, "You are an experienced agent, Malone, so please don't take offense if I state the obvious, but I feel compelled to be thorough."

James tilted his head toward Bimal and listened.

"We're not offering her anything other than the chance to prove she wasn't involved in the attacks. We have told her the purpose of the neural link will be to ascertain whether she has told the truth in this regard. However, if you can get into her head, you are authorized, at your discretion, to go beyond the scope of those objectives, up to and including use of non-injurious coercion, to uncover other potentially relevant information."

James experienced a squirt of adrenaline at these words, but felt Renée's eyes bore into him. Conduct in the fetish sites qualified as extremely rough, so his primary objective with the detainee had better be restraint, notwithstanding the enticing wiggle room Bimal had bestowed.

"It is my sincere hope," Bimal continued, "that you do not find anything that will put this young woman into more trouble than she tells us she has already incurred by her illicit identity business and her unfortunate proximity to someone else's much more serious crime. But if she knows anything that will advance this investigation, I want you to dislodge it."

"Understood," said James. "What's her true name?"

"That's a matter of perspective, at least so far," answered Renée. "She says her birth name was Rachel and that she was born to a family of Aggressives named Guidreaux, all of whom are either dead or long gone. We're trying to verify that now. For the time being, we're referring to her as Moss because that's the ID that is most heavily documented and the one she was using when we arrested her."

"Even though it's fake," said James.

"It's not yet clear what's real and what's fake," shrugged Renée. "Perhaps you can sort some of it out."

James accepted the working file on Gillian Moss and went to his office to prepare.

Forty-five minutes later, James and the detainee faced one another across the interrogation room table, each wearing a quantum array wired to a Micromedium node. They both connected to the node via a text-command channel to control and calibrate the equipment, and a broad quantum channel to form the neural link.

James and Gillian were both experienced at using the quantum interface to form a neural meld. After a few minutes and adjustments, they simultaneously darted into eye contact as their minds interpenetrated and became almost as one.

"Yes," thought James when he sensed Gillian's familiarity with his face. "I've seen you before too."

Gillian observed James in auditory and cognitive silence. This took James somewhat off guard. He had never encountered anyone so capable of noiseless conscious awareness. Sensing his surprise, Gillian smiled with hostility.

James tried to knock her off kilter a notch with a pulse of cold aggression, something he had honed to a dark art during his forays into the abuse sites. To his satisfaction, Gillian noticeably flinched, and it was James who smiled. She rallied after a beat and regained her composure, but James had shown his teeth.

"Where have we seen each other?" was Gillian's first verbal thought.

James showed her an image of her appointment calendar, part of the loot the arresting officers seized when they picked her up. He mentally zoomed in on an entry date from the previous May: Cleague Social/Evelyn Malone 2:00 p.m. Images of his great-grandmother's estate and the party they had both attended filled his thoughts.

"Ah," she replied.

"Do you call them Cleagues when you accept their payments for your, mmm, services? Miss Moss, is it?" thought James.

Gillian was unfazed by the snide query. "Of course not," she thought in response. "That would be in rather poor taste."

"To say the least," James thought in reply.

He interrogated her for the better part of an hour regarding her birth identity, childhood, and adolescence among the members of her native Aggressive community, as well as her acquisition and use of false identities and her career as a broker for others seeking to do the same.

James perceived her answers to be fresh and candid. However, when he tried to extract names and identifying information for people who helped her procure fictitious personas, she insisted she knew them only by aliases. When he tried to pry these loose, he was astonished that she could limit his access to what she wanted him to see. He told her this undercut the utility of the interrogation and its potential to exonerate her.

"I agreed to let you verify I wasn't involved in the bombings," she pushed back. "I was told this is not an interrogation regarding my Citizen-identity business. I will not assist you in persecuting my associates. I've told you as much as I'm willing to for purposes of showing you what I've said is true. If you insist on pursuing that, we're done."

A ringtone in James's earpiece told him Renée wanted his attention, so he blunted the quantum signal and listened.

"James, Lauren queried the DII liaison about using the equipment for interrogation purposes under the pretext of needing the information for your parasitic abuse investigation. Lauren suggests you induce the subject to revisit the day of the attacks in her mind and allow you to explore her associated thoughts and feelings. This will serve two purposes: You can evaluate the veracity of Moss's story, and when she opens up to allow this while focused on such vivid memories, you can listen for background thoughts she might be trying to hide."

James severed the audio signal without changing expression and restored the quantum signal to full capacity.

"Plotting?" came Gillian's thought.

James ignored this. "I know this will be difficult"—he swaddled the thought in a soothing tone—"but I want you to take me to the day of the explosions. If you share your memories from the day of the incident and reveal enough for me to experience your feelings and thoughts, I should be able to determine with a high degree of certainty whether you're telling me the truth. If I find that you are, I will persuade my colleagues of it."

She accepted the challenge, and closed her eyes.

James saw vividly with his mind's eye the interior of a café from the perspective of standing behind the counter. Sun streamed through the front windows and, across the street, he saw the undamaged Board of Classification headquarters, its majestic arches intact.

Leo Baksh walked up to the counter and ordered a coffee. James found it momentarily disorienting to see a familiar face in the context of someone else's memories, but dismissed that thought and stayed focused on her perspective. He felt the barista's mind fill with a sense of warmth and sympathy toward the advocate. He heard her mind race through several commiseratory sentiments regarding his recent defeat before the hearing officer in the high – profile Anna Dao case, then decide voicing them would be unprofessional. She didn't know Baksh, after all. She settled on a gesture of friendly surrender, doing her best to convey empathy but not pity. Baksh shrugged an acknowledgement, paid, and left to find a table.

All of this felt authentic to James. However, as Gillian began retrieving the memories from this traumatic day, he had a clear sense that there was another distinct line of thought that she was concealing from his purview. He could hear it, like clamoring voices, loud on their own side but faintly audible to him, as though he were listening to them through a thick concrete wall.

As Leo Baksh left the counter, James saw in Gillian's mind's eye that she turned to the back of the café to grab a washcloth. A blinding flash of light burst from behind her and she fell to her knees. A terrible, percussive crash sounded, and a geyser of glass blasted across the counter over her head and spattered the wall she was facing.

She stood and turned around to see the café windows shattered, the Board's headquarters in flames, and the café interior cast asunder with patrons bleeding and screaming. Then, she saw a great concrete projectile arcing toward the café from the building across the street. She ducked back to her knees and hid behind the counter as the massive object crashed into the sidewalk, quaking the earth around her when it struck and heaving another torrent of dust and debris over her head.

James attended closely as Moss let him see all the subsequent events. Leo Baksh bloodied but conscious, beckoning her to help him get the others to safety. Vaulting over the counter to assist him. Helping the wounded escape the blast zone. The paramedics. The police.

"OK, stop," commanded James.

The scene dissolved in their shared consciousness. As Gillian's mind calmed, James again sensed she had cordoned another line of thought from her central awareness.

"I'm sorry you had to relive all of that," he thought to her.

"I relive it every day, if not in conscious thought, then in my dreams," she replied. "But thank you."

James had scrupulously avoided alerting her that he was aware she was hiding something. He kept his mind free of verbal thoughts and compartmentalized his own suspicions to conceal them from her. He did not allow himself to consider whether she detected voices calling from behind his barrier as he detected hers.

"Please go back to the morning before the incident and show me your day prior to arrival at work."

Gillian closed her eyes and James's mind's eye filled with a vision of her apartment. As he had hoped, when Moss strained to remember these mundane details, the background noise of the thoughts she didn't want him to hear got noticeably louder. He asked her to slow down and walk through in detail.

When she complied, James visualized a wall in her mind thinning, becoming translucent and porous. He listened deeply and words slipped through under the primary narrative. James adopted a state of open receptivity and focused his attention on the secondary throughput. He heard, and saw spelled in his mind's eye as though he were viewing it on a Micromedium screen, the word "Subterraneum."

He took a gamble and interrupted her. "What's Subterraneum?"

He felt a cold chill go through her mind, then saw a rapid-fire sequence of word segments breaking through the surface. She strove to suppress them, and he struggled to make them out. From the jumble he discerned a fragment that looked like "-gresser," as well as "DII," "nested spheres," and the alphanumeric sequence "Tr8." He also saw and heard "Hackizen," which startled him and caused his scrutiny to waver momentarily.

James grabbed hold of himself to avoid any revelatory response to this familiar moniker, but Gillian exploited his split-second lapse and subverted her involuntary information dump with a strong intentional thought: "I said you promised not to do any subterranean excavation. You're prying into my subconscious. Stop it or we're done."

"Clever," thought James in return. "But it definitely wasn't Subterranean I saw. It was Subterraneum."

She yanked the array off her head, threw it on the table, and crossed her arms. The neurally interfaced interrogation apparently was over. James and Gillian stared at one another, absorbed in their own thoughts for several moments.

James left the room. He stuck his head into the observation booth and spoke to the group of expectant agents. "She's telling the truth. The explosion was a traumatic surprise. She had nothing to do with it and doesn't know who did."

"Anything else?" asked Renée, but James had already turned to leave and did not respond.

Noting the other agents' impatience, Chief Mills said to Renée, "Let him collect himself and prepare a report." Renée tapped her watch crystal but assented. When they turned their attention back to the young woman in the interrogation room, she was chain smoking again and looked considerably less composed.

James replayed the scraps of information in his mind. He grabbed a note pad and wrote:

Subterraneum
-gresser-
DII
Nested spheres
-TR8-
Hackizen

Inclusion of the final item on that list both intrigued James and put him in a bind. He had heard the pseudonym before, in connection with a different false-identity broker whose services he had utilized on behalf of someone dear to his otherwise rather barren heart.

"Baby sister," he said aloud, "Is there no end to the troubles I endure for loving you?"

Five years earlier, James arrested a man on a gun charge who disclosed during interrogation that he also worked as a broker in a false identity enterprise. The timing was serendipitous because, on command of the Malone family matriarch, James was in search of a quick means to secure Citizenship status for Wendy.

James's and Wendy's fathers were cousins. James's dad enjoyed an untarnished history as a full Citizen, like his forebears. Wendy's dad, discontent, hotheaded, and rebellious by nature, ran afoul of the law in his late adolescence, and was exiled to an Aggressive ghetto. There, he married Wendy's mother, also an Aggressive, and they conceived her. Wendy inherited their presumptive status but spent most of her childhood cloistered away with her great-grandmother, Evelyn Malone.

When Wendy was in her early teens, her parents were killed in a riot at the ghetto barricades during a period of unrest, and James's parents took her in.

She already bore the Malone surname and was related by blood, so informally adopting her did not attract undue attention. To formally adopt her would attract official scrutiny even of as orthodox a branch of so august a family. They needed to modify her records to make her a Citizen, both to facilitate the adoption and to secure for her a habitable future. Going through a formal process would have associated her with her radical Aggressive parents, which the Citizen Malones wanted to avoid at all costs. No point in resurrecting *that* scandal. They needed a little harmless subterfuge, and James was on the lookout for an opportunity.

Never one to waste the resources of a person whose freedom he controlled, James struck a bargain with the arrestee. James offered to bury the arrest and steer the authorities clear of the false identity enterprise, and the broker agreed in exchange to take Wendy as a client in the strictest confidence. The stakes were high for both men, assuring mutual destruction if either blinked, which neither did.

The man was shrewd, which James considered an essential job qualification. The downside was that this meant he was tight-lipped regarding his coconspirators. James's wiliest interrogation techniques extracted from the broker no more than that he worked with an individual known as Hackizen to execute the identity modification. The broker conveyed this claim with a cocked eyebrow, as though he were dropping a name James should know meant the transaction was safe. James had never heard of the individual and could not find him in any department database, but let on at the time as though he had.

He resisted the urge to dig deeper because exposing the ring, or even spooking the players, would jeopardize Wendy and himself. Once he received proof that Wendy's Citizenship records were in order, he let the matter drop.

Nevertheless, he was not one to forget a name. He had repeated the alias to Evelyn and Wendy, the former because she was the only person in the world who could charm James and the latter because she made her payment for the costly transaction contingent on hearing all the details. Of these, James was privy to embarrassingly few, but she accepted those he offered and funded the successful change to Wendy's official status.

Now, the same appellation had surfaced in the mind of Gillian Moss, a.k.a. Allison Flanders, the mystery barista, amidst an intriguing little trove of word bits. *Is it the same person?* James wondered. "Who are you, Hacky boy, and what are you up to?" he whispered.

Department procedure mandated he immediately disclose all these details to his DDI colleagues. However, the presence of Hackizen's moniker rendered proper protocol unacceptably risky for James. He wasn't handing Renée any maps that could lead back to his unlawful procurement of Wendy's papers and associated improprieties. "Out of the question," he proclaimed aloud.

He pored over the list of information from his interrogation of Moss, trying to decide whether to bury it. The problem with doing that was Moss knew he had seen at least some of it. If she ever disclosed that, it could cause problems.

The presence of Hackizen's sobriquet made sense given Moss's claimed profession, but that did not explain the other tantalizing items or Hackizen's relationship to them, if there was one.

James decided his itch to see where these clues led dovetailed with his need to have a plausible excuse for withholding them from his colleagues if they ever discovered he had. He soundproofed his office, deployed a scatterbug, and opened an encrypted Micromedium voice link to his back-channel DII contact, Agent Baikal.

"I had a higher duty to share information involving International with that agency and allow it, in its expertise, to determine its national security significance before releasing it to agents at Domestic, Your Honor, Madam Delegate, Madam Chief Executive, blah, blah," he rehearsed aloud as he examined his fingernails and waited for Baikal to reciprocate the link.

Any uncertainty James harbored about the wisdom of his choice dissipated when he summarized the situation to Baikal. The International operative was acutely interested in the intel and made James go over it several times until he was satisfied James had disclosed everything he knew. Then, the agent admonished James to keep the information secret and alert him if there were any talk of changing Moss's custody status before she was in International's clutches.

"I don't think that will be a problem," said James, savoring the scent of expanding career options.

"Excellent work, Agent Malone," said the DII operative. "I will be in touch."

James whistled to himself and read the list one last time for good measure. Then, he placed it in the shredder and began preparing a redacted report for his colleagues.

29

HALF A DAY. THAT WAS how long Leo remained at the office before he was crashing so hard he had to flee. For several weeks after he wrote the stellar draft in the conditional-permit case, Harlan cut him slack, but Leo's decline was precipitous. Everyone could see it but no one wanted to disrespect or embarrass him with a confrontation.

He bounced back and forth between harrowing efforts to wean off the drug and giving in to increasingly extreme binges. Every time he ran out of dope, he surfaced into a situation marked by greater chaos due to his neglect and misdirection of resources. Try as he might, the point always arrived when inhaling more of the toxic smoke felt necessary for survival. So he got high again.

After a night spent sucking on the pipe and wired into the twisted thoughts of Aggressives at the fetish sites, Leo grabbed an hour of sleep, got up, and hit the pipe anew. Before getting ready for work, he hopped on the Micromedium to see whether his favorite Aggressive, Domin8U, was around.

Half an hour later, he admonished himself. "You need to leave for the office in thirty minutes. Go shower." He picked up the pipe for a little energy. Five minutes later, he had cleaned out the rig and was sitting in a partial stupor, wired into the array and hyperfocused on scanning the room participants for someone whose aggressive energy he could tap and siphon.

He looked at the clock an hour later and said, "You're late. You needed to leave thirty minutes ago. Go!"

Then he hit the pipe again.

An hour later, he faced the fact that work was a lost cause and said to himself, "You have to call in sick." An hour after that, he ran out of dope again. He sheepishly called Harlan, left a rambling and choppy message, then hung up and set out to find his dealer.

He spent three hours caught in a drug eddy at the dealer's house, where people passed a pipe and held forth at length regarding subjects relative to which they imagined they held great expertise and penetrating insights. Eventually, the dealer needed to make a delivery and kicked everyone out. Leo took his bag of

Elidrine, secured on a burgeoning line of credit, and headed home. Blasted on the drug and sleep deprived for weeks, he was unfit to drive, which he demonstrated like a champ by getting into a minor collision on the way. Fortunately, the other driver was uninsured and did not want to make a police report. Leo proceeded home, his tailpipe dragging and sparking on the pavement.

Franz was yowling forlornly as Leo entered the apartment. The cat was emaciated. His fur had fallen out in large patches, and the only emotion he shared when touched was distress. Leo meant to feed him but decided he needed a hit to calm his crashing nerves first, so went to his den and sparked up the pipe. Inevitably, he redonned the array and navigated to his now favorite site. He had stopped questioning why he found the dark venue so compelling when high on Elidrine. The combination was intoxicating and anaesthetizing, a pain-obliterating rush. The two had become so linked in his mind that as soon as his lips touched the pipe he was thinking about the site and the extra punch it would give to the euphoric delirium.

Domin8U was not there, but another person hailed him, using the moniker GressUDown. Leo responded to the greeting, and the two formed a link. Leo found his presence familiar but GressUDown assured him they had never met. Leo marked it up to true Aggressives having a common neural pattern and delved into the connection.

GressUDown said he had an extensive collection of QFRI-enhanced recordings, which he described in brutal detail to Leo: prisoners of war, domestic violence, street fights, and beatings of institutionalized Vulnerables. He had recordings fitting every conceivable power imbalance, all of them capturing acts of abuse, the vicious rush of the persecutor, and the fear and pain of the recipient.

"I don't care," Leo said after a while, sick to his stomach and losing interest in the neural link as the descriptions mounted. "Whatever flips your switch. Nothing too extreme, please. No violence if you can get into anything shy of that."

James Malone sat wired into his array at the dedicated work station at the DDI Capital Region headquarters and drummed his fingers as he awaited confirmation from the tracer program. Preliminary data suggested that the person behind the moniker VulNeedsLesson might be none other than ...

A ring tone in his earpiece intruded. He dialed down the neural channel, doubled checked that the current session was still concealed from the department's monitoring and backup subroutines, and sent a text line:

> **GressUDown:** Be right back.
>
> **VulNeedsLesson:** OK

James's encrypted voice line alerted him he had an incoming call. He sealed the room, bug proofed it, and reciprocated the link.

"Agent Malone," came the caller's voice. "Cormack here."

"Yes, Mr. O'Brian," replied James, not concealing his annoyance.

"I know you are busy, so you'll excuse me for being brief and to the point?"

"I prefer it," replied James, with a sigh that said Cormack had already wasted his time with superfluous pleasantries.

"I'm calling to find out whether you've dug anything up on Leo Baksh."

James had agreed to this favor when Cormack requested it at Evelyn Malone's garden party, partly because his work was theoretically symbiotic with Cormack's confinement services and lobbying efforts, but mainly out of respect for the old man's longstanding friendship with his great-grandmother. This rationale was somewhat at odds with Cormack's request that James not tell her he was doing it. Then again, there was no point in agitating the old bag about things she was too senile to understand even if they were explained to her, he reasoned.

He didn't give a damn about Leo Baksh when Cormack made the request, but that changed when Baksh started showing up in his dreams. This baffled him at first. Now it looked as though the explanation for this uncomfortable phenomenon might soon converge with the other little detail he had all but nailed down.

"I told you I would let you know if and when I did, Mr. O'Brian," James said in a politer tone that he would have were this not Evelyn's friend. "Interrupting me delays my work."

"Yes, sorry," said Cormack sounding uncontrite, "but my need to incapacitate him has become rather urgent. He is serving as legal advisor to the classification board's chief adjudicator. This means Mr. Baksh is in control of the Board's developing law."

"I'm sure you overestimate his influence," said James.

"I don't think so," replied O'Brian. "Harlan Durell is a blustering wreck. Yet, I have learned he is about to author a groundbreaking decision authorizing Aggressive parolees to live among Citizens during their rehabilitation."

"Who cares?" said James.

"A lot of people care. I, like you, am not one of them. More crime means more lockups."

"It won't cause more crime. Read some statistics."

"I have read them and you're right, it probably won't. However, most people think it will, which is enough to get tougher sentencing laws passed."

"*Ka-ching*," said James, flatly. Cormack's fixation on money was tawdry, as far as James was concerned, when the investigation and prosecution of crimes involved so many more stimulating features. James eyed the screen and noticed his chat target was getting impatient.

> **VulNeedsLesson:** ???

James typed out a reply:

> **GressUDown:** Hold tight, digging up some good stuff.

"Sounds like you think Baksh is acting in your interests," James said to Cormack. "Why are you taking my time?"

"The point is he wrote that decision, which gives him power and clout at the appellate division. That's significant because the Board has accepted a more troubling case that argues incarceration of Aggressives and institutionalization of Vulnerables should be limited to extreme cases, and that the current rate of confinement impinges on fundamental rights to due process."

"No kidding?" said James. "Surely they wouldn't issue so radical a ruling on the heels of the conditional-permit case."

"It would be political suicide, I agree, but that doesn't mean they won't do it. It's the kind of decision worth sacrificing one's career to shove down my throat."

"You think Baksh is gunning for you?"

"No, not really. I think the man believes he is acting from principle. That doesn't matter. His involvement is threatening my family's prosperity. I tried to enlist him to help me find a profitable way to modify the confinement business at a sustainable pace, but he forwent the chance. I think he believes he can cut me off at the knees."

"Perhaps he isn't thinking about you at all," prodded James.

"That alone is reason to dislodge him from his position of influence."

James saw an icon flashing on his screen.

"I don't want to see the man suffer unduly," said Cormack. "I actually rather like him. But I want his appointment reversed and I want him out of the public debate."

James clicked on the icon and the tracer program confirmed the preliminary results. He could not help laughing. "I don't think Leo Baksh will be a problem for you much longer," he said cheerfully.

"And why is that?" asked Cormack, surprised by the sudden shift in James's demeanor.

"Sorry, that's classified information. You know about that, yes?"

"Naturally."

"This conversation never happened."

"What conversation?"

Click.

James reached over to reengage the neural link but stopped before his finger touched the screen. Wendy's face appeared in his mind, wounded and angry. He chewed on a fingernail, knowing that what he was about to do could cost him her trust, which was the one thing in life he valued for its own sake and not as a means to some other end. "She'll never know," he said aloud, and pushed the thought aside.

Taking a stomach-lurching hit of acrid smoke, Leo felt the neural signal charge back up and sensed the mind of GressUDown interpenetrate with his own.

"Listen," thought the GressUDown part of the shared mind, "I'm sorry to do this, but, I have to go."

Leo was disappointed. He found this person's energy potent and intriguing.

"I'd like to hook up again if you're interested," thought GressUDown.

"Sure," replied Leo, hitting the pipe again.

"Here's a couple hot recordings in the meantime," thought GressUDown, initiating a transfer protocol to send a copy of two files to Leo's Micromedium terminal.

"I can't view those unless I experience them with someone else in a link," thought Leo.

"So share them with someone," encouraged GressUDown. "These fit the range you described. They both involve Vulnerables being abused by Aggressives, but only through verbal and psychological coercion."

Even the thought of this turned Leo off, though he knew he would enjoy the rush it could trigger in a neurally joined Aggressive partner.

"Consider these an apology for bailing early and an invitation to hook up soon."

"OK," said Leo and signaled acceptance of the files.

"Until next time then," thought GressUDown.

"Ciao," Leo mentally verbalized in reply, "and thanks for the gifts."

"No problem. I intend to collect next time we meet," said GressUDown before his signal vanished.

When the session ended, Leo became conscious of his surroundings. He heard Franz's sorrowful voice calling from the other end of the apartment.

"Come here, Franz!" he yelled, scanning the chatroom participants. "I'll be there in a minute. Come here, baby."

Leo started to get up to check on the cat when he heard a ping on his Micromedium terminal. A message popped up:

> **Domin8U:** I'm pissed off and I need to thrash someone in here before I do it for real.

Leo redonned the array, swept everything off his desk, hit the pipe, and wrote:

VulNeedsLesson: `You're in luck.`

They formed a link and exchanged the usual preliminary banter, aligning their signals for maximum shared intensity.

The Domin8U part of the shared mind said, "I need to see something new."

Leo told him someone had given him a couple of recordings but he hadn't seen them and couldn't vouch for them. He repeated the descriptions and Domin8U said, "Could pack a charge. Let's see."

Leo launched the first recording. He felt a rush of aggression from Domin8U as the sequence began. The pleasure centers in Leo's brain lit up from the energetic pulse and he inhaled more of the evil smoke. As was his practice, Leo didn't pay attention to the canned sequence. He was wholly focused on Domin8U's aggressive response. Part way through, however, something tugged at the edge of his awareness and he turned his attention to the recording.

It depicted a man pinning a woman down amidst a tumble of boxes in a warehouse. He was screaming at her and she was begging him to let her go. Both wore elastic headbands around their skulls. Leo felt Domin8U's aggressive response intensify, then surge as the man in the recording raised a hand threateningly and both Leo and Domin8U palpably sensed the attacker's aggression and the Vulnerable's rising fear.

Intoxicating as Domin8U's aggressive energy was, Leo's shock was even greater as the thought dawned on him that this might be the recording at issue in Jeaneane's assault case. He saw Jeaneane in his mind's eye and shut the recording down in shame and horror.

He sensed amusement from Domin8U. "You know her?"

"No," said Leo. "But I don't like that one."

"OK," said Domin8U. "Let's look at the other one."

Leo said he wasn't sure he was up for that, but Domin8U plied him with fantasy scenarios accentuated with tightly focused bursts of aggressive energy. He said he still needed to vent his rage. Leo's neurons, juiced on Elidrine and primed by his previous session with this Aggressive, fired brightly at these words, a fact palpable to Domin8U. Domin8U amplified this response with provocative taunts and colorful threats. These triggered Leo's urge to outwit the jerk. When Domin8U sensed this upshift, he hit Leo hard with a surge of aggression he wasn't expecting, which first scared him, then made him angry.

Resolved to turn the tables and play this pig for his own gratification, Leo sparked the pipe once more, said, "OK, buddy," and launched the second recording.

Leo focused his attention on Domin8U, creating a layer of insulation so he could absorb the buffeting from the Aggressive's vengeful outbursts and ride the surge of his raw neural energy. He took no notice of the recording's early moments, other than a vague impression of a figure creeping down darkened hallways.

Domin8U's signal was strong and alert, as though he were poised to pounce. Leo attentively investigated this throughput, finding it both mesmerizing and disconcerting, until his attention snagged on a voice from the recording and he turned to observe it in greater detail.

The visual component depicted a person cloaked in a black, form-fitting bodysuit, prowling through an old house. A woman's voice echoed from beyond, faint and plaintive. Someone apparently was recording from behind and, though not visible, must have been wired to an array because Leo felt a rising neural presence bleed into and overlay the audiovisual signal.

Leo turned his attention back to Domin8U and felt his excitement rising, though he wasn't sharing any thoughts and nothing new was happening in the recording.

"Have you seen this before?" asked Leo.

"No, shh," replied Domin8U.

Leo felt Domin8U's aggression spike and, in the recording, saw a lock of dark brown hair whip around the corner at the end of the hall, with the stalker in hot pursuit and gaining ground.

Domin8U's aggression surged through Leo's mind so fiercely, Leo strained to prevent it from hurting him. Just when he thought he might have to abort the session, the pursuer in the recording turned into a cul-de-sac and kicked open a door at its end. It slammed ajar onto a room where a tall and well-muscled woman pinned a strong but smaller struggling woman's arms behind her back, as the black-clad figure wrestled to force a crude nodal array onto her cranium. The captive was head down and fighting, her thick, tangled hair thrashing as she squirmed and kicked in vain to stave them off.

Leo began to pull away from the scene but Domin8U projected a vibrant rush of energy and thought, "This is hot. Let's check out what happens together."

"You like it?" Leo asked, though he felt the answer already.

"Oh, yes," replied Domin8U.

Leo felt sick to his stomach but was transfixed by Domin8U's potent response. He appeared to be surrendering to his aggressive reaction. It was at once revolting and consuming.

The abuser, also a woman as Leo could now see, bound the prisoner's feet and snarled threats and cruelties into her ear. Though the audio signal was poor and choppy, Leo pieced together that this was a home invasion, that the perpetrators had stalked and haunted this poor woman for days to shatter her nerves before they broke into her house, and that her communication devices were disabled and exits blocked. She was at their mercy, and they clearly intended to show her none.

During this, the array on the captive apparently went live, because Leo felt her explosive emotional energy pour into the neural mix. She was terrified, furious, and sorrowful, an amazing temperamental range. There was something familiar about her, though the sequence was moving too fast for him to stop and think.

Somehow, the tormenters knew what the woman most feared and threatened her with it in escalating rhythm: to take and harm her loved ones, throw her unprotected into a crowd of violent Aggressives, strand her in a war zone to go mad amidst the cries of the injured and dying.

Leo felt the captive's rising terror when she recognized at the most intimate levels of her psyche that this attack was personal and targeted. As this thought ricocheted around her panicked mind, the captors activated a device attached to her array.

She screamed and pleaded for them to stop. By way of her recorded neural signal, Leo perceived that they were pummeling her with neural impressions from the victims of a massacre. As she reached the cusp of hysteria, the output merged into a mind-splitting signal, piercing the neural field like a deafening auditory feedback loop.

Leo convulsed in shock from the merest echo of this phenomenon. He had never encountered anything like it. The signal fanned out from the center of the captive's mind like soul-destroying radiation, wave after wave of violently malevolent neural energy, of a toxicity and magnitude Leo could barely tolerate even from his remote, thrice-removed distance. He could not imagine what she was experiencing as she wailed from her guts, shrieking and howling in demonic fury.

"That's enough," spoke a disembodied, deep-alto voice. "We have what we need."

Then, the captive stopped fighting and the tone of her emotional energy turned cold and deathly quiet as the weapon fell silent and she recognized the voice of her assailant. "You," she growled, her voice reflecting horrific violation and betrayal. Slowly, she lifted her head toward the person from whose vantage the recording was made, and shook the hair from her face.

There, staring at and into Leo through his joined mind's eye, her cheeks streaked with tears of sorrow and rage, her face set in an expression of stone-cold hatred, younger than he knew her but unmistakably herself, stood Anna.

Leo's shocked scream caught in his throat and gagged him. He pulled off the quantum array but before he ripped it loose, heard Domin8U think with glee, "Got ya."

Leo jumped up from the desk and knocked his chair over. Overcome with nausea, he lunged for the door and tripped over the chair, crashed to the floor, crawled to the toilet, and heaved up his guts. His throat burned as shock waves pummeled his mind and body. "Oh my God," he said. "Oh my God, what have I done?" He rocked back and forth, chewing on his hand, paralyzed with loathing, shame, and dread.

For a long while, he didn't move. After the initial impact subsided and his Elidrine intoxication lowered from the psychotic levels he had smoked, he became aware of his surroundings and flushed the toilet. He went to rinse his mouth but nothing came out of the tap. His addled brain puzzled over this until he realized the toilet tank wasn't filling either. The water must have been shut off because the bill had gone unpaid.

Leo reached for the hallway walls as he staggered to his bedroom. He sat on the edge of the filthy bed, panic rising in his chest. Thoughts tumbled through his mind: responsibilities he had neglected, wreckage he had caused, and the perils he faced as a result. Troubles rose like a dust storm.

He wandered around the apartment, surveying the damage. The kitchen stank of rotting garbage, dirty dishes, mildew, and cat urine and feces wafting in from the bathroom. He stood in self-absorbed turmoil, then realized Franz had neither food nor water. He went to the tap with the dry bowl and discovered once again that the service had been interrupted.

"Franz," he called in a dry, cracking voice.

"Franz," he called again, louder.

"Where are you, baby?" Waves of anxiety crashed and intermingled into a mounting dread.

"Franz!" he called again, his voice fearful. He knew this was not the way to coax a cat out of hiding, but his need for something to hold on to impelled him forward. He searched under the couch, in the clothes hamper, in the corners, in the linen closet. No Franz.

Back in the bedroom, he sat on the bed to collect himself and, to his great relief, noticed Franz curled up against his pillow, giving him a well-deserved dose of indifference.

"There you are," he said, his anxiety subsiding somewhat. He knew Franz would be cross, but even a cantankerous squawk would be music to Leo's fearful ears.

"I'm sorry, sweetheart" he said tenderly as he stroked the bony old back.

The cat's flesh was cold and unyielding.

"Franz?"

Leo yanked back the blanket. Franz lay frozen, clutching the sheet by his brittle old claws, eyes open, mouth peeled back in a tortured rictus. The poor animal had died. Cold, starving, thirsty, and alone, clinging to the space where his beloved Leo once slept before he went blind, deaf, and mad.

"No," Leo pled in sorrow. He put his hand on the stiff, cold body, fell onto the pillow, peered into his friend's dead eyes, and wept.

His tears turned to sobs, and his sobs into moans. He buried his faced in his pillow to muffle his cries and his moans gave way to feral screams. He roared as grief rained down and rolled over him like a celestial holocaust, crushing the life out of him and pounding him until all he could do was surrender to the truth of its enormity and bellow from the depths of his soul.

He wept for Franz's precious life, for the horrible injustice of having his flawless loyalty, love, and friendship rewarded with heartless abandonment, murderous neglect, and cold indifference as he lay dying.

He wept for Anna, for the wounds she had suffered all her life, for the ghastly violence she endured and hid from the world in solitary silence, for her courage in trusting him to help her, and for his unspeakable betrayal of her tender heart.

He wept for his utter failures as a human being, for time wasted, resources squandered, warnings unheeded, friendship dishonored, and good fortune taken for granted and burned into ashes like rubbish.

He wept for his lost innocence, incinerated in a glass pipe and transmuted into sordid filth by his craven descent into the darkness of his own shadow.

He screamed in impotent rage at the savage and unforgiving inexorability of time for pulverizing everything he held dear and everyone he would ever love irretrievably into the dust of oblivion.

He cried at the futility of his own sorrow, and the void he screamed it into.

He went over the preceding weeks, remembering Franz calling him, his voice sorrowful and lonely, beckoning Leo back from the brink to save them both.

He hadn't listened, and now it was too late.

Too late.

His sobs eventually subsided as the first wave of grief cudgeled him into submission. Tears came and went, new flows snaking down through salt-encrusted tracks with each aftershock. After several hours lying in a nearly catatonic state and staring into Franz's empty eyes, Leo wrapped his old friend in a piece of fine cloth.

He needed to talk to someone. He desperately wanted loving understanding from Jeaneane. Problem was, though she surely would understand his grief, he could not imagine telling her its cause. He decided to call John instead.

When he picked up the receiver, the phone was dead, as was his mobile device, which used the same account. The apartment was so cold he could see his breath in the twilight seeping through his window. He reached for the lamp to determine what was wrong with the heater and got his answer in the form of continued darkness. No power. He had aligned the billing cycles for his utilities to fall near payday, then smoked up all his resources. Cold and alone in the dark with his dead cat. He almost laughed at the extremity.

All cried out and finally hurting more from the damage of his drug abuse than he was from withdrawal, he left the pipe alone and drifted into fitful sleep.

He woke every couple of hours and lay in the dark, remembering Franz's death, the sickening QFRI recording of Anna's abuse, and the wreckage of his life. This was how he passed the night, between waking moments of despair and jagged stints of troubled sleep, haunted by foreboding shades, and portents of calamity.

30

AFTER MONTHS OF EXPERIMENTING AT the social sites and careful planning, the hacktivists finalized their strategy and scheduled a virtual meeting to execute their mission. Liam mentally checked off names as each of his coconspirators appeared in the secret Micromedium venue and hailed one another.

All but one. As the minutes ticked beyond the designated hour, they got nervous.

> `**Infiltr8org:** Where's Subterraneum?`

No one knew. They compared notes and agreed their compatriot's absence was troubling. Sleeperagent thought they should abort. Aggresserable disagreed. They had trained extensively for this run, and everything was in place. Calling it off could set them back for weeks. By then, the DII might have adjusted the security infrastructure or protocols in a manner that made compromising the hub impossible.

They all knew there was another consideration motivating Aggresserable's argument. After his initial foray into the shield, Liam had disregarded the frightening dream that followed, and had formed another nondual link with a sentinel. Hackizen had tunneled through it to the DII hub. He had spent the duration of that connection exploring and mapping the DII mainframe, then spent weeks with the others devising program code for his arm of the mission.

Rather than abating, Liam's nightmares had worsened to include multiple entities scrutinizing him. "You're on their radar, Tr8," Hackizen had argued. "They have your neural scent. They've probably been dreaming about you too. Plus, their minds are linked, so maybe they are all dreaming about you or overtly discussing you. You shouldn't have gone in again after your first dream. Someone else must do it now. Too risky for you to go back in, not just for you, but for all of us, and for the mission itself."

Much as he hated it, Liam knew Hackizen was right, and the group decided another hacker should take over the job.

The others continued training in neural espionage at the social sites, forming nondual links with other minds, tunneling through the entangled arrays, and commandeering the targets' computers.

Aggresserable had the greatest success at forming nondual connections. More than the others, Aggresserable could achieve mental silence sufficiently complete to merge centers of consciousness with the target and entangle their arrays for one of the others to tunnel through.

The problem was, Aggresserable didn't have the others' stamina. Aggresserable's signal faded faster than theirs. They could compensate for this by boosting the output from Aggresserable's array, up to a point. To everyone's dismay, rather than gaining stamina over time, Aggresserable appeared to lose it. No one felt comfortable asking too many questions about why this might be, since it was critical they remain anonymous in case their ranks included a double-agent, one of them suffered arrest or counter-espionage, or someone intercepted their communications.

Their objective was ambitious to the point of absurdity: they had to outwit the neural shield, establish a stable channel into the hub, and keep it disguised long enough to use it.

Here was the plan they developed: Aggresserable would do as Tr8 had, namely penetrate the DII sentinel shield, travel to its inner layer, and form a nondual link with one of the sentinel sources. Tr8 would remotely monitor Aggresserable's Micromedium terminal and adjust the settings as necessary to keep the QFRI neural field projection strong and stable.

Meanwhile, Hackizen would remotely monitor Aggresserable's terminal and communicate with Tr8 to determine when Aggresserable had established a nondual link. Then, Hackizen would tunnel through the entangled arrays, penetrate the hub, implant a fictitious agent identity, and find the current passcode sequence for gaining overt access to the hub.

Once he completed these tasks, he would transmit the information to Sleeperagent, who would approach the sentinel shield from the outside, using the passcode and fatuous identity, and formally request access to the hub. If this succeeded and the sentinels approved a data stream through the shield, Sleeperagent would tether it to a Micromedium node for future access, power down, and disappear. From inside the hub via the quantum tunnel, Hackizen would ensure the data stream was secure and would insulate it from the DII's ongoing validation subroutines. Then, he, too, would power down and signal Tr8 that the hardwire was in place. Tr8, in turn, would remotely power down Aggresserable's array, and they would hold their breath for a few days before trying to access the hub through the stable data stream connection.

Subterraneum had practiced all the roles in this scenario and was prepared to provide backup in case anyone could not fulfill his or her function. Subterraneum also had agreed to monitor all communications between the hacktivists and hold vigil for issues they might not catch when focused on their individual tasks. Subterraneum, however, was missing in action.

Time was of the essence because the game could change without notice and Aggresserable's ability was fading. They argued at length about the range of possible reasons for Subterraneum's absence, from the mundane to the sinister. Aggresserable finally called the question:

> **Aggresserable:** If you want me to do this, it must be now. You have to trust me. I can't wait any longer. If we don't do it now, one of you will have to do my part.

In the end, they decided to proceed, though they had their reservations.

Aggresserable purged all verbal thought and piloted the QFRI signal to the DII quantum neural shield, then deftly maneuvered through the outer layers and waited within the inner sphere until the sentinels executed a shift change. As the source whose shift was ending faded and the sphere began to close the resulting breach, Aggresserable aligned signals with the sentinel's replacement source to form the entangled link at the beginning of the sentinel's eight-hour shift.

Liam remotely monitored Aggresserable's signal and communicated with Hackizen as the run unfolded. The signal remained strong throughout the first stage, and Liam did not have to boost its output, to everyone's relief. When Aggresserable's terminal showed the signal had achieved stasis, Liam concluded that a nondual link with the target sentinel source had been established.

Via the quantum neural signal, Aggresserable's and the target's minds had become one, centered on the same point of consciousness. The physical arrays the quantum fields streamed through became entangled at the quantum level and were not two, despite the physical separation on the macro level.

> **Infiltr8org:** Hardware entangled. Proceed.

Upon receiving this welcome report, Hackizen executed the tunnel, and via the entangled arrays, connected to the DII hub. Relieved to find that the programming architecture had not changed significantly, he located the current passcode, accessed the agent database, and implanted a fictitious profile for the identity Sleeperagent would use as a disguise. Reasonably satisfied he had achieved these tasks undetected, Hackizen transmitted the passcode to Sleeperagent and gave the go-ahead.

On cue, Sleeperagent hailed the sentinel shield with the passcode. The outer field responded immediately and allowed Sleeperagent to penetrate the outermost mantle. Sleeperagent performed the role flawlessly and, after two rounds of colloquy, was floating in the shield's menacingly quiet inner membrane.

Hackizen's connection to the hub flickered.

Hackizen: The tunnel is destabilizing.

Infiltr8org: Stand by.

Sweat dripping down his forehead, Liam willed himself to remain focused and prohibited himself to rush. Carefully, he remotely boosted the output from Aggresserable's array, notch by notch, until the signal regained stasis.

Hackizen: Better.

Inside the shield's inner layer, Sleeperagent felt the sentinels go on alert. Intentional search beams crisscrossed through the field. Automatically implementing the protocol the hackers had rehearsed for such a contingency, Sleeperagent silenced all thought and waited. Eventually, the atmosphere cleared and the inner sentinels performed the final round of scrutiny.

Hackizen monitored the process from inside the hub as the shield sentinels accessed the agent database and verified Sleeper's fictitious identity against the fraudulent profile he had implanted.

Everyone held their breath and, whether they believed in a supreme being or not, prayed like hell.

After several tortured minutes, the joined mind of the sentinel shield's inner layer informed the fictional agent Sleeper portrayed that access was approved. A conduit emerged from the center of the sphere, pierced the shield's layer, connected to the Micromedium node coordinates Sleeperagent provided, and went live.

When the task was complete, Hackizen remotely dialed down Sleeper's array, and Sleeper's neural projection vanished from the sentinel shield.

Sleeperagent: Data stream established. I'm out.

Her moniker disappeared from the virtual meeting place as well.

Working inside the hub via the entangled arrays, Hackizen launched a program to insulate the data stream from the DII hub's troubleshooting and verification systems, then severed the tunneled connection.

Hackizen: I think we've got it.

Liam raised a fist in victory, but before he had finished the gesture, his terminal flooded with alarms. He scrambled to figure out what was happening and alerted Hackizen.

Infltr8org: I'm detecting an anomaly in Aggresserable's signal.

Hackizen: I'm out.

Just then, Liam's terminal registered a massive power surge from Aggresserable's terminal, and the signal went dead. Momentarily stunned, he hesitated before executing the agreed response to anomalous behavior, which was to physically disconnect from the Micromedium. He regained his senses after a beat but it was too late. A klaxon told him his terminal had been compromised.

Panicked, he directed a warning to Hackizen:

Infltr8org: `I'm hit!`

But Hackizen was gone.

Liam ripped the cable out of the Micromedium node and crammed equipment into his case. He had carefully chosen the site for his uplink. Another shuttered office building in an obsolete industrial park. There were no residences nearby and he was confident his foray into the decaying commercial graveyard drew no notice. Only kids on drunken rampages and homeless people passed this way.

These facts yielded little comfort. The DII had traced his signal. Liam strained to quell his rising fear. He wiped the hair back from his sweating brow and surveyed the room. Seeing no stray items, he grabbed the handle of his equipment valise and beat a hasty exit. No telling how soon the DII goons would arrive with their truncheons and torture devices.

Liam furtively darted down the halls and out of the building and ran to the car he had hidden in some brush overtaking an adjacent lot. Deciding speed was paramount, he skipped the usual scans, and screeched out of the lot and neighborhood as fast as he could drive.

"Get rid of everything," he instructed himself aloud to calm his nerves. He pulled over and retrieved from the rear floorboard a dual-pouched bag that, when the contents were mixed, produced a caustic, quick-set cement. He broke the seal and mixed the ingredients, then ripped open the end and tossed it into his equipment case along with some lead weights and a powerful magnet to scramble his drives.

As he started to close the case, he noticed an important item that it should not contain: the DNA-degrading fogger, which in his haste he had forgotten to deploy.

"Shit!"

He slammed the valise shut, shook it violently to distribute the cement, and secured it with sturdy steel mesh straps. Minutes later he drove onto a bridge he had preselected for the purpose during more lucid moments and, at the center of the span, hurled the case over the rail into the swift channel that ran beneath.

Riding the slight relief this act afforded, Liam turned for home. On the way, his head clearer now, he mentally revisited his exit from the hack site. He was reasonably sure he had collected everything. He had tunneled through to a remote Micromedium intersection when he hooked up. Even though the DII had traced his signal to his terminal, that didn't mean they knew where it was physically located.

Even if they found their way to the room, there would be no fingerprints.

The chances of them finding any DNA were miniscule. Skin flakes at best, intermixed with filth and debris. He was probably safe.

"Liam, it's me. Pick up if you're there."

Wendy crouched on the steps below the terrace on Evelyn Malone's estate, holding her mobile device with one hand and wrapping her midriff with the other arm, as though to keep herself from blowing apart.

"Liam!" she shouted.

"I'm here," came the startled and ragged voice on the line. "Shh. I'm here."

Wendy burst into sobs.

"What's happened?"

Relieved to make contact, Wendy cried a while longer, then wiped her nose, heaved a deep breath, and said, "Great-Grandmother is dead."

Liam was silent.

"Liam?"

"I'm sorry. I'm just ... in shock. She seemed so well last time I saw her."

"She *was* well. I went with her to her last checkup. She was in excellent health. Francesca found her when she brought her morning tea."

"I'm so sorry, Wendy."

Wendy fell silent for so long that Liam asked if she was still there.

She hissed into the phone, "Something isn't right, Liam."

"How do you mean?"

"Francesca found her fully clothed and lying on top of her bed, which had not been turned down. The doctor said he thinks she died of a massive stroke." Wendy paused, then continued in a squeak, "Her *face*, Liam," she covered her mouth until she could finish, "she looked terrified."

"I imagine a stroke would be scary."

"The expression on her face was beyond fear." Wendy stifled sobs. "It was like she was staring into hell. I've never seen such horror, not even in movies."

Static prickled Liam's skin. "It couldn't be," he whispered.

"What?"

"When does the doctor think she died?"

"Based on her body temperature, about 2 a.m."

Liam didn't respond.

"Which is part of why it's so weird that she was dressed. She always gets into her night clothes by nine."

Wendy thought the call might have disconnected. "You still there?"

"Was there was any strange ... equipment near your great-grandmother when Francesca found her?"

"Equipment?" Wendy laughed despite her grief. "Like a vibrator?"

"No," Liam snapped, his disregard of her joke and shortness of temper whipping Wendy to attention. "Like a wired device for someone's head."

"You mean one of those quantum interface things?"

"Yes."

"Not that I've heard. I rather doubt it, why?"

"Just a crazy idea. The timing and your description of—"

Liam was cut off by the sound of splintering wood.

"Liam!" she screamed.

The connection had been severed.

Wendy called Patrice on the way to her car, intent on driving straight to Liam's. Alarmed, Patrice made her remain stationary and explain the situation. Wendy hoped for words of comfort and perhaps an offer to accompany her to Liam's. Patrice said instead, "Wendy, listen to me. I need you to trust me and do as I say, even though you don't know why I'm saying it. Do not go anywhere near Liam's apartment. Go take a snapshot of your great-grandmother's bedroom with your mobile and come directly to my place."

Wendy stopped in her tracks, incredulous. "What the hell?"

"Stay calm and do as I say. Right. Now."

The final order was delivered in a dictatorial tone unprecedented in Wendy's experience with Patrice's already forceful personality. She shivered.

"I'll see you in ten minutes," she said, numb from overload. True to her word, she knocked on Patrice's door shortly thereafter with the snapshots of Evelyn's room in tow.

Patrice ushered Wendy in. After she closed the door, she scanned the area with a device for detecting electromagnetic fields and sonic wave patterns, but saw no signs of surveillance. Wendy bore witness in shocked disbelief.

"Come on," said Patrice, pulling her toward the bedroom. Once inside, she deployed a device she called a scatterbug and questioned Wendy about every detail of Evelyn Malone's death and her conversation with Liam.

Satisfied Wendy had disclosed everything she knew and could remember, Patrice reflected for several minutes, then took her hand. "There are things I need to tell you. I've tried to insulate you from this, but I think you may already be unwittingly involved. You may even be in danger."

Wendy raised her brows and laid fingertips on her sternum.

"You may be what brought us together. Even if you weren't, we have you in common, which could be just as bad for you."

Wendy started to speak, but Patrice gestured for silence.

"For the past year, I have been part of an anonymous group of activist hackers that has trained together to compromise the Department of International Intelligence Micromedium hub. We did exactly that, last night."

Wendy regarded Patrice wide-eyed a moment and started to run with the joke, but trailed off when Patrice's expression did not waver.

"Great-Grandmother was involved how?"

"I don't know that she was. But there are some things I know and things you've said that make me think she might have been one of us, implausible as that might seem."

"You can't be serious."

"I am serious."

Patrice told Wendy about each of the hacktivists' monikers, skills, and limitations. She described the history of their acquaintances, the development of their plan, Subterraneum's disappearance, the decision to proceed, Aggresserable's role and issues with stamina, as well as Infiltr8org's leadership role and seemingly limitless wealth.

"The run last night seemed to go off without a hitch," said Patrice. "We established a stable, insulated data stream through the shield and I powered down and disconnected. But I got a message from Hackizen ten minutes later telling me Infiltr8org had reported an anomaly. Hackizen didn't stick around to find out what it was. He unplugged, and neither Tr8 nor Aggresserable has surfaced."

Wendy repressed the urge to lambaste Patrice for undertaking the suicidal mission, but she knew about Patrice's activist heart, and the deed was already done.

They lay together, side by side, and sorted through the details. Wendy had confided in Patrice that her Citizenship status was forged. Patrice had persuaded her to arrange a meeting with the false-identity broker James had hired to assist her, because one of Patrice's political associates desperately needed such services. When Patrice made the arrangements with the broker, they also conducted a cryptic exchange through which she telegraphed political proclivities and technical expertise the broker suspected his contact, the person known as Hackizen, would find intriguing.

The broker facilitated a virtual meeting between Patrice, who introduced herself as Sleeperagent, and Hackizen. After interrogating her to his satisfaction, Hackizen told her an activist group was forming to explore possible uses of Micromedium technology for opposing and exposing some of the government's covert atrocities in hopes of triggering more widespread public resistance.

Wendy listened to Patrice's story in growing distress.

"Who else knew about your Citizen-status forgery?" asked Patrice.

Wendy told her that James had arranged it, Evelyn had funded it, and Liam—her former lover and dear friend—had been her confidante.

From these facts, along with the timing of Evelyn's death, Liam's frightful disappearance, the questions Liam asked Wendy right before he disappeared, and what they knew about each of them—Liam's wealth and rebelliousness, and Evelyn's vibrant mind, complex perspective, sheer chutzpah, and age—Patrice and Wendy speculated that Evelyn Malone was Aggresserable and Liam O'Brian was Infiltr8org.

It also appeared that the lynchpin was not Infiltr8org, unbeknownst probably even to him. The grouping and operation hinged on Hackizen. Each participant, they hypothesized, had met him by way of their association with Wendy, though she had no idea she had served as a catalyst.

"Supposing that's accurate," said Wendy, "Then we know who three of you are, and we know Hackizen is who you have in common, all by way of knowing me. But who is Subterraneum?"

Patrice said, "Must be someone who knew Hackizen by means other than through you. Or maybe one of the others brought Subterraneum in. Either way, he or she apparently was a mole."

"Or maybe a torture victim."

Patrice winced in acknowledgement of this chilling possibility. Though each thought it, neither voiced the fear that Liam might be suffering a similar fate, as if saying it aloud might increase the prospects of its truth.

Shifting back to the evidence at hand, Patrice transferred the images of Evelyn Malone's bedroom from Wendy's mobile device to her Micromedium terminal and began manipulating them with filters and effects to accentuate contrasts and details. After several modifications, she said, "There." She cropped and enlarged a section of carpet between the bed and the back wall, where a tapestry hung. Men's shoe prints and linear depressions were clearly visible in the enhanced image.

"Couldn't those be artifacts of the filters you used?" asked Wendy.

"No. The filters enhance what's already there. Those are not random shapes. Someone dragged something from the wall and picked it up."

"Something?"

"Someone, would be my guess," said Patrice softly. She pecked Wendy lightly on the lips to show her sympathy.

"But the drag marks, if that's what they are, start right at the wall," said Wendy.

"I agree. They look as though they came through the wall."

Patrice clicked around the image. "Have you ever peeked behind that tapestry?"

"Not that I recall," answered Wendy.

Her curiosity piqued, Patrice said, "How well do you know Francesca?"

"I'm not especially close to her, but Great-Grandmother trusted Francesca with her life. Great-Grandmother was shrewd as a snake."

"Yes," said Patrice, and a tear rolled down Wendy's cheek. Patrice wiped it away and handed her a disposable phone.

Wendy left the signal-blocking bubble of Patrice's apartment, went to the crowded art bazaar, and called Evelyn Malone's personal assistant at her private number. After exchanging comforts and confirming that Francesca was alone, Wendy asked her to go into Evelyn's room and peek behind the tapestry.

Francesca reported that there was a flaw in the wall. She poked at it and discovered that a rectangular piece had been hastily patched. At the center was a three-eighths-inch circular hole, and at each of the rectangle's four corners was a smaller hole. The holes were filled but the material inside them was slightly concave to the surrounding surface, as though patching plaster had shrunk when it dried.

"Like a switch box was there before?"

"Yes, like that," said Francesca.

"Do you know what used to be there?"

"No."

Wendy weighed whether to disclose more or probe. Francesca's tone was serious and unsurprised, which told Wendy she at least realized discretion was in order. Wendy decided not to push. Instead, she asked whether there were any other features behind the tapestry.

Francesca said there were seams in the shape of a larger rectangle, "About the size of a door frame," she said with a slight note of conspiratorial confidence.

"How odd," said Wendy.

"Quite."

"Can you give it a little push?"

The line was silent a moment before Francesca said, "Solid as the rest of the wall, I'm afraid."

Wendy thanked Francesca and asked whether she would have a problem forgetting they'd spoken.

"Last I recall seeing or hearing from you was when we said goodbye this afternoon," Francesca replied.

"Thank you, Francesca."

"I'm sorry I couldn't be more help."

Wendy considered a few sly replies, but her sober grief washed away the spy-intrigue drama and she simply said goodbye.

Back in bed at Patrice's and cloaked in electronic scramblers, Wendy and Patrice reviewed everything they knew.

"What now?" asked Wendy.

"I don't know," confessed Patrice. "For the moment, all we can do is wait."

Though she knew it would be pointless, Wendy begged Patrice to abandon any thoughts of pursuing the hacktivists' mission further.

Patrice reacted angrily at first: "After the sacrifices it took to get this far? The death of Evelyn, and Liam's abduction?"

Wendy regarded her in disbelief. "You didn't know either of them. Those are *my* losses. How dare you?"

"They are my losses, too," Patrice said more gently, "though of a different kind. I'm sorry I spoke like that. I'm scared too."

"I knew Great-Grandmother was near the end of her life," said Wendy, "but to go like this? So ... horribly."

"She chose this, Wendy. We all knew this could be the last thing we did. She lived one hell of a life. If she was Aggresserable, she chose a spectacular closing act. If I have anything to do with what follows, she'll go down in history as the hero who gave her life to pull the mask off the world's worst state terrorist enterprise, festering under the Citizenry's noses right here at home."

"I'd rather have her," said Wendy, "and now I'm supposed to lose you too? I can raise a toast to the revolution and the death of everyone I ever loved with a single glass. How economical."

"Thanks for the vote of confidence," parried Patrice, "but I'm hoping it won't come to that. The most urgent matter is to locate Liam and figure out if we can help him without compromising the mission."

Wendy dropped her jaw with open incredulity.

"He wouldn't have it any other way," said Patrice. "I can assure you. If we screwed the mission to try and spring him somehow, he would consider all our lives to be failures. In the end, they would get us all anyway. The mission comes first."

Wendy covered her eyes. "Liam."

"Don't torture yourself. We will find him somehow," she said, though she sounded unsure.

"And?" asked Wendy.

"I don't know yet. Like I said, for now, we wait."

Wendy turned to her, "And to think how conflicted he was about meeting you, when all along you didn't know you already knew each other."

"Anonymously and in a limited capacity, but yes, that's oddly true."

"A capacity that placed both your lives at risk and may have cost him his," Wendy shot back like a curse. "Pretty intimate. Not exactly strangers."

They regarded one another and contemplated the web of entanglements that had existed between and among the three of them and who knew how many others for months without any of them knowing it.

They held one another. Made love. Slept a few hours. Eventually, they spoke of practicalities, agreeing to part temporarily for Wendy's safety in case the DII found a path back to Patrice. Patrice instructed Wendy on how to engage in encrypted Micromedium voice communication so they could talk unsurveilled.

"You have to be strong for us," she admonished Wendy.

Wendy stood in the doorway and gazed into her lover's eyes. What could she say? Bereft of wisdom and unable to summon words of comfort that sounded like anything other than trite aphorisms, she hugged Patrice, turned resolutely, and strode away, praying that their lives would not be forfeit for this reckless mission she had unwittingly helped launch.

31

Leo awoke in a cold sweat, tortured to the edge of madness by the neural effects of the Elidrine abuse and withdrawal. He had sucked the last of the residue from his pipe when fists began pounding on his front door.

"DDI! We have an arrest warrant! Open up now!"

Leo's first thought was about the illegal drugs. He threw his pipe under the bed, then slipped and staggered over debris as he made his way to the door in a panicked blur. When he reached the front hall, he realized he was nude, having made it halfway through changing from one dirty outfit into another. He turned back for a robe, but the pounding became more insistent and a man's voice shouted, "Open up or we'll break down the door!"

"I'm naked," Leo said meekly.

The voice, stern but somewhat less ferocious, said, "Just open the door, Mr. Baksh."

Leo unlocked the door to three officers—two women and one man—pointing two guns at his chest and one at his head.

Leo raised his hands. Emaciated, dehydrated, naked, trembling in fear and clearly unarmed, Leo presented no threat of resistance or flight. The officers pointed their weapons toward the ceiling and advised him to step back. They followed him in and demanded he sit on the couch.

Agent Drey interrogated Leo while the others, a woman with an unruly mane of frizzy curls and a man with steely grey eyes who felt oddly familiar to Leo, tore apart every corner of his apartment and seized piles of his belongings. Drey asked him if he was intoxicated. Jacked up on his last hit of Elidrine, Leo's judgment and intellect were eclipsed by both fear of drug charges and an irrational belief he could talk his way through the situation, so he said no.

Drey was a skilled interrogator. After a half hour of questions, Leo began to understand that he was in their crosshairs because of illegal Micromedium activity, not drugs. Drey turned on the charm, sharing with Leo that she too had earned her way from Vulnerable to Citizenship status. She told him he seemed like a good guy and that she wanted to help him get the mess straightened out.

All she needed was a clear sense of the situation so they could resolve what surely must have been a misunderstanding.

Still high, Leo fell for this ruse despite his legal training, neatly tying a prosecutorial noose around his own neck. By the end of the interrogation, he had confessed everything.

Agent Drey placed him under arrest. Soberer now, Leo asked for legal representation but it was too late to do him any good.

Eight hours later, after Leo had been fingerprinted, photographed, and left to rot in a filthy holding tank equipped with a cement bench, stainless steel toilet, and a constant stream of ice cold air, a guard unlocked the door. "He bailed you out."

"Who?"

"How the hell should I know, asshole? Someone."

The guard directed Leo down a series of dimly lit hallways and through several secure doors, releasing him into a more colorful and picturesque reception area, where he found John Hanes waiting. Overwhelmed by the ordeal, he hadn't thought about how grey, cold, filthy, and dull his environment had been until he stepped back into the free world with its rich textures, colors, and sparkling shine. It was like passing from a black-and-white photographic negative into a color print.

Neither John nor Leo spoke. Together, they walked to John's car (whose seats Leo found unbelievably cozy) and made their way to Leo's apartment. Upstairs, John stood in the wreckage of Leo's living room and regarded the wraith that had possessed the life of his old friend. John's face bore an expression blending extreme seriousness, disappointment, and embarrassment. Or perhaps pity. Leo could not meet his eye.

John moved some debris so he could sit on the couch, and asked Leo to tell him how he had come to this terrible juncture. Leo cleared another space and sat, telling him about the downward spiral he'd ridden on opiates and Elidrine to his current state of depletion and depravity. John regarded Leo with intense scrutiny.

As Leo finished, John remained still with a hand over his mouth and examined him. After an uncomfortable interval, he finally spoke: "We need to get your utilities and means of communication restored. Then, you need to get into inpatient addiction treatment. You'll need an advocate."

Leo opened his mouth to speak, but John continued.

"I take it you've burned through all your money."

"Yes," Leo confessed, ashamed.

"You'll need a substantial chunk of cash to get on your feet. I can loan you some, but you better call your folks or Jeaneane or anyone else you can think of. Like, now."

He handed Leo his phone and crossed his arms.

"Now, Leo."

Leo tried to think of a way around it but could find no options. Tremulously, he called his parents. To his tearful relief and deep shame, they responded with love and concern. They said they would wire one hundred credits to John, lest there were liens on Leo's account.

Leo told John he could not call Jeaneane.

"Why the hell not?"

"Please don't make me explain," said Leo. "I cannot ask Jeaneane for help right now."

John eyed Leo with suspicion but honored the request until Leo was stabilized enough to survive having the full truth throttled out of him. "Get me a copy of your bills," said John. "While I get you hooked back up, find your health insurance policy and the customer service number so you can get a treatment referral."

Easier said than done amidst the wreckage, but Leo complied.

Hours later, they stood under a willow tree at a nearby park that Leo had chosen as a burial site for Franz, and John rested a hand on Leo's shoulder as he wept.

As Leo wiped away the last of this round of tears on the back of his hand, John glanced at his watch and said, "It's time to go." The two friends, one tall and strong and the other crumpled and weak, walked back to John's car. As John pulled away from the curb, Leo flipped on the macroaudio A newscast was underway:

"... arrested by the Department of Domestic Intelligence on charges of distributing recordings of his own client's abuse.

"Amidst demonstrations decrying the arrest as a politically motivated smear maneuver, DDI Agent Drey described the crime, which purportedly involves startling new technology that allows perpetrators to feed together off the victim's mental anguish."

The segment cut to the voice of Lauren Drey:

"The technology captures an impression of the victim's mind during the abuse such that the criminal directly experiences her suffering. It is a parasitic consumption of the victim's person or identity."

A reporter asks:

"Advocate Baksh participated in the illicit experience of an assault on Anna Dao?"

Drey responds:

"He did more than that. He distributed these enhanced abuse recordings and joined with others to relive Ms. Dao's abuse together for illicit gratification. Unfortunately for him, one of his distributees was an agent of our department."

The segment cut back to the main newscaster.

"For more on this new technology, we're joined by Dr. Felix Binhoff from—"

John snapped off the audio.

"Anna?" John said in disbelief. "Anna? Really, Leo?"

Leo told John how he had come into possession of the recording and explained that he did not know its contents before he shared it because one must experience the QFRI-enhanced recordings in a neurally joined state, and the donor had not viewed it with Leo before logging off.

John snickered coldly. "Classic setup. How could you be so fucking stupid?"

Leo flinched, both over John's nasty tone and the chilling possibility he had voiced.

John softened his voice somewhat, saying, "I'm sorry, Leo. I know you don't need that. I'm worried about you. But I'm also angry."

"I understand."

"I will stand by you through this every way I can," said John. "But I can't protect you from my staff without resigning my post. I would consider doing that if I thought it could help you, but someone else would step up. Then you and I would both be out of a job."

Leo reflected on John's words, realizing that among the many disasters that lay beyond the immediate crisis, his career was over.

"No point in that," Leo replied. "What the hell am I going to do?"

"For starters," said John, pulling into a parking spot, "Get your head straight. We're here."

John escorted Leo into the treatment center.

"I'll get your place cleaned up and find you an advocate while you're here," said John as he hugged Leo goodbye.

Leo considered protesting but he knew he had no choice but to accept John's assistance if he had any hope of survival.

"Thanks."

John held Leo by both sides of his head and pressed their foreheads together. "You need help. Let these people guide you." He kissed Leo on the cheek and left.

Leo took a long shower and changed into clean clothes the staff provided. A nurse gave him something to calm his anxiety and he crawled into bed.

The next morning, he awoke disoriented and gradually remembered the catastrophe underway. He walked to the front desk where a pleasant but stern nurse told him meetings would start at 7:45 a.m. in the main conference room. And no, caffeine was not allowed.

Sipping a wan cup of decaf coffee, Leo went back to the front desk to get directions to the site for the first meeting. The nurse was busy at a filing cabinet and said she'd be right there. While her back was turned, Leo spied a copy of the *Capital Times* at her work station. He turned it to the front page. In large, bold font, John's paper blared the morning's scandal: Baksh Arrested for Mind-Raping and Pimping own Vulnerable Client Dao.

The nurse caught him. "Now, now, none of that. They shouldn't have let that in," she said. In a quieter voice and with a wink, she said, "I'll make sure none of the other patients see it."

Leo stared at her, numb with despair. "It's over," he said. "My life is over."

She patted his hand. "Don't jump to conclusions, baby. Sometimes endings are beginnings in disguise."

Leo gave her the once-over and thought she must be insane or stupid.

"I'm not saying you aren't about to weather the mother of all storms," she said. "But it won't last forever, and storms can be cleansing."

Leo was speechless.

"Give it time," she said softly.

32

IN A TWIST OF BENEVOLENT irony common to recovering addicts, Leo's total defeat created the opening for his rebirth into a person fully alive, both humbled and empowered, relieved of petty, self-centered obsessions and released into a communion with the creative power of life itself.

During treatment, Leo made a few feeble attempts to rationalize his behavior or portray his life circumstances as incomprehensibly and uniquely intractable. To his surprise and gratitude, the counselors found his machinations most pedestrian and dispatched them deftly. Exposed and vulnerable, he trusted that his guides were equipped not with platitudes as he had feared, but with tools and insights borne of years living through life's travails in sobriety and helping others awaken from their addictive death spirals to embrace life in its full measure and on its own terms.

He emerged from treatment after four weeks, his mind clear, bloodstream clean, and full of hope that his total collapse might, indeed, prove to be a beginning in disguise. When he turned the key to his apartment, he found the place immaculate. A bouquet on the dining table filled the air with the fresh scent of hope. A card read:

> Congratulations old friend. I'm proud of you. Stay strong. Go to a meeting. Call me. There is work to do. John.

The final sentence poked a pinhole in Leo's dirigible of relief, reminding him that consequences set in motion before he entered treatment had barely begun to play out. Leo turned his attention to the papers that had accumulated during his absence. Mercifully, someone had organized everything into categories of urgency and discarded unnecessarily disturbing items.

The most important piece was a letter from Lance Wilson, the advocate John had hired for Leo. Leo knew Wilson by reputation. He was considered one of the country's most successful criminal defense advocates, and Leo blanched at the thought of what his services must cost. Wilson's letter advised Leo that he had spoken at length with the advocate general's office and, he was sorry to report, they intended to pursue charges. They also refused to allow Leo to present himself for the arraignment, so the letter advised he should be prepared as best one can for arrest at any time.

Leo's stomach lurched.

Wilson closed by advising Leo to make contact as soon as he received the letter and to refer any questions by law enforcement to him. Leo felt a familiar impulse to escape these frightening prospects. He reminded himself that would be inconsistent with the path he had committed to walk, and where was there left to hide?

"Nowhere," he said aloud, then left a message for Wilson telling him he was home from treatment.

In the kitchen, he found the refrigerator well-stocked. *Thank you, John.* Franz's food bowls and mat were gone, with a shiny waxed floor in their place. Leo felt a twinge of irrational anger, underlain by lamina of sadness and regret. He said a silent blessing for Franz and dialed John.

"Well, hello there," came the answer. "Someone must be home."

"Yep," confirmed Leo, "just got in. I can't believe what you did here."

"Don't mention it."

"I don't have words to thank you properly."

"Don't use words," said John. "Show me."

"How?"

"By handling your shit."

"I can do that."

"I know you can. Now do it. You're in for a pile of it, so you'll have ample opportunity to display your appreciation."

"Thanks."

"You're welcome."

After that essential call, Leo ate, showered, and left for a meeting. Afterward, he returned home, meditated for half an hour, and retired. No one knows the blessedness of a simple night of natural sleep as well as an emancipated addict.

Next morning, Leo awoke with a gasp to what felt like the resumption of a nightmare. Fists rained down on his door. "DDI, we have an arrest warrant. Open up now!"

This time, peacefulness descended over him as he awakened. *This is it*, he thought. The storm. He said a silent prayer for strength and hope that this would all result in a better life ahead, donned a robe, eased open the door to the same three agents who had arrested him the first time, and raised his hands.

The officers, who clearly sensed Leo's tranquility and could see the healthy state of his abode, reciprocated his vibe and politely informed him they were there to arrest him and transport him to the court for arraignment. Leo said he understood and asked if he could dress. They accompanied him as he threw on some clothes and a pair of flip-flops, cuffed his hands, and paraded him past his peeping neighbors to their vehicle.

The DDI agents were jocular on the ride downtown, assuring Leo it would be a short proceeding and that they were sure he'd be home by lunchtime. Leo thanked them for their decency, and Lauren Drey responded by saying, "We're human beings, like anyone else." The others voiced accord. Agent Drey tried to ask Leo about his employment status, but Leo politely told her he was represented by counsel and was not comfortable communicating with them outside his presence.

"I don't like talking to her either," said the other female agent, whose name Leo gathered was Melissa something. Everyone giggled, though the sound of amusement from the agent named James felt chilly to Leo. Everything about James felt chilly, but also magnetic and strangely familiar, though Leo was sure they had met during his first arrest. As he reflected on this, a few barely discernible forgotten dream fragments arose to Leo's mind from his subconscious. It dawned on him that this might be his fetish site compadre, Mr. Domin8u, in the flesh. Leo and James made eye contact as this thought formed. Leo blushed, and James regarded him with something between a smile and a leer before turning away. Leo felt like he'd been injected with ice water.

At the arraignment, reporters furiously scribbling notes filled the courtroom. The adjudicator read the charging document, which alleged two counts of distributing QFRI-mediated parasitic abuse recordings, and three counts of possession. On the advice of his advocate, Leo pled not guilty. The court turned to the question of Leo's custody status. His advocate told the adjudicator about Leo's successful completion of addiction treatment, long record of public service, and strong community ties. He also advised the court that, through him, Leo had offered to present himself for arraignment but that the prosecutor, without any rational justification, had insisted on inflicting the trauma and indignity of arresting him again and dragging him into court for the arraignment in handcuffs.

"It's nothing short of an abuse of her power and a tawdry supplication to the media," said Advocate Wilson. "Totally unjustified. Frankly, it borders on grounds for sanctions."

The prosecutor, none other than Leo's adversary in Anna's case, Ms. Alecia Cheung, showed no concern. In a voice devoid of discernible emotion, she played her trump card: "The Citizenry believes a full hearing will be necessary to ascertain the defendant's proper custody status and eligibility, if any, for bail, Your Honor. Seventy-two hours."

"Your Honor," began Wilson, but the adjudicator cut him short.

"We all know the score, Mr. Wilson. My hands are tied. The prosecutor has absolute discretion to require a seventy-two-hour custody before a bail hearing"—he turned toward Ms. Cheung—"whether or not I think it's justified," he added pointedly. "The matter is continued for three days."

Leo was thunderstruck. As the National Police escorted him into custody, Wilson said, "There's no way to prevent this. She's got the power and she's abusing it. Try to relax. The time will pass and we'll get you out at the bail hearing." Leo wanted to ask more, but the officer firmly directed him through a door back into the photographic negative world of dirty cement, steel bars, and flickering fluorescent light.

Leo shivered on a stainless-steel bench in the courthouse holding cell for two hours. Police then escorted him to a transport vehicle where he joined a dozen similarly manacled detainees, bound for a local jail.

Leo and his fellow transportees were funneled into a filthy holding cell with standing room only, where they remained for five hours. After that, they were routed into a larger, louder holding tank, populated with street Aggressives jacked up on Elidrine, jabbering without surcease about their criminal exploits.

For thirty hours, he tumbled along the streams of incarcerated humanity as they converged into deeper, wider channels, until he was a tiny speck floating on a great river of the detained, each reduced to a number and a half-rotten bologna sandwich. People used toilet paper rolls as pillows and tried to sleep where they could. Most stood. The jailers provided no trash receptacle, but the inmates, in an ironic display of civility surpassing their confiners, corralled the garbage into the corner next to the single toilet to preserve the illusion of sanitation.

Leo stood against a wall, avoided eye contact, and fought panic as the thugs he was standing inches apart from vowed to kill any "Vulbusers" in their path. *That's rich*, thought Leo. Most of these jewels were in custody for violent crimes or for dealing Elidrine, a drug that triggered many forms of Vulnerable abuse and annually killed thousands by overdose, intoxication-related accidents, or violence. Yet somehow they were the self-appointed morality police.

When the conversation got around to the QFRI parasitic abuse phenomenon, the detainees milked every remaining Elidrine-induced amp to proclaim their righteous bluster and murderous intent. As the confinement rolled past the twenty-four hour mark, the great impotent warriors crashed off their Elidrine highs so badly they passed out in drooling heaps on the grimy cell floor.

About twenty-five hours into his ordeal, Leo was facing interrogation by an officer who determined rather belatedly that Leo should not be in the general population and placed him alone in another cell. After another two hours, two peaceable and self-possessed inmates joined him.

Three hours after that, he received a bedroll, towel, and a comical hygiene kit. Leo was examining the little toy razor that looked as though it belonged in a doll house as the guard opened the steel door and escorted him into a triangular housing pod with two tiers of cells surrounding a common area with cement benches and four macrovision screens. Shower stalls with symbolic privacy doors were visible on one flank. The walls on each tier bore old-school macrophones at their centers.

The guard brought Leo to a cell and opened the door. A handsome, muscly, and compact blond fellow hopped up from his bed, gave Leo a head-to-toe, and shook his hand. They exchanged a few pleasantries and small jokes while the escorting guard conversed outside the cell with the unit officer. When the guard stepped back into the room, the inmate, whose name was Mark, said, "This one can stay." He and the guard both snickered and the guard locked them in.

"The guy who was here before you was a real asshole. I made him call the unit officer and tell him he needed to move to a different cell. He left ten minutes before you got here. That's what that was about."

"Ah," said Leo. "I promise I won't trouble you."

"I'm not worried," responded Mark. "Your vibe is peaceful. Want some coffee?"

Leo's eyes lit up. After thirty hours enduring icy holding tanks, lack of sleep, and coffee deprivation, he had a blazing migraine. "Yes, please."

He watched in fascination as Mark took an empty potato chip bag open at both ends and slid it through the crack between the closed door and door jamb, catching the attention of an inmate who was cleaning the common area. The inmate walked over with a pitcher of hot water and poured it in the end of the potato chip bag. Mark collected the water into a cup as it seeped out the bag's other end inside the cell, and used it to make the coffee.

"Prison ingenuity," Mark said to an impressed and amused Leo. "Gourmet it isn't," he continued, handing over a lukewarm cup of thick instant coffee, "but it packs a punch."

Leo accepted the cup gratefully, took a sip, and shuddered.

Mark slapped him on the back as though he were choking. "House specialty. Good stuff, huh?"

"Delicious," croaked Leo, forcing down another swig. As he waited for the caffeine to hit his bloodstream, he climbed into the upper bunk, arranged the sparse bedding on the thin rubber mat, and lay down. "Oh my God, that feels so good. Soft, warm, dry, clean. Heaven."

"Interesting how your standards change when you go through that, isn't it?"

"Amazing."

Leo and Mark were friends at once. Mark gave Leo stuff to read, coffee to drink, snacks from his commissary stash, and a caring and sympathetic ear. He taught Leo where to sit and to avoid trouble, how and when to use the phones, protocol for showering, the schedule of daily operations and feeding, the skinny on the guards and other inmates. By evening, this companionship gave Leo a measure of peace, and he welcomed a healthy night's sleep.

Next day, Leo and Mark read and spoke intermittently. Mark had been confined in that cell for three months, fighting a fraud case. He had no idea yet when his fate would be adjudicated or how much time he was facing. He had developed a routine of exercise, reading, writing letters, and sleeping to hold on to his sanity.

Leo told Mark about his struggles with addiction and, eventually, about his case. Mark received the information without judgment. Leo later realized Mark probably already knew about his charges from media coverage that slipped past the less-than-diligent jail censors.

They talked about friendships and families, and about people's attitudes and reactions to a person facing criminal charges. "Let me tell you something," said Mark during one such exchange, "As you go through this, you'll find out who's in your corner and who isn't, and it will surprise you."

He didn't know it at the time, but Leo would revisit that thought during the years ahead and conclude that truer words were never spoken.

After choking down a few meals so vile he nearly threw them back up and watching a little macrovision with Mark in the common area, Leo spent a third night in jail.

At 2:30 a.m., the jail staff rudely awoke him and told him to get ready for transport to court.

"Wash up and shave," Mark advised.

"Maybe I should let them see the impact of this ordeal."

"Trust me, they do not care one bit about the impact. If anything, it arouses their bloodlust. All they care about is appearances and decorum. Show them the best face you can."

Leo accepted this advice and pulled out the "razor" from his hygiene kit. He had to hold the one-square-inch tool between thumb and forefinger by a plastic nib. Leo eyed the thing skeptically and repeatedly scraped his face with it. Leaning toward the scratched stainless steel "mirror," he examined his face by the dim light. His efforts had accomplished nothing.

"They gave me an anti-shaving razor," said Leo. "My toothbrush might be more effective."

Mark gave him a wry smile. "That's the only kind they provide. Here, let me show you."

Mark took the ridiculous toy and practically drove it into Leo's cheekbone, stretching the skin off his jaw in the process, and forced the dull little metal strip into Leo's epidermis.

"Like that."

Sure enough, there was a bald patch. Leo regarded Mark doubtfully, then brutalized his face as instructed until the razor ceased to perform even when forced with such extremity.

"That means you're shaved," explained Mark.

Leo felt the remaining stubble and shook his head. As he toweled dry and combed his hair, the officer opened the cell door. Mark shook Leo's hand firmly and wished him well.

"Much as I like you, I hope I don't see you again."

"Same to you," replied Leo with a tinge of sadness.

After another seven hours in holding tanks and riding in a bus with legs shackled and hands cuffed and chained to his waist, Leo entered the courtroom for his bail hearing. As the officers escorted him to the defense podium next to Advocate Wilson, Leo scanned the room: John Hanes was there, Jeaneane, several other advocate colleagues, his parents and siblings, Jeb and, next to him, Jamie. Leo frowned, but Jamie gave him a signature dorky thumbs up. This tickled Leo's ribs.

Advocate Cheung was the first to speak after the court opened the hearing:

"Your Honor, the charges at issue in this case are extremely serious. The defendant knowingly and deliberately obtained, consumed, and distributed QFRI-enhanced recordings of his own client's horrific abuse. He also distributed an abuse recording we believe is at issue in an assault lawsuit being litigated by his friend and colleague, Jeaneane Spence." Cheung peeped over her shoulder at Jeaneane for effect.

Jeaneane was off-guard as all heads turned to her, then absorbed what the prosecutor had disclosed and turned to Leo with a visage of ice. Clearly this was the first she had heard of this unfortunate detail. Leo surveyed the other faces and saw James Malone observing Jeaneane with interest.

Leo's stomach churned and skin crawled.

"He is a dangerous predator," Cheung continued, "A trafficker in his own client's misery and exploitation. As such, he is a threat to Vulnerables and to all the victims in this case, specifically Ms. Anna Dao, on whose back he rode to fame before he peddled her recorded incident of abuse for others' illicit consumption."

Wilson objected to the inflammatory litany. "Your Honor, none of this has been proven. The police reports indicate Mr. Baksh did not know the identity of the persons depicted in the recordings at issue until after the fact. It is absurd to characterize him as a 'predator.' He did not 'peddle' anything, if by use of that word the prosecutor is attempting to fraudulently represent that my client was engaged in a commercial enterprise."

"Your Honor," Cheung objected.

"Stick to bail issues, Mr. Wilson," the adjudicator admonished.

"More importantly for purposes of this hearing," Wilson continued, "Mr. Baksh has been out of custody and proactively overcoming his addiction. This good man is a fearless champion for Vulnerables, and is on a lifelong productive track he temporarily strayed from while under the influence of a dangerous and debilitating drug. He is doing everything the Citizenry could reasonably ask of him to ensure that he will remain in his right mind and stay on track. Custody is beyond unnecessary. It would be harmful and counterproductive."

Cheung dug in even more fiercely and did her best to paint Leo a deranged monster who gorged without restraint on his vulnerable, innocent client.

As she unleashed this tirade, Leo whispered in Wilson's ear, "Not to minimize my conduct, but since when does Ms. Cheung give a damn about Anna's welfare or the plight of Vulnerables? Up until several weeks ago she was painting Anna a dangerous psychopath who should be isolated from the Citizenry. If I'm a menace, why did she wait a month to arrest me? What's the sudden public emergency?"

"She's an unprincipled opportunist who wants to use your eye socket as a rung in her career ladder," Wilson covered the microphone and whispered back. "As you are no doubt aware, she's not nearly as bad as many of her colleagues."

"I know," said Leo. They held eye contact briefly before turning back to the front.

The advocates jousted at length until the court interrupted: "I'm not worried about him fleeing but I'm concerned about him losing control. I will allow release on a one-thousand-credit bond, subject to electronic monitoring, curfew, drug testing, counseling, and gainful employment."

Leo's advocate reported that John Hanes would take a lien on his house to fund the bond. Leo turned toward him, and John winked.

As the advocates and court sorted out the details, Leo tried to catch Jeaneane's eye so he could mouth "I'm sorry." She was no longer paying attention to the hearing. Instead, she had her eyes on James Malone. Leo watched as James turned to Jeaneane and returned her gaze for an inappropriately long interval, his expressionless mien twisting into a smirk at the last moment. When Leo turned his attention back to Jeaneane, she too looked intrigued.

"That's it," said Lance Wilson, snapping Leo back to the proceeding. "It will take a while to process you out but John Hanes will meet you when you're released."

Hours later that night, Leo lay in his bed and cried. Exhausted from the horrific ordeal, he slept, despite the bulky and uncomfortable ankle monitor strapped to his leg.

Two days later, in between mandatory meetings with a pretrial release officer, his new therapist, and the employment agency, Leo received a text message from Jeaneane:

"Why haven't you called?"

"Why haven't *I* called?" said Leo aloud to his mute device. "Um, because I was in jail you ass. Why the fuck haven't you?" Instead, he wrote, "Sorry, overwhelmed with court-ordered appointments." Jeaneane didn't respond.

Seated at a restaurant, Jeaneane glanced at her mobile device, hit delete, stuck it in her handbag, and took a sip of wine. Over the rim of her glass she stared into the steely grey eyes of James Malone.

"Anything important?" he asked, sipping his own wine and nestling his leg against hers under the table.

"No," she replied. "Nothing."

33

"DAMN, WENDY, I'M SORRY, OK? Lighten up."

Wendy gripped the edge of the pass-through to the pub's kitchen.

"I'm sorry, Vito," she said to the exasperated cook. "I'm not myself lately."

Vito regarded her soberly. "I know, sweetheart. We all know. What's going on?"

Wendy shook her head. "Just … stuff," she said, forcing a smile and pretending to arrange her unfixable hair.

"I'm here if you want to talk," he said evenly. "*Talk*," he barked. "Not bite my head off." This he followed with a fake expression of fury and retrieved the plate containing the wrong order from the pass-through ledge. "I'll have the mushroom caps ready in five minutes."

"Thanks, Vito."

Wendy swerved back into action. It was a busy night at the watering hole and Wendy had to devote twice her usual energy to keeping track of customers' orders and socializing appropriately, so tortured was she by worry over the dangers her loved ones faced. The outburst at Vito was the inevitable release of subterranean volcanic emotions, however undeserved.

Distracted as she was, she had still sensed that the man in the back corner table had been watching her. She darted a peek from the corner of her eye. He made no effort to pretend he didn't notice. When her coworker Tye said he needed a break, she jumped at the chance to cover his tables, which included the one where the intriguing stranger presided over a barely touched beer.

As she approached the table, Wendy caught her breath. Regarding her with unabashed interest was positively the most exotic and beautiful man she had ever seen. Though seated, he was tall, long limbed, and well but not overly muscled, all of it wrapped tastefully in a sport coat and fine, creamy chemise. His skin was a dark mahogany tinged with rose. Thick chestnut hair with threads of auburn was woven into tight braids and bundled back from a high, broad forehead into a loose pony tail. His features were as though chiseled from the finest wood—narrow nose with flaring, almost equine nostrils; graceful, sensuous lips; square, solid jaw; long, muscular neck. But his eyes stopped her in her tracks for a breathless moment. Unlike any she'd ever seen, his irises were deep-black veined with gold, like slices of obsidian near the pupils, fading into and surrounded by luminous amber a shade darker than her own, and ringed by a rich, rusty ochre. They pierced her with their feral intensity, yet glittered like precious jewels through a shimmering stream. He radiated strength and cool confidence. Wendy flushed under the power of his gaze and, to her embarrassment, stammered when she spoke:

"Tye, I mean your server, the other guy—"

He beamed warmly and she relaxed, making light of her own tongue-tied predicament.

"—is on break," she resumed with more characteristic panache. "You're stuck with me for the moment."

"Thank God," he said. "I thought I'd have to pay the bill and start over at a new table."

He spoke in a deep, sonorous voice that reminded her of water in a dark cave, through an accent somehow at once clipped yet languid and velvety. His expression conveyed foreign birth, though she couldn't tell from where. The islands, perhaps. He likely had an opulent upbringing, or at least education.

"To what do I owe the pleasure of such attention?" she asked innocently as she straightened items on his table.

"To your remarkable beauty and irresistible charm," he replied, "among other things."

She turned down the corners of her mouth and rotated her head while continuing her make-work task. "Flattery with a cryptic finish," she observed.

"Mm," he acknowledged. "Just so. Might I interest you in a round of something more private once your workday is finished?"

Why not? she thought. The rules with Patrice permitted it. God knew she needed a release. He could be a serial killer, but her instincts said his intensity derived from other than sociopathological sources. She opted for reckless abandon:

"I'm through here in an hour."

"Just when I was planning to be done with my beer."

"You haven't touched it."

"That's because I hate it," he said, crisply snapping his Ts.

"I'm flattered," she rejoined, "But your chivalry needn't involve drudgery."

"To the contrary," he said, caressing the back of her hand with an index finger, "I've indulged in the viewing of you. What more would I need?"

"A palatable beverage wouldn't hurt." She stood and withdrew her hands to her hips before they attracted attention.

"Actually," he said, shifting gears now that they'd crossed the threshold, "Perhaps I'll take a walk and end up out front when you're leaving."

"I'll get your check," she said without missing a beat. Into his ear, she added in a whisper. "Be sure to give Tye a good tip, since I seem to have cut short your visit."

He slapped a fifty-credit note on the table, said "See you at ten," then arose with the grace of a panther and padded out of the pub.

Wendy followed him with her eyes, excited enough to have forgotten her troubles for the moment. Tye walked up behind her and said with mock scorn, "Excuse me, tart, but I have other tables, and so do you."

She donned an expression less contrite than smug and pointed to his tip.

He gasped. "That clearly was left for you."

"That would be most unseemly," she scolded good-naturedly. "I'm certain it's for you."

"I like this arrangement," he replied as he tucked the bill into his pocket. "Your customers can pay me to pick you up anytime." He put finger to his forehead in mock epiphany. "But that would make me your—"

She slapped a hand over his mouth and pretended to twist off his nose. "You're welcome."

"Thank you," he said when she allowed him to speak.

She gave her best glare of stern warning, then took stock and began ministering to her neglected customers until quitting time, which could not arrive too soon.

Their lovemaking was fit for the history books. They naturally fell into a rhythm and intermingled in such a profound range, from heartbreakingly tender to epically gymnastic, that they collapsed into a heap of astonished joy when they were through.

Wendy and her lover lay in her bed in post-coital bliss, he on his back and she curled against his side with her cheek on his chest, her fingers rising and falling like arpeggios as she ran them up and down his abdomen.

As their breathing calmed, she tipped her head up toward his face. "I'm Wendy."

He turned to her, his eyes radiating an intoxicating blend of fierce animalism and almost supernatural intelligence, and fixed her with his gaze. She waited patiently, wondering as he lay silently regarding her whether he would reciprocate the gesture.

"Anaku."

"That's a sexy name," she replied, "as it should be."

He lifted her chin to kiss her. "We have things to discuss."

She laughed, her voice like wind chimes.

"So soon? I've just learned your name."

"You learned rather more than that," he rejoined. "But that's not what I mean, much as I'd like to do this every day forever."

"I knew it was too good to be true," she sighed. "Time for the cryptic part."

"I'm afraid so."

She disentangled her lithe form from his, put on a robe, and moved to the end of the bed. "It's been a rough week. If you're making it rougher, I'd rather you leave me in the dark."

He crossed his arms. "Though some of it may be hard to hear, I do not believe knowing what I have to tell you will make things any worse. To the contrary, I can help you. Or, rather, I believe we can help each other."

She closed her eyes and massaged her temples. Help she could use. "OK," she said, giving him her full attention and bracing internally. Nothing could have prepared her for what followed.

"It has come to my attention that you either are, or are connected to, the point of intersection between the members of a group that has until recently been engaged in a rather dangerous game."

Wendy's eyes widened.

"Their group is one of many that have sought to breach the Department of International Intelligence Micromedium hub, but they have the distinction of being among the three most capable cells and the only one that the DII is aware succeeded in surveilling its quantum neural security shield."

Wendy's heart raced but she forced herself to remain still.

"The people I believe are associated with you breached the shield ten days ago. Unfortunately for them, one of their members, a young woman they knew as Subterraneum and known in her public life, among other names, as Gillian Moss, was arrested on suspicion of involvement in the terror attacks on the capital last year. She foolishly tried to clear her name by forming a neural link with an agent of the Department of Domestic Intelligence. During that session, she inadvertently spilled scraps of information related to the group. Unbeknownst to her, the Domestic agent she accidently shared these mysterious details with was working on the sly with a Department of International Intelligence operative.

"Based on those bits of intel, International tracked their Micromedium activity and correlated it with anomalies the neural shield agents had perceived. Ten days ago, one member of the group breached the hub's shield while another individual assisted her by calibrating her Micromedium equipment remotely. The hub security agents detected the intrusion and summarily executed the person who breached the shield with a massive, traumatic neural pulse."

A tear slid down Wendy's cheek.

"Since she was a wealthy, powerful, and well-connected woman, her disappearance would have been problematic. Accusing her of having breached the DII's advanced security barrier would have been … a tough sell, since few knew the scale of this woman's rather remarkable personal strength and fortitude, hmm?"

Wendy laughed through her tears.

"Agents confiscated her equipment and arranged things so the effects of the pulse, which mimics a massive stroke, would appear natural."

He let her absorb this before he continued. "Her fate, though likely terrifying, may have been kinder than that of the person who was remotely assisting her."

Liam's face flashed through Wendy's mind and she bit her lip.

"The agents traced his signal to an abandoned office site, where they found enough fresh human DNA to identify the individual who is now in DII custody."

"He's alive?"

"Yes, though I'm not sure he's better off for it, I'm sorry to say."

"Thank God he's alive," she said, "poor Liam."

"Yes, poor Liam," he said softly. "And poor Gillian. Both are undergoing brutal interrogation at an extraterritorial DII site."

"You mean they're being tortured?"

"I'm sorry. Yes."

Wendy broke into sobs.

Anaku pulled her into his arms, stroked her hair, and held her until she calmed.

"May I continue?"

She gave her assent, comforted by his heartbeat and the resonance of his voice.

"I am also aware of a third member I know by pseudonym, Hackizen, through others he interacts with. He is an adept and well-protected operator. I have arranged for him to receive technology and training critical to the group's mission, though I have never met him and I don't know whether he has any sense of who I am."

Wendy pulled away and resumed her post at the end of the bed with knees protectively to chin. "You were part of this group's activities?"

"Not as such," he answered, "but yes, in the sense that I"—he straightened out the hem of the bedsheet—"fulfilled some of their needs. I have provided similar support to each of the three most viable groups."

Wendy turned her head to the side and held his gaze, flying mentally through possible scenarios, from heroic to sinister. She remained mute rather than risk sharing information with someone who had not yet proven himself an ally, notwithstanding his delectable gifts in certain areas, she thought with a momentary grin.

Anaku resumed: "Other than the unfortunate disclosures she made during her neural interrogation by the DDI, Gillian Moss, a.k.a. Subterraneum, has proven surprisingly immune even to the most coercive techniques, and has disclosed no additional information about the hacker cell.

"The DII team charged with eliminating this group has surmised that the individual known as Hackizen remains at large. Based on forensic Micromedium data, they opine that there is likely at least one other member unaccounted for. After my own analysis of the evidence, I am inclined to share their assessment."

Wendy deployed her best poker face.

"I'm afraid there is a rather urgent race afoot—"

She cocked an eyebrow, afraid to speak lest she reveal anything she would regret.

"—between the DII agents who want to destroy them, and I, who want to help them complete their mission."

He let her take this in before he continued.

"I strongly suspect you can help me determine several crucial facts. First, who the unidentified group member is. Second, how to contact the individual known as Hackizen. Third, whether they achieved more than the aborted penetration of the neural shield before the agents"— he shifted to a softer tone—"ended your great grandmother's courageous and likely historic life and abducted your friend Liam."

Wendy pulled a sheet over her knees. "Why on earth would I share such information with you if I had it?"

"Because there may be no other way to save Liam's life, not to mention Gillian Moss's, though I don't know if you know her. It may also prevent the eventual capture, torture, and execution of Hackizen and other at-large members of the group—"

Wendy cringed as Patrice's face passed through her mind, a visual cue she knew Anaku did not miss.

"—and help them complete their mission of revealing the inner workings of the most monstrous state terror enterprise in history, which, if unfinished, would make the sacrifice of all these brave lives nothing more than a well-intentioned act of suicidal futility."

Wendy slipped away to crank up the thermostat on a wall heater, and it hissed to life. After soaking up some warmth, she crawled back under the sheet.

"As much as I want to believe you would pursue those objectives," she said, practically validating Anaku's assumptions. "I need to know more about your stake and role in this and how you know all these things."

He clucked his tongue. "I would expect no less from such a fierce woman with so formidable an ancestry."

She wagged a finger at him. "No flirting."

He feigned a pout.

Wendy resisted the urge to jump on him and wrestle. "Spill it if you want it."

He raised his eyebrows and turned his head, but hewed to a serious path as instructed, lest he be scolded again.

"You don't know it, but by telling you what I have, I've already placed my life in your beautiful hands. I have revealed that information and what I am about to share with you at risk of lethal consequences."

She held up her hands in response to this weighty pronouncement, but he persisted. "I trust you not to hurt me. I want you to trust me not to hurt you. There's no better way."

"That's more responsibility than I can handle," she protested. "I've just met you."

"Too late."

She was incredulous. "Why would you trust me with that kind of knowledge and power?"

"Because the stakes could not be higher and time is of the essence."

She shook her head. "Why should I believe you?"

"Whether you choose to trust me is going to turn on your instincts."

She licked her finger and stuck it in the air as though testing the wind, and he continued:

"I am an agent employed by the DII. But that is just an item within a tool chest I employ pursuant to what I like to believe is a higher calling."

Wendy's head quivered in disbelief. "A spy?"

"I have spent the past five years identifying, assisting, encouraging, and equipping individuals and groups I believe are laboring toward our collective evolutionary development."

"As part of your job?"

"Yes and no. Gathering information on political activism is part of my official duties. However, I have rigorously filtered what I report both to keep the DII off the scent of true activists and to assist the groups where I can. That part is," he gestured as though granting a point, "extracurricular."

Weirder by the minute, thought Wendy.

"At heart I seek to facilitate the transcendence of existing oppressive social structures and underlying obsolete belief systems."

"You're a DII agent and a revolutionary?" she asked with a tinge of ridicule.

He took no offense. "In a manner of speaking and in one aspect, I hope so."

"Were you involved in the terror attacks?"

"Certainly not," he said with obvious distaste.

"You're a nonviolent, revolutionary DII agent," she said with increasing irony.

"If I'm a revolutionary, that would mean I'm nonviolent."

"I think the Restruct types would disagree."

"I'm sure some of them would," he replied, "which is why they are not true revolutionaries. Violent revolution is an oxymoron."

Wendy went slack in theatrical disbelief. "Interestingly put. But violence has been necessary for every revolution, bar none."

"I disagree. The world has yet to see a true revolution. At best, violence rearranges how oppression is administered and who wields power. Only nonviolence can be truly revolutionary because it redefines what power means."

Wendy chewed on that nugget a moment. "Interesting," she said, tipping her head from side to side. "Not sure if I agree, but OK."

Anaku nodded respectfully, then resumed his tale.

"Two years ago, the DII began working with quantum neural interfacing technology. Agents at my level were trained in using the equipment, ostensibly in preparation for its utilization as an interrogation tool."

"Charming."

"Yes, isn't it. The provenance of this technology is classified and shrouded in lore, but it almost certainly was designed by university research scientists using secret intelligence infrastructure development funds. Though its origins remain a secret, even to me, the technology itself leaked out like water through a sieve. Despite efforts to control its production, companies began clandestinely manufacturing it in various shapes and configurations, both here and abroad. The DII seizes unauthorized equipment and manufacturers wherever it can, but a surplus of the devices persists."

Wendy crawled over and lay back against Anaku as he continued.

"I am certain that the DII is using this QFRI technology for purposes well beyond garden variety interrogation. I do not know the details of how, but persistent rumors within the agency and on the Micromedium suggest the neural arrays are being used for severely coercive interrogation and infliction of pain."

"You mean torture," said Wendy.

"Yes, I mean torture," he replied. "There is also talk that the agency is weaponizing the technology somehow, a rumor it would appear your great-grandmother's death corroborates. I do not know the mechanics or extent of that application, but I fear the worst."

She shivered, and he wrapped his arms around her.

"As you might surmise, I have cultivated many sources of information. I learned of several hacker groups conspiring to breach and expose the DII's secret operations.

"It is my firm conviction that disease breeds in secret. Exposure to light, both literally and figuratively, purifies and promotes life. I view the objectives of these groups as progressive and cleansing. The DII can only perpetrate its atrocities in the dark."

Wendy tapped him on the chest. "Why don't you go public yourself?"

"First, I don't have a high enough security clearance to access sufficiently damning information to make a difference. Second, if I tried to gain access to that information from within the agency more aggressively than I already do, I would be detected, stopped, and likely killed. I am willing to commit my life to cleansing the world of the DII's disease, but I prefer not to throw it away in a symbolic gesture that yields no benefit. I can be more effective by passing information and technology to skilled activists working anonymously, and by sheltering them as best I can from official scrutiny. The time may come for me to go public."

Wendy fiddled with one of his braids as she absorbed these details. "Is this your modus operandi? Screw first and disclose earth shattering facts later?"

She bounced against his chest as he laughed.

"Not as a general rule. Would you have spurned my advances if I had told you these things first?"

"Guess we'll never know," she said airily. "But there is a little matter of respect," she said through playfully clenched teeth, elbowing him in the gut.

"It's not a question of respect," he countered. "I needed to know if I could trust you."

"Sleeping with me settled that question?"

"It showed me more than mere conversation would have revealed."

"You've obviously never been burned by a lover."

"We've all been burned, but this was the best way to get a read on you short of forming a neural link."

"Hmm," she said skeptically.

"Plus, you're hot."

"Well," she said with mock relief, "I'm glad to hear that figured in somewhere." They both smiled. "So are you, for the record." She patted his arm.

Wendy's smile quickly faded, as the weight of the topic at hand settled back onto her like a lead smock at the dentist's office. "How did you get information and equipment to this group?"

"I learned through several intermediaries of their existence. By way of one, I provided QFRI arrays to the person known as Infiltr8org, who I believe was Liam O'Brian.

"Through another, I provided equipment to a talented group of techies devoted to reverse engineering the arrays and devising ways to spy on neural links undetected. This group trained the individual known as Hackizen, but they also served as a wall between us. He is skilled at getting what he wants while hiding behind a fictitious identity. I had several opportunities to try to force a meeting with him, but the intermediaries jealously guarded their relationships with each of us, probably out of a healthy paranoia, given their endeavors. It was more expedient to supply his needs through the others, let him equip the hacker cell, and see what they accomplished."

Wendy resisted the urge to explain how she was connected to the person known as Hackizen, and why that placed her in proximity to so many members of his group. Sensing her struggle, Anaku resisted his own urge to push her, and opted instead for patience and further disclosure.

"Hackizen and I no longer have the leisure of working anonymously together through intermediary strangers. I need to communicate with him as soon as possible so we can maximize whatever inroads he and the others achieved. Not only are Liam's, Hackizen's, Gillian's, and," he let her squirm, "others' lives at issue, the opportunity to rip the mask off whatever the DII is up to will pass if we do not strike immediately. I believe the DII is up to some very dark business indeed, business so repugnant that revealing it could precipitate a profound cultural shift."

Anaku allowed Wendy to wrestle with herself at length. Eventually, she formed a tentative decision and reached for a robe.

"I need to make a private phone call. *Private*," she emphasized. "Can you honor that?"

"Of course," he assured. "Would you like me to leave?"

"Not if you can mind your business here while I speak in the other room."

Anaku pulled an audio device out of his bag and donned earphones. Wendy shook a finger at him in admonishment, and he held his palms together in a gesture of sacred promise. She threw a skeptical squint and adjourned to a nook in the next room to place an encrypted Micromedium voice call to Patrice.

Anaku relaxed to the soothing sounds of a mediation audio mix while Wendy made her call. When she was through, she awakened him from his semi-trance with a brush of the lips. He checked his watch as he pulled off the earphones. Forty-five minutes had elapsed. He pulled her onto him, breathed in her delicious scent, and brushed back her hair tenderly.

Wendy broke the silence: "The additional group member you correctly have guessed to exist is named Patrice. I have convinced her to speak with you via encrypted Micromedium voice link. If she trusts you, she'll share what she knows and assist you."

Anaku sighed with relief. "Thank you, Wendy."

She placed a silencing finger across his lips. "I suppose it pales in comparison to the issues you have to discuss, but there are a couple things you need to understand if you want to avoid causing a lot of heartache and torpedoing your chances of earning her trust."

His eyes registered patient attention.

"Patrice is my dear friend and primary lover. The rules of our relationship permit what you and I just did, but that does not mean it's OK to rub her face in it. I let her know the circumstances we met under, as a matter of basic decency. Please be mindful and gentle."

Wendy explained how she was remotely associated with Hackizen due to his involvement with securing her forged Citizenship status, and how the hacktivists had met him through her. "I'm a hub by accident," she explained, "He's the real hub. I'm the gateway, though I didn't know it. I've never even met him, as far as I know."

"How fortunate for me," replied Anaku, running a finger down her spine.

After establishing the encrypted link, Wendy handed the headset to Anaku. They instinctively positioned themselves respectfully apart, as though Patrice were in the room with them. Anaku spoke kindly to Patrice, told her all he knew, and requested her assistance. Patrice described the hacktivists' run on the DII sentinel shield, told him of the quantum tunnel they established through the entangled arrays and the stable, cloaked data stream into the DII hub they secured.

"Ingenious," said Anaku. It was more than he had allowed himself to hope.

Patrice also agreed to pass along Anaku's request for an introduction to Hackizen.

Anaku pledged his knowledge, connections, and resources toward helping them maximize the data stream's utility. He desperately wanted to connect to it and rip open the hub, but disciplined himself to build a rapport with the two still-free hacktivists first. These individuals were extraordinarily talented, both technically and in the art of survival. Their chances of success would be greater if the three cooperated. Besides, they alone knew the coordinates for the data stream's access node. Patience, he told himself.

Rather than try to dislodge that information before they were ready, Anaku applied his formidable powers of persuasion to convincing Patrice she should leave the country for a safe location he would arrange. She resisted at first, but passing the headset back and forth, Wendy and Anaku brought her to her senses.

Anaku gave Patrice Micromedium coordinates where she could reach him unsurveilled and arranged passage and shelter for his new coconspirator. Within a half hour, he had equipped her with a new identity, passport, travel reservations, and a guide to receive her and escort her to the island safe house.

Once all this was complete, Anaku and Wendy crawled back into bed. Nothing for it but to wait until he could speak with Hackizen and the three of them could plan their strategy. What better way to pass the time than swimming in pools of bliss?

Later, Wendy asked Anaku, "You said your DII gig and supporting these hacktivists groups were just one of the tools you use in your grand quest to liberate humanity."

Anaku feigned shock at the jab, then winked. "Yes, that's roughly what I said."

"Can you tell me what some of your other tools are? Or would you have to kill me?"

"I'm a lover, not a killer," he said, tickling her until she cried foul.

"Yes, yes, lover. Stop that!"

He adopted a partially facetious air of seriousness. "I use many means to urge people on the verge of awakening to open their eyes and wield their creative potential. Among other things, I have trained people in various positions of influence over the political system, adjudicatory bodies, and popular culture how to use the QFRI arrays for purposes of interfacing neurally with others."

"What does that accomplish?"

"It reveals what is hidden, and fosters intimacy and understanding."

Wendy reflected on this. "Nice in theory. Has it worked out that way?"

For the first time in her admittedly brief, albeit intimate acquaintance with him, Wendy saw emotions of sadness and worry cross Anaku's features.

"Not in every case. No."

She lay her chin on his chest and observed him until he was prepared to elaborate.

"One person I provided with an array and taught how to form a neural link is an advocate I'm sure you've heard of, Leo Baksh."

Wendy recoiled, "I know him personally and am a lifelong friend of his former client and now victim, Anna Dao."

Anaku met her gaze with genuine surprise mixed with sympathy and, to her annoyance, a slight tinge of amusement as he realized the reason he found her face familiar when first he met her was because he must have seen it among the memories in Leo's mind. "I continue to be amazed at the interconnectedness of it all," he said in response to her irritated expression. "The human fabric is so tantalizingly interwoven that it seems we should decipher a message in its patterns. Half the time I don't think there's a story to be discerned other than that we all are part of each other and of a living whole."

Wendy was in no mood for sententious rumination. "I'm sure that's profound," she said in an angrier tone than she would have liked, "but you're philosophizing about a situation that is devastating to many people, including one close to me."

He listened patiently. "I'm sorry. It's devastating to me as well."

This cooled her jets. "I still can't believe what Leo did. I don't understand it. Totally at odds with everything I perceived about him. A gentle and caring exterior, yet a monstrous core?"

"No!" Anaku's deep voice percussed, startling her. "Leo is a sensitive, generous, and empathetic person. That is his core."

"How can you say that?" she asked.

"Because I know it," he answered without reservation. "I have directly experienced his mind. It is because of this truth that I find what happened so heartbreaking. That, and because I feel partly responsible for his dissolution."

He massaged his brow.

"I taught him to use the equipment because I perceived him, accurately I still believe, as having the potential for greatness. He possessed a native recognition for the plight of the oppressed borne of his personal struggle to transcend the wounds and fears from his own experience as a sapient Vulnerable. He built a career out of deploying those assets to champion the interests of Vulnerables and challenge the Citizenry to strive for a higher, truer expression of its own potential. He was a natural ally for my mission, a living exemplar of post-nonviolent-revolutionary Citizenry.

"When I linked with him neurally, I detected a deep wound in his heart, as well as strength, intelligence, and creative power he had yet to tap. Leo has a beautiful soul. When I had the privilege of directly experiencing it, I could not respond with anything other than love."

Wendy flopped down on the bed. "That's consistent with my perception," she admitted. "Or was. What happened?"

"A tragic retreat from the brink of awakening into the illusory safety and fatal trap of anaesthetizing drugs is what happened," replied Anaku. "I felt him pulling away and falling apart. The last time we exchanged words, I found him in a fetish site, wired in via quantum interface. I could see that he was self-destructing, but he rebuffed my attempt to engage him. There was nothing I could do but pray he got through it alive.

"One effect of forming quantum neural links is persistent entanglement of the participants' minds after the session. Not consciously, but on deeper levels. It is common for people who have formed nodal links to dream about each other."

"I've heard," interjected Wendy.

"I found myself plagued with increasingly disturbing nightmares about Leo. I tried to send him healing light through meditation, but he felt shielded in darkness to me. Eventually, I had to train my own mind to screen him out so he didn't pollute me. One of the most difficult and painful decisions I ever made. But it was necessary."

Wendy felt a chill and pulled a blanket over them. "The drugs don't excuse what he did."

"I didn't say they did. Knowing what I do about him, I doubt he would say so either."

Wendy ran her fingers through the tangles in her wild locks.

"It wasn't your fault," she offered.

"I was part of it. I supplied one of the tools of his self-immolation."

"That doesn't make it your fault. The tool you supplied was neutral. You did it for the purest of reasons, if all you say is true. You had no way to know he would use it so irresponsibly. Did you give him drugs or suggest he take them?"

"Certainly not."

Wendy kissed his palm in response.

"How is Ms. Dao handling the news?" asked Anaku.

"Anna is far less pissed off than everyone else," said Wendy.

"Interesting."

"Perhaps she's romanticizing her abuser," said Wendy. "Victims do that."

Anaku tipped a finger back and forth in the negative. "I doubt it." His T's snapped like sparks.

Wendy smiled despite her fraught feelings around the situation. "It's true that Anna is not one to identify with her oppressors," she conceded. "She hasn't discussed it with me much, other than to tell me how surprised she is by her advocate's sudden portrayal of Leo as someone she now claims she always knew was damaged goods."

"Public calumny produces interesting shifts in alliance," Anaku observed.

"Mm hmm, well, her advocate's private perfidy has done little to endear her to Anna."

"That speaks volumes about each of them,"

"Yeah, well, Anna's no bendy straw, that's for sure."

"So it would seem," said Anaku, amused.

Wind shook a window in its frame.

"I always liked Leo," said Wendy, "But I cannot get my head around him screwing both Anna and the victim in Jeaneane Spence's assault case like that."

"Leo's advocate said he didn't know the contents of the recordings until after the fact," Anaku reminded her. "I'm sure there is a more to this case than we know. Maybe he was set up."

Wendy flicked away the thought. "My brother James was the investigating officer."

"Ah, yes," said Anaku. "The illustrious James Malone."

"You know my brother?"

"I know *of* your brother. Enough to know he is dangerous and can't be trusted."

Wendy considered taking offense but knew there could be reasons for such an opinion. "I don't know why he would want to set Leo up," she said. "Even if he did, how could he have done it?"

"There are ways," said Anaku. "Have you asked James?"

"Repeatedly, but he says he can't discuss it."

Anaku let the silence stretch. "Hmm," he said in staccato.

In truth, Anaku knew that James was the agent who interrogated Gillian

Moss and tipped off the DII to the hacktivists' existence. Anaku suspected there was more to James's relationship with his backchannel DII contact, a person whose identity Anaku had yet to discover. He wondered whether that relationship is what stopped the DII from zeroing in on Wendy as a source of information. Whatever the reason, Anaku was grateful for it and would do all he could to keep her safe.

Anaku concluded it would be cruel and unwise to share with Wendy what he knew about James's involvement in busting the hackers. The last thing he needed was for an aggrieved Wendy to confront James while in possession of Anaku's secrets. Despite his general belief in the healing—even revolutionary—power of transparency, he kept mum, vowing to explain it to her once he could do so without jeopardizing his larger mission and hurting her unnecessarily.

"Well," Wendy said after mulling things over, "I may not have misperceived Leo, which comforts me on some level. I knew Elidrine can tear some people apart but God almighty, what a disaster."

"Truly," replied Anaku. "We'll see what his advocate argues. Exposure to the fetish sites through a neural interface under the prolonged influence of that destructive drug probably caused Leo's unmanaged negative emotions to metastasize into a malignant addiction. He poured dark energy into his own shadow and it eclipsed the better parts of who he is. I encouraged him to use the interfaces in neurally joined meditation sites so he could investigate his inner wounds and heal them, or at least make peace with them, through gentle awareness. He threw Elidrine into the mix, though. When you go spelunking into your own spiritual nether regions under the influence of that drug, you get lost in the dark."

"Don't make me say poor Leo," Wendy cautioned.

"You may say just that before the government is through with him."

"They say he may be imprisoned for a long time under the new law," she said with a cringe.

"Yes, I believe that is the prosecutor's objective."

"Can you help him?"

"I don't know yet. I'm waiting for an opportunity. I hope so."

"At least he's sober now, according to his advocate."

"Yes, thank the Gods for that. Let us wish for him to stay that way."

Wendy slid the tip of her index finger down Anaku's abdomen. As she passed his belly button, Anaku's mobile device rang. He answered to the voice of Patrice, grabbed a notepad, and scribbled down a set of Micromedium coordinates, then hung up.

"Sorry, lover," he said. "Hackizen is ready to talk and I may need quick access to other resources. I need to jet."

He jumped up and began to dress. Wendy was more accustomed to being the one who danced away sweetly after a dalliance, leaving her partner wanting more. She did not relish the thought of being on the other end of that dynamic.

"Is that it? I've served my purpose?"

He flashed a grin. "Hardly, love. You don't honestly believe I could cut you loose after what you've shown me of your," he darted a playful glance, "delights." He savored the word like a nectar.

"People have," she replied coolly.

He set down his things, knelt on the bed, and cradled her chin delicately in his hand. "They were fools undeserving of a moment's thought." He kissed her gently and resumed his preparations to depart.

Anaku extracted from Wendy a solemn vow that she would not reveal his identity or the contents of their conversation to anyone. Once she agreed, he said, "I'll call or come see you as soon as I can. If you need to reach me, use these coordinates and the encryption method Patrice taught you."

They each touched fingertips to their lips and cast a kiss to the other as he turned, graceful as the moment she first laid eyes on him, and vanished.

Two nights later, Wendy missed a call while working at the pub and scolded herself for wondering whether it was Anaku. "Don't get mushy on me now, girl," she admonished herself in the restroom mirror during a break.

When she went back on duty, none other than Leo Baksh himself walked into the establishment, looking far healthier and more pulled together than she had seen him in a long time. Patrons stopped talking as he passed, but he proceeded undaunted. Wendy stepped before him, impressed by his courage, heartened by the physical evidence of his sobriety, and rather less angry after weighing Anaku's analysis and finding it plausible.

Her willingness to communicate with him solidified as she recognized in his eyes the unmistakable mark of deep shame. Despite his obvious discomfort of facing her, he held his ground and politely gave her the opportunity to decide whether he would be invited to stay. After a moment, she gave him a grim smile, hugged him, and gestured to a table. Voices gradually bubbled back up and the pub returned to normal operations on the unofficial authority of Wendy's ruling.

She was pleased when he ordered a root beer, passing on the tempting array of spirits.

"New leaf?" she observed with approval.

"Yeah," he replied. "Inside and out, top to bottom."

As the last of these words crossed his lips, into Wendy's view appeared the enigma who had rocked her already vertiginous world two nights before.

"Anaku," she whispered. Leo's eyes widened and his head snapped around to see where she gaped, but Anaku had spotted Leo first and aborted his entrance. Leo saw tips of braids disappear beyond the door frame.

He turned back. "What did you say?"

"I said responsibility is a-knocking. I have to make my rounds. What'll it be?" She gave him her best blank dizzy blonde, but he knew better than that.

He squinted at her. "No, I think you said 'Anaku.'"

She feigned confusion and shrugged. "No idea what that means. Shall I surprise you?"

"Surprise me?"

"With culinary delights."

There was no point in trying to persuade Wendy Malone to disclose anything she wasn't prepared to share.

"Yes, please."

When John Hanes arrived, the three of them attempted to perform their time-honored roles. None of their hearts were in it, and Leo wondered sadly whether any of the sweetness of his old life would survive the tempest that was twisting into view.

34

OVER THE NEXT TEN DAYS, Anaku, Patrice, and Hackizen conferred regularly via encrypted Micromedium link and exploited the cloaked data stream to eavesdrop on the Department of International Intelligence's Micromedium hub. With Anaku's knowledge of the agency's structure and protocol, and the others' extraordinary programming and hacking skills, the new team efficiently mapped the hub and cataloged the operations connected to it.

Though they had to overcome advanced security measures, they eventually penetrated processes within the hub related to the newly activated hybrid facility south of the capital. Anaku knew the site included a particle accelerator and advanced computer, but he did not know its purpose. The three ascertained that the facility possessed computing power far greater than the DII hub itself.

After three days and several near detections, the team hacked into the larger hub. Overwhelming and baffling, the facility appeared to be the processing center for a massive, nationwide surveillance matrix, with additional arms reaching beyond national boundaries. To their shock, this superhub was not crunching Macromedium and Micromedium communication streams for key words. Instead, it appeared to be receiving data from quantum neural eavesdropping equipment deployed nearly everywhere.

Within the superhub, the quantum neural streams were organized into larger analytical categories. The ad hoc team accessed control programs available to agents operating it and figured out how to parse the data by location and graph the gradients of Vulnerable–Aggressive temperamental throughput for each chunk they examined. They zoomed in the analytical lens all the way to the physical and neural configuration of a room full of people, and out to local, regional, and national combined temperamental spectra comprising the web of surveillance streams.

Anaku and the others brainstormed a panoply of possible purposes for the massive quantum neural surveillance, but needed to test their hypotheses. So, they developed links to the superhub's analytical tools and planted spy programs to monitor how the DII operatives were routing the neural field energy.

While their spyware tracked the throughput, the hackers exploited the superhub's central mapping program to catalog the sites where the neural arrays had been installed. They found the devices were collecting neural data in most national public venues, which was consistent with a domestic spy operation, though they could not see how crude neural impressions would yield sufficiently detailed information for intelligence purposes.

Sleeperagent: What is International doing in domestic intelligence?

Anaku: The DII is a national entity charged with ensuring the country's dominance and persistence through espionage, covert war, assassination, and torture. Don't let the name fool you. Department of Ubiquitous Intrusion would be more fitting. They are acutely interested in anyone or any group that is amassing power, regardless of geographic location.

Hackizen: In other words, they have their noses up everyone's asses.

Anaku: Probes in everyone's brains, it appears. But yes.

Sleeperagent: They're monitoring for aggregations of aggressive energy? Vulnerable weak points?

Anaku: Yes, it appears they are doing that at the least. The question is why?

Hackizen: To facilitate control.

Anaku: But how?

Hackizen: By identifying potentially destabilizing trends in collective temperament?

Anaku: That is no doubt one of this system's functions. I'll wager we've yet to grasp its primary purpose or range of applications.

Patrice executed a data sort and pulled up a new mapping quadrant for the others to view.

Sleeperagent: Why would they be monitoring the prisons?

Anaku: Why indeed? One would expect to find colliding aggregations of Aggressive energy in

> those wretched sites. Containing aggression is their stated purpose. What is there to monitor?

The team didn't know, but the superhub's map showed that a substantial portion of the surveillance equipment had been installed in prison facilities.

Unable to figure out the site's purpose without more information, the team let their automated systems track the flow of energy and data, hoping that would yield larger and more revealing patterns over time. Meanwhile, they focused their efforts on hacking into encrypted links to the DII hub and superhub, and on searching for Liam O'Brian and Gillian Moss.

Those two quests converged three weeks into the mission when they pierced an unusually protected quantum-neural, multimedia stream originating from overseas and feeding into the DII main hub. The first component they intercepted was a bundle of video streams. Each recorded an individual restrained, battered, and subjected to torture. Never had any of them, including Anaku, seen such horrors. They divvied up the streams and skipped through them until they found Liam and, using an image Anaku provided, Gillian.

Both were strapped to chairs, badly bruised, shaking violently, and drenched in perspiration and streaks of blood. Both had neural arrays strapped to their heads. Their eyes registered sheer terror. Someone was subjecting them to neural shock. With each jolt, they convulsed as though electrocuted.

Anaku dislodged Hackizen and Patrice from momentary paralysis in the face of such atrocity:

> **Anaku:** Focus! Make sure we're capturing all of this. Hackizen, track the signal's origin. Sleeper, get the audio stream online. I'm going to surveil the quantum neural signal.

The others tried to dissuade him from taking the risk, but Anaku was resolute, assuring them he was best trained to avoid injury and asserting that as a rogue DII agent, he most deserved harm should it result. They both had reservations on his final point but it ended their objections long enough for him to take the initiative and proceed.

Anaku steered his neural array to dip into Liam's QFRI stream, centered his mind as best he could, bled his field into the periphery of Liam's, and listened. Liam's mind was terribly chaotic, though he somehow still maintained partitions within it. Liam was clinging to an anchor in the center of his own consciousness, bracing.

Suddenly, Liam lurched back in his seat as a signal drilled into his awareness like a laser. Microscopically focused at first, it rapidly expanded until it blasted malevolent force, like a demonic chorus roaring in apocalyptic rage and hatred, vomiting death and destruction into Liam's mind like caustic sewage.

Patrice connected the audio feed during this pulse, and they heard Liam screaming.

Then it stopped. Into the silence that followed, Anaku directed to Liam's awareness a simple message: "Help is coming." Liam's eyes widened, and Anaku prayed the interrogators, if they heard him, attributed the words to Liam's own desperate mind.

Fearing continued interpenetration with the field might arouse suspicion, Anaku disconnected his array. "What in the name of all that is sacred?" he asked aloud, grasping the arms of his chair and willing down nausea.

Anaku: Are we recording all of this?

Hackizen: There is too much quantum neural data to capture.

Anaku: There's no point in recording that. One must experience it through real-time link, though I don't advise it.

Sleeperagent: I have all the audiovisual data.

Anaku: They are being tortured with QFRI technology. I have no idea how. That was not the mental signal of an interrogator. Not one from this world. I've never experienced anything so monstrous.

Sleeperagent: What do we do?

Anaku: Record everything we can for now.

Liam lay in the dark on a cement slab, trembling. His brain cracked and popped, and his body jerked and twitched, but these were almost peaceful compared to being wired into the torturers' arrays.

He was pretty sure he hadn't given anything up, but they had taken plenty, including all but the last shred of his hope for survival.

Liam pressed his face against the cold slab, listened to water trickle down the walls, and felt insects scurrying over his body—but he did not move.

He was beyond tears. Beyond rage. Beyond even fear.

Help is coming, he thought but did not believe, carefully refusing to let himself speak the words aloud, lest he give these monsters anything they could add to their arsenal.

35

WHILE THE REMAINING HACKTIVISTS SURVEILLED the country's main purveyor of espionage and torture, criminal defense advocate Lance Wilson finished analyzing Leo's case, conferred at length with the government's advocate, Alicia Cheung, and delivered to Leo a bracing dose of professional tough love. Under the new QFRI-Mediated Parasitic Abuse law, Wilson informed him one sunny afternoon, he faced a mandatory minimum sentence of ten years in prison and a potential maximum term of thirty years.

The government had surrendered no evidence to corroborate Leo's claim that his addiction predated and precipitated his descent into the Micromedium's darker reaches. Nor had the government yielded anything to support Wilson's suspicion that a DDI agent supplied the recordings to Leo in the first place. Absent corroborating evidence, Leo's defenses boiled down to assertions and speculations.

At best, they could mitigate the impact by humanizing Leo to the court and documenting his work in addiction recovery and therapy. To limit Leo's exposure, Wilson negotiated a deal with the government's advocate. Leo would plead guilty to one count of distributing a QFRI-mediated parasitic abuse recording, and the government would agree to a ten-to-eighteen-year potential sentence.

Leo was struck numb by the devastating reality that his best-case outcome would be ten years in prison. Wilson was willing to take Leo's case to trial, but it would be ugly. All the gory details would be paraded before the public. Anna might be forced to testify. He would probably lose. Without the constraints of the plea deal, the government would seek the maximum thirty-year sentence for its trouble trying the case.

"That's fucking insane," said Leo.

"It is unfortunately the situation we face," replied Wilson. "I'm sorry. The decision is yours. If your goal is to minimize your term of incarceration, I suggest you take the deal and we'll focus on mitigation at sentencing to get you the low end of the range."

"I can't believe Alicia Cheung won't consider pursuing a lesser charge," griped Leo. "She knows goddamn well this wouldn't have happened if I hadn't been out of my mind on Elidrine."

"As near as I can tell," replied Wilson, "she is a reptile with ice water for blood. I've yet to see evidence there's human DNA in her genome."

Leo smiled grimly. "That's a cruel thing to say about snakes."

"Take a week and think it over," Wilson advised. "Talk it out with people you trust. Call me any time if you need to."

Leo consulted with John who dispassionately told him to take the deal. "The political situation is boiling over, Leo. Lock in your potential jeopardy now. If you drag it out, the delegates could try to push through an even harsher law and make it retroactive."

Leo blanched at this unimaginable prospect.

"There's no way to tell where it's all headed," John continued, "but I would not rule out the possibility of getting help from the chief executive."

"You mean a pardon?" Leo asked incredulously.

John shrugged. "Perhaps not quite that much help. Maybe a partial commutation of sentence. It's a long shot and it wouldn't happen right away. Unless you accept responsibility for your actions and take your punishment on the chin, it will never happen."

"Those are high stakes and long odds."

"I'm not saying you should depend on it. That would be ridiculous and a recipe for suicidal disappointment. You should plead guilty with the intent to get through the whole term and use it to grow stronger. I'm saying that we can't predict the future. Things are slipping into massive flux. Anything is possible. Don't assume this choice will foreclose a life worth living. You may find this crisis leads to possibilities you never let yourself imagine."

"That platitude is beginning to chafe," retorted Leo.

"It's not a platitude. You can only see a few feet down the road right now. Don't give up hope just before it bends in a direction still hidden from view."

"I don't consider a decade short-term."

"In the context of a lifetime, it is," John persisted. "Especially when the road you were on when this disaster struck likely would have ended your life altogether in short order."

Leo had no retort. He regarded John in silence. "True," he said at last, "but I don't think the CE will soil her hands and her party's political prospects by meddling in my case."

"Not now, she won't. We don't know where things are going."

Leo eyed John curiously. "Is there something you're not telling me?"

"I need to run, old friend," John said. "Stay strong. That's the most important thing you can do right now. Don't lose your head."

Leo wanted to push but he knew it would be a waste of time.

Instead, he solicited feedback from the therapist he had been seeing since his initial arrest, a tough and smart practitioner who cut Leo not one millimeter of slack. His advice dovetailed with John's. "When you consider you were hurting people and destroying yourself, what's a felony conviction and some years in prison?"

"I've been working hard at cultivating acceptance," Leo said. "But things keep getting worse—"

"That is not the way acceptance works. If you place conditions on it, it's more evasion," the therapist said.

No place to hide with this brute, thought Leo.

He wanted to talk it through with Jeaneane, but she had ignored all his attempts at contact since his bail hearing. He considered showing up on her doorstep the way she had done to him on multiple occasions but decided he could live without her wrath and judgment, much as he missed her love and wise counsel.

Ultimately, the clincher turned out to be examining the choice through the lens of addiction recovery. In consultation with some battle-scarred veterans, he concluded suffering the consequences of his behavior was essential to taking responsibility for it, beginning to make amends, cutting loose the past, and forging a new path.

"You want to be a better man?" one old-timer asked him, "then face your fears and own your shit. There's no other way."

After a couple more days' reflection, he resolved to take the deal and asked Lance Wilson to set a hearing for change of plea.

As the hacktivists wended through the DII labyrinth and Leo prepared to face his penance, Agent Drey wrestled with a professional, ethical, and strategic conundrum.

The case against Leo Baksh could not have been more neat and tidy. He had handed an expertly tied noose to an undercover agent and politely placed his neck within its loop. Never had she seen a perp serve himself up so efficiently for quick prosecution.

Or so it seemed at first. After Alicia Cheung secured an indictment and formally charged Leo, a couple of loose ends appeared. Lauren wasn't sure what to do with them.

First, Renée Stephens approached her. While investigating a tip regarding black-market munitions distribution, agents under her direction stumbled on a major Elidrine sales operation. The dealer kept meticulous, undisguised records of his customers and their accounts, which presented a wrinkle in the case against Leo because there in black and white were logs of his Elidrine purchases, organized by date and quantity. The account book also showed that Leo carried a heavy debt, reflecting the extremity of his addiction.

"Damn it," snapped Lauren when Renée delivered the news. "Did you have to tell me this?"

Renée tipped her head, more in disgust than disbelief at the implications of Lauren's question. "Yes, if I give a damn about my professional integrity, the honor of our work, or any semblance of respect for the truth."

Lauren rolled her eyes and snatched the report out of Renée's hands.

"Surely this won't screw the case," offered Renée.

"It could if his advocate presents a diminished capacity defense."

Renée raised her hands in surrender. "Sorry, Lauren. Reality's a bitch."

Lauren compared the entries to James's logs of his chat sessions with Leo and, right up through the night Leo transferred the recordings he was charged for, found a perfect match.

"Damn it," she said again. Lauren rushed to Melissa's office. "We have a problem with the Leo Baksh case."

"You already know?" Melissa replied with surprise.

"About the drug records?"

"Drug records?"

They beheld each other in confusion.

"Please tell me there's not another problem," said Lauren.

"I've found an anomaly in James's reports. I scoured his final narratives sequentially and everything was in order. But when I examined each separately, I found what looks like an earlier draft containing a reference to the file name for a recording Baksh distributed."

"And that's a problem because?"

"It predates the night we say Baksh distributed the file to James."

Lauren collapsed into a chair, stunned. "Have you asked James about it?"

"No," said Melissa. "You are leading this investigation and you asked me to be on lookout for inconsistencies in his reports. I thought I should tell you before I did anything."

"Maybe he prepared rough drafts of the reports at the same time and it's a simple mix-up," said Lauren.

"Could be," said Melissa, "but all we'll have to go on is James's word because he says he destroyed all his contemporaneous notes."

"I instructed him to preserve his notes."

Melissa shrugged.

Lauren's pulse raced. She wanted to stomp into James's office and sock him in the mouth for his insolence and insubordination. After a tick, she deescalated the scenario to marching into the chief's office and filing a formal complaint. A few moments later, she decided to wait until she felt more collected to question James.

"You still think James has a good side we've yet to see?"

"Yes, I do," Melissa replied, "but that won't stop me from doing my job."

Lauren shook her head. "Make a copy for me and lock up the original."

Lauren opened James's office door without knocking and slapped the discrepant document on the desk, hoping to catch him off guard.

"Uh, good morning?" James said with undisguised distaste.

"This document is at odds with your final report. It also predates your report regarding Leo Baksh's distribution of the QFRI recordings, yet it appears to memorialize your receipt of one of them prior to when you say you first received them from Baksh."

James eyed her coldly. "Number one," he snarled, "You have no authority, nor is it appropriate by any stretch, to address me like an interrogee in one of your investigations."

She started to object, but he cut her off.

"Number two, my final draft of each report is the one I sign, which means it is the one that accurately memorializes the relevant facts. That's the point of successive drafts. They supersede the ones that precede them and correct errors.

"Number three, we all collate information from notes into multiple reports simultaneously. I do it. You do it. Don't try to tell me you don't. Sometimes things get crossed in the process and if we do our jobs they get straightened out in the *final report*."

"Did you supply Leo Baksh with the recordings you claim he gave you?" pressed Lauren, refusing to let James shout her down.

James's eyes said he would gladly snap her neck, but he remained still as a statue.

"Are you accusing me of falsifying a report, Drey?" he said with deathly cool.

"I'm asking you a question of fact."

"My report speaks for itself."

"Which one?" she shouted, yanking the sheet out of his hand and waving it in his face.

Lauren thought he would strike her, but he held still as they glared at each other.

"How dare you speak to me like that?" he said with icy rage. "Get out of my office."

Lauren considered pushing him further, but his position was clear enough: The draft was an error and he stood by his final reports. Nevertheless, she refused to give him the satisfaction of ejecting her before she was ready to leave. "I instructed you to preserve your notes," she said evenly. "Those should help clarify the"—*fraud*, she thought—"potentially problematic inconsistency in your reports." She held out her hand.

"I don't take orders from agents of equal rank," said James. "My longstanding practice is to destroy notes once they are memorialized in a report. It helps prevent unfocused agents from cooking up mythical problems to sabotage their airtight cases."

Lauren smiled mirthlessly at his audacity. He smiled back defiantly and snatched the document out of her hand.

She leaned across the desk and whispered, "It's a copy."

As she turned to leave, James said "Mind your choice of enemies. You're a cop. He's a perp. Don't get distracted."

She paused at this semi-threat and considered a few retorts, but left without comment.

Her confrontation with James heightened Lauren's suspicions and deepened her dilemma. After running mental circles for half an hour, she made her way to the agent who, though neither of them ever spoke of it, was the closest thing she had to a mentor.

"Got a minute?"

Bimal shifted from the reading to distance regions of his bifocals and gestured her inside.

Lauren took a seat and regarded Bimal across his desk as she collected her thoughts. He gave her his full attention and waited patiently.

"I have learned of two pieces of evidence bearing on the Leo Baksh case."

"I'm aware of the drug dealer's log," he preempted.

Lauren bowed her head once. "In addition to that item, which the defense presumably would use as part of a diminished capacity argument—"

Bimal nodded acknowledgement of this possibility.

"—there is a document that raises questions about the,"—*veracity*, she thought—"completeness of James Malone's report detailing the events the distribution charges against Baksh are based on."

Bimal raised his eyebrows and Lauren handed him a copy of the page in question. As he examined it, she explained how Melissa discovered it and told him how James reacted when she confronted him.

Bimal took in her disclosure with characteristic poise. "What's your analysis?"

She felt like a teacher had just picked her from the sea of raised hands in a high school math class. Unlike many kids, she had always relished the pressure. "The discrepant document may have been a simple mistake that James corrected in his final draft. However, my gut tells me otherwise, and James cemented that instinct by reacting as he did. The document raises serious questions about his reports. We have a duty to disclose it to the defense advocate."

"Would it absolve Baksh of criminal liability if agents were both his suppliers and recipients?"

Lauren considered the question. "No, as long as he possessed the intent to receive and distribute the recordings on his own."

"Correct. But?"

"But that doesn't mean he couldn't use the document's existence to argue James falsified his report and supplied the recordings to Baksh in the first place."

"That alone still wouldn't prove entrapment."

"No, but it might turn off an adjudicator or jury and raise questions about what James was hiding. The defense advocate could suggest all sorts of exculpatory possibilities."

"James is a skilled witness."

"A document like this could still seriously undercut his credibility. An advocate like Lance Wilson could shred our case with a loose end like that, no matter how good James is on the stand."

Bimal granted the point. "Is there any other evidence to support a claim that James supplied the recordings?"

"Not that I'm aware of," Lauren said, throwing her hands up in frustration. "But the day's only half over."

Bimal silenced an incoming call. "If you found out James provided the recordings and falsified his final report, even if he did so because there was some irregularity in his own possession of them," he let the silence stretch, "would you believe Baksh was innocent of the charged crime?"

"No," Lauren replied after a moment's reflection, "but I would have concerns about the integrity of the process leading to his conviction, and serious concerns about Agent Malone."

"As well you should," said Bimal.

"My opinion also might change if I found out James had actively seduced Baksh to accept recordings he would not otherwise have possessed."

"That's the rub, isn't it?" said Bimal.

"What do I do?"

"The drug-sale logs and the errant draft report page are potentially," he peered over his eyeglasses, "consequential in the proceedings against Mr. Baksh, regardless of whether they are legally significant."

"Exactly."

"It's a close call whether we have a duty to disclose them. However, the integrity of the adjudicatory process is potentially implicated. If we don't obtain convictions fairly, then upon what do we base our moral authority?"

"On enforcing the law," countered Lauren.

"Without a fair adjudicatory process, law enforcement can devolve into abuse of state power," Bimal said. "Not all agents possess our omniscience to render optimal decisions before the fact."

"True," she conceded with a sigh. "So I should disclose the new evidence."

Bimal held up a finger. "I believe you must report it to the government's advocate. It is up to her to determine whether to produce it to the defense."

"In other words, pass the buck."

"In other words, discharge our duty and entrust it to her professional discretion."

Lauren did not like this answer. "Alicia won't disclose it unless she has to. All she cares about is putting Baksh away. I share that goal but I don't like resolving ethical problems by handing them off to people who don't care about them."

"Neither do I," said Bimal, "but to do otherwise would exceed our authority. There may be a time and place, perhaps even in this case, to sidestep the government's advocate. But I don't think this situation merits that sort of showdown. Do you?"

Lauren considered the career consequences of sabotaging a pending criminal prosecution, particularly with evidence of ambiguous significance, and saw Bimal's point.

"No."

"However," Bimal continued, "the implications for Agent Malone are another matter."

Lauren crossed her arms and listened.

"Allow me to be blunt: I don't like Malone."

She was startled by his candor.

"While I admire some of his remarkable skills, I do not respect his values or trust his motives. To hear that he has threatened you—"

Lauren started to qualify but Bimal held up his hand.

"—surprises me only in its lack of guile. You must have taken him quite off his guard." He allowed Lauren to reflect on this. "If I had the power, I would long ago have stripped Agent Malone of his badge and sentenced him to five years hard labor to beat into his arrogant skull a rudimentary sense of humility."

Lauren yelped, then cupped a hand over her mouth.

Bimal smiled thinly. "Alas, I lack such power. I must content myself with scrutinizing his behavior and assembling an arsenal to take him down should the need arise. This little item"—he held up the errant draft remnant—"could prove useful. You won't mind if I retain it?"

Lauren couldn't believe her ears. After a moment of internal fluster, she answered, "Not at all."

"I thought perhaps you'd feel that way."

"I have logs of an earlier discrepancy in James's reports regarding this investigation, which triggered my request that Melissa watch for further inconsistencies. Would you like a copy of that as well?"

"Please."

They adopted neutral expressions and discussed the matter no further.

"Thank you for helping me think things through," said Lauren. "I'll advise Alicia Cheung about both new discoveries."

"Do it through a formal report," advised Bimal. "Retain multiple backups."

"Wouldn't want the buck pushed back if things went badly." She pretended to garrote herself.

"No, we would not want that," he agreed.

Lauren spent the afternoon detailing the evidence and her concerns about its potential consequences in a report to the government's advocate.

When Alicia Cheung opened her micromissive account later that day, two items carried greater urgency than the rest. One was a note from Leo Baksh's advocate Lance Wilson advising her that Leo was prepared to accept the plea deal.

The other was Lauren's new report. Alicia read Lauren's narrative thoroughly and tapped a pen on the desk as she thought. She picked up the phone to call a Micromedium technician who owed her enough favors to keep his mouth shut.

"Chad, how hard would it be to permanently erase any record of a micromissive?"

"Not difficult at all, but the sender will have a record of its dispatch."

She weighed it out and decided that would have to do.

"Can you do me a favor?" she asked.

"Of course," he replied.

36

"TO THE CHARGE OF DISTRIBUTING a QFRI-mediated parasitic abuse recording, how do you plead?"

Leo turned toward the back of the crowded courtroom. He recognized John Hanes. *Who are all the rest?* He glanced briefly at his advocate, then turned to face the adjudicator.

"Guilty."

The room remained silent as a tomb.

The adjudicator engaged Leo in a colloquy to ensure he was entering a change of plea voluntarily. Hardly, he wanted to retort. *I've been strong-armed into it by a vindictive prosecutor harnessing public hysteria through an insane statute passed by a corrupt Council of Delegates.*

"Yes," he responded instead to each question, sealing his fate. The court set the case sixty days out for sentencing and turned to the question of Leo's custody status.

True to ice-blood form, Alicia argued that Leo should be remanded to custody immediately, offering the disingenuous rationale that it would ensure he did not relapse or harm himself while awaiting the frightening eventuality of sentencing. *As if she gives a damn about either possibility*, Leo thought bitterly.

Wilson argued valiantly that Leo should be left free to get his affairs in order and continue therapy. His arguments did not carry the day, however, and the adjudicator ordered Leo taken into custody.

"Every day counts toward service of your eventual sentence," Lance told him as the courtroom deputies gripped Leo by the arm to escort him out. "Stay focused. I will visit you soon so we can plan for the sentencing hearing."

Back to jail Leo went, this time with no release date in sight.

Because of the prosecutor's feigned concern that Leo might be a suicide risk, his jailers placed him in solitary confinement, a perplexing response given that it could drive even a stable person to the brink. They released him into an empty common area for one hour every other day to shower, make phone calls, select reading material, and take his turn at distributing hot water through potato chip bags to similarly segregated inmates. The other forty-seven hours he was locked down in a cold cell. The ambient racket made normal sleep impossible, so he grabbed a few hours when he could, but usually awoke from nightmares to a disembodied voice shouting obscenities into the grey void. The ordeal before him stretched like an endless, treacherous wasteland.

Wilson met with Leo a week into his confinement to prepare for the sentencing hearing. This amounted to compiling evidence of Leo's character in hopes of limiting his term of incarceration to no more than ten years.

Three weeks into Leo's confinement, Wendy came to see him. Due to his unnecessarily harsh custodial status, the guards placed him in leg irons, cuffed his hands and chained them to his waist before escorting him to the visiting area. Leo saw Wendy through tempered glass in the visitation booth. He felt like a ghost, rattling his chains as he perched on the tiny stool.

Wendy regarded him sadly before picking up a grimy telephone.

"It's kind of you to come see me," Leo said.

She pressed her lips together grimly. "Don't mention it. Why in God's name are you in chains?"

"Apparently I'm a dangerous criminal."

"That's absurd. You're already in jail."

Leo shrugged.

She banished any signs of pity.

"I assumed you would be too angry to have further contact with me," he said.

"Of course I'm angry," she replied. "We're all angry at you."

"I'm angry at myself."

"That's why people are willing to forgive you. Provided," she emphasized, shaking a commanding finger at him, "You learn your lessons and it never happens again."

Leo's cross-the-heart gesture was impeded by his chains, but Wendy got the point.

"Is there anything you need?" she asked.

"No, thank you. John Hanes has generously put funds on my commissary account and is sending me the newspaper and books."

"I can't imagine that reading the papers is too good for your emotional state."

Leo torqued his features into a caricature of madness. "Yes, I've become the demon du jour."

"A public menace," she confirmed.

"The very reason we need harsher laws."

"You've gone from advocate for the oppressed to poster child for the oppressors."

"Yep, and they're trying to undo everything I accomplished before my arrest."

As Leo went through his ordeal, the conservatives exploited his charges to justify an attack on the provisional residential permit case he wrote for Harlan Durell. They also set out to stop the Board from placing limits on the government's power to confine people, due to Leo's employment when the case raising that issue reached the Board.

"They're trying to thwart my professional achievements and prolong my incarceration in one and the same stroke."

"Don't follow the mess in the papers. You'll drive yourself nuts. Focus on your strength."

Leo pretended to flex his pectorals, but couldn't muster much humor or enthusiasm, no matter how wise he knew her advice to be.

"How are you?" he asked.

"I've been better," answered Wendy. Leo started to ask what was wrong, but she held up her hand. "We don't have much time before they haul you back out, so let's skip the courtesies."

"I didn't ask you out of courtesy."

Wendy closed her eyes and shook her head. "That's not what I meant. Thank you for asking, but I came here for Anna."

Leo felt a chill.

"How is she?" he asked. "I know she's terrible but how is she?"

"All things considered, she's solid," Wendy replied.

Leo exhaled. "Thank God."

"She told me to tell you she forgives you."

This cut Leo's heart like a scalpel. He wiped away tears on his shoulder.

Wendy turned down the corners of her mouth sadly and placed her palm on the glass. "She also told me to tell you that while she's glad Jeaneane Spence is her advocate, she wouldn't want her for a friend after seeing how she turned on you."

"Turned on me how? She ignored all my calls and no doubt has made me fodder for her gossip mill. Is there more?"

"You don't know?"

Leo shook his head.

"She's fucking the DDI agent who busted you."

He flinched as though slapped. "What?" he shouted.

Wendy placed a silencing finger across her lips. Leo gritted his teeth to restrain the torrent of invective.

"He is my brother, as you must know by now," Wendy offered. Leo said he did. "I love him," she continued, "but he routinely destroys people caught in his trance. They deserve each other. You can rest assured the situation will contain its own punishment for Jeaneane."

Leo stifled expressions of cruel pleasure at that prospect. "Thank you for telling me. Let's get back to Anna."

Wendy eyed him carefully. "The prosecutor wants her to testify at your sentencing."

"What?" Leo screamed again.

Wendy clenched her jaw and glared at him to calm down.

Leo clenched his fists and willed himself to comply. Through a voice ragged with fatigue and suppressed rage, he said, "God fucking damn it. That's one main reason I pled guilty. To avoid dragging her through a trial."

"Let me finish."

Leo relaxed his hands and gave her his attention.

"She told Alicia Cheung to get screwed."

"No she didn't," Leo swatted at Wendy and his chains jangled on the counter.

"Perhaps not in so many words, but she has refused to testify."

Wendy pulled a small written note out of her bag for him that read: "She has recurrent nightmares of suffering the abuse. When she lifts her head to the person who is recording and directing it, she sees you."

Leo's stomach dropped.

Wendy flipped over the note. On the back it asked, "Have you been having reciprocal nightmares?"

He nodded.

"She told Alicia she doesn't have anything bad to say about you and she doesn't feel that your crime has harmed her," Wendy said aloud, in case they were being monitored and recorded.

On another piece of paper, she showed Leo these words: "It's an aftereffect of all neural entanglements. She doesn't blame you, and she doesn't want to give the prosecutor a chance to question her about it and use it against you."

"Maybe she should," said Leo aloud.

"She knows you are not the monster they are painting you to be," said Wendy. "She refuses to assist such a distorting characterization. She thinks those recordings harm users too."

"But," he began to object.

Wendy gave him the stop sign. "She knows who she is. She has made up her mind."

Leo cherished the thought of Anna's stubborn determination. Nevertheless, he had grave misgivings about her downplaying what appeared to be quite tangible effects from his viewing the recording of her abuse.

He wanted to ask whether Anna dreamt of James Malone as well. James regularly starred in Leo's nightmares, often associated with scenes of abuse Leo had never encountered during his forays into the fetish sites.

Wendy or Anna apparently anticipated the question because another scrap of paper read: "The person she hates is my brother. He haunts her dreams like an icy specter."

Leo shivered.

Wendy resumed speaking, shifting to a less dangerous subject. "Jeaneane doesn't want to pursue Anna's appeal in the light of publicity around your prosecution. She has advised Anna to withdraw it."

"But that's crazy," protested Leo. "Anna can't possibly want that. It's giving Alicia Cheung the across-the-board victory she wants."

Wendy started to respond, but Leo continued. "It will arouse Cheung's bloodlust," he said with disgust. "She won't rest until she gets Anna reclassified as an Aggressive and ensures her self-destruction in an Aggressive ghetto."

Wendy suffered the tirade, unmoved. "Are you through?"

"For the moment."

She waited to be sure Leo stayed mute. "Jeaneane has reached a tentative agreement with Cheung. The government will take no action against Anna if she enters guided development."

"That will destroy her."

"No it won't," said Wendy calmly. "It didn't destroy you, did it?"

"I'm not so sure," said Leo, rattling his chains.

"You did that to yourself," she said coolly.

Leo considered a complex defense that his old emotional wounds made him vulnerable to addiction and his behavior was the result of Elidrine-induced temporary psychosis. But his therapy and work in recovery kicked in, and he took her admonishment in stride. "True."

"Also, the reprogramming is more competently individualized now than when you went through it," she continued. Leo tipped his hand from side to side in partial agreement. "The government will allow her to go through an accredited private provider, so she can choose her poison."

"Anna can't afford that," countered Leo.

"No, but I can," said Wendy. "My great-grandmother set me up rather well."

Leo cringed. "I've never had the presence of mind to tell you how sorry I am about your great-grandmother. She was a magnificent woman."

"You knew her?"

"Not personally, no. I knew of her charitable work. I respected her."

"Thank you," said Wendy, resisting tears. *You don't know the half of it*, she thought.

"You can pay for Anna's treatment, education, and therapy?"

"Can and intend to," she said.

"You are something else, Wendy."

"So I'm told," she said, amused and sad at the same time.

"Now that you're a properly well-heeled Malone, no more waiting tables?"

"I haven't decided," she replied. "It's a great way to meet people." Anaku's face flashed through her mind.

"I hate to see Anna give up her case," said Leo. "I'm disappointed in Jeaneane and furious at her."

Wendy shrugged. "Anna is resolved to this, though. Learning how to stop fighting might be the more powerful choice."

Leo contemplated that a moment. "I suppose that could be true."

"In any event, it's the path she's chosen, so I will encourage her to make the most of it."

"Please tell her I'm so sorry," said Leo. "For everything."

"I will," said Wendy. "She would visit you herself but it's prohibited."

"Yes, I know," said Leo, wondering if he would ever see her again.

"As for you," said Wendy, opening her bag in preparation to leave, "People out here are pulling for you. Do not give up hope, no matter how dark it gets in the short term, do you hear me?"

Leo gave a thumbs up but eyed her curiously.

"Things are not always as they appear," she said, using a variation of what Leo had come to view as her favorite cryptic quip. "People are," she tucked away the scraps of paper, "looking into what can be done."

"What?" he started to ask, but she gave him the *Shh* sign.

"Large forces are at play. Everything is in flux. Right now, you're being crushed by it. Stay tough. Think like a diamond." She clicked her fingernail on a glittering pendant resting on her sternum. "Miners are excavating as we speak."

Her features registered gravity, seriousness, and a touch of playful mirth. The combination gave Leo an ineffable sense of hope.

"OK," he said. "Thank you."

Wendy kissed her fingertips and touched them to the glass. With a wink, she arose and took her leave.

Later that night, Leo awoke from an emotionally intense dream he could barely remember, save for a calm, loving presence telling him to be patient.

"Anaku," he said aloud, and drifted back to sleep as tears slid down his temples.

37

IN THE WEEKS FOLLOWING THEIR breach of the DII superhub, Anaku, Patrice, and Hackizen analyzed data from the automated surveillance programs they had implanted. As Anaku had surmised, the superhub and its continent-wide spread of quantum neural tentacles appeared to have a far more nefarious purpose than surveillance.

Patrice zoomed out a map one chilly morning and the pattern before her eyes triggered a moment of hacktivist satori:

> **Sleeperagent:** `They aren't just eavesdropping. They're harvesting and concentrating aggressive neural energy.`

She transferred the map to the others, and they agreed.

> **Anaku:** `Now` *`that`* `makes sense.`

As their map of the DII quantum neural web developed, they tracked the path of these concentrated signals into other protected areas of the superhub and then through Micromedium channels to sites overseas. They hypothesized that the DII was somehow using this distilled cocktail of neural rage and hatred in its torture of Liam, Gillian, and who knew how many others.

They became preoccupied for a time with trying to uncover the DII's mechanisms for blending, concentrating, controlling, and delivering neural energy in such tightly controlled, potent bursts. Unsure where their investigation was headed or when it might be stymied, they documented their discoveries and hid their intel in caches throughout the Micromedium.

To their partial relief, the DII left off torturing Liam and Gillian several days after the trio first intercepted the multimedia stream. Though they were traumatized and uncomfortable, Liam and Gillian appeared to be experiencing a respite from the neural abuse. No one knew why this was, but the hacktivists wished desperately to liberate the detainees before the torture resumed.

Anaku began compiling a statement to accompany mass revelation of the atrocities they had uncovered, along with a detailed analysis of the superhub's collection, concentration, and weaponization of the aggressive quantum neural energy. He was polishing this multimedia act of suicidal whistleblowing when Hackizen, who had returned to analyzing the superhub's operations, hailed him.

Hackizen: We uncovered another layer of activity.

Anaku: ?

Hackizen: The aggressive energy is flowing both directions.

Anaku: Meaning?

Hackizen: They are not just collecting it. They are piping it into the domestic venues, too. In some cases, they pour a little in, which triggers an uptick in aggression, then harvest the amplified result.

Anaku quietly absorbed this for a beat.

Anaku: Fascinating.

Sleeperagent: Fucking twisted.

Hackizen: Precise and deliberate.

Sleeperagent: To what end?

Anaku: Their main purpose is always control.

Sleeperagent: Introducing aggression into public venues seems like a risky way to maintain control.

Anaku: The goal is a balance between stability and chaos. They need enough chaos to keep the public scared into accepting control. Too much chaos can trigger political resistance. Too much stability and the public starts to question restrictions on its freedoms. The sweet spot for the DII is a public that is scared but not desperate.

Hackizen: How should we proceed?

Anaku: For now, let's try to map and chart how the DII is routing the aggression and correlate it with activities at the venues to the extent we can. Think in terms of parsing it into easily grasped graphics and snapshots.

Anaku checked his watch.

Anaku: `Baksh's sentencing is about to begin. Can you get me the coordinates for the courtroom?`

Hackizen consulted the map he and Patrice had compiled and connected Anaku to a user interface for monitoring the QFRI surveillance equipment installed in the courtroom where Leo was to be sentenced.

Anaku activated a macrovision set in his home office and tuned to a station scheduled to broadcast the proceeding. As the station's host blithered preliminary nonsense to fill time before the hearing commenced, Anaku switched back and forth from the video feed on macrovision to the neural output from the courtroom via his clandestine user interface to the DII superhub, and tried to match the neural signals to the figures on the video screen.

Across town, Leo sat in a chilly holding cell on a stainless-steel bench, awaiting his fate. His heart was pounding. Breathing exercises curbed his fearful tremors to a steady thrum. After ninety wretched minutes, a metal clang signaled the courtroom deputy's entrance to retrieve him.

"It's time," the officer said, opening the cell door. "I don't need to cuff you, do I?"

Leo made eye contact. "Of course not."

The officer consulted his time-honed instincts, then took Leo by his upper arm without restraining him and escorted him to the proceeding.

Back through the mirror Leo walked, from grayscale to woodtone, and glanced around the packed courtroom. His parents were making their best attempt at reassuring smiles. John Hanes was seated in front and greeted Leo with a sober nod. Jeb, Jamie, Wendy, and several of Leo's colleagues were there, but not Jeaneane.

Adjudicator Conrad Hutchinson allowed Lance Wilson to go first. Wilson had filed a psychological evaluation report concluding that Leo's main problem was his Elidrine addiction, now in remission, and associated mental degradation at the time of his crime. Wilson had also given the court a stack of letters from people who knew Leo well, all attesting to his peaceable and responsible character, valiant work on behalf of Vulnerables, and assertions that his crime was an aberration that would not have occurred but for the addiction. Wilson had bolstered this with logs documenting Leo's drug treatment and recovery, and accompanied these documents with an impassioned brief arguing that the court should sentence Leo to the lowest possible term.

In court, Wilson reiterated these arguments and called two witnesses: John Hanes and Leo's father, both of whom vehemently testified Leo had learned his lesson and they would help him stay on track. Leo's father did not understand that Leo had already agreed to serve at least ten years in prison and begged in vain for the court to release his son. Leo wiped away tears of shame as his father pled for compassion Leo knew the court was powerless to provide.

After the defense made its arguments, Alicia Cheung turned to Leo with a cold sneer and proclaimed, "So far, everyone has focused on the defendant and his alleged virtues and forgivable weaknesses. I want to focus on his crime, a revolting and heinous act of exploitation, violation of his duties of office and position of power, and commission of an act of parasitic abuse so vile and corrupt he should be imprisoned for life if we were to accomplish justice in this proceeding."

Wilson started to object on the grounds that the parties were bound by their plea agreement to a ten-to-eighteen-year range. Cheung cut him off: "The most we can achieve is to send him away for eighteen years," she argued. "But even the maximum sentence available is a slap on the wrist compared to what this monster deserves."

Outrage erupted from the audience, but the court bellowed them into silence. "The next person who interrupts these proceedings will be removed."

With order restored, Cheung outlined her argument. She had hoped to call the victims in the case, Ms. Anna Dao and Ms. Jane Doe, the plaintiff in the assault case whose recorded abuse Leo had distributed. "However, Ms. Doe's advocate, Jeaneane Spence, has refused to subject her client to the trauma of testifying."

Wilson eyed her suspiciously.

"Anna Dao, Mr. Baksh's former client, has refused to testify because that man"—she jabbed a finger at Leo—"terrified and violated her to the point she could not bear to be in the same room with him."

Wendy jumped to her feet. "That's bullshit!"

"Silence!" the adjudicator howled. He dispatched the courtroom deputies, who seized Wendy by the arms. As they roughly escorted her from her seat, she strained toward Alicia Cheung and snarled, "You are a filthy liar."

As he witnessed this spectacle via macrovision, Anaku relished her indomitability.

The courtroom's occupants froze in stunned silence as Wendy was removed. All eyes turned to Cheung, who smirked and shook her head, undaunted. "There is no evidence that drugs had anything to do with the defendant's criminal behavior, other than self-serving statements he made to his treatment providers and hired psychological evaluator."

Lauren and Melissa turned toward one another in shock. They resumed poker faces, but not before Wilson made note of their surprise. James did not flinch.

Wilson started to interject that the psychological evaluator's professional opinion on the role of Leo's addiction was authoritative evidence. The court ordered him to save the point for closing remarks.

With the floor passed back to her, Cheung called her star witness,

Department of Domestic Intelligence agent James Malone. Impeccably dressed and groomed, and moving with characteristically forceful poise, James cut an impressive figure as he took the stand. Cheung established that he had operated undercover in the fetish Micromedium sites as part of an investigation into the newly proscribed crime of QFRI-mediated parasitic abuse. James described the neural interface phenomenon, chatroom dynamics, and the shared experience of QFRI-enhanced recordings. He described interacting with the person identifying as VulNeedsLesson and forming a relationship with him. He explained how he used a tracer program to identify the person behind the moniker as Leo Baksh.

"He's a sadistic Aggressive," James testified flatly. "He lives to abuse Vulnerables. He cannot get enough of it."

He characterized Leo's part of their interactions as involving predatory consumption of the Vulnerables' suffering. "I just observed," James proclaimed. "It was shocking and offensive, and I will always suffer wounds from having been exposed to such obscene cruelty."

Leo turned to his advocate slack-faced, but Wilson registered acute concentration.

Cheung appeared satisfied. "I see," she said. "Now, please tell us about the night of the charged offense."

At his workstation, Anaku turned from the audiovisual macrovision coverage of James's testimony to the superhub's depiction of the courtroom's quantum neural configuration. He used his neural array to mentally text the others:

> **Anaku:** I see two aggressive spikes in the room, but I can't tell from this interface who they correspond to.
>
> **Sleeperagent:** I'm trying to access a graphic display of the signals' spatial origin, which should answer the question. One of those spikes should be coming from the defendant. I don't know about the other one. I'll get you a definitive map in a minute.
>
> **Anaku:** While you're at it, is there any way to determine whether neural energy is being routed into the room?
>
> **Hackizen:** We're working on a plug-in for your user interface for that purpose. Stand by.

Meanwhile at the superhub facility, unbeknownst to Anaku and the others, a senior DII agent was training a subordinate in operating the quantum neural equipment using Leo Baksh's high-profile sentencing hearing as an educational exercise. The senior agent showed his student the neural readings coming from the room, and the student considered them against the room's physical configuration depicted on the macrovision coverage of the hearing.

"He must be facing a serious charge of aggression," said the student.

"Yes," replied the senior agent, "Distributing and consuming a QFRI-enhanced recording of his own Vulnerable client's severe abuse."

"These readings are off the charts," exclaimed the student as he scanned the room's neural signals. "This guy's a fiend. How can he look so unthreatening?"

The instructor concealed his amusement.

In the courtroom, James described the night of Leo's crime, explaining that Leo had offered to jointly view QFRI-enhanced recordings of Vulnerable abuse. James said he did not know at the time who was depicted in the first one, but that Leo's neural signal showed he found it thrilling.

Then, James testified, Leo showed him the recording of Anna Dao's abuse. James said he was shocked when he realized who was depicted. He said Leo's interest was more intense than it had been in any other recording James had experienced with him, and that he detected in Leo's mind both acute excitement and what James said he could only describe as pride. James said he was sickened by this, and that Leo devoured the recording and unceremoniously severed the link once his neurons had achieved satiety.

James said Leo was the most cold-blooded and heartless sociopath he had encountered in his career. Leo's parents wept tears of rage at this patent falsehood, but held their tongues, lest they suffer the same fate as Wendy. John Hanes observed the proceeding with cool detachment, waiting to see Lance Wilson work his art.

Cheung finished her examination of James and the floor passed to Wilson. "Mr. Malone," he began, "I am handing you the text the government's advocate claims accurately reflects your conversation with Leo Baksh the night of the events he is being prosecuted for."

James took the text and eyed it perfunctorily. Wilson had him read it into the record and authenticate it as accurately reflecting their exchange.

"It's true, isn't it," Wilson continued, "that you asked Mr. Baksh to show you, quote, 'something new.'"

James admitted this was true, but said it was because of Leo's past propensity to offer new recordings.

"But you initiated the conversation, the neural session, and the use of the recording."

James attempted to quibble over the meaning of "initiated," but Wilson disengaged and let the point's significance echo into the silence as he prepared his next question.

"You say my client was excited by the first recording."

"Yes," James replied.

"But that's clearly not true, is it?" Wilson made James read aloud the text showing that Leo cut off the recording and said he didn't like it.

James said, "All I can tell you is that I was directly connected to his mind and he lapped it up like ice cream."

"Why did you have to badger him into launching the second recording?" asked Wilson.

"I didn't," snapped James.

"Didn't you, now?" Wilson showed James a statement from Leo Baksh on the day of his arrest, attesting that the person identifying as Domin8U had teased, taunted, invited, and cajoled Leo into viewing the second recording over Leo's clear statement that he'd had enough.

James eyed the report but dismissed it as self-serving dissembling. Leo sent the recordings of his own accord, James insisted, and his neural signal clearly reflected his interest.

"For that we have nothing but your word," countered Wilson. "Mr. Baksh's contemporaneous statement clearly contradicts your account. Furthermore, the Micromedium terminal he used captured parts of your exchange as text files, and those fragments support his version, not yours. Isn't that true?"

The government's advocate started to intervene, but Wilson withdrew the question, though not its taint. "The forensically recovered text speaks for itself in black and white," he said flatly, staring James in the eye.

James's expression grew dangerous, but Alicia bared her teeth in warning and he did not argue.

Out of nowhere, Wilson tried to catch James off guard by asking, "Where did you first obtain these recordings?"

James was unfazed: "From Leo Baksh that night, as evidenced among other places, in the text you're holding."

"I mean before that," said Wilson, raising his voice. "Who gave you the recordings?"

James regarded him coldly. "I've already answered that question."

"I don't think so," shot back Wilson. "What I'm asking is who gave them to you *before* you gave them to Mr. Baksh under another undercover moniker?"

Cheung rose to her feet and shouted an objection: "Your Honor, there is no evidentiary basis for this line of questioning."

The court pivoted to the defense advocate, "Mr. Wilson?"

"My client received the recordings from an individual he'd never met minutes before Agent Malone logged in under his usual moniker. My client found the donor's energy signature familiar. It is fair to inquire whether this was Mr. Malone under another identity."

Cheung erupted in outrage. "Mr. Wilson's hunch is not in evidence, is uncorroborated, and does not provide a foundation for this defamatory line of interrogation."

The adjudicator eyed Wilson, who held his ground and stared down James. James's eyes showed not concern, but cold hatred as he returned Wilson's gaze.

"Let me rephrase," said Wilson.

"Proceed," said the adjudicator, and Cheung slowly returned to her seat.

"How do you believe Mr. Baksh came into contact with the recordings?"

"I have no idea where he got the first one," responded James. "From some other pervert, no doubt."

"No doubt," Wilson pointedly replied.

James ignored the jab. "As for the second one, for all we know he created it himself."

The audience erupted in fury over this allegation. As the court struggled to regain control, Melissa and Lauren exchanged a long glance.

Wilson observed this and, when he turned back to Malone, saw that he was glaring at his colleagues with barely concealed rage.

Patrice tore Anaku away from the coverage of this drama.

Sleeperagent: We're plugging the new applications into your interface. There may be a brief interruption, but you'll have a graphic map of the room's neural configuration and readings for flows into and out of the room.

Over at the superhub, the DII student turned to his supervisor. "These aggression readings are way above average. Baksh is well within the Aggressive range. He's screwed."

The supervisor regarded his student with impatience. He clicked on an icon to activate a graphic map of the room's neural signal configuration.

Sleeperagent: If I'm reading this correctly, the most intense Aggressive signal is coming from the witness, not the defendant.

Anaku: That's no surprise to anyone who knows these people.

Sleeperagent: But the whole point of this proceeding is that the defendant is allegedly a violent and dangerous Aggressive.

Hackizen: And? I thought we long ago agreed that the classification system was fraudulent.

Sleeperagent: Yes, but even by its own rules these readings make no sense.

"—and the other spike is coming from the prosecutor," said the DII student as he matched the video feed to the graphic map.

The supervisor eyed him and smirked.

"According to this screen," said the student pointing to another monitor, "you are routing neural energy into the room." He looked back and forth between the screens, then up as recognition dawned.

Sleeperagent: Someone is routing aggressive energy into the arrays streaming through the brains of the prosecutor, the witness—

Anaku: And the adjudicator. Are we recording this?

Hackizen: Yes. I can patch you into the link they're using to route energy into the room if you want to try and influence it.

Anaku: Tempting, but no. Becoming part of this manipulation would destroy our authority to denounce it.

Hackizen: Too bad. Next best option: I think I can sever the link and cut off the inflow.

Anaku: Excellent. Do that if you can.

At the superhub, the DII instructor's merriment fell flat as the quantum neural conduit he had configured to feed aggression into the courtroom went dead. His fingers flew over a keyboard and clicked through screens, but he couldn't restore the signal. Aghast, the student watched his mentor struggle in vain to reinsert his invisible hand into the minds of the prosecution team and the arbiter of Leo Baksh's fate.

In the courtroom, Cheung was midstream through a question to James on redirect when she abruptly stopped speaking. Cheung, James, and the adjudicator were visibly disoriented, as though they had just become aware of their surroundings.

Wilson and Leo exchanged a perplexed glance, as did Melissa and Lauren.

"Um," Cheung resumed, "No further questions."

The judge shook his head. "Mr. Wilson?"

Lance was unable to decipher the abrupt temperamental shift and disjointed behavior. "No more questions for this witness, Your Honor."

"Very well," said the adjudicator, regaining his judicial demeanor. "Mr. Malone, you may step down, but please remain in the courtroom."

James stumbled on his way back to the seat next to Melissa, a most uncharacteristic breach of grace.

The adjudicator turned to Lance Wilson and asked whether the defendant wished to address the court. Wilson said he did, and Leo stood at the microphone, not as advocate for someone else like so many times before, but to speak on his own behalf. He had prepared notes but barely consulted them as he voiced responsibility for his failure to manage his emotional issues, irresponsible and catastrophic failure to get help for his drug problem, and horrifically depraved criminal acts. He pledged to absorb the significance of his punishment and harness it to grow stronger and wiser, so that when he was released, he could spend his life making amends for his actions and helping others avoid the same mistakes. He closed by telling the adjudicator he trusted him to render a fair sentence and that he would do his best to work productively with whatever the court deemed appropriate.

Sleeperagent: The defendant's neural signal registers in the Vulnerable range, and the prosecutor still registers in the Aggressive range, even without the intrusive boost.

Anaku: This surprises you?

Sleeperagent: Yes. I thought that the reason he is the defendant and she the prosecutor was because he is a dangerous Aggressive and she's a well-tempered Citizen.

Anaku: That's how the law portrays it and society views it.

Sleeperagent: What a fucking joke. Check out these readings. We could strap arrays on them, record this farce, and the neural aggression junkies would lap it up at the fetish sites Cheung claims she's trying to eliminate.

Anaku: Colorfully put. I would say the law is crude and does not grapple well with the reality of human complexity.

Hackizen: If the Citizenry gave a damn about abuse of power and Aggression, this prosecutor should be confined on the spot. She's doing what she is supposed to be eradicating.

Anaku: Perhaps not confined. We have too much of that already and it's not helping. Viewed as having issues of her own and abusing her official power? Yes. With that I would agree.

Sleeperagent: It stinks of hypocrisy. We have it all recorded.

Anaku: Perhaps we can help the public recognize that Mr. Baksh is not the only perpetrator of pathological aggression in this drama.

Hackizen: Good luck convincing these comfy Citizens that their pillars of justice are criminals in disguise.

Anaku: We can frame the issue more skillfully than that. What Leo Baksh did was wrong and deserving of punishment. But that does not mean Cheung isn't also perpetrating an offense against the values underlying the definition of Citizenry. It will be tricky, but we must try to include a critique of this when we make our public disclosure of the larger atrocities. We will have one shot to unmask the classification system and its abuses. Let's make it count.

Back in the courtroom, Alicia Cheung decided it would be imprudent to harp after Leo's sincere mea culpa. She declined to make further remarks for the moment.

Wilson summarized the evidence he had presented and, though he impugned James's credibility, stopped short of arguing he had entrapped Leo, both because he lacked proof and because he feared it would work against Leo's acceptance of responsibility. Nevertheless, he had raised the question in the adjudicator's mind and hoped it would weigh in Leo's favor. Wilson closed by imploring the court to impose the minimum available sentence.

Once the parties completed their arguments, the adjudicator made the startling move of denouncing the statute and mandatory sentencing minimum as disproportionate to the offense and unduly harsh. "This man has already learned his lesson and taken the steps necessary to restore his sanity and functionality as a Citizen. I see little to be gained by separating him from his family and community or confining him with Aggressives in a setting where most people get sicker, not better.

"Unfortunately, neither the statute nor the plea agreement give me the latitude to go below the mandatory minimum. Mr. Baksh, you are on track. Keep it that way. Engage your mind every way you can. Your family, friends, society, and if you're true to your word, even victims of the kind of crime you committed are depending on you to stay strong, get through this cleanly and intact, and leverage what you learn to make amends for your errors. Do not let them down."

Leo held back tears. "Yes, your Honor."

Annoyed by this turn of events, Cheung stood and said, "One more thing, Your Honor. In addition to the term of imprisonment, the Citizenry asks that you order Baksh summarily reclassified as an Aggressive."

Wilson jumped to his feet. "That is not part of the plea agreement."

"The agreement is silent on this point," said Cheung, "and the government believes reclassification is necessary and appropriate."

"Ms. Cheung's opinion on that subject is beyond the scope of this hearing and, no disrespect to Your Honor, likely outside this court's jurisdiction. At the very least the matter must be continued for briefing and argument on the point."

The court looked weary. "I will leave questions of the defendant's Citizenship status to the Board of Classification. Putting Mr. Baksh in prison is sufficient for today, Ms. Cheung."

She started to object but the adjudicator raised his hand and sentenced Leo to ten years in prison.

As the deputies escorted him from the courtroom, Leo's parents broke into sobs. He lifted a hand in sad farewell to them and scanned the faces in the room. The last eyes he saw were those of Jamie Tesh, who regarded Leo with a steady calm as the door slammed shut forever on Leo's life as it had been.

38

Jeaneane pressed her lips together and daubed her lipstick with a tissue. She smiled at her reflection, gazed into her jeweled eyes, fixed an errant strand of copper-gold hair, and pronounced herself gorgeous.

Satisfied that she was polished for the evening's festivities—an award dinner for advocates where she expected to receive an honor—she made one last attempt to reach the man she hoped would be her date. This time he answered.

"Yes?"

Jeaneane's instinctual response to such a terse reception ordinarily would be to turn on the ice, but to her annoyance and titillation, James was better than she at that maneuver. She opted for warmth.

"Hi, it's me. I'm so glad to catch you."

No response. Jeaneane felt a blend of longing and anger, but maintained her tone.

"Did you get my messages about the award dinner tonight?"

"Yes," James said again, brinking on collapse from the tedium.

Jeaneane's anger began to overtake her desire, but she didn't want to lose her head. She found James's detached manner and intelligence intoxicatingly erotic, and with his ridiculously good looks, he would make an ideal companion as she basked in the evening's spotlight.

Guilt surely would not work. Snotty was out. Needy would be a turnoff. Straightforward stood the best chance, she decided.

"I would be honored if you would accompany me to the dinner," she said in her best stab at playful pseudo formality. After a moment, she added somewhat less confidently, "I think the keynote speaker will be entertaining. It's catered by Élan so the meal will be exquisite."

Not a peep from James.

Out of Jeaneane's abdomen, a frightening desperation rose, one she had experienced on occasion with other men, but never so acutely or disquietingly. James called it forth on command through increasingly diverse means, including the timing of his silences. She had the eerie sense that he had dispassionately collected information about her weak points and learned to play them like a harpsichord. The ground was dropping out from beneath her, and she wanted to leap into his arms to keep from falling. Not knowing if he would catch her compounded her sense of need. On one level, her instinct told her to slam down the phone and forget his number. Then she remembered the last time they made love. She wanted more of that. Besides, who was he to send her running like a scared child? She was Jeaneane, goddamn it.

"I'm sure we could slip away early for a private celebration," she half whispered.

At first, she thought he was continuing the silent treatment, but he had begun to laugh—a humorless, cynical sound.

"How many times have you called me this week?" he asked coldly. "Five? Ten? Did you think I'd forgotten how to speak English? Did you fear I'd lost the use of my index finger?"

Jeaneane's shock overwhelmed her ability to shift gears and she was stunned mute.

"Here's a little tip that seems to have eluded you: When people don't return your calls, it means they don't want to talk with you."

Jeaneane was too disoriented by this sudden viciousness to react with anger at first. "What? Why are you speaking to me like this? Did I do something to offend you?"

"Hardly," he snapped. "You couldn't offend me if you tried, Ms. Spence. I've grown bored if you must know. It was good for a few rolls, but your company has ceased to interest me. I have no need to lie with you again, and I certainly have no desire to be your escort."

"How dare you!" Jeaneane roared, her anger surpassing her shock. "Who the hell do you think you are? Cop trash. For the record, you were never anything more to me than a cheap toy."

James laughed again, with amusement this time. "Whatever you say."

"Bastard!"

"Oh, please," James shot back. "You're the jewel who has been boffing the cop who took down her own friend. Spare me the attitude, honey pie. You and I are just alike." Jeaneane drew a breath to object, but James continued in a quiet snarl: "But unlike you, I don't enjoy fucking my own reflection."

Jeaneane slammed down the phone, balled up her fists, and erupted in rage. She shook from head to foot, and her fury slid into panic. Trembling, she wrapped her arms around herself and growled a few curses before stomping back to her mirror and patching up her mask. As the shock waves subsided, she promised herself she would not let James Malone ruin this important evening. He had shaken her, though, and she rehearsed scathing comebacks as she drove to the award dinner, perfect *coups de grâce* she would never deliver.

Two hours later, after graciously accepting her award and downing a few cocktails, Jeaneane presided over the table of honor, surrounded by friends and devoted colleagues.

John Hanes, who also had received an award that evening for his paper's coverage of law and politics, sat at an adjacent table with several politicians and luminaries in the advocates' guild. He had avoided Jeaneane's table, but was too close to prevent hearing her voice.

His efforts to screen her out failed when he heard Leo's name cross her lips. He abandoned the effort and scooted back his chair to hear her clearly.

"... I always knew he was a mess," she told the occupants at her table. "He could never manage his finances and he was always in one crisis or another. I knew he used drugs too, but I assumed he had gotten a handle on that."

John gritted his teeth. His skin crawled as Jeaneane then launched into the publicity about Leo's case.

"Can you imagine? His own client. Anna's devastated."

"I'm sure," one of Jeaneane's friends who had always liked Leo interjected meekly, "but wasn't his addiction a major factor in his crime?"

"Is that supposed to be an excuse?" Jeaneane snapped, indignant.

"No, but—"

"I'm sorry," Jeaneane said, reaching for her wine glass, "but wasn't he responsible for trying the drug in the first place?" She took a triumphant draught of Bordeaux.

"Lucky for her she didn't come from an alcoholic family," said a woman holding a glass of sparkling water to her similarly abstemious neighbor. They clinked glasses.

Jeaneane, who had not heard the comment, accepted their gesture as applause. No one dared correct her.

Thinking she had been cheered on, Jeaneane resumed her attack on Leo, commencing to dissect his failed relationship with Jeb. At this, John stood up, threw down his napkin, stalked over to her table, reached between two diners sitting opposite Jeaneane and slapped his hand on the table so hard the cutlery leapt and fell in a dissonant metallic chorus. Jeaneane's glass of wine toppled, throwing a crimson stain across the pristine linen and splashing on her dress. Conversations screeched to a halt and heads turned toward the disturbance.

"Excuse the interruption," John growled, "But your social cannibalism has spoiled my appetite and I want to pay my respects before I leave."

Jeaneane looked up from her ruined gown and held her head high. "How dare you?" she bellowed imperiously.

"How dare I?" John spat back. "I see right through your veneer, Jeaneane. I know it's hard for you to wrap your pretty head around this, but unlike your circle of sycophants, I don't give a damn what you think of me. Here's a bit of honest feedback: You never deserved or recognized the value of Leo's friendship.

Your smug, self-righteous vilification of him, and your disgusting efforts to isolate him when he is facing a predicament that nothing in your pampered little life equips you to imagine proves what was already apparent to anyone paying attention: You are selfish, cruel, disloyal and arrogant, and you haven't the faintest clue what friendship means."

Jeaneane opened her mouth to parry but John didn't give her the chance. "Why don't you cut the charade and go back to your trailer in bumfuck wherever you're from. Maybe they'll still buy your shtick, but don't whip it out around me. I see you for who you are: A greedy little girl who thinks her daddy didn't treat her like the princess she was born to be and who views the world as existing to paper over the flaws in her pretense to royalty. Get over it, babe, you're a small-town yokel in the big city, feeling like an imposter and using everyone else to compensate for your insecurities." John bent over the table, his fingertips splayed as though he might leap across it. "Leo saw these things clearly, but he was too loyal to speak of them with others and too decent to point them out to you. He accepted you and loved you for who you are, a concept that clearly eludes you."

Jeaneane's eyes filled with tears of rage. "I did not grow up in a trailer."

John smiled cruelly. "We both know you might as well have. Here's a little secret, Your Majesty: It's nothing to be ashamed of. If you could grasp that, maybe you could begin the process of becoming a human being. Perhaps then you could develop some real relationships instead of screwing over people you profess to love and surrounding yourself with flatterers who lack enough identity of their own to call you out for the self-centered glutton that you are."

This precipitated several indignant gasps at the implications of John's tirade for the table's other occupants.

"I'll leave you to your courtiers." John continued without apology. "Maybe one day they'll figure out that what you're doing to Leo you'll do to every one of them too, if you haven't already." He glanced around the table. "Wake up, people. Your function here is to serve as flattering mirrors. Falter in that role and you'll be carved up on her plate with your blood dripping down her chin. Don't expect the other minions still standing to let her see it. That's not their job"—he turned to Jeaneane and hissed—"is it, princess?"

Jeaneane threw down her napkin and rose as though from a throne. "I've got a newsflash for you, Johnny," she drawled. "You're not the first man who couldn't handle a powerful woman. You shouldn't let it make you bitter. Forget about it. God knows I did." She gauged her audience and threw John a smirk. "It's nothing to be ashamed of," she snarled, mocking his advice regarding her humble roots. "Face it," she concluded in a breathy whisper. "Not all your performances deserve an award."

More gasps. A few laughs. "That's not what I heard," said one sparkling-water drinker to the other. Again, Jeaneane took the amusement as applause and laughed too at her own disgraceful performance.

John registered no emotion. He considered telling her the turnoff wasn't her power but her lack of integrity. Instead, he declined her tawdry bait and shook his head in disgust, anger giving way to pity as he realized he must have deeply hurt her to arouse so desperate and inappropriate a retort. Perhaps one day he would apologize but not tonight. He begged pardon from his shocked tablemates, and left without another word.

Jeaneane retook her seat, and the woman sitting next to her put an arm around her shoulders and said, "Good for you. That was horrible. What a beast. You didn't deserve that."

"No," said a man to her right, "You were being honest about Leo. People can't handle the truth." He stroked her back, snapped his fingers at a waiter and pointed to her wineglass.

The women who had kept their sober wits about them throughout the evening's antics apparently found merit to John's critique, however, because they sat out the round of condolences to Jeaneane and announced they were calling it a night.

"Bye," Jeaneane said brightly as they left. "God, what bores," she said after they were out of earshot. Everyone tittered dutifully as Jeaneane waved a final farewell to her departing guests.

Gradually, conversation bubbled back up, most of it centered on John Hanes' scandalous breach of etiquette and embarrassing departure. Jeaneane accepted words of comfort from passersby as the evening wound down, but she was still fuming over John's rant, and irritated at him for making her think about what Leo was enduring.

39

Hackizen: `We're good to go.`

Anaku flipped through his notes. For several weeks, he and the hacktivists worked together to produce a multimedia presentation to expose the Department of International Intelligence's nefarious activities. They hoped to plant among the Citizenry grave doubts regarding the legitimacy of the classification system itself and unleash a firestorm of resistance.

All we can do is show them, he reminded himself. We can't control how they react. Though Anaku remained convinced that transparency bred accountability and that an educated electorate made wiser choices, he could not deny a nagging fear that exposure of the corruption could result in violent resistance and a brutal governmental crackdown.

He saw no way around it.

If it were his final contribution to the world, he was determined to rip the façade off the DII. He hoped it could save Liam O'Brian, Gillian Moss, and all the other DII torture victims. He also hoped that the horror of those people's plights would not obscure the more subtle manipulations the DII was perpetrating within the country's borders. Much would depend on the public's reactions to these lesser offenses, not the least of which to Anaku's heart being the fate of Leo Baksh and people like him deemed Aggressives by a system immeasurably more violent than the crimes it purported to abjure. If the public scrutinized the grounds for imprisoning Aggressives, perhaps it would also cast a critical eye on the justifications for confining Vulnerables and for defining Citizenship so narrowly. Or so he hoped.

Anaku and Hackizen worked back-channel connections into Macromedium news and entertainment outlets to implant means for interrupting regular programming with a pirate signal. Once they'd installed these conduits, the hacktivists deployed their best skills to insulate them from disruption by the government. It would be a race to get Anaku's report out before the DII or its proxies severed his access to a public audience.

Regardless of how long he maintained a live signal, Anaku had transmitted a text version of his report to John Hanes in a file that would open in his

Micromedium terminal just as Anaku's clandestine broadcast commenced. If all he did was state his name, credentials, and purpose, Anaku would have succeeded in hooking the public's attention and introducing his report. It would be up to Hanes to get the rest of it out. Anaku felt some reticence about putting the journalist at risk, but Hanes enjoyed legal protections and celebrity status that would make it difficult for the government to shut him up, much less harm him. Hanes also had a reputation for navigating the legal system adeptly. Anaku assumed the scoop would be adequate compensation for the danger it carried. Provided the civil government did not collapse, that is.

The hacktivists timed their intrusion to occur ten minutes into the evening broadcast. It would rudely preempt coverage on five macrovision channels and three macroaudio stations, as well as live-stream into several Micromedium news and political venues. Unless the government managed to locate Anaku's hidden broadcast location, the hacktivists believed it would be impossible to overpower the broadcast outlets before he had completed his presentation.

Leo scooted his plastic chair to make room for another inmate who, being large in stature, provided shelter from the more aggressive members of the population. They greeted one another and tuned their audio devices to the frequency posted on the macrovision screen as the evening news broadcast began.

During the first commercial break, Leo felt a hand clap him on the shoulder. He turned to see Mark, his friendly and helpful cellmate from his pre-bail hearing odyssey, crossing his path again at the low-security prison. Leo removed his headphones and was exchanging pleasantries with Mark when several men, unaware they were speaking loudly because their head phones obscured their own voices, shouted confusion and irritation over the sudden interruption to their evening broadcasts.

Leo and Mark turned frontward and saw all three macrovision screens carrying the same feed: a striking man with braided hair and intense eyes, seated in a high-backed chair, speaking. The two exchanged expressions of surprise and redonned their headphones. Leo found the speaker's face eerily familiar. He was puzzling over this as the man finished a sound check and spoke in a sonorous bass-baritone with clipped diction:

"May I have your attention, please."

"Check," Leo said, turning to his neighbor, who fanned himself over the speaker's beauty.

"This is an unauthorized interruption of regular broadcasting on multiple macrovision, macroaudio, and Micromedium stations. What I am about to tell you is of the gravest importance to both the Citizenry of this great nation and people worldwide. I do not know how long we can keep this broadcast going, so please listen closely."

A few inmates laughed and said it must be a come-on. When they changed stations, they kept encountering the same broadcast. Eventually, the majority shouted the noisemakers down. The inmates turned up their audio receivers.

"My name is Anaku."

Leo gasped.

"I am an agent of the Department of International Intelligence. I have learned that the DII, in violation of national and international law, has installed throughout our public venues a web of devices that spy upon, collect, concentrate, and control the flow of quantum neural energy. Most of our public facilities—courts, administrative offices, board rooms, police offices, prisons—are wired with devices that stream subatomic particles through our brains, monitor our mental activity, and harvest aggressive energy."

Macrophones and mobile devices rang throughout the country and world as word of the broadcast spread like lightning, and millions tuned in.

The video of Anaku shrank to one-quarter of the screen as Patrice coordinated audiovisual footage to accompany his presentation. A map zoomed in and out as Anaku described the extent of the intrusion and web of conduits. He explained how the DII was using the superhub to collect aggressive neural energy, weaponize it, and deploy it in concentrated form for torturing Citizen detainees at secret sites overseas. Patrice punctuated this segment with footage of Liam O'Brian strapped to a chair, wired into an array, bruised and bleeding, and screaming in agony and terror.

Cormack O'Brian, who watched the broadcast in his office, roared in impotent rage at this grisly sight. He had been furiously trying to locate his missing son, unearthing cryptic and foreboding rumors he hoped and prayed could not be true. But here it was on national macrovision. "My son! My precious child!" he howled. "No!" He broke into ragged sobs.

Tears rolled down Wendy's cheeks as she sat paralyzed in front of the macrovision screen in her apartment. She shook her head, refusing to believe this was real. If he was still alive, Liam was being tortured. Patrice was in grave danger. The country had been hijacked by the nation's international terror agency, and her new lover was throwing away his life to lay bare its lies. She wanted to smash the screen and run away, but she made herself keep watching.

"This calculated and deliberate concentration and criminal misuse of aggression is the most brutal manifestation of a widespread and intricate strategy of fraud and manipulation perpetrated by this terror agency on the Citizenry and world," Anaku continued. "The DII is using the harvested energy as a weapon and method of torture, as well as regulating the flow of aggressive neural energy into domestic public venues and destabilizing and distorting public proceedings by streaming aggression into the minds of officials and participants in administration of the government."

Patrice cut to a video stream from Leo's sentencing on one half of the screen and graphic representations of the neural configuration and flows of aggressive energy both from and into the participants' brains on the other half.

"As you can see—"

A loud blast overloaded the audio signal and the video went black.

Hackizen immediately switched settings and video began streaming from above Anaku. Three figures, masked and clad in black body armor, viciously beat Anaku and shot him with high voltage disablers. One assailant put a hand to his ear, craned toward the live camera overhead, and sprayed it with black paint.

Hackizen shifted settings again and another camera began collecting feed from below. Blood ran from Anaku's nose, foam poured from his mouth, and his eyes rolled into their sockets as his body twisted into a seizure. The intruders grabbed him by the arm pits and dragged him out of view.

Prison guards stormed into the common area and ordered the inmates to their cells. "Lockdown! Move now!" Leo was frozen in shock at the horror they had witnessed. "Now motherfucker!" a guard screamed in his ear. Leo's viewing neighbor and friend Mark hauled him to his feet and out of the room.

Wendy slipped into a catatonic state and stared blankly at the screen as the station regained control and scrambled to package and market the incident as a news product.

When the pirate signal went dead, John Hanes, who had watched it at the office, turned his attention back to his Micromedium terminal screen. It displayed the text file and cache of the video feeds and exhibits Anaku had implanted remotely. John's heart pounded as he reflected on the enormity of this dangerous gift. This could change the world. Or at least win him a lifetime achievement award, he thought with an ironic smirk. It also placed him squarely within the crosshairs of the Department of International Intelligence.

"Thanks, Mr. Anaku," he said aloud with more than a tinge of resentment, a juicy dollop of excitement and, he had to admit, a chilly ripple of raw fear.

He copied the file onto a mini drive and mailed it to Lance Wilson. "Sorry, old buddy," he said as he sealed the envelope. "Looks like we're taking on the big dogs." He then hid a copy of the cache in the newspaper's encrypted Micromedium vault.

Having taken these precautions, he put his hands behind his head and contemplated how best to utilize this powerful information.

PART 3

International Intelligence Director Trent Hobson knew things he could not share with Belinda Mosgrove, the chief executive he reported to and who ostensibly held the position of highest power in the civilian government.

A war was afoot, one that was dissolving the line between the mental and physical. The QFRI technology a secret branch of his agency had installed into public and private venues throughout the country and overseas was but one facet in the emerging conflict. The real war resided in the consciousness of the species, and conventional means could not contain it.

Civilian politics was a necessary luxury and Hobson believed it was his job to preserve the illusion of a safe space for it. This required him to fight a battle he could not even allow the electorate and its representatives to know existed, because their fear would make the privilege of ordinary civil life impossible.

The quantum neural interface technology allowed the DII to peer into the minds of hundreds of millions of people worldwide. What Hobson saw in the initial reports made him wish he had never accepted his appointment. Despite the patina of a world organized into nations and orderly political subdivisions that supported a commercial system generating global prosperity, the underlying reality he saw through the QFRI lens was utter chaos.

Were it simply a matter of countering Aggression, Hobson could have brought his findings to the CE and the Council of Delegates, but the truth was not so tidy. The more Hobson analyzed the quantum neural data, the more dangerous and unstable the world appeared. Not only were foreign nations and rogue organizations weaponizing aggressive neural energy, but the nation's resolve at home was rotting from within. There were blank spots in the neural field the DII was surveilling and mining, impenetrable zones that registered neither in the Aggressive nor Vulnerable spectra, and the mind of the nation was riddled with these gaps like a piece of moldy Swiss cheese.

Hobson had seen the result of the QFRI equipment's misuse by enemies overseas, had seen it used for indiscriminate torture, fomentation of riots, and experimental mass killings. It was just a matter of time before foreign agents and their domestic operatives made another run at the civilian government, not through manipulation of an election as they had accomplished through their placement of Belford Thorsch at the helm prior to Mosgrove's ostensibly legitimate election, but through a brute-force attack on the minds of the public and its officials. If he could not protect the public from its own ignorance, the next attack would render the notion of democratic control a quaint anachronism. Raw neural combat would remain, and slavery would be the result.

He would accept the heat if it would keep the world safe for Belinda Mosgrove's naïve political gamesmanship. She had no idea her executive stage itself was in danger of being swallowed by a chasm the likes of which she had never seen in her worst nightmares. He did not want to disabuse her of this utile delusion. Ultimately, the most important variable was belief, and he intended to do all he could to keep these kids playing in the fairytale of self-governance.

Unfortunately, Agent Anaku's arrogant and reckless usurpation of information control had put Hobson in a bind, and though Mosgrove had no way to know it, she could not afford for him to step down or yield control of the forces he marshaled in defense of the nation, from threats without and within.

40

Anaku's broadcast struck the Citizenry's collective mind like an apocalyptic bell that vibrated the country apart at its joints. Spontaneous demonstrations erupted in every major city. Crowds poured out into public squares from coast to coast and, for the first time in living memory, activist groups across the political spectrum found themselves standing next to each other instead of separated by lines of riot police. There was no organizing force or unifying leadership, just opposition to an enemy so extreme it temporarily drove their differences into the background.

This unprecedented unity-by-default yielded no stability, however. To the dismay of the moderate activists and the delight of those who believed massive chaos would give birth to something better, many of the makeshift congregations channeled their collective fear and anger into violence and looting, breaking glass and vomiting spray paint with no discernable message other than rage and confusion.

News media scrambled to cover the disintegration and weave it into a coherent story, but even the most adroit spin doctors could not paint a comfortable veneer on the rising sense of hysteria. Placards, political rally megaphone snippets, and graffiti exemplars rolled across macrovision screens like a psychotic ticker tape. "Democracy first!" pulled into the foreground, but could not shake calls to "Burn it down!" The most obvious focal point for the collective hatred was Director Hobson, whose fate ranged from burning effigies to the more genteel "Arrest Hobson now!" Neither aspiration would prove attainable, however, as events would soon reveal.

There were amnesic claims that "Thorsch was right," referring to when the former chief executive had publicly denounced Hobson and the DII. How that jived with "Democracy first!" was a mystery, since Hobson had been the one to unmask Thorsch's corruption of the electoral process using help from overseas. The main gripe the protestors had in common was that they had been collectively mind-raped by an agency beyond their control.

Within five days, ad hoc delegations converged in a march on the nation's capital, with millions of enraged Citizens and excluded class members surrounding the offices of the chief executive. Celebrities, delegates, law enforcement officials, community activists, labor leaders, civil rights advocates, and representatives from moderate and radical social movements put aside differences and railed at Belinda Mosgrove's administration to abolish the rogue intelligence agency.

The only discernable common demand was that the government get its probes out of the public's brains, though there was no unity as to whether that should be accomplished by prosecuting the perpetrators or tearing the country to its foundations.

As these voices roared beyond their protective environs, the chief executive convened a meeting with key advisors.

"First order of business is to calm down that mob," advised National Police Chief Alex Fortas.

"Obviously," said Vice Chief Executive Nick Cushman. "We have to take Hobson into custody. That mob—I assume you mean the cross-section of our populace—will settle for nothing less, nor should they."

"*Can* we arrest Hobson?" asked Mosgrove.

"We can put together the paperwork to try," said Advocate General Orya Talbot. "No one has ever tried to arrest a sitting head of any national agency, much less a head of an intelligence agency. Even if we find an adjudicator brave enough to issue a warrant," she turned to Fortas, "the real question is, would you enforce it?"

Everyone knew Fortas owed favors to the political and religious conservatives. Mosgrove kept him on board in no small part due to his favor among her political adversaries. Now, the locus of his loyalty could be critical to her retention of power.

"I follow the chief executive's commands and am committed to the integrity of our government," replied Fortas. "However, the Department of International Intelligence is protected by some of the most deadly paramilitary forces in the world. I do not think we would succeed, and our failure would turn that mob into something none of us could control without sacrificing our reasons for trying."

Cushman scoffed. "I don't think we're quite tracking the scale or pace of these events. If the National Police are wincing at the thought of removing one of your subordinates, Belinda, declare martial law and send in armored troops."

Mosgrove acknowledged this outburst with eye contact but remained silent.

"Hobson is an asshole and a power whore, but he's not crazy," said Talbot. "Much as I would love to help drag him before an adjudicator at gunpoint, I agree with Chief Fortas. You should try to maintain a semblance of civil process."

"He's not returning calls," said Mosgrove.

Cushman could not believe his ears. "This is a threat to the continued existence of this administration and this form of government. Are we all living in the same dimension? An intelligence agency appointee has been wiring the country to control our minds. Our freedom is at stake, and that is no hyperbole. This is war. Declare martial law and attack the superhub."

Mosgrove turned for input to Blaine Sitkin, chief of the Joint Armed Forces. Mosgrove had secured Sitkin's appointment because she knew he would not flinch at any military contingency, even a domestic one, but possessed an admirable lack of bloodlust. She trusted him to give principled advice.

"I believe a declaration of martial law would be premature, Madam Chief Executive," he advised, to Cushman's dismay. "The public mistrusts this administration. They are in no mood to accept even temporary military rule. You have to show them that you and they face a common foe before you can expect anything but open rebellion. We can maintain order at a far lower cost, both human and monetary, if you exhaust diplomatic options first."

Cushman's temples throbbed. "But—"

"However," Sitkin said, "I agree with Mr. Cushman that the superhub facility must be neutralized as soon as possible."

"How do you propose we accomplish that, Mr. Sitkin," Mosgrove asked.

"Negotiations in the foreground, special forces in the background. If that fails, *then*, declare martial law and attack the facility."

"With what?" asked Mosgrove. "Bunker-piercing munitions on domestic soil?"

"For a start," said Sitkin, "though I doubt they would be sufficient."

A chill ran through the room.

"If I may," chimed in Domestic Intelligence Director Mara Brock. Mosgrove had invited her to the meeting over the objections of Cushman, who feared collusion between the intelligence agencies. "We have multiple liaisons with International."

"No doubt," snapped Cushman, "which leaves one to wonder why you didn't see this coming and alert your superiors, meaning the others in this room."

Mosgrove clicked fingernails on her chair's armrest. Tact was not her deputy's strong suit.

"Good question," responded Brock evenly. "I have begun an internal investigation on that subject, but we can't wait for answers before using all available means to open channels with International."

"With all due respect, Ms. Brock," replied Cushman, "I do not think you should even be attending this meeting. You clearly do not have control of your own agency. Critical information isn't getting in, and we have no way to trust that even more critical information won't leak out. I see no reason to believe that Domestic's involvement would help more than it hurts."

"Nick," said Mosgrove. "She is here. Hobson isn't. We have to trust our friends to assist in this crisis." Turning to the full assemblage, Mosgrove said, "Hobson hasn't made a public appearance or issued a statement. The public no doubt assumes we are either in on the scheme or trying to work out a solution. We need to negate the first assumption and let the public believe the second one until we are sure there is no possibility of a diplomatic mend."

Cushman shook his head.

"No one in this room will reveal that Hobson is incommunicado, is that clear?"

All assented.

"If he dares to openly disavow the supremacy of the central government, he will leave us no choice but to use legal and, if necessary, police or military force. However, to match his silence with such a move now would place the onus of the crisis on this office. For now, we prepare for all contingencies."

"His silence?" balked Cushman. "He has wires in our brains. Isn't that a sufficient disavowal of this government's supremacy?"

"Not yet," Mosgrove replied curtly, "unless we react to it as such."

All but Cushman agreed.

"Perhaps you should tap Thorsch's base," offered Talbot. "Throw them some crumbs. Say in light of recent events, Thorsch had a point."

Mara Brock made no effort to conceal her shock at the advocate general's suggestion. "Need I remind you that Thorsch is why we are in this mess?"

Talbot was unswayed. "Whether Thorsch created the rift or not, Hobson must be neutralized and we need all the allies we can get."

Brock threw down her pen. "We have every reason to believe that Thorsch colluded with our enemies overseas to secure his post. Hobson called him on it. That's why Thorsch hates him. Bringing in Thorsch and his supporters to thwart Hobson would be like shooting ourselves in the head to cure the flu. We don't need enemies from without to get control of one from within that they and their *agent* Thorsch manufactured."

"I think it's an overstatement to call Thorsch a foreign agent," said Mosgrove, "but I agree. I was elected by a majority that recognized him as a threat to our sovereignty due to his foreign corporate and governmental ties. We cannot pander to his garrulous base without sacrificing the legitimacy of our own position."

"Legitimacy?" said Talbot. "Belinda, you have got to be more pragmatic."

"How's this for pragmatic," interjected Cushman, "Thorsch's diehard supporters are impervious to facts and hate Belinda even more than Hobson.

They wouldn't buy it, and her own base would feel totally fucked over. Brilliant plan."

"He's right," said Mosgrove. "Besides, Thorsch's base already thinks Hobson is a threat. We won't get more from them than that. Claiming sympathy to Thorsch would also destroy any hope of negotiations with Hobson. I appreciate your creativity, Orya, but no. Even though he has brought us to this brink, I must believe that Hobson is driven by his commitment to the safety of our country as he understands it. That makes him a lesser evil than Thorsch, appearances notwithstanding."

The chief executive was good at delivering definitive commands, a crucial power for the nation's highest decision maker, and one of the strengths that got her elected at each stage of her ascent. Even as she filled that role in the new act unfolding, however, events were moving too fast and were of too unprecedented a nature for any of her advisors to have an objective perspective.

"Prepare an application for an arrest warrant," Mosgrove ordered the advocate general, "and a legal memorandum regarding declaration of martial law. Those are second-to-last and last resorts, but if they become necessary I want the guns in my holster."

She turned to Sitkin. "Deploy your best advanced team to assess whether the hub facility can be compromised, and prepare a short list of escalating options." She looked at Cushman. He was unsatisfied, but nodded.

"Work your connections," Mosgrove directed Brock. "Trusted connections. See if you can get anything about Hobson's priorities and exit strategies. Figure out who we can use to leak creative intel if that becomes useful."

Brock started scribbling down thoughts.

Mosgrove directed Cushman to contact high-ranking committee members from the Council of Delegates and assemble a delegation to physically approach the building where Hobson kept his offices. "We'll try knocking," she said with undisguised irony. "On macrovision," she instructed her media guru.

"You can't be serious," Cushman said.

"We need a mandate to use all available means to take Hobson out, if that becomes necessary."

"They are already burning him in effigy and demanding his arrest."

"Yes," acknowledged Mosgrove, "but they do not understand what those demands would mean, and apparently neither do we yet. The public must view whatever aggressive action we take as unavoidable. Drawing the first punch puts us at the advantage, Mr. Cushman."

After issuing her orders, Mosgrove appeared in the Executive Mansion rotunda on national macrovision, broadcast on huge screens for the demonstrators to see.

"The existence of this public expression demonstrates the strength of our values," she proclaimed with a tone that bespoke both gravity and empathy. She assured the crowd that her administration was concerned about the recent revelations regarding secret installations of quantum neural equipment in public venues. She promised that all options were under review, but asked for the public to be patient, lest haste borne of fear produce avoidable misunderstandings or legally erroneous responses that made a soluble problem more complicated.

"Now, more than ever, we need cohesion as a people," Mosgrove said. "That is our greatest strength. Let us show any one who chooses to identify as an enemy of our great nation, whether here or abroad: We are unshakable because we stand as one."

Most of the crowd cheered, hungry for unified leadership and a reason to believe the rot was limited to one agency. Under this somewhat manic surge of hope, angry voices could be heard decrying the administration as complicit in the mass-scale neural intrusion.

Trent Hobson, ensconced deep within the bowels of the DDI headquarters, observed this performance and convened a meeting with advisors of his own.

Hours later, he sipped an iced tea, having years ago stopped indulging in liquor, and reflected on what to do. He took Mosgrove's call for calm as a signal that the hotter heads in her administration had lost the opening scrimmage in forming her strategy.

"Wise choice, Belinda," he said aloud. Hobson regretted having failed to give her a chance when she entered office. Maybe she could have handled a little more truth, even if it meant admitting her role was a scripted palliative. He cursed Anaku for dragging destabilizing distractions into the mix, and clenched his fists at the thought of wringing the man's neck. Not that he hated Anaku or failed to grasp his point. Were the world as civilized as the poor fool imagined, his revelations would be relevant. Revolutionary, even. Hobson sniggered.

He activated a secure channel. "I need a good playwright. Someone who can rearrange things into a form Mosgrove and I can use to end this. Otherwise I will be forced to argue this was an unauthorized action by a cancerous cell within the department and determine who we might safely place on the funeral pyre. Get me workable scenarios."

Civil war was the last thing Hobson wanted, but he was even less willing to surrender his post. He viewed himself as a bulwark against an even greater disaster for the country, though Mosgrove was, thanks to his protection, too blissfully naïve to know it.

41

"And, we're ready."

"This is Monica Andrade with Capital Macrovision on location at the Department of International Intelligence's main entrance."

The camera lens zoomed out to encompass an ad hoc diplomatic entourage standing astride Andrade, somber but determined as they prepared to request formal audience with the rogue international intelligence director. Heads of the delegates' intelligence, military, and adjudicatory committees were there, as was Vice Chief Executive Nick Cushman.

"This coalition of government leaders is about to call for open discussions with Director Hobson regarding recent allegations of quantum neural espionage, not to mention collection, concentration, and weaponization of aggressive neural energy from unwitting members of the public, Citizens and non-Citizen populaces alike, in public venues nationwide."

Andrade gestured toward the sterile edifice. "Through this broadcast, you will be with them as they call for answers to the disturbing questions raised by the former agent known as Anaku in his illegal broadcast."

Wendy stopped between tables at the pub and viewed this surreal spectacle with disbelief. The government had fractured into armed factions. A "delegation" was openly attempting to broker "negotiations" with an agency that should be reporting to the chief executive, and Capital Macrovision was serving it up as just another interesting day in the madcap world of the country's political process.

John Hanes also saw the broadcast and found the warped theater disturbing. However, he was sure there was a point to the play, and he cringed at the thought of what it might presage.

Andrade turned to Drake Esty, head of the Delegates Intelligence Committee. "What do you hope to accomplish today?"

"We are calling upon Mr. Hobson to go on record with the public he serves and explain where he stands," said Esty bluntly.

"And then?" asked Andrade.

"I can't answer that until we hear him out," said Esty.

"Of course," said Andrade. "Nevertheless, a delegation of public figures as prominent as you and your colleagues for such a mission is unprecedented. Wouldn't this ordinarily take place behind closed doors?"

"Yes," said Esty.

Andrade waited for more, but Esty wasn't offering it.

Nick Cushman stepped in front of the camera. "Director Hobson, if he still holds that title legally, is being given a generous opportunity to parlay with this group of representatives from the legislative and executive branches of our government and with the public we all serve, to explain why the full force of law and arms should not be brought to bear upon him and the agency he directs."

Andrade did her best to appear unruffled. "I see. Wouldn't he have done that already if he were so inclined?"

Cushman eyed her with amusement. "Yes, I believe so."

"Is this just a fool's errand, then?" she had the temerity to ask.

"Not at all," Esty answered. "We are asking Mr. Hobson, on behalf of and under the eyes of this great country, to demonstrate the courage and integrity around which we have structured our laws and society. It is not too late. If we get past the rumors and determine the DII's true intent then perhaps we can find a solution to this breakdown in communication."

Nick Cushman tensed from head to foot but held his tongue.

"Breakdown. In communication," parroted Andrade. "Is that what this is?"

"We're about to find out," answered Cushman.

The group assembled on the steps in front of the DII entrance. Each of the officials called upon Hobson to join them before the cameras and brief the public on the agency's response to Anaku's allegations. They urged him to pledge his allegiance to the administration he reported to and to the public he was sworn to protect. They prevailed upon his honor, his love for his country, his basic decency as a human being.

As the speeches wrapped up, it was clear that Hobson would not be making an appearance. No DII spokesperson even deigned to peek out the main door, much less send the director's regards.

"Left at the altar, it appears," Andrade remarked shrilly. She was new to the beat and had the mixed luck of cresting famous at a time when the country's bedrock appeared to be shattering.

The Macromedium and Micromedium alike frothed over this blatant rebuff. Mosgrove had expected the insult, and it served the exact purpose for which she had been willing to suffer it: The public was aghast at Hobson's arrogance and called upon the chief executive to rein in the madman her predecessors had unleashed on the world. Either that, or move out of their way and they would do it.

While the delegation carried on the public performance, Mosgrove received briefings from the chief of the Joint Armed Forces, informing her that the DII headquarters and the superhub facility were impregnable through conventional military means.

"Special forces could take out perimeter guards, but there is no way into those facilities without compromising the DII staff. We are working with Domestic to determine whether any International agents are willing to assist, but it will take time. You may be able to exploit the tailspin within those walls, but there will be no entry by stealth or moderate force at present."

Domestic Intelligence Director Mara Brock's briefing was potentially more encouraging. Her sources gleaned that Hobson was taken off guard by agent Anaku's public disclosure. It appeared he had no intention of standing down, but no one yet knew whether this was because he had dictatorial aspirations or because he could not see how a rapprochement was possible after revelations of such a nature. "He may not see a way out," said Brock. "Can we give him one?"

"*Should* we?" asked Nick Cushman.

"In time," said Mosgrove, "but not yet. We need to make sure there's a fire burning in the hall behind him before we let him think there might be a door into anything other than a jail cell."

"Or a gas chamber," said Cushman.

Mosgrove ignored that. "We have to reach terms we can live with."

"To get that we have to make him uncomfortable first," acknowledged Cushman, more soberly.

"Exactly."

The next morning, Monica Andrade stood in the Capitol Rotunda to broadcast her live report. "Early this morning, in the wake of yesterday's rebuff, a legislative summons ordered International Intelligence Director Trent Hobson to appear before the Council of Delegates for questioning. Hobson has not made a public appearance or statement since the individual known as Anaku made his disclosures ten days ago. The Council of Delegates has promised Hobson safe passage if he honors the edict, and the question on everyone's mind is will he show?

"Last night, Chief Executive Belinda Mosgrove held a press conference and ordered Mr. Hobson to obey the summons and appear as commanded."

The screen switched to a recorded excerpt of Mosgrove. "Although it is unprecedented to compel testimony from a sitting intelligence agency head, these are unprecedented circumstances. It is a lawful summons and, as chief executive, I am directing Mr. Hobson to attend the hearing in accord with its terms."

Andrade resumed: "Keep in mind that Hobson reports to Mosgrove, and he has a legal duty to keep the Delegates Intelligence Committee informed regarding threats to national security as well as operation of the agency, which is funded by the public fisc. Hobson's response will answer one important question: Does he still consider himself subject to this government's laws?"

Back in her office, Mosgrove turned from the broadcast as Mara Brock entered.

"He isn't coming," she said.

The CE clicked off her macrovision set. "I'm sorry to hear that."

She turned to Advocate General Talbot. "As soon as the non-appearance is officially recorded, secure an arrest warrant and hold a press conference. Feel free to rattle sabers."

Talbot made as if unsheathing a sword before leaving to launch this escalation.

Arrest warrant for hobson inked the front page of the *Capital Times.* News of the development set the pundits squealing with lurid excitement and the streets crying for blood. Mosgrove's approval rating shot up overnight and Capital Macrovision ran constant news streams on the historic significance and constitutional dimensions of the crisis.

Stationed in front of the DII headquarters in her new position as chief correspondent to the crisis, Monica Andrade moderated a sparring match between two pundits—Leon Fetterly, a retired prosecutor, and Demetrius Greer, a retired adjudicator—on the subjects of Mosgrove's and Hobson's likely intentions and the repercussions of Hobson's various potential responses. Fetterly and Greer were Capital Macrovision fixtures who could always be trusted to disagree with each other over the day's legal and political issues.

"She has put him in an impossible position," said Fetterly. "Hobson cannot submit to common criminal status, nor can he refuse the warrant without seceding from the government. She might as well bring in the troops now."

"Oh, good God, can you be more dramatic?" countered Greer. "Hobson can make a general appearance via counsel and negotiate terms for a civilized arraignment fitting a person of his stature. These situations are workable. She has challenged his contempt, as she must. He has resisted, as he must, and he has sophisticated legal staff that can help him solidify his increased power without tearing apart the government. This is all theater. The real negotiations are happening off camera. They will come to a peace. They have to."

"You are hopelessly naïve if you honestly believe—"

"Excuse me gentlemen," interrupted Andrade, "but I'm told that Hobson has responded to the warrant."

The camera cut to the Department of Adjudication Capital Division.

"What's happened?" asked Andrade?

"Well," responded the reporter on the scene, "not only did Hobson decline to offer himself into National Police custody, International filed a motion in the Department of Adjudication to quash the warrant, arguing the director is immune to judicial process."

The screen returned to Andrade and her commentators. "What does that mean?" she asked.

They were momentarily stunned.

"It is tantamount to gentlemanly declaration of civil war," said Fetterly, who was too shocked even to appear smug. For once, Greer, who looked quite troubled, did not disagree.

The country fell for a day into deathly quiet as everyone took stock.

Mosgrove held further conferences with the delegates' intelligence, military, and adjudication committees. Nick Cushman, at her behest, had several off-the-record (and technically improper) communications with law clerks serving the nation's highest court to gauge its willingness to back her invocation of executive authority. The National Police, Department of Domestic Intelligence, and military chiefs briefed her on a joint protocol for maintaining order. As confident as she could be of support from these sectors, Mosgrove crossed the line she had hoped to avoid: she declared martial law, and imposed a curfew.

As she was speaking on national macrovision to announce the measure, the military and National Police began seizing control of major public venues to remove the QFRI arrays. Mosgrove's media secretary worked with the major macrovision networks and utilized several Micromedium channels to stream video feed of the military action as Mosgrove wrapped up her remarks.

The public did not receive the news well, and there were predictable skirmishes on the streets as armed forces ordered crowds to disperse and head home before curfew. While the media covered this fearsome drama and did its best to calm the public, a bigger conflict was brewing.

Off camera, troops surrounded the DII superhub and confirmed there was no way to reach its subterranean links to the Micromedium.

Mosgrove met with her advisory team.

"Belinda, you have got to order the military to shut that thing down, whatever it takes," insisted Nick Cushman. "Hobson could be running this meeting, for all we know." Cushman's eyes darted around the room.

Mosgrove was relatively confident she was not being pumped full of manipulative aggressive neural energy, though she was beginning to have doubts about her deputy. "I believe I still have the power to make my own judgments, Mr. Cushman," Mosgrove coolly responded.

After further consultation with Blaine Sitkin over military options, Mosgrove tried one penultimate maneuver before leading the country into domestic armed conflict. "Ms. Brock," she addressed the DDI director, "I want you to leak intel to Mr. Hobson through the interagency channels you have determined you can trust."

"What sort of intel?" asked Brock.

"Tell Mr. Hobson I am prepared to order use of a tactical nuclear device to disable the facility."

"Belinda, I didn't mean ..." began Cushman.

"Have you lost your mind?" erupted Advocate General Talbot, then caught herself. "You're considering use of a nuclear device before even attempting to achieve your objective through police or conventional military force? We've gone beyond domestic constitutional law into war crimes jurisprudence here. As your chief legal advisor, I must strongly object to this proposal."

"If I order the use of military force, you can object, resign, and seek an indictment against me," said Mosgrove.

Mosgrove's advisors were beginning to fear that Hobson might be eavesdropping on their communications, or that there might be a mole among them. Mosgrove had to be bluffing.

"If you cross that line, that is exactly what I will do," Talbot promised.

Glances were exchanged but no one spoke, and Mara Brock took her leave to direct the threat of domestic nuclear war through the intelligence agencies' labyrinthine back channels.

Unfortunately, the conduits between the agencies either were not as secure as Brock believed, or Hobson himself directed that the leak seep into the general public's purview.

Demonstrators broke curfew to protest the chief executive's threat, viewing it as an insane escalation with potentially disastrous public health and environmental consequences. Among their ranks was Ishwar Palam, the renowned physicist who had briefed Lauren Drey and her colleagues on the QFRI and neuro-interfacing phenomena. Palam had tried to secure an audience with the chief executive through his contacts at the DDI, but her staff denied the request.

After he was introduced and his qualifications summarized, Palam ascended a makeshift stage, and cameras carried his face on live macrovision to homes around the world.

"We cannot know the full repercussions of a nuclear strike against this facility," he warned. "I fear it would go beyond the already unsupportable risks of radiation poisoning and environmental degradation, not to mention the utter moral catastrophe such a mad act would represent. Grave as those consequences would be, there may be more immediate concerns. No one yet knows the extent or reach of this hub's quantum neural tentacles. Nor do we know the potential consequences of emitting a massive pulse through the arrays connected to it and streaming through who knows how many human beings' brains."

Palam's voice was drowned out by earsplitting audio devices as the National Police bore down on the assemblage and ordered the demonstrators to disperse. The line between police and protesters disintegrated into a blur of batons, pepper spray, fists, and broken glass.

Palam screamed in vain, begging for calm. The National Police issued a final command to stand down, and when the demonstrators refused, opened fire upon them. In full view of macrovision cameras, dozens of activists were gunned down before the world's eyes. Among them was Ishwar Palam, who took a bullet to the head.

"Goddamn it!" yelled Hobson from the depths of the DII headquarters, slamming down his fist so hard he cracked his desk. He did not view Mosgrove's threat to use nuclear force as credible, but this blunder necessitated a public counterpunch if a rapprochement were ever to be taken seriously. "Get my press man."

The morning after the tragedy, a DII spokesperson appeared on national macrovision to convey Trent Hobson's first public statement since the crisis began.

"International Intelligence Director Trent Hobson sends his condolences to the families of the Citizens gunned down by Mosgrove's administration in cold blood for exercising freedoms fundamental to a just society.

"The illegal broadcast by the individual calling himself Anaku that triggered the current crisis was the product of a domestic terrorist enterprise. While Director Hobson understands that images included in that broadcast were disturbing to many, the criminals who issued it strategically omitted information crucial to understanding its significance. Liam O'Brian is no victim. He is under arrest and interrogation for having masterminded an intrusion into the nation's intelligence infrastructure and for orchestrating the vicious terror attacks on domestic targets in the capital last year.

"Chief Executive Belinda Mosgrove has proven beyond all doubt her incompetence to protect the public against this homegrown threat. Worse, she has abused her office to obliterate the very civil liberties the Department of International Intelligence has fought without surcease to protect against destruction by violent extremists, like O'Brian and his international coconspirators.

"Rather than lead a unified government against this terrorist threat, Mosgrove has aligned herself behind the rogue agent called Anaku, a traitor who betrayed this agency and his country to the radical anarchist Restruct movement.

"Director Hobson calls upon the Council of Delegates to initiate the impeachment of Chief Executive Mosgrove for dereliction of duty, allowing a domestic terrorist threat to arise under her steerage, attacking the nation's intelligence community—our best defense against such threats—and for turning lethal force on her own Citizens because they dared to question the use of nuclear force within our borders and against our own most effective defenses.

"Our country is on the brink of collapse. We must replace Mosgrove with a leader equipped to protect our sovereignty and wipe out the extremists with overwhelming force. Mosgrove would rather attack her own Citizens than do what it takes to keep them free. If she remains in office, what is left of our precious republic will be doomed."

Mosgrove turned from the broadcast to Nick Cushman who sat beside her in her chambers. "That's what's known as a backfire," said Cushman. "I told you military force was our only option."

"Don't jump to conclusions," advised Mosgrove. "But I agree, it doesn't look good."

The killing of Ishwar Palam and the massacre of Citizens who had braved a confrontation with the National Police to protest nuclear action against the superhub fragmented resolve across the political spectrum. Progressive activists who had stood behind the chief executive but who could not back Hobson found themselves without an official champion. The Citizens Action League officially took up the rallying cry for Mosgrove's impeachment, but the group's membership was far from unanimous on the subject. Internal squabbles hemorrhaged into public skirmishes, and the organization's façade of conservative unity fractured.

With even the country's stalwart authoritarians divided, the public's sense of urgency grew severe, and people began fearing war, if not self-inflicted collective annihilation.

Cormack O'Brian leaned back in his leather office chair, swirled ice cubes in his fifth tumbler of scotch, and tried to decide what to do. He knew his son was an activist at heart, but he did not believe Hobson's claim that Liam was a terrorist. Cormack was certain one of the ruffians he'd used and paid to execute the attacks would have let him know if Liam had been involved in the bombings at the capital.

It was all too possible, however, that Liam had played a role in the DII security breach that resulted in the game-changing disclosures that were ripping apart the country's paper-thin veneer of stability. This Cormack could believe. He was sure the fact could be leveraged for Liam's salvation, since the public was so outraged by what had been revealed.

He drank off the last of his scotch and wiped his lips on the back of his hand. "What a mess," he said to the empty office. *Nothing is ever as simple as it seems*, he thought. The QFRI industry was staggeringly lucrative. How could a self-respecting businessman eschew its bounty? He had received handsome remuneration for allowing installation of the QFRI arrays throughout his private facilities. He knew the DII was using the technology to foment instability and intensify punishments, but that dovetailed with his interests as a purveyor of confinement services. Doubly lucrative. How could he say no? In a moment of half-drunken self-honesty, he admitted he had long suspected the agency was using the equipment for more violent purposes, perhaps as a torture device or even a deadly weapon. It's a rough world. These things exist. He was just trying to keep the cash flowing for his family and legacy.

Now, however, his legatee was victim to the agency's abuse of this powerful technology. Worse, Cormack had served up a significant portion of the aggressive neural energy they were using for purposes of torturing Citizens, including his own son. That would not do.

Whatever route he took, he would have to disclose his involvement in the attacks and sacrifice himself to save Liam. The remainder of his life in prison or death by execution was not what he had in mind for retirement, but it appeared necessary to spare his son. Unless ...

At the DDI regional headquarters, James Malone tuned in as Bimal Gurung and Renée Stephens briefed their colleagues on the latest developments in their investigation into the terror attacks at the capital the previous year.

"You may recall that, prior to our arrest of Gillian Moss, we had detained two individuals with radical ties, using charges based on explosives found during a traffic stop," began Renée.

"You said those charges wouldn't stick," James recalled.

"That was our initial belief, but the prosecutor was confident she could nail them for plotting a terror attack. We assessed their value as informants first, using the threat of indictment as leverage."

Bimal assumed the floor. "At the time, we were trying to identify the mystery barista near the explosion at the Board of Classification bombing site. We hoped these two detainees, Jamal Blain and Jessice Mead, would lead us to knowledgeable individuals within the Restruct movement, including the barista if she was involved, which we now believe she wasn't."

"Where is Ms. Moss, speaking of?" interjected Lauren.

Bimal gestured to Renée, who flushed. "According to Jill Blatsky at the *Capital Times*, Moss is undergoing 'coercive interrogation' as part of the same operation DII Agent Anaku revealed. Blatsky won't disclose how she knows this."

The ceiling fan whirred to life and papers fluttered on the conference table.

James narrowed his eyes, wondering what else Blatsky knew, and how.

Lauren was furious. "International supersedes our jurisdiction, countermands our findings, and renders our detainee to a torture site, and we learn about it through a reporter at the *Capital Times*?"

Renée mirrored Lauren's outrage, but held her tongue. It was Melissa who voiced the next question on everyone's thoughts: "If James probed her mind and reported she was not involved in the attacks, why would International have taken her? What was she involved in?"

Eyes fell on James, but he held up his hands and shrugged. No one pushed, but his protestations of ignorance raised a host of unspoken questions. James's could feel his wiggle room shrinking.

The chief intervened: "This briefing concerns information from these other two informants?"

"Yes," Bimal resumed. "We tailed Mr. Blain and Ms. Mead for several months. We didn't arrest them, but we kept them conscious of the jeopardy they faced, hoping they would take steps to extricate themselves."

"Risky," said Lauren.

"Obviously," replied Bimal. "But they neither fled nor self-destructed, thank goodness."

James hoped no one saw him roll his eyes. Who cared if these trash blew themselves up?

"Unfortunately, they also never led us anywhere useful. We presented them with a draft indictment last week. They hired advocates. Yesterday Coreen Jacobs, representing Mr. Blain, contacted Renée with a troubling claim."

"According to our two would-be bombers," said Renée, "the attacks last summer were executed by three separate cells of Restruct-affiliated terrorists, coordinated by a single woman, who worked at the request and with the assets of one Cormack O'Brian, president and CEO of Protection Inc."

The agents inhaled a collective gasp.

"Impossible," James barked, though his mind found the scenario all too plausible.

The agents spent the next hour debating theories and grilling Bimal and Renée for every detail they possessed.

"Can you haul in O'Brian based on what you have?" asked Lauren.

James held his breath.

"Yes," said Bimal, "but we believe it would be premature."

James exhaled.

"O'Brian is a formidable adversary," Bimal continued. "We need to hit him with everything we've got before he sees us coming."

"Work out an immunity deal with the prosecutor for the Restructors," advised the chief. "Not one word about this to anyone. Is that clear, agents?" Solemn affirmations circled the table. He held their attention a moment longer to drive home the seriousness of his command. "Very well. Meeting adjourned."

To avoid arousing suspicions, James chatted with the other agents and spent twenty minutes with Lauren discussing ongoing parasitic abuse investigations. When he felt a sufficient duration had passed, he casually walked to his office.

Once inside, he locked the door, bug-proofed it, and placed an encrypted call over the Micromedium to Agent Baikal, his contact at International. "They think Cormack O'Brian is responsible for the terror attacks," he unceremoniously announced when Baikal answered.

Baikal pumped James for all he knew, and secured a promise James would funnel all new information without delay. They discussed how to insulate themselves from suspicion over the QFRI intrusion, and explored Cormack O'Brian's potential utility in formulating a solution to their deepening fix.

Ignorant of these developments, Cormack opened an encrypted Micromedium voice channel and pinged his contact at the Department of International Intelligence. He left a recorded message.

"It's Cormack. I'll save us time and be blunt. Your associates have possession of my son. I know some problematic facts about your identity and involvement in the torture program. I'm sure your employers are trying to decide whom to throw to the sharks, yes? I'm confident we would both rather it weren't you."

Cormack examined a snapshot of Liam on his desk.

"I don't know whether you're a father, but let me unveil a little irrational truth that goes along with such a relationship: My son's life is more important to me than my own, so I'm willing to sacrifice mine to save his. If that's what it takes, I'll do it, and you'll come with me. I prefer a solution short of such unpleasantries, as I would imagine do you. I've got a few ideas. I'll wager you've got your own. We need to talk. Immediately.

"By the way, if you decide to eliminate me, the information I possess will automatically become public knowledge." Cormack was lying about having made such arrangements, but it sounded plausible. "You can deprive me the satisfaction of saving my son, but it won't save you. Let's keep our heads and work something out, Mr. *Sandoval.*"

Cormack had never disclosed he knew the identity of his contact. Doing so now added a little rush to the game he hoped would retrieve Liam from the monster's jaws before it was too late.

Forty-five minutes later, as Cormack was pouring himself yet another scotch, an encrypted call pinged his Micromedium terminal.

"That was quick," he said with a smug grin. He swirled ice cubes around the amber liquid and took a warm-cool sip, then reciprocated the voice link. "Yes?"

"Allow *me* to be blunt," said the DII operative without preamble. "The reason I didn't answer was because I was receiving a report that the Department of Domestic Intelligence has credible evidence and willing witnesses connecting you to the terror attacks last year. Actually, 'masterminding' and 'funding' were the words my liaison used."

Cormack swallowed slowly and set down his glass. "That's absurd," he feebly bluffed.

The agent ignored him. "You have a gun to my head, Domestic has a gun to yours, we both want to avoid getting holes in our skulls, and we have urgent needs the other can help satisfy, wouldn't you agree?"

"Provided my son is still alive, it would appear so."

"We'd better think this through carefully," said Sandoval. "Domestic isn't planning to arrest you yet. I have influence over advocates at the prosecutor's office. However, our little problems are nested within a significant standoff between my agency and the national government, and the advocate general herself appears loyal to Mosgrove. Whatever we come up with must fit into a larger tradeoff or it won't matter one bit what you and I do."

Cormack thought in silence for several beats. "Agreed."

"Delighted to hear it. Here is what I propose."

In his cell, Leo dreamt of Anaku. He couldn't see him or hear his thoughts, but he sensed his presence, like light from a flickering candle in the cavern of his mind.

42

It was driving Wendy nuts. Everywhere she turned, she saw Anaku. Not just in the expressions of people on the street or in her mind's eye, though she saw him there too. Anaku's image had become ubiquitous. Activists silk-screened multicolored renderings of his face on banners, T-shirts, and political placards. A troop of guerilla artists painted a spectacular mural in honor of the man and his heroic quest on the backdrop of an amphitheater in Memorial Park. Graffiti artists plastered his visage on urban surfaces large and small.

Wendy stood regarding a masterful fifteen-foot rendering in multiple hues of spray paint, one with such virtuosic shading and perspective that it appeared as though Anaku were reaching out from the wall in three dimensions, his beatific features exaggerated and semi-cartooned into something between superhero and deity. She soaked in this grandiose tribute, noting its effect on her mind and body, until her attention faltered on the rumble of a public disturbance. At first it sounded like a run-of-the-mill demonstration, but this one was rapidly escalating. She feared being caught in a riot. "That's it," she snapped aloud. "I'm getting out of this goddamn city."

As the DII and national government faced one another across the chasm of civil chaos with muscles tensed and pupils constricted for battle, demonstrations had begun erupting anew on the streets, and political speech dotted the Micromedium like mold spores on the surface of spoiled juice. Short of shutting down the communications infrastructure—which would hobble the government and might be impossible given the DII's control over parts of it—there was no way to silence the growing dissent.

After the initial demands for dismantling International proved impossible to meet without the use of devastating force and loss of life, activists shortened their gaze and began calling for the agency to produce Anaku so the public could verify he was alive and unmaimed. The DII refused, and word spread that International had murdered him, which the agency neither confirmed nor denied. Wendy feared the worst. One thing was certain: The DII's cryptic evasions did nothing but amplify Anaku's public apotheosis.

Wendy gave the rapidly growing assembly wide berth and headed home to pack a bag, reserve accommodations at a bed-and-breakfast on the coast, and schedule a chauffeured car to take her there. "Thank you, Great-Grandmother," she said softly as she completed these tasks without concern for their cost.

Seated in the plush backseat of her comfortable transport, Wendy listened for news of the demonstration to find out how serious a situation she had left behind. She was startled alert when a newscaster said Chief Executive Belinda Mosgrove was about to address the public: the central government and the DII had reached an agreement to break the deadlock and restore civil order.

Forty-eight hours prior, International Intelligence Director Trent Hobson broke the standoff and contacted Chief Executive Mosgrove, armed with an audacious and complicated proposal hatched by one of his midlevel agents and other interested parties.

"He doesn't lack for ambition," said Mosgrove after briefing her staff on what she already viewed as a troubling approach.

"Just take him into custody when he gets here," said Nick Cushman.

"I promised him safe passage," said Mosgrove. "We will hear what he has to say, though I don't like the overview."

"I'm sure he has a plan to avoid his own imprisonment," predicted Advocate General Talbot, whose presence Hobson had requested.

"He will destroy you," said Cushman to Mosgrove. "Maybe he won't take away your title, but he'll have your soul before he's through, and the country's with it."

"That may be," acknowledged Mosgrove, "but if we still have a country, at least we will have a fighting chance at redemption. If we go to war, all we will have are ruins."

"It won't be the same country," said Cushman.

"That's already true, Nick," said Mosgrove.

An electronic chime sounded.

"Hobson insists on armed escort," announced Mosgrove's chief of security over a secure line.

"Out of the question," snapped Cushman.

"That's fine," said Mosgrove at the same time.

"Goddamn it, Belinda. You are the chief executive. You will not place your life at risk to accommodate this megalomaniac. I cannot allow it."

"Our entire way of life is at risk," she said calmly. "I didn't work as hard as I did to get to this office just to worry about my own backside at so critical a juncture. Did you?"

"The sanctity of your office *represents* our way of life," he replied. "Without that, without you, it's all over."

"Then let's hope this bet pays off." She put a hand on his shoulder. "Trent won't harm any of us. I don't believe he wants go down in history as an assassin. He wants to negotiate from a position of strength. We can't deny him that if we want him to agree to acceptable terms."

Cushman was furious and frightened. "My objection stands."

"Noted," said Mosgrove. "Match his agents with our own and escort Mr. Hobson in," she directed her chief of security.

Hobson entered the chief executive's inner sanctum in a cocoon of armed officers, both his and hers. Tensions were high and it was not clear who was being protected from whom. The only thing certain was that Hobson would leave unmolested when he was ready, or exact a cost worth far more than his own arrest.

Impeccably framed in charcoal business attire, the man stood trim and solid six-foot-five, with broad shoulders. His silvering hair was neatly groomed, and square facial bones supported weathered good looks. He scanned the room thorough sky-blue eyes, seizing everyone's attention by his presence as much as his position. Hobson carried himself like a man who believed he was born to command the world.

"Trent, how kind of you to pay a visit," said Mosgrove and offered him a seat.

"Thank you for hosting, Belinda," he replied with equally incongruous decorum.

Hobson signaled the security agent in charge of his phalanx, and Mosgrove mirrored the gesture. The two armed units filed out of the office while Mosgrove and Hobson took seats at her conference table, joined by her advisors.

Hobson glanced around the room and its occupants. He greeted no one else.

"We need a way to back down from our current stalemate with minimal attrition," he began. "Neither of us intends to go down without a fight, and neither of us wants to inflict the consequences that would entail."

Mosgrove listened attentively but offered no response.

"We both love this country, Madame Chief Executive, and we share a commitment to its survival. Our most important focus should be our pledge to protect our nation and its people. I will not waste time persuading you that my approach is a necessary component. There are threats so horrific and severe that you could not imagine them, and if you heard about them you would never enjoy another peaceful night's sleep. We protect you from that."

"You are speaking to the nation's chief executive," said Cushman through clenched teeth. "*You* report to *her*. How dare you presume to keep matters of national security from her."

"I have the utmost respect for the chief executive and her office," replied Hobson without turning from Mosgrove. "However, no one can do everything. Were she burdened with the things I know, I daresay not even as great a being as she could do her job. I have no desire to take on her responsibilities." Hobson turned to Cushman. "I have enough to manage keeping your sniveling ass safe." He turned back to Mosgrove. "No single person can handle both jobs, Belinda. I can't do yours and you can't do mine. I do not apologize, nor do I intend to abandon my post."

"You've made that quite clear," said Mosgrove. "We all know the stakes, and time is of the essence. Let's focus on specific proposals."

"Agreed," said Hobson. "Now everyone pay attention." Hobson cracked his knuckles. "As you know, a great deal of uproar surrounds our detention and interrogation of an individual named Liam O'Brian. The public is concerned for his safety and fate. As I'm sure you also know, Liam is the son of Cormack O'Brian. Cormack O'Brian is prepared to assist us in orchestrating a mutual retreat from this precipice, at great cost to himself, but subject to significant conditions. Properly executed, these two public figures can serve as proxy for the reconciliation of my agency with this administration, and restoration of public acquiescence, if not trust, in both of us."

Mosgrove looked at Talbot, whose role would be key to the drama Hobson's underlings had concocted. She turned back to Hobson. "Proceed."

"First," said Hobson, "the DII will release Liam O'Brian to the custody of civilian authorities, who will charge him with hacking into the DII hub and planning last year's terror attacks."

Talbot maintained a neutral visage as she listened.

"Those are capital offenses," said Hobson, "which we must emphasize to make clear the seriousness of his crimes."

"Execute Liam O'Brian and you will have a revolution on your hands," said Chief Fortas.

"Obviously," agreed Hobson, who indulged Fortas with a glance before turning to Talbot. "I'm confident the advocate general could cook up a way to reduce those charges to unauthorized release of classified information, which would spare the younger O'Brian's life."

"And the purpose of this charade?" Cushman asked.

"Placing O'Brian in the civil government's hands would show our good faith and validate your administration's authority," said Hobson.

"How generous," scoffed Cushman.

"Yet filing terror and espionage charges against him would validate the legitimacy of his initial detention and interrogation by the DII," said Mosgrove, who understood the gesture.

"Not to mention the righteousness and indispensability of the DII's official mission," added Cushman.

"Exactly," replied Hobson, ignoring the sarcasm. "Transferring Liam O'Brian in this manner would mollify the public in mutually beneficial respects."

"And then?" said Mosgrove.

"Cormack O'Brian will be arrested and indicted for attempting to overthrow the government by coordinating installation of the QFRI surveillance and manipulation equipment."

"That's preposterous," balked Cushman. "You can't possibly think you can dump your agency's culpability onto one man, even a rich greedy bastard like that one."

Hobson glanced disinterestedly at Cushman. "To make it plausible, O'Brian senior will also be charged with conspiring to commit treason with an unnamed DII agent. However," he said, again directing attention to Talbot, "the government will block identification of that agent on state secrecy grounds."

"How nice for you," said Cushman.

"That would thwart the conspiracy charges against Cormack O'Brian," replied Talbot.

"Exactly," said Hobson. "I believe you could use that development as a reason to reduce Mr. O'Brian's potential jeopardy from death to life without parole, which is a condition of his willingness to participate in this scenario."

"I could still make a case that attempting to overthrow the government is punishable by death," began Talbot.

"I understand that," said Hobson, cutting her off. "It's not a question of what you can do. It's a question of what the public will accept and whether you can deliver it. Sparing O'Brian's life would meet less public hostility if they believed he was being scapegoated for agents who acted with impunity."

"In other words, if they knew the truth," said Cushman.

Hobson shrugged. "For now, bear with me. Is it something you could do?"

"In theory," Talbot said after a moment's reflection. "There is enough leeway for us to seek a penalty less than death for an attempt to overthrow, depending on how we framed it. Perhaps we could recharge a lesser sabotage."

"Perfect," said Hobson. He predicted the public would settle for O'Brian's conviction and eventually abandon its cry for exposure of involved DII agents.

"I doubt that," said Cushman. "The public wants your agency dismantled."

"That is not an available option," countered Hobson, who spoke to Mosgrove as though Cushman were not physically present. "To sweeten the deal," he added, "we will make a great show of removing the QFRI equipment from public venues."

"And the superhub facility your errant agent exposed?" said Mosgrove.

"That must remain intact," said Hobson.

Cushman opened his mouth to rail, but Mosgrove gestured for silence.

"Why would Cormack O'Brian agree to take the fall for the surveillance intrusion instead of saving his own skin by implicating coconspirators at the DII?" she asked.

"Because in exchange," replied the DII director, "the government will not charge him with masterminding the terror attacks he is believed responsible for."

"That could be a problem," said Talbot, who knew the DDI Capital Region had solid evidence of Cormack's involvement. "We're dealing with an independent bunch of cops who would not take kindly to ignoring serious crimes or hiding damning evidence."

"Then we will have to impress upon these upstanding Citizens the nature of the stakes," said Hobson. "If they insist on pursuing terror charges against Cormack O'Brian, he will cease to cooperate and the scenario will collapse."

The CE and her staff were suspicious. "The public will not accept a scenario in which no one is held responsible for the terrorist attacks," she pressed.

"Nor should they," said Cushman, who could barely contain the tirade raging in his head.

"We have a solution to that problem too," Hobson assured, ignoring what he considered Cushman's naïve and petty ethical afflictions.

"Which is?"

"We will reveal that the terror attacks were coordinated by a Restruct operative named Gillian Moss."

Talbot narrowed her eyes. "According to the briefing I received from Domestic after their initial interrogation, we wouldn't have enough to secure a conviction against this individual."

"We won't have to," Hobson replied. "She's dead."

Talbot registered mild surprise. She folded her hands and showed the barest hint of a smile as she saw the whole picture. "So we accuse Liam O'Brian of planning the attacks, then save him from the gates of death by blaming Moss, who has already passed through them."

The negotiators regarded one another soberly. It could work. Liam O'Brian's prosecution in civilian court would legitimate both the DII and the central government. Cormack O'Brian would take the fall for the surveillance intrusion, protecting the DII agents from identity exposure, execution for treason, or extradition to international war crimes tribunals. Both O'Brians would avoid prosecution for the terror attacks Cormack funded, which would keep Cormack compliant and Liam alive. Responsibility for the attacks would be pinned on the tortured corpse of Gillian Moss.

Meanwhile, Mosgrove and the government she headed would remain in power and Hobson would continue at the DII. That would require some additional theatrics, but those shouldn't be so difficult to stage.

“There’s one hitch,” said Hobson. “As Ms. Talbot indicated, the DDI Capital Region believes Moss was innocent in the attacks. Luckily for us, the main source of that belief was a neural link performed by an agent named James Malone.”

Talbot pursed her lips. “Perhaps we can work something out.”

“Getting Malone on board shouldn’t be difficult,” agreed Hobson, “but convincing his colleagues will take some doing.”

Mosgrove adjourned her staff to an adjoining room to discuss Hobson’s proposal. When they reconvened a half-hour later, she laid out her conditions.

“If we were to consider participating in this,” said Mosgrove, “we have some items that must also be addressed.”

Hobson gestured for her to continue.

“First, you will do more than make a show of removing the QFRI surveillance equipment from public venues. Every single installation from government locations will be identified and eliminated.”

“That is acceptable,” said Hobson. “The alleged manipulation of public proceedings was not officially sanctioned.”

“Oh, come on,” started Cushman.

“Be that as it may,” interrupted Mosgrove, “it must be stopped.”

“Yes,” said Hobson. “I’m sure you’ve already verified this, but none of the equipment was installed in your headquarters, nor did any agent attempt it.”

Mosgrove raised a peremptory brow at Talbot and Cushman, then turned back to Hobson. “Were it otherwise, we would not be having this discussion.” She slid a document toward him. “Second, you will honor the subpoena I ordered you to obey and you will testify before the Council of Delegates.”

“Possibly,” said Hobson. “Subject to certain assurances.”

“Thirdly, you will disclose the status of the agent known as Anaku.”

Hobson shook his head. “That issue is a matter of internal agency administration.”

“Hardly,” said Mosgrove. “That individual is of national interest.”

“Global interest,” said Cushman.

Hobson placed a hand on Mosgrove’s armrest. “The identity, status, and disposition of that person are matters of internal agency administration. This is not negotiable. You’d better decide if it’s important enough to close off this narrow opportunity to avoid something irreversible.”

Cushman could barely restrain himself from yanking Hobson’s hand off Mosgrove’s chair.

“We will get back to you,” said Mosgrove, unruffled.

An equally placid Hobson replied, “While you decide, we should figure out how to get Domestic on board. Just in case.”

The parties agreed to huddle separately and reconvene after Mosgrove had time to reflect.

Hobson left the meeting confident that Mosgrove would see the wisdom of the plan and settle for a version of her own conditions that he could live with.

Mosgrove found Hobson's solution repugnant. Bringing the proposal to fruition would require the complicity of law enforcement and prosecutorial authorities, not to mention perpetration of a massive fraud upon the public. Not only was this riddled with unforgivable ethical offenses, it would be nearly impossible, given the number of participants and level of coordination it would require. However, she could not readily dismiss the results Hobson predicted: If executed, the compromise would pull the nation back from the brink of civil war, Mosgrove's administration would remain in power, the DII would stay intact with Hobson at its helm, none of his agents would face prosecutorial incentives to rat out the others, and it would likely quell the threat of populist revolt.

With the abstention of Cushman, Mosgrove's advisors persuaded her the ruse was necessary to save the country from implosion and that history would view her as a once-in-a-century leader capable of operating beyond the dictates of peacetime propriety to make the existence of civil society and its privileges a continuing possibility for the people she served.

She didn't like it. She feared she could not persuade her subordinates and coordinate branches of government to fall in line, and she wasn't sure she could face herself when it was over. Despite that, keeping the country together had to be her highest priority. So she forged a pact with the prodigal international intelligence director and turned her attention, staff, and resources toward serving up the concocted reality with theatrical cunning.

Before this phantasm could take flight, Mosgrove and her staff had to get the Department of Domestic Intelligence on board. Advocate General Talbot, DII Director Hobson, and Chief Executive Mosgrove met in secret Micromedium conference with Domestic Intelligence Director Mara Brock, and DDI Capital Region Chief George Mills.

Brock said she wouldn't order Mills to cooperate with the ruse, but said she agreed with the others it was a workable course for the country, no matter how distasteful.

"We'll have Cormack O'Brian out of the game for life," she told Mills, "and the public won't be the wiser. Moss has no known living family to mourn her disgrace and death, to our knowledge. She spent the last years of her life hiding in a maze of false identities, engaged in multiple criminal enterprises.

The terrorists will be stopped and the public will get its red meat. That there is a rather," she thought for a half second, "*convoluted* relationship between the two is of little significance."

Chief Mills, a principled but pragmatic man, agreed with his director's assessment and scheduled a meeting with his staff. He rarely felt tense before briefings, but he strained to maintain his usual calm as he prepared for this one. He would be demanding his subordinates' loyalty in a form they would view as conflicting with their own moral principles. Yet, without their participation—or at least silence—the deal would not work.

The agents sat stunned as Chief Mills unveiled the proposed plan's outlines. "Excuse me," said Lauren when he was done, "but as I recall, our colleague who dipped into Gillian Moss' mind informed us that she had nothing to do with the attacks."

Everyone turned to James. Unbeknownst to Mills, just prior to this fateful meeting, James's backchannel contact, DII Agent Sandoval, speaking at the behest of his director, had persuaded James to tell his colleagues he had reflected on his mind meld with Moss and concluded he was mistaken regarding her innocence. James rattled this off disinterestedly, casting a cursory glance at Mills, who regarded James with both relief for the fiction and deep concern about his fealties.

Lauren and Renée were livid. Melissa remained quiet, but studied James intensely during the exchange that followed.

"What is this, James?" asked Lauren.

"Neural links are complex," he said dismissively. "I could tell Moss was walling something off from me, but little bits seeped through. It took a while for the pixels to form a picture in my mind." He shrugged.

"You expect us to believe that?" said Renée.

"Why don't you form a neural link with me and find out for yourself?" he asked, mixing hostility with mock flirtation.

Renée clenched her jaw. "No thanks."

"Everything about this feels wrong." said Lauren. "I don't want any part of it. My duties do not include participating in conspiracies to absolve criminals and falsely accuse the innocent."

James covered a smirk.

"Maybe it's time to consider whistleblower protections," said Renée.

Chief Mills remained calm in the face of this threatened mutiny. He told Lauren and Renée he would respect their decisions, but exhorted them to recognize that a greater concern was at issue, namely keeping the country from collapsing. "The things you are focusing on, though of great importance under normal circumstances, will have no meaning if we don't resolve the current crisis."

Ultimately it was Bimal Gurung who bridged the gap, persuading Lauren and Renée that queering the great bargain by vindicating Moss would throw the country into catastrophic conflict to champion a woman whose claim to virtue was having committed slightly less serious crimes than the one attributed to her.

"Slightly less serious?" Lauren retorted, aghast. "Identity theft?"

Bimal gestured for calm. "It is safe to assume she was mixed up in something more consequential than that to have attracted such"—he glanced at James with disapproval—"lethal interest by International."

James refused to meet their eyes.

"We will do Ms. Moss an injustice," Bimal acknowledged. "Cormack O'Brian will unfairly retain his life because Moss cannot defend her own. There are no real innocents in this mess. The country's survival is at stake. Do you consider that an acceptable cost?"

It sickened them to cosign this fraud, but by the time the CE walked before the cameras to announce the deal, Lauren and Renée were cooperating, albeit under protest. Neither the chief nor James were confident the two could be trusted, but that was only one of many potentially disastrous variables in this precarious scenario.

As the press conference commenced, the CE's image radiated presidential authority from macrovision screens across the nation and in public squares at the center of every major city and town, and on Micromedium screens of every shape and size. Behind the CE and to her left stood Trent Hobson, endorsing the deal with his presence and by his apparent submission to the possibility of arrest. To his left stood Director of Domestic Intelligence Mara Brock and, next to her, chair of the Council of Delegates Intelligence Committee, Drake Esty. To the chief executive's right stood Chief of the Joint Armed Forces Blaine Sitkin and National Police Chief Alex Fortas. The message of this tableau could not have been clearer: A deal had been struck, the government stood united, and the public had best stand down.

That image conveyed much more than the CE's terse opening words. She assured the public her administration had worked with the nation's military, law enforcement, and intelligence departments, including the DII, to restore the public's trust without compromising the nation's security. She said details were still being worked out but voiced confidence that the broad framework they had erected would support the country as it restored balance.

She asked the public for patience and faith. She couched the plan as a step in healing rifts that predated her administration, and as reflecting a greater unity that would keep the country stronger against foreign influences. She waxed eloquent about the nation's long history and survival in the face of epic challenges in the past. She promised her administration viewed protection of civil liberties just as important as enforcing the Citizenry's security. "Otherwise," she asked, "what would we be protecting?"

"Good question," said Wendy aloud as she listened to the broadcast over macroaudio in the back seat of her transport to the coast. Absent the visual theatrics, she found the speech heavy on aphoristic theme and light on substantive detail.

The CE continued, "This process of reconciliation will begin, and I repeat, begin, with the following three measures that will help rebalance authority among the branches of government, ensure the public's right to democratic self-determination, increase public agency transparency, remedy unlawful privacy intrusions, and bring parties responsible for recent violations of the public trust to justice."

"Wow," said Wendy skeptically. "Amazing. Anything else?"

"First, the Department of International Intelligence will release detainee Liam O'Brian to the custody of domestic law enforcement. Mr. O'Brian's condition and the circumstances of his detention will be evaluated by qualified health care, law enforcement, and prosecutorial professionals, in a fair and humane setting. Whether and upon what basis Mr. O'Brian faces charges will be at the discretion of national legal staff and any disposition will take place through open and public proceedings in the Department of Adjudication."

Wendy's heart pounded as she listened. "Liam's alive," she said with a cry of relief. "Turn around!"

"I don't think we can," replied her driver. "Dispatch says the roads back into the city are blocked."

"He's alive," she assured herself again. That would have to be enough for now.

"Second," the CE said, "Cormack O'Brian has been arrested by the Department of Domestic Intelligence on suspicion of conspiracy to commit treason and overthrow the government by coordinating and funding the illegal installation of quantum neural field technology throughout the public sector."

Wendy gasped, and roars erupted in public venues across the nation.

"The advocate general and the director of domestic intelligence have committed to bringing the full weight of justice to bear on Mr. O'Brian, and to hunt down and punish anyone, within or outside the government, with whom he may have conspired."

Viewers and listeners nationwide exploded in cheers, their collective voice rising and crashing in manic waves of relief and hope, with an undertow of thirst for bloody revenge.

"Third," said the CE, "International Intelligence Director Trent Hobson will honor my directive and testify without legal representation before the Delegates Intelligence Committee in open session. The hearing will be broadcast live, and representatives from community groups will be chosen by lot to submit questions as well."

John Hanes sat in his office with a hand over his mouth and listened. It was too early to decipher the trade-off this charade served to disguise, but he had his suspicions.

"These investigations are certain to reveal more information," continued the CE.

"I'll bet," John said aloud.

"These measures will restore oversight of the DII to the government and the public it serves and protects."

"Right," scoffed John. Grumbles of skeptical discontent bubbled up between manic cheers.

The CE wrapped up her speech by assuring the Citizenry that domestic law enforcement and prosecutorial authorities would wield responsibility for investigation into the allegations against the O'Brians and related matters without interference by the DII, and closed with a few final buzz words about the rule of law, public trust, and the fundamental value of human liberty.

John laughed without humor. He not only doubted the DII would keep its hand out of proceedings inimical to its interests, he doubted the CE believed her own words. "A mere prologue to the script they've already written," he guessed aloud.

Lauren Drey viewed the CE's speech with her lips pressed together so tightly they had begun to tingle from oxygen deprivation. As the macrovision coverage cut to a panel of analysts, Lauren felt a hand settle gently on her shoulder and discovered, to her great surprise, it belonged to Bimal Gurung.

Blood seeped back into her lips as she smiled grim thanks for the uncharacteristically tender gesture.

"Having second thoughts?" he asked.

"Trying not to," she replied.

As John Hanes had correctly surmised, the CE's speech concealed more than it disclosed. The O'Brians' prosecutions were meticulously foreordained, requiring carefully orchestrated compromises in professional judgment and integrity by myriad and disparate players throughout the criminal justice infrastructure. Even setting the stage for this imposture by selecting initial charges required a nearly inconceivable assembly of de facto coconspirators, many of whom required a great deal of persuasion, not the least among them being Lauren Drey and her colleagues at the Department of Domestic Intelligence Capital Region.

After watching the CE perform the chimera's opening scene, Lauren bristled anew. "This is wrong," she said.

"On one level of analysis, yes," Bimal replied. "On another level, necessary."

"Yes, I know the rationale—"

"Listen to me. I do not believe the government's dutiful peons will be able to control the course of these events. Too many variables, players, interested parties, and *potential leaks*."

Lauren gave him her full attention.

"I have a few ideas about how some of the stratagem's greater injustices might be," he cleaned his glasses with the edge of his shirt, "mitigated. Would you like to hear them? In the strictest of confidence, of course."

Lauren repressed a shiver at the implications of these words. "Yes."

"Good," he said. "Come with me."

43

After Mosgrove's speech, controversy sounded from all quarters. Despite the panicked hunger for a solution, many were skeptical of the purported deal's sincerity or realism.

When the DII produced a living and superficially undamaged Liam O'Brian, however, and when the DDI released footage showing Cormack O'Brian's dramatically choreographed arrest, the streets calmed. Riding the shift, the Macromedium and Micromedium alike exploded with political debate, speculation, learned analyses, conspiracy theories and, despite the cryptic nature of the CE's remarks, a collective sigh of relief.

With help from the entertainment and news sectors, the public turned its attention from excruciating fear of civil collapse and revolutionary fervor to the more palatable, politically charged, and luridly dramatic prosecutions of Liam and Cormack O'Brian.

"Tonight," blared one evening macrovision tabloid program's teaser, "Our investigative reporters will spare no expense to talk with the people that knew them best. The O'Brians. Two men. Two countries. And a war over who we are as a people."

The scenario's media value seemed inexhaustible. Father and son operating outside the law on opposite sides of a political divide that nearly tore the country apart. The father masterminding the greatest surveillance intrusion in human history and laying infrastructure for torture by the world's most advanced intelligence agency. The violent, activist son risking his life to unmask said agency as a terror organization and becoming victim to the very abuses he opposed, fueled by neural energy his own father had enabled the agency to amass. News organizations, gossip publications, and pulp fiction purveyors alike seized on the salacious drama, and a majority of the beleaguered Citizenry took refuge in viewing the political crisis through the lens of adroitly scripted, soap operatic farce.

On the surface, at least.

Ultimately, both Mosgrove and the DII knew the government would need more than theatrics to keep the public compliant. Nevertheless, the unplanned tabloid frenzy lent precious time to coordinate the real production, to be presented in three overlapping acts.

Just as the ratings dropped on the family drama, Government Advocate Cheung opened the first scene by securing an indictment against Cormack for conspiracy to commit treason and overthrow the government. Capital Macrovision's ratings soared anew as viewers settled in for the legal pyrotechnics.

For maximum effect, two National Police officers escorted a handcuffed Cormack into the courtroom. Cormack's Citizens Action League allies spoke with reporters and condemned the treatment as ill-befitting a prominent Citizen, no matter how serious the charges. Others praised the decision as a heartening equal application of the law without regard to money or status.

In any event, the image was powerful. Cormack appeared stoic. He pled not guilty, and the prosecutor held a press conference to pledge her zeal in bringing O'Brian to justice.

Days later, John Hanes sat in his office and read notes from his intrepid investigative reporter, Jill Blatsky. An anonymous tip from the advocate general's office suggested Cheung was considering granting Cormack partial immunity if he named coconspirators in the Department of International Intelligence.

Such a development would be standard fare under ordinary circumstances, but John doubted Cormack would sacrifice any agents. Nonetheless, the purported tip had found its way to other news outlets, so John had no choice but to publish the manipulative and carefully managed storyline, whose terminus only the purveyors of the titrated information knew.

Two weeks later, another ostensive leak indicated that the advocate general had secured up to three sealed indictments naming Cormack O'Brian's DII coconspirators. Again, John viewed the pseudo news with distrust and directed his staff to lowball the announcement and keep their reporting lawyerly and terse.

The less traditional information outlets latched onto the rumors and amplified them until rags at the grocery store checkstands began running headlines like O'BRIAN TO BRING DOWN SPY MASTERMINDS and DII AGENTS MAY FACE EXECUTION.

Fervor over the expected disclosure peaked with demonstrations outside the courthouse before a pretrial conference in Cormack's case. Alicia's face glared out upon the world through macrovision screens with a mien of cold authority, and quiet swept the country as she rose to speak. "Your Honor, the government is prepared to unseal and file three indictments—"

Adjudicator Hutchinson preempted her. "I am duty bound to inform the parties that the administration of Chief Executive Belinda Mosgrove has invoked executive authority to bar on state secrecy grounds the disclosure or production of any DII agents Mr. O'Brian may have been involved with." Hutchinson made no effort to conceal his displeasure.

Cheung feigned shock. "Your Honor, we do not believe invocation of state secrecy is proper when the proposed defendants have engaged in criminal conduct that threatens the continued existence of civil government itself. State secrecy does not legitimately extend to shielding saboteurs from within national borders."

The judge's expression betrayed his suspicion that Cheung was merely performing her assigned role for the cameras. "Good point, Ms. Cheung," he remarked coldly. "Perhaps you should take the matter up on a writ and find me some authority to proceed notwithstanding Ms. Mosgrove's assertion."

Cheung did not flinch. "We will definitely review the relevant authorities, Your Honor, and proceed accordingly."

"You do that," the adjudicator said. "Apparently for now, Mr. O'Brian will face this jeopardy alone."

The advocates and court staff were trapped in the Department of Adjudication building for hours after this proceeding, held in place by a spontaneous siege. Eventually, they were escorted through the melee by armored transport, but even the thick steel could not insulate them from the roar of fury.

Mosgrove waited two days to assess whether to continue implementing the plan.

"How are people taking the news, Chief Fortas?" she inquired.

"The initial response has been violent. Three hundred were arrested in the capital after the hearing. Many more in outlying cities."

"Casualties?"

"Mercifully few," replied Fortas. "Reports indicate no more than five deaths attributable to riots."

"Damage to infrastructure?"

"Broken glass. Fires. Graffiti. Blocked roads. One of our precinct buildings has been destroyed, along with five of our vehicles from gasoline grenades. Reports of looting in most cities. All peripheral. The civil government's spine is well intact."

"The predominant contribution on the guerilla-art front appears to be various permutations of you in erotic embrace with Trent Hobson," Nick Cushman noted in a tone suggesting he found the depiction fitting.

"Not my type," said Mosgrove. She turned to Mara Brock. "Has Domestic identified anything more dangerous in the works that should cause me to reconsider?"

"Our field agents are monitoring meetings of the activist hubs. Lots of bravado. They are trying to subvert your administration but none of the ideas are new. The groups are angry and full of conviction, but none of them are armed to pose a genuine threat."

"In the near term that may be true," said Cushman, "but a well-organized public can challenge control without violence."

"True," said Mosgrove, "but that sort of challenge may be what saves our country in the long haul."

"What about Micromedium threats?" Cushman asked.

"Anything on that front would ordinarily be cause for concern," answered Brock, "but at the moment, those efforts are a bigger problem for the DII than for the central government."

"Perhaps the DII protects us after all," said Fortas. Cushman turned to the chief with scorn, but Fortas winked.

"I don't think there's any question that they protect us," said Brock. "The question is whether the dangers they create exceed the ones they repel."

Mosgrove scanned her advisors. "Fortune appears to have blessed us, and public reaction is within acceptable limits. Any suggestions on how to reinforce this fact?"

"Show a little less unity," advised Brock. "Get the delegates to appoint a special prosecutor to challenge your decision in the appellate division. Have a public fight with Drake Esty."

Mosgrove turned to Orya Talbot.

"It's a good idea," said the advocate general. "Not even the high court will override your assertion of executive privilege. The skirmish will be a good distraction."

"You are all whores. You know that, right?" said Cushman.

No one wasted time on retorts.

The Adjudicatory Committee of the Council of Delegates had little difficulty convincing the legislature to appoint special counsel and challenge Mosgrove's assertion of executive privilege to conceal the DII agents who assisted Cormack. The ensuing court scrimmages provided both good theater and hope to the public that law, not raw power, might govern resolution of the nation's great crisis.

As that sideshow proceeded, Alicia Cheung appeared to shift gears, announcing that a deal had been reached that would allow Cormack O'Brian to plead guilty to thousands of acts of domestic wiretapping and a charge of attempted sabotage of government infrastructure. The charges were serious, but they fell short of conspiracy to commit treason. Consequently, Cheung regretted to report that the best punishment she could seek for Cormack O'Brian would be life without the possibility of parole, rather than the preferred sentence of death. The lesser penalty was unfortunate but unavoidable, she said, since Mosgrove had suppressed the identity of his coconspirators.

Cormack's change of plea and sentencing hearing were a media event to rival the richest of royal weddings, albeit adorned in sinister black rather than gold and lace. Though there was great controversy over the ultimate penalty, Cormack's official demise served as a great collective catharsis, and the public somberly vomited up reservoirs of fear and hopelessness as the great villain took his lumps and headed off to a well-deserved lifetime of misery in prison.

In the masquerade's next act, launched while Cormack still awaited sentencing, Liam O'Brian was initially charged with perpetrating the terrorist attacks on the capital the previous year.

FATHER AND SON, TERRORIST TAG TEAM screamed one conservative tabloid. The majority of outlets, however, having spent fortunes to cast Liam as tireless activist and anti-dad rebel, were skeptical of the new charges. The *Capital Times* took the lead in turning scrutiny back upon the DII and its interrogation techniques. All but the most conservative apologists followed suit. Activist groups held vigils outside the facility where Liam was held, and public officials began going on record to question the wisdom of the prosecution.

Cheung played her role well, publicly insisting that the DII's purported excesses did not absolve criminals of responsibility for their heinous acts and that only enforcement of the law could restore the country to order. A month after Liam's indictment, however, the DII disclosed with crocodile contrition that it had determined the attacks were perpetrated by a Restruct activist named Gillian Moss who, the agency regretted to report, suffered from a congenital heart condition she hadn't disclosed and died during her interrogation.

In light of this "disclosure," the prosecutor secured a superseding indictment that charged Liam with breach of the DII Micromedium hub, a crime that carried a possible sentence of life in prison. However, in recognition of the rough treatment he received and the public's outrage, he was allowed to plead to unauthorized disclosure of classified information and was sentenced to ten years.

Parallel to and coordinated with the O'Brian prosecutions, International Intelligence Director Trent Hobson testified before the Delegates Intelligence Committee and fielded questions from legislators and community organizations alike. Hobson, as head of the DII, took full responsibility for any agent's involvement in installing QFRI equipment in domestic public venues. He refused to answer on state secrecy grounds whether the agency had expressly authorized the surveillance intrusion. However, he assured the delegates that Donald Chou, head of the Office of Legal Counsel, had produced a thorough legal memorandum advising that use of aggressive neural energy for interrogation was legal under national law and international standards of war, which applied because the country was protecting itself form guerilla terrorist threats.

Director Hobson acknowledged that his agency, in its zeal to protect the country from the threat of extremists, may have been complicit in a blurring of the boundaries between government domains, not to mention the Citizens' reasonable expectation of privacy in the activity of their brains. For these transgressions, Hobson assured the delegates he was sorry.

One headline in a second-tier newspaper read IS THIS A JOKE?

Apparently, it was not. If the Citizenry expected Hobson's blood as sacrifice for redemption of his agency and resurrection of the public trust, they were sorely disappointed. Through one means or another, some entity had scared or bought the delegates into soft-peddling their interrogation. Though outrage blazed across the Micromedium, the questions Hobson faced from the community organizations, supposedly chosen by lot, were equally conciliatory.

It took demonstrators being arrested by the hundreds in front of the Council of Delegates' chambers on national macrovision before a delegate from the capital city itself pressed the issue of the superhub.

Hobson was prepared for the question. "With the ubiquity of the QFRI arrays and their use by increasingly sophisticated and organized insurgents and enemy combatants, it is essential to the nation's security that the DII process enormous volumes of quantum neural data." To do that, he assured the delegates, the agency must retain the superhub. Beyond that, Hobson refused to provide further detail on grounds of state secrecy.

Various delegates called for Hobson's impeachment. There was some talk of appointing special counsel to prosecute him on behalf of the Council of Delegates, sidestepping the advocate general and Mosgrove to hold him to account.

In the end, the delegates settled for imposing on Hobson an act of public censure and extracting from him a solemn promise that the DII would cooperate with domestic law enforcement in removing the QFRI equipment from all domestic public and quasi-public venues.

The DII delivered on that pledge, and with great flourish, working with the National Police to identify and dismantle the QFRI surveillance-manipulation arrays. The nightly news willingly assisted this apparent penitence, colorfully packaging in commodified chunks the frightening equipment's ongoing purgation.

It appeared the three-act fraud might carry the day.

The demonstrations died down, civil law was restored, and the veneer of normal life congealed on the country's surface like a fragile skin on scalded milk.

44

John Hanes tracked the unfolding developments as he presided over his paper's reportage, assessing how to leverage the power Anaku had bestowed upon him.

He saw wisdom in the central government making peace with the DII and using the O'Brians' prosecutions as stand-ins for larger institutional problems that were being worked out behind the scenes. However, nowhere in the diorama did the main parties resolve the other component Anaku had begun to expose: manipulation of public proceedings, including the criminal action against Leo.

John apparently was not the only one who found this omission troubling. The Micromedium bubbled with truculent suspicion and recurrent calls to action. Though the country paused to draw a breath after the initial rapprochement between Mosgrove's administration and the DII, the threat of destabilizing activism was smoldering below the country's new civil surface. John fired up the embers with a bucket of gasoline, lest things should solidify with the domestic issues Anaku had so bravely identified still obstinately ignored.

Anaku's full report revealed: criminal prosecutions contaminated with piped aggression blared the *Capital Times*' headline. In a front-page article by Jill Blatsky, part one of what promised to be a two-part exposé, the *Times* summarized new information from Anaku's report, featuring a detailed account of Leo Baksh's sentencing hearing, its manipulation by the DII, and the fact that, by the superhub's own readings, the worst Aggressives in the hearing were not Leo but the prosecutor and her star witness.

Demonstrations erupted anew at these revelations, with even middle-of-the-road Citizen activists questioning whether the entire classification system was based on lies and manipulation. Demands to see Anaku gained renewed momentum, as did sanctification of his image and the lore surrounding his name.

Capital Macrovision did its best to cover the new disturbances as after-ripples from the now-resolved crisis, but the characterization didn't quite fit the footage. "He's a hero," said a young man with tight braids, an homage to the errant agent. "His work has just begun," continued the earnest commentator. "We can't let these hypocrites off the hook. It's up to us. It's our minds were talking about here." He turned to the camera and emphasized, "Our *minds*, people."

The camera panned back to show a stenciled, stylized image of Anaku that seemed destined for the perennial pop-culture lexicon. Behind him a crowd chanted, "Transparency now! Rip out the wires and open the jails!"

The Citizens Action League made an intrepid effort to stem this tide, characterizing the iconography of Anaku as heretical idolatry, the man himself as a double agent working for Restruct, and both he and Leo as cancers to be eradicated before they metastasized into the nation's sociopolitical marrow.

This recycled tirade never gained traction, however. When the government was unable to dispel claims Leo's sentencing was contaminated by neural manipulation, the lead progressive organizations harnessed pressure from the street and waxed united in a demand for review of all potentially tainted legal proceedings. Moreover, they raged in one voice, was not the QFRI equipment still in place when Liam O'Brian met *his* judicial fate? How high did the conspiracy go? Was the entire Mosgrove–Hobson deal nothing more than a scripted farce?

Mosgrove's advisors did not take this growing critique lightly. "We can't afford this, Belinda," warned Nick Cushman. "It's a brush fire."

The CE dispatched Mara Brock and Orya Talbot to meet Hobson and suss out what else Anaku's disclosures might expose.

Predictably, Hobson refused to indulge the inquiry. "Rather than play twenty questions, our time would be better spent staunching further publication of former agent Anaku's claims," he countered.

Fearful of the whistleblowing that might be gurgling up the steam pipe, Brock acceded to Hobson's approach and, together, the agencies sought a court order requiring the *Capital Times* to refrain from further publication of the material and disclose its source. At John's directive, however, the paper aggressively fought the move, and the Department of Adjudication began a series of hearings to analyze the conflict between freedom of the press and the government's prerogative to control the release of classified information.

Orya Talbot invoked the standard national secrecy and public safety arguments. To the government's consternation, the brave presiding adjudicator defied the executive administration and refused to issue an injunction against the paper while these issues were sorted out. John Hanes appeared on Capital Macrovision after the ruling and vowed to disclose Anaku's findings.

Mosgrove and her cabinet met for damage assessment.

It was a matter of public knowledge that Liam had been tortured with concentrated neural energy. The mere suggestion his purportedly reconciliatory civilian prosecution might have been tainted by the same technology could spell disaster if not neutralized. This did not fit neatly in the prescribed script, and behind the Mosgrove administration's ministerial façade, the CE's staff and DII liaisons scrambled to hold the deal together.

Research polls suggested even authoritative government assurances that the proceedings against Liam were untampered would be unlikely to assuage the public. Emboldened by the judicial support, the mainstream media broadcasted more critical analyses, calling upon Mosgrove to step aside, publish transcripts of her meetings with Hobson, and hold a general election for her replacement.

"You have got to get control of this debate," advised Cushman. "The people need to know you hear them or the conservatives will exploit this to drive you out."

"What do you suggest?"

"Use your clemency authority. It will piss off Hobson, which adds to its value."

She considered the proposal. "You're right, Hobson would be furious."

"Naturally," scoffed Cushman. "All the more reason not to involve him. He won't be pissed enough to scuttle the deal and it will send him an important message, that like him, you intend to survive this crisis. The bastard won't even tell you what else Anaku's report might contain. Fuck him."

Unable to refute this logic and hearing no cogent objections from her other advisors, Mosgrove rolled the dice and granted Liam a full pardon. Appearing on macrovision to announce the decision, she cited the importance of Liam's actions in bringing to light unlawful activities that threatened the country's continued existence as a free society. She also characterized the forgiveness of his crimes as a stage in healing the nation's wounds, and called upon the warring factions to find common ground.

Liam's pardon precipitated yet another volley of protests. The conservatives labeled him a dangerous terrorist and the CE as complicit in his crimes. The progressives condemned the Citizens Action League as apologists for state terrorism and the suffocating surveillance state, not to mention a neurally raped judicial system. Overall, the split was status-quo, and unlikely to amount to more than the latest iteration of an age-old spat.

Mosgrove's gamble paid off, and even Hobson viewed the move as strategically prudent, not to mention reflecting mettle he was glad to know she still possessed.

After his sentencing, Cormack O'Brian was designated for confinement to a high-security, government-owned prison in the country's eastern region.

As arrangements were being made to move him, John Hanes received a troubling tip from an individual at the Department of Domestic Intelligence Capital Region's office, and he cleared his desk to throw together a story.

Later that night, the National Police collected the elder O'Brian under cloak of darkness for transport to his new, rather less comfortable abode. As Cormack was boarding the transport vehicle, the *Capital Times* was uploading an early Micromedium edition of an article slated for print distribution the next day, quoting an unnamed source who claimed there was credible evidence Cormack, not Liam, had been involved in planning the terror attacks the previous year.

Protesters converged on the holding facility where Cormack had been imprisoned, calling for his case to be reopened. The warden held an impromptu press conference and announced Cormack O'Brian was on his way to another prison and that his destination and itinerary were classified for security reasons.

The *Capital Times* was modifying the print version of its article when a breaking newsflash blazed across macrovision and macroaudio stations in every city: The caravan escorting O'Brian had been attacked with explosives and gunfire. Miraculously, not a single law enforcement officer was seriously hurt. When the smoke cleared, Cormack O'Brian was nowhere to be seen.

The Department of International Intelligence immediately attributed the attack to Restruct and recharacterized O'Brian as a Restruct collaborator.

Outrage over the government's failure to connect these dots sooner and keep Cormack secure prompted coalitions to bridge previously intraversible chasms. People claiming affiliation with Restruct pointed out that the group had consistently condemned the terror attacks as senseless barbarity and disavowed any association with Cormack O'Brian or his confinement industry. The moderate progressive activists, who had forged a shaky peace with the radicals in their common opposition to the DII's abuses, rallied behind Restruct and called for a formal inquiry into the allegations against O'Brian.

At the Citizens Action League headquarters, the organization's top brass read the direction of the political winds and made a strategic decision. Opposing terrorism was a pan-partisan issue. The CAL could align with the moderate progressives and even the radical reformists on this point without sacrificing its own conservative bona fides. Joining forces with traditional adversaries could strengthen the CAL and enhance its credibility. In the process, the conservatives could deflect troubling questions about Cormack O'Brian's associations.

The Citizens Action League leadership made the unprecedented move of standing shoulder to shoulder with Respect, Spectrum, Pro'gression, and Restruct, publicly condemning Cormack O'Brian and calling upon the government to bring the dangerous fugitive to justice.

Cormack sipped a fruity cocktail on the lanai at his tropical getaway, observed the political theatrics, and seethed. Apparently, the Citizens Action League leadership either believed he was too scared to challenge them, or thought the best way to protect themselves was to so thoroughly discredit him that anything he said would be viewed as a desperate attempt to divert blame. They likely assumed he was out for the count, that the DII never would permit his rearrest, and that everything could therefore safely be laid at his feet.

"I think not," he said aloud.

This was not part of the deal he had struck with the DII. He was to escape custody and fade into obscurity. In light of the ill-timed and unplanned leak from someone at Domestic associating him with the attacks, Cormack could understand International's quick decision to blame his escape on the phantom Restruct movement. That was strategically prudent, provided the DII didn't follow up by arresting him. Fortunately, none of the radical movement's genuinely terroristic elements would dare draw attention to themselves by pointing fingers at Cormack. Besides, the DII needed his silence. If he remained free, he would not turn a light on the agents he had agreed to help conceal.

The Citizens Action League was a different matter altogether.

He could understand why CAL officials who helped him plan the attacks wished to see full responsibility follow Cormack into his social death. Unlike with the DII, however, Cormack saw no quid pro quo for such a sacrifice. These people planned to use his social corpse to preserve for themselves the liberty he had forsaken? No, he decided. That would not do. Cormack had nothing else to lose, or at least nothing these petty actors could take from him. They did not grasp this truth. But they would, he decided, draining his glass. They would understand that most palpably before he was done rewarding them for their arrogance and disloyalty.

Marta, the young woman he had joined at this hiding spot, popped out of the lagoon and onto the lanai, her water-sheened tattoos glistening. As she toweled her hair, which had grown out during her months of voluntary exile, she narrowed her eyes. "You're scheming."

"Just a little house cleaning," he replied. "That's all."

"Hmm," she said, making no effort to conceal her suspicion.

"Don't worry. Your part was done a long time ago. I'm a man of my word, if nothing else."

She eyed his empty glass and continued to towel off. Cormack reached over to touch her but she slapped his hand and scooted out of reach.

"Still?"

"I haven't decided yet."

"You do realize I could throw you to them, don't you?"

"I don't advise it," she answered coolly before leaving him alone on the deck.

Smart girl, Cormack thought. She likely had arranged to expose the location of his hideaway should anything happen to her. This wily independence was why he chose her to coordinate the attacks, and why he still craved her. Nevertheless, it did not make for a comfortable cohabitation in exile. There were solutions to such problems, but Cormack had bigger lessons to dispense first.

45

JOHN HANES STARED AT HIS Micromedium terminal screen, gobsmacked. Another scoop winked at him naughtily, a scandalous tell-all with attached audiovisual files confirming it was a message from Cormack O'Brian.

"I want you to run a Micromedium *Capital Times* extra edition to publish my introductory letter," spoke the jowly exile in the first video file, titled *A Gift for Mr. Hanes*. "As soon as it hits the readers," Cormack continued, "I want you to deliver the other video in this bundle, containing my full statement, to a friend of mine at Capital Macrovision. I've enclosed a transcript for your review."

Cormack had gambled that giving Hanes the scoop might provide incentive to publish the story before he turned the tape over to the police. Cormack also sagely predicted Hanes would pass a copy on to someone he trusted before turning it over to the cops, lest law enforcement discredit the print report and trash John's office. If the elder O'Brian had sent the recording to a macrovision studio, they would have been forced to decide whether to consult with the authorities before broadcasting it. If there were already a print account of the highlights, the government would have a hard time justifying a gag order for the video. Cormack was staking his chances on John's journalistic zeal and hunger for glory.

"You bet well," John said aloud after exploring all the situation's political and legal contours. "Nicely played, you old bastard."

In the introductory *Capital Times* article and excerpt of Cormack's statement that hit the Micromedium that night, Cormack avowed responsibility for inciting the attacks on the Board of Classification headquarters, the offices of the Citizens Action League, and the advocate general's building, but he claimed his role was part of a larger conspiracy involving prominent Citizens and public servants whose names he would disclose and roles he would explain in irrefutable detail.

The Macromedium went wild. Ratings soared as Capital Macrovision preempted ordinary broadcasts and turned its best talent to harnessing and magnifying the hype. "Will we finally hear the full story?" asked one lead into the broadcast of Cormack's video the next day. "Cormack O'Brian: criminal, fugitive, hypocrite, monster. Can he be believed?"

The lead cut to a previously recorded statement from a representative of the advocate general's office: "Publication of the fugitive's propaganda is illegal. We are confident the court will issue an emergency injunction to prevent it. Anyone involved with this broadcast had best be ready to spend time in prison."

After a rapid-fire montage of Cormack images, superimposed by an enlarged archived newspaper headline saying INJUNCTION DENIED, published when the DII and DDI last tried to silence the *Capital Times*, the screen cut to a representative of the Spectrum movement. "Where is the advocate general's concern for justice?" he asked indignantly. "As for the threat of an injunction and prison for the news industry"—he faced the camera defiantly—"your track record isn't nearly as scary as your haircut, sir."

Belinda Mosgrove resisted fervent advice from National Police Chief Alex Fortas and Advocate General Talbot to use armed force to block the event. "I'm not declaring martial law over a macrovision broadcast," she announced, "and I will not send in guns to suppress the media in the absence of a declaration of martial law. That would undo all we've built."

"Exactly," agreed Nick Cushman. "Besides, I suspect whatever he has to say will hurt our foes more than ourselves."

"Let's hope so."

Cormack's face filled the screen, and there in living color, he spoke the words the *Capital Times* had quoted, proclaiming in his own voice that he had been responsible for the terror attacks. It was viscerally shocking to see him confess.

True to his word, Cormack began to lodge hooks into disloyal former associates and drag them down in his wake.

"Maintaining a narrow definition of Citizenship and a healthy flow of inmates into prisons and Vulnerable confinement facilities were goals I shared with several other key actors," he began. "Some of these fine individuals have recently claimed alliance with their ideological enemies in the Restruct movement to condemn me. To survive, I will have to live in hiding. I have nothing left to lose. I've done some soul searching and it's time to set the record straight. For the good of the country. To protect the innocent. To pull off a few disguises."

Cormack poured himself a glass of scotch, and commenced his tale. The newsroom at the *Capital Times* was eerily quiet, as were gathering places throughout the country. Though the message was recorded, the experience of viewing it was collective and live.

"This all began when Alistair Coyle, president of the Citizens Action League, asked me if there might be a way to influence Closun Mbeza, a hearing officer at the Board of Classification, to obstruct the famous Miss Anna Dao's

Reclassification Petition, which Coyle thought presented a threat to both our interests. Coyle sat on the board of directors for my company, Protection Inc., and Coyle and I sat together with several other CAL executive members on boards for companies serving the confinement industry, as well as several companies involved in manufacturing quantum neural arrays for the government, including Interlink Technologies and Polytronics Inc."

Cormack took a sip off his tumbler of spirits, leisurely swallowed, and resumed.

"Bribing Mbeza was easy. We knew one another socially. I had money to spend, which Mbeza craved, but the CAL had leverage to fast-track his career ascent, which he desired even more.

"Unfortunately, Mr. Mbeza's susceptibility to bribery was not paired with skills in discretion. I learned too late that he had carelessly conversed with me on one occasion within earshot of his research assistant, the dearly departed Richard Heller."

Cormack paused. His expression a combination of fatigue and concentration.

"The late Mr. Heller was independent and principled by nature, to a fault as far as Mbeza was concerned. Heller had the gumption to refuse to draft a ruling against Ms. Dao." Cormack indulged a silent chuckle over this. "They fought bitterly over this insubordination," he continued, gesturing at the camera with his glass of scotch. "Mbeza threatened to fire him, and Heller said he would go public about the bribery. This would have spelled disaster for Mbeza, and would have given me a rather unpleasant headache. Mbeza excused Heller from participating in the case, but secured in exchange what he told me was an unnervingly ambivalent pledge to hold off on public renunciation." Cormack shook his head in paternalistic disapproval.

"While our plans for Ms. Dao's case were threatening to unravel, her case had become the point around which ancient social divisions had begun to pivot. As these street skirmishes grew more frequent, Coyle and his vice president Paul Graham feared we were on the brink of an historic juncture," Cormack raised his eyebrows and proclaimed with mock dire, "a cultural shift that could pull the plug on the confinement industry and rob the conservatives of their control over the moral vocabulary." Cormack stared at his audience with pregnant neutrality. "We could not allow such a sea change without a vicious fight. The three of us, each in consultation with others I am prepared to identify, set about finding a way to stymie and discredit the so-called progressives."

Sounding a bit drunk, Cormack continued.

"At one meeting about a month before the big hearing in Ms. Dao's case, talk went beyond the usual strategies of sabotaging protests and triggering riots, and crossed a threshold into questioning whether we couldn't accomplish a more powerful assault on the social movements: framing them for a terrorist attack of unprecedented horror." Suddenly Cormack seemed quite sober.

"Once the thought crossed lips and eardrums, it soon consumed all our minds through its sheer audacity, potential impact, and ruthless guile."

Though Cormack was allegedly in confessional mode, he appeared to savor the intrigue.

"The main plan was simple: associate bombings of key targets with the ruling against Anna Dao, fan the implied suspicions, and watch the social movements self-destruct."

Capital Macrovision froze Cormack's face at these words, and a commentator cut in: "We are viewing a recorded statement from former president of Protection Inc. and fugitive Cormack O'Brian. He has accused Citizen Action League President Alistair Coyle and Vice President Paul Graham of conspiring with him to compromise the proceedings in Anna Dao's reclassification case by bribing Hearing Officer Closun Mbeza, as well as framing the social movements that backed her for the attacks, in an effort to destroy the conservatives' political enemies. These are incredible allegations. The country is spellbound."

Video footage switched to shocked audiences, watching in silence in public squares, barrooms, and in one case, a stadium.

"Capital Macrovision has not yet reached Mr. Coyle or Mr. Graham for a response. We'll be back after a brief break," promised the commentator in a near whisper.

"Are you worried about quantum arrays?" began a commercial.

"They're in our minds," exclaimed a harried looking woman. "Those devices could be anywhere."

The screen cut to a man wearing a construction hardhat with work overalls: "The government says there're getting rid of them, but how do I know?"

"New, from NexiSolutions, your Micromedium technology experts: the Quantum Array Detector."

The screen filled with a sleek, black, handheld object, festooned with buttons, lights, and a metallic protrusion at the end.

"Light weight, portable, and elegantly designed, you can activate the Quantum Array Detector anywhere and find out if there are subatomic particle guns streaming spy-rays through your brain. No more wondering if your thoughts are private. No more questioning if you are being manipulated like a marionette. Take charge of your brain and send the eavesdroppers packing."

Over footage of the no-longer-harried woman confidently scanning a room with the trusty device, the commercial concluded with a speed-talking sotto-voce post-script: "May not detect latest versions of the quantum array technology. NexiSolutions is not affiliated with Interlink Technologies or Polytronics Inc."

Cormack's face once again filled the screen, superimposed with O'BRIAN

REVEALS ALL. The Capital Macrovision commentator gave another synopsis, and Cormack's account resumed.

"We couldn't decide where to plant the explosives, and we argued over the potential symbolic and strategic value of various targets," Cormack explained with mock boredom, as though he were recounting a couple's stalemate over whether to dine at this restaurant or that, "but two events made the choice clear: Closun Mbeza told me that his research assistant, Mr. Heller, was threatening to alert the authorities, and Coyle received word that two individuals in the Citizens Action League's evangelical wing had learned of the conspiracy to influence Ms. Dao's case and objected on ethical grounds. These were *schooled* theologians," Cormack emphasized with eyes wide, "who also believed there was a doctrinal basis for expanding the criteria for Citizenship in a manner consistent with Ms. Dao's claim. Like Heller, these devout souls threatened to go public."

Cormack indulged a sloppy chortle. Time and intervening events apparently made the concerns that drove the trio to monstrous acts appear droll in retrospect.

"This could have propelled Ms. Dao's case to success and opened a rift within the Citizens Action League itself," he explained. "With so many groups denouncing the organization and its platform, the CAL could not risk disunity."

"Three birds, one slingshot," Cormack recalled Coyle saying. "After Mbeza ruled against Anna Dao, bomb the Board's headquarters and make sure Heller was among the casualties. Bomb the Citizens Action League's evangelical offices and make sure the dissenters were silenced. Bomb a third target—the advocate general's offices—to scare the living bejesus out of the Citizenry and make the anarchist implications impossible to miss. Then, pin the whole thing by implication on the groups backing Ms. Dao's case. The CAL would be consecrated as victim, the public would be scared into even more restrictive control and use of confinement, and the social movements would be tarred as chaotic terrorists." Cormack crossed his arms. "It was perfect."

Cormack said he had little difficulty enlisting the services of a well-connected radical whose acquaintance he had made through means he preferred not to disclose. "Gillian Moss is as good a name as any, I suppose," he said, shrugging. Off camera, Cormack's tattooed coconspirator Marta crossed her arms and shook her head.

"Ms. Moss made arrangements for the bombings. I paid her generously. Mbeza made sure his research assistant was in his office and he himself was out. Coyle ensured the uppity evangelicals were piously ensconced at their offices. Moss's associates let it rip."

Having implicated top brass at the CAL and Closun Mbeza as terror conspirators, Cormack took the liberty of isolating them and jettisoning any remaining political cover: "The people who planted the devices—I do not know their identities—and Ms. Moss, who served as liaison and coordinator, would call themselves members of the elusive Restruct movement, but their values do not reflect those of that loosely knit organization's majority, most of whom abhor violence and actually believe, bless their naïve hearts, that people are capable of governing themselves and caring for one another. In other words, dear Citizenry, there is no terrorist organization called Restruct. There are simply lunatics among us, the most active and organized of whom wear the banner of law and order, and others like myself who make a living inflicting misery on anyone who threatens their control.

"I hope this clarifies things," he said in closing. He raised a glass in salutation, took a sip of scotch, and held up a remote device to cut the camera.

An advocate representing the Citizens Action League appeared after the broadcast, denying categorically all his claims. Conservative pundits followed suit. Yet, neither of the high-ranking CAL executives appeared on his own behalf to refute Cormack's allegations.

WHERE WENT THE CLEAGUES? jabbed an evening issue of one tabloid.

John, from his office, and Leo, from the inmate macrovision room, both wondered what Cormack still wasn't revealing, and why.

In truth, Cormack knew additional significant details about the Micromedium technology companies' involvement in experiments with the quantum arrays, including two incidents that culminated in the QFRI-enhanced recordings for which Leo Baksh was prosecuted. Cormack sorely wished to do Leo the favor of revealing this information, but doing so would implicate his allies at the DII who had commissioned the experiments. So far, unlike the cowards at the Citizens Action League, Cormack's DII associates had kept their word and kept him safe. If this remained true, Cormack would have to leave those matters to some other brave soul.

Belinda Mosgrove felt sucker-punched by the DII, but Director Hobson insisted his agency had nothing to do with Cormack's escape (which was a lie) and was as blindsided as she by Cormack's public unmasking of his terror coconspirators (which was true).

Hobson, who dealt with real problems, had no love for the Citizens Action League or its top brass. He considered their moral rhetoric contemptible and their involvement in the terror attacks fittingly gutless. He was no fan of the progressive movements, either, however. Enmity between the political factions kept attention off the DII. As a bonus, though he did not endorse violence in the homeland, the horror surrounding the terror attacks supplied an enormous surplus of aggressive and fearful energy for the DII's neural arsenal, not to mention willingness to tolerate and fund massive law enforcement.

Cormack had wisely omitted mention of the DII or its operatives, which could still spare his life. Nevertheless, he had put Coyle and Graham in a desperate pinch, whose resolution they might foolishly believe involved inculpating members of Hobson's department, which would not do. Unbeknownst to Mosgrove, Hobson intended to design a colorful fate for Cormack in the event his unauthorized contribution to the public debate scuttled the nascent remarriage between the central government and the DII, or if his revelations led back to any of Hobson's agents. Fortunately for Cormack, Hobson had a few moves left that might avoid the need for such punishment. For now, the order of business was damage control.

Department of Domestic Intelligence swat teams simultaneously stormed the houses of Alistair Coyle and Paul Graham to detain them for questioning regarding Cormack's allegations.

"DDI! Open up now!" shouted agents at both locales, followed by forced entries with guns drawn.

The police drama provided excellent media juice from outside the house, but events off camera inside were both sickening and disappointing. The lead agent at Coyle's house found the Citizens Action League president seated in a desk chair, with his back to the door, wired into a quantum array. "Mr. Coyle, you are under arrest. We are going to dial down your neural equipment. Please raise your hands and do not move."

The agent signaled to one of his fellows, and the two slowly approached their target from either flank. Coyle didn't move or respond and, when the agents reached him, they found his eyes were open and unseeing, his dead face twisted in fright. The Micromedium terminal to which he was still wired was unresponsive and damaged, as though fried from a power surge.

"Coyle's dead," announced the agent to his colleague in the parallel mission.

"Ditto for Graham," responded the other.

A medical examiner concluded that the men had died by traumatic neural pulse, delivered through quantum arrays their own companies manufactured. The DDI forensic team recovered on each individual's Micromedium terminal several QFRI-enhanced abuse recordings, including the two for which Leo Baksh had been prosecuted. Other evidence showed the two were neurally linked at the time of their deaths, and the incident was provisionally categorized as a twisted double-suicide.

It struck most people as implausible that the men would choose such a petrifying and humiliating finale. After Cormack's allegations, one could easily imagine any number of players who might want them silenced. The scenario's illicit undertones and seeming poetic justice provided sensationalist fodder for well-oiled media commodification of the ongoing political theater. There were few public tears over their deaths, even if crucial information had died, or been killed off, with them.

In contrast to that literal dead end, the third individual Cormack identified, Hearing Officer Closun Mbeza, was arrested without incident. Unfortunately, the DDI agents who interrogated him, both through conventional and, though the public didn't know it, quantum neural means, concluded Mbeza had communicated with no one other than Cormack and knew nothing about the other conspirators' identities, associations, or actions.

This was maddening to the public, who had momentarily dared hope that a larger and more nefarious enterprise would soon be denuded and dismantled. With that prospect dashed, the activists turned their attention to other potential uses for Mbeza's exposure.

"It is unfortunate that the criminal imprisoner and terrorist Cormack O'Brian's revenge did not extend to his most important fellows," announced a spokesperson for the moderate progressive activists at a press conference. "Apparently the war criminals at the Department of International Intelligence and Mr. O'Brian are still protecting each other. However, Mr. O'Brian's revelations also make clear another troubling fact: Hearing Officer Mbeza rejected Anna Dao's reclassification petition on illegal grounds. We demand that the case be reopened and assigned to a principled jurist for readjudication."

The shaky cross-partisan coalition between the progressives and conservatives that had formed to condemn Cormack O'Brian shattered in the shock wave of his disclosures regarding the Citizens Action League. The progressives' renascent interest in Anna Dao's case made the renewed enmity mutual. No longer possessing a common foe with the Cleagues and back to viewing them as the enemy, Respect, Spectrum, and Pro'gression, represented by a team of progressive advocates, filed a petition seeking an order to reopen Anna's case. Restruct, which viewed incremental change as nothing more than reconfiguring an unjust system, sat this one out, but neither opposed nor publicly critiqued the demand.

Trembling from Cormack's allegations and the loss of their top leadership, and enduring the indignities and intrusions of official scrutiny, the Citizens Action League attempted to cash in on surefire political currency by characterizing Anna as the original seed that had grown into the monstrous crisis under which the nation still quaked.

As it turned out, perceptions had changed almost as quickly as events, and the move backfired. Throngs of protesters emerged out of the Citizenry to support Anna and, by their sheer numbers, made any Board involvement seem a quaint formality. As institutions are wont to do, the instruments of government moved expeditiously to preempt their own irrelevancy by hijacking the populist momentum and imperiously bestowing official notice of the potentially prejudicial irregularities in Mbeza's rejection of Anna's claim. The Board, on its own initiative and without clear statutory jurisdiction, placed Ana's case on its docket for reconsideration.

The progressives knew they had won the scrimmage, notwithstanding the judicial trappings, and proclaimed victory on macrovision and in the streets. "Let her in! Let her in!" rang out like a war cry.

Anna herself, however, wanted no part of it. She was well underway in her guided development, working with a skilled private provider whose services Wendy had retained on her behalf. To her surprise, Anna found the therapeutic aspects healing, the educational aspects intriguing, and the prospect for wielding authority within the classification system empowering. When Cormack unmasked Mbeza and the public cried for Anna's case to be revisited, she was in the midst of preparing what appeared likely to be a successful application for advocates school. Like Leo more than fifteen years earlier, she was too far along a conventional path to sacrifice her investment on the altar of antitraditionalist activism. Not now, and not as the person whose life would serve as the test case. Someone else could carry that banner. If all went well, she could be the courageous individual's advocate. Her days as controversial petitioner were over. Besides, she had a few scores to settle, and an advocate's license was a perfect weapon for the task. Who had time to be a party in litigation?

Sans Anna, Jeaneane Spence appeared before the Board of Classification and reported that her client respectfully withdrew her petition.

Unsurprisingly, activists imagined invidious plots must underlay Anna's decision. The tabloids cashed in on the paranoia: DAO LOBOTOMIZED INTO NEURAL MARIONETTE and DAO: BRAINWASHED AND IMPRISONED.

She considered making a public statement to dispel the roiling gossip. Fortunately, the Department of Adjudication stepped in to calm things down by ordering the Board of Classification to review all of Mbeza's rulings for the two years preceding Anna's case. The court also invited advocates for Vulnerables and Aggressives confined during the same period to petition for readjudication of their client's court cases if there was any credible evidence the proceedings were tainted with quantum neural manipulation.

Drawn by this shift, the progressive activists turned their attention from Anna toward the larger systemic issues, and focused their efforts on getting all the potentially affected cases dismissed. The prosecutor's office pushed back, arguing that mass dismissal would have disastrous consequences for the Citizenry. The advocate general further argued that neural manipulation, even if it occurred, likely had no material effect on the cases' outcomes. Absent case-by-case evidence of actual prejudice, it would not justify dismissal. In response, activists demanded legislation limiting prosecutorial discretion and narrowing grounds for confinement.

The parties hunkered down into a more conventional battle over allocation of power between the public and its government, one with potential for genuine, though likely not paradigmatic, change.

46

LEO WAITED ANXIOUSLY TO BE called in for his visit. These few hours would be the highlight of his month, and he had begun preparing for them the night before, pressing his "nice" uniform, arising early to shower and shave, limiting his liquid intake so he wouldn't be at the guards' mercy for permission to urinate, thumbing the aspirin in his pocket he planned to swallow just before he went in so bending over the little tables in the visiting room didn't kill his back, and double checking to be sure his pockets were otherwise empty.

When he heard keys jangling, he downed the aspirin, made a final pit stop, and stepped in line. After a pat down, Leo walked into the visiting room and scanned the occupants until his eyes lit upon the sweet face of his most steadfast visitor: Jamison Tesh, who had achieved his dream of becoming a media consultant. They exchanged waves. Leo maneuvered between rows of chairs, and Jamie rose to greet him.

"Hi," they said simultaneously as they engaged in a brief and prison-appropriate bro-hug. They settled into plastic seats, facing one another across an eighteen-inch-high plastic table. *Prison is nothing if not infantilizing*, Leo often reflected.

After exchanging pleasantries and inquiring into each other's wellbeing, Jamie turned their conversation to current events. "I assume you've followed all the drama with Cormack O'Brian, Closun Mbeza, and Anna Dao."

"Rather hard to avoid, yes," Leo said.

"My feelings are all over the place," Jamie said. "I'm guessing yours are complicated too."

Leo tipped his head from side to side. *Complicated indeed.* Jamie listened patiently as Leo sorted his thoughts and emotions like tangled skeins of yarn. When the separate colors were unknotted and neatly bundled, he realized he couldn't change the past. Anna was on a path with less mythic drama than the original one, but who was to say it would be less heroic? Maybe she would find peace.

"I'm betting she'll inflict a few fearsome bruises before she's done," Jamie predicted with mock fright.

Leo pictured Anna in his mind. "No doubt. Anna has a long memory. God knows what's in store for me," he said with eyes wide.

"Better you than me, buddy," said Jamie. "Want something to eat?"

Leo felt inclined to say he wasn't hungry or that Jamie shouldn't undertake the expense, but they had been through this before and it always ended with them sharing a meal.

"Sure," said Leo. "Surprise me."

Jamie winked and headed for the vending machines and microwave ovens. He returned with hot and cold treats balanced in a pile, which he neatly arranged on the diminutive furniture.

Jamie was solidifying into the man Leo knew the former intern would one day become. The shifts were subtle: a more calm and confident demeanor, steadier eye contact, greater comfort with silence, a squarer jaw, more pronounced cheek bones, deeper brow, and ruddier complexion.

"What?" Jamie asked when he noticed Leo's scrutiny.

"Nothing," Leo replied. *You're beautiful,* is what he was thinking. *You've gone and finished growing up into a beautiful man, inside and out. How could I have been so short-sighted?*

Leo shook his head to clear these useless thoughts, and asked Jamie about his work. They chatted amiably as Jamie regaled him with peppery vignettes. Leo did his best to reciprocate the entertainment, laying out stories of his own which, though bleak by comparison, carried their own measure of pith, spice, and sardonic humor.

Leo mentioned he'd been having weird dreams. He'd meant it as a comma in the narrative, but Jamie mentally flagged the topic and, when Leo finished his batch of tales, circled back around to revisit it.

"What kind of weird dreams?"

"Hmm?"

"Weird dreams. You said you've been having weird dreams."

Leo shifted uncomfortably in his chair. His features grew fretful, like a sunny meadow turning damp and chilly under the shadow of a passing cloud. Jamie was sorry to see signs of distress, but sensed this was important and held his tongue while Leo collected his thoughts.

"Yes," he said after a moment.

Jamie raised his eyebrows in gentle curiosity, but did not otherwise push.

From the corner of his eye, Leo saw a guard berate a couple for trying to sneak an intimate moment. "Some are good-weird and some are creepy-weird, but they're persistent and intense."

"Let's start with the good ones," said Jamie as he tore open various microwaved repast.

Leo scooted back his chair and relaxed a bit. "I keep dreaming about the neurally joined meditation groups I participated in. It's always a variation on the same theme: I'm wired into the group and we're mentally repeating a mantra. It's calmingly rhythmic," he said, snapping his fingers in a languid beat as the memory took hold, "and I can feel myself dissolving into the shared mind. Just before I get there, though," he said as the snapped metronome halted, "I panic, and the harmony fragments. I wake up and realize it's a dream, but the feeling of being connected to the group persists. The dreams are luminous, vivid. More like," he shook his head, "a visitation than a dream."

When he was sure Leo had finished, Jamie said, "Maybe it is, in a sense. A visitation. Maybe you're still linked to them on some level and they're reaching out to you."

Leo swallowed a gulp of coffee. "Maybe."

"Are you meditating during the day?"

"No."

"Maybe you should."

"Perhaps," Leo conceded. He had been thinking the same thing.

"Why not try it and see whether it affects the dreams?" Jamie nudged.

"Probably a good idea, regardless," said Leo.

Jamie snapped apart a candy bar and handed half to Leo. "What about the creepy-weird ones?"

Leo frowned. "I keep dreaming about James Malone. Or, more like I'm dreaming through him. I'm aware of his presence, but the dreams are grotesque montages of parasitic abuse, some of which I experienced with him, I'm sorry to say, but others I've never seen before."

Jamie's expression registered mild alarm. "Could they just be subconscious spew? You're probably still purging that stuff from your mind."

"Always possible," acknowledged Leo. "But this is some specific shit. It feels foreign. Like a movie."

"Like you're seeing what's he's seeing?"

"Yeah. It's vile and polluting."

"Have you discussed it with the psych staff?"

"They say it's unresolved guilt and unprocessed trauma."

"But it doesn't feel that way to you."

"No. It's like the dark twin of the meditation dreams. Like James Malone is linked to my mind and I'm seeing the horrors filling his."

Jamie shivered. "If you and he are still linked, can you complete the circuit somehow? Stream light from the group meditation into the darkness of James Malone's shadow? If you're dreaming of him, maybe he's dreaming of you too."

Leo regarded Jamie with frank interest. "I don't know," he said, "but that's an intriguing thought."

Jamie threw his hands into a *Ta-da!* gesture, displaying enough vestigial dorkery to assure Leo he was still dealing with the same person. Leo laughed but his visage darkened. "I have to confess I find the thought of helping James Malone rather distasteful."

"But you'd be helping him while helping yourself. Besides, if you don't mind me saying, that thought is beneath you."

Leo coughed in mild surprise. "I'm not sure whether to say screw you or thank you."

"Yes, it was one of those," Jamie confirmed.

Leo accepted the admonishment. "I'm not sure how to do it, though. Complete the circuit, as you put it."

Jamie turned pensive. "I don't know either, but I imagine you would need an anchor strong enough for both of you. And lots of light."

"Meditation," said Leo.

Jamie pointed at Leo in approval.

"Perhaps some creative visualization," thought Leo aloud.

Jamie shrugged. They contemplated this before turning to lighter subjects. After a few exclamations over a book they had finished reading in tandem over the previous weeks, Jamie raised a question on both their minds: "Are you going to petition for readjudication of your case?"

"Lance is preparing the papers. Unfortunately, he doubts it will get me anywhere. I did confess, after all. He expects the prosecutor to successfully argue that I wasn't prejudiced by the intrusion."

"But Anaku's exposure of the manipulation in your case blew the whole thing open."

"That doesn't change that I'm evil incarnate."

Jamie threw down a bag of chips. "It doesn't seem right."

Leo picked up the bag and handed Jamie a chip, and the two munched on junk food in frustrated silence. Thinking about his incarceration and the people he knew who were soon to be released turned Leo's attention to another subject that had been eating at him: "Do you know the status of the conditional-permit decision I wrote for Harlan Durell?"

After Leo's arrest and prosecution, the Citizens Action League raised hell over the Board of Classification Appellate Division ruling, authored by Harlan Durell, in which the Board held that confinement parolees were entitled to consideration for conditional residential permits to live among Citizens while they worked toward restoration of their Citizenship. The conservatives complained it had been written by Leo Baksh, a convicted criminal, and was nothing short of an Aggressive insurrection into the sovereignty of the Citizens' residential territory. They challenged it in court, arguing that it conflicted with national rules establishing the rights and privileges of Citizenship. Leo's access to information was frustratingly limited and this was the last he heard.

"Good news," answered Jamie. Rather than babble everything he could think of to cheer Leo up, Jamie held back motes of favorable information like a bag of firecrackers, which he doled out and set off to light up Leo's eyes at opportune moments. This new pattern evidenced the fellow's wily maturation.

"Is that so?" said Leo, crossing his arms.

"Yes," said Jamie. Leo was tickled to see he was being required to wait.

"Word is that a deal has been struck between the Council of Delegates and Mosgrove's legislative liaison to push through a compromise bill. Long and short, they'll create a new national zoning authority to carve out transitional buffer neighborhoods on the periphery of the Citizen territories. People working toward Citizenship, whether from a nonincarcerated excluded-class status or while on parole, could live there. It's still being worked out whether people transitioning from Vulnerable class status would live in the same communities or be segregated into other transitional zones."

"But no 'unrepentant Aggressives.'"

"No. Which should help create a more therapeutic environment."

"Mm hmm, but still not among Citizens."

"No, which should steal some of the Cleagues' thunder."

"But still—" Leo protested.

"However," Jamie cut him off, "Citizens wishing to live with transitional non-Citizens would have the option of doing so in the new zones."

Leo's eyes widened.

"If that's what the Citizen and the former and future Citizen wanted," Jamie concluded.

"That would be an enormous sacrifice for such a Citizen," said Leo.

"Depends on who he was getting for his trouble," Jamie replied with a mischievous grin before jumping to his feet to fetch coffee from the vending machine.

When he got back, they left the touching suggestion implicit and unspoken. Unless something changed, it would be many years before Leo was eligible for parole.

"This bill is likely to pass?" asked Leo.

"It appears so."

They smiled soberly but said no more on the topic for the remainder of their visit.

James Malone awoke before dawn with the remnants of an unsettling but not altogether unpleasant dream luminescing like a fading chimera in his mind. He concentrated to solidify the remains into waking memory before they vanished, and skimmed up three elements: the palpable presence of Leo Baksh, the chilling image of prison bars, and a piercingly beautiful pinpoint of light shining through them—or through the mind that was perceiving them—James couldn't say which. Glorious, opalescent white, yet perceptibly containing all colors. James knew this was true as a matter of optics, but in his dream, he sensed energy beyond visible light, as if the whole electromagnetic spectrum were incandescing from a single point.

As he focused on the lingering image, he remembered that in his dream he wanted to fan the light to greater intensity. He felt that if he could set it afire, it would consume him.

He was jarred out of this reverie by the jangle of a macrophone chime.

"Yes?"

It was DII Agent Sandoval. "Have you seen the news?"

"No. I just woke up."

"*Capital Times* has released the rest of Anaku's report."

"And?"

"Read it." *Click.*

"On," James said to his Micromedium terminal. As it fired up, he set coffee to brewing. While he waited, his gaze settled on the coffeemaker's tiny status beacon. It reminded him of the light from his dream, but juxtaposed to his waking mind, he found the memory irritating despite its sublime nature a short while earlier.

"Ready," said a sexy female voice from James's Micromedium terminal.

"Time to change that audio," he muttered as he sat down and pulled up the *Capital Times*' node.

ANAKU'S REPORT, PART TWO announced the splash line. A brief introduction explained that the material would be presented in four articles. Two of them summarized information Anaku and unidentified others obtained through their surveillance of the DII hub and superhub. The other two derived from inside information Anaku possessed due to his connections with the DII.

James shivered once and scrolled down to the first headline: SOCIETY MATRON ASSASSINATED. The first article reported that a cadre of hacktivists had worked together to penetrate the DII hub and establish the link through which Anaku and his confreres had collected the information that so recently set the country ablaze. Among those group members was Liam O'Brian, whose involvement was already a matter of public record, but also prominent socialite, beloved Citizen, and elder stateswoman Evelyn Malone. Contrary to the coroner's report cited in Evelyn's obituaries, she did not die of natural causes, according to Anaku, but by way of a massive traumatic neural pulse delivered by the DII through the quantum array she used to pierce the shield protecting the agency's central computing infrastructure.

James rocked back with mouth agape. "No," he barked, more in disbelief than despair, at least at first. He read through the whole article, first thunderstruck by the scenario's improbability and his utter blindness to Evelyn's personal power and intellectual potency.

"Holy fucking shit." He laughed aloud as the immensity of her courage and audacity materialized in his belated understanding.

Once the initial shock subsided, other feelings surfaced, layer by layer. First, a smoldering rage that his DII connection had concealed this immensely personal cost of the equipment installation he enlisted James to facilitate. Then a nagging sense of guilt at his involvement in the mechanism of Evelyn's death. When that ebbed, something more primal and far less comfortable came into view. To his shock, James felt tears roll down his cheeks, as a simple, child's sadness washed through his heart.

"Great Grandmother," he whispered.

He wiped tears on the back of his hand and stared at them in barely comprehending astonishment, as though they had dripped upon him from some alien dimension.

As if all of this were not bad enough, his next thought was of Wendy, and his role in inflicting this heartbreak upon her. "I'm sorry, baby sister."

The cold observer in James beheld this sentimental display with mild disgust and tapped him on the shoulder. Heeding the familiar perspective's timeworn utility, James shook his head to clear the superficies, wiped away his tears, poured a cup of coffee, and moved on to the next article.

DII: DRUG TRAFFICKER? zinged the headline. *This should be good*, thought James. According to the article, Anaku's report contained detailed allegations that the DII was integrally involved in the manufacture, distribution, and large-scale sale of Elidrine. Not only did this raise enormous revenues for the agency outside its official funding, but, according to Anaku, top-level management at the agency had recently circulated study reports indicating Elidrine both enhanced and distorted use of the QFRI arrays. The DII dumped massive quantities of Elidrine onto the streets, while simultaneously monitoring its effects on the quantum neural energy the agency was tracking and collecting.

Anaku said he himself had clandestinely made QFRI equipment available to individuals and groups that could use it progressively. Just before he prepared his public report, he learned that others in the DII were distributing the mind-warping poison.

The most visible case in point for this deadly addictive intersection of drug and technology, said Anaku, was Leo Baksh, an individual he had supplied and trained to use a QFRI array, and whose mind was corrupted by the drug's accentuation of the technology's darker capabilities.

As if to validate this point, the *Times* embedded amidst the text of this article a short side-bar reporting that Anaku and his associates had discovered within the superhub a cache of QFRI-enhanced recordings, including the two Leo Baksh had been prosecuted for.

The axes of DII-sponsored evil seemed to intersect right through James. He felt ashamed and enraged. He had little compunction about doing what was necessary to advance his interests, but to be used unwittingly for larger atrocities that harmed people he loved and may have harmed his own mind? That was a different matter.

He gulped down the remainder of his coffee and moved on to the fourth article: TERROR ATTACK AT 'POWER PLANT' WAS NEITHER: COGNITIVELY IMPAIRED MAN FRAMED FOR ACCIDENT AT DII PROTO-SUPERHUB. In a blistering exposé, Jill Blatsky reported that, according to Anaku and consistent with forensic reports by experts retained by the *Capital Times*, the alleged terror attack at a power plant in the capital two years earlier was in fact a massive accident at the DII's first attempt to build the QFRI superhub. Welds on the superconducting magnets in the facility's particle accelerator failed, causing a chain of blowouts. This damaged the cooling system for the entire superconducting structure, resulting in a massive explosion.

The article lambasted the DII for its lies, machinations, and arrogant disregard for the constraints on its authority. Where, asked Blatsky at the end of her article, is the individual falsely accused of this nonattack? And what is the agency planning to do to make amends to him and to the public whose trust his persecution so flagrantly mocked?

When he finished the last article, James poured more coffee and took time to think. He found the revelations troubling, something he was not accustomed to feeling.

A moment later, his Micromedium terminal signaled an incoming encrypted voice link from Agent Sandoval.

"Not now, you prick," James snapped at the mute device. He powered down his terminal and took the unprecedented step of calling in sick to work. If he didn't call Wendy within the next few minutes, she would either call him or show up. James chewed on a fingernail. What would he tell her?

For the first time since his encounter with the QFRI arrays, James couldn't glibly dismiss discomfort with the abuse recordings and his role in propagating them. He knew he hadn't ingested Elidrine, but people he linked with and shared the QFRI-enhanced recordings with had, and not just Leo Baksh, poor bastard. Had their drug-altered minds affected his neurons? "How could they not have?" he thought aloud.

Each line of thought led him back to the DII. He was far from innocent in these affairs, yet it was becoming clear that he was more plaything than player in this nefarious drama. That pissed him off and caused him to question his judgment. About everything. And that gave rise to something with which he had next to no experience: bald-ass, lizard-mind, proto-human fear.

And what about these goddamn dreams?

James was not pleased.

47

As James gnawed on his cuticles and wrestled with what to tell Wendy, she was not, as he imagined, reeling in shock over news regarding Evelyn's cause of death. She was conferring with Patrice over encrypted Micromedium link, wondering what she should tell James, and whether she could pull off telling him nothing.

"Anaku swore you to secrecy," reminded Patrice.

"But it's all out now, and Anaku's—"

"We don't know his status," Patrice calmly interrupted. "Besides, your acquaintance with Anaku is not public knowledge. It needs to stay that way, for all our sakes. James is the last person you should tell."

She was right.

"I don't know if I can pull off acting like this is news. James is intuitive."

"You can do it, Wendy."

I'm not part of your damned conspiracy, Wendy wanted to scream. *Then again, that is no longer quite true*, she thought with a mixture of fear, anger, and resignation. By being who she was and loving whom she did, she was smack dab in the middle of the mess.

This was the first time in weeks Wendy and Patrice had spoken. After Anaku's violently aborted live report, Patrice and Hackizen agreed their work was done and that further contact between them would be unwise. Neither had any idea who the other was or where he or she was physically located. Patrice waited two torturous days before risking contact with Wendy, and they limited their communication until the political situation reconfigured to give them hope no one was stalking Patrice. Two months had passed without incident.

"How is Liam?" asked Patrice, temporarily tabling the subject of how to handle James.

"Withdrawn. Says he's OK, but he's not the same. How could he be?"

Patrice asked whether he was receiving treatment for his traumas.

"He's undergoing an experimental treatment for post-traumatic stress disorder. Sounds horrible but it's the latest. They trigger flashbacks in a therapeutic setting, then administer a drug that prevents reconsolidation of memories in the amygdala."

"Is it helping?"

"I don't know. Like I said, he's withdrawn."

"Is the government providing the treatment?"

"No," said Wendy. "Liam is paying for it."

"I'm glad he's not at the mercy of government shrinks after what he's been through, but it must cost out the ass."

"His advocates got a lot of Cormack's publicly known assets transferred to him."

"Do those include ownership of Protection Inc.?"

"What's left of it, yes."

Patrice hissed coldly. "How ironic."

"Very," agreed Wendy. "The government retained most of Cormack's assets to compensate victims of the terror attacks. Still, Liam's pretty sure he can hang on to the company."

"He wants to?"

"Yes, he said he has spent time thinking about something my great-grandmother said about the potential influence of institutional power like the kind his father's company wields."

"Influence?" Patrice spat. "I'll say."

"This is Liam we're talking about," Wendy reminded. "Relax. I don't know the details, but he's going to appoint a new board, purge the executive staff, buy out the minority shareholders if it comes to it, and use the company to press for reform in the classification system and in the rules and manner of confinement."

"I thought you said he was withdrawn."

"He is emotionally withdrawn from me, but that doesn't mean he isn't still scheming. It's the main reason I'm letting him have his space. I can hear his heartbeat."

"Infiltr8org has infiltrated his father's company and wants to make it eat its own tail," mused Patrice.

"More like point it in a new direction," said Wendy. "Just destroying the company wouldn't change anything. Another would take its place. I think he has something more challenging in mind. We'll see."

Returning to the more pressing subject, Wendy said, "I'll do the best I can. With James, I mean."

"Thank you," replied Patrice with relief. "No one can ask more than that. I've yet to see your best be anything but more than enough."

Wendy tapped her foot. "Are things OK, wherever you are?" She had gathered from a few cryptic clues that Patrice was someplace warm and beautiful, but scrupulously avoided asking for endangering details.

"Better than OK," said Patrice. "If it weren't for being separated from you, they would be close to perfect."

"When can we see each other?"

"Let's give it another six months and talk about it."

Wendy massaged the frown line between her brows. "Six more months?"

"Maybe longer. I can't risk—"

"I know," Wendy snapped. "I'm just," she swallowed, "alone," she said with weary grief.

They fell quiet and allowed their emotions to undulate.

"I know," said Patrice. "So am I. I hate it for both of us."

"Me too," said Wendy, biting her lip and thinking she didn't know how long she was willing to be part of this situation.

As though reading her mind, Patrice said, "If you want me to stop calling, I will understand. It would be difficult but I can't ask more of you than you've already given. I had no right even to ask for that."

Wendy said, "I'm not ready for that."

Patrice exhaled in relief. "Then I'll call in a week."

"OK," said Wendy.

"Love you."

"Love you."

They severed the link.

Wendy sparked up a cigarette, a bad habit she had picked up recently to calm her thrashed nerves. She watched lungsful of smoke jet from her lips and billow into a hazy cloud pierced with beams of sunlight, and braced herself to speak with James. Extinguishing the cigarette and opening a window to clear the noxious fumes, she thought for the hundredth time *I have to quit smoking*, and dialed her brother's number.

James answered on the third ring. After confirming that they had both read the news about Anaku's report and his claims regarding Evelyn's cause of death, James told Wendy he was home for the day and asked her over. Wendy worried that a face-to-face encounter would be harder to pull off and considered making excuses, but something in his voice gave her pause. Rather than investigate it over the phone, she went to take a closer look.

When she arrived, she found James uncharacteristically disheveled. She paused at his threshold and scrutinized him before accepting his invitation to enter. If he noticed the critical appraisal, he didn't say anything, which was as unusual as his messy hair and wrinkled shirt. She supposed it could be grief, but this was James ...

They hugged and voiced their astonishment over Evelyn's purported activities and demise. When they parted and sat down, Wendy noticed, to her further surprise, that James looked genuinely upset. James realized that Wendy seemed more concerned about him than the news, which made him feel like such a louse that he didn't stop to think about what her apparent equanimity might mean.

"There are some things I have to tell you," he began. "I won't make you promise to keep them secret because I owe it to you to tell you regardless of consequences. But my life may depend on you keeping this between us, and if not my life, my job and liberty for certain."

Wendy threw up her hands. "You too? Why does everyone feel compelled to confess life-threatening secrets to me?"

James raised his eyebrows in curiosity.

"Don't even think of asking, Jimmy," said Wendy, wagging a finger. "You want me to keep your secrets? You will have to accept that I'm someone who knows how. Can't have it both ways."

Yes, but I'm your brother, he considered saying, but he was about to test that relationship, so he decided invoking it at the outset wouldn't play well. Besides, who knew what privileges these other confidantes might enjoy? He broke her gaze as he realized with surprise that this possibility aroused telltale symptoms of jealousy. He frowned as he added this odd disturbance to the growing list of anomalies.

Wendy studied the subtle outward manifestation of James's mounting inner turmoil during the strangely long pause before he spoke. This did not fall within the range of her lifelong experience with him, and she felt reciprocally nervous. Determined to keep her wits, she turned within, calmed her mind, and gave him the most soothing expression she could muster. She was further disconcerted when he grasped for comfort in the gesture. This was not the James she knew.

He regained composure with difficulty and said flatly, "I killed Great-Grandmother."

As Wendy puzzled over what this could mean, to her shock a tear spilled down his cheek. She had never seen James cry, and she would have been unfazed to learn he was neurochemically incapable of the function.

"Tell me right now what the hell is going on."

So he did. He told her all about his backchannel connection at the DII, his involvement in what he thought was a surveillance intrusion, and his realization that he had helped assemble the equipment the DII used to execute Evelyn Malone. James appeared somewhat less tense for having confessed his crimes, and for that she was thankful.

"You didn't kill her," she said at last.

The response surprised James.

"One, you didn't know it was a weapon system."

"I suspected."

"Then shame on you. But two, you didn't fire the pulse that killed her.

And three, if Anaku's report is accurate, Great-Grandmother deliberately broke the law and risked her life to help expose the DII. That was a suicidal act of heroism. You can't blame yourself for what the DII did. I'm sure she wouldn't, and neither do I."

This undeserved forgiveness was like a crystal dropped into a supersaturated solution, and James's mind slivered into layers. One level observed in cold astonishment as another steeled to keep from breaking into sobs.

Wendy continued, "But how the hell could you be so selfish and irresponsible?"

"Irresponsible?" This was not an accusation to which James was accustomed. Ruthless, yes. Disrespectful, excessively zealous, insufferably cocky, governed by his own rules and social convention be damned. But irresponsible? Never.

"Yes, irresponsible," she repeated through clenched teeth. "To the country, your family, the world. You participated in what still may prove to be a death blow to our republic. Does that mean nothing to you, Mr. Law Man? What did you think you were protecting with your work? Your own nest? Your fucking ego?"

Irritation stepped partially into the foreground as James received this critique. "I thought I was protecting us, Wendy. Our family. You."

"Sorry, Jimmy," she countered, shaking her head. "That's way too simple and you know it." When he didn't respond, she pushed on with an edge that sounded almost snide: "You were high on power," she realized with revulsion as she said it. "That's it, isn't it? You're a power junkie. An addict."

James flinched, not because of his history of abusing official power, but because of his fears about having neurally interfaced with Elidrine fiends. "I am not an addict," he said as much to himself as to Wendy. "It's not just about power. There is more to me than that."

"Is there?" she asked, searching his eyes. "I always believed so. But is there?"

James began thinking this visit was a mistake.

"I've always cherished the special place you reserved for me," said Wendy, "and the shelter it afforded me from your brutality. I focused on your heart and saw the sweetness in you, despite your trail of wreckage and devastated lives." She regarded him fiercely. "I told myself I saw the real you and everyone else saw your protective shell. But you've hurt me, James. Hurt us. Hurt everyone. You selfish bastard."

James moved back to the couch next to Wendy, but something about his disintegrating composure made her uncomfortable, and she stood up and moved away.

She stared out the window "I've never seen you like this," she said a moment later. "You're scaring me." She eyed him over her shoulder and then gazed back out the window.

James got off on frightening people, but scaring Wendy made him feel ugly, not powerful. "*I've* never seen me like this," he agreed. "My seams are coming unstitched."

She turned around and propped against the window sill, examining him. "When did this start? This can't just be about Great-Grandmother. You and she weren't exactly close."

"She was still my GaGa."

Wendy cringed sadly at this childhood nickname she had not heard anyone use in decades and could not believe had just left his mouth.

James brushed a lock of hair off his forehead with his fingertips. "I feel like a monster for having had a hand in what happened to her. Who wouldn't? But you're right. The thing I feel shittiest about is the impact of her death on you." Even as he said it, though, he realized she was more neutral about the recent news than he was. For the first time, he stopped to wonder why that might be. He eyed her with colder interest, but Wendy ignored it.

"Don't make my grief about *you*," she said in partial jest. "Since when have you become so empathetic?"

"Be nice or you might hurt my feeling," he replied with a quick smile.

"Just the one?"

"I don't want to overstate things."

Wendy cracked a grin but turned away so he couldn't see it.

"As for this mental entropy, I don't know when it started but it's been happening for a while."

"Like discovering when you start puking that you've been coming down with the flu for days," offered Wendy.

"Yes, like that."

The two were quiet a moment.

"I've also been having strange dreams."

She wasn't used to James sharing personal information. The more he offered, the more serious the situation seemed.

"What kind of dreams?"

He described them and Wendy's curiosity grew. "Those could be important." She mulled over this revelation in light of his unprecedented discomposure. "Maybe it's an awakening."

James shivered. "They are vivid," he confirmed. "But I don't like what they do to me. It feels like they're connected to this," he curled a lip, "disorder."

Wendy laughed. "You mean this unkempt business of having emotions? Yeah, being human's harder than it looks, Supercop."

He eyed her without amusement. "It's not just about having feelings. My focus is faltering. It's like when a Micromedium signal gets interrupted and the picture on your terminal cracks into pixilated noise. That's how I feel. My screen keeps breaking up and jerking around."

It was hard for Wendy to maintain unadulterated anger towards James when he was displaying this uncharacteristic vulnerability. Then again, she admonished herself, people were always chasing after James's elusive vulnerability. Remembering that rekindled her anger at the misdeeds he had confessed. She decided to see how he would respond to a crack of the whip.

"I don't know what you expected when you started using those goddamn things," she scolded. "Any idiot would have known they came with a price."

James didn't answer, and Wendy regarded him in frosty silence. "Not the exception to the rule this time, eh Jimmy? Must be tough for you."

"You have no idea."

"You have got to stop using the arrays, at least until you," she ran through words in her mind, "stabilize." She figured he wouldn't like hearing that, but it was the most diplomatic term she could muster.

"Probably sage advice," he conceded. "But they're integral to my job duties."

"Job duties?" she sneered. "You mean hunting and assisting prosecutorial overkill on people like Leo Baksh?"

"Leo Baksh is a—"

Wendy held up a finger. "I know Leo, James. And a lot of other people who know Leo."

"I neurally—"

"Some of whom," she barreled over him, "connected with him neurally, just like you. He is not the monster you people portrayed him to be. Plus, let's not forget that you were being manipulated with neural aggression from outside your own brain while you testified. I love you, Jimmy, but I don't consider your opinion reliable on this subject. If you've got half the courage you claim, try questioning your own judgment for once."

"He confessed."

"I know. What Leo did was horrible. He deserved to be held responsible for it, drugs or no drugs, but that sick freak Alicia Cheung is a filthy liar and a sadistic pig, and you damn well know it. You people didn't try to punish Leo for his crime, you tried to destroy him. Excuse me for pointing this out," she said, stepping toward him and locking eye contact, "but you played a role in what he did. How intimate a part, only you know," she added, raising her voice, "but if you're dreaming about cosmic light emanating through prison bars from his mind to yours"—she stood right up into his face and snarled—"I'd say it was pretty goddamn intimate."

James felt like he'd been slapped. Before he knew what was happening, he had gripped Wendy by the shirt and nearly lifted her off her feet. His breath singed her face, and his eyes blazed with rage. "Let me go," she commanded through her teeth, glaring back at him with reciprocal fury. But he held tight, his body trembling. Sadness seeped through the anger in his eyes. He pulled her closer, and just before his lips touched hers, Wendy wrenched herself free, nearly falling over.

They gaped in mutual shock.

"You should leave—"

"I'm going—" they blurted simultaneously. Wendy flushed with conflicting emotion and sensation, and surprisingly not all of it unpleasant.

"Go," said James.

"Quit your job, Jimmy. Get some therapy." When he didn't respond, she added, "Don't call me until you do."

She grabbed her bag and fled, leaving James feeling as though he had destroyed the one thing he held sacred.

The next day, James requested a two-week leave of absence to grieve the loss of his great-grandmother and get some much-needed rest. Chief Mills was startled by the request, but suspected the neural abuse investigations were causing James stress. It was understandable that the recent revelations about Evelyn's death would exacerbate any ambient tension. For an ordinary man, anyway, which James was not. Nevertheless, the chief concluded a leave of absence would reduce friction in the office. He granted permission.

When Mills stuck his head in Lauren's office to break the news about James's leave, her she was slack-jawed. "James is dropping his pending investigations?"

"Temporarily, yes."

Neither found it necessary to verbalize the obvious degree of atypicality this development bespoke. Lauren closed the file she had been reviewing, placed it on a stack, and reached for another. "We will make the necessary adjustments."

"Thank you, Agent Drey," said the chief, skipping his eye around the neatly organized labors on her desk to highlight his recognition before he moved on to other tasks.

In truth, it was a massive inconvenience to Lauren and Melissa. Neither was equipped to assume James's undercover identities nor keep his investigations hot.

"Damn it," Lauren said aloud. She did not like depending on James for anything, and this sudden halt in the quantum neural abuse investigations heightened her disconcertion.

During James's fortnight of leave, a newly minted task force from the Capital Region's office landed its first promising leads: Two low-level security officers working for SecurePort Inc. claimed they had helped install some of the quantum surveillance arrays concealed in the walls, floors, and ceilings of various public venues. After proving their inside knowledge by leading the DDI agents to previously undiscovered hidden arrays, the two informants began identifying other SecurePort security and custodial staff they claimed had participated in the nationwide criminal intrusion. As the DDI questioned its widening pool of interrogees, the confessions converged on one man: SecurePort's director of labor relations Fredrick Luttrell, the man who—unbeknownst to anyone other than James, Sandoval, and Luttrell himself—James had used to coordinate installation of the arrays.

James would have remained blissfully and perilously ignorant of the wildfire closing around him like an incendiary noose had he not stopped by the office one afternoon to touch base with Lauren and mitigate the impact of his absence. During a pause in their conversation about James's cases, Lauren mentioned offhand the developments in the QFRI intrusion investigation and told him the chief was at that moment securing an arrest warrant for Fredrick Luttrell.

James, whose life already was in tectonic shift, failed to conceal his shock with characteristic inscrutability. Lauren did not know what to make of his surprise amidst all the other signs that James was suffering an existential crisis. Her investigatory instincts momentarily alerted her to pursue the matter, but her compassion and discretion superseded that impulse, so she decided not to pester him, though she intended to mention it privately to Bimal.

James erected a mask of relative sangfroid and hoped he maintained it long enough to quell any dubiety on Lauren's part. When he detected a conversational interstice suitable for bringing their exchange to a close, he seized the chance and made his farewells. After ensuring no one was following, he ducked into his office and made an encrypted Micromedium voice link to DII Agent Sandoval.

For two days, James waited in white-knuckled anticipation for news of further developments in the QFRI intrusion investigation. He restrained himself from calling Sandoval or his own colleagues at the DDI Capital Region, partly out of superstitious fear that doing so would draw trouble like lightning to a weather vane.

Finally, the story broke across the Micromedium and Macromedium news and information conduits: A covert DDI manhunt for a person they believed coordinated installation of the QFRI surveillance and manipulation equipment ended abruptly when Fredrick Luttrell's body washed up onto a rocky beach near the capital. James felt a sickening blend of guilt and relief at this news. "Sorry, you stupid bastard," he said aloud. "Thank God," he added in a whisper.

Unless Luttrell had told someone else about James's involvement, the only people who knew were DII Agent Sandoval and Wendy. Sandoval was apparently still protecting him. He doubted Wendy would throw him to the wolves no matter how angry and disgusted she felt. Of course, that made her complicit in his crimes at this point as far as the law was concerned, but he doubted she saw it that way. He also had the sneaking feeling he was just one of many felons to whom she served as well-intentioned accomplice after-the-fact, and probably on both sides of the rift he had helped cleave through the nation's sociopolitical substrate. Unfortunately, none of that gave him any sense of absolution for the harm and jeopardy he had brought upon her.

In the past, James had little difficulty dismissing guilt over even the most ruthless acts of disrespect toward others, not to mention emotional and physical abuse he had inflicted. His assault on Wendy, however, was a different matter altogether. He had always protected her, and he knew this was connected to the best part of him, a place he kept cordoned off from the rest of his life and concealed from others' view. He could not stop revisiting the incident, wondering how it could have happened, against Wendy of all people, yet finding himself unable to puzzle out an answer.

To his further consternation, when struggling with remorse over having violated this sanctum, James encountered random memories of times he'd felt as though his colleague, Melissa Benton, had x-ray vision and was staring right through his most granitic barriers. He had dismissed those sensations in the past with a flirtatious wink, but she always responded with a quiet and steady gaze that took neither the bait nor any apparent offense. Thinking about it now increased a sensation that the platform on which he had built his strength was sliding off a disintegrating sand dune.

The day before his two-week leave was to expire, James forced himself to meet with a therapist Wendy had recommended. After ensuring his secrets would be preserved, James summarized enough of his shifting predicament that the doctor all but insisted he take an extended sabbatical to stabilize and to investigate the nature of his mental dislocation. When James resisted, the shrink informed him that, although he certainly would not break James's confidence regarding his past actions, he would alert George Mills if he felt James were unfit to return to active duty.

James vividly imagined himself strangling the doctor, but another part of his awareness said this violent urge proved the doctor's prescience. Over his own objections, James yielded and informed Mills he wished to take a six-month sabbatical.

Chief Mills was stunned mainly because he had perceived James as something other than human. "Take all the time you need," he said in a kind but scrupulously unpatronizing tone that James appreciated. Bimal and Lauren were suspicious, but they kept that between them.

And so, the ruthless James Malone found himself face-to-face with an alien. It had volcanic sub regions, haunting regrets, and a lunatic urge to ponder dimensions beyond the physical, which he believed had something to do with his existential entanglement with Leo Baksh. Exploring this mess, he realized to his amused unsurprise, would require greater courage than it took to be a DDI agent. The task would be more daunting than any he had previously undertaken: investigating the contours of his own true self, which recent events suggested might be both smaller and greater than he had imagined.

48

LIAM KEPT VIGIL OVER A cold cup of coffee at a sidewalk café near the Heartwood Pub and waited impatiently for Wendy's arrival.

Having been unmasked as a radical activist, survived torture, endured prosecution and imprisonment, and been released as a pawn in a larger game he minimally understood, he refused to surrender any remaining moments of his life to emotional paralysis. Instead, he channeled his wounding into renewed activism, though of a more seasoned and lawful variety. The work was far less exciting and dangerous. Fortunately, he had big tools. After settling claims against his father's legally divested estate, he assumed the helm of Protection Inc., replaced the executive officers, strong-armed or bought out minority shareholders, and set about steering the great ship into battle.

During his recovery process, he had distanced himself from nearly everyone, including Wendy, though for her, his heart's most treasured friend, he periodically sent up smoke signals, a privilege he denied others. She had visited him at the treatment center, but he was so heavily medicated at the time, he barely remembered it.

Wendy slid her arms around Liam from behind and kissed his neck. He turned to see her, and she locked his pupil for the split second it takes old friends to confirm that their connection remains intact.

"Hi, handsome," she said softly.

"Hi," he replied, and kissed her arm.

Wendy slid into the chair opposite Liam. No words could capture the enormity of what they had been through.

Liam had aged.

She broke the silence. "How are you feeling?"

His baseline expression bespoke deep fatigue.

"I'm fine."

Wendy felt out the answer.

"How are you really?"

"How the fuck do you think I am?"

She pressed her lips together. "I'm sorry," she said after a beat.

"No, I'm sorry. There is no point in dredging through it. I'm alive. You're alive. There hasn't been a revolution. There is work to be done. Let's move on."

"If you say so, sweetie, but is that sustainable? Can you plough past all of that trauma?"

"More sustainable than a bullet to my temple, or someone else's."

She didn't like the sound of that, but she decided her impulse to probe was for her own assurances, not out of respect for his needs.

"OK," she assented, "tell me about your work then. What are you doing with Lock-Em-Up Inc."

He smirked at the moniker. "Turning it into Fix-Em-Up Inc."

"Oh, yeah?" she said, snapping her fingers at a waiter.

"Yes," he said. "Big changes."

"Cappuccino. Hot," she barked.

Liam turned down the corners of his mouth. "Look who's all tough now."

She dismissed the comment with a flick of the wrist. "When you're the best, you don't settle for slack," she explained.

Liam barely registered the quip. Apparently, her charms no longer had the same effect on him. They silently mourned the innocent complexities between them that used to seem so important.

She scooted her chair closer. "So? Tell me."

He told her the first steps he took were purely internal. "I can't shorten anyone's term of confinement, but I can change it. We're lowering population density and shifting the emphasis to treatment and education."

"Glad to hear it," she replied. "How?"

"Well," he said, warming to the subject, "we've commissioned three new state-of-the-art facilities, designed to mimic normal life and help people transition back to functional living."

"I'm sure the Cleagues love that."

"No," assured Liam, "which is a bonus."

They both smiled.

"I hired a pack of architects to put multipurpose spaces into the older facilities for socializing, therapy, recreation. All that good stuff that no one wants to pay for. We're also overhauling the medical departments, making university courses available, improving nutrition, expanding treatment options."

"Do you have enough reserves to do that and keep the company profitable?"

"I have the resources to get it rolling. As for the long-term profitability, that's part of my larger evil scheme for major systemic changes. *Mwah ha ha*!"

"Ambitious," she said with a grin of approval. "How are the staff reacting?"

"The unions were resistant, but when they saw how much money would flow into new positions, they started working with me to reconfigure. I fired a few throwbacks. We're fighting over that. The bigger tussle will be over my plan to tether pay increases to inmate success in the programs and reductions in recidivism."

"They'll definitely go to the mat over that," Wendy said.

"Hopefully they'll throw the fight if the checks they get when they do their jobs right are big enough."

"That all sounds great," she said as enthusiastically as she could. Wendy was past caring about big reforms, but she could not see Liam being satisfied with creating less horrible conditions of confinement. This was a guy who penetrated the Department of International Intelligence hub to help expose a torture regime. If he wasn't at peace inside, she figured he would need something pretty substantial on the external front to keep him occupied.

"Don't worry, love," he said in response to her tone. "That's just the platform. I've brought in nonpartisan auditors to monitor and document the effects of these changes. I'm optimistic that the data will be useful ammunition for some bigger battles."

Now that sounds more like Liam, she thought. Wendy exhaled with relief.

For six months, James Malone plumbed the alien depths of his own psyche. The shrink forbade any amorous entanglements during this time, so he passed the weeks largely in solitude. No skirts to chase or criminals to hunt. The deeper he examined himself and the longer he abstained from his "investigations," the more he believed he was entangled, not just neurally or on a quantum level, but psychologically and experientially, with the people he was officially empowered to bust. The line between hero and perp blurred when he zoomed in the lens. Questions about the virtue or even legitimacy of his role, which he ordinarily would dismiss as so much liberal hand wringing, began to trouble him.

James frequently dreamt of the abuse recordings he had experienced, often with the disturbing sensation that he was connected to the victims' minds in real time. Unlike at the fetish sites, though, he felt no energizing power surge. Instead, he sensed the victims' fear, humiliation, and rage. Inconveniently, it bothered him and made him think of Wendy.

This was almost enough to make him fear sleep. Sometimes, however, these nightmares morphed into dreams where he was connected to Leo Baksh, with little dots of light pulsing in the center of their chests. He wished for those dreams, and when he was in one, he focused into his own center, willing the light to expand. He carried thoughts of both kinds of dreams into his day, and with them a deepening rift in his perceptions.

As he entered the final week before he was to return to work, James was teetering on a razor-sharp line between two universes. One had a dark, addictive allure that promised an intensely fierce and salty pleasure, but he increasingly believed it was life-consuming and evil. The other contained a wellspring of possibility, and in it he felt the prospect of liberation from the dark side's illicit pull and forgiveness for having tarried there at all—perhaps even the hope of fulfilling deeper yearnings he delusively sought to satisfy there. As he perched on the ridge and surveyed these two worlds, he realized the main reason he drank the dark land's smoky liquor was because he had lost faith in the light side's healing and invigorating nectar.

Hewing a wholesome path was a fearsome prospect that would require total self-honesty and exposure. This existential nudity was tougher than the ugliest of battles at the office or risks in his investigations because it left him, well, vulnerable. Once he acknowledged this deep fragility, he realized everyone else was probably scrambling to hide and protect it too, even the freaks in the fetish sites. He suspected the solution to the whole quantum abuse recording disease lay not in further isolating the already-deluded and off-balance participants, but in something like the self-exploration he was undertaking.

He wasn't sure what he could contribute toward fixing the problem but he knew he wouldn't find it in the fetish sites, which meant he couldn't return to his investigations.

All but resolved to quit his job, James received news from Melissa on the final night of his leave that cinched his decision. James did not know Melissa well, but he found her quiet strength notable and he sometimes felt inexplicably visible to her. His perplexity that she called him gave way to greater surprise when she spoke:

"I don't know all the details but Bimal and Lauren have been talking about you. Lauren has intimated that Bimal has documentation of inconsistencies in your reports regarding Leo Baksh. He's also asking questions about your relationship with Fred Luttrell. I think they are building a case for driving you out of the department. Or maybe something worse."

James was chilled by the implications of these words, but also puzzled as to why Melissa would show him this courtesy, and habitually suspicious someone else had her do it for strategic reasons. Something in the gentleness of her voice—a fact he would in the past have seen as an exploitable vulnerability but now found reassuring—cut against those thoughts. He minded his tone and said, "Melissa, I appreciate the tip, but why are you telling me this?"

"I assume you're working through something difficult." She fell quiet. "I thought you might want to know," she concluded without further explanation.

James let her words and the awkward sweetness of her voice ripple around in his mind. Unsure what to make of it, he accepted her gesture at face value. "That's kind. I don't deserve it. But thank you."

In a tone somewhere between declarative and interrogatory, she said, "See you tomorrow."

"Good bye," he answered without confirming.

James's primal urge to fight lurched to the foreground. "How dare you try to kick me when I'm down and force me out, you arrogant piece of shit," he snarled at the walls. On deeper reflection, he decided Bimal's campaign merely dovetailed with his dawning concerns about the investigatory work. He needed out. Why fight? The change might lead to a more habitable future. There would be opportunities enough to fight down the road if he retained a taste for combat.

That didn't mean he had to turn stupid now though, he reminded himself. James placed a call to Bimal and made it blunt: "You want me out and believe it or not, I want to go, but for reasons unrelated to yours that are none of your goddamn business. All I need to know is this: Would my departure from the DDI get you off my ass?"

James drummed his fingers.

"Permanent departure?"

James swallowed. "Yes."

There was a long silence on the line.

"Yes," Bimal said finally. "Several more urgent matters require my attention, James."

To his annoyance and puzzlement, James detected kindness in Bimal's voice. Resisting a disconcerting urge to confide his struggles, James severed the call without closing courtesies.

At war with himself and in unspoken trepidation seasoned with hope and twinges of self-doubt, James contacted Chief Mills and tendered his resignation, praying it would yield a more sane and meaningful path, and that Bimal Gurung would be true to his word and consider James's preemptory resignation to be victory enough.

After a year of Liam's reforms at Protection Inc., the independent auditors published a report showing that the results were favorable. Inmate violence and rule violation fell to unprecedented lows in the prison facilities, and behavior at the Vulnerable confinement centers stabilized significantly. Confinees in both settings made accelerated progress toward greater functionality as measured by standard tests of fitness for Citizenship.

Armed with these data, Liam formed a task group to brainstorm ideas for development of Protection Inc. and larger reforms to the classification system.

To his dumbfoundment, Wendy suggested he invite her brother. Liam was skeptical, but he trusted Wendy and, though it seemed impossible, she insisted James was experiencing a personal awakening and needed an outlet to work for progressive reform in the country's response to criminality. She argued that James's history lent a type of influence and credibility money could not buy.

On this last point Liam agreed. Fundamentally pragmatic by nature, he conditionally set aside his misgivings and gave James a chance.

At their first meeting, Liam's apprehension gave way to fascination as he took in the changes to James's demeanor. Less self-assured, more open, less pushy, yet still wielding a palpably intense presence. In some ways, Liam saw his own deep mental wounds reflected in James's eyes, which he could not fathom but corroborated Wendy's claim that James had gone off a life-altering cliff. Liam remained instinctively wary of James, but they fell into a dynamic working relationship and, by the end of their first meeting, both had concluded it would be a fruitful collaboration.

The task group hired legal counsel and a lobbying firm and began pressing the Council of Delegates to broaden the definition of Citizenship and create an incentive system to reward both public and private confinement providers when recidivism rates dropped, rather than by default when inmates returned to prison or institutionalization.

The public-sector prison guard unions fought the move, as did several smaller companies that provided private confinement services. That changed, however, when Protection Inc. secured a contract from the national government to provide security, therapeutic services, medical and psychological care, and educational programs in the newly minted transitional zones where ex-confinees lived while working toward restoration of Citizenship. As the colossal monetary value of this contract became apparent, stakeholders throughout the confinement industry recognized that the changes Liam spearheaded need not interrupt their income streams, and they scrambled to catch the wave.

As Liam toiled to shift the country's confinement policies and practices, Leo adapted to surviving under its longstanding rules. His life became rigidly routinized. He learned to hold his tongue and follow orders when guards spoke rudely to him, and to accept that he had power over almost nothing except his own mind. Over that, he regained and expanded control.

The other recurrent features of his life behind bars were setbacks and disappointments, his ongoing consequences intersecting with the human frailties of people he counted on in the free world, as his life path disentangled itself.

As Mark had predicted years earlier, Leo's predicament showed who was in his corner and who wasn't. And it did indeed surprise him. For months that stretched into years, Leo wrote Jeaneane, sharing his insights, making apologies, describing the work he was doing to grow well, and pleading with her not to end their friendship.

After ignoring his missives, Jeaneane finally responded in a note hastily scrawled on a cheap card she'd no doubt received for free from a charitable organization's fundraising drive. Leo had received the same card from his mother and cherished it, but Jeaneane's stylish cards were among the indicia of her personal élan. He didn't miss the petty slight.

"Leo," she wrote, "I'm glad you're well. I miss you sometimes, and there are things about you I love. But I cannot go back there."

"She needs to get the fuck over herself," Mark sniped when Leo showed him Jeaneane's terse kiss-off. "There are 'things' she loves about you? How big of her. Call me old-fashioned, but you either love a person or you don't. Screw her, Leo. Good riddance to cheap trash."

"It's not that she doesn't care about you in her own self-centered way," John Hanes tepidly offered during a visit a few days later. "It's that she defines her existence by other people's opinions, so she can't imagine being associated with a convicted felon. It doesn't cast the right light on her cheekbones."

"Jeaneane is not that shallow," countered Leo.

"I didn't say she was shallow," John replied. "Just damaged, and lost behind her fortress of mirrors."

Leo appreciated the attempt but couldn't buy the script. He missed Jeaneane terribly and regretted all the ways he had let her down. Nevertheless, he was furious over her proud, self-righteous abandonment, and her blindness to her own shortcomings. He let his blood cool for a few days, then faced facts, scrawled out a short note, and reciprocated her farewell.

After a few months of brooding, Leo realized his indignation over people who had left him was blinding him to the wonderful people who were standing by him and, in some cases, like Jamie, had become even more solidly present than before he was locked up.

On Leo's behalf, Lance Wilson petitioned for Leo to be resentenced in light of the evidence Anaku had revealed that his sentencing hearing and who knew what other stages of the proceedings against him were tainted by quantum neural aggression piped into the participants' brains by the DII.

As expected, the court agreed with prosecutor Alicia Cheung that Leo's confession on the day of his initial arrest amply supported his penalty. The neural manipulation didn't determine the outcome or warrant overturning Leo's sentence. Wilson sought an evidentiary hearing to question Cheung and the DDI witnesses under oath regarding their knowledge of the QFRI technology and its origins. Cheung argued the issue was irrelevant and, in any event, involved protected state secrets. The court agreed.

"I won't be getting out any time soon," Leo told Jamie when next they spoke.

"Disappointing," he replied. "I still think something will break. I don't believe you'll be in there for the whole term."

"Anything's possible," said Leo. "I can't hang onto that though. It makes the time even harder."

"Don't give up hope."

"Hanging tough," Leo replied.

To get through it, he hunkered down and learned a new form of strength: not the kind one needs to carry great weight, but the kind that allows a person to bend without breaking.

As Leo's failed attempt to get a shorter sentence played out, Anna Dao started her second year of advocate's school and became certified to practice under the tutelage of a licensed advocate while she completed her studies.

Her first act was to bring a lawsuit against the individual who had orchestrated her neural assault and the QFRI recording of it that figured so prominently in Leo's prosecution. According to her complaint, the perpetrator was Lydia Phrane, a therapist Anna's family had hired when she was a teenager to help her decide whether to submit to reprogramming for Citizenship.

"Rather than serve as trustworthy confidante and guide," alleged the complaint, "Defendant Phrane mined information about Plaintiff Dao to use against her in a malicious attack, calibrating the QFRI weapon and choreographing the assault to exploit her most tender vulnerabilities."

Due to Anna's notoriety, the case spattered across the Macromedium and Micromedium news and gossip tableaux, thrusting her back into the public eye and dragging Lydia Phrane with her into its glare.

Phrane's advocate filed an answer denying the allegations and held a press conference to refute Anna's claims. The thin man in rumpled suit, his few remaining hairs adorning an otherwise bald and freckled head, peered through wire-rimmed glasses and opened his mouth to speak. His voice whined like a rusty hinge, greased but unfortunately not silenced. After proclaiming his role and credentials, he offered a sterile assessment of the case:

"Although the therapist–patient relationship is sacrosanct under most circumstances, Ms. Dao has placed it at issue by bringing this lawsuit. Consequently, my client will be forced to disclose important facts about Ms. Dao she would prefer to keep in her confidence. For now, we will say that the case has no merit. Ms. Phrane had no role in the assault on Ms. Dao or its recording, and the real issue here is the plaintiff's degraded psychological state. That is what should be of concern to the courts and the Citizenry."

Anna gritted her teeth as she listened to her adversary's plan of attack. So much for keeping her private life out of the public maw.

"I also note that the allegations are preposterous on their face," continued the defense advocate. "The complaint offers no plausible explanation as to why a seasoned therapist would perpetrate such a sadistic and self-destructive act. Not only will we get this case thrown out, we will pursue a cross complaint against Ms. Dao to hold her accountable for this outrageous defamation."

Unbeknownst to Phrane and her advocate, Anna had sent an advance draft of her complaint to John Hanes before she filed it so that he would have a story ready when she struck the match. Unknown to Anna, John had launched an investigation into Phrane's background.

As Phrane's advocate was finishing his press conference, the *Capital Times* published a Micromedium news blast linking the therapist to Polytronics Inc., one of the Micromedium equipment manufacturers Cormack claimed was part of the conspiracy to thwart Anna's reclassification petition. According to the article, an anonymous source said Phrane was working with the company on secret experiments investigating the technology's potential as a weapon.

"Given Agent Anaku's claims regarding misuse of this technology by the Department of International Intelligence," said an anonymous commentator in an accompanying sidebar, "one cannot help but wonder whether Polytronic's research was conducted at the agency's behest."

The *Times* article also hinted a connection to Jeaneane's assault case, which involved an employee of Interlink Technologies, the Micromedium equipment manufacturer Cormack had identified that was governed by corporate directors in common with Polytronics Inc., the company associated with Phrane, as well as Cormack's—and now Liam's—confinement business, Protection Inc.

"As previously reported in the *Times*, Polytronics Inc., Interlink Technologies, and Protection Inc. had several common corporate directors, among them Citizens Action League President Alistair Coyle and Vice President Paul Graham, both of whom perished under suspicious circumstances after Cormack O'Brian's exposé." How and why, asked the article with mock innocence, could the Department of Domestic Intelligence never have investigated these companies' activities? Were the intelligence agencies in collusion?

After reading this report, Anna amended her complaint to add the DII and DDI as defendants. She subpoenaed representatives from both agencies regarding their involvement with, or knowledge as to, the Micromedium technology companies, her former therapist, and experiments using the QFRI arrays for infliction of pain.

"Anaku's Improbable Legacy: Anna Dao Sues the DII" read one Macromedium lead that evening.

"Just how far and wide did this conspiracy go?" asked a retired Aggressives defense advocate on an evening news program.

"It's a combination terror–confinement system that keeps everyone imprisoned in one form or another," opined an interviewee on the street who declined to state his name. "We're either behind razor wire, skewered with neural death rays, or blinded by belief in the Cleagues' and government's lies. Even the private reprogrammers are involved in weapons development and torture? No matter how you slice it, they have us trapped." He stuck his face in the camera. "And it's making them rich."

Conservative pundits tittered at this sound bite and argued that judicial scrutiny of Anna's claims would put to rest such extremist prattle.

The government itself apparently had less confidence in the mechanisms of justice. A deputy advocate from the advocate general's office intervened in the lawsuit the next day, filing a motion to quash Anna's subpoenas on state secrecy grounds and dismiss the case in the interest of national security.

This sent a cold chill through the Micromedium, which gave birth to a firestorm on the street. "Corporate–DII Conspiracy" was spray-painted across the courthouse façade and reproduced on Macromedium and Micromedium screens nationwide. MOSGROVE ADMINISTRATION COVERUP? ran one macrovision headline that afternoon.

With the help of her supervising advocate and a pile of friend-of-the-court briefs from advocates representing organizations across the moderate to liberal spectrum, Anna fought the advocate general's move. Picketers provided rowdy backup outside the courthouse on the day the court was to rule. "Justice for Dao, justice for all!" became the predominant chant.

These official and organic efforts were in vain. The court agreed with the government advocate that the case was too dangerous to proceed and—based on information neither the public nor Anna ever saw—granted the motions to quash the subpoenas and dismiss, and tossed Anna's assault case against her therapist straight into the trash.

Appeals were announced, but the case—and the naive hope of inroads into the DII's nefarious web—came to a screeching halt.

John Hanes refused to accept that a simple judicial pronouncement could suppress public outrage over the recent spate of revelations. Hoping to keep the activist communities inspired and focused, he strategically linked the rulings in Leo's and Anna's cases into a symposium in the *Capital Times* addressing the government's ongoing refusal to come clean over its involvement in developing and using neural weapons on its own Citizens, and its deliberate evisceration of the civilian adjudicatory process through intrusive use of the quantum arrays.

As John had hoped, several professors from Anna's school weighed in and linked the issues. In the words of one: "The government's intransigence regarding use of the technology, combined with unlimited prosecutorial discretion and the leverage of mandatory sentencing minimums that not even judges can override, means that the intelligence agencies and the power interests they serve can use prosecutors and exploit the courts to eliminate political enemies by fiat.

This leaves the public with an invulnerable prosecutorial machine serving the interests of what increasingly resembles a paramilitary regime armed with mind-flaying technology. Whither our pretense to democracy, due process, and the rule of law?"

The more activist of the academics said the thinnest plate in the machine's armor was prosecutors' absolute immunity from civil liability. "They don't police each other," summed up one educator, "and the public can't sue them. Changing that would provide a powerful lever to disrupt this abusive system."

The activist groups got the message and turned their attention to the prosecutors. Respect, Spectrum, and Pro'gression, having built ties during the tumultuous aftermath of Anaku's original report, formed an ad hoc political and legal action group to propose and lobby for reform legislation. Liam and James anonymously infused the new group with massive donations, and James recruited a former prosecutor—whose intended whistle blowing Alicia Cheung had silenced with threats several years earlier—to help the group draft specific legislative proposals.

On this organization's initiative and with its support, a group of liberal delegates introduced a spate of reform bills. Progressive Caucus Chair, Yosuf Sisulu, held a press conference to announce the legislation:

"Recent events have made it clear that our criminal justice system has become lopsided and unjust. In tandem with ongoing efforts to immunize our adjudicatory venues from quantum neural manipulation, our caucus is responding to overwhelming public demands for limitations on the power of the advocate general's office and its deputies by introducing the following proposed measures:

"First, we will eliminate mandatory sentencing minimums so that judges, not the advocate general's office, will have the authority to determine a fair sentence on the merits of each case.

"Second, we will modify prosecutors' immunity from civil liability, such that they can be sued in court for gross violations of their professional duties.

"Third, we will create a Citizen's review panel with subpoena power to investigate prosecutorial abuses and recommend discipline.

"Finally, we will empower the Council of Delegates to appoint a special prosecutor, outside the advocate general's office, to pursue criminal charges against severely malfeasant government advocates."

The moderate liberal activist coalition praised the proposal and public polls showed strong approval. Predictably, the Citizens Action League was not pleased. Backed by the DDI, DII, national and local police, and unions representing law enforcement officers and prison guards, the conservatives argued that the legislation would dismember the rule of law, hamstring the prosecutors, and unleash instability so extreme that recent events would appear minor in retrospect.

A lobbying and PR war waged for months. John kept the heat on the government and stoked the street-activist fires with periodic symposia on DII and prosecutorial abuses. Eventually, a moderate majority in the Council of Delegates concluded that giving the public some power over the prosecutors would be better than continued public demands for exposure of state secrets or another crisis between the DII and the central government.

Belinda Mosgrove agreed. Nearing the end of her tenure, she waxed courageous and signed into law the prosecution reform bill, divesting government advocates of their treasured immunity from oversight, not to mention civil and criminal liability, for abuses of their powers.

The formidable forces she thwarted with that act joined hands and vowed to remove her party from power in the next election. To drive home how deeply they reviled her actions, they ran International Intelligence Director Trent Hobson on the conservative ticket.

Polls consistently showed Mosgrove's chosen successor, Progressive Caucus Chair Yosuf Sisulu, with a healthy lead. On election night eight months later, however, as Sisulu was preparing to deliver his victory speech, anomalous returns began rolling in. Hobson was the victor by a slim margin.

Protests erupted across the country with fiery allegations that the election process had been hijacked through manipulation of the voting and tallying equipment, if not outright intrusion into voters' brains. The *Capital Times* ran investigative pieces and speculation raged across the Micromedium.

In the end, there was no proof, and the nation's High Adjudicatory Tribunal, several of its members Mosgrove appointees, concluded the country could not endure another constitutional crisis and blessed the election with its judicial imprimatur. Progressive activists wept tears of rage when the ruling was announced. After the initial shock subsided, their grief phase-shifted into a deep foreboding, prompting renewed calls for organizing and, if necessary, economy-crippling civil disobedience.

The political factions squared off for another fight, this time with the former Department of International Intelligence head poised to assume the nation's office of chief executive.

Cormack monitored these developments from his self-imposed covert tropical exile. He had used his time relatively wholesomely: drinking less, eating less, exercising a little, relaxing. He felt rejuvenated and invigorated. He had even bedded Marta a few times, though he never forgot to mistrust her. Well, maybe for a moment here and there. *She is mightily gifted in many ways*, he thought with a sneer. But almost never.

When the electoral political tide shifted—or was shoved—Cormack contemplated orchestrating a return to public life. He would need assurances of immunity, but he knew a few potentially leverageable items of information. If he played it right, it might be possible, he thought with a rush of the old adrenaline.

Marta spied on Cormack through a crack in her bedroom door as he compiled his list of contacts and formulated his strategy. When she was reasonably certain he would remain engrossed in his scheming, she locked her door and tapped the space bar on her Micromedium terminal. With her encrypted chat session revived, she networked her terminal to Cormack's and patched the hacker who shared her virtual space into Cormack's private data.

It took only a few minutes to crack open files containing account locations and information. By the time Cormack scratched on Marta's door, the deed was done. She powered down her terminal, pulled off her robe, and greeted the old criminal in the buff to keep his mind on fleshly concerns.

Later, she poured him a fruity concoction she had customarily served up after treating him to her amorous delights. Cormack nestled into a chaise longue, sipped the nectar through a straw, and watched waves roll into the hideaway's lagoon.

Ten minutes later, he dropped the glass, spilling half the contents.

"Strong drink," he said through slurred speech.

"I wanted to celebrate," she said with an edge of hostility he was too impaired to detect.

"Our return to society?"

"No. My freedom and prosperity," she corrected, zipping up her bag as a boat pulled up to the bungalow's lanai. He hadn't even seen it enter the lagoon.

Cormack had enough consciousness left to feel a moment's fear as his eyes crossed. He watched two Martas give him a fingertip wave, and saw a lithe young man and his doppelgänger help the Martas into the boats. Two wakes intersected in the blue as they sped away and Cormack's vision faded. His final disintegrating thought fragments were not so much anger as amusement that he should end up bested by this beguiling, tattooed ruffian.

49

When it became clear Trent Hobson would be Mosgrove's successor, Anna heaved a sigh of relief that she would not be at the center of the culture war's crossfire. She was in her second year of advocate's school, one year and an internship away from full Citizenship and a license to practice in the Department of Adjudication. Hordes of activists would need representation when the new chief executive began his assault on civil liberties. She hoped she could help the activists turn his abuses against him so deftly that his eventual downfall would drive the conservatives from power for a generation and trigger completion of the progressive swing to which his electoral theft was a desperate and hopefully unsuccessful backlash.

Her lawsuit having foundered on the rocks of official secrecy, Anna hunted for a new project to fulfill the supervised-practice portion of her curriculum. It infuriated her that both her life and Leo's had been so viciously lacerated by the government, and that their potential remedies disappeared behind the cowardly veil of bureaucratic cover-up and government-wide complicity, if not conspiracy.

With Mosgrove on her way out of office, the minimal hope one might extract from her paltry political remains was about to wink from view. Anna fretted over how to exploit the outgoing administration's lame-duck powers until, in a moment's clarity, she tripped upon a plan. It was poetically elegant, deliciously controversial, and politically defiant:

She, the official victim of Leo's crime, would represent him in a petition for executive clemency.

She relayed the idea to Wendy.

"Seriously?" responded Wendy. "Do you think that will play well? Haven't you had enough fighting with the Cleagues?"

"Not even," scoffed Anna. "They won't know what do with this. It's perfect. I can't imagine a clearer Fuck You. We have to get it done before that monster takes over."

Wendy sighed. "You and Leo are cut from the same cloth, you freak."

"In some ways," Anna said a little less enthusiastically. "I'm still pissed at him, but we're both being screwed and he can do more to grovel at my feet in servitude out here than in there."

"True," acknowledged Wendy.

"I can't visit him in prison," said Anna, "so I need you to tell him."

"You mean ask him?"

"I mean tell him."

Wendy partially obeyed, visiting Leo to tell him Anna's idea.

"That's out of the question," he replied.

Wendy told him Anna was hell-bent for glory to do it, and not just for him. "She feels like it's an across the board Screw You—to the spies, prosecutors, courts, Hobson, the Cleagues, fear mongers in the Council of Delegates. Let her do it. She's already frothing at the mouth. I haven't seen her so amped up in ages."

"It's going to draw their fire."

"They are coming for all of us, whether we resist them or not. We have to push back, and we need to start before Hobson is inaugurated. You're no help to anyone in here. If Mosgrove lets you out, it will give the progressives hope and send a shot across Hobson's bow. Don't become institutionalized for God's sake. You want to make amends to Anna? Get out of prison and work for cheap in her advocate's office when she gets licensed."

Leo reflected ruefully. "We never know how the wheel will turn, do we?"

Wendy shrugged. "No, but at least there is movement. As long as that's the case, anything is possible."

"Things are not always as they seem," he said, parroting the adage she used to entice and cajole him with.

She giggled, then turned serious. "You have a sliver of an opportunity to get out now instead of in eight years. We need you. Anna wants to help you, and together, you guys can make one hell of a splash in the process."

Leo cringed at the thought of Anna using her provisional student advocate's credential to seek his, her official parasitic abuser's, release. Technically, she did not need his permission to proceed. He wasn't sure whether she'd sent Wendy as emissary to seek his blessing or give him fair warning. Either way, his activist heart felt a stick-it-to-'em rush.

He decided it could not get any worse for him. As for Anna, it would establish her credibility as an audacious fighter before she even entered the professional ring. If Anna started challenging sacrosanct assumptions before she was even licensed, she could wield an aura of independence and courage that would make her future adversaries think twice before glibly dismissing her as a professional greenhorn.

Though she hadn't technically asked for his permission, he gave it, along with a pledge to lend his strength to hers should their paths cross sooner than Cheung had anticipated.

That threshold crossed, Leo felt a steady resolve, partly due to surviving horrors that dwarfed the mainstream concerns he used to take seriously, and partly due to having soaked up some unflinching and dispassionate focus—and perhaps a significant vein of cool aggression—from James Malone. Leo was more intrigued than fearful as he contemplated the struggle ahead.

As soon as Anna filed Leo's clemency petition, conservative news outlets attacked: BATTERED CLIENT SYNDROME? VICTIM DAO TRIES TO SPRING HER ABUSER. Anna tried to ignore the headlines, but Leo didn't have that option. The trashier of his fellow prisoners, especially ones locked up for drug dealing instead of the Vulnerable abuses they had gotten away with, peppered Leo with insults and threats.

The Citizens Action League rushed to leverage the development. "This goes to show why the criteria for Citizenship should be tightened, not eased," claimed a CAL spokesperson.

Lest that perspective gain traction, the *Capital Times* spilled a little grease in the bullring by publishing conveniently timed revelations. An anonymous government source claimed that the prosecutor in Leo's case buried evidence that the Department of Domestic Intelligence had supplied him with the QFRI recordings he was convicted of distributing, as well as documents in the government's possession that proved Leo was telling the truth about the impact of Elidrine on his actions, and that the prosecutor knew it.

Capital Macrovision's commentators slobbered over the claims, speculating that the "source" was someone within either the DDI itself or the advocate general's office. No one stood up to take credit for the leak. Outside public view in the privacy of his office, Bimal Gurung celebrated with a middle-finger salute.

Lance Wilson filed papers to reopen Leo's case yet again, and Anna amended Leo's clemency petition to cite the scandalous new allegations.

Belinda Mosgrove gazed out her office window with arms crossed as she received her morning briefing. The closer she got to yielding her desk to Trent Hobson, the harder it was to endure the daily summaries of political intrigue and harrowing threats from without and within. Today, she felt as though she might wheel and scream, "What the fuck difference does it make?"

Nick Cushman remained with her after the others had left.

"I'm tired of this," she said.

"Which part of it?" replied Cushman.

"All of it."

"Belinda, it's almost over. You've done a wonderful job. No one could have done better."

"No?" she asked. "I've let the intelligence agencies take me places I would rather have died than go."

"You did the best you could with an impossible situation."

"You would have handled it differently."

"I would have driven us off a cliff. You've always had a cooler head at the poker table. You avoided civil war and preserved a strong executive power."

"Against what?" countered Mosgrove. "A political coup by the director of a spy agency who has stolen my post through a hijacked election?"

"Yes," conceded Cushman, "from one perspective."

"Some legacy."

Nick put his hand on her shoulder. "Our government is still intact. At least there was the pretense of an election. It would have gone worse without the compromise."

"Yes, yes," she said, dismissing the coddling but offering a smile of thanks nonetheless.

"There is one rather colorful thing you could do before we snap shut our valises."

Mosgrove turned to him. Such teasing introductions usually preceded suggestions so outrageous that they reminded her why she was the chief and he the deputy.

Cushman handed her a file. She peeked at the cover sheet: "Petition for executive clemency. Petitioner: Leo Baksh. Submitted by: Anna Dao."

Mosgrove and Cushman exchanged an amused glance.

"I've done my best to avoid the coverage of this," said Mosgrove, "but I suppose the final decision rests with me."

"I believe that's how it works," replied Cushman, who poured them both a cup of tea as Mosgrove sat to review the file. Her legal staff, as with most such petitions, recommended summary denial. They advised that this was particularly appropriate in Leo's case given that it had become such a political rallying point.

Her pardon of Liam O'Brian had indeed drawn fierce criticism, but what was there to lose now?

She read Anna's petition, including the allegations of withheld evidence and neural contamination of the proceedings, a subject Mosgrove knew far more of than did Anna or the *Capital Times*.

Nick kept mum as she flipped through the pages and closed the file.

"Well?"

"I'll sleep on it."

Next morning, as her departure from the chief executive's mansion neared, Mosgrove signed a clemency order commuting the remainder of Leo's sentence. She already was hated for clipping the prosecutors' wings by signing the reform bill, why not undo one of their abuses? She also shared Anna's urge for a poetic middle finger to Hobson and his backers on her way out of office.

"That's for hijacking my administration," she said aloud as she penned her name.

She stopped short of a full pardon, however, which would have restored Leo's Citizenship and maybe his advocate's license.

Anna was disappointed, but John Hanes, who visited Leo after the announcement, wasn't surprised. "Who knows? Maybe she thought exonerating you would reflect badly on her for signing the law they used to prosecute you."

"She probably wanted to mitigate the political backlash," said Leo.

"Can't blame her for that," said John.

"She might think my crime was so horrible that it doesn't merit full forgiveness, even if the proceedings were tainted."

"Maybe she thinks it would do you good to earn back your Citizenship the hard way."

"I doubt she's that interested in me."

"Probably not, but you never know. She's a great woman."

Whatever Mosgrove's reasoning, she only granted part of what Anna sought on Leo's behalf, but it was the most important part: his release from prison.

James Malone whistled when Mosgrove announced her decision. It was a relief, provided whoever leaked the tip made sure it didn't lead back to him.

He knew that Leo's interest in the activity they shared was anything but wholesome. He had fed the darkness in Leo, fertilized the seeds of potential evil with radioactive effluent from his own cavernous subregions.

Had he stopped a criminal in the process or created one? Lain bare criminal propensities or dragged a good man down into his own worst possible deformed manifestation? James didn't believe he had created the darkness in Leo, but neither had he helped him overcome it. He had joined him in catalyzing its metastasization. He wasn't proud of that, despite the tingles of pleasure memories of it sometimes brought.

James could not view his collision with Leo Baksh as a bad thing, on balance. They were puzzle pieces that fit one another to their mutual downfall, and if played right, their salvation. Leo may have absorbed traits from James, but James had absorbed traits from Leo—and they weren't all bad.

Leo's release seemed a favorable portent.

On a lark, James called Melissa to share these thoughts and get an off-the-record peek at how Leo's commutation was playing at the DDI regional headquarters.

"Lauren was apoplectic," said Melissa.

James couldn't help but laugh.

"Hey," said Melissa, who wasn't happy about the clemency decision either, but who could understand James's amusement with Lauren's fury. "Be nice. These quantum neural abuse investigations have been the mainstay of her career for years."

"Yes," said James. "And yours. And mine."

They ended up talking for an hour. As the conversation wound down, neither wanted to say goodbye. James mustered courage he had never needed when dealing with women, and asked if she would let him take her to dinner.

Neither spoke for a long interval. James was about to shrug it off as an inappropriate idea and make apologies when Melissa said, "Let me think about it."

He considered a thousand retorts that bore his well-worn aloof disdain, but he refused to give those a voice and said "OK." Though he felt like a convict at the gallows pleading for mercy, he added, "I hope you call."

"Take care," she said.

"You too," he replied, and clicked off.

Wendy, who had restored contact with James after he showed signs of genuine growth, teased him mercilessly when he told her he was awaiting Melissa's answer to his invitation for a date. "Not used to that, eh big brother? At the mercy of a pretty girl."

"No," he agreed, parrying her playfulness and resisting the urge to sarcasm. "I'm more accustomed to the other end of this equation."

"Let's hope it's not the same equation, Jimmy. I'm all for karma, but I hope yours doesn't come in the form of a female version of you."

James mugged fright. "I don't think she'd be as brutal as that, whatever she decides."

"No way to tell by the first kiss, lover boy."

"Thanks, I feel much better."

They were laughing amiably over this when James's phone signaled an incoming call from Melissa. Unbeknownst to him, though he had assumed it likely, Melissa had conferred with Lauren and Renée regarding his invitation and both were scandalized that she would even consider it. She explained that he was living through profound shifts, but they were unreceptive. Both colleagues icily told her she should do whatever felt right, but that they would consider it cause for concern if she put herself in his line of psychological fire. Melissa trusted her instinct, albeit with a mindful skepticism she promised not to forfeit absent corroborating proof that James had changed, and resolved to accept his offer.

When James switched phone lines and learned of Melissa's choice, he felt a layered surge of emotional energy: an habitual rush of predatory victory, nervousness, and a small voice singing with excited hope—by far the most promising of the three. He silently vowed to keep that level in focus, no matter how faint or nascent.

It took a few months to get the paperwork and bureaucratic tangles worked out, but nearly three years after he lost his freedom, Leo made final preparations for his release from prison. He gave away the conveniences he had purchased or inherited during his stay. The night before his departure, Leo's friends prepared a farewell banquet, forged from commissary items, black-market supplies from the chow hall, microwave cookery, and inmate culinary ingenuity. There were laughs, hugs, and in a few cases, tearful partings, before the evening was done.

Early the next morning, Mark helped Leo carry the remainder of his belongings to Receiving and Discharge, hugged him fiercely, and said, "Don't come back." Leo ruffled his hair and they held up hands in goodbye as an officer opened the door to Leo's transition into freedom.

An hour later, oddly calm, Leo emerged from a double-locked sally port through the final gate into the prison's public lobby, where Jamie Tesh and John Hanes waited. Leo hugged each in turn, and together they stepped into the relatively free world. John had to leave for an appointment but said he would call later, once Leo was settled in.

Jamie opened the passenger door of his car for Leo and hefted his sad box of property into the back seat.

"If you need rest, we can head to the apartment. But if you're up for it, I thought you might enjoy a trip to the grocery store. Or we could go to a restaurant."

"I'm way too wound up for rest. Grocery store could be fun."

Jamie slapped the dashboard. "Probationer's choice. Pick your poison and I'll do my best impression of cooking."

Leo stroked Jamie's cheek with the back of his hand. "Let's go," he said, and settled into the ergonomic seat, the comfort of which seemed extraordinary after years of plastic chairs and cement benches. When Jamie pulled out onto the road, Leo's neurons sang in tangy pleasure over the burst of motion, shape, and color after trudging down the same cluster of dimly lit halls and jogging around the same track for so long. He would adjust, but the initial sensation of freedom and variety was drug-like, and he soaked it all in.

Though he was wearing civilian clothes when they walked in the grocery store, Leo felt like everyone could see and smell prison on him. Logically he knew it wasn't true, but he was too accustomed to prison khakis to feel invisible in this environment.

"You OK?"

Leo turned to Jamie's kind face.

"Yeah. Just a lot of sensory input."

Jamie scanned their surroundings. "It's just a grocery store. You'll be used to it again in no time."

"It's quite green," observed Leo.

"I've never noticed," said Jamie, "but you're right." He stroked Leo's back.

Leo alternated between feeling too shy to select anything and wanting to buy everything he saw. Several times he picked something off the shelf to admire it and, when he started to put it back, Jamie yanked it out of his hand and threw it in the cart.

"I hope you like the place," Jamie said after they'd finished shopping and were en route to the transitional neighborhood where he had secured an apartment for the two of them.

"Trust me," said Leo, "after where I've been, it will feel like heaven. No razor wire or jangling keys? Perfect."

"It's a little nicer than that," he tepidly assured. "But I can shake keys at you if you get disoriented."

"Thanks, smart ass," said Leo, amused.

They each hefted two paper bags of groceries, with baguettes, ruffly greens, and a cluster of tomatoes peeking over the edges, up a flight of stairs.

The place was modest but charming. Hardwood floors, pane glass windows looking out on a park, a futon couch, dining nook, some decorative wooden boxes, a blown glass vase, and a couple of woven tapestries. Lots of healthy plants. And a rather skeptical cat. Leo placed his bags on the floor and clicked his tongue at the feline, who chose flirtation over aloofness and drew Leo into pursuit around the room before coyly accepting a few pets. Leo was smiling broadly by the time he was allowed this privilege.

Jamie observed, still holding a bag of groceries. "It's small but it has an office nook where you can write and it's near the rail line ..."

As Jamie apologetically recited the place's redeeming features, Leo stepped toward him. He did not answer, but holding Jamie's gaze, he gripped the bag of groceries by its other edge and tugged. Jamie's speech trailed off as he released his hold. Leo carefully placed the bag on the dining table and, without a word, at long last, took Jamie into his arms.

Later, they lay partly covered in sheets, Leo sitting up and leaning back against a pillow, and Jamie lying next to him on his stomach, propped up on his elbows, both sipping tea as a fragrant afternoon breeze puffed through the open window and caressed their moist skin.

"My God," said Leo. "I don't know whether I've been locked up too long or you're the dynamo you seem to be, but if I'd had any idea that was an option, I never would have tried Elidrine in the first place."

"I tried to tell you," said Jamie, holding the hot mug against Leo's side for a second to scorch him in punctuation.

Leo pulled away from the heat and feigned injury. "Yes, you did," he conceded. "But the timing wasn't right. I wasn't ready."

"Neither was I," agreed Jamie after a moment's reflection.

"You were still a kid," Leo said.

Jamie ran his fingertip around the rim of his mug. "Not anymore," he said softly.

"No, not anymore," Leo agreed.

The teacups kept company on the nightstand as the celebration of Leo's freedom resumed.

50

Among those surprised by Leo's change of fortune, the most ill prepared was Jeaneane. He had hurt and disappointed her, and it was easy to pretend he stopped existing when he was tucked away in prison.

The act of executive clemency substantially ameliorated Leo's pariah status, and she could well cross paths with him. "Why is nothing ever easy?" she asked aloud.

Who knows, she thought, he might turn his experience into an ironic form of social cachet. Plus, she did love him, she thought with a sigh.

"Wait and see," she advised herself aloud in the mirror as she touched up her mascara.

Leo felt like he was laboring against a mighty river current. As he executed multiple tasks to reestablish himself in a more-or-less normal life, he reminded himself—and when he forgot Jamie reminded him—that the beginning would be hardest. Nonetheless, it took a few months before his feet found purchase on solid rock, albeit slippery and unstable chunks of it.

In addition to getting Leo out of prison, Anna hooked him up with a job. Issa Zimmerman—under whose tutelage and license she sued her abusive former therapist and filed Leo's clemency petition—knew Leo by reputation from before his collapse, had participated in a conference panel with him years earlier, and liked him. Zimmerman already had hired Anna part-time as a research assistant, and had invited her to complete the internship portion of her curriculum at his firm. Anna enthusiastically accepted.

He was cautious when Anna first suggested pulling Leo in with her. He wasn't scared of controversy and he shared her contempt for government abuses, but Anna had her sights on establishing her own firm, and he figured Leo would go with her when she left.

They were both talented, and in Leo's case, experienced. They were also a bargain, because neither one had an advocate's license. Zimmerman knew they would give it their all because both needed a professional foothold, though for different reasons. They shared a drive to fight the forces that had harmed them, individually and together. All of this would fuel the bonfire of their creative passion while they worked in tandem with him, even if it rocketed them into escape velocity after a few years in his orbit.

Overall, Zimmerman felt it was a good investment in the short term and longer if he helped them stay on trajectory and burn to their own interstellar heights in the fullness of time.

Leo awoke early on his first day of work to find Jamie's side of the bed empty, except for their adolescent feline, Anaku. Leo kissed the purring furball on the forehead and made his way to the kitchen, where he encountered a steaming cup of fresh coffee, and his companion leaning back to avoid having his corneas spattered by the eggs that hissed in an overheated skillet.

"I never said I could cook," said Jamie.

Leo stood behind Jamie with one arm around his waist and, with his other, turned down the flame under the pan and kissed his neck. "You're doing great. It takes practice. Thank you for making breakfast. My turn tomorrow." He held Jamie and rested his chin on his shoulder as he fished the crisped eggs onto platters and helped assemble the meal.

"Are you nervous?" Jamie asked as they ate.

"A little," said Leo. "I'm just glad for the job. Zimmerman is doing me a good turn."

"He's also buying your skills off the auction block. He's no dummy."

"I know," said Leo. "But still. We like him."

Jamie agreed.

When Leo arrived at Zimmerman's offices, the support staff greeted him warmly and helped him equip his new workspace, a small office with natural light and a houseplant looking for love. Zimmerman arrived shortly thereafter and summarized several research and writing assignments, which Leo promptly organized and commenced.

A week later, as Leo put finishing touches on a draft brief, Zimmerman called and told him to head home for the day. "Hobson's inauguration is tonight and protesters are already filling up the streets. You can't afford to get caught up in any trouble, and I don't want to lose you before we even file your first brief. Get inside and lie low."

Leo accepted the sage advice. Much as he loathed Hobson and all he represented, and though his activist blood fizzed like sparkling water, he could not risk being construed as violating his parole.

When he left the office, protesters already were assembling on both sides of the street and soon would spill onto the thoroughfare and cut off the flow of traffic. Chants were audible from multiple directions. Leo felt a surge of exhilaration and fear, and picked up his pace to get home.

As he double-stepped toward the nearest light-rail station, he phoned Jamie to suggest they rendezvous at home early, for safety's sake.

"I can leave in an hour," said Jamie after a moment's consultation with his coworkers.

"I'll order something delivered," said Leo.

"We can console each other through the inauguration," offered Jamie.

"I'd rather see a movie. Or roll around on crushed glass. But I guess watching the bastard take office is the least we can do if we're not throwing ourselves into the gears."

"The gears have ripped you up enough for one lifetime," said Jamie. "Let's figure out some less damaging ways to chime in, OK?"

"Okaayyy," said Leo with feigned ennui, and they clicked off. Leo pocketed his mobile device and was still smiling to himself when he turned forward and saw a halted figure facing him on the sidewalk ahead. Leo's eyes mirrored the surprise in hers as the initial shock wave of seeing one another broke across their sense fields.

"Hello, Jeaneane," said Leo coolly.

"Hi," she replied with equal tepidity.

Leo felt an impulse to put them both at ease and build a bridge. He resisted the urge. Jeaneane regarded Leo in frosty silence, but realized she would have to initiate conversation. Apparently, he did not plan to grovel at her feet in penitence.

"Congratulations on your early release."

"Thanks."

"Are you working?"

"Yes, as of a few weeks ago."

Jeaneane waited for more, but Leo just studied her.

"I was surprised to hear you were getting out so soon," she said.

He raised his eyebrows in amusement but said nothing.

"I have unresolved feelings about the things you did, Leo."

Join the club, he thought.

"I don't know whether I'm interested in having contact with you," she offered. Leo suppressed a laugh, having not suggested anything of the kind. "I might want that," she continued imperiously, "but if we do, you'll have a lot of work helping me resolve my feelings. Your situation has been hard for me."

For you? thought Leo, resisting the urge to shake his head.

When he didn't reply, Jeaneane said, "If you decide you're ready to take responsibility for that, I'm willing to allow you to call me. I might be interested in talking."

A dozen oft-rehearsed retorts and brutal final words played across his mind, from "you seem to have mistaken for someone who cares what you think" to "fair-weather friends are a dime a dozen" to "the loss of respect between us became mutual years ago."

He was surprised to discover he couldn't utter them. He had said all he had to say in his final letter to her. He had nothing to add and, apparently, neither did she.

Instead, Leo centered his mind and honestly beheld Jeaneane, his long-harbored resentments evaporating like the remnants of a desert rain. All the festering ruminations over her betrayals, abandonment, and self-righteous judgment; all the heartbreak and fury he had projected onto her memory flaked off like old paint, and she stood before him a person. Despite her radiant surface, he recognized her as only partly beautiful. She was also disgustingly ugly, which placed her in good company with all the other shit-filled, decomposing, inconsistent, and contradictory skin bags walking the planet, including himself. He doubted Jeaneane would derive as much relief from this revelation as he did, so he kept it to himself with a smile she could not read.

Seeing her this way, he could forgive her, even as he was beginning to forgive himself. That didn't mean he wanted her back in his life, though. There was too much sewage under the causeway for Leo to entertain the thought of new life chapters with Jeaneane. She would have to work through her feelings without him just as he had been forced to work through his without her. He was stuck with himself for as long as he lived, but she was a different story. He bid Jeaneane a permanent farewell with neutrality, which was as much kindness as he could generate, and the best she deserved.

"Thanks, but I'd rather not. If you'll excuse me, I need to get off the streets. Be well. Stay safe. Goodbye." He resumed his trek to the rail station without looking back.

Leo had food arranged on the coffee table in front of the couch when Jamie got home so they could munch as they viewed the inauguration travesty on macrovision.

The media buzzed and cooed as aides scrambled over the banner-clad dais where Hobson was to take his oath of office and deliver his inaugural address. Leo and Jamie could hear protests rumbling on the streets, yet there was no mention of unrest in the mainstream coverage. A few commentators weakly acknowledged the "controversy" that surrounded Hobson's election, but strained to construct a narrative of reconciliation in which the high court had served as universally respected constitutional umpire and given the Citizenry a legitimate path forward. It sounded positively genteel to hear the macrovision commentators tell it. As Hobson's appearance neared, outrage on the street grew louder and more violent.

Leo looked out the window to assess their level of safety and found to his relief that the immediate area appeared calm. He closed the window to diminish the noise and scooted back next to Jamie as the media prated in hushed whispers that Hobson was about to take the stage.

With poker face, Belinda Mosgrove introduced the chief executive elect, and Hobson walked on stage to a blaze of camera fire and canned applause. Towering above and behind him, his image shined in titanic proportions on a giant macrovision backdrop screen. Rage on the street outblared the apparent mirth at the official site, giving the tableau a surreal chill for anyone viewing it from outside the cordoned and secure inaugural theatre.

After Hobson waved down his applause with pompous faux-humility, Mosgrove introduced High Adjudicator Alyssa Brannice, who was charged with administering the oath of office. Hobson and Brannice faced one another solemnly, both in human scale on the stage and in Olympian grandeur on the screen behind them.

Hobson raised his right hand.

If Brannice felt anything other than respect and confidence in the face of this magisterial personage, it didn't show in her carriage. "Please repeat after me: I, Trenton Nygaard Hobson do solemnly swear to honor and respect the constitution and laws of our great republic ..."

Hobson had no sooner begun to parrot these hieratic words when the microphones went dead.

The two maintained their composure and glanced around minutely, and even the clamor on the streets subsided as staff attempted to diagnose the problem.

"There seem to be technical difficulties at the inaugural venue," observed a Capital Macrovision commentator.

His colleague nodded, but the two darted a moment of eye contact. All the equipment at the event site had backup systems, and should have been failsafe. "Something's not right," whispered a voice in the newsman's earpiece.

The scene on the macrovision screen behind the dais shattered into a kaleidoscope of image fragments. The video of the dais and its rapidly disintegrating political drama continued, but broken into shards. The pieces of video swirled in a random pattern for several seconds, then coalesced into a moving, composite image. The fluid mosaic was mesmerizing, as a piece of art, a technical triumph, and an act of political sabotage so colossal it pierced the central government's image of supremacy and control. When the image stabilized, a collective gasp sounded.

"I am Anaku!" thundered a voice over the audio system.

Though it vibrated in familiar deep bass, the audio signal sounded digitized, marred with infinitesimal lacunae, and oddly sterile. While the shifting visage formed from the shattered video of the devolving scene on stage was clearly of Anaku, it was also abstract due to its form. The composite Anaku moved as he spoke, but it was like an animated representation. As to whether that was connected to a live feed was anyone's guess.

The crowd didn't care. A roar concussed across the continent.

"The government will shut this down shortly, so I'll be brief and to the point," the image roared back.

"Hobson is a war criminal who has seized power through a political coup. The election is a sham, sabotaged with quantum neural technology, manipulation, and subterfuge.

"He has no legitimate claim to office, contrary to the high court's attempted whitewash. He should stand trial in international criminal court for crimes against humanity.

"Don't let the media apologists fool you. The government may have the guns, but you have the power, because the government is a mirage born of our collective belief. We can believe something better into existence.

"The current juncture could not be more critical. This is a matter of life and death, for our republic and all it strives to be, for the concept of freedom and human evolution beyond our cyclic descents into barbarity, ignorance, and spiritual death.

"If this matters to you, I tell you the most meaningful and important moment of your life is at hand and you must resist! Do not pay your bills. Do not pay your taxes. If your work feeds our outdated idea of government, find something else to do. Form food and resource exchange cooperatives. Serve your community's immediate needs. Do all you can to shut the national economy down completely.

"The state terrorists will fight you. They will try to convince you with bullets and truncheons that violence is power. But hear me well: Violence is not power. It is the tool of cowards who live in fear."

Cheers from the inaugural crowd merged with those from the street and people began surrounding the giant macrovision screen to stop anyone from cutting off the feed. Riot police stormed the stage and formed a wall of shields around the political figures, then began pounding and hauling away the rogue agent's impromptu coconspirators.

"You cannot let them sell you this lie," continued the Anaku video mosaic. "Meet violence with violence and you feed their ugly machine your souls and life energy. Fight them with arms and they will already have won, no matter the outcome of any battle. The antidote to fear is courage and this is what you must teach, even unto death if we are to show the world a new way.

"This is the truth and the state terrorists know it: Cutting off the energy supply to the evil beast that has stolen our political reins is an act so powerful and unprecedented it can abort this historic catastrophe before it even draws a full breath. *That* is true power, and it is yours to wield.

"Stand shoulder to shoulder, Citizens and members of the excluded classes. Focus your resolve, own your power, and shut this country down until Hobson is impeached, arrested, and draped in chains as he deserves."

A battle cry raged from coast to coast. National Police ushered away the dignitaries and finally succeeded in cutting cables to the giant macrovision screen. The media feed from the inaugural site went black. Stations across the country cut to scandalized commentary and scrambled to cobble together a threadbare patina of professionalism and normalcy.

Leo's mouth was agape. "He's alive?"

"Was that really him?" asked Jamie. "It could have been computer generated."

Leo shrugged and shook his head with eyes wide. "Whoever it was, they just shut down the CE's fucking inauguration."

Leo and Jamie gaped in disbelief.

"Holy shit," said Jamie. "What's going to happen now? A revolution?"

"Anyone's guess. I hope they heard the part about nonviolence."

"It'll be a bloodbath," predicted Jamie.

"Let's not put energy into that thought," Leo admonished himself as much as his companion.

"What do we do?" asked Jamie.

"Lie low and see what happens," replied Leo, "and hope no one burns down our house."

51

After Anaku's first illegal broadcast—the one that ended with him being dragged away by armed agents on national macrovision—the National Police, military, intelligence agencies, and local law enforcement departments scrambled to lock the country down. This time they were ready.

Signs appeared in all cities:

Curfew: 7:00 p.m. to 6:00 a.m.

"Public Assemblies Of More Than Two People Unrelated By Blood, Adoption, Or Marriage Are Prohibited."

The same messages ticked along the bottom of every macrovision screen, and blared from PA systems in public transit cars and government buildings.

Despite those efforts and Anaku's call for nonviolence, skirmishes between protesters and riot police sparked. Hundreds were arrested and scores were killed by official firepower, but the news media were barred from covering it. Instead, official propaganda from Hobson's administration appeared on news channels. Political speech critical of the government was characterized as criminal conspiracy and treason. Off camera, National Police began hauling political dissenters into custody without a hearing.

The only viable organizing conduits left to progressive activists were word of mouth and the Micromedium. The DII and DDI constantly strove to monitor Micromedium communications, but hacktivist cadres raced to devise encryption and cloaking programs. Through these shifting data links the government could not eliminate, spontaneous groups heeded the inaugural-night call to bullet-less arms, launching one nonviolent action after another and dealing tangible and disruptive blows to the flow of commerce and the course of basic infrastructure administration.

After a few weeks, the guerilla economic protests began to take their toll on the economy. Hobson's administration, though well-armed, was no better equipped than any other government to withstand a protracted economic downturn. He called for normalization of commerce, backed by executive orders that purportedly outlawed food collectives and mass electronic communications, but the act was viewed as desperate and the resistance grew. It became clear a period of austerity in one form or another was inevitable. Despite Hobson's threats and periodic offers of stimulus money for organizations that would work with the government, a growing segment of the public opted for self-imposed material limitations rather than permanent surrender to an illegitimate and militarized security and surveillance regime.

Rogue broadcasts erupted on the Macromedium, their existence mocking Hobson's bombastic show of force and suppression of speech. "Dig in!" became the battle cry, sprouting like bamboo through cracks in the pavement.

This was not good news for Hobson.

Tensions rose and the country grew poorer, but a collective sense of lean determination emerged. The executive administration and its tools of violent oppression hunkered down on one side, and an increasingly resolute and unified public crouched down on the other, both aware that something deep was shifting, subterranean girders were torqueing and moaning, and that a force more consequential than money or even guns was driving the continental drift.

Zimmerman, Anna, and, off the record, Leo worked feverishly through the turmoil, finding advocates for detained activists and filing lawsuits against the Hobson regime to highlight its abuses and throw judicial roadblocks in its way for as long as the courts remained even superficially relevant.

"How long do you think they'll indulge us?" Anna asked Leo one afternoon as they reviewed a new motion demanding hearings for detained activists.

"For as long as they think letting us bitch in court does more to placate the public than rile it up, I would imagine," replied Leo. "Anyone's guess. It would be difficult for the government to maintain order for long without at least the veneer of judicial process."

"A few years ago, I thought advocates were the true warriors," said Anna, "but I'm starting to think it's the street activists who drive this thing."

Leo shrugged. "We all have a part. Without them, we have no tide to harness. Without us, they have no interface with the machine. There are no superheroes. Just a bunch of people deciding which way to push."

"What about Anaku?"

Leo considered the question. "Without us, he would be nothing but a digitized megalomaniac."

Anna gasped in mock shock at this sacrilege. "I thought you were one of his worshippers."

"I was," replied Leo, clicking keys to bring Anna's document onto his screen. "I'm just not much into worship these days."

Anna pulled a chair up next to him and opened her research file.

"I am still a big fan though," he added. "If he still exists."

"Maybe his part's done," said Anna. "It's not him we need. It's what he said."

"It's more than that. It was the spirit carrying the message that gave it strength."

"True," acknowledged Anna, "but—"

"I understand what you mean," said Leo. "He probably would agree with you, which is why he carried such authority."

They were quiet a moment.

"I doubt we've heard the last of him."

"If he still exists," Anna replied.

"Regardless," said Leo.

Anna squeaked, and they turned to the task at hand.

As the months of steadfast resistance wore on, the public gained a growing sense that the radical inaugural address spoke truly: If the people could stay focused, their power would make the government's presumption of unshakable supremacy, arrogant disregard for its founding principles, hypnotizing iconography and bureau-speak, cavernous jail cells, torture chambers, and dizzying array of weaponry look like the amateur theatrics and stage props they were. Unified nonviolent resistance would unmask Hobson's violent tactics as no more than the obsolete tantrums of developmentally stunted evolutionary throwbacks. The more coordinated the public's passive resistance grew, the clearer this became, and both sides knew it.

Six months into the crisis, it was clear that even a full-scale domestic military occupation might not break the public's resolve. Conservative leaders in the Council of Delegates soberly assessed the situation and concluded that, given the depth of resistance, use of massive force would be even worse for commerce than the perennial boycotts and strikes.

Preston Flynn, chair of the Conservative Caucus, met with top leaders within his party and a key potential ally from the Progressive Caucus in closed strategy session over whiskey. "We've never had a clearer mandate," said Flynn to the others. "We have to break ranks with Hobson."

"He will destroy us all," objected Drake Esty who remained chairperson of the Delegates Intelligence Committee at the behest of the Progressive Caucus, which barely held onto its majority after the political firestorm that burned Hobson into office.

"He will destroy our party if we don't remove him," countered Flynn. "I don't expect you to care about that, Drake, but he'll take the rest of the country down with it."

"I don't mean he'll destroy us figuratively," said Esty, swirling ice cubes in emphasis. "He will fry our brains."

"Can he?" asked Neil Gascon, Alistair Coyle's successor as president of the Citizens Action League. Flynn had invited him to the meeting. "You're the top intelligence point-person, Drake." He regarded Esty with a hint of disdain. "Are there neural weapons in the delegates' chambers or not?"

"I wish I knew," said Esty, eyeing Gascon who, as Citizens Action League head, Esty suspected had closer ties to Hobson than he would reveal.

"Subpoena the new DII head and find out," replied Gascon, meeting Esty's gaze but declining any implicit challenge to the purpose of his presence at the meeting.

"That would be lovely," said Aksel Pao, general counsel for the Conservative Caucus, "provided we wanted to put on a meaningless show for your audience. International does what it wants. Face facts: The DII has become a sovereign entity."

"Hardly," objected Flynn.

"Not in law," said Pao, "but in fact, yes, of course it is."

Flynn hoped for support from Esty and Gascon, but neither seemed to disagree.

"The DII does not have the resources to run this country," said Flynn in retort, "especially if our economy collapses, which is a possibility. Sovereign entity or no, it needs us."

"Provided we play along," said Esty, "and removing Hobson is not likely to earn the agency's favor."

"Well and good," chimed Gascon, "but we have to do something. This resistance, movement, revolution, whatever it is, isn't going away. We have to harness and redirect it before it puts us out of our houses."

"You mean co-opt it."

"Call it whatever you want. History will view you as saviors if you play it right, and the only way we can bring these disrupters to heel is to serve up Hobson."

"Through what?" balked Pao, "criminal charges? We don't have the power to charge the chief executive."

"No need for anything so untoward," said Gascon as he watched the liquor swirl around his glass. "Impeachment would suffice." He tipped back a sip and regarded the others.

The three registered no reaction.

"We do have sympathizers within the agency," admitted Esty. "But they are afraid."

"If we weaken Hobson, will they gain courage?" asked Flynn.

"I'm sure they would," said Esty, "but enough to build momentum against him even within the agency?"

"Impossible to predict," said Flynn. "We have to take the chance. Our republic is collapsing."

Esty looked him up and down. "You're going soft."

"Don't be ridiculous. Have you read the delegates' budget forecast?"

Esty poured himself another nip. "Yes."

A clock on the mantle ticked as the four reflected.

"The worst part is we'll have to forge a pact with your Progressive Caucus to pull this off," said Flynn, gesturing with his glass to Esty, who raised his in mock toast.

"All the more reason for you to take the lead," said Gascon. "You'll be the bringers of peace, law and order. A one-stop political party."

"I may be sick," said Pao.

"You'll survive," replied Flynn. "More importantly, I'll survive."

The four chuckled.

"Impeachment it is," said Flynn.

They clinked tumblers.

When the impeachment proceedings convened, anger shifted back to fixation on scripted media political drama, and the flow of ordinary civil life ran more freely. Progressive legal professionals like Zimmerman and his crew shifted from triage to longer-term strategy in hopes of harnessing the shifting political tide and funneling its force into lasting institutional reforms. At the end of ten, sixteen-hour days at the office, Zimmerman, Leo, and Anna had no new clients or emergencies for the first time in half a year. Distrusting this caesura could last, they took advantage of the relative civil peace and enjoyed a long weekend of rest and relaxation.

Jamie swept all tasks off his calendar as well, and he and Leo headed by rail to a beachside cottage for some frolicking in the surf.

Carrying backpacks loaded with treats, books, playing cards, music, candles, and sundry unguents for a weekend's leisurely retreat, the couple boarded a light-rail down the block from their abode and began a series of legs to their destination. They turned out not to be the only cabin-fevered denizens venturing out on the tentacles of public transport during the ad-hoc truce. The train was packed.

Leo grabbed a vertical support rail, and Jamie gripped an overhead hand loop as the coach lurched out of the station. Crashing into each other slightly, though not unwelcomely, they smiled conspiratorially and hefted their backpacks onto the floor. Leo rested his weight against the rail and pulled Jamie back against him. They excitedly discussed the sites they wanted to take in and trails they wanted to hike during their getaway.

Three stations later, after hordes of passengers debarked and boarded, Leo and Jamie hauled their packs over and stood in front of the closing doors, positioning themselves to step off first at the next station, where they planned to make a quick connection to another line. The train stood motionless for several minutes, and Leo reviewed the stops on their printed itinerary. He snapped alert when Jamie clamped his forearm with a vise-like grip. Leo reacted with surprise and Jamie darted his eyes toward the glass door in front of them. Leo turned just as a man standing opposite him on the platform rotated his gaze from a woman with long frizzy curls and faced him through the glass.

For the first time since the sentencing hearing, Leo Baksh and James Malone faced one another eye to eye. Neither flinched, blinked, or averted the other's gaze. They regarded one another frankly. Though the encounter crackled with static, neither man felt anger or aversion.

A tone over the PA system signaled that the train was about to pull out, and both men realized the moment would soon pass. Each in his own way sought out the point of intersection he had experienced in his dreams of the other. On instinct, Leo steepled his fingertips in front of his heart. James blinked minutely and gracefully reciprocated the gesture. The two men bowed to one another, holding eye contact and smiling subtly, until the train moved and they slid from each other's view.

As the train left the station, Jamie regarded Leo with nervous inquiry, but could see that he was at peace. The two rode on without speaking.

Back on the platform, James turned to Melissa. She studied him uncertainly until his features broke into a placid smile. She returned the expression, scooted closer, put her hand into his back pocket, and laid her head against his shoulder. James brushed back her hair with his fingertips and softly kissed her forehead, then caressed her with his cheek.

"Movie or botanical gardens? If it's the movie, we have to catch the express."

"I want to do whatever you want to do."

The words clearly surprised him when they crossed his lips as much as they did her. He examined his feelings and realized he meant it.

As the next train pulled into the station, Melissa raised her voice over the squeal: "I'd like to check out the ancient textiles exhibit at the museum, if you must know."

James cocked his head in interest at the suggestion. "Then we needn't catch a train at all."

"No."

James offered her his arm. "To the museum then."

Melissa took his arm as they wove their way through the crowd and left the platform.

A third of the globe away, Marta bodysurfed into shore on a turquoise wave so pristine her companion on the beach could see through it like a piece of liquid glass. She landed on her feet as the wave broke and waded through the receding waters, then jogged across the firm sand and hot-footed it over the searing powder that lay beyond.

Sitting on a blanket, her friend shielded his eyes from the sun with a lazy salute as the vision of body-art raced toward him, glistening and lithe as a cheetah. Marta dove onto him, and he fell back to receive her weight, the two laughing as she drenched him in sea water and they kissed and wrestled.

She sat up and swung back her hair in a great arc, revealing a face aglow with health and a nose peeling from weeks of exposure to the salt and sun.

"Any news?" she asked.

"Nothing certain."

"Life's never certain."

He didn't reply.

"Was it him or not?"

"I'm not certain."

"I believe we've established that. What do you think?"

"I think the specs I received on the upgraded neural shield, accompanied as they were by details from our surveillance of the superhub, could only have come from Anaku."

"Directly?"

"Either directly or by extraction under compulsion."

"Which is possible."

"In theory. But he was a tough customer."

"They have big tools."

"So does he. He probably also had allies."

"So?"

"So I need to confer with Sleeperagent and some others to see if we can figure out a way to test what I've received without undue risk of falling into a trap."

"I think he's alive."

"Maybe."

They spent the afternoon swimming and romping in the tropical sunshine, amply funded by Cormack O'Brian's pilfered assets, heaped together with mountains of other illegally procured hordes. The sun dipped over the horizon and Marta's cohort, the person sometimes known as Hackizen, advised Patrice via encrypted Micromedium chat of the suggestive communiqué he had received. Each decided to consult with trusted associates and meet via avatar the next day to formulate a plan.

After they conferred, Patrice felt duty bound to tell Wendy, despite the twinges of jealousy this aroused in her gut. Then Wendy, who tracked down Leo at the beach, took Anna along for the ride and drove out the next day to deliver the news unsurveilled, after correctly surmising that the brief interruption to the weekend's seclusion would add to its beauty.

"He's alive," said Leo.

"Maybe," said Wendy.

"Then there's reason for hope," said Jamie.

The other three swapped glances.

"I'm not sure I'd go that far," said Anna.

"Cynical bores," said Jamie. "Then how about reason not to give up?"

"Yes," agreed Leo. "There is always reason for that. You never know what's around the corner."

All four recognized the truth of this as they reflected soberly on what they and their countrymen had been through.

"Maybe we'll find him around the next one," said Anna.

"Maybe," said Wendy softly.

The four held one another in the afternoon breeze and said a silent prayer. Kisses and hugs were exchanged all around and the women headed back to Wendy's car. After buckling in, Anna rolled down the passenger window, stuck her head out, and pulled down her sunglasses. "Don't forget to get some rest this weekend, boys."

"Play is restful," Jamie retorted.

"Just remember to get a little sleep," Anna said, her laughter floating like piano notes on the air as Wendy pulled away.

Back at their island hideout, Marta and her scofflaw paramour lay in a pretzel of limbs and luxuriated in the gentle trade winds wafting through the mosquito net draped over their pleasure nest.

"If you don't mind me asking," said Marta as they caught their breath, "since we've become so intimate and everything, and since you know who I am, and since I've more than paid my share of the rent—"

"With Cormack's money and my help," he reminded.

"By incurring a karmic debt many cultures view as punishable by eternity in hell," she countered.

"You had scores to settle with him long before you wanted to chip in on this playpen," he retorted. "This wasn't exactly your first track meet."

"Regardless," Marta said with semi-mock sternness, "It's fair to ask who you are, Hackypunk."

He gaped at her audacity. "Surely you do not take me for such a fool as to trust a terrorist and assassin with information so essential and sensitive as that."

She lifted a shoulder in playful dismissal. "You've got more on me than I do on you."

"Hardly."

"I can already make your life difficult."

"If you say so."

She held his gaze. "Come on. Who are you?"

"Sorry, babe," he said, rolling on top of her. "I have to keep a few secrets."

"You don't want to get on my bad side," she said, giggling as he tickled her.

"Likewise, *assassin*," he replied. "Besides," he added, "the fight's not over and I still have a few good tricks up my sleeve. You'll have more fun riding with me than trying to knock me off my horse."

"Hmm," she said as the wrapped her legs around him, "We'll see."

Later that night, Leo and Jamie lay on the beach and gazed at the star-filled sky. Points of light, thousands beyond counting, pierced the darkness.

"I think a graffiti artist has commandeered an interstellar transport," said Leo. "I see Anaku."

"I see him too," said Jamie.

A wave nipped their feet.

"Tide's coming in," said Leo.

"Time for sleep."

"Time to dream."

"We don't need sleep for that," said Jamie.

"No," Leo agreed, "we do that best when we are awake."

"Come on, then. We'll dream some more tomorrow, when we're fresh."

"Sounds good," said Leo as Jamie pulled him to his feet.

They shared a kiss, and made their way across the cool sand.

Meanwhile, thirty floors below Memorial Park at the nation's capital, a circle of DII agents reclined in ergonomic pods, wired into a constantly expanding neural field that soon would span the globe, and listened.

"Those gaps in the field are getting larger," said one agent to another as they debriefed after completing their shifts.

"I know what you're referring to," responded the other, "but I wouldn't call them gaps. They are energetic. Something is going on in them."

"We can't penetrate them."

"No, we can't."

"Until we know what they are, Hobson's right, we must assume they are a threat."

The second agent sighed. "Agreed."

"Now!" commanded the instructor. The virtual circle of neurally wired meditators solidified their focus. "Now," they thought together in return, and joined their minds in radiant silence.

ACKNOWLEDGEMENTS

This project took years of labor and I could not have completed it without the loving support of friends, family, and professional associates.

I am delighted to have met and worked with Heather Jacquemin of HJ's Editing Services, a brilliant editor who hadn't the least compunction about slashing thousands of extraneous words from my manuscript, honing edges, and showing me where to work harder.

Heartfelt thanks to my father Barry Borgerson, Steve Uhrig, and Connie Morris for safekeeping my handwritten draft and moving it into digital form, not to mention providing support through the difficult life chapter I was living when I wrote the first draft, and beyond.

Deep thanks to Karl Sikkenga and Nancy Karmiller for reading early and penultimate drafts and giving me detailed and invaluable feedback and input. Thanks also to Peter S. Goodman for reading my first draft and giving me candid feedback that helped shape the work's development to completion.

Great thanks to my mother, Sybil Bailey, for reading my early drafts with her heart and brilliant mind, and showing me with her visceral reaction to the characters that I might be onto something.

A special thanks to Michael Nava, an author I have long admired and with whom I have had the privilege to become acquainted in recent years. Michael kindly read a late draft, gave me incredibly helpful feedback, and engaged me in conversations that helped me take the work to a higher level during my last substantive revision.

Gratitude also to Daniel D., Mike B., Eric H., John L., Stephen R., and Stephan S who read the first hand-scrawled draft as I peeled it off notepads in serial form. Their enthusiasm and encouragement helped me trust my own voice. You guys have enormous strength and I miss you.

Thank you to the aptly named Gary Wise for the author photo and friendship, Alex Kronz for her beautiful original illustrations, and to Jessica Bell for her wonderful cover designs.

Respect and gratitude to Gene Faurie Jr., for his courage, loyalty, and unwavering support during my darkest hours.

Thanks to Hans P. Fleischner, Marvin H. Weiss, Kenneth Balser and Thomas Grossman for cheers and sustenance as I neared the finish line.

Last but not least, thanks go to Robert Hildebrand, who knocks me off my high horse and hands me a clean shirt. You are a good man.

ABOUT THE AUTHOR

Eric Borgerson has been a writer in one form or another since junior high school in Oakland, California. He completed degrees in philosophy at Reed College and law at U.C. Berkeley. His career has included work in labor and civil rights law and politics, as an organizer, attorney, writer and journalist. He is also a fan of good science fiction, an avid science enthusiast, loves backpacking, music, film, and literature, and is a lifelong student of philosophy and spiritual traditions. *When the Eye Sees Itself* is Eric's first major work of fiction. While it is neither biographical nor autobiographical, it is informed and animated by Eric's extensive experience with politics and the law, as activist, participant and exile. Eric lives in the Palm Springs, California area.

Made in the USA
Columbia, SC
05 April 2018